The Memoirs
Of Saint John
No Greater Love

Richard Edmondson

Once There Was a Way

OTWAY BOOKS

This is a work of fiction. Names, characters, places, and incidents are the products of the author's imagination or are used fictitiously. Any resemblance to actual events, locales, or persons, living or dead, is entirely coincidental.

Published by OTWAY Books
Fairview, TN 37062

www.memoirsofsaintjohn.com
www.leftwing-christian.net

Excerpts from "Thanksgiving Day in the U.S." are taken from *Threatened With Resurrection: Prayers and Poems from an Exiled Guatemalan*, by Julia Esquivel, © 1982, 1994, Brethren Press, Elgin, Illinois, www.brethrenpress.com. Used with permission.

ISBN 978-0-9678909-0-6

Richard Edmondson
P.O. Box 923
Fairview, TN 37062
info@memoirsofsaintjohn.com

Printed in the USA by Lightning Source

Acknowledgements

The author would like say special thanks to Anne Knauff, Paul Griffin, Eileen Flemming, and Israel Shamir for reading the manuscript and offering comments and suggestions.

Greater love has no one than this,
that he lay down his life for his friends

—Jesus

Table of Contents

Foreword

In an author's note to *Out of Egypt*, the first installment in her *Christ the Lord* series, novelist Anne Rice comments on a curious anomaly encountered while doing research for her book, to wit the prevalence of New Testament scholars who seem to exhibit a visceral antipathy to their chosen field of study. It's a phenomenon I also found in the course of researching this work. Rice referred to it as "skeptical scholarship," conducted by "those who claimed to be children of the Enlightenment" and often with the objective of portraying Christ negatively or refuting his existence altogether:

> Many of these scholars, scholars who apparently devoted their life to New Testament scholarship, disliked Jesus Christ. Some pitied him as a hopeless failure. Others sneered at him, and some felt an outright contempt. This came between the lines of the books. This emerged in the personality of the texts.

Rice goes on to compare other fields of study, observing for instance that Elizabethan scholars don't pepper their works with snickering comments about Queen Elizabeth I, or spend their careers trying to undermine her historical reputation. She then adds: "But there are New Testament scholars who detest and despise Jesus Christ."

Rice very diplomatically doesn't name those scholars to whom she refers. But we might pause a moment, just for the fun of it, and engage in some idle speculation. Could one of them have been Robert Eisenman? Eisenman is a professor at California State University Long Beach, Visiting Senior Member of Linacre College, Oxford, and author of the books *James the Brother of Jesus* and *The New Testament Code*. In an article published on *The Huffington Post* December 19, 2007, Eisenman expressed his belief that the writers of the gospels had fabricated the character Judas Iscariot out of motives of anti-Semitism. "The creators of this character and the traditions related to him knew what it was they were seeking to do and in this they have succeeded in a manner far beyond anything they might have imagined and that would have astonished even their hate-besotted brains," he writes.

Eisenman was responding to an op-ed piece by April DeConick, religious studies professor at Rice University, which had appeared December 1 in *The New York Times*. The piece concerned the Gospel of Judas, or more specifically the National Geographic Society's translation of that text from Coptic to English—*faulty* in DeConick's view. Among Eisenman's complaints was that Judas Iscariot's "heroicization," as he termed it, had been proceeding along nicely until DeConick had messed things up with the publication earlier that year of her book, *The Thirteenth Apostle*, and then with her commentary in the *Times*.

Far from being a villain, Judas was in reality a hero, the most trusted of Jesus' disciples—this, according to National Geographic, was what the Gospel of Judas conveyed. And when he handed Jesus over to be killed, he was actually doing the latter's bidding. A much-publicized TV special, and later a book, were dedicated to this reexamination of a man reviled through history and whose very name had become synonymous to betrayal. A new Judas seemed to be the order of the day. Ah, but not so fast, said DeConick, who found that the National Geographic translation team, consisting of Professors Rodolphe Kasser, Gregor Wurst, Marvin Meyer, and Francois Gaudard, had made "translation choices" which fell "well outside the commonly accepted practices in the field," leading to a presentation of Judas that was completely opposite, in certain key respects, to what the text said in Coptic. For instance the National Geographic's transcription referred to Judas as a "daimon," which the team translated into English as "spirit."

"Actually," said DeConick, "the universally accepted word for 'spirit' is 'pneuma'—in Gnostic literature 'daimon' is always taken to mean 'demon'."

Other examples of such questionable "translation choices" can be found in the pages of the Rice University professor's book, *The Thirteenth Apostle*. The long and the short of it is this. The Gospel of Judas was composed by Sethians, a group of second-century Jewish Christians to whom the rather catch-all term "Gnostic" has been applied. The Sethians regarded themselves as the offspring of Seth, the third son of Adam, but rather than portraying Judas as a good guy and friend to Jesus, they actually branded him a demon who would "not ascend to the holy generation," as DeConick's translation phrased it.

In his *Huffington Post* rebuttal, Eisenman fumed that DeConick "wishes to check the heroicization of Judas that ensued and return to portraying him as the Demon (Daimon) incarnate—in Gnostic, as she puts it, 'the Thirteenth Apostle.'" Not only was the character of Judas wholly manufactured by the "Gospel artificers" of the New Testament, the same might be said of Jesus himself, Eisenman seemed to feel. He hints in fact that future historical research may well prove this to be the case, and one way he underscores this point is by placing quotation marks around the name "Jesus" throughout a good portion of his piece.

Scholarly research to prove or disprove the historicity of the Christ of the gospels is nothing new. There have been numerous "quests for the historical Jesus" embarked upon over the years, one notable example being the Jesus Seminar. Begun in the mid-1980s, the Seminar consisted of a series of twice-yearly conferences in which scholars attempted, by means of popular vote, to rate the authenticity of various gospel passages. A color-coded system was devised under which red meant the passage in question was deemed a fairly accurate representation of what Jesus said, while black designated the opposite, with pink and grey representing varying shades of certainty in between. The Seminar's findings were presented in several books published mainly in the 1990s, perhaps most notably *The Five Gospels* by Robert W. Funk—and there the matter presumably might have been laid to rest.

But in December of 2008, one year after the *Times/HuffPo* crossfire between DeConick and Eisenman, came the launching of yet another "quest," this time under the title of "The Jesus Project." Like the Jesus *Seminar* before it, the Jesus *Project* consists of a colloquy of scholars who announced plans to hold periodic meetings in a "renewed quest for the historical Jesus"—this according to the Amherst, New York-based Center for Inquiry (CFI), the sponsor of the project. The initial meeting took place December 5-7 in Amherst, and one of the presenters was Eisenman. Others included Bruce Chilton, professor at Bard College and author of *Rabbi Jesus: An Intimate Biography*; James Tabor, author of *The Jesus Dynasty*; German author and academic Gerd Lüdemann; and Robert Price, author of the somewhat mordantly titled *The Incredible Shrinking Son of Man*. Also listed as Project Fellows on the CFI web site: Justin Meggitt, senior lecturer at Cambridge University; Gary Greenberg, president of the Biblical Archaeology Society of New York and also a consultant on National Geographic's *Science of Bible* series; and archaeologist Dorothy Lobel King.

Though invited, DeConick declined to attend, mostly it seems out of differences over method, coupled with the belief that "another quest for what we can know about Jesus will turn up nothing new." (posting, DeConick's

Forbidden Gospels blog, Feb. 5, 2009). But CFI reassuringly pledged the "highest standards of scientific and scholarly objectivity" in the effort, and Project Chair R. Joseph Hoffman said he believed an important question to finally explore is "the possibility that Christianity arose from causes that have little to do with a historical founder"—this while acknowledging what he referred to as "Jesus fatigue" among the public. But from Hoffman's perspective, the work of the Jesus Project was needed in order to correct shortcomings of the Jesus Seminar, which he believed had "raised more questions than they answered," producing a Jesus somewhat akin to "a talking doll with a questionable repertoire of thirty-one sayings. Pull a string and he blesses the poor." ("Rocks, Hard Places, and Jesus Fatigue: Jesus Seminar and Jesus Project," *Bible and Interpretation* web site.) The Jesus Project, he seemed to feel, would do better.

Perhaps the scholars in attendance at that meeting in Amherst were too absorbed in their Jesus research to take much note of an intensive assault launched later that month by Israel against the Gaza Strip. Few seem to have commented publicly on it, despite many of them maintaining blogs and web sites of their own—a case in point being Richard Carrier. Carrier, author of *Sense and Goodness Without God*—who is also listed as a Project Fellow on the CFI web site—posted a two-part report on his blog describing some of the scholarly presentations and other events at that early December meeting of 2008. One of his posts was dated December 26, one day before the Gaza attack began, the other January 10—four days after Israel had carried out a missile strike on a U.N. school. In neither posting did he mention events transpiring in Gaza, even though he occasionally blogs on political issues (he was an Obama supporter in the 2008 election). Question: are scholars, so seemingly obsessed with proving or disproving what happened in Palestine 2000 years ago, oblivious to events taking shape there currently? Are they really unconcerned about the slaughter of innocents in today's "Holy Land"? Or do they remain silent for another reason?

The Israeli invasion went on for twenty-two days and killed approximately 1400 Gazans, roughly 300 of whom were children. It was during the Gaza siege that I was completing the final chapters of this book. Sitting at home, I would write through the morning and early afternoon hours, and then around three in the afternoon switch over to the Internet where I would read of white phosphorous explosions, of hospitals overrun with victims, and of people taking shelter for days in bombed out basements with the corpses of their relatives. Gaza of course was the enclave through which the infant Jesus and his parents would have passed when fleeing to Egypt. Did the family perhaps journey smack dab through the area now called Ezbt Abed Rabbo, where Khaled Abed Rabbo saw two of his daughters shot dead while the girls' grandmother carried a white flag attached to a mop handle? Or could they have paused to rest with their donkey at Zeitoun— maybe at that very spot where four small starving children, too weak to stand, were found next to the bodies of their dead mothers by rescuers, rescuers who had been trying to reach the neighborhood for days after it came under Israeli attack?

There were, of course, those who very much did *not* remain silent during the siege of Gaza. One of these was Irish human rights activist Caoimhe Butterly. Butterly was in the costal enclave at the time the attack started and spent the ensuing days working with Palestinian ambulance paramedics attempting to reach the dead and wounded. While Israel kept the media out until the killing was over, it was not able to stop reports such as Butterly's from slipping through to the outside world. And in an article that appeared January 16 on the web site *Counterpunch*, she provided a vivid account of the agony.

> The morgues of Gaza's hospitals are over-flowing. The bodies in their blood-soaked white shrouds cover the entire floor space of the Shifa hospital morgue. Some are exposed, heads blown off, skulls crushed in. Family members wait outside to identify and claim a brother, husband, father, mother, wife, child. Many of those who wait their turn have lost numerous family members and loved ones.
>
> Blood is everywhere. Hospital orderlies hose down the floors of operating rooms, bloodied bandages lie discarded in corners, and the injured continue to pour in: bodies lacerated by shrapnel, burns, bullet wounds. Medical workers, exhausted and under siege, work day and night and each life saved is seen as a victory over the predominance of death.
>
> The streets of Gaza are eerily silent—the pulsing life and rhythm of markets, children, fishermen walking down to the sea at dawn brutally stilled and replaced by an atmosphere of uncertainty, isolation and fear. The ever-present sounds of surveillance drones, F16s, tanks and apaches are listened to acutely as residents try to guess where the next deadly strike will be—which house, school, clinic, mosque, governmental building or community centre will be hit next

and how to move before it does. That there are no safe places—no refuge for vulnerable human bodies—is felt acutely. It is a devastating awareness for parents—that there is no way to keep their children safe.

As we continue to accompany the ambulances, joining Palestinian paramedics as they risk their lives, daily, to respond to calls from those with no other life-line, our existence becomes temporarily narrowed down and focused on the few precious minutes that make the difference between life and death. With each new call received as we ride in ambulances that careen down broken, silent roads, sirens and lights blaring, there exists a battle of life over death. We have learned the language of the war that the Israelis are waging on the collective captive population of Gaza—to distinguish between the sounds of the weaponry used, the timing between the first missile strikes and the inevitable second—targeting those that rush to tend to and evacuate the wounded, to recognize the signs of the different chemical weapons being used in this onslaught, to overcome the initial vulnerability of recognizing our own mortality.

Though many of the calls received are to pick up bodies, not the wounded, the necessity of affording the dead a dignified burial drives the paramedics to face the deliberate targeting of their colleagues and comrades—thirteen killed while evacuating the wounded, fourteen ambulances destroyed—and to continue to search for the shattered bodies of the dead to bring home to their families.

Reading of these events while at the same time working on a book such as this left me, in a certain sense, with a feeling of the past colliding with the present, with Palestinian mothers such as Sabah Abu Halima forlornly emerging as modern day Rachels, weeping for their children. Ms. Abu Halima's home came under what appears to have been a white phosphorus shelling in early January. Her story was reported, oddly enough, by the *New York Times*—and that was one of the peculiar things about the Gaza war: that at least in terms of the *categories* and *types* of crimes committed, "mainstream media" seemed to verify much of what so-called "alternative" or "left wing" journalists such as Butterly were saying. Thus *Times* reporter Ethan Bronner reported on January 21:

> In Gaza Ms. Abu Halima said that when her family was hit, "fire came from the bodies of my husband and children."

"The children were screaming, 'Fire! Fire!' and there was smoke everywhere and a horrible suffocating smell," she said. "My 14-year-old cried out, 'I'm going to die. I want to pray.' I saw my daughter-in-law melt away."

Dr. Nafez Abu Shaban, head of Shifa's burn unit, said the family's burns, which he and an assisting doctor from Egypt had treated, were of a kind he had never encountered, reaching to the muscle and bone.

Despite such gruesome occurrences, *widely* reported, at least on the Internet, U.S. scholars maintained their silence. In this I'm not singling out only they of the Jesus Project, for that would be grossly unfair. The fact is, the vast majority of U.S. academics have had little to nothing to say about the Palestinian-Israeli conflict, a rather curious omission given the role played by our government in supplying the money and weapons that help perpetuate this festering sore. Yet the rule of silence is the one that seems to prevail whenever yet another armed conflict breaks out involving that Middle East country to which American taxpayers hand over an estimated three billion dollars per year, the same Middle East country that imposes a system of blockade and apartheid rule upon those it has colonized. This is not to say there haven't been some exceptions. There have. One which emerged during the Gaza siege, one who, sort of, in a roundabout way, broke the rule of silence, was Kenneth Ring, Professor Emeritus of Psychology at the University of Connecticut. During and immediately prior to the 22-day attack, Ring posted online two collections of excerpts from emails he had received from friends in Gaza, one entitled "Gaza Voices, American Silence," the second simply "Letters from Gaza." Both ended up making the rounds at a number of websites, including *Antiwar.com*, where site visitors were able to discern for themselves the tragedy then unfolding, as described in the words of those living it. One of Ring's correspondents wrote to him as follows:

Thank you so much for your concern and your noble feelings, I really appreciate them. You can say that I am fine but my people are not, you can never even imagine the destruction and the horror we're living in, circumstances are the worstest, we haven't had electricity for two days, and we just got some, It's actually 4 o'clock after midnight, and it is an awful night. F-16 planes are joining our children with their dreams or what have become nightmares.

Ring by the way is a prominent researcher into the phenomenon of near death experiences (NDE), having authored several books on the subject. Not surprisingly, the NDE issue has entered the theology debate. With literally thousands of these experiences reported, it would hardly stand to be otherwise. The reports typically involve an "out-of-body episode" in which NDEers experience a tunnel and a light, encounters with deceased loved ones, a life review, etc. Many have also spoken of coming into the presence of a spiritual entity, often described as bearing unconditional love toward them. Skeptics of course abound, and one favored argument is the neurological one. Thus Carol Zaleski writes in the *Oxford Handbook of Eschatology* (2008, Oxford University Press, p. 619):

> The second caveat is that the dying or nearly dying person is a fortress under siege, experiencing the mind-altering effects of drugs, anesthetics, sensory isolation and confinement, oxygen deprivation, or a host of other physiological and psychological stresses. Endorphins rush in to mute the pain and anxiety, sometimes resulting in ecstatic feelings; the temporal lobe creates a storm of fireworks, triggering panoramic replays of childhood memories and geometrically patterned visual hallucinations.

To such criticisms, NDE researchers have responded with accounts of "veridical" NDEs, episodes in which some aspect of the experience is verified by third-party testimony. A comatose patient, for instance, might later accurately report a conversation between doctors or nurses or even family members sitting out in the waiting room. In his book *Lessons from the Light*, co-authored with Swiss researcher Evelyn Elsaesser-Valarino, Ring relates the story of "Maria," a migrant worker who suffered cardiac arrest at Harborview Hospital in Seattle. The following day, having been resuscitated by doctors, she described for hospital social worker Kimberly Clark an out-of-body episode she underwent during the moments she was clinically dead. Maria claimed to have floated outside the walls of the hospital where at one point she became distracted by an object sitting on the ledge of the building's third floor—a tennis shoe. In considerable detail she described the shoe—it had a worn place in the little toe, and as it rested on the ledge, one of its laces lay tucked underneath the heel. Confused about the vision and desirous of knowing whether it had been real or simply a figment of her imagination, the patient pleaded with the hospital social worker to go and see if the shoe were there. Ring writes:

> I have been to Harborview Hospital myself and can tell you that the north face of the building is quite slender, with only five windows showing from the third floor. When Clark arrived there, she did not find any shoe—until she came to the middlemost window on the floor, and there, on the ledge, precisely as Maria had described it, was the tennis shoe.
>
> Now, on hearing a case like this, one has to ask: What is the probability that a migrant worker visiting a large city for the first time, who suffers a heart attack and is rushed to a hospital at night would, while having a cardiac arrest, simply "hallucinate" seeing a tennis shoe—with very specific and unusual features—on the ledge of a floor *higher* than her physical location in the hospital? Only an archskeptic, I think, would say anything much other than, "Not bloody likely!"

But for the archskeptics, it's still not enough—and in a strange sort of way the debate over NDEs mirrors that involving the historical Jesus.

Scientists would doubtless find Gaza fertile ground for NDE research, but as I write this, the world seems rather less interested in out of body episodes than war crimes. As 2009 wore on came the release of the 575-page Goldstone Report, implicating Israel in violations of the Geneva conventions, including strikes upon hospitals, civilian homes, and U.N. facilities. The report (predictably) was rejected by Israel, and repudiated (equally as predictable) by the trained seals of the U.S. Congress. As the year came to a close, Gaza remained under blockade, its people still unable to rebuild, and on December 11, a group of Palestinian Christians released *The Kairos Palestine Document*, presented as "a word of faith, hope and love from the heart of Palestinian suffering." The Greek word *kairos*, like the word *chronos*, means "time," but as opposed to *chronos*, which refers to chronological time, *kairos* designates a special, or opportune time. In the Gospel of John, in chapter 7 verse 6, the term is used twice, as Jesus speaks the words, "My time has not yet come, but your time is always here." The authors of the *Kairos Document* call upon peoples of the world to support the boycott, divestment and sanctions movement to end the occupation.

But to get back to the Gospels, how much of what they tell us can be regarded as historically accurate? Were they written by "artificers," as Eisenman terms it, people with "hate besotted brains" intent on promoting their own agendas through the creation of myths? Perhaps we should pose these questions from a slightly different perspective and ask, "How well, in terms of overall truthfulness, do the gospel writers stack up against, for instance, today's mainstream media? Could their minds be any more hate filled than the pundits who relentlessly pound the drums for one war after another?" Fables about Saddam Hussein's weapons of mass destruction and similar fictions have been cleverly sold to us. They continue to be sold to us. Can we, then, reasonably assign to the gospel authors more credibility at least than that? I think we can—which is not to say they got everything right. These were not journalists or historians in the modern sense (perhaps not a bad thing!), and certainly there are discrepancies in the different narratives they have left us. One thing we can say in their favor though is they did not advocate for war. On the contrary. If we take the quotes they attributed to Jesus as expressions of their own views, it would appear they would have us love our enemies and turn the other cheek.

But what are we to make of the virgin birth, the resurrection, or stories of Jesus performing miracles? What are we to make, for that matter, of the thousands of near death experiences reported? For those who have never experienced miracles in their own lives, the natural tendency is to believe such things cannot and do not happen. But for people like Maria, the notion that a man might heal the sick or walk on water is perhaps not that tough of a sell. Modern day Indian saints such as Paramahansa Yogananda have in fact told us similar stories.

Yes, it is true, there *are* passages in the New Testament which portray Jews negatively. It is also true that the Talmud contains tractates in which non-Jews do not fare especially well either, and that there are halakhic laws that "inculcate an attitude of scorn and hatred for Gentiles." (Israel Shahak, *Jewish History, Jewish Religion*, Pluto Press, p. 110). What is hoped for, of course, is that we might move beyond all of this, and to come to realize, before it is too late, that when we look into the eyes of another, we see ourselves. Something of the sort is indeed expressed in *The Memoirs of Saint John* by the aged Jewish hero of the story, to his young Gentile friend:

> This doing away of divisions amongst humanity, learning
> to love one another as brothers and sisters—it *must* come,

and it *will* come, for in a very real sense it is *inevitable*, Quintus. For when the sun is darkened, when the moon no longer gives off her light, and the stars fall from the sky, when *all* the tribes of the earth mourn, then the notion that we are Jew as opposed to Gentile, Greek as opposed to Roman, or this as opposed to that, will be seen for what it is—an *illusion*. And when that day comes, God, the God of love, will wipe the tears from the eyes of his children.

If we fail to do this, that is to see beyond these artificial separations, then we risk falling into an abyss, the vertigoes from which may be matched only by the human mind's rather considerable capacity for justifying evil, a trait that seems to run through all ethnic races and branches of humanity.

What seems clear, at least to my own satisfaction, is that *something* happened in the first century. We may not know exactly what. But whatever it was, it was sufficiently stirring to the human heart as to compel people to begin relating narratives about it, composing songs, giving public performances, and eventually putting it all together, the factual, the speculative, as well as the interpretive, into written texts, and here I'm referring to the texts which later made it into the New Testament, as well as the many that did not; the apocryphal stories as well as the Gnostic treatises; the gospels of Matthew, Mark, Luke and John, as well as those of Thomas, Philip, Mary, and the rest; the Sethians, the Valentinians, the orthodoxies, the heterodoxies, and the in-betweens. Added to the references to Jesus we find in the writings of Tacitus and Josephus and it becomes a sizeable body of evidence that "something" did indeed occur, and that people were moved in dramatic ways by it.

What I've tried to write in the main here is an historical novel. The premise that Jesus existed I've of course taken as a given. That he furthermore said and did things that upset people in authority also seems clear, and the radical champion of the poor is very much the sort of Jesus the reader will encounter in these pages. Other historical facts, such as the Emperor Tiberius' comment that, "Gorged horseflies suck less blood than fresh ones," are also weaved into the story, but as in the case of any novel of this type, the kernel of historic facts that underlie the story are combined with much that is purely the product of the author's imagination.

One other thing I feel obliged to mention is that I do not speak Aramaic, the native language spoken by Jesus, but there are a number of scholars who do, and three of these in the main I've relied on: Neil Douglas-Klotz, George

Lamsa, and Rocco A. Errico. The explication of the Lord's Prayer in chapter fifty-one is in fact drawn almost in its entirety from Douglas-Klotz's *Prayers of the Cosmos: Meditations on the Aramaic Words of Jesus*. It may come as a surprise to many westerners, but there are remarkable, almost uncanny, similarities between the different Semitic languages. Take, for instance, the respective words for God, the root for which is usually *El* or *Al*. In Old Canaanite we have the word *Elat*; in Hebrew, God becomes *Elohim*; in Aramaic, *Allaha*; and in Arabic, *Allah*. As Douglas-Klotz comments, "If this simple fact became better known, I believe there would be much more tolerance and understanding among those who consciously or unconsciously perpetuate prejudice between what are essentially brother-sister traditions."

I would also like to mention the work of Elaine Pagels. It was roughly eight or nine years ago I read her book, *The Gnostic Gospels*, stumbling upon a copy of it in my local public library, and it completely galvanized my thinking on early Christianity. But Pagels isn't alone. James M. Robinson's *The Nag Hammadi Library* is another valuable resource for those interested in learning more about the amazing diversity of early Christianity. Other scholars whose works I've found useful include Richard Bauckham, Helmut Koester, N.T. Wright, and Raymond Brown. I would be remiss if I did not also mention the website of Ramon Jusino, which too, as in the case of Pagels' *Gnostic Gospels*, I likewise stumbled upon quite by accident some years ago. His article, "Mary Magdalene: Author of the Fourth Gospel?", is what first got me to thinking about the Gospel of John possibly having been written by the woman whom, we are informed, went to anoint Jesus' body on the third morning after the crucifixion. It appears Jusino actually wrote the article in 1998, which would mean it would have preceded the publication of Dan Brown's *Da Vinci Code* by some five years. Essentially what Jusino does is make a strong case that Mary Magdalene, and not John the disciple of Jesus (or any of the numerous other possible candidates), was in reality the "Beloved Disciple" of the Fourth Gospel.

Christianity is a broad, multifaceted topic, but what it comes down to in a nutshell is *inclusion*. The teachings of Christ were and are a doctrine of inclusion, rather than exclusion. The kingdom of God was open to anyone who knocked. In the first through third centuries, that basic foundation, having been established, began to develop into many different strains and beliefs, but one thing they all seem to have shared in common is this characteristic of inclusiveness. Poor people, the dispossessed, even slaves, were welcome. Those in need were provided for. All of which probably accounts in no small part for the steady growth of the faith. Even the Gnostics, often lambasted for their "elitism," posed few barriers, or obstacles, to the extent that anyone seeking entry was willing to apply him-or-herself to the path of knowledge. The concept of Divine love for humanity had been born, and it was a powerful idea. Under "The Way," as Christianity initially was called, a poor widow with no more than two mites to her name could find herself more honored in the kingdom than a man of great wealth. Earthly wealth did not matter. It was of no consequence. For in the eyes of God we were all equal.

Richard Edmondson,
January 7, 2010

Scrolls

From the newswire of the Atlantic Media Corp.

[1]

Ancient scrolls
Discovered in Syria

DAMASCUS, Nov. 17—A cache of papyrus scrolls, possibly written by a contemporary of Jesus Christ, has been discovered by a British archaeological team working in Syria, near the border with Iraq, officials said yesterday.

The find is the result of an excavation spearheaded by the University of Martinsburg's highly renowned Department of Archaeology.

"It's an amazing find in its own right," said Dr. Arthur MacBride. "But if it proves to be as old as I think it is, it could well have some far-reaching implications for our understanding of the historical figure known as Jesus."

MacBride heads up a team working in eastern Syria at the site of Dura-Europos, which at one time was an ancient Roman garrison on the banks of the Euphrates River, near what is today the village of Salhiyé. Team members include students from several countries.

MacBride said the scrolls were found sealed inside a clay jar.

[2]

Scientists Date Text as
Possibly 1,900 Years Old

DAMASCUS, Dec. 12—Radiocarbon testing carried out on a papyrus scroll recently dug up in the Syrian desert has placed the artifact to within a hundred years of the time of Christ, scientists said.

According to Dr. Arthur MacBride, head of the Department of Archaeology at the University of Martinsburg, researchers have subjected the material to a radiocarbon analysis of the variety known as AMS, or accelerated mass spectrometry—a newer, more advanced method of dating archaeological discoveries.

"Our test results point to this article dating back more than eighteen centuries, possibly to some time around the late first or early second century of the current era," MacBride said.

The document purports to record certain events surrounding the life of Jesus Christ, as told from the point of view of one of the 12 disciples, MacBride said.

"Does that mean this is a genuine bona fide historical record written by none other than the *apostle John*? That's a question we don't have an answer to at this time."

[3]

Professor Hails Archaeological Discovery

GLASTONBURY, ENGLAND, Feb. 19—A set of ancient scrolls uncovered by a British team in the Syrian desert may be the find of the century.

So says Martin Kleesman, Professor of Ancient Christianity at Hollis College.

"This written manuscript is an extraordinary find," Kleesman said. "Its attention to detail goes far beyond anything we see in any of the gospels."

The scrolls were acquired by an archaeological team from Britain's University of Martinsburg.

"The incredibly rich texture of the narrative, the attention paid to detail—make it abundantly clear this is the work of an eyewitness to the events described," Kleesman said. "Essentially what we have here are the memoirs of a man who actually knew Jesus of Nazareth. The question then becomes who was he?

"If you are asking for my best guess—and that's all I can really give you— I would say he is exactly who he presents himself as in the manuscript: John, the son of Zebedee, the apostle of Christ," he added.

[4]

Experts Search for Clues
About Mystery Manuscript
As Controversy Heats Up

LONDON, March 8—Scientists and other experts continue to pore over a series of ancient scrolls that some have alleged challenge prevailing views of the historical Jesus.

Unearthed near the ancient settlement of Dura-Europos, on the Euphrates River, the find consists of a clay jar containing scrolls written in Greek.

"The scrolls are in rather good condition, although we had to go to Syria to carry out our work," said Enders Thenatakios, Professor of Classical Studies and Socio-linguistics at the University of Exeter, who has translated a portion of the text.

Thenatakios said the Syrian government has refused to allow the discovery, which has become the subject of growing controversy, to leave the country.

"They are written in the most beautiful of language, and the story they tell is extremely moving," said Thenatakios. "And I'm extremely upset at the censure of Professor Kleesman on this issue."

Professor Martin Kleesman was fired from the staff of Hollis College last week following published comments on the manuscript. Kleesman had theorized that the ancient author of the text was "exactly who he presents himself as," namely "John, the son of Zebedee, the apostle of Christ."

Hollis officials dismissed Kleesman's remarks as "ill considered" and based upon "irresponsible speculation."

Biblical Text Rests at Center
of International Dispute

DAMASCUS, March 12—Scholarly efforts to unravel the mystery of a series of scrolls, possibly written by an eyewitness to the crucifixion of Christ, collided with the realities of war and international politics yesterday.

Researchers believe the scrolls, discovered in Syria last year by a group from Britain's University of Martinsburg, date to the first or second century CE.

"Access to this artifact will continue to be made available to Dr. MacBride and his team of experts. In this we have pledged our full cooperation and assistance," said Ayman Daoud Sigrist, Syrian Minister of Culture. "But this discovery came from the Syrian land. It belongs to the Syrian people."

The find was made near what was once Dura-Europos, an ancient outpost of Rome that later fell to the Persians, and the scrolls have come to be referred to as the Dura-Europos scrolls. The area of Syria in question lies near its border with Iraq—a region U.S. officials charge has been used by foreign insurgents to infiltrate into Iraq.

The Syrian government has been on the receiving end of blunt U.S. criticism for its failure to stop the cross-border infiltrations.

Emerging after two hours of meetings with government ministers here, Dr. Arthur MacBride, head of the university's Department of Archaeology, said, "The dispute that has occurred is unfortunate, but I think at this point we have a working relationship, and I'd like to thank Minister Sigrist for the role he has played."

In addition to the international flare-up of the past week, the series of controversies surrounding the scrolls has included the firing of a Hollis College professor, and a frenzy of speculation in the British tabloid press.

"What's important now is that we get back to work," said MacBride. "People's reputations have been smeared. Also allegations have been raised regarding our methodology, particularly insofar as the dating of the document. I have requested additional testing that I hope will mollify the critics as well as lead to a greater understanding of this unusual find."

[6]

Clay Jar 1900 Years Old, say Scientists

LONDON, May 10—Scientists using a method known as thermoluminessence dating have determined that a clay jar uncovered from the Syrian desert was formed sometime around the end of the first century CE.

"We believe this pottery vessel was heated sometime around the year 100—give or take 25 years in either direction," said Dr. Sylvia Oneska of the University of Northampton.

The jar had contained ancient papyrus scrolls that reportedly describe certain events in the life of Jesus Christ, including the crucifixion.

"Up to now we had focused all of our attention on the manuscript," said Dr. Arthur MacBride, head of the British archaeological team which made the discovery. "But this test now gives us some insight into the clay vessel which contained the manuscript."

According to officials, thermoluminescence dating is especially suited to determining the age of pottery vessels.

"It works on the principle that soils and clay contain radioactive isotopes, such as uranium, in low concentrations," Oneska said. "The electrons in these minerals emit light after being heated."

Scientists then extract these light-emitting minerals from the pottery sample, stimulate them under laboratory conditions, and measure the luminescence.

"The temperatures involved range up to 500 degrees centigrade," Oneska said.

The unearthing of the Dura-Europos scrolls, purportedly written by a disciple of Jesus Christ, has been hailed by some as a discovery comparable in magnitude to that of the Dead Sea Scrolls.

Satellite News Network-Live Interview, June 18:

[7]

SNN Anchor, New York: Good evening, joining us live now from London is Dr. Arthur MacBride head of the Archaeology Department of Britain's University of Martinsburg. Dr. MacBride's team has come across a collection of scrolls that has been described as one of the most important archaeological discoveries since the Dead Sea Scrolls, and possibly having links dating all the way back to the time of Christ. Dr. MacBride, welcome.

Arthur MacBride, London: Thank you.

SNN: Dr. MacBride, place this into perspective for us—why is this such an important discovery and what does it tell us about the historical Jesus Christ?

MacBride: Well what we have here is an ancient manuscript that seems to tell a man's life story. It's the story of a man who lived in the first century, but it seems to have been put down on papyrus at a time when he was quite advanced in years.

SNN: There have been reports that this may have been written by one of Christ's disciples, what about that?

MacBride: The manuscript is written in classical Greek, by someone who was obviously well educated. The writer, that is to say he who put pen to papyrus, so to speak, is a man who identifies himself as a Roman citizen. He apparently was imprisoned for harboring dissident views of some sort against one of the emperors. When we say the writer of the manuscript, or perhaps a more accurate term would be scribe—*that's* the person we're speaking of. The manuscript itself tells the story of someone else, an individual who lived and traveled throughout much of the Roman Empire, and he may even have been present at the time it was written down, or the text would seem to suggest such. But in answer to your question—yes, it *does* purport to be the story of one of Christ's disciples. Again, however, I want to emphasize that we don't know for sure. The issue of lacunae, that is to say lines and words within the manuscript that are indecipherable due to erosion of the papyrus, is always a problem when you're dealing with a document

Scrolls/9

this old. But we have a team of experts, and one thing they have going for them is that the text is in remarkably good condition. The area from which it was recovered has a very dry climate, and consequently the scrolls, there are twenty-five of them, are extremely well preserved.

SNN: Can you tell us more about this area—because there have been charges coming from the U.S. State Department that some of these areas have been used by terrorists who've been smuggling weapons to the insurgents in Iraq?

MacBride: Well, I've been heading up an archeological dig at a site called Dura-Europos, in eastern Syria. As far as insurgents or terrorists using this area, I can't really testify other than to say I haven't seen any. But there's been a lot of confusion about where this artifact was found, and who it was found by, and I'd like to clear that up. The clay jar and the scrolls contained therein were not found by our team in Dura-Europos. The've been called the 'Dura-Europos Scrolls', mostly I think for lack of a better name. But the jar containing the scrolls was actually found by two Bedouin tribesmen in a remote region known as Sahl Khaba'ir al Hāmidah, part of which does indeed lie near the Iraq border. Now the jar and its contents ended up in our hands by means of the owner of a curio shop in Damascus, a kinsman of one of the tribesmen, who initially approached us at Dura-Europos and offered it for sale. There have been inaccurate reports in the media saying that we dug up the scrolls ourselves, but that is not the case, and I wanted to clear that up.

SNN: Thank you for helping us clarify that. So give us your opinion, Dr. MacBride, how does this discovery stack up against others that have come before? Is it as big of a find as, say, the Dead Sea Scrolls?

MacBride: Well that's hard to gauge, and I'm not a biblical scholar in any case, but yes, I would say this is a very important discovery. But again, keep in mind, the study of these texts is a process that will take time—we're talking years. The Qumran scrolls, that is to say the Dead Sea discoveries, surfaced in 1947, and there are scholars today who are still evaluating what they tell us.

SNN: Dr. MacBride, thank you for being with us on SNN.

MacBride: Thank you.

Email Correspondence:

Subject: International team

Date: June 24 12:21:52 – 0700

From: Arthur MacBride <amacbride@umartinsburg.co.uk>

To: Martin Kleesman <mkleesman943@hotmail.com>

Dear Dr. Kleesman:

After our phone conversation the other day, I began thinking about something and wish now I had brought it up with you. What is being put together is an international team of about 20 or so scholars which would operate perhaps under the aegis of UNESCO and the Syrian government. The purpose would be to thoroughly evaluate the text with, hopefully, a view toward gaining a better understand of what it tells us. The team would be comprised of scholars of various nationalities. The first order of business would be to put together an authoritative translation and publish it. I would like very much, if you're not involved in other pursuits, to consider being a part of this effort.

One scholar who will definitely be a part of the team is Dr. Dominic David LaSalle. He is American, a Jesuit, though he has spent most of his years in France, and currently is on teaching assignment in Rheims. We are in fact old friends, and spent a good bit of our youth rambling about together in the south of France. David is a priest, but one with a rich background in academia, and I trust him implicitly to keep the team's work free from the taint of politics and religious bigotry. I feel also you could be of great help to him in the realization of that goal.

The Syrians have requested to play a role in the team's work, though their main fear right now is of their country being attacked. One may well understand such concerns. The scrolls must be kept secured at all costs—this we have tried to impress on them, and to their credit they have spared no expense in this effort. Of course one must ask the question: how much control would they retain in the event an invasion of the country occurs? The ultimate nightmare scenario, at least from an archaeological standpoint (leaving aside the human catastrophe for the moment), would be a replay in Damascus similar to what occurred at the Baghdad Museum. Whatever happens, be it war or peace, the loss of this treasure would be unthinkable. I hope you will be able to join the team. Let me know of your decision.

Sincerely,

Arthur MacBride

Email Correspondence:

[9]

Subject: The Beloved Disciple and other matters

Date: June 26 01:42:45 –0800

From: Martin Kleesman <mkleesman943@hotmail.com>

To: Arthur MacBride <amacbride@umartinsburg.co.uk>

Dr. MacBride:

Again let me say thank you. Your support has meant a great deal to me in this difficult time, and I would happily assist in whatever manner I can. Your offer comes as a shining light in my present bleak circumstances. I've made applications to several teaching institutions, but so far have secured no offers of employment. I currently make ends meet by helping out in a bakery. Amazing as it seems, religious wars aren't fought only in places like Belfast and Baghdad. They can also be waged in the halls of academia.

It was a pleasure meeting you, and I, like yourself, greatly enjoyed our subsequent phone conversation. To elaborate on some of the questions you raised, first of all, it's widely accepted today that large portions of the Bible are pseudepigraphal, that is to say written by someone claiming to be someone else—usually a person more famous or influential. There were a variety of forms and methods of this. Take for instance the Pauline corpus in the New Testament. Many scholars today hold the letters of First and Second Timothy, Titus, Colossians, and Ephesians to be pseudo-Pauline.

There's no mystery here. Let's say you're an average sort of fellow, a quiet, unassuming chap, but you want to make the point that women shouldn't teach or hold authority over men, as the writer of First Timothy does. Well you write a letter saying women must be modest, submissive, never speak in assembly—you know, the usual—and sign Paul's name to it. That's one form of pseudepigraphy.

Another form would be that which results from the growing up of schools or communities around a central individual or wise teacher. A body of writing is produced purporting to be the wise man's actual words, spoken or penned by he himself. In reality, only *some* of it may be his, while the remainder could merely be the words of his adherents or followers, some of whom may not even have been born yet when the learned one breathed his last. Nevertheless it's presented as being, shall we say, "in the spirit of" the great man. No distinction would be made between this, and the words of the great man himself. It was quite a common practice. The Book of Isaiah, and particularly its component parts, Deutero- and Trito-Isaiah, are believed to have been produced in such a manner.

Whether we like to face it or not, redactors and editors, some of whom came along well after the fact, had an enormous hand in shaping the Bible into the form in which it comes to us today. Changing someone's written or spoken words, forging a well-known person's name—for people in the ancient world these were not by and large major integrity issues, and in fact were more or less in line with ancient notions of "authorship." That's not to say there weren't those who objected to such practices. There certainly were, and some most strenuously. Thus we have in the final chapter of the Book of Revelation the author calling down God's wrath upon anyone who might add or subtract from the words there written. Strong stuff, to be sure.

Now we come to the Gospel of John. A somewhat unusual piece of writing. It breaks the mold, so to speak. First of all the writer never identifies himself. In fact, the name "John" is never mentioned other than in reference to John the Baptist. But then appears a mysterious character, "the disciple whom Jesus loved," who *also* never is identified by name. In reading the gospel one generally assumes this "Beloved Disciple" to be the writer of the book. Christian tradition has long held that person to be John the son of Zebedee, the disciple of Jesus. But why? What internal evidence is there to suggest this might be the case? The answer is very little.

In fact, quite a bit of internal evidence would seem to point to the contrary. In chapter 18, on the night Jesus is arrested, Peter and an unnamed disciple—we presume it's the Beloved—follow Jesus, who is then in the custody of the soldiers. They go to the house of Caiaphas, the high priest. Peter at first is left standing outside. But the scripture tells us the unnamed disciple, being known at the house, not only is admitted but once inside is then able to persuade the person at the door to allow Peter in as well. The high priest was appointed by the Roman prefect—Pontius Pilate in the time we're talking about. Pilate was subordinate only to the Legate of Syria, who in turn answered directly to Caesar. So we ask ourselves: how did a poor fisherman's kid from Galilee come to have such connections in the household of the high priest? Who is, or was, the Beloved Disciple? Was he really John the son of Zebedee? Or possibly someone else? Could *he* in fact have been a *she*?

Intriguing yes, but there's more. Alone among the four gospels, the Gospel of John hints at a strong emotional bond between Jesus and Mary Magdalene, the suggestion of which has fired the imaginations of artists, writers, poets, and composers for centuries. Auguste Rodin depicted the two as lovers; Rainer Maria Rilke saw them as having a child together; Verdi and others have brought Magdalene-like characters to the opera stage; and the list could go on—all the way up to the latest pulp fiction bestsellers of today. People can be forgiven for latching onto the romantic viewpoint; it's the natural human tendency. But is there, in reality, any sound basis for supposing that Mary Magdalene, rather than John the son of Zebedee, was the Beloved Disciple? Certain Gnostic texts would seem to suggest there may be. The Gospel of Philip for instance, a late second-century Valentinian text, has her and Jesus kissing, apparently quite passionately.

But of course Mary isn't the only alternative to John the son of Zebedee as candidate for the title of Beloved. Scholars have also nominated Lazarus, John Mark, others have suggested a church elder also named John, and then we have the theory that it was really only a fictitious character, a sort of "idealized" follower of Jesus. But those who have postulated an actual historical figure, and that is probably the majority, tend to believe that, whoever it was, he/she was the founder of what today we think of as the "Johannine Community," the group of Christians which produced the Gospel of John. If so, it would tend to mean this 'Beloved Disciple' was indeed the gospel's author—"author," that is to say, at least, in the ancient sense of the word. This much we can assert with a fair degree of reliability.

But looking back on it, the Johannine Community, as a group, does not seem to have had an easy time of things. Evidence would suggest internal dissent. Some commentators, notably the late Catholic scholar Raymond E. Brown, have even theorized a schism occurring over a number of issues, the group's relationship to Judaism for one, as well as whether Jesus was human or God. In Brown's thesis, the split most likely occurred in the latter first century, probably after the death of the Beloved Disciple, with one party of adherents gravitating toward the orthodox branch of the church, while the other— Brown believed the larger in number—went over to the Gnostics. Interesting grist for the mill perhaps, but of course the question still remains—*who* was the Beloved Disciple? Why was that person's name deliberately redacted out? It's a mystery that has lingered for centuries. Postulations and guesses are all we can offer today. But is it possible, we might now ask, that the Gnostics had it right all along, that it was indeed Mary Magdalene?

The *Gospel of Philip* isn't the only Gnostic tract to assign a key role to Mary. In *Pistis-Sophia* she becomes "the inheritor of the light," while the *Gospel of Mary* has her consoling the grieving, fearful disciples following the crucifixion, and in *Dialogue of the Saviour*, she is elevated into "the woman who knew the all," the one who reveals the "greatness of the revealer." Could the Johannine Community possibly have been founded by such a individual? If so, it would mean the Fourth Gospel was authored by a woman—and herein we perhaps have a motive at last for the redacting out of the Beloved Disciple's name. Would the early Church ever have accepted a gospel from a female author? The answer is unequivocally no. It would not have mattered that the woman herself may have passed away some years previous. As we read in First Corinthians, the head of every man is Christ, and the head of every woman is the man. A gospel authored by a woman, and a group whose founder and spiritual leader was a woman, would have been deemed irremediable and of scant worth.

Of course the irony here is that the gospels depict none other than Jesus himself as holding egalitarian views toward women. Take yourself back 2,000 years. It's early morning of the third day after the crucifixion. The resurrection, arguably the most important event in human history, if indeed it occurred, has just taken place. Out of all possible candidates, to whom does the newly-arisen Christ first choose to reveal himself? Why, Mary Magdalene, of course. But wait. Take yourself back even further, let's say a year or so. Jesus delivers the Sermon on the Mount, a remarkable address for a lot of reasons, although especially striking is the manner in which he completely overturns traditional thinking on the sin of adultery. Whoever looks upon a woman in lust, he tells the crowd, has already committed adultery with her in his heart. The upshot, as the scholar Susan Haskins has noted, is that it places the burden of the sin upon the beholder, rather than upon she who is beheld, essentially shattering the "woman as temptress" stereotype. And of course we read of women followers, some of whom supported the group financially. From all the evidence, it's hard to imagine that Jesus would ever, in a million years, have issued a decree forbidding women from speaking aloud in his church. Yet by early second century this was precisely the direction in which the church was headed.

By contrast, the Gnostics were far more disposed to equality between the sexes, and some even seem to have had women leaders, which may be why the orthodox wing of the church so despised them. Early church fathers, such as Irenaeus and Hippolytus, had absolutely nothing to say in their favor. In fact, up until 1945 most of what we knew about the Gnostics came from these, their chief enemies—the so-called "heretic hunters" of the early church. But then in 1945 came the discoveries at Nag Hammadi in Egypt, a veritable "library" of written tracts produced by the Gnostics themselves. Suddenly, for the first time, the "heretics" were able to speak for themselves. The result? The modern age made the discovery that Christianity in its formative years was infinitely, *infinitely* more diverse than ever previously suspected. And now comes your discovery in Syria, which, unless I miss my guess, stands to shake up the world as much, if not more.

Finally in closing, I'll address one other point just briefly, namely the crucifixion and the role played in it by Pontius Pilate. Rome of course was the imperial occupation power. No one, but no one, wanted to get on their bad side. In pondering the crucifixion we must remember above all that this was an execution ordered by the highest Roman official in the land. Accounts of the event would need to have been handled very delicately. To say this wasn't on the minds of the New Testament writers is to be willfully naïve. Thus in the gospels, Pilate comes across as a mostly-benevolent buck-passer, bowing to the will of the Jews, mainly in the interest of preserving order. Yet this picture of the man is sharply at variance with one provided by Herod Agrippa I, who in a letter to Caligula characterized Pilate as "inflexible by nature and cruel because of stubbornness." Agrippa and Caligula were friends. They grew up together in Rome. Would Agrippa perhaps have felt freer to speak candidly about this man, Pontius Pilate, than the gospel writers? Moreover, when Agrippa accuses Pilate of "graft, insults, robberies, assaults, wanton abuse, constant executions without trial, unending grievous cruelty" might we not perhaps at least give it equal weight with the accounts left by the gospel writers, who seem to find no particular fault with the Roman governor? None of this of course is new. These are all arguments which have been made in the past and which might logically also explain the negative portrayal of the Jews we find in the gospels, which for the most part were written in the years just after the first Jewish revolt.

Of course the tapestry here is rich, and all we can do as scholars is examine one small section at a time and try and formulate some assumptions. It's hit or miss. Mostly, or in all too many cases, *miss*. And the notion that we will ever be able to step back and examine the tapestry as a whole, in all of its grandness, is probably nothing more than wishful thinking—although these scrolls you have come across do seem, on the surface of things, to add an interesting, heretofore unnoticed perspective.

Sorry for rambling on so, but I hope this has been of some help. Again many thanks for the opportunity to be a part of the international team. I look forward to working with Dr. LaSalle.

Sincerely,

Martin Kleesman

LaSalle 1

Rheims, France

Dr. Dominic David LaSalle, SJ, ended his last class of the day by winding up his lecture on Manichaeism and the Sassanid Empire and giving his students an assignment. Then he closed the window and announced, "class dismissed." The captive audience that was his 2 o'clock period wasted no time liberating themselves from their desks, a few quite literally leaping to their feet.

"*Je vous verrai Lundi*, I will see you Monday—and do not forget your exam." He added with wry humor: "*Si vous savez ce qui est bon pour vous*, if you know what is good for you."

The toiling young scholars responded with good-natured smiles, along with a melodramatic chorus of groans, as they clustered out the door, until at last he stood alone in his classroom. Pausing for a moment, he slipped his notes in his satchel, zipped it, and made his way out to the corridor, at last exiting the building through the outer courtyard and setting a diagonal course across campus. Dressed in collegiate khaki and tweed, with soft-soled shoes, he didn't look like a Jesuit priest, but then he had never cared for clerical collars and priestly black garb, leaving such outfits at home in the closet whenever possible. Besides that, it was July, a time of year far too warm for starched vestments. Leaving campus, he soon found himself in the thick of the city of Rheims. Even in the heat of summer, the air in this part of France seemed to have a robust, slightly tingly quality, a gentle reminder perhaps of the region's most famous product: sparkling wine. The Champagne-Ardenne area of northeastern France—it was five years ago he had taken his teaching assignment here, and in that time he had come to view it as home. Something about it, he had to admit, grew on you.

Dominic David LaSalle was the offspring of a French father and American mother. He held dual citizenship in both countries, and while he was fond of America, he had adopted France as his home long ago. His life was here. Here he had achieved considerable success in academia. Being the author of three books on ancient Christianity, also numerous articles in scholarly journals, had earned him something of a respite from the "publish or perish" pressures that normally beset university professors. Now, in his mid forties, he had to admit he had arrived at a station in life he found comfortable and satisfactory.

Of course, it had not always been that way. During and after his tertianship he had served with a Jesuit-run refugee center in Thailand. Four years. It was a time that had tested both his faith and his stamina. What could a small group of people do when inundated like that? Simply cope the best they could. Mostly it had been Karen tribal people, fleeing the military junta from across the border in Burma. The poverty, the hunger, the dazed look in the eyes—it had given him a certain perspective as he came face to face with injustice on a scale vaster and more monstrous than anything he would ever see in civilized France. Yet somehow those simple people kept on, unbowed. Where did they gain such strength? It had humbled him, and it had also brought him closer to God, closer in a way he had never imagined possible, for there was, it seemed to him, something perpetually surrounding and guarding the human spirit from the powers of this world that seek to beat it down. That "something" might perhaps be thought of as a transom bridge, a transom which led the journeyer safely through a wall of fire. How else could you explain the ability of those simple people to carry on? But yes, it had humbled him. And he had sought to learn from them, to gather their spiritual and psychological resources and make them his own. He had also learned the art of Buddhist meditation, finding it wholly compatible with the writings of such Christian mystics as Meister Eckhart and Teresa of Avila. LaSalle, in short, had emerged from Thailand a different person. Even his friends had remarked the change. But then that was what life was all about, was it not?—changing and growing.

Crossing the Canal de la Marne and entering the Quartier Courlancy, almost like a drop of water into a fountain, he paused at the Chaussée Bocquaine, waited for the light to change, and then crossed into the park, wondering as he did so if he would meet the "elderly jogger" today. He found himself here most days around this time. It was a verdant place, where one could stroll and ruminate, yet on his excursions, he almost invariably encountered the "elderly jogger." The priest thought of him by this name for he knew him by no other. But for weeks now they had run upon each other, quite by happenstance. LaSalle had never spoken to the man, not really, or he to him, yet after so many encounters, and always by blind chance, they had come to the point of never passing each other without exchanging greetings.

There was a human, almost comical, element to it. It's funny how people's daily habits become so set. Here he knew virtually nothing of this man, yet their respective schedules brought them irretrievably to this spot in the city of Rheims at precisely the same time every day; it was also funny how someone could become a part of your life without your ever even knowing their name. LaSalle looked for him...and sure enough, there he was! The man was elderly. That was no exaggeration. In his seventies at least. As he jogged, there was an about-to-run-out-of-steam-any-minute quality to his gait which you would certainly expect from one his age. Yet undeterred by waning strength or long-gone youth, he was out here every day, jogging, pumping his spindly legs, with a haggard determination LaSalle could not help but admire. As he approached, the Jesuit flashed his warmest smile, a smile that seemed to say, "Yes, here we are again today!"—a sentiment reflected back through the elderly jogger's own smile, which always, somehow, managed to arise through the vortex of his strained exertion.

"Bonjour."

"Hi again!"

And then all in a single, magical, summer's moment, they were past each other, continuing on their respective ways. "I only hope I am in that good of shape when I get to be his age!" he thought.

LaSalle had an abiding love for the French people. They were warm, generous, and sincere once you got to know them, although he had taken a merciless ribbing from his French friends after "freedom fries" fever had swept America. Bottles of French wine dumped into gutters, cafeterias and restaurants changing their menus, deleting the word "French" before "fries", almost as if it were France, and not Iraq, America was preparing to invade— the news had given it all a fair amount of play, and his friends had made merry at his expense. "Eat your freedom fries, David! *Mon bon camarade*! It is every American's duty!"

Smiling, he had sometimes reminded them he was only *half* American, though of course it had all been in good fun. Moreover, he had to admit that in the cross-Atlantic insult game the French had given back as good as they had gotten, renaming American cheese "idiot cheese." But all that had been in the prelude to war, and it had been followed by the ongoing bloodbath of the war itself; the French government, to the relief of the majority of France's citizens, had stayed out of it.

Leaving the park, he sauntered for some ways down the Rue de Courlancy, coming at last to the orphanage, which had been his destination all along. It was a Jesuit orphanage, the only one in this part of France. Entering the glass front doors, he strolled through the foyer past the great, gleaming cross on the wall, looked about for Sister Denise, spotting her finally, holding a clipboard, by the unlocked brass cabinet fixture. Clad in a soft, beige turtleneck, she was in her early forties, with hair cut short and sloping down her studied forehead. Her whitened nails tightly gripped the barrel of an ink pen, but as he drew near, she looked up from her clipboard and smiled. "David." It was one of those tireless smiles one occasionally encounters, a smile that seemed to support heaven by means of its ability to nourish so many. He had a great deal of esteem for this woman, the work she did, and her own unique brand of renunciation.

"How is she today?" he asked.

"Doing very well and in good spirits." Sister Denise placed the clipboard on a countertop next to a vase of flowers and began to walk beside him. "Though as always looking for you, and hoping this will be one of your days to visit." They were discussing one of the wards of the orphanage, and the word "looking" was to be taken figuratively, for the girl in question was blind. Born with a congenital defect, she had never known sunshine other than as a sensation of warmth on her skin, never known, except by touch, the face of her mother, a French actress who had committed suicide. Now at the age of thirteen, Cateline had spent the last four years of her life here at the orphanage. As for her father, nothing was known of him, not even his nationality, though LaSalle had made concerted efforts to find out something of the man, who he was, if he were still alive, but to no avail. It seemed the mother had made some concerted efforts of her own—to cover up his identity. The father's name had been left off the birth records, apparently deliberately.

LaSalle and Sister Denise walked the bustling corridor, coming at last to the large day room. Brightly decorated, it housed some twenty-five children who at first glance appeared normal as any. Upon closer inspection, however, the casual observer noticed most were affected with a disability of some sort. This, however, did not prevent them engaging in a variety of games and play, for such is the irrepressible adaptability of the very young. And something else one noticed: the facility had the highest of standards. Though many of these youngsters suffered from the two-fold disadvantage of being orphaned as well as having special needs, these were some of the best-cared-for children in France. Sister Denise had seen to that. She was a nurse by training, and LaSalle had been instrumental in recruiting her as chief administrator.

So many children, each with a unique story, each with a precarious thread to a place of his or her own in the wider world—yet there was one child in particular LaSalle had come to see. He paused, glanced around, past the great monstrosity of a potted palm in the center of the room, a stately and metabolizing presence which had grown up with an enduring resilience and become a deliberative and attending spirit, spreading its frondage until it created its own little sacred lodge in the center of the room where children sometimes played games of hide-and-seek—paused, yes, until he saw her, just beyond the plant, beyond the game table, beyond the cappuccino-shaded settees, her frail, inconspicuous form somehow, as usual, not completely commensurate to the surroundings. Upright she sat, propped in a chair by the open window, alone. Sister Denise called out, "Cateline, you have a visitor!"

The girl brightened. "It's Père David! I know it is!"

"*Oui* Cateline," LaSalle answered.

"I *knew* it was you!!!"

"And how did you know that?"

"I heard you coming. I always know your footsteps."

"I don't see how you can hear *anything* above the thunder of that TV set," the priest quipped in mock disapproval. There was indeed a television in the room, usually on this time of day, a large screen Toshiba occupying one wall of the day room. Monopolizing its remote control, the group of children seated about it seemed oblivious to whomever they might be drowning out.

"You forget," Cateline replied. "I have *very* sharp ears! It's only my eyes that are useless!" She reached a pair of trembling hands toward the sound of his voice, doing so with a fetching luminosity that was almost part of the curvature of her lovely and childlike face. LaSalle knew of course what she was reaching for: his hand. Obligingly he gave it. "I am *so* glad you are here, Père David! It has been a wonderful day. Sister Denise and I went for a walk, and I have so much to tell you!"

"Well you must tell me all about it, and don't leave anything out!" *Only my eyes that are useless.* Jokes at her own expense—it was her particular brand of humor, part of her patter and charm, and though she was a beautiful child, LaSalle knew she had virtually zero chance of being adopted. Something else he knew as well: she had developed an emotional attachment to him, a tie of affection she had shaped and fashioned carefully out of the raw material of her penumbral darkness, adorning it with all the embellishments she could conjure and conceptualize. It was an attachment which ran deep—*too* deep, LaSalle had reflected more than once. *Too* deep given his teaching duties, his devotion to the priesthood. Of course, such bonds of affection were not uncommon among children here. She had sought in essence to make him her substitute father. Many orphans developed such fixations, and usually it was nothing to grow concerned about. But why him? This had puzzled him. There were other staff members around. Other male staff members, and yes even other priests. Yet for LaSalle and LaSalle alone she seemed to dream away the hours. Or, that is to say, for he and Sister Denise alone, for her attachment toward him seemed in some way to have made a horizontal trajectory outward to include the orphanage director as well. Within Cateline's young heart, there dwelled the surreal imagining that he and Sister Denise would one day get married and become her real parents. A child's infatuation, to be sure. But there it was. And of course both he and Denise were aware of it. Moreover, it was not as if they had not grown fond of her. They *had*, and both had begun to cast about for ways of making her life better, but neither knew how, and part of the problem lay in the fact there was more going on with Cateline, other forces clashing inside her body, than sightlessness alone. Even more disturbing, the doctors had no explanation or answer for the bizarre symptoms she had shown.

"Why don't we go out on the terrace?" suggested Sister Denise. "It will be much quieter."

"That is a *great* idea!" LaSalle answered, injecting a note of hearty concurrence. The girl smiled agreeably, fumbling for her cane, while the Jesuit resisted the temptation to assist her. Always, he thought, there was this urge to offer an arm, an elbow, help in some form, but he knew it was counterproductive, and he knew also she was fully capable of maneuvering around the orphanage on her own, had even managed excursions on the street. Tapping tentatively at first, she turned toward Sister Denise, then to LaSalle, and together the three made their way out onto the open-aired terrace.

"Père David?"

"*Tout' à vous.*"

"Did you know that in reality *no one* ever escaped from the Château d'If?" With a coy smile, she tapped her way along until they reached the latticed deck chairs.

"Is that right?" As they seated themselves, he wished there were some way she could see the bright, ambrosial sprinklings of flowers around the terrace, to know, or at least have some idea, of the companionable diorama of her surroundings.

"Yes that's right. I'm reading *The Count of Monte Cristo*."

"The Count of *Monte Cristo*?" LaSalle shot Sister Denise a quizzical glance.

"Yes, well...it–it was what she *wanted* to read..." the sister shrugged, "so I procured it from the Braille Library."

He quipped, "You couldn't have just found her an audio book?"

"David stop!" she laughed. "It had to be Braille. You *know* she must practice reading. She is in Grade 2 Braille now and she has to work at it."

"Okay, okay, so it's *The Count of Monte Cristo*. Are you enjoying it?"

"Yes, very much!" Cateline replied mater-of-factly. "But when I get through with it I want to read one of *your* books, Père David."

"One of *my* books? Oh, I don't know...I think compared to Monsieur Dumas you would find my books quite boring!"

"Nonetheless, I want to read one! I want to read them all!"

"Listen I have some work to do." Sister Denise smiled, beginning to rise. "You two enjoy your visit." Something about the sister's body was both hard and soft, her movements graceful as she rendered stillness into motion, LaSalle watching her walk away for a moment before turning his attention back to the girl. The latter, with a matchless exuberance, described the plot twists in *The Count of Monte Cristo* before transitioning, with hardly a pause, into the outing she and Sister Denise had made earlier in the day.

"And we went all the way to the Esplanade Capucins!"

"And was it very crowded?" he asked.

"Yes, there were many people about, and birds—I could hear birds. I think they must soar with a heavenly light, Père David, and when they fly, the clouds part for them and simply let them go by. That is how I imagine it. Imagine being a bird, Père David! Imagine having wings, and being able to find the sun by means of the trees!"

She seemed reasonably happy, and in fact LaSalle had often noted her behavior in general, other than a persistent aloofness from the other children, was not so unlike any other thirteen-year-old girl. So where, he wondered, had the mania, the depression, and the rest of it come from? What had brought them on so suddenly and why had they passed equally as suddenly? But most crucially, what strange thing had caused the bleeding from her eyes? If there were no medical answers, what then *were* the answers? Or, stated differently, were there perhaps answers from which the doctors, as well as he and Sister Denise, had deliberately turned away?

It had been three years ago, in the early part of December. The girl had commenced to grow sharply withdrawn—not unusual in orphaned children with recollections of lost family members. Depression, said the psychiatrist. Medication was prescribed. But the symptoms had not only persisted, they had grown worse. By middle of the month, the depression gave way to manic episodes, in which Cateline grew increasingly agitated. The medication was increased, but again the symptoms worsened, morphing at last into scarcely-fettered screaming, her natural loveliness, as if dragged far away from comity's reach, giving way to a mask of terror. In attempting to keep her calm, the staff had provided even-handed, round-the-clock attention. But wits' end had quickly been reached. Then it began happening. *Whoever knows the truth is free.* Cateline, in her more lucid periods, would talk of "seeing" a wall; moreover, in her description of it, the wall contained "faces of the dead." But such moments of seeming coherence gave way to fits of screaming, which could continue for minutes or hours. Eventually, however, calmness would return, at which she would again speak of the wall she claimed to be able to see. But was not the girl blind? What "wall" was she talking about? How could she "see" anything? Yet a detailed description she was able to supply. A vast wall. Faces of dead people in the wall. Some of the faces decomposing in putrefaction. Very clear, she insisted.

Clear to her perhaps, but thoroughly mystifying to everyone else. The doctors dismissed it as a phobia. But then on the morning of December 25 events took a bizarre turn. That was when the bloody tearing started. Cateline began to cry ceaselessly, but mixed with the tears was bright red blood. Sister Denise called him at home and he rushed over, finding her screaming and thrashing, the front of her shift soaked with blood. Torrents of it had seeped from her eyes. Her pillow and bed linens had been changed twice, and staff were about to change them again. It was as if she had been dragged into the midst of a nightmare. A *bloody* nightmare. Promptly they had taken her to hospital.

The tearing persisted through Christmas day. On December 26, a doctor at the hospital had begun a complete workup. It was the same day an earthquake, its epicenter far away on the other side of the planet, generated a tsunami in the Indian Ocean in what became one of the deadliest disasters in human history. More than 200,000 people were killed.

The doctor had at first suspected diabetes, though this was ruled out, at which point specialists were called. But even for the specialists, diagnosis proved elusive. The blood from her eyes appeared dangerously low in clotting particles, and immediately a type II platelet disorder was suspected, but subsequent tests ruled that out. More specialists were called, whereupon it was thought the girl suffered from a condition known as von Willebrand disease, a disorder of the bloodstream characterized by a deficiency of a protein called von Willebrand factor, or vWF. Samples of Cateline's blood plasma were examined in an effort to determine both amount and functionality of the vWF protein, but again nothing out of the ordinary turned up. "We did a conjunctival biopsy with imaging, ran blood and coagulation profiles, checked serum and hormone levels, and ran a Factor VIII analysis. Everything turned up normal. We've been able to determine no cause for Cateline's condition."

In the end, the doctors had probed and irrigated the nasolacrimal system and sent her back to the orphanage. LaSalle had heretofore taken an interest in the girl, her avid nature, so much like a stalk of grass, her ability to negotiate her independence and breach the walls of her blindness in ways some would find remarkable, but at this point she began increasingly to occupy his thoughts. What was wrong with her? If there was no medical explanation, what *was* the explanation? The bloody tearing, of course, brought to mind all those ridiculous stories one hears about statues of the Virgin Mary and suchlike. But this was no statue. Cateline was a living human being.

The bleeding eyes and the rest of the symptoms continued with a winding crookedness, weaving in and out through periods of relative calm, over the next month, but then in early February it stopped. Without warning, with no clear reason, the symptoms ceased. The media at this time continued carrying news of the devastation suffered in the Asian countries struck by the tsunami, a terrible tragedy of course, yet so wrapped up in his university schedule had he been, not to mention concerns over the girl, that LaSalle had followed events on the other side of the globe sporadically at best. But suddenly one day, on the Internet, his attention was drawn to a photo on a web site, a photo of a wall. The picture, according to the caption, had been shot outside a police station in Sri Lanka. The wall was covered with what at first appeared to be a jumble of shadows and blots, though after a moment these resolved themselves before LaSalle's eyes into human faces. Men's faces, women's faces, even children. But something was amiss, for the faces did not look normal, and in fact they weren't. They were the faces of corpses. The tsunami had exacted an enormous toll in human life. With death on such a massive scale, authorities had taken to photographing the bodies and then disposing of them with quick burial. But then, with the aim of helping family members identify missing loved ones, the photos were posted on the wall outside the police station. LaSalle stared at the gut-wrenching image in disbelief. A wall containing *the faces of the dead*. He blinked, looked away, but his eyes raced back to the image. It was as Cateline had described it, down to every detail. Though blind from birth, had the girl nonetheless somehow "seen" the wall in Sri Lanka? Moreover, had she seen it from a distance of *space* as well as *time*, for of course, as he remembered, she had begun speaking of the wall before the tsunami had even struck?

In eastern spiritual traditions, human beings are believed possessed of a *chakra*, or spiritual center, thought to lie at the center of the forehead between the eyebrows. The *Ajna chakra*, as it's called, though others have referred to it as the "third eye." Ostensibly, through deep meditation, it is possible to open this eye, and in doing so, one attains to an ultimate state of awareness, the realization of a spiritual world said to exist beyond the senses. Some have called it "god consciousness," others "Krishna consciousness." Buddhists think of it as "Nirvana," a place of eternal and incomprehensible peace, yet at the same time comprising the ultimate reality, a point or place of being separate from the spurious world of ignorance and illusion. Medical science of course looks askance at anything pertaining to "spirit" or "god," yet even medical science speaks of a "proto-eye" within the brain, represented by the pineal gland, believed to be a vestigial remnant of a larger organ, much in the same way the appendix is thought of as the evolutionary remnant of a larger digestive organ. Or an "atrophied third eye," as the pineal has come to be thought of in popular mythology. This *glandula pinealis*, as the Latin would have it, is cited in the voluminous medical writings of the ancient Greek, Galen. The Renaissance philosopher Descartes had called it "the principle seat of the soul." Others have drawn similarly imaginative conclusions.

Was Cateline's third eye (assuming such a thing even exists) opened at the time of the tsunami? And was this the means by which she had seen the wall in Sri Lanka? Was such a thing possible? Or was it all a coincidence? LaSalle was inclined to believe the latter, though at the same time he had no answers for any of it, the bloody tearing, the mania, her speaking of the vision she had presumably seen. He had had none then. And he had none now.

"Listen, Cateline. I have enjoyed our visit greatly, but I'm afraid it's time I must go."

"Oh please, Père David, not yet!"

"Now, now, no arguing. And besides that, it is dinner time and I would not want you to miss your dinner on my account. Would you like me to walk with you down to the dining room?"

"That would be nice, Père David! And Père David?"

"Yes Cateline?"

"Any time you want to take my arm it's okay." She fixed upon him her wide yet unseeing eyes, at the same time injecting into her voice a discreet note of confidentiality as she whispered, very adult-like, "I know you sometimes think you shouldn't help me get around, but *really* it is okay. In fact, anytime you wish to offer me your arm, I would *very* much like it if you did so."

"We shall see," he said, overcome with renewed amazement at how much of the world she was able to sense and understand—and then he held out his arm.

Together down the corridor they walked. "Will you come back sometime this weekend?" she asked.

"I will try."

"Promise?"

"I promise I will try. That is all the promising you're going to get out of me now!" She grinned, counting it a victory.

Yes, he wished he could help her, and in some more substantial way than offering an arm. But how? Here she had the best available care. What else was to be added beyond that? The most he could ever seem to do was visit, say goodbye, and promise to return, but somehow the girl seemed to regard it as more than sufficient.

LaSalle stopped at the office on his way out, finding Sister Denise once again absorbed in her paperwork. He didn't intend to stay long. Hearing him enter, she looked up, remarked, "I have two new children coming in tomorrow. That's going to put us at maximum capacity."

"Better that than nine over as it was in March."

She smiled ruefully. "They *do* seem to keep coming, don't they?"

An attractive woman, Sister Denise. Yet even in the warmth of her smile, he had always sensed something reserved about her. LaSalle knew she was dedicated to her work, and that for all intents and purposes she existed wholly and completely for the children in her care.

"I am going to London in a few weeks," he said. "I don't know exactly how long I shall be away; it could be a matter of weeks, it could be longer."

"That won't be easy for you-know-who."

"Yes I know. It can't be avoided though. I've committed to helping the British research this thingy-ma-bob they've stumbled upon in Syria."

"Oh that scroll thing—yes it's been on the news."

"I won't be leaving for a while yet, but before I go I'll give you a number where I can be reached in London, and you've got my cell; and if we go into Syria, which I anticipate we'll do, I'll keep you posted." He turned and started to leave. "If anything should come up here do not hesitate to give me a call."

"I will. Goodnight David."

"Goodnight Sister."

"And David?"

He turned, "Yes Sister?"

"You look tired. Try and get some rest."

With a grin and a wave, he turned once more toward the door.

Home at his flat, LaSalle brewed a cup of coffee, seated himself comfortably in his cramped kitchenette, and began to sip at the steaming liquid. Sister Denise had been correct. He *was* tired. For the past three weeks, he had labored on a translation of the scrolls Arthur and his team had acquired in Syria. It had been exhausting work, but as he sipped the pleasing brew he had whipped up on his stove burner, he began now to feel rejuvenated. He always took his coffee black. It was one American habit he had yet to cast off, and never planned to. In the mornings, of course, but also invariably a cup in the evening as well—he always made time for it, and never worried about it keeping him awake. He was a night owl anyway, and didn't plan to be in bed for hours yet. The coffee was a rich roast, and as he drank, he ruminated on the girl, the mysterious scrolls, and a host of other things. Across the room, over by the closet door, an amorphous quantity of newspapers and magazines, some out of date by as much as a year, smothered his worn-out armchair, hiding very nearly from sight its arms, seat, and back. The unruly heap needed to be tidied, or better yet disposed of altogether, but it was a task that always got put off. From somewhere in the middle of the boggy mass, a picture of the pope stared out. Whatever one might say about the Holy Father, it could not be claimed he lacked scholarly grounding or that he was an unintelligent man. Yet from the start there had been fears over the direction he would lead the church, fears that in large part had been unfounded. For most of a year, a certain papal predilection for Gucci sunglasses seemed the most the media could find and fixate upon or chatter about. But then had come the inexplicable speech in Budapest in which the pontiff had managed to inflame the passions of virtually the entire

Muslim world. There had been criticisms, criticisms that were well justified, said some, but of course the church survived. Moreover, LaSalle's opinion of the pope had not really changed. While the Holy Father may have his faults, he was at heart a good man. This LaSalle felt sure of.

But the priest had more on his mind just now; finishing his coffee, he placed the cup in the sink, strode into the sitting room, and powered on the computer. Then with two fingers, he keyed the brass switch on his old Tiffany desk lamp. Old—yet still colorful and bright. It had once belonged to his father, a family heirloom he had hung on to for practical as well as sentimental reasons. Attendantly now it cast a wedge of pastel light over his keyboard and papers as he waited for the computer to boot up. His friend, Arthur MacBride, had posted photographic facsimiles of the papyrus scrolls. Other than the various lacunae, the documents had been clear enough to read. The neat, two-inch stack of copier paper on the desk beside his monitor represented his English translation of the text thus far. He had printed the stack out before leaving for campus this morning and intended mailing it off to Arthur first thing tomorrow. Even though LaSalle planned being in London, possibly as soon as next month, he knew it was desirable Arthur get his hands on this material right away. Much was at stake.

LaSalle was a specialist in Greek and Semitic languages. The papyrus scrolls had been written in classic Greek, and while he had had little trouble deciphering them, he knew that what lay before him was not necessarily a definitive translation; other scholars on the team would need to be consulted, and major disputes could, and often did, break out over the translation of a single word. It was simply the nature of the business. So no, what he had was not definitive—but it was close. Briefly, he thought of alternatives to sending the text by mail. He could email the files, or save them in PDF format and post them online. That way Arthur could click on them at his leisure. But he decided against it. Putting this material on the internet, even on a secured page, risked the possibility of someone unauthorized gaining access, and what he had rendered into English was potentially too explosive for such a risk. He looked at the stack again. The media reports had essentially been right. The document *purported* to be the life story of John, the son of Zebedee, the disciple of Christ, but was it really? That Hollis College professor had possibly been right. The ancient text may well be exactly what it claims, though of course it had not been especially wise to make the statement he had. The answer may never be known conclusively, and certainly it was unprofitable to speculate until a *lot* more study was done. A trip to Damascus, by LaSalle and the other team members, would undoubtedly be in order. The scrolls themselves, as opposed to the facsimiles, should be examined in minute detail, every square centimeter of every stem, piece and section. A further excursion, to the Sahl Khaba'ir al Hāmidah region where the find had been made, might prove useful as well. Did something else perhaps yet lie in the ground? It should at least be checked.

Certainly, Arthur was correct about one thing. The greatest danger was of the war in the Middle East shifting into Syria. In such an eventuality, how would the archaeological treasure be protected? About the mysterious text there remained many unanswered questions, but one thing LaSalle was sure of. If it were determined conclusively the tractate had been composed, at any rate narrated, by John the disciple of Jesus, and if that same "John" turned out to be the author of the Book of Revelation as well, the fallout would be considerable. It would impact the world in ways that were unpredictable, possibly unimaginable. Whatever light the Dura Europos scrolls might shed on the writing of the Gospel of John, if any, would be of academic interest—primarily to scholars and theologians. The real flash point would be the Book of Revelation, the final book in the Christian Bible…also known as the *Apocalypse of John*.

With the computer fully booted now, LaSalle checked his email—the usual. Nothing from Arthur, at any rate, which is what he had been looking for. But then, after all, the ball was in his court. He clicked the "compose" button and began a message.

Subject: A Work in Progress
Date: 3 Août, 20:22:26
From: LaSalle <dlasal@oceanet.fr>
To: Arthur MacBride <amacbride@umartinsburg.co.uk >

Dear Arthur,

The facsimiles proved effective. I've translated a portion of them and will post out to you that which I've completed so far. You should receive the packet by Tuesday or Wednesday at latest. The translation is still very much a work in progress, and it will be helpful when I'm finally able to consult with other scholars on the team, but what I'm sending you will give you a fairly clear idea of what you've uncovered. I've arranged to take a year's sabbatical starting in two weeks and plan to devote the entire year to the team's work. As you will see, the tractate is remarkable. It is more than remarkable. But beyond that, perhaps we should hold off discussion until we meet. I plan to be in London by no later than September 4. I look forward to seeing you then.

Yours,

David

LaSalle hit the "send" button, waited for the "message sent" cue, and leaned back in his chair. Out the window, in the streetlight below, he could see a young couple slowly walking up the sidewalk, swaying, leaning close to one another, as they disported with the friendly spirits of the darkening street. For a moment, he watched them, turning at last back to the stack of papers on his desk. On impulse, he decided to methodically check through the translation one more time. In three weeks of effort, he had painstakingly assembled what he had so far, and he felt reasonably satisfied with it, though of course, anything could bear a final scrutiny, and maybe that's what he should spend the evening doing.

As he reached for the first page, it seemed to quiver as if under a draft of wind. For a moment he paused, his mind in thought, his hand stilled just above the paper pile. To read the story in the original Greek left one feeling wholly caught up, spellbound in a sense, yet even the English translation, he realized, exercised a gambit, a certain demarche, upon the mind, and for a moment, with hand yet poised above the paper pile, he experienced something eerie. It was a feeling of kinship with the writer, but even more than that, it was a sense that he had, in some way, *looked upon* the face of the man who had composed these pages—a man who had lived and died some nineteen hundred years ago.

Flamboyance and Thunder

Quintus

hat morning it was only the third hour but already the sun was up high in the sky. I and seventeen other banished souls of Patmos were shackled together and loaded onto the ship for what was to be our trip to freedom. A new emperor was on the throne and decreed thereby was an amnesty of certain prisoners, particularly of the Flavian era. We were to be transported to the mainland, turned out upon the harbor of Miletus, and set *free*—to the extent that anyone can be so deemed in a world so thoroughly and irrevocably dominated by Rome's reign of the mad.

As the hatch closed, the fetid stench of the hold bored up into my nostrils. Little sunlight filtered down, and I could scarcely make out the visages of my fellow convicts. The iron bonds pressed at my wrists and ankles as, with great difficulty, I positioned my eye to a small notch just to the rear of my left shoulder. Visible through the tiny crack was a translucent blue, rippling glassily outside the hull. The decrepit, leaky old boat shuddered slightly, and began to move. We were drifting, *uncia* by *uncia*, away from the island.

"Praise be to Apollo," I thought, and I hoped I had seen the last of the place. By all rights I should not be making this trip; by all rights I should be dead. A random memory carried me back to that day my leg had been crushed, now nearly four years ago, but I remembered as if yesterday: the faces of prisoners and soldiers alike gathering above me. On each of their features, a message I could read even through the fog of my pain and terror— I was being stared down upon by eyes which had already mentally consigned me to the grave. The collapsed marble pediment had ripped tendons and shattered bone as it rolled over me, leaving my nearly severed limb folded in unnatural directions. Reflecting on my pitiable state, I had wondered at the irony of it all; here I was, dying, in this obsolete backwater of the world, after a life that had begun to hold such promise for me. But no more. I was now a forlorn, tragi-comic Briseis, with my lifeblood spilling out. The "swine of

Rome" would be no doubt pleased, he who had sentenced me to this banishment.

But then it happened. That strange old man. I had seen him a time or two since my arrival on the island, a peculiar denizen of a peculiar land of lost souls. He was a *monachos*, a solitary one, with a face as aged as the wheel of Chronos. Never had I exchanged a word with him, not so much as a mere commonplace, yet through my delirium I suddenly became "conscious" of him as I lay on the ground, aware that he was kneeling at my side, though in my state of shock I had no idea how long he had been there. Looking up at him, however, I found the eyes riveting. "*Parakletos ego eimi*," he spoke, and touched my face with his hand. I'm not sure how, but it was then I knew, with utmost certainty, I was not going to die that day. Upon my ruined leg, he placed his hands, stanching the blood, with the result being that the flesh seemed almost to begin repairing itself. Was I dreaming this, or was I going mad? But judging from the faces of the other prisoners, I was neither.

They had carried me that evening into the camp and lay me upon a mat within one of the *iasis* huts. After two days, I was again ambulatory, and in a week, no trace of the wound remained. I sought out the old man for to offer thanks. He obviously was a healer, a physician of some sort, with a power obtaining to the curative arts, an ancient, learned one from one of the great schools of medicine, Laodicea perchance, maybe Corinth, or even Rome; but what remedy had he applied upon me? I still did not know. *Anthropos mysteria*. Why such a man as this had been exiled to this place of woe I could not guess. Doubtless another fiat decreed by he of the sovereign snout and charged upon yet another of our noblest of citizens. The world forever retained its rancidity and rankness, yet here was one, this learned, this wise old man, who had done me a wonderful, nay a marvelous, turn. It was a favor I considered I should never be able to repay. "See here, Johannes..."—for in the course of my inquiries I had discovered he was named Johannes, "in the name of whatever god guides you, I humbly offer my thanks. You have saved my life."

He dismissed my words with a thin, bony hand. "Nay, I did not. Do not thank me, but Him. *Tēn doxan autou*," he said. "We have beheld His glory."

Beheld *whose* glory? I wondered. I had not the slightest idea to what, or to whom, he referred, though later I learned he was a follower of the Nazarene, that is to say a member of that sect so viciously despised by the noxious and the efficacious alike, a group which above all had been deemed perilously seditious by the anti-republican holders of power in Rome—and so perhaps was not *all* bad; one must, after all, keep an open mind on certain matters. In any event, it was said he had been banished to Patmos not once, but twice, both occasions for long periods of time. Finally, one other discovery did I make: the prisoners, as well as our guards, harbored a fear of him. It was rumored he held magical powers. Leery of becoming the object of a sorcerer's hex, most residents on the island shunned him, a paradoxical state of affairs given his frailty and advanced age. I dismissed it, all of it, as an anomaly, mostly to be forgotten in the daily struggle of staying alive on this island prison. That, as I say, was four years ago, and it all had occurred within the first few months of my banishment to Patmos. It was my twenty-third year of life, and the eighth year in the reign of the Emperor Domitian, whose disfavor I had incurred. I am Quintus Cintugnatus, branded an enemy of that beast known as the *Pax Romana*, a distinction I wear with pride, all the more so given who it was branded me as such: the silly and pompous son of Vespasian and former title-holder to the royal jowl, self-proclaimed Lord, Master, and Sovereign Deity himself—the Emperor Domitian. Who is now the *late* Emperor Domitian, praised be Apollo.

And what was my crime? First, I shall mention what it was not: I did not assassinate a public official; I did not set fire to the city of Rome; never once have I boiled little children in oil, or chewed upon human flesh, either with or without seasoning from the Far East. No. When my eulogy is delivered such things cannot, with any degree of veracity, be applied to my list of achievements in this life. My crime, that of which I plead guilty, was the taking up of a calamus, that instrument of writing, friend of playwright and poet, that has given birth to various accomplishments, as well as ill-accomplishments, of the versecraft-inclined. With aforementioned device in hand, I had proceeded to employ the art of satire upon a sheath of papyrus. While the resultant musings aroused a wholly unexpected degree of public hilarity, I regarded merely that I had set down a few simple and unadorned truths. Though earlier Caesars, going all the way back to Augustus, had on the whole been content to be worshipped as deities only if the stupid, sheep-like citizens of Rome so *wished* (a gesture of genuine benevolence by the standards of the mad criminals more recently elevated to that office), Domitian, on the other hand, perhaps feeling inferior to his predecessors, had given *orders* that he be worshipped. That's right. Orders. All of Domitian's subjects, on pain of punishment, were to address him as *Dominus et Deus*, Master and God. This new policy was mandatory, proclaimed by imperial fiat, a matter that was beyond dispute. The decree, most assuredly, *had* been issued. While I had merely noted that which was uncontested fact, it was perhaps my coining of the phrase "the swine of Rome" that became my fatal undoing. The only one seemingly not amused was the *Dominus et Deus* himself. I was accused of harboring "republican sympathies" (a charge to which I freely and hereby plead guilty) and packed off on a galley bound for Patmos, deemed one of the most notorious of the empire's inexpungeable and innumerable dungeons and penal colonies. After a life once so full of promise, in which at the age of twenty-two I had seen my first play performed to widespread acclaim, I was now to make my home in a place in which one group of murderous animals (the soldiers) held omniscient, god-like power over a second group of murderous animals (the convicts). Damnable misfortune, perhaps, that I was consigned to membership in the latter rather than the former; at any rate, here it was I spent the next four years, and quite likely would have remained for all of eternity but for Domitian's having the good grace to die, a fortunate occurrence that surely could not have transpired were he the immortal being of his mind's fancy. Yes, quite so…and now that he was dead, I was to go free.

Just after *solis ortus* this morning those of us marked for reprieve had been informed of our status and given order to prepare for boarding. Gratified had I been to note that the *monachos* was included. At least the old fellow would not die on Patmos, I thought. And now here we were, shipboard, the currents carrying us further and further away from that wretched island. Hoping to obtain some idea of where we were, I again positioned my eye to the crack and was just able to make out what appeared to be the Asian coastline coming into view. On deck above I could hear the soldiers, those vitiated specimens of humanity, engaged at their usual bantering, their obnoxious voices mingling with thump of luff and spar, the sound penetrating down here into the muscat of the hold. It was quite singular, that bantering of our keepers, a noise I had come to know well and detest over my four years of captivity. It was the sound of human voices smugly satisfied and oblivious to the reality of human misery. In fear and hatred does one's blood course through one's veins in its presence.

"May I forever be rid of that tare and dross of humanity," mumbled one of the prisoners, though in the shadowy light I could not make out his face.

"Pray the gods be kind and slay them and all of their children," another muttered.

"And cast their filthy remnant into Hades!"

"Don't speak so loudly, for you might yet end up with the fishes, and us with you."

"Aye. Curb your voice. I seek to rejoin my wife and children."

"Fool! Your wife and children have long forgotten you!"

"What do *you* know!"

"Old one!" This latter came from one whose voice I *did* recognize—a Greek named Hierax, a man of brute strength and cruel disposition. "What do you plan to do when we make land? What seek you first, a fine *meal*—or a fine *woman*?"

"Dung! What money have you for either?" someone retorted.

But the bellicose Greek seemed to have determined to while away the time by making sport of the old man, Johannes. "Come on old one! Give us a hint! Tell us your first endeavor at appeasing your appetites. Shall it be a banquet of the table?—or one of the sleeping room?" Salacious laughter rose in his throat: "I think it perhaps may be the latter!"

"You're contemplating banquets, Hierax, and with what? You've not a *denarius* to your name!" shouted someone in an effort to shut the ignoramus up.

"Perhaps the old man's god will spread one before us. And perhaps of the finest flower at that!" The Greek's voice suddenly became noticeably louder, "Could that be so, old man? Does your *god* provide you with such comforts?"

"His god is the *Christos*. Shut your foul mouth."

With a sudden violence Hierax lunged at the speaker of this last, drawing his leg irons to their full length. The chains held, thus restraining him from physical combat, yet the force of effort caused the hull of the vessel to vibrate with the power of his demonic fury, prompting one of the guardians on deck above to hurl an ill-tempered denunciation down our way. "Maybe when we are freed from these irons I will duly kick your teeth in!" sneered the Greek, oblivious to reason. "*Old man!*"

"Your pompous mouth is a burden and an oppression," said a prisoner, his comment prompting others now to chime in as well:

"Yeah, leave the old man alone, Hierax!"

"The old man is sick. Leave him alone."

But the barbarous Greek ignored his critics. "Old man! What kind of sorcery did you lay on Porfirio?"

"Cease these idiotisms, Hierax."

"Don't think for a moment you will succeed in stemming his words," opined another. "His brains are of marble."

"Old man! I asked you a question! What method of sorcery did you lay upon Porfirio?"

The old man, who up until now had been silent, bestirred himself, his ancient voice beginning totter. "From the very beginning, the message that we heard was that we should but love one another…" At first it was unclear to me whether he was endeavoring to answer Hierax or merely was rambling in the senselessness of the extremely aged. "I am 93 years old, and I can tell you that there is nothing in life more important than this. That which you describe as sorcery is none other than the *Logos*, the Word. The Word is God and of God. It is the sound that brought forth all sound and light."

Something here struck within me a responsive chord, but before I had time to ponder what he was saying, my thoughts were interrupted by yet another outburst from Hierax, who continued laboriously to press for an accounting of the aforementioned Porfirio. With regards the latter I should perhaps here pause in digression, for it is a most curious tale. A murderer was he. Just five new moons ago he was freed, but some number of weeks before the termination of his bondage he had begun taking meals with the old one, spending numerous hours in his company. It was a strange tarrying of two men who could not possibly have been more dissimilar in temperament, and it worked within Porfirio a change remarked upon by all. A man who had ruled others through terror, he seemed no longer to have heart for endless hostilities toward his fellows. And when he departed the island, this after serving a lengthy sentence, it was said he'd carried a letter of some sort written by the old man. To whom it was addressed, or where it was to be delivered, no one knew. It was, as I have said, quite curious.

"Old man, what of this *Christos* you worship but that you so seldom speak of? Pray you, impart some information regarding this strange deity." Not from Hierax, but from one of a usual reticence came this last. It brought in reply another just-audible flow of words from the old man:

"He was of light himself, and did many times heal the sick, and cause the blind to see again. He spoke often of justice for the poor and freedom for the captive, and of a new world, a kingdom which is to come, a kingdom which is here even now, and that is even within you. It is a kingdom other than Rome, and wherein wonderful things may come to pass."

"I believe you, old man," said he who had spoken earlier of rejoining his wife and children.

Hierax on the other hand was dubious. "Bah! You are suckling bilge!"

Johannes seemed to consider this for a long moment, then replied to the Greek, "You speak of banquets. Ask not of God what you already possess. It is in your hands. If you desire to obtain mercy, you must be merciful yourself. Yeshua did tell us this many times."

For once the Greek had no rejoinder, neither one of wrath nor mockery. In fact, a pall seemed to settle upon us. For my own part, my thoughts turned toward that given promise by the immediate future—freedom. Freedom from the bonds which had held me for four years. Fastening my eye once again to the crack, I was rewarded with a handsome sight, the inlet forming the entrance to the great northern harbor of Miletus; on either side, standing watch, as it were, two huge stone lions gazed forth upon the passing ships, our own among them. We were about to arrive. I was upon the verge of being disgorged from the penal system, umbilical cord cut to a mother of hideousness.

It was still dark in the hold, but I could sense the ship being docked, and could hear the frothy cries of our keepers as the mooring cables were tied. A Roman soldier came down into the dank hold and shouted, "Vermin! Prepare yourselves!" He then proceeded to disenfranchise us from our ironage, at which we were ordered to fall in line for deboarding. The old man Johannes fell in immediately to my rear. On the way up to the deck, we passed a soldier standing at the hatch; upon me he rudely stared, though by contrast quickly averted his eyes from the old one coming up just behind me.

Down a steep ramp we were marched, being deposited at last onto a quay, here setting foot for first time upon the Asian continent. All in all, we made for a bedraggled contingent, yet we managed to assemble ourselves, somewhat formally, as a centurion proceeded to read from a scroll: "By the grace of the Emperor Nerva, and by arrangements thereof, it has been ordered and decreed: that there should this day be carried out, in the interest of mercy and compassion, commutation of your just sentences. This by imperative authority of Nerva, *Numen Augusti*, the Divine One, whose genius, divine will, and life-force bless us all. *Roma Aeterna*. It is hereby done." The centurion rolled up the scroll. "Go your way in peace."

We were officially free. Wasting no time, I left the dock. It was the last I was to see of Hierax and the others, not that I had any sentimental desire for lingering in their company. It was also to be the last I would see of the old man—for a while. By and by I found myself on the Avenue of Columns. I was now in the Asian city of Miletus! Sights and sounds collided fantastically with my suddenly liberated body and its equally-as-suddenly liberated senses, noisy market stalls rarifying the atmosphere with a fermenting abundance of goods, but I was empty of purse. Pausing at the door of a shop, I appealed to the charity of the merchant, receiving a stream of invective rather than the poor round of barley bread for which I had dared hope. Angered, I spat venomously in reply to his unwarranted abuse, "You howling monkey! Keep, then, your execrable fodder!" At this, he pulled out a curved sword, its blade of fearsome size, rounding upon me, though not quickly enough fortunately; at top speed, I exited his squalid little place of commerce, hastily merging myself into the throngs on the street.

For two tiresome days, I tarried in Miletus, wandering its doggedly crowded avenues, while taking refuge at night in a dank shed to the rear of the bouleuterion. Finally, with no luck improving my lot, and being of enormous hunger, I departed south. Around the Cape of Monodendri and past the Altar of Poseidon I made my way. At a pilgrim's haven by name of Panormos a kindly woman offered bread, dried figs, and olives, which fare I ate of ravenously. From Panormos the road was flanked by reclining stone lions and various other statuary, including likenesses of the branchides, the priests of the sanctuary, the Temple of Apollo, located in the city of Didyma, where the southern road led me at last. Here I made obeisance to the God and found employment in the service of a tanner. It was disagreeable work, accompanied by the most atrocious of smells. After two weeks of steady toil, for which I was paid 12 *denarii*, I took route across the Plain of Meander, returning at last to Miletus, from which I hoped to obtain passage to Rome.

At just past noon I found myself once more in the city's vast and teeming agora, whereupon I stumbled on a most unexpected sight. In front of a scent merchant's shop, near the Ionic Stoa, a cluster of pedestrians had gathered, giving ear to a gesticulating little man standing in front of the doorway. Curious, I pulled closer, jostling my way judiciously toward the head of the crowd so as to get a better view, hereupon making another discovery—the figure of a *second* man, lying prone upon the street, presumably either drunk or unconscious. "It was this morning initially I laid eyes on the poor fellow!" The little scent merchant directed his comments to no one individual but more or less collectively at the gawking crowd at large. "He did not ask for alms, only for permission to rest in front of my door. I–I am a generous man! And a compassionate one! And this I did not deny him!"

Wedging closer, thinking to be of assistance, I looked down, glancing upon the face for the first time—and here received something of a start, for it was none other than the old man Johannes, he recently of Patmos, the very one who had saved my life four years ago.

"Maybe the *aedile* should be sent for," suggested someone.

"Two lanes over there is a man who has ass and cart," offered another, discerningly rubbing a tuft of chin whiskers.

The little scent merchant continued to fret, "At about the third hour I looked out my door, whereupon I thought to myself, 'that old fellow has gone to sleep!'"

"I know this man," I said.

"Then at the fourth hour, when I looked again," the scent merchant resumed, scarcely skipping a beat, though now aiming his remarks at me in particular, apparently deciding I had some sort of role to play, and that such relieved him of further responsibility in the distressful affair, "I thought, 'his sleep is long, poor man, may great Jupiter provide rest for the weary...'"

I pressed three fingers to the large vein of the old one's neck. He was alive and did breathe, but barely. The scent merchant had not finished, nor did it appear as if he ever would, "...and then at the fifth hour when, as before, I looked once more through my door and found him still there, I thought, 'This man does not appear to be merely *sleeping*!'" Slowly I gathered the old one into my arms. It was at this point, amidst the scent merchant's continued verbal spillage, that some kind bystander directed us to a nearby medical dispensary. The place turned out to be a distance of about a furlong and a half. I am not now, nor ever have been, formidable of size or powerful of limb, yet at this time I found the old man scarcely of any weight to speak of. I judged he had not eaten for a number of days.

At the dispensary, he was given oil mixed with wine, as well as some other potion I have not the name for, and fed a thin soup. On the following day, he was much improved. "To turn him out causes me great pain," confided the physician. "But we are overcrowded. Many citizens of this city seek cures here." Aesculapius was kept busy. The Britanians, the Germanians, the Druids, the Parthians—all these and more could testify as to Rome's propensity for the waging of endless wars, into which were poured incalculable talents of gold. But as to the empire's own sick and needy—these must depend invariably upon some mythical God of healing, thought I bitterly.

"Do you know his age?" the physician asked.

At first, I drew a blank, then recalled: "Ninety three."

"Yes…hmm…were it in my power I would have him linger in our care for at least three days longer, but there simply is no room." He produced a medicinal amphora. "See that he gets three swallows of this each day. When it is empty, return here and I will replenish it."

I paid him two *denarii*. The old man and I departed. "Johannes," said I after we had stopped to rest at the noisy Portico of Tiberius, "Have you any family to care for you?" He was still of weakened state, yet to my surprise inclined to talk; he knew not, with any certainty, the whereabouts of any relatives, though as he spoke, I gathered there had been some once—in Ephesus. As we sat there in the portico in the midst of the milling crowds, I began now to ponder various strategies, including the possibility of embarking for Ephesus for purpose of seeking out these possible relations, but deducing him too weak at the moment to make the journey, I dismissed the idea for now. Maybe in a week or so, I thought. If he continued to gain strength. We would see.

"Nay, it will not be so," he said, as if reading my mind.

"What did you say, Johannes?"

"I have lived long. It is my time to die," he said in that voice of Chronos.

"You must not die, Johannes!"

"Burden not your heart, *meus amicus*. In the faraway terebinths, the dove sings. For me it is time now to go and listen to her song. For you it is different. You are the *hazzan*, the blower of the trumpet. It is your turn in life."

"Do not be so sure." Considering what must be done, I began to collect my thoughts: first and foremost I had to find shelter. Not only for him. For *both* of us. I could not let him die. Not after he had saved my life. So shelter. Yes. But where? I had only ten *denarii* left, and I was pretty sure he had not even a single *pruta* to his name. It was still my intention to return to Rome, and briefly I thought of simply abandoning him to his fate, but I knew I could not do so, for there was that debt. I might have served four years in prison, but I considered myself, if nothing else, an honorable man. As I pondered the choices before me, I turned to him once more: "There is something, Johannes, that for a great long time I have desired to ask you. That day I was struck down, the day my lifeblood moistened the earth—how was it that I lived? What transpired?"

When his answer finally came, it was of no real sense, "A long, long time ago, I stood at a place called Golgotha, known as the place of the skull. In time and distance it is far away, and I have traveled many miles, but in some ways I have never left there."

Suddenly I was of much curiosity. Certainly, he was old enough to recall the Tiberian era, and probably even carried memories of the time of Augustus. Such a life spanned a large fragment of history. He was a Jew. About him I knew that much, though little else. What did he recollect, I wondered, of the persecution of his people by Caligula? Or of the ruins and depravations of Nero? And what of the destruction of Jerusalem by Titus—in the name of Great Apollo, would he have, *could* he have, been witness to *that*? Of these things I now questioned him, and it was at this point he began a rather astounding tale. Not far had he gone with it, however, when suddenly my mind was made up. I told him to hold off speaking, for now, and roused him to his feet; together we made our way, slowly for he could not walk very well, to a crumbling *insula* block near the harbor. Here I paid out another five *denarii*—for a room not much larger than a box. On a mat I helped him to lie, gave him a swallow from the amphora, and tried to make him as comfortable as possible. The building was noisy, odorous and disgusting, populated with a lamentable clientele of riffraff, but it was shelter, at least of a sort. Protection at any rate from the winter rains, and these were soon upon us. In fact, it turned out to be one of the worst winters seen in this region for many completions of the calendar. The year was 856 *ab urbe condita*. Or, put another way, it has been 67 years since the death by crucifixion of he referred to as Jesus the Christ.

These things I do now record, they having been told me by he of many years, at a time of misfortune, and under direst of circumstance. Yet to set it down I thought mainly worthwhile. "I have seen things you would not believe..." he began, and indeed, certain things of which he spoke defied explanation, at least in his relating of them. "I have also known sorrows of a deepness I once could never have imagined..."

And thus began the tale to spill out. I implored he should start at the very beginning, for I had decided to write it all down, having carried with me since leaving Didyma a calamus and several sheaths of papyrus—those very items which had landed me on Patmos to begin with. But writing was in my blood. Thus, fool that I was, I began faithfully to record, at risk of utter ruin and a return trip to Patmos, the words and life events of he, who, like myself, had been branded for subversion by the powers of Rome. They who dare criticize that excrescence of a farce known as *Pax Romana* do ever so court personal disaster, yet compelled did I feel, possibly by reason of something embedded deep within my own nature, to tell the old one's story. This labor transpired over a period of fourteen days, and what follows is gravid with details, for often I did stop him to ask clarification on this point or that. Whether the truth resides in every single bit and parcel of this story, I cannot say. At the very least, however, I believe it to be the truth as he remembered it, a faithful and sincere attempt, in the last fading moments of his life, to bare record of all things that he saw.

The words you are about to read are his and his alone, he being named Johannes, a disciple and follower of the Christos.

Quintus Cintugnatus

Chapter One

O ut of all the species of life on earth, I'm inclined to believe that the most lowly, conniving, and tragically miserable is the human. If you did but take the entire lot of us, put us within the confines of a giant olive press, and applied pressure, I doubt you would squeeze out more than a few drops of truth. Truth is sought or known by only a few, while it cannot be denied there are those who shun truth, still others who are its bitterest most unrelenting enemies. But *pante rei*, as the Greeks say, all flows.

I remember the day in Jerusalem, very long before your time, my young one, when a certain magistrate uttered the words, "What is truth?" It was a question I certainly was not capable of answering. My own actions on the eve previous had been less than exemplary, in a manner of speaking cowardly. There was one, however, who had been a fountain of truth, who burst the bar of illusion, and traversed this miry road that silts its way to the open sea. That one was put to death, and as for the aforementioned magistrate, I do not know if he ever found the answer to his question, but somehow I doubt it. He ended up being recalled to Rome after slaughtering a group of peaceful Samaritans on Mount Gerazim. *Cum tacent clamant*, when they remain silent they cry out.

But since you have asked to know certain things about me, dear Quintus, I will tell them to you. For 93 years I have lived on this earth. During that time, I walked with a man who said, "Love your neighbor as yourself," and who lived it. I knew the love of a beautiful woman. I stood in the same room with the Emperor Nero, and I saw human beings torn apart by wild beasts in the Circus Maximus. I beheld the smoke of Mount Vesuvius, and watched my children scattered by the winds, from Masada to Britania. Such is inherently the nature of our passage on this earth. It is a long and winding path we travel, a path almost inescapably of suffering, of searching, as we grasp for the invisible threads which connect us to the All. But I'm getting ahead of myself, while you have asked me to start at the beginning. In this I can oblige, for while this circle that we refer to as life has no beginning and no ending, and for many no entrance and no exit, there is indeed a beginning to this story.

***

I was born in Bethsaida, where the Jordan River wanders south on its way to the Lake of Gennesaret, which lies not too far distant. At the age of five I started school at the *beth ha-sefer*, or "house of book." It was behind the synagogue, and the master was Rabbi Hamul, a bombastic, rotund man who drummed the lessons into our ears with an impatient earnestness. He was assisted by a young Rabbi by the name of Joel, a gentle, unassuming soul, virtually Rabbi Hamul's opposite in decorum, speech, and manner. Together they drilled us in the Torah, language, grammar, history, geography, and everything else we knew of the world being taught to us principally from the scriptures.

In those early years of my schooling, a boy named Hodi became my chief source of torment. He was six years my senior, stocky of build, and had a mean streak the size of an ox. Leader was he of a rowdy group of boys who one and all seemed to think that even his dung was of the sweetest smell, and all manner of fiendish pranks and tricks they played upon me. A special delight of theirs was confronting me in a noisome, bothersome manner that was impossible to ignore, and with my attention thus preoccupied, to have one of their number creep up to my rear upon hands and knees, positioning himself immediately aft, his body forming a trip; at this point, the ruffian facing me would plant hands upon my chest and administer a treacherous shove, landing me upon my backside in the dirt amidst a chorus of laughter.

Around the time of my birth a man named Judas, a Galilean, had led an armed revolt against Roman rule. We Jews should never have mortal masters, he had preached, for we have God as our Lord. For us to acquiesce or become subservient to the laws of others was an insult to God most high, who had led us out of Egypt. Judas' followers eventually, in later years, came to be known as the *Zealots* (as they liked to refer to themselves), or *Sicarii* (which the Romans came to call them), and they have a very great deal to do with this story. But as to the matter of this revolt started by Judas, it was joined by many willing souls whose one desire was to free our land and restore our sovereignty. Rome responded as Rome always does, with unmatched mayhem and destruction, and we lost the best of the nation. Thousands were slain in battle; hundreds more were crucified. Those were years in which terror and violence wracked the land, and I think it was some of this spirit that had rubbed off on Hodi and his followers, for there was an innate cruelty about them. Lacking anywhere near commensurate size and strength, I was incapable of standing up to them, or rather, such resistance as I *did* offer served no purpose than to arouse their hilarity. Of course, I wasn't their only victim. There were others, invariably boys who, like myself, were smaller and weaker.

Curiously, one who could seem to find no fault, with either Hodi or his friends, was Rabbi Hamul. Forever was the good school master unable to perceive their true nature for the excellent reason that in the rabbi's presence Hodi and his disciples conducted themselves in the most exemplary of fashions. Of course, this deference to the head master did not extend to his assistant. For Rabbi Joel the group reserved some of its most fiendish pranks, including the theft of his sandals upon one occasion, and the placing of a rotting fish in the folds of his cloak upon another. Too meek and gentle to exert discipline, the rabbi's response was to laugh away these provocations good-naturedly. Thus, in my conflict with Hodi, I found myself with no available recourse to authority.

And so it was, after the letting out of school one day, my antagonist hailed me in an insulting and demeaning manner. "Hey *Muma!*" The name *Muma* had been the gang's special designation for me. The word means "spot"—and in those days, I had been not much bigger than one.

"Well, well, it's the little Muma!" Hodi walked up and stuck his chest in my face.

"It's the little Muma!" one of the underlings repeated obsequiously.

"Leave me alone!" I tried to sound brave, but I was shaking from my head down to my sandals.

"Muma, I've been thinking of some things I want you to start doing for us." And there ensued a list of demeaning endeavors I was to perform in their service. The bully's followers were enjoying themselves immensely, and no doubt were serious, that I should either become their dutiful servant or have my face pounded in the dirt. Up to here, the eipsode had gone like so many of my *other* encounters with Hodi, but this time things were to turn out differently, for suddenly down the lane, upon wide, loping strides came a lanky, broad-shouldered youth, and judging from his pace, he was in something of a hurry—though *not*, as it turned out, too much of a hurry to notice the intimidation to which I was just then being subjected. Something else became apparent as well: that unlike Rabbi Hamul, he knew full well Hodi's real character. "How is it, Hodi," he inquired as he changed course, veering suddenly in the bully's direction, "you have the nerve to call another a 'spot' when you yourself are the most unseemly blemish on the countryside?" His thick hair hung down to his shoulders. He was an older boy. I actually had seen him around before, recognizing him as one of those who of late had begun keeping company with my older brother James. Even by himself he was a match for Hodi and his gang, and the entire pack of brutes were incensed at his cheekiness.

"Stick your nose elsewhere, Simon, this does not concern you!"

"Don't be so confident of that, Hodi."

"You are the offspring of a whore of the stinking *am ha'aretz*. Go and filth yourself!"

"Do not worry yourself so much about my origins," replied Simon. "Far more profitable you were to ponder the curvature of my *fist* as it comes at your face!" And with that he larruped the bully a staggering blow squarely upon the mouth. Caught by surprise, Hodi screamed in outrage—"Get him!"— yet it was a scream delivered through cracked and bloodied lips. A great deal of huffing and wheezing then ensued as the whole band of them swarmed about Simon, who, unperturbed, retrieved from the ground a fat stick, which he began using as a bludgeon. Holding it by the middle, he thrust the cudgel alternately here, there, knocking the sacred countenance off the face of one attacker, before turning, rather masterfully I thought, to meet another. Unused to an opponent who actually fought back, the ruffians scattered, but their parting cries left little doubt as to their intent for revenge.

"Stinking *paniym ha'aretz*—you and all your family!" bellowed Hodi from afar.

"Stinking *am ha'aretz*!" the underlings repeated obsequiously.

We stood there in the middle of the road till their curses and shouts faded at last in the distance. Finally, with a great deal of timidity, I confided to Simon, "You'd better be careful. They'll come after you."

He tossed the stick down. "They are nothing." Leaving me with my mouth agape, he then turned and hurried once more on his way. In my young life, it was one of the most impressive performances I had ever seen, and in open admiration I stared after him.

A few days afterwards, I learned he was the son of a man named Jonah. And while his formal name was Simon, there were some about, close friends and confidants, who called him Cephas, which means "rock," although in the Greek tongue this would be rendered "Petros," or simply Peter.

Chapter Two

In those days were certain rabbis about who told a parable concerning a "perfect son." It relates the tale of a man blessed with a very loving and respectful son but who one day, in a moment of wrath, takes hold of a sandal and unjustly strikes the boy with it. As he does so, the sandal flies from his grip. Keeping in mind God's commandment to honor his father and mother, the son retrieves the sandal from the far side of the room, returns, and kisses his father's hand as he lays the object back in it.

I had heard the parable often, and I mention it because in a way it was the sort of obedience my father expected from his own children—of whom there were three. My brother James was the oldest; my sister Susanna came next; and then I—I was the youngest. Father was stern toward all of us, though I'd have to say it was James who had it toughest. Being eldest, he tended to be the focal point of Father's expectations. My father was head of the Bethsaida Fisherman's Guild. His name was Zebedee, but among his friends he had another name, *Nasha Hadad*, or Thunder Man. It was a name he lived up to with no trouble. As the *bukhra*, or first-born son, James would one day take over our boat and fishing business. For this purpose he had been groomed since birth, and because of this Father had a tendency to demand much of him. He demanded much—but he also received much. James knew he had been planted as a seed in a garden of perseverance, and he tried, he really tried, to live up to the standard set by the boy in the parable. Times were he fell short, however, or at least in the eyes of my father, the thunderer, he fell short.

Our house was built around a small courtyard, in the center of which was a fire pit and oven where my mother, Salome, did her cooking, and beyond this a stall for our donkey, while on the other side of the courtyard was a large, walled-in area where we lived. There was no privacy. My mother and father slept in one bed; Susanna in a second; James and I in the third. And we were among the better off families in town. In the summer months when it was hot, we slept on the roof.

The fisherman's guild functioned as a great heart, with all the crews pooling their catches. In this manner, better prices could be obtained from the salters and wholesalers who came up from Jerusalem, and it was testimony to the esteem in which my father was held that the men of the guild had chosen him as their *rishi*, yet he was of iron and not much else. The obedience he demanded of his children, particularly James, he for the most part received, though at times my brother's independent nature got the better of him. Clashes, when they erupted, usually occurred over Father's rigid application of Jewish law in our family life. For Father, the Law was everything. It was his reason for getting up in the morning. His reason for going to bed at night. And if truth be known it was probably even his reason for going to the *beit chara* and relieving himself as well. Not that Father was by any means the only devotee to the Law around; certainly, other men in town exhibited comparable levels of piety, but Father, at least in his own mind, was one of the most pious, and it wasn't just the written law either. We were obliged to uphold, in all of its various nuances, the oral law too. James was required to say the *Shema* twice a day, to wear the *tefillin*, and observe the standard purification procedures. As a fishing family, it was also necessary for us to be mindful of what fish could be sold to Jews, and which were to be reserved only for Gentiles, who, other than for purposes of trade and commerce, were on the whole to be avoided. In fact, a Jew could become defiled by the mere act of entering a Gentile's house. And it wasn't only contact with the persons themselves. If a knife had been handled by a Gentile it had to be re-ground, while pottery vessels touched by Gentile lips were disposed of. Shop owners might sell milk from a cow owned by a Gentile— but not to Jews. And so on and so forth. It was a challenge just keeping track of all the requirements, which is why we had doctors of the law who were experts on the matter, and when in doubt, you simply asked, although the answers could vary depending on which one you consulted. But as I was saying of my brother, James for the most part detested these restrictions. Little about it he did not regard as pointless.

As for my sister Susanna and I, we often escaped the Law's more whimsical demands; girls were not supposed to say the *Shema*, for instance, while I was below the age of thirteen, relieving me of a number of obligations shouldered by my older brother. With Father and James, however, things were different, and one morning quite early, the acrimony reached a head— over my brother's refusal to say the *Shema*.

The *Shema*, in case I neglected to mention, is a prayer. It was taught to the children of Israel by YHWH, who commanded it be recited often, and Father was adamant that this be faithfully executed by James. For the most part, James complied with everything Father demanded, but there was an imperious tone, quite distinctive and characteristic, that crept often into Zebedee's voice in his dealings with his oldest son, and it was on display that morning. So one might say it was this which brought the crisis on—this, plus a flickering desire for freedom that I knew burned in my brother's own heart. Maybe also a little bit of stubbornness on both their parts. At any rate, James, for one of the rare times in his life, directly disobeyed his father. *Aukama*. It was a blackened pathway. Zebedee thundered like an immortal, accusing my brother of behaving as one of the lowly *am ha'aretz*, or as the term applies literally, "people of the land." Being so lumped and branded placed you amongst "the rabble who know not the law"—in other words people who were not Jews. Or at least not strictly observant ones. *Am ha'aretz*. It was about the worst insult you could pay anyone.

"You are *not* one of them! No son of mine is!" thundered Zebedee.

James was trembling, but there was something inside him rushing forward, rising out of the fire of his young heart's yearning. "All of my life I have given the Law its due! I only wish you would do the same for me!" It was risky to speak to Zebedee in such a manner. In essence, James was letting it be known he had no intention of saying the *Shema* that morning. It was not a particularly wise move on my brother's part, though I suppose after a lifetime of chaffing under Zebedee's hand he had reached a boiling point, but if he had reached the boiling point, so, too, had Father.

"Why must you be always so unruly? You are going to learn one way or the other!"—and with that Father swung and hit James a savage blow. No mere sandal being flung across a room this. It was an act of brute violence, and it took us all by surprise; my eyes saw but the blur of my father's fist, followed by my brother lying on the floor a moment later. At the age of fifteen, there was no way James could hope to prevail against Zebedee. As head of the family, Father had the right of *tura tsa*, that is to impose correction or discipline, but there had been a level of savagery to the act wholly unexpected. He was a lank, sinewy man, my father, with the rough, indurated hands of a Galilee fisherman, hands that were cut and scarred with a chaotic and confused calligraphy, etched into the callused flesh by a lifetime of hard work. He was in reality a "man of the land" himself, although of course he would never admit it. By turn, his eyes could easily convey piety, studiousness, or sharp rebuke, depending upon the occasion, and in those days his beard was still mostly black, lending him an air of purposeful gravity. When he spoke in that imperious tone he was inclined to, you knew he was of utmost seriousness. A dutiful, faithful provider—he was always this. Though we were not rich, none of us had ever gone hungry, but human warmth did not come easily to him. There was a shadow substance in his soul that, despite his amorousness for Jewish Law, made an idolatrous offering to the gods of thunder. Like them he was hard, cold, unyielding.

Salome, on the other hand, was of quite different material, and it was not in her nature to sit idly by when someone, especially members of her own family, acted rashly. My mother, to put it quite simply, was one in whom the soul doth thirst. It was her eternal desire to make the world a better place, and to that end she had devoted herself to improving the lot of all the girls in our town. This she hoped to accomplish by sending them to school, more about which I shall mention later. For now, however, it is enough to say that upon seeing her eldest son beaten to the floor she was by no means content to remain silent.

"Stop this!" Rising to her feet, she inserted herself between Father and James; Zebedee continued to bark imperiously, though backing off a few paces. Slowly my brother picked himself up from the floor, the back of one hand wiping a trail of blood that dribbled over his chin. But Salome had not done. "This house has taken leave of its senses! For the sake of the Lord, control your temper! Do not strike your son!"

"If there is one thing I will not tolerate in this household it is irreverence for the Holy One!" growled the Thunder Man.

"Cannot the Holy One make his way in this life without such ever-faithful assistance from you?"

"Woman, be silent!"

"Husband, I do not ask you should forego the respect that is due you from your family, only that you should remember that your son is just exactly that—your *son*—and that your actions be tempered with love and understanding."

"Presume not to tell me your foolish opinions!"

"I do so presume."

"You are as insolent as he. James, put on the *tefillin* and say the *Shema*!"

"I will not!"

Zebedee advanced a step, however my mother again purposed to intervene herself, eliciting an ominous response from Father: "I have warned you!"

"You have. And now hear me well. If you attempt to strike your son again, then prepare to strike me as well!"

When it came to my father, the only person I ever saw get the best of him in a contest of wills was my mother, which she did that day. Our God, whose name we were not supposed to pronounce, is a God nonetheless of many pseudonyms. We know him as *Elohim*, the Strong One; *HaKodesh*, the Holy One; and *Adonai*, Lord. He was the God of Abraham, Isaac, and Jacob (he obviously had a preference for men), and he was the God of my father, Zebedee, though maybe, just maybe, he had smiled on my mother that day. Or maybe it was simply my mother's indomitable will, for truly she did have something of the sort about her. She and Zebedee glared furiously at each other, but at last it was my father, mindful of the violence he would have to wreak in order to prevail, who spun on his heels and stalked from the house.

We were waiting dinner when he returned that evening; James remained completely silent through the meal; only later, with an air of contrition, did he make his way, tentatively and cautiously, to stand before Father. It had come to this. All day long, I had noticed, since the episode this morning, he had been fighting an inner battle with himself, and now, with head bowed slightly, standing before his father, he began to recite the *Shema*.

Hear O Israel, the Lord our God, the Lord is One....

James was trying to be the perfect son in the parable, and he offered up the prayer as a giver of splendor. Many times throughout our youth, my brother was to find himself torn just so, between his father's demands and his own yearnings for independence; this time the perfect son won out, but it would not always be that way...

Later, the entire family gone to bed, long after James had fallen asleep and whilst I was *pretending* to sleep, I could still hear my parents talking quietly, and what I heard was my mother's voice, "You will catch more flies with honey."

"What do you mean by that?" countered Zebedee.

"A lesson you should learn," she replied coldly, and blew out the lamp.

My memory of that day is one of the main memories I have of my father and the one that usually comes to mind before all others. And it had all been over Jewish law, toward which my father hearkened himself in all matters. In this respect, at least, he was not so very different from other Pharisees. And oh yes, in case I forgot to mention it, my father, Zebedee, counted himself a Pharisee.

Chapter Three

Very near to Bethsaida where we lived, at a bend of the Jordan, the waters widen into a pool deep enough for swimming. Here the river wears the apparel of its lush, canopied banks, here sprigs of herbs, wild bananas, and terebinths grow as if purloined from Demeter, offering to the eye a patina of mystery.

"It is mush," said Simon Peter, standing in waist deep water, although it wasn't the water he was referring to.

"It is *not* mush. It is beautiful," answered my sister Susanna from a rock where she sat with feet dangling in the river.

That denounced as "mush" by Simon Peter, and defined as "beautiful" by my sister, was the story of a young maid who lived in a tower and who's name was Hero. Each night she was said to have lit a lamp which served as a guide to her lover, a young man by the name of Leander, who swam nightly a body of water known as the Hellespont in order to be with her. But tragically one evening Leander drowned in a rough sea, and in grief, Hero threw herself from her tower onto the rocks below, joining him in death. It was a story of the Greeks. Thanks to Rabbi Joel, Susanna had learned to read. She had in fact become a rather voracious reader; under the rabbi's tutelage, not only had she studied the formation of Hebrew letters, but Greek ones as well, learning to read both languages, and developing in the process an ardent passion for the Greek poets. I mention all this because it was not the usual custom for girls to learn to read and write. Many rabbis opposed it, some quite vehemently. "It would be better to see the Torah burnt than to hear its words on the lips of women!"—this had been one particularly indignant pronouncement on the matter. Indeed, had you looked closely, you would have noticed that our school, the *beth ha-sefer*, was made up entirely of boys. Fortunately for Susanna, however, Rabbi Joel was one of the small minority of rabbis who saw no objection to teaching a girl to read, or who at least could be cajoled into it. Precisely this had my mother undertaken to do, for Salome believed in the depths of her soul that her daughter possessed as much right to learning as either of her two sons, and she had made private arrangements with Rabbi Joel in the amount of six *denarii* a month to that end. Aside from being disposed toward fairness between the sexes, the rabbi was also a poor man and needed the money. But in deference to sensibilities of the time, Susanna could not sit in class with the boys; her lessons had to be conducted in the privacy of the rabbi's study, while my father refused to pay for it.

"What would be the point in it?" he asked.

"So she can *read*," my mother blithely replied.

"Girls have no need of reading," he said, dismissing the entire enterprise as folly.

"From where comes all this lofty talk of Jewish independence! It is not the Romans who forbid Jewish women from acquiring learning; it is Jewish *men*!" Even though she had to pay the six *denarii* a month out of her own sewing money, my mother stood her ground, and Susanna began lessons in reading, writing, and mathematics. And yes, as I mentioned, the learned young rabbi instructed her in Greek as well, and in the process opened up the world of the Greek poets to her. It was nourishment of a sort. Susanna, as it turned out, was a phenomenally bright girl, and in each and every subject, though especially in Greek, she outperformed us all.

The other part to this story has to do with my mother, for so successful were her endeavors with Susanna, she set out to make it possible for other girls to avail themselves of the same opportunities. In the process, she discovered there were other women in town who thought similarly on the matter—much to the consternation of many of the town's *men*. But Salome had a way of always, or *almost* always, coming out on top, and she had, in her own small way, started a social revolution in Bethsaida. Rabbi Joel was kept busy, now tutoring not only Susanna but three other girls as well.

For his own part, Rabbi Hamul officially frowned upon teaching "Greek influences" to the children, or anything else for that matter, excepting it be from the scriptures, though he rather regarded the Greeks especially as propagators of "a lot of heathen tales." Rabbi Joel, however, was a dreamer, prone to let slip a mention now and then, and thus we had become privy to the story of Hero and Leander and their ill fated love; Susanna, being of romantic bent by nature, who could so readily fly upon the wings of her imagination, was quite taken by the tale, finding herself, in a word, captivated.

The brackish, murky waters of the Jordan were doubtless a far cry from those magical currents that had buoyed the Greeks in the days of the Trojan

War. Nonetheless, our own swim that afternoon, perhaps inevitably, brought to mind the lovers' sad account.

"How could he earn his living after doing all that swimming every night?" Peter wanted to know, posing the question with a scoffing air.

"If," remarked James, "he swam across the Hellespont every evening, spent the overnight hours locked in the throes of passion, then swam back every morning, he would not be fit for hoeing even a single row the next day!"

They were teasing Susanna and having great fun at it. In this jest I also partook, keen to prove my mettle with the older boys. "He must have been sleepy," I supplied. "They probably called him 'Sleepy Leander.'"

"Sleepy Lee!" laughed Philip, another boy from our town who had joined us on this afternoon.

In Susanna's view, we were all *mōrŏs*, which was Greek for stupid. And underscoring her sentiments on the matter, she slipped a foot into the Jordan and sent a splash of water directly into Peter's face. This prompted much laughter and a response from my brother, James: "You have encountered my sister's wrath. Steer carefully your course lest calamity befall you, Simon Peter!"

Filled with romance was Susanna's heart. She was fourteen years old at this time, and had spent a large share of her life assisting Salome in my care, to the point where "mothering" me, I suppose, had become second nature to her. This of course was to my supreme annoyance. At the ripe age of ten I considered myself eminently grown up and wanted no care or assistance from her, yet it seemed there was little escaping whenever she took a notion to "help" me with something. She and my brother in fact both had a tendency toward over protectiveness, none of which, as I say, was to my liking especially, yet at the same time Susanna also possessed a streak of independence, something I think she picked up from all the poems and stories she read. Or maybe she had inherited it from our mother. But whatever it was, it lent to her nature an element of the untamable. In all manner of things she viewed herself as equal, in every way, to the boys. Unlike us boys, however, reading was her passion in life. She lived and breathed her Greek poets. In her young heart they had kindled a fire, a fire I could sense even when she was busy mothering me, for I would see it—for there would come to her eyes at odd times, without warning, a look, a spell almost; into this she would fall for as long as a moment, sometimes two, and it would seem as if that other world, populated by its heroes and heroines, gallant and brave though sometimes tragically flawed, were calling out to her in a voice only she could hear. Yet as pertains to Susanna and motherhood, I should state emphatically, for I believe it to be true—that had she lived she would have one day excelled at it.

"Fair maiden, may I offer to you my apology?" Having had water sloshed in his face, Peter, it seemed, sought to make amends. Had the teasing, perhaps, gone too far? I should mention that Peter, by this time, had become our firm and fast friend. More than a year had it been since he had saved me from Hodi and his gang, and in that time we had, in many respects, become his proxy family. His father, Jonah, was an old man who had sired two sons, both at a relatively advanced age, yet even so, Jonah, ironically, had outlived his young wife, who had passed away when Peter was still small. Consequently, Simon Peter had grown up roaming the countryside with little anchor or support. And maybe that's what he had come to see in us—an anchor, something to belong to and be a part of, a presence to still, at least partially, his unabated restlessness. And so he had become our closest friend. But we had also become his. After that initial tussle with Hodi, Peter, together with my brother James, had sought out the entire mob of ruffians. Working in tandem, they had inflicted punishment on the lot of them. The foray solidified a firm friendship between Peter and James; it worked out pretty good for me as well. I no longer trembled in dread when Hodi walked by. Others did. But I was now free of the bully's reign of fear.

"To show you how sorry I am, I shall swim the Jordan across and back. Three times. I will be Leander, and you shall be Hero." Furthermore, added Peter, he would swim to the very rock upon which Susanna sat, which for purpose of the exercise would serve as her "tower."

Was Peter in love with my sister? I don't think so. I think he was just making sport, yet nobody was sure how to take this. Was it a romantic parry—or a mocking peonage to a dreamy young girl? Susanna herself, for once, was speechless. It was in fact Philip who broke the silence, "Yes, but do not forget, you must swim *naked*."

This brought laughter, for indeed, as the story went, Leander made the nightly swims clothed only in his bodily glory. The thought of Peter swimming the Jordan likewise was deemed uncommonly funny, by everyone except Peter himself, whose face took on a dignity-swindling redness. This coloring faded momentarily, but then recrudesced with a vengeance with the sudden appearance of my mother. Whether Salome had actually overheard Philip's remark about swimming naked I could not say, but being a mother of sense and sensitivity, she immediately set about putting us at our ease. Few rabbis would have approved of young people our age socializing outside the presence of an adult. My mother, however, as we all knew, held a more open-minded view. Assuming our basic goodness, no opprobrium did she voice. "I was out gathering wild bananas and thought I might find some down here by the river." There was indeed a woven basket on her arm, and as so often in our midst, her eyes were robed with nothing but friendship.

We young ones in a very real sense had come to regard Salome as "friend" or "companion"—almost more so than as "mother" per se—which is not to say we held her in low respect or esteem, only that we had come to think of her as an equal sharer in the feast of life's wisdom.

"Our corn has grown tall and before the summer is over we shall have some melons as well!"

As she chatted, she smiled upon us one by one, each in turn, until her eyes came to rest upon Susanna, whereupon suddenly, "Cover yourself child!" The words flew with a chafed urgency, as all heads turned toward Susanna; still upon the rock my sister sat, her feet, even now, dangling in the water, yet at some stage in our childish bandying, her himation had drawn and bunched itself up to a point well above her knees. As I say, Salome tended to be rather open minded, though on the subject of her daughter forgetting to keep herself modestly covered, she was stern in the extreme. Moreover, this was not the first time she had reprimanded Susanna on such. "My word, girl," she sighed, "you at times have the most unpersevering and foolish mind!"—whereupon Susanna, with a sense of penitent hastiness, began to arrange herself. "You children be home in an hour. Dinner will be ready!" Salome finished, and departed from us, following the river south.

As for us, we continued claiming title to our little swimming spot, turning our attention once more to the pressing matters of youth. Late summer had lavished the land with its gold and tawny-hued sinecures, effusing into our young souls a spirit and thirst for adventure. Because of my mother's good heart, we had been left to linger on, here in the dense shade of heaven—where we most desired to be.

Chapter Four

"**W**hat do you think of this yellow wolf?" asked James as we continued on in the rose-apple solitude of our river sanctuary.

"In the Roman language it would be '*lupus croceus*,'" said Susanna, trying to remember to keep her knees covered though having once more allowed her feet to dangle in the current.

"*Lupus*-what?" asked Peter.

"*Croceus*. It means yellow." My sister, having mastered Greek, was taking up the Roman tongue as well, so it seemed.

"In other words 'yellow *wolf*,' knave!" said Philip, who did *not* speak Latin, but who had at least grasped the meaning of the words *lupus* and *croceus*.

By now our topic of conversation had shifted from the tragic plight of Hero and Leander, though not entirely had we left the subject of legends. The new object of our speculation was a creature known only as "the yellow wolf," the lore of which had sprung not from the Greeks, but the Egyptians, who of course, it was well-known, worshipped animals. Only in this case, the particular Egyptians who had promulgated this story of a wild *lupus croceus* lived not in Egypt, to the south and west of us, but in the desert to the east, where, sooner or later, those of a certain bent and temperament eventually habited themselves, ostensibly in the search for God. Little was known of this small group of wayfaring Egyptians other than that they had come to call themselves "The People of the Light." Given the aforesaid quest for God, for all we knew, it could be said that their stories had sprung less from the land of Egypt than the brilliances of the barren desert sky.

"So what about it, do you suppose this yellow wolf is real?"

"There may be such a thing. I don't know." Philip shrugged. "What does Rabbi Joel say?"

We listened intently. The young rabbi was our one and only source of information on things like desert sages and Greek fables, the things which generally fascinated us most.

"The yellow wolf is real. Of that I am sure!" announced Andrew, silent up to this point but now commencing to speak with an air of authority. Peter's younger brother was an imaginative youth, much prone to curiosity, one who often seemed to get carried away in enthusiasm for some new thing or fashion. It was a trait that made him susceptible, when he grew older, to philosophies and ideas far outside the considered norm. Yet he was basically a good-hearted boy, even if perhaps a tad bit eccentric. "It supposedly comes directly from God! Rabbi Joel says the story was passed onto him by a man of the Essenes."

Now everyone knew whom the Essenes were, a sect of Holy Sages who lived far to the south at the Sea of Salt, the waters of which, though I had never been there, reputedly were both salty and odorous. As to the Essenes themselves, the "pious ones," as it would be said, whether salty or odorous I could not say, and few were those in our town of Bethsaida who had actually met one; what was reported, though, was that they possessed something called the *Book of Solomon*, a written treatise on the secrets of healing, and that additionally certain numbers of them held the power of actually seeing into the future. Now the notion that there might be those correctly able to predict future events, fortune tellers if you will, excited our imaginations all the more, even if the fortune tellers lived at the foul smelling Sea of Salt. Maybe *especially* if they lived at the foul smelling Sea of Salt. And if the Essenes were truly able to foretell the future, what powers, pray tell, did the supernal and vatically mysterious "People of the Light" possess?

"How can a wolf come from God?"

"How does *anything* come from God, including you? Did not God create them?"

"Do you know much of these People of the Light?"

"No," replied Andrew. "But of the Essenes—*them* I have heard much."

"What have you heard?"

"They live in the desert, by the Sea of Salt. It is said that they own nothing individually, but rather hold all things in common, and there are those who say that no flesh do they eat of any living thing."

"Why do they live down there?" asked Peter. "And if not flesh, then what sort of things do they eat?"

"Whatever is not flesh, knave!" Philip responded sardonically.

"Rabbi Joel says they measure time by the movement of the sun, rather than the moon," broke in Susanna. "He tried to explain why, but I didn't really understand it. But the yellow wolf supposedly is mentioned in a book held by the People of the Light, and the Essenes, I don't know—" she shrugged abstemiously, "have seen the book, I guess."

This announcement heightened our sense of intrigue.

"But is the wolf not an animal to be feared?"

"Not if it's all yellow. Then it becomes as the heifer that is all of red—that being of a total pureness," said Andrew.

"And besides that, wolves are sacred to Apollo," explained Susanna.

Philip at this point added his own rather limited expertise on the matter, "Some people say there has never been a wolf that was completely yellow; others say there is one now that makes his home on Mount Hermon, and that he is the first yellow wolf to appear in more than a thousand years."

"No!"

"That is what they say! I'm only telling you what I've heard."

"They say that about the red heifer too," said James with a yawn.

Yet it was Andrew who dispensed the most startling news of all.

"The wolf is as fleet of foot as the very mind of God," he declared. Then lowering his voice, he expounded further: "And they say that those who are lucky enough to see him will receive a special blessing from God."

"Andrew, where do you obtain such absurd notions?"

"What nonsense!" exclaimed his older brother Peter.

"It is *not* nonsense!" Andrew retorted.

"We should ask Rabbi Joel."

"Rabbi Joel says exactly that! It is he who told it to me!"

"Knave! You are full of foul-smelling dung!"

"He *did*!"

Suddenly James stood up and stretched.

"I do not know about the rest of you, but I am going in for a swim."

"Perhaps you will see the yellow wolf," Peter supplied with a grin. "Perhaps he swims with the fishes!"

We didn't observe any wolves swimming at the bottom of the Jordan that afternoon, but the next day when we saw Rabbi Joel we prodded our young teacher for every single fact or hearsay he could pass along about the mythical creature.

"The yellow *wolf*, do you say!" Tidying a collection of papyrus scrolls while cleaning dust from a shelf, he paused. "The yellow wolf...hmmm..."

"Andrew told us this wild story about blessings from God, and he said he got it from you, so we wanted to know, well, if any of it's true or not."

"He's a good boy, Andrew. Very bright, that one."

Rabbi Joel was in his thirties. Though a gentle soul, he had a tendency to solitariness, a diminutive Osiris-in-passage, who seemed to reside perpetually in his own rhythmic peculiarities. We'd see him wandering the lanes of our town sometimes, hands clasped behind his back, ruminating absently to himself. Not from Bethsaida was he, but Egypt. I had heard that he was an Alexandrian Jew, in fact one of the Therapeutes, or a displaced one at any rate. He had arrived in Bethsaida six years before, as if having drifted in on some random current of the Jordan, a being constituted with an odd mixture of penance, self-mortification, and a dreamy sort of worldliness. As I've already mentioned, my mother had enlisted him as her somewhat unwilling accomplice in the teaching of girls, though the road had not been easy for either of them. One major obstacle had been Zebedee, who had remonstrated to no end on the evils of interfering in the business of others.

"Let them raise their daughters as they wish!" he had fumed.

"But it is not fair for the boys to learn to read and write, while the girls remain ignorant!" my mother had protested.

"Why must you persist in thinking it's your place to change matters? Desist and stay out of it!"

"What can be stayed away from is only that which cannot be impelled by prayer. How does wine become wine but with the help of God?" Salome retorted.

I guess you could say that was another argument my thundering father lost. And while my mother had been up to handling the criticisms of her own husband, the husbands of other wives, the father's of the girls she was trying to help, had been a far different matter. Teaching a girl to read and write was considered largely tantamount to starting her down the road to moral depravity, at least that was the view held by some. The fathers for the most part were not happy with what my mother was doing, and while Salome had tried to shoulder most of the criticism herself, Rabbi Joel had not been spared completely. As I've previously mentioned there were, counting Susanna, a total of four girls now receiving instruction. For my mother it was a victory, yet the number would have been five had not Caleb the miller steadfastly refused even the first letter of the alphabet should be taught to his daughter. She was a young thing of eleven whom the miller had ferreted out at the school building one day, subsequently dragging her off toward home in a torrent of tears. It had been a few nights later when, encountering Rabbi Joel on a lane near the edge of town, the miller, a dull-witted brute who had little in the way of learning himself, had imparted upon the teacher a look of implacable hatred.

"So what about the yellow wolf," prompted James.

"Well," answered the rabbi. "There are different views on the matter, and it's mostly speculative; few, if any, have actually seen it, and none that I know personally."

"Have the People of the Light seen it?"

"Hard to say for sure, but yes, that is the story. What has been told is this: that the wolf is in essence a manifestation of the divine mind. Think of him as a spiritual wolf, as a heavenly being, that is to say from above. If there is a 'primal man,' as the Phrygians would have us believe, can there, the People of the Light would ask, not also be a primal wolf? Such at any rate is the thought on the matter." The rabbi's arms were now filled with wax tablets collected from benches across the room, tablets used by us students for writing; gathering them up, he stacked them neatly upon the now-dusted shelf, then turned, propping himself on one corner of his desk while allowing a sandaled foot to dangle loosely. "The theory on the wolf is that the spirit of God is in it. There are those who say the last yellow wolf lived more than a thousand years ago, but it's also rumored one is alive today and living upon the Mountain of the Snow, which is to say Mount Hermon. The story is that one may perchance glimpse him if one goes there and is very lucky."

"Do you really receive a blessing from God if you see him?"

He laughed, softly amused. "This creature holds much fascination for you, I see."

"We were just wondering, is all. So *does* it?"

"Well, this is the belief. It may not be the blessing you expect, nay, one that you might think even desirable at the time, but a blessing of some sort nonetheless." Then with a wistful smile he added, "What we know for sure is that it says in the *Book of Noah* we are to acquire wisdom and understanding. And then there is the prophet Isaiah, who tells us of what is to come when he says, 'the wolf shall dwell with the lamb, and the leopard shall lie down with the kid, and the calf and the young lion and the yearling shall live together, and a little child shall lead them.'"

"That's beautiful," murmured Susanna.

"What I think it comes down to is this: when you look into another's eyes, what you must see is yourself. That is the way."

"So where does the wolf come from?" asked Peter.

"*Shmaya*," he replied. "Heaven."

Chapter Five

Being young and of that spirit of the breaking up and turning of new earth, we decided to head for the Sacred Mountain of the Snow to see if we could find the yellow wolf. It was the coming-to-end of summer. Young people and summer go hand in hand, both being racers. That summer in particular we had seemed to be racing something, attempting to catch up to what forever lay just ahead of us. It was a time of volant wonder, filled with the flamboyance of youthful growth, with the ardent thunder of exploration, and it was a fitting close to the summer, we felt, that we should no less than seek out the mysterious yellow wolf, to find out for ourselves if the legend were true.

"But how do we get to Mount Hermon?" asked Philip.

"Look to the north," replied Peter.

"I think you get there by following the Jordan," said James.

"It is a long way."

"It is many furlongs off, many miles even. And even if we make it that far, how will we know where to find the yellow wolf? It is a large mountain. It is actually three mountains," supplied Philip.

"If God is in the wolf, and the wolf is on the mountain, we cannot help but find him," asserted Andrew, perhaps a bit too confidently.

"That is speculative! We should try to be certain."

"We should ask Rabbi Joel. Maybe he knows the part of the mountain the wolf is on."

"He doesn't know if the wolf even exists or not!"

"Well he at least knows how to get to the mountain; we should *ask* him!"

"Well one thing is for certain," announced Susanna. "If you go to seek the yellow wolf, I go with you."

This threw the discussion into confusion.

"Nay! You are a girl! It is too dangerous!"

"I can climb a tree as good as any of you, and I can read Greek *better*!"

It was true, she could climb a tree pretty well, and in all things Greek she excelled beyond the lot of us. Every poem and play in Rabbi Joel's collection she had devoured with an insatiable appetite. That year her breasts had begun to bud, and there was a magical lightness to her eyes as she performed her chores, mothering me, studying her books, all the while trying to remember to keep her legs covered; she had also begun to wear her hair pinned back, in the manner prescribed for "proper" young ladies, this too at my mother's insistence, yet as in the matter of her himation, always there seemed stray wisps and strands that furrowed their way to freedom.

"What do we need of any Greek-reading capability on this journey?" asked Philip.

"That shows what you know!" my sister retorted. "Suppose you get to the top of the mountain, and suppose thereon you uncover some stone tablets written in Greek. Suppose these stone tablets relate information concerning the whereabouts of the yellow wolf? You, with your pitiably inadequate knowledge of the language, would be unable to decipher them."

"That is a good deal of supposing."

"It makes no difference to me whether you say, 'Come with us,' or 'Don't come with us.' If you leave, I will simply follow you. *All* of you."

"No, Mother would never allow you to go," replied James.

"Let us face facts, *none* of our mothers or fathers shall ever allow *any* of us to go," replied Susanna.

"Yes, she is right about that." Philip's voice was suddenly conspiratorial. "If we are going to go we simply must up and leave."

"The two of you are speaking lunacy!"

"We should all be in trouble when we return."

"Trouble may be our lot, even if we *don't* go," Andrew theorized now.

"How so?

"Well, supposing one day we find ourselves on a battlefield. And suppose we are surrounded by a million bloodthirsty Parthians. And suppose we are all out of arrows. And suppose at that very moment, just before we finally are overcome by the enemy, we think back to that day, long, long ago, when we saw the yellow wolf, and we remember, so thinking back, 'I, fortunate fellow that I am, still have one last blessing from God remaining to my credit!'"

"We have crossed back into the 'Land of Suppose' again! In the name of the heavenly host!"

"Do not be overly dramatic, Andrew!"

"Think it can't happen!?" protested Andrew.

"Yes and a pig can fly like a bird!"

On the crest of a giant slab of basalt, looking somewhat regal as the wind blew back his hair, perched Peter, with James, my quiet, strong brother, a cubit or so below him. Philip and Susanna leaned against the base of the rock, Susanna with her himation drawn up, leaving her knees exposed once more, while Andrew and I sat cross-legged on the ground a short distance away. We were near the spring in the center of town, where the road came together with two others. A retaining wall had been built, with stone benches for people to rest on, but we preferred the giant rock. From the center of the retaining wall, however, spring water gurgled, supplying us with a tranquil melody as it flowed out of the pipe. With it not being a market day, we had the place pretty much to ourselves, or so we thought. Suddenly, however, from the north side of the square a man with donkey and cart approached noisily.

"It's Caleb the miller," said James.

"Greetings Caleb!" Peter hailed through cupped hands from the top of the rock.

"Sshhh!" admonished Susanna. "Don't speak to him! He's that disputeful fool who dragged his daughter out of school and beat up his wife."

It was true. One night, not long after forcibly removing his daughter from Rabbi Joel's class for girls, the miller had gotten into a most spectacular row with his wife. It had been a dreadful affair. The poor woman had taken blows from her husband's fists, the entire town awakening to the ruckus, but what really left people shaking their heads in wonder was Caleb's binding his wife and leaving her chained all night to a stout tree trunk—although this aspect of the affair had not been discovered until appearance of the sun next morning. Rabbi Hamul had issued a sharp rebuke, upon which the miller had sheepishly freed his wife, but that had been the extent of protection the rabbi could offer the woman. Less than a month later, Caleb had declared her "unclean" and written her a bill of divorce. She was sent packing. He had not even paid the *kethuba*. The divorce left her destitute. A week later, Caleb had proceeded to marry a woman fifteen years her junior.

"Yes. He's kind of a stern one, Caleb is," remarked Peter.

"'Stern?'" repeated Susanna. "Far be it from me to cast aspersions on your learned assessments, but I hardly think 'stern' be the correct word to describe a man who ties up his wife like he was tying his donkey."

"Nay," Peter grinned. "His donkey probably receives the better of the treatment."

"Jest not! It is not a lighthearted matter!" Susanna retorted.

"Think I was jesting?"

Came now the noise of the rattling cart as Caleb drew nigh. Politely we wished him peace, *shalom alekh hem*, as he passed us, except for Susanna, who pointedly looked away. From the opposite side of the square by chance my mother appeared, carrying two water pots for filling at the spring, and as luck would have it, she and the miller crossed paths. "Hello Caleb." But there was no warmth in her voice; it was in fact quite cold, my mother fixing upon the miller a gaze leaving little doubt of her contempt. In reply, the miller offered a contorted "hrrrmmph" while proceeding on past in disdainful repudiation, much as if my mother were something unclean. It was at this point we kids *tried*, we truly tried, to control our laughter, for to laugh at such moments is indecorous and rude, but of course we were children, and controlling laughter when one is young is not an easy thing to do; and so our mirthfulness spilled forth.

All we could see of Caleb at this point was his petulantly retreating back. It was to be safely assumed, however, he was not amused, causing us to laugh the harder. But if Caleb was unamused, Salome was even less so, which struck us as somehow not quite as funny. After greeting us, *somewhat* more politely than she had the miller, her pots she began to fill, though as her eyes fell on her daughter, a renewed look of exasperation swept through her face. "For the love of the Lord, girl, cover your legs up!"

One and all we glanced at Susanna, only to discover that, yes, it had happened again; the hem of her himation was once more in high flight, leaving exposed not only her knees, but a curvaceous section of bared thigh, doubtless duly taken note of by Caleb. Stung by her mother's rebuke, my sister carefully rearranged herself...as Peter's eyes followed her movements in wistful longing.

"And *keep* them covered, for the love of the Lord." Fresh off the encounter with the miller, Salome was in no trifling mood. "Listen, all of you! I made a cinnamon cake and I want you to take it over to Naava, the widow of Eliab. Her rheumatism has been acting up again and she can't even get out of bed now. Get moving, all of you! Father will be home and dinner will soon be ready!"

We helped Mother carry her water pots back to the house, took the cake to Naava the widow, and then, as the sun sank, returned home for dinner. But the next day we were once again plotting our journey to the Mountain of the Snows.

"We will need to take food," said Peter.

"And bedding and clothing that are of a thickness to keep off the wind. It is likely to be cold on the mountain."

"Are you jesting? It is *hot* now!"

"Nay, not on the mountain! It will be cold!"

"We should take nuts. Nuts fill the stomach and will stay fresh."

"I know of a field where there are pistachios growing. Let's go and gather some."

"How many should we take?"

"A great many."

"We should maybe gather some for Naava the widow too," suggested Susanna.

"Come on, let's go!"

Suddenly we were on our feet, racing out of town, past the northern hedgerows, into the rolling hills beyond, our arms, our legs, our whole bodies, proudly proclaiming themselves to sun, sky, and extended space. In the hills outside of town we found sheep grazing, as well as a field of barley, languishing like a freed slave under the late summer sun. Skirting these temporary impediments, we came at last to a stone wall rising up on our right like some protective minion. Following it until it intersected with another like it, we eventually found ourselves in a familiar maze of identical stone escarpments, all taller than we were, an area in which we had played many times in the past. Usually it was abandoned. Today, however, we found it occupied. Rounding from one maze passage into another, we came face to face with a rather frightening specter—a man. He was lanky and tall, dark and brooding; he was in fact a smoldering requiescat of quenched fire, and had we not known better, we might have suspected him a shade, freshly emerged from some abandoned necropolis, but of course we had all seen him before. Our only surprise was in running into him here.

The man was known by the name Rogah. Unsettling in appearance, his hair and beard were of an untamable wildness, the clothes he wore scarcely more than rags. Encountering such an apparition most anywhere would cause fright, but running into him here, in a place we customarily had to ourselves, threw us into an unnerved silence. He was the nettle of many names, the cast aside cloud of Khepera, as he stood there, swaying in his angst, his heavily furrowed brow devouring gravid felicity's offspring as he regarded us with eyes of deepest, blackest turbulence. Nobody in the village knew much about him. Other than of course his name. Rogah. And while seldom seen in town proper, he was known to haunt the hill country around the northeast shore of Gennesaret. Something of a familiar figure he had always been, yet even so, his sudden materialization here in our secret sanctuary threw us into a temporary state of confusion, as we stammered a plea of forgiveness, *washboqlan*, for having disturbed him. To this apology, he voiced no actual words as such, yet much as if in reply came a gravel-throated snarl, miasmic in tone, only part-human-sounding. This was attended by a perilous and bewitching contortion of the features which shaped his visage into a look of malevolence so startling it was suggestive almost of a total abhorrence of all life. Yet immediately upon establishing itself there on his face, it dissipated wretchedly into an apotheosis of despair. At this point, he stood before us in a cloud of ague and gloom, arms bent, fingers trembling.

Squelching our fright, we filed by in orderly manner, giving him as wide a berth as possible amidst the narrow confines of the maze. Then, safely out of sight, with no further pretense to decorum, we took off running as fast as we could. Out of the maze and down the hill we flew, further and further, until deeming ourselves safely away from that specter-ridden berth. "I think we lost him," said a breathless Peter when we at last stopped at the base of an acacia tree. "When we got out of the maze I looked back, but I didn't see him."

"I wouldn't put it past him to try and sneak back up on us and kill us," remarked Philip.

"That's silly!" replied Susanna, her budding young breasts heaving beneath her himation. "We probably scared him as much as he scared us."

"He looked awfully mean."

"They say he is demon-possessed."

"It is perhaps a thing to be believed!" laughed Peter.

"I saw him down by the Lake of Gennesaret one day as Father and some of the others were pulling in their nets." This from James, who seldom spoke to excess and was on the whole quiet by nature, yet when words perforce did cross his lips they usually added some useful or sensible perspective, which was the case now. "There was a large gash over his eyes, and I could hear him mumbling something. It was almost like he was speaking to himself. He seemed in fact not to see any of us, or to be aware we were even there."

"Maybe Rogah is a sage."

"In the name of the heavenly host! He cannot be demon-possessed and a sage too!"

"I heard," said Andrew, "that there was once a shepherd named Azgad, who used to frequent these parts to graze his flocks. They say that one night Rogah killed him and cut off his head."

"I have heard that rumor too," answered James. "I do not believe it is true."

"Then how come Azgad has never been seen since?"

"Who knows? Shepherds come and go."

But Andrew remained unconvinced. "They say Azgad rose from the dead, and that he wanders the hills at night searching for his lost head."

"Fool! Do you believe everything you hear?"

"Well no but it...*could* be true!" protested the always-truth-seeking Andrew.

Recovered from our fright, we proceeded to gather a full jute sack of pistachios and almonds, taking some of it to Naava, along with another cake and some roasted pollan our mother had made for the ailing widow; at last, we returned home.

But over the next few days we continued to prepare for our journey, gathering breads, nuts, fruits, dried fish, along with two full wineskins of water. At last, determining our provisions sufficient, we took one further precaution. We went to see Rabbi Joel. Having talked it over amongst ourselves, we had decided to take him into our confidence. It was a decision not reached lightly, but we were in dire need of directions.

"How is the best way to get to Mount Hermon?" we inquired, having found him in his study, surrounded, as usual, with his books and tablets.

A quizzical smile formed itself as he replied, "You would follow the road north as it goes along the Jordan—why?"

It was Andrew who divulged the news.

"We are going to find the yellow wolf!"

The smile vanished. "N-n-no, I-I wouldn't do that—"

"And then when we find him we shall receive a blessing from God!"

"But-but-but—it's dangerous," were all the words our dear Joel could deliver. In his face were rain clouds of disapproval, but we knew it was a dry thunder, and we were much too excited to be talked out of anything at this point. We had become clandestine wayfarers, though wayfarers not altogether certain how to reach our destination, and after tricking him into telling us the way to Mount Hermon, we swore him promptly to secrecy.

"But-but-but..."

"Don't you want us to receive a blessing from God?"

"Well yes but..."

Before he could finish we were gone, leaving our stammering, unwilling confidante stammering to an empty room.

I have no doubt that throughout our absence from Bethsaida Joel did reproach himself for having "filled our heads with a lot of heathen tales," as Rabbi Hamul might have put it. But true to his word, he kept our secret—out of a desire for self-preservation, you might think. But I have always believed it was more than that. With the possible exception of my mother, he was closer to us in spirit than any adult we knew.

And the next day before sunup we started out.

Chapter Six

I t already smelled of fall that day in the month of Tammuz, though there could still be felt a redolent trace of summer's warmth. Without so much as a farewell to the guardians of authority, we commenced our journey, severing our hindrances in the entrancing bliss of our nomadic *bereshith*. Two jute sacks of food we carried, including three loaves of my mother's course barley bread. In number, we were eight: Peter, James, Susanna, Philip, Andrew and myself, our usual group, plus the cousins of Philip, Nathanael and Perpetua, who were from Cana and Capharnaum respectively.

A disparate band we made. Nathanael was big, strapping, stout, and ruddy-cheeked, his youthful step marked by a distinctive bounce, this despite the fact that he carried around a fair amount of excess weight, or perhaps rather because of it, and before long I noticed something else too: that at home on his face was always a ready, eager smile, a wonderful fixture which waxed and waned to a degree but never departed completely, even, as we were to discover, under the most adverse of circumstances. The other cousin, Perpetua, was a dreamy-eyed girl who spoke little but ever so often broke forth into giggles over some seemingly pointless remark, as if whatever had been said were of an unsurpassed humor. She was forever stubbing a toe, losing her balance, or encountering some other difficulty, and overall required a great deal of assistance. For two hours we walked, much of it uphill, resorting to frequent stops so as to accommodate her various exigencies.

"Which way should we go?" asked Susanna when at last the river and the road diverged from one another, a divergence posing no small quandary, since Rabbi Joel had told us to "walk the road as it follows the river." But now the road was going one way, the river another. Furthermore, the river itself seemed to branch as well, offering us two possibilities in its own right.

"Well...the rabbi said to follow the *road*."

"Yes, but now road and river part from one another, and the river divides in two separate directions as well. So what should we do?"

"In the name of the Holy One, it does seem a perplexing question!" Philip mused, scratching his head.

"Maybe the road goes someplace other than the mountain, possibly a village somewhere. Most likely the river, however, will go to the mountain, for that is probably from where it runs."

This seemed logical...somewhat.

"Then we should stay with the river?"

"Yes—perhaps," Peter answered doubtfully. "But then it is to decide which of these is the *main* river, and which is only a branch."

"How do you tell when they both look equal in size?" wondered Andrew.

Confused, we stared at the scene, listening to the murmuring of waters as we tried to discern the Finite Jordan from the Infinite Jordan.

"I think it is that one," said Philip, pointing. "It seems to lead in a direction closer to where the mountain lies."

Far away, the mountain that was our goal rose like a diadem above the horizon, its peaks enjoying a familiarity with the clouds. Great was the distance, and a vast stretch of forest and crag-studded estates lay between us and it, yet afar it could be seen, asserting its existence, as it seemed to whisper to us with the strength of heaven.

"Let us stop and drink some water."

"Yes, and eat something. I am hungry."

Though hardly a banquet of the gods, the food we took was most welcomed after our long trek, its taste upon my tongue reminding me of home.

"How much farther do we have to go?"

"Not far. Maybe another two hours."

"Don't be deceived! The mountain only *looks* that close. It is in reality a great many miles off."

"What blessing do you think we will receive after laying sight upon the yellow wolf?" wondered Andrew.

"How would I know?" replied Philip.

"Perhaps you will be granted the opportunity to see Azgad looking for his lost head," Peter theorized humorously.

"Stop it! That is not funny!" Andrew protested.

"Think this may be the tallest mountain in the world?"

"Not even close! There are many that are taller."

"Rabbi Joel says there is a land called Raetia, where there are many tall mountains, taller than Mount Hermon."

"Where is this place? Maybe we should travel there next."

"Knave! It is too far away. But it is said that the mountains there are called 'alps' and that they are very tall."

"How tall?"

"Tall enough for you to fall off and break your head," said Peter, as Perpetua began to giggle.

"Maybe we should stop here for the night," suggested Nathanael.

"No, there is much daylight left. We should go on."

"But which way? To the right or the left?"

"I still think the right fork is the correct one," said Philip.

"But what if it turns out to be wrong?"

"I think it is the right way."

"You have confidently spouted that opinion three times now!"

"If the right branch proves to be incorrect, we can backtrack to here and take the left," suggested James thoughtfully.

This seemed a good idea, but after an hour or so the branch we had chosen narrowed into a sluggish stream and soon riffled out altogether into a dried bed of scree. Instead of backtracking, however, at Peter's urging we set out overland in what was judged a more direct course for the mountain, or as direct as possible, for many obstacles lay between us and it, rock formations, thickets defying all but the most determined penetration; by evening when we made camp we were lost.

"We are lost."

"We are not lost," disagreed Peter. "We know the Jordan is somewhere to our left, so stop speaking like a *raca*."

"Yes, but how far to the left?"

"We are not lost. We'll find the Jordan tomorrow."

"We are lost."

The night streamed upon us like a bellows, confirming the Vulcanalia of the stars, as a crystalline chill clung to the air. Having made a fire, we ate some more of our food as the call of a wolf rang forlornly in the distance, its cry immediately followed by a chorus of others.

"It is the yellow wolf!" posited Andrew.

"Knave! How can you know the color when it is dark and you cannot see twenty cubits beyond the campfire? Besides we are not even at the mountain yet!"

"Well maybe he comes down from the mountain occasionally."

"For the love of the heavenly host!"

"Well, if he *is* the yellow wolf he has a large number of companions," said James, as the distant pack of carnivores continued to raise their cries in the night.

"What if we are attacked by wolves?"

"We will beat them off with a stick."

"What if we are attacked by bears?"

"Then we will use a bigger stick!" said Peter, prompting a fresh spray of giggles from Perpetua.

At last, we slept, though in the middle of the night I awoke, becoming instantly conscious of a shroud of fog covering the land. And something else as well—a noise in the distance, a milch-fleecy, fitful sound, as if something, an animal perhaps, were rooting around in the darkness just beyond our camp. Somewhat uneasily, I rolled closer to my brother James, who lay asleep beside me.

"Think it is the Jordan?"

"No, it is too small."

It was the next day and we had walked three hours, coming by midday to a swift-flowing rill. It was not the main river we had been seeking, yet we parted company with our sandals and waded in, Susanna holding the hem of her himation high above her knees. Availing ourselves of this opportunity to wash the dust away, we shared the stream with a flock of herons that seemed eminently companionable toward us. Concluding our dip, we set out once more. Over the next few hours, our feet grew sore, and by sundown, we once again made camp.

"Think we have enough food to get us to the mountain and back?"

"Most likely."

"If we see something edible along the way we should probably stop and gather it, though."

The fire cast moving shadows on our faces, although the darkness beyond taunted us with an air of mystery as it grutched and breathed with the forest life around us, sparring with the fire's relatively feeble light. From somewhere out in that impenitent darkness came suddenly a sharp noise—*Crack!*—much like a breaking branch.

"Did you hear that?"

"Yes."

"What do you think it was?"

"It was a branch."

"For the love of the heavenly host! I *know* that!"

"Then why did you ask?"

"Knave! I meant, what *caused* it?"

"Then why did you not say so?"

"*Raca!* Must you give ear to everything in a literal manner?"

At this point two additional noises gripped the night. Much louder than the breaking branch of a moment ago, they retained an eerie, almost unearthly quality. One, a wrenching, baleful howl, not exactly the howl of a wolf, but something crisper, more guttural, came from just to the west, while the other, a piercing, gorgon-like screech, flew at us in short repetitive bursts from the north and east.

"What in *gehenna* was *that*?" quavered Philip.

Replied Peter, "Go out and see and when you've done so come back and report to us fully," arousing Perpetua once more to giggling.

"It is probably an owl of some sort."

"Owls do not break branches."

"Then what do *you* think it may be?"

"Evil spirits maybe."

"What is that passage from the Psalter, Philip? You know, Rabbi Hamul's favorite?"

"It goes: '*You sweep men away in the sleep of death; they are like the new grass of the morning.*'"

Rabbi Hamul was known to suspect himself beset by demons, and it was rumored he took particular care to avoid sleeping in his own house alone at night least he be attacked by Lilith the She Devil, for lone men were ever said to be vulnerable to her clutching embraces. He also tied a red rag to his donkey every day, allowing the cloth to hang just between the animal's eyes, for a red rag hanging on a donkey's forehead was known to ward off falls. Such were the rabbi's superstitions, and all of us had laughed and jested over them before; no one, however, was jesting now.

"Why does Rabbi Hamul speak that particular passage from the Psalter?"

"Haven't you heard?"

"Heard what?"

"Well..." Philip lowered his voice. "Some of the rabbis teach that that verse exercises a sort of sovereignty over demons, and that if you recite it, you will be afforded protection from the spirits. It is a verse that is carried in the *tefillin* by the doctors of the law."

"'You sweep men away in the *sleep of death*?' What does it mean?"

"Demons are the spirits of the dead."

"I still say it was an owl."

"Maybe it was an owl that has somehow become inhabited by a demon."

"A 'demon-possessed' owl? You have a fertile imagination."

"The Romans," Susanna confided now, "say there are such things as lemures—spirits of the dead—and that they go about at night and haunt and terrorize. And each year the Romans hold a feast, called the Lemuria, during which they make midnight offerings to appease these spirits, who are said to be very angry and malicious."

"It is all a bunch of rot. There are no such things as lemures, demons, or any of it!" asserted Peter.

"I'm not so sure."

"Yes. Those sounds—what if they really *are* demons? And what if they come into our camp later when we're sleeping?"

"Good point. Maybe we should say the verse. After all, it couldn't hurt."

"That settles it then. Say the verse, Philip."

"What verse?"

"You know—the verse."

"What verse?"

"For the love of the heavenly host! The verse from the *Psalter*, knave!"

"Oh. That verse." Philip shrugged. "So say it then."

"I do not *know* it!"

"Perhaps *you* should say it, Philip, since you seem to be the one who knows it," Susanna suggested with a fatigued sigh.

Philip shrugged, faced to the right, left, then paused, raised his voice and orated grandly: "**You sweep men away in the sleep of death; they are like the *new grass* of the morning!!!**"

Howwwwwwwllllllll! Screeeeeeeeechhhh! Shrieeeeeekkkkkk! The noise burst forth this time with a disconcerting tumult.

"This isn't funny," Perpetua murmured, her giggles departing as she became frightened for the first time.

"I do not think the demon is very intimidated by your verse," said Peter.

"It's not my verse; it's from the Psalter. And I never said it would work."

"I am going to see what the nature of this is," said James, rising with a stout stick in hand.

"I'll go with you," announced Peter, arising similarly armed.

Boldly I declared, "I go also!" though like a windlestraw was yanked down by Susanna, who promptly issued an order: "No, John! Stay here!" It was that annoying mothering she had been inflicting on me my whole life! With a newly-unfolding insight common to boys my age I was growing heartily sick of it, yet so accustomed to her authority was I, I allowed myself to be pulled back down.

James and Peter went out scouting the darkness, leaving behind the camp and its friendly fire, as the rest of us waited anxiously, their shadowy forms somewhat visible out in the distance as Peter's voice at one point demanded, "Who's there?" in the stern clip of a gallant imperator. No reply came.

"What did you see?" queried Susanna when they had returned.

"Nothing," said James.

For a long moment silence. Then Philip spoke:

"That means it's an evil spirit—because evil spirits are invisible."

"Your *brain* is full of evil spirits! It was an owl!"

Again silence as we tried to absorb the possible explanations.

"Did you see any owls out there?" Perpetua asked, hoping at least not to eliminate that possibility though fearing what the answer might be.

"No. None," replied Peter.

"Maybe it was just the wind," said Nathanael, his good-natured smile undiminished.

Yes maybe it *was* the wind...but somehow that didn't seem convincing.

"There may be a way we can tell if it is a demon."

"How?"

"Well," confided Philip, "it is said, that if by night you put sifted ashes on the threshold of your house, and a demon is in or about, the demon, though invisible, will leave his footprint in the ashes; then the footprints may be seen in the morning, in which case you will know that you in fact have a demon."

"We have no threshold."

"Knave! We have no *house*."

"No—but we have a camp. A house. A camp. It is the same thing!"

"For the love of the heavenly host! How can a camp and a house be the same thing?"

"For this purpose they are identical," countered Philip defensively.

"Aye, identical, except one has roof and walls and one does not."

"Roof and walls are not needed. Only a threshold."

"What are you—pretending to be a *specialist* on demons?"

"I'm only telling you what I heard!"

"You heard that a camp and a house are the same thing...and that a speech-bereft demon will *announce* himself by stepping in your ashes?"

"Nay! You are twisting my words!"

Perpetua was back into giggling mode again.

"Maybe there is something to what he says," James intruded now. "Sift some ashes from the fire and lay them somewhere."

"But where—where should we lay them?"

"Beyond that broom sage over there is a large flat rock," said James. "That can be our threshold."

"Where? I do not see."

"No," he said. "You can't see it from here. Come, I will show you."

We got up, followed my brother. In the flickering shadows on the edge of camp, just this side of a spiny acanthus bush, a large flat rock exerted itself like an anvil across the pale, interposed moonlight.

"Here," said James. "Spread the ashes here."

Chapter Seven

Sometime during the night, I awoke, hearing, as upon the previous night, a rustling sound in the trees beyond camp. This time I did not dismiss it so easily for an animal. Moving closer to my brother, I shook him by the shoulder. "James," I whispered. "Do you think it is the demon?"

He was asleep. "Hhhmmmph," he mumbled. I shook him again. "*James*," I whispered more urgently, and when finally he was sensible, repeated the question.

"Do I think *what* is the demon?" he replied tiredly.

"*That*," I said—but the sound had stopped.

"I do not hear anything. Go to sleep, John." He placed an arm over me, and we drifted off to slumber once again.

With a dove's cry came the sun, the Eye of Ra, the next morning. Trying to imitate the relaxed-but-methodical movements of the older boys, I began rolling up my blanket. I had gotten no more than halfway through this task when suddenly Andrew appeared.

"There is a large footprint in the ashes."

Dumfounded, we all looked around at each other, blinking in bewilderment.

"You are stuffed full of dung, knave!"

"Nay! There is a footprint!" he insisted. "If you do not believe me, then go over and see for yourself!"

To the flat rock where, the night before, we had laid the ashes, we now as a group ran. Sure enough at one end of the rock was a lengthy, diffuse, ash-occluded imprint of a human foot.

"Holy *Shmaya*!"

"Alright! Who got up in the middle of the night, came over here and stuck his foot in the ashes?"

"Not me," whispered Philip. "It is bigger than my foot."

Peter, standing close to the edge of the rock, propped up an appendage for comparison. Gazing down with an analytical eye, he commented in surprise, "It's bigger than *my* foot too." When we realized the print was bigger than all our feet, a new concern, one more acute even than that of the night before, swept over us. The great unmitigable truth we had to come to terms with was that someone, or some*thing*, possibly at this very moment, was observing our movements.

"Holy *Shmaya*! Let's get out of here!"

"Yes! Let's be gone from this place—as quickly as possible!"

For two hours we walked. In the face of this discernable danger, even Perpetua seemed to have far fewer toe-stubbing incidents, and after some time, the lay of the land became markedly more elevated. At one point, we startled a herd of ibexes grazing fastidiously on those latticed and primordial heights, realizing with a sense of triumph that we were, quite truly, in the high country now! The mountain, too, in size and scope was noticeably closer, not like the previous day when we had walked for hours seemingly with no appreciable closing of its distance; now it loomed majestically.

"We are going to climb *that*?"

"Yes, man!"

"How? It is too high. We will never make it to the top!"

"It is not so high."

"Maybe we should turn back," said Nathanael doubtfully.

Glancing at Philip's cousin from Cana, I found myself wondering how he would ever carry all that excess weight up to the top of such a mountain.

"Turn back?" Peter demurred. "Surely you are jesting! After we have come this far?"

"Maybe the yellow wolf resides at a point lower than the top," suggested Andrew hopefully.

By mid afternoon, we had drawn close enough to see the outlines of a town, lying, as it turned out, at the mountain's base. The little settlement seemed to waver in the late gold of the sun, and while making for it we regained the Jordan—at a point where the river cascaded superbly into a roaring waterfall. Staying close to the river's churning waters, we followed the trail north and east, arriving at last at the town, whose name, we discovered, was Panias. A paved walkway led us past the seeded and inutile shadings of a crowded market, where a vacuous sort of glory seemed to shine amidst the scent of burning incense. The walkway, as we followed it further through some trees, deposited us at last upon a large square, in fact a temenos, dominated by two massive temples, and here a great many people seemed to be about, wandering to and fro in lazy oread.

"Look at these temples!"

"Truly they must do a great deal of worshipping here!"

Led by James, we made our way to the west end of the acropolis, the side closer to us, here coming upon a spectacular edifice built around a huge grotto or cave. Carved just above its mouth was a wide niche, *inside* of which stood a stone sculpture, of a *creature* of some sort. It was half man and half animal, possibly a goat, though I could not say with certainty. Inside the grotto, lo and behold, was an underground spring, the spring, as it turned out, feeding the very headwater we had followed into town! We had, for all intents and purposes, made our way to the source of the Jordan River! Up at the grotto, with its peculiar half-man/half-beast carving, we stared in some curiosity; below the niche was an inscription...written in Greek.

"What does it say?" asked Philip.

It was here Susanna's prediction of our journey's requiring the services of an accomplished Greek reader came to fulfillment. "It reads," she now informed us, "'The Court of Pan and the Nymphs.' This temple is dedicated to Pan. In fact you could say the whole town pretty much is, which is why it's called Panias."

"Pan? Who's Pan?" wondered Andrew.

Susanna rolled her eyes.

"Greek God of the woods and fields, knave!" She shoved him playfully. "Also known to have had the sexual habits of a goat."

The temple pediment was held aloft by massive stone columns, shouldering its weight with an apathy as well as an unmoving life wind. The other temple, on the opposite side of the grotto, was dedicated to Caesar Augustus, and it was here one might make an offering and pay worship to the Roman emperor. Built it had been by the late king, Herod the Great, known to have been somewhat less than heedful of Jewish law. Herod could never have gotten away with constructing such a temple in Jerusalem, but this was the land of Gaulanitis. Here things were different, *very* different, as we were beginning to perceive. We were now in a Gentile city!

Up the steps toward the Temple of Pan we made our way, arriving at last at its entrance. Technically, in the eyes of Jewish law, we were now defiled, but rather than compelling us to turn back, the thought gave rise to a tingle of the forbidden. In the lofty and recondite pronaos a woman spoke to us. "Where are you from?"

"Bethsaida."

"All the way from there? How long have you traveled?"

"Three days."

"We are going up to the mountain," said Andrew, "to seek the yellow wolf."

"Yellow wolf?"

"It is told of by the People of the Light. The yellow wolf lives on the mountain, and if one lays eye upon it he will receive a blessing from God."

"*She* also will receive! You seem to forget, two of us are women!" Susanna reminded him.

At this point, the priestess smiled.

"My name is Pompeia. You look very tired. Why don't all of you come to my house and rest up from your travels?"

Though hesitant, we accepted, a wise decision as it turned out; her hospitality was of an exceeding graciousness. Not only were we able to bathe, but also to dine in the rich comfort of her triclinium upon a flavorful and succulent fare, a veritable lintel of comestibles, affording our tongues a liberating respite from the exiguous substances, now grown stale, from our jute bag. In the course of a delightful meal, we learned that two others shared the house with her—also women.

"We are priestesses in service to the God Pan."

It was another way of saying they were extremely high-class prostitutes. The way the temple system worked was this: the weary traveler came to pay his respects to the God; if his donation were especially generous, Pan might show his appreciation by favoring the worshipper with the company of one of his nymphs. In addition to providing sexual favors for pay, the priestesses played musical instruments and tended a fire, all in tribute to the goat-man deity, who, though having at one time caused "panic" among the Persians, is thought perhaps to have been less a warrior than a lover. It was said that he spent the greater part of his days wandering the forests of Arcadia playing the pipes and pursuing a redoubtable bevy of nymphs, including the nymph Erato, who became his prophetess.

"If," said Pompeia with a smile, "you come during festival time you can attend the holy rites of the Bacchanalia."

"What is that?" asked Susanna.

"Oh…" our hostess shrugged, "a lot of people wearing animal masks and cavorting naked through the forest, all while consuming vast quantities of wine, of course."

"You can certainly count me in for the next one!" said Philip, as Pompeia regarded him, amused.

"Your kindness is most excellent," Susanna said. "Had you been with us in the place we camped last night you would know how truly welcomed are the warmth and safety of your hearth."

"How so?"

"We kept hearing strange noises," said Philip.

"Aye," put in Andrew. "Horrible sounds, such as you never heard before."

Here the face of the priestess darkened a shade as she commented, "It is said that there are evil spirits ranging in the forest."

"See!" Philip remarked, triumphant. "Did I not *say* so? But would you believe me? 'No!!!' you insisted obtusely. 'It is only an *owl!*'"

"Stifle yourself, knave! What do you think, you've received divine verification of your genius or something?"

"What is your own opinion?" James inquired now of Pompeia. "Do you believe these evil spirits are real?"

The priestess shrugged. "I do not know. All I can tell you is that a year ago a man, a traveler not of these parts, came into town one night in a terrible fright. He told of rustlings in the wood and a number of other strange occurrences, and a few days later, he went completely mad. Staring mutely, he refused all food and one night when the moon was full took himself to the edge of town, climbed to the highest part of the cliff, and threw himself off."

We pondered this news in constrained silence.

"The Psalter has a verse in it that supposedly wards off evil spirits, and we tried saying it, but the demon, or whatever it was, did not go away."

"The *Psalter*?" replied the priestess. "You are Jews, then?"

"Yes we are."

"Have many travelers stopped here on their way to seek the yellow wolf?" inquired Andrew.

"I have not heard of this yellow wolf of which you speak," replied Pompeia. "But it is said that the mountain is sacred to people of many religions. It is also said that it holds the three worlds, the heavens, the earth, and the underworld, within its grasp, and that the snows it wears are its celestial garments. Perhaps you will find what it is for which you search."

I wondered if we would. The mountain lay just beyond the town, under a day's journey away. What would we find when we reached it, and would it come anywhere near what we had conjured in our imaginations?

"In climbing the slope step with caution," the priestess said the next morning after a delectable breakfast of fresh cherries, salted bread, eggs and cheese. We had had a long, blissful sleep. How wonderful to make a friend in the most unexpected of places! She had captivated us with her hospitality, favoring us with a priestly pinacotheca of lordly fare—not something any of us were soon to forget. "The trail up is steep and treacherous in places. Go with great care."

"Thank you again! Your hospitality has meant everything to us!"

That day we climbed to a point whereat we could look down and see the town of Panias, with its two pagan temples, now in miniature, and its people making their way along their tranquil walkways; much like a demarcation of ants they appeared from this height. The air here was of a noticeable thinness, our breath coming heavily, and after a while I found myself tiring as much from the climb as from the taking in of deeper and deeper draughts of air. The sun gradually faded, finally disappearing altogether as it left us substantially in blackness lasting longer than an hour—until an eerie moon jumped at last from behind the towering peaks. It was a moon which seemed to greet us with a jauntily raised hand and a gloating, slightly sinister smile.

Chapter Eight

Our progress was slow the next day as we made our way up one ridge cleft after another until it became clear the mountain was comprised of not one, but three major peaks, not unlike three beauteous maids. No snow could be found on the upper elevations, for it was still summer, but as predicted, it *was* cool. Of course, we had no idea where the yellow wolf might be. Mindful as well of what the priestess had said about evil spirits, we kept our senses keenly sharpened for hint of demonically possessed owls and what not. Nothing of the sort did we see. Yet something peculiar *did* present itself. As we ascended yet another ridge, there came upon us in that abysmal stillness a crashing boulder, a gargantuan thing, asserting its mastery by force as it burst upon us with a malign peevishness; with no warning it appeared, and had its trajectory been so much as a fraction of a cubit to either right or left it should have caused us unimaginable calamity. Even in our sidestepping of its ground-quaking bullishness, Susanna had been forced to grab Andrew by his tunic, yanking him backwards with not a moment to spare.

"You grabbed me too hard!" he complained afterwards with a frosty petulance.

"Knave! You would have been flattened into a wheat cake had I not!"

The fact of the matter was we were tired—and by day's end more so. Fatigue brought with it pessimism, making us increasingly ill of temperament with each step. The encounter with the boulder had, at least for one terrifying moment, brought us to an acute awareness of our mortality, an awareness to which ones as young as us were not normally susceptible. Our thoughts took an unusual turn as we grappled for the first time with the idea that we were on unfriendly terrain and that we could lose our lives here on this mountain.

"Maybe we should give up trying to find the yellow wolf."

"Yes. Maybe he does not wish to be found," said Philip.

And so we began entertaining notions of turning back. But this was complicated by a storm which in the early evening commenced to brew.

"Think we should try climbing down if this is still falling in the morning?"

Under a rock overhang we had taken shelter, huddled in a circle while holding blankets over our heads in an effort to protect ourselves from a cheerless, apathetic rain—*shelter* of a sort—but it had not dissuaded the night's stodgy wetness from soaking clear through our clothing all the way to our skins.

"It'll stop."

"But what if it doesn't?"

"Then we shall walk down off the mountain in the rain."

"It will be very slippery," Philip pointed out.

"Knave! Is it necessary for you to always state the obvious?"

Another hour went by and the rain continued.

"I have been having a thought. It keeps passing unendingly through my mind," Philip declared in a deeply troubled tone.

"*Well*?" Peter replied after a long and extended silence, "are you going to *tell* us your thought...or are you simply announcing the *presence* of one in your tiny noggin?"

At this, Perpetua gave birth to a malnourished, rain-drenched giggle.

Philip answered with annoyance, "My thought is *this*, and it keeps coming back to one question: *where* did the boulder come from?"

"What do you mean?"

"Did you not notice? The boulder which nearly killed us—that it seemed to come from nowhere?"

"It was a rockslide."

"A rockslide of only one rock?"

"Who knows? It was a rockslide. Rockslides are normal in these parts."

"Knave! How do you presume to know what is 'normal' in these parts? You have never set foot on this mountain before!"

"So where do *you* think the rock came from, Philip?" asked Nathanael.

"I do not know," he answered quietly.

"Knave!" bellowed Peter. "Why bring it up then?"

"Only just to say...that it was kind of strange."

There being nothing anyone could offer to dispute this, we fell into a moody silence, broken only by the sound of the abrogating rain. Susanna's arms encircled me, and for once in my life I was *glad* of her mothering, for I was scared—scared, wet, and miserable. Eventually I fell into a fitful sleep.

Dawn arrived, and the rain slacked off, becoming more of a foggy mizzle than an ongoing, persistent shower, nonetheless, we were cold and dispirited; making matters worse, our food was soggy, having transformed itself overnight into a sodden, amorphous cosmogony. We deigned to eat only a few unappetizing morsels before rising to meet our challenge: getting down off the mountain in one piece. For yes, we had decided to relinquish our quest to find the wolf.

"I think if we go down this way it will be easier." Peter pointed to a declension through a ridge that seemed to provide, at least initially, an easily negotiable pass toward the lower elevations.

"But that is not the way we came. We should go back the way we came up," Philip advised.

"The way we came is very steep. I do not relish reversing our steps and going back that way, especially with the ground as wet as it is." Peter continued to insist we would get down more quickly by following the declension, yet Philip adamantly favored the same route we had taken upon our ascent, thinking, I suppose, the perils we knew preferable to those we did not; in the end, however, it was Peter who prevailed. We started down the pass, it beckoning at first gently to us, though after an hour the terrain changed markedly, as we found ourselves entangled in a knitted bundle of basalt formations, a series of jagged and daunting escarpments we were forced to mount awkwardly, so that in many cases we found ourselves obliged to climb *upwards* before actually making any downward progress. Such hand-holds and toe-holds as we could obtain were slippery, crepuscular, glistening piteously in the dim morning wetness. Finally, around the fourth hour we came to a drop-off into a deep gorge, a chasm of almost dizzying dimensions that seemingly offered us no choice but to turn back. The distance down was so far we could not, in the fog, make out the bottom. The sole exception to this was a rough outcropping some twenty cubits down, and extending maybe four cubits outward as it jutted, meniscus-shaped, from the cliff's otherwise vertical face. Below that—nothing. Looking over that edge gave me a dizzying sensation of fear.

"We will have to turn back," said Philip. In his voice I could perceive no trace of satisfaction in having been right, yet Peter was unwilling to concede the point.

"If we turn back it will take all day! There's another way. I can jump across."

"Nay!" said Philip.

"See that tree trunk on the other side? When I get over there I can maneuver it into place. We can stretch it over the top of the rim and the rest of you can walk on across. It will be just like walking over a bridge."

Indeed, the abyss before us resembled nothing so much as a deep and limpid crevice carved into the soul of the mountain, and was not so wide as to preclude any thought of making such a leap, and while there were not many trees growing at this height, there was indeed a fallen one on the far side, a tree which seemed, as Peter remarked now, to have been left there for just such a purpose. But to actually answer that call, to leap into the time-light of that chasm, required a casting aside of reason and prudence. The penalty for failure would be dreadful in the extreme; even so, Peter was determined to try. "To turn back is to spend another night, maybe two, on this mountain."

"Peter, it is too risky," said Susanna.

"It is not that risky, and it will save us a lot of time and effort."

"Nay, Peter, do not!" Philip responded, growing angry now.

There is no sin in the mistakes we make unintentionally, and even if we are not born of wind and clouds, never could we pass the eternal regions of Light without at least a momentary urge to reach. Disregarding our pleas he should consider otherwise, Peter gathered himself into a spry and manifest principium—and then flew like Icarus. His leap was a sharp and vigorous salute, propelling him to the opposite rim...yet not far enough to achieve the platform of secure footing for which he had aimed. Seeking the effulgence of the cliff's level top as one might seek the Great Holy Nourisher, he scrabbled now, his hands grasping for a hold, even as the trunk of his body slid slowly but relentlessly downward. Desperately he sought to regain his equilibrium, to stop an erratic displacement of his legs and trunk, but to no avail. In the end, there was nothing to grab onto but filaments of moss-covered rock. Scraping his face against the very ledge where his feet should have been planted, he went flailing terrifyingly into space as Perpetua shrieked in horror.

"Peter!" screamed Andrew.

"Nay!" Susanna wailed.

Standing upon that dentilated precipice, we watched in horror as he plummeted. But the abyss did not claim him, not completely. Suddenly his fall into what surely would have been the house of death was halted with an abstemious impermanence, an impermanence that had perhaps bowed to the deity of the great mountain, as Peter's body slammed, with a terrific force, into the rugged, meniscus-shaped outcropping below. Had he been spared the descent into full Eternity? We held our breath, for suddenly it looked as if he might lose this perch as well. Over the side and downward he went once again, but this time his arm, like the sovereign monarch of a minor kingdom, was able to gain claim upon a rock—a rock which refused to slide or budge. Daring to hope he might yet live, we looked on in suspense as he realigned himself painfully into a secure position in the recess of the outcrop. At this point, ornamented with a very peculiar and loosely fitting mantle of life, a scream tore itself from his throat, echoing up through the chasm.

Gazing upon that lawless void, with Peter's scream echoing, I saw several lammergeiers soaring on graceful wings; it increased my sense of disorientation, like a clematis in the desert, to see birds actually flying *below* me. "Oh my God, what are we going to do!"—this from Perpetua, who, giddily, with eyes afire, gazed down into the gulf as if sublime recognition of the Eternal had been suddenly expropriated through the pores of her skin.

"We'll have to drop a rope down to him," said James. "One of us will have to go down." Then he called over into the foggy chasm with a ferocious urgency: "Peter! Can you hear me?"

"Aye," the distant reply floated up, followed by a tenuous wave of the hand.

We indeed had thought to bring a rope with us—only one. This we uncoiled now as Nathanael moved to fasten one end to a rock.

"I'll go down," said James, testing the line.

"James be careful!" said Susanna.

"It might not be long enough." Philip strained his senses downward, trying to judge the distance. James dropped the rope over the side, at which Philip assessed emphatically, "No, it is not long enough!" Indeed the line extended for only a little over half the necessary distance.

"We need another rope."

"No other do we have!"

"Then we'll have to make this one longer," said James, pulling the line back up.

"Make it longer? How?"

"We'll tear some blankets into strips and add the strips to the rope. It will increase the length."

"It will never hold!"

"It will have to. There's no other choice. We just have to double them and tie them very tightly."

The rest of us began following my brother's instructions, employing a knife as we rendered a blanket into strips that were two hand widths in size. After shredding the first blanket in such manner, we set to work on another.

"Tie them tightly!" said James.

"I'm tying them tight," said Philip.

"Then tie them even tighter!" Susanna ordered crossly. "We cannot afford to have this give out!"

"I'm tying them as tight as I can!" Philip retorted angrily.

"Hang on Peter, we're coming down to get you!" James shouted down the chasm.

With the rope lengthened by a good six to eight cubits we lowered it once more—but it was still too short.

"This is the last blanket." My brother looked grimly into our eyes. "When we cut this up we will have no possibility of keeping warm." The idea of being here on the mountain without even a single blanket between us was an unpalatable prospect, yet there was no question we would make the sacrifice for Peter.

Andrew began to cry, as James picked up the knife and started to cut. The rest of us took the strips and tied them together. Finally, the rope was lowered once more. We had no protection now from the mountain's debilitating chill, but the sacrifice paid off. This time the line dangled a scant distance above Peter's head, maybe three cubits.

"I am going down," James said. "When I get there I will tie the rope about his chest; when I signal, the rest of you pull. After you get him up, untie the rope and drop it down for me."

Philip nodded, a methodical, cool-under-pressure nod of understanding. Resolutely my brother strode to the edge of the precipice. As I looked on in fear, he took hold of the rope and eased himself, with a sky-diminishing obscurity, over the side. Would the line hold with its added-on lengths? I didn't breathe, I don't think any of us did, until his feet landed on the rocky proscenium where Peter lay. We could not hear what words were exchanged, for the two of them were much too far below us, but Philip was quick to assess the problem. "It's *still* not long enough!" he said of the rope. "Your brother will somehow have to get Peter onto his feet before he'll be able to tie it around him."

Even as Philip spoke, James began assisting Peter to a sitting position, an effort which went well up to a point, but when Peter attempted to stand, another scream, like an Erinys' cry, tore its way from his throat. James looked up and shouted, "His leg is broken! He can put no weight on it!"

Hearing this, Perpetua dropped to the ground with a sullen thud—sullen though not defeated—as she importuned quietly of the gods, "What are we going to do now?"

As if in answer, my brother's voice echoed again, "Someone must come down and hold him upright. Only then will I be able to wrap the rope around him and tie it!"

"I will go." Philip barked the words with crisp decisiveness. Without waiting for a reply, he grabbed the rope, shinnying himself swiftly and monkey-like over the side. Andrew was still crying. I looked at Susanna, scared. We watched Philip's form grow smaller and smaller as he descended.

"Oh God please help us," Susanna breathed a weary sigh.

The line had proven itself once, and it was reasonable to presume it would do so again, but at this point, a new thought occurred to me: how would that little rock outcropping respond to the weight of yet a third person? We were about to find out. Philip aimed himself downward, downward, until at last he gained a footfall. "He's down!" Susanna reported unnecessarily. To my enormous relief, the substratum held. Death, for the moment at any rate, was slighted.

With Philip supporting Peter's weight, James began tying the rope. But it would end up taking us a full hour to hoist Peter out of that chasm, and while we would all breathe a sigh of relief once it was done, there was yet one other catastrophe to befall us that day.

Peter was standing now. We watched as his broken leg sagged, the rope now holding the bulk of his weight. All seemed ready. Our three companions gazed up at us; the rescue effort had now come down to the five of us remaining on top. Did we possess sufficient strength to pull Peter up? There were two girls. And two boys, who were scarcely more than children. And then there was Nathanael, who, to be sure, was stout, large, and strong. I looked at Nathanael now. He radiated something, a simplicity of heart that seemed to grow out of that ever-present smile of his. A curious exception he was to the mode of behavior normally prevalent in our little group. In all of our trading of mock insults with one another never once had I heard him call anyone "knave" nor proffer any harshness of discourse, even in jest. His contributions to our scoffing, wastrel rhythms were usually limited to his friendly, ever-present smile and the dropping of a few virtuous, good-natured annotations. As I looked at him now, I was profoundly glad he was here with us on this mountain.

"We are ready!" James shouted up.

Susanna took off her sandals, her bare feet affording better traction on the wet rocks. Andrew had stopped crying. Nathanael voiced soft encouragements to the rest of us and took hold of the rope. We followed suit. "*Abwoon, nehwey tzevyanach*," he said, "God's will be done." We began to pull, but suddenly were forced to halt our efforts as another scream tore loose from the abyss, "Aaarrgggghhhh!"

"Nay! Nay! Nay!" came the shouts from below, the frantic cries rising up through the nostrils of the wind. It was James and Philip, and they were screaming in unison: "Desist! Desist!" Up on top, we were a number of paces back from the edge of the precipice, unable to see what the problem was, though *something* obviously had gone wrong. Puzzled, we dropped the rope and made a dash for the rim…

And it was in that moment that the day's *second* disaster fell upon us, fell upon us even as the shouts of James and Philip persisted. "Desist!" It was a disaster so sudden, so complete, and so jarring it left us impotent to make sense of the peculiar, folly-laden sight that now met our eyes: a jute sack, along with spilled contents, diving downward through space, end over end, like some wine-sotted fowl. Befuddling was the sight. My eyes simply could not make sense of it. I knew only that it was a jute sack, floating inexplicably in mid air. A jute sack with a strangely familiar look. Then it hit me. It was *our* jute sack, *gatha d'Alaha*. O cry of God! And something else as well: the objects it was disgorging in a haphazard gallimaufry, sending them drunkenly into space, were what remained of our food supply. The food we had taken with us when leaving home—how many days ago now? Following the rain of the night before, it had become little distinguishable from mud, yet it was all we had; there was nothing else to sustain us for the journey down. In dismay, we watched as it plummeted in majestic emancipation, out of human reach forever.

"Desist! We must retie the rope!"

But the words echoed hollowly as my mind suddenly conceived the chain of events which had become our undoing: that the rope encircling Peter's chest had become ensnared; that the jute sack had been left close, carelessly close, to the edge of the precipice; that Nathanael, in his haste to determine the cause of the cries from below, and overlooking the sack's eminent consummation upon the couch of the clouds, had accidentally given it the nudge needed, which after all was not much stronger than a wind's breath, to send it over. Little was to be said. It was but one more thing gone wrong in a gone-wrong day. Recriminations would not be worth speaking. Even if anyone had wanted to point an accusing finger at Nathanael, there was no time. For one monumental task lay yet ahead: getting Peter, followed by James and Philip, out of that gorge.

The rope tied around Peter had indeed become knotted and ensnared high up on his chest, under his arm, resulting in his scream of pain the moment we had begun to pull. James and Philip, aware of what had just happened to the jute sack, dolefully retied it. At last they signaled to us. We were ready to try again. Nathanael, along with the rest of us, once more took hold of the rope.

While Andrew, Susanna, Perpetua, and I did what we could, it was clearly Nathanael who made the difference. Gradually Peter began to emerge from the chasm. As his head neared the top of the precipice, we anchored the rope, locked arms around him, and pulled him the rest of the way up. "Peter! Peter! Are you alright?"

Wincing, but smiling weakly, he said, "What took you so long?"

We then pulled Philip out, lastly James.

In the day's waning light, and quite miraculously, we found a shallow cave in which to take shelter. We were exhausted and night was falling, but we were united once more. However, our situation, as we took stock of it in the gathering gloom, was a grim one. On a mountain peak we were stuck, with no food, no blankets, and one of our number incapable of walking. And to make matters worse, the rain began once more.

"James," I heard Susanna whisper in the darkness of the cave. "What are we going to do without food?"

"I do not know."

By this time, the rain was falling heavily.

Chapter Nine

"God, the Eternal One, creator of the heaven and earth, giver of life, all-merciful, all-powerful, giver of the Torah to the Children of Israel, O please deliver us..." We could hear Philip's voice, but it was too dark in the cave to see his face, yet in silence we listened to his prayer. The rain stopped for a time, but in an hour or so started up again, and sometime in the late hours, as the temperatures dropped, it turned to snow. Huddled together in a circle, with Peter, in some considerable pain, laid out in the center, we tried to sleep, but none of us did. With the coming of daylight we discovered, looking out from the mouth of the cave, a world starkly transformed under a blanket of snow.

"We have to get down off this mountain!"

"But how will we get Peter down?"

"I do not know," Philip answered quietly.

"The first thing we need to think about is finding food," said James.

"Where? How? Everything is covered with snow."

"Perhaps we can find some leaves and boil them."

"Nay, no fire will burn with all the rain that has fallen."

"You all go," said Peter, still in much pain. "Go down the mountain and save yourselves."

"Nay, Peter," dismissed Perpetua. "We will not leave you!"

I'm not sure exactly when, but at some point during our journey Perpetua had begun to fall in love with Peter. Throughout the night she, more than any of us, had held his head in her lap, caressing his brow, offering him such warmth from her body as she could muster.

"Then go and seek help, and return to me when you find it," said Peter.

Even as he spoke, the snow began falling once more.

"That is not a bad idea," Philip appealed quietly to the rest of us.

"That is a *terrible* idea," disagreed James. "If we leave him here he will freeze to death."

"I will not leave him!" Perpetua announced defiantly though in hushed tones so as Peter would not overhear. "No matter what any of you do! I will not leave him!"

"We should scout around." James walked to the mouth of the cave, where flakes of snow blew into his face. "Perhaps we may find something nearby that would be of assistance."

"Yes, maybe there are some berries to eat," said Andrew, who was ashamed of the tears he had shed before us yesterday.

Perpetua and Susanna remained in the cave with Peter; Nathanael, feeling unwell, elected to stay as well. The rest of us, James, Philip, Andrew, and I, forayed out into the silent, white world, and though somewhat hopeful on starting out, my spirits soon sank. Everything was frozen! How would we find anything to eat? Moreover, with landmarks obscured by snow, nothing looked the same as it had yesterday. My bearings were quickly confused, and I found it impossible to determine with any certainty the path we had traveled previously. James and Philip walked ahead, their frosty breath trailing out behind. I hoped they knew where we were, because I didn't. "Stay together everyone!" James called.

A quarter of an hour later, we came to a snowfield that looked totally unfamiliar. On its far side was a thicket consisting of some stubby, snow-covered trees. It was the only ground cover around. Approaching the thicket from afar, we spied what might have been movement from somewhere deep inside, a barely-perceptible stirring in the undergrowth, but then it ceased.

"Did you see thee anything—over there in those trees?"

"No!" replied Philip dourly.

But then it happened again, a slight disturbance of a branch, and this time Philip saw it too. A moment later, through the fir boughs, we detected, very shadow-like, what might have passed for a human form. There *was* someone there...someone within the thicket!

"*Shlomo*!" James called out.

All of a sudden, framed by needles and bark, a face appeared. It was for only the briefest of moments. So quickly did it vanish, I could make out little more than the blur of a man's hair and beard.

"*Shlomo!*" we called again. But by now all movement in the thicket had ceased.

"Where did he go?"

"Look!" Andrew pointed.

On the far side of the copse was a barren rise leading up toward a distant ridge, and there, up this snowy embankment, we saw a man dressed in dark clothing, retreating rapidly, ethereal-like, galloping from us on long, graceful legs. Nothing but his back was visible, and this only for a moment, as he loped up the hill, disappearing at last over the ridge.

"For the love of the heavenly host!" whispered Andrew. "Where's he going?"

"He's running from us! Why?"

"Come on!" cried James, breaking now into a sprint.

The rest of us followed, or tried to, though we found ourselves making slow progress because of the snow's considerable depth, James himself faring not much better. But of the four of us, I seemed to be struggling most of all. Part of the problem was my sandals accorded me little protection, and my feet were of a monstrously painful coldness. In snow up to our knees, our sluggish exertions stood in marked contrast to the easy, almost graceful strides exhibited by the—man, spirit, phantom, or whatever it was, we had witnessed a moment earlier. Reaching the thicket at last, we found it, of course, abandoned. Or *almost*. On the ground, beneath one of the trees, amidst a patch of trampled snow, lay a jute sack.

"Look! What do you suppose it is?"

"He must have dropped this in his haste to be away."

"Open it up and see what's in it."

"Nay! I will not touch it! Suppose something awful is inside! An adder, perhaps!"

"Knave! Snakes lie fallow in the winter."

"It is not winter! It is only winter up here! Down there it is still summer!"

"I will see what is in the bag," James announced and picked up the jute sack; for a moment, I was afraid Philip was right and that a snake would spring out. It was a fear quickly dispelled. "Olives!" cried James, upon untying the sack. "Olives—to eat!" We rushed forward. Sure enough, inside the sack were ripened olives, not enough, to be sure, for a full meal for eight people, but enough to secure some relief from the pangs of hunger.

"Do you think they are safe to eat?"

"Why wouldn't they be?"

"Suppose they are poisoned?"

"Knave! Who would carry around poisoned olives on top of a snow-covered mountain?"

"Wait!" said James. "There is something else to think about. The man who dropped these—he probably needs them as much as we do. If we take them, then *he* will be hungry."

"Just what do you propose to do about it?" inquired Philip suspiciously.

James shrugged. "We should try and find him, to share them with him."

"No, knave!" Philip erupted volcanically. "If we find him, then he will claim them! They are rightfully his! Then *we* will have none!"

"I still think we should try. If we ourselves are cold and hungry, think of him!" James, ill at ease over the matter and still carrying the bag, left the thicket, walking now in the direction of the ridge where we'd last seen the man. Philip watched my brother go, then shook his head, "For the love of the heavenly host!" and started after him. Andrew and I fell in behind. The four of us followed the mysterious man's tracks, calling out ever so often, "*Shlomo!*" but the snow was falling so rapidly that by the time we reached the ridge top nothing was left of the trail; the tracks were completely covered in by new snow. No sign of our quarry could be seen.

"*Now* can we go?" asked Philip dourly.

Abandoning the attempt, we returned to the thicket and cut some firewood. "It will be too wet to burn now, but we can dry it out in the cave," theorized James. "We should also cut some of these fir branches to put over the entrance. They will at least help keep some of the wind out." All in all, the little thicket had afforded us much. Back we started for the comfortless cave where we had spent the previous night.

"Where did the olives come from?" inquired a gladdened-though-puzzled Susanna on our return.

In hurried tones, we filled her in. Though much needed doing, hunger was first and foremost on our minds, and we allotted ourselves two olives apiece. Everyone ate except Nathanael, who apparently could eat nothing.

"He has been vomiting," Susanna confided. "Twice he has left the cave to empty himself. I don't know what to think about it, but he seems very ill."

The snow was falling harder. James looked up for the sky, which was nowhere to be seen; what met the eye instead was a white, whirling frenzy. Ribbons of the stuff had begun accumulating on our shoulders and in our hair. We were becoming walking snowmen. "We should secure some branches over the mouth of the cave."

"I'm for that!"

First laying in several armfuls of wood, we next began to cut and hone spruce branches, tying them together to block off the entrance. Hopefully the firewood would be dry enough to burn by morning. But after deliberation we decided our fuel supply would be inadequate should the snow continue another night and day; prudence seemed to dictate another trip to the thicket. To this end, three of us now set out: Philip, Susanna, and I. Once again I experienced a sense of confusion, for in such a short time had so much new snow fallen. "It is this way," said Philip.

"Nay, I think it is this way," I argued, but I wasn't sure, and in the end we followed Philip. It was a good thing. With an unerring sense of direction, he led us back to the thicket where we had found the olive bag, only this time, upon our arrival, a new surprise awaited us. No more than a few paces from where we had found the olives, there now lay a blanket. Moreover, it was a blanket which had not been cast aside in a rush, as we had all along assumed with the olives, rather it had been folded neatly, almost daintily, and left sitting on top of the snow, much as one would find a blanket carefully emplaced at the foot of a warm feather bed. For such was suggested by the casual yet tidy, almost loving, way it had been left.

"This wasn't here before!" Philip now sputtered. Then added as if unsure of himself: "*Was* it?"

"Nay," I shook my head.

It was difficult to hear ourselves over the wind, yet we stared at the sight in no small wonder. What did it mean? There seemed no explanation for it, but little time could be spared to ponder the matter. We needed wood and we needed it quickly. After cutting as much as we could carry back to the cave in one trip, Philip stooped to retrieve the blanket.

"We can't take it!" I said urgently.

"What do you mean!"

"It is his! It belongs to him! He will need it!"

"Bah!" spat Philip.

"Nay!" cried Susanna. "He is right! Maybe this is his home! Maybe we shouldn't even *be* here!"

"What do you mean to do, go back to that cave and freeze?" Philip held the blanket firmly in his reddened, chapped hands.

"Nay!" Susanna attempted to tear it away, but he thrust her roughly aside.

"Come on!" And with an impatient growl he started for camp. But Susanna had other ideas. Stubbornly she swung in the opposite direction, leaving us standing, as, like a stray leaf grabbed by the wind, she exited the thicket into the open snowfield. "There is something here…" her eyes scanning the surrounding peaks. Peevishly Philip overtook her, pointing out that it would be dark soon.

"*Go* then! I will stay!" she shrieked.

"Nay! You will come!" Though attempting to grab her, his efforts were defeated by the headstrong willfulness of my sister. Brushing him furiously off, she stalked further into the open snowfield. It was at this point Philip tried a new tack—and in doing so demonstrated signs of the robust man of ideas he was to become. Pursuing harmony by a more indirect means, he gave vent to a declaration that was, in itself, all too obvious: "The others need this wood." Then adding somewhat mournfully: "I cannot carry it all back myself. They will be miserable with no fire…and *very*, *very* cold!"

Realizing she had lost the argument, Susanna conceded, and we started back for camp, each carrying a turgid armload of wood, Philip sauntering along with the blanket balanced triumphantly atop his own. But as we made our way away from there I could not help thinking of the strange man whose path we had crossed twice now. First we had taken his food. Now his blanket. And like my brother and sister, I felt no small measure of unease, but then a new thought occurred to me. Had we, strictly speaking, *stolen* these items? Or had they perhaps been *deliberately* placed in our path? It was an enigma. But the pondering of enigmas, as so much else in life, is subject to heat and cold, pleasure and pain; my pleasure just now was to avoid further exposure to the elements, and the only way to do this was by returning to camp as quickly as possible, for by this time my feet, clad only in their sandals, could no longer remain quiescent to the snow's gnawing and numbing cold.

"Take some of this wood inside to dry," James directed when we got back. "By morning we'll have a fire."

It was certainly a thing to be wished for, but even without a fire, our plight on this second night was markedly improved. We found that our new blanket, when spread out and draped over the lot of us, provided a modicum of warmth. Moreover, the branches we had tied over the mouth of the cave afforded us additional shielding from the elements. Despite little let-up in the snow, we considered ourselves better off than on the previous night.

Better off, that is, in some respects, though not in others—for upon me there now arrived a discomfort so rampagingly excruciating it made every single discomfort I had experienced heretofore seem agreeable by comparison. My feet I am speaking of. They were cold. They were beyond cold. They were frozen stiff. And no matter how much I rubbed them I could not seem to inspire normal feeling to return. Regarding it manly to bear my condition in silence, I did so, this as Perpetua apportioned out some olives for dinner, but when I tried to eat, the food turned moribund and unwholesome on my tongue.

"I am glad we found these! We would have nothing otherwise," said Philip, happily stuffing the succulent fruits into his mouth, chewing vigorously, and spitting out the cores. Other than Nathanael, everyone ate something. "You must eat!" Philip urged him heartily. "You will need your strength to get down from this mountain!"

But the big strapping youth insisted he was not hungry. Fine otherwise. Just not hungry. We were not so sure, for something seemed to have come over him, a sickness or malaise of some sort. While it was troubling, no one commented on it. Perpetua set aside enough olives that we would have three apiece in the morning. Night fell, and it was once again so dark in the cave we could not see one another's faces. Yet this did not prevent us discussing our prospects for reaching home and safety.

"How will we get Peter down from the mountain?"

"I have been thinking about that." It was James, his voice now probing its way through the darkness. "I have seen the Romans place their wounded on a wooden frame of sorts. It is essentially a moveable bed. They lay the wounded man upon it, then pick it up by poles at the ends; through such means they are able to move their wounded from place to place. We will make a similar thing for Peter."

"Will it work?"

"Of course! If it works for the Romans, why not for us? All that is needed are branches of wood. Tomorrow, when it is light, we will go back to the thicket and cut the rest of those trees. Their branches we will then lash together to form the moveable bed. After it's built, we will place Peter on it and carry him down the mountain."

Philip belched and expelled an exasperated sigh. "Well, if Nathanael gets any sicker we may have to put him on it too!"

"I can walk," asserted Nathanael in the darkness. "I just don't feel like eating."

As it happened, Nathanael wasn't the only one with lost appetite. My own had gone astray as well. Two olives had been all I could manage. Now, curled up, hoping for sleep, I rubbed my feet, trying to ignore the feeling that my toes seemed about to break off. Tiredly, with thought of escape, I closed my eyes...

Sometime later in the night, I awakened. The others were asleep, apparently soundly. At first, I had no notion of anything amiss, could not even fathom why I had awakened. It was only after several moments of consciousness, in which some part of me bargained unsuccessfully for an unrestrained pathway back to the land of dreams, that I sat bolt upright. Simultaneously, a poisonous knowledge hit me: I was in mortal *agony*. My feet. At some point as I had slept they had fettered themselves back to my body's sense of feeling, yet to no normal or regular sense of awareness had they returned, but to an extraordinarily ripened one. Having been frozen before, they were now, quite incongruously, burning!

"Do not thrash about so, John!" said Susanna, who, in my distress, I awakened. But I was in an unrelenting sea, my thrashing body refusing to lay still. The torment in my feet was worse than any pain I had ever known. Suddenly I could not help it, I began to cry. Hoping to provide some comfort, Susanna took my feet in her hands, but it had the barest effect upon the raging fire eviscerating them. In desperation, she elevated them a notch further, to the celestial flesh underneath her cloak, lodging them against her stomach, just below her breasts. The warmth was of some help, but I was still in agony.

"Take it easy, John," said James, also awake now. My brother had taken charge of the other end of my body, cradling my head in his lap. But despite his reassurances, I could take nothing easy. I was in a kingdom of affliction, a land far away, where the voices of my brother and sister came and went like elusive shadows.

"What else can we do for him?"

"I don't know," answered Susanna tiredly. "Nothing I guess. Just try and keep his feet warm."

And so they tried. Throughout the night. I got no more sleep, nor did Susanna or James, nor, I suppose, anyone else in the cave. But by morning the pain had begun to subside. I was exhausted, but markedly improved. In the pale light, we ate the last of the olives. I felt tired and spent, even while the others, as if strung together by some invisible thread, made preparations for our departure. The first order of business was getting more wood—for the moveable bed. I began to don sandals, thinking to accompany them back to the thicket, but Susanna intervened. "Nay, little one. Remain here. Keep warm!" She kissed my cheek, pushing the blanket back up to my chin so that I was covered. "Rest easy. We will be back." There she went…mothering me again! But after my ordeal of the night before, I was perfectly willing to be mothered, and at this point I looked up at her with a vicarious and unspoken gratitude.

And so it was decided, I would remain in the cave with Peter and Nathanael while the others went out in what was hoped would be the last excursion to the thicket, which of course was considerably pared down and not so thick any more. During the night the storm had broken, the snow had stopped, and the sun, praise God, was visible in the sky—palely, but visible nonetheless. Out through the entrance the others went, but not far. Even from inside the cave I heard the cries of "for the love of the Lord!", the indrawn breaths, expressions of astonishment given so generously to the fair wind one would think they had stumbled upon a string of jewels the length of ten oxen! Something, I realized, had transpired, apparently just beyond the cave. Wincing at the thought of stepping into snow again, I nonetheless clasped on my sandals, hurried to the mouth of the cave, and cried, "What is it?"

Perhaps ten paces away, they were all clustered about in a circle, though a circle literally pullulating with excitement as they crowded round, gazing one and all at some object lying in the snow.

"What is it?" I called again.

Andrew looked up, "Come and see!"

"*No*, John! Stay in the cave!"

But ignoring my sister's proscription, I made my way, whereupon I, too, cast eyes down no less in wonder, for what lay dormant on the snow, there at our feet, was a quail, its neck broken. It had been freshly killed, too, for upon someone's picking it up it was discovered that its body was still warm.

"But where did it come from!" someone asked.

"Can you not guess?" replied Susanna. "It is from he—the mountain man."

Chapter Ten

"It is like he is watching us."

"Or watching *over* us, maybe."

"But why? What are we to him?" Philip wondered dubiously.

"Who cares what his reasons are?" answered Perpetua. "I'm just glad he dropped this off!"

We had roasted the quail—on a fire made from our newly dried wood. The flesh of the bird made but a paltry portion for the eight of us, or rather seven of us, for once again Nathanael was too ill to eat, but it was of some help, and such sustenance as it *did* provide was direly needed by our bodies. The wood, we found, had burned with some difficulty. But it *had* burned. Presently, as we ate, the fire succored us with a degree of comfort not experienced since before our troubles began. My wretched feet were propped, drawing in its blessed warmth. Tranquility. Bliss. The wood gathering expedition had been accomplished now as well, although the moveable bed had yet to be assembled. Our hunger was still with us, but thanks to the mountain man, it was not as great now.

"Think we have enough wood to make the moveable bed for Peter?"

"Yes, plenty," said James. What he did not say, however, and what I knew he was thinking, was that once we had lashed the stout strips together we would no longer have a proper rope. Or any rope at all. We would simply have to trust to fortune that a negotiable path off the mountain would be found, and hope that no one fell into any more chasms along the way. "We will start down after first light in the morning."

"I do not like the fact that someone is out there watching us," said Philip. "It is like he is observing our every move."

"It certainly is a mystery," agreed Peter, his leg propped up and his pain somewhat abated.

"Had he meant us any harm he would certainly have done so by now," commented Perpetua. "The Lord knows he has had ample opportunities!"

"Likely we have caused him more harm than he shall ever cause us. After all, we have grown fat on his meat and his olives, and warmed ourselves with his blanket."

"You consider this 'growing fat?' Truly, I would hate to abide a thinness!"

"How do you know he has *not* tried to cause us harm?" came the rejoinder from Philip. "Maybe the boulder was caused to roll upon us by someone. Perhaps it was he."

"You are surmising much, Philip."

"Aye, too much."

"It is possible!" Philip persisted.

"Yes, and perhaps he also performed an evil magic that caused Peter to jump into the chasm. Or maybe the snow or rain could not have fallen without his help, and maybe, while he was about it, he grew this mountain out of the earth, too! You are deranged!"

"Get some sleep, Philip," Susanna put in tiredly, "and when you wake in the morning, perhaps you will feel better."

If sleep had been disturbed last night by the terrible agony in my feet, tonight it was Nathanael who kept us up; at some point during the long period of darkness, his sickness grew worse and he sought to leave the cave so as to void himself in the snow. James, fearing he should not venture out alone, left with him. I listened as their footsteps crunched forlornly off in the darkness. Looking upon the embers of our dying fire, I thought of my mother, and I wished I were home. I wished we were all home. At home there was plenty to eat. There were no treacherous trails where one might misstep into calamity, no evil spirits, no mysterious denizens of the wild lurking in shadows. Since we had ascended the mountain, I had had the feeling we were caught up at the epicenter of vagrant and unknowable forces.

Presently, Nathanael and James returned to the cave. Neither spoke. Nathanael groaned as he rolled into a tight but very large ball. I began to wonder at the nature of this sickness that had come upon him, and as I did so a curious thought struck me. It was that he had somehow—I'm not sure how to say it—but that he had in a sense *willed* it upon himself to become sick. So sick he could not eat. And I wondered if he had done this as a means of self-punishment for having caused the loss of our food supply, though certainly no one had blamed him. Yet the thought would not leave me. Could a man cause himself to become sick simply by means of willing that it should be so? I did not know. It was a strange thought, and perhaps, as I say, I was only imagining it. And also perhaps he was simply foregoing food for another, more practical reason: so the rest of us would have enough. Yes, that was possible. But at the same time I sensed about him a need for performance of penance, and assuming that was the case, I wondered at what kind of strange yearning would drive him to such a thing. What could motivate such a voluntary sufferance of penalty? And the more I thought about it, I thought, too, about his perpetual smile, and his reluctance to ever hurt anyone or to refer to anyone as "knave." And the conclusion I came to was that that thing inside of him, the thing that was driving him to sickness, was *love*—a love so strong it did literally cause him to grow ill and cease eating. Such were my ruminations, fanciful to be sure, when James finally broke the silence in the cave.

"We saw the mountain man."

His words, though softly spoken, were startling, yea, we could not have been more startled had it been announced the moon had just fallen from the sky and now lay resting upon the earth.

"Nay! You did not!"

"Yes...we did," sighed my brother, though at this point he paused, as if deliberating what to say next, or perhaps, more accurately, as if pondering what we, his listeners, might be prepared to accept or believe. "We went out behind that large rock. Nathanael was very sick, but wanted to go further from the cave, so on we walked, maybe another twenty paces or so. Everything was covered with snow, but the moon was very bright; that was when we saw him. As I say, the moon is full, and in its light I could make him out very clearly. He was standing on that ridge close above us. Standing there, very still and straight."

"What did you do?"

James shrugged. "I just looked at him. He saw me at the same time. Then he turned and started moving away, but unlike when we saw him before, this time I got a clear look at his face."

"And?"

"Well—" James paused, choosing his words carefully. "This may sound strange, but I think it was Rogah."

"Who?"

"Rogah—you know, the solitary one. Remember the day we went to gather the nuts?"

"Nay! It is not possible!"

"You cannot be serious!" spat Philip. "*That* man? The *raca* who goes about muttering things to himself?"

"Do *not* call him a *raca*!" Susanna answered fiercely. "He cannot be an empty-headed fool if he can find food on this mountain, whereas we, in our helplessness, cannot!"

"Bah! You're addled!"

"Nay," countered James with a tired sigh. "The moon is full and because of the snow everything is white. I saw the face very clearly. I am certain it was he."

"How came he, assuming it *was* Rogah, to be here on the mountain?" wondered Peter.

"I do not know the answer to that," replied James. "How is your leg?"

"Not so bad I guess," Peter replied. But this was not true. His discomfort had ebbed and flowed all day, forming at times into acidic beads of sweat on his forehead; he needed medical attention badly.

"Try and get some sleep," my brother told him.

Sleep. We were actually *all* in need of it. I curled up like a mouse next to a hearth…and blissfully it came.

The morning brought with it another gift from the mountain man, more quail, only this time, lying upon the snow, were not one, but four, warm, freshly-killed carcasses. Philip, far from being gladdened by the find, was annoyed. Yea, all along his reaction to the encounters with our elusive visitor had been of a far different nature than our own. Whereas we had regarded it all more or less with a sense of wonder, Philip on the other hand, with each new "gift" left in our path, had succumbed to a toxic and weltering antagonism. As we stood outside the cave in the frosty air, this rancor reached a festering and ugly head.

"Who *are* you?????" he screamed with a manifestation of the heavy clouds accumulating in his soul, and I found myself wondering if he were not becoming, in a manner of speaking, unhinged. We live, my dear Quintus, by hearing, and continually hearing, God's name, though there are times when we succumb to the nullity and God is no longer recalled. This was the case with Philip now. "Why are you doing this!!!!!!!" The stems of his legs, along with a feckless rodomontade of words, carried him aimlessly as he gave vent to pent-up choler, demanding that the mountain man should speak. The snow-shrouded heights remained muted, however.

We likewise were at a loss for words. What had brought this ominous change in Philip? Would his erratic behavior grow worse, and if so, how would it effect our getting off the mountain? We already had Peter's broken leg and Nathanael's sickness to contend with; was this some new misfortune come upon us? Perhaps, even more pertinently, had the mountain thus provided us with additional evidence, as if any were needed, of its ability to cast its varied spells over us? Later, as we ate the newly-delivered meat, Philip remained morose and silent.

This time our bellies were filled with a roaring abundance. Renewed, nourished, and strengthened, we set to work, and before long, the moveable bed was assembled. Our plan was to get Peter off the mountain and as far as Panias, and while my feet were once more stinging with cold, I shouldered my share of the work with a stubborn determination, feeling, along with everyone else, reasonably buoyed at our prospects for success.

"I am sorry to be such a burden on you—all of you."

"Nay Peter!" replied James. "Do not think that!"

But it was Perpetua who most refused to hear such talk from Peter, and in fact put a quick end to it by giving him a playful punch. "We think you are worth it!" Leaning forward, she then planted a kiss on his mouth. "You are worth that and much, much more!" she whispered, a husky fire burning in the back of her throat. Perhaps it was something about his helpless condition that had kindled such a passion in her. I don't know. But whatever it was, Perpetua had fallen deeply in love with Peter. She began now, with a proprietary air, directing his placement upon the moveable bed, imploring he should be strapped for safety, with an additional binding securing his broken leg so as to prevent any movement or displacement of the limb in transport. Her instructions were sensibly spoken...and indeed acted upon. At last, we were ready.

The moveable bed, with Peter upon it, was quite heavy, though we found, distributed amongst the seven of us, the weight was manageable. Despite it being his fourth day without food, Nathanael too assisted. I detected a slight wobbliness in his stance, yet even in his obviously weakened state, a commanding power seemed to pour forth from him, his muscles straining as his great breadth bent now to the task at hand. We had done it. We had actually done it! And working together now, we raised Peter into the air. All good so far. The southern slopes were the direction we intended to take, these having the advantage of affording at least a more direct route back to Panias, but moments after setting off, we stopped, confronted with something wholly unexpected, a sight of such richness that the astonishment it wrought upon us held very nearly the capacity to smite us where we stood. Helpless were we to do anything but put the moveable bed back down and gaze upon the thing in copious, star-alluring wonder. It was up on the ridge, the same ridge where, the previous evening, James and Nathanael had seen the mountain man, but no mountain man was there now. What *was* there was no less breathtaking and astonishing however, for it was a wolf. Moreover it was a wolf that was all over a solid color, that color being *yellow*.

"It's the yellow wolf!" whispered Andrew in reverence.

"*Lupus Croceus*," murmured Susanna, moved no less to watery wonder. We were all moved, staring at the being enthralled. It scarcely glanced in our direction, yet there was no doubt in my mind it sensed our presence. Even so, its majestic gaze was fixed not upon us, but upon the protracted, far-dazzling distances, its pose studied, as if pondering flowing streams of holy oil, its rich pelage highlighted by the fiery, falcon-gladdening sun.

"For the love of the heavenly host!"

At a loss were we for any other words.

And as suddenly as the wolf had appeared, it turned, with an airy, form-annihilating recompense, and disappeared over the ridge.

"We shall surely now receive a blessing from God!" whispered Andrew reverently.

Chapter Eleven

B y the second day, we had made our way down past the snow line. I breathed a sigh of relief, for the torture to my poor feet was over. And while we had left the snows on the upper elevations, we had not left the mountain man. He was still with us. Provisions continued to be left in our path...and on the third day, we saw him. This time, truly arousing our sense of wonder, he appeared before all of us.

Descending down out of a draw with a line of tall trees to our left, I had at first only a vague feeling of his presence, this being hampered by the fact that it was impossible to see through the tree line due to the position of the sun. Yet I knew, somehow, he was there, just as surely as one knows the presence of a caterpillar upon a leaf. Peter's weight on the moveable bed made our progress interminably slow; it was an enormous strain carrying him, and we were worn down to a blood-congealing fatigue, yet so acutely did I sense the human presence through the trees that for a time I even stopped feeling the pain in the shanks of my legs as my eyes scanned that luminous barrier. In this I was still occupied when James called a halt to our progress, deciding we all needed a rest. "There is something in those trees over there," said I after we had seated ourselves on the ground with Peter and his bed alongside us.

"Aye," sighed James tiredly. "I have seen it. He has been following us for the past hour."

No need explaining who "he" was; we all knew. Though my body felt much too tired to exert itself, my eyes nonetheless scanned the distance. With a hand raised to block the sun, I suddenly saw something—not the mountain man, but Susanna. She was some distance off on a sloping flexure overgrown with dewberries, slowly making her way upward...upward...toward those hither-beckoning trees. When had she slipped away? Presumably the moment we had lowered the bed, yet somehow, her absence had gone unnoticed—until now. We watched, all of us, as she navigated her way up a talus-strewn slope, persevering in her slow, careful steps, ever upward, toward that sun-praised forest line. It was only as she reached the top we saw him. Boldly he emerged, pillorying out into the open smoothly, like a gourd floating on water and blown gently by the wind. "What in thunder!" Philip blustered. "It is your sister and the *raca*!" In the next moment, they stood facing each other. "For the love of the heavenly host!" he persisted. "What is she doing? He could kill her!"

"Nay Philip," answered James tiredly. "He will not."

Though some distance off, we could see them as they stood frugally before one another, the young girl and the mountain man. Clearly, James had been right. It was indeed Rogah, the unhappy creature we had encountered on the day of our nut gathering. Yet at the same time it was a different Rogah, an ancient Rogah, standing in an emerald field, carrying the sky on his back, and though dressed still in rags, he was somehow vulpine, the sovereign ruler of the mountain, become effused and at one with the wailing and weeping of its wild winds. With Susanna standing before him, a darkened, ragged palm he reached forth, and with it gently touched her face, a caress from which she did not flinch, but seemed to yearn toward, staring upward into the sequestered gloom of his gaze. I remember the sky at that moment being the color of cerulean, and the air permeated with the fragrance of terebinth.

Then as suddenly as he had appeared, he turned; Susanna remained standing, motionless, as, with that same ease of gait he had displayed that day in the snowfield, he glided toward the trees. Reaching the tree line, he veered—*upward*—aiming himself back...back...toward those *lupus-croceus*-haunted heights from whence he had safely delivered us. I thought about that often in the years to come. How is it that a man, who, when seen in and about Bethsaida, could be thought of only as destructively anguished, of having a demon even—how could such a man have done what he did for us on that mountain? He had mysteriously joined the palms of his hands to ours, and in so doing he had saved us, and then just as mysteriously, he had vanished. That mountain—was it a realm beyond heaven? Clearly it was, for him, a place of life, of blossoming, but even more than that, it was as if God, in bestowing its snowcapped peaks upon him, had handed him a filled chalice of fasting and purification, of gnosis, a chalice that was his to drink from, but only as long as he remained on its heights. Come down and the chalice was rendered empty, to be refilled when, and only when, he returned to that windblown dominion. Maybe I'm presuming more than is warranted here. But that's the way it would seem to me, especially later in light of what was to transpire in Bethsaida.

When we reached Panias late that afternoon, the Goat God was doing a brisk business. Entering the temple doors, we found Pompeia presiding along with two other half-naked priestesses. Peter's leg by now was swollen, causing him severe pain. Briefly, we described our travails upon the mountain. Pompeia issued crisp instructions, hastily wrapped a cloak about her shoulders, and sallied forth, returning a short time later with the town doctor. Our friend, the priestess of Pan!

"He should be fine," said the doctor after setting the leg in a splint. "Just keep him off it. I will check back and see how he is tomorrow. It's amazing that you were able to carry him all the way down the mountain." Then with a smiling appraisal, he added: "You are friends indeed!"

Again, we were welcomed into the priestess' home. Another feast we partook, the fare this time including some exotic fruits I had never heard of before, called *mandarins*. "The tetrarch had them brought from India," Pompeia explained, hastily offering us more of the tasty fruits. They had a curious bitter-sweetness, quite moist and tangy on the tongue. Even Nathanael broke his fast, his smile beginning to reassert its accustomed home on his face. We told Pompeia of our adventures, including our sighting of the yellow wolf, and for the next three days, we remained her houseguests.

Old Jonah, Peter's father, rented two mules and a *reda*, a covered passenger wagon, and eventually we got Peter back to Bethsaida in it. My mother was in the house alone when James, Susanna, and I walked in. One look at Salome's face told us we were in plenty of trouble, though we knew the majority of the trouble would not be coming from her. "My children, why have you done this to us? Your father and I have been so terribly worried!"

Chapter Twelve

We had no explanation for our behavior. We could only say we were sorry. And we did say it. Over and over. My mother of course, being the kind woman she was, was more than willing to forgive, but in Zebedee's eyes we were fully deserving of divine retribution. In trying to explain where we had been, we tactfully neglected to mention the Temple of Pan. Being a Pharisee, it was to be presumed my father would not take kindly to notions of goat gods and such. But of course it was common knowledge that Panias, just 200 furlongs to the north, was a "heathen city," with all kinds of wicked goings-on; if we had been anywhere near the place, Zebedee was convinced, we had been sifted by Satan.

"This is what happens when girls are filled with book-learning, taught to read, and such!"

In defiance of logic my father blamed it all on Susanna's having acquired an education, this despite the fact that it was James, not Susanna, who was eldest, and who, of course, also knew how to read. But James, unlike Susanna, was not the sort that would traipse to a mountaintop on a whim. He would had to have been talked into it by others. In this much, at least, Father was correct. Where he erred, of course, was in thinking our northward excursion had had a thing to do whatever with Greek poets, Satan, idolatry, or *anything*, for that matter, other than our own yearning to share in that great basket of life known as Freedom. Coming down from the mountain, though tired and ragged, we had entered the city of Panias with a feeling of elation, the kind of elation felt by the young when they have crossed a magical boundary. We had negotiated the first perils of adulthood; we had faced hardship; feasted our eyes upon a forbidden temple; survived what nature had hurled at us; and successfully applied our wits to pull ourselves out of a dangerous situation. And on top of all that we were now Children of the Wolf. Would we receive a blessing from God? I did not know, and maybe it didn't matter. The mountain had changed us in a profound sense—and maybe *that*, after all was said and done, was the blessing. But trying to make Zebedee understand any of this was pointless. He shouted. He raged. He roared like *Nasha Hadad*. But shouting and roaring were not enough. Somebody had to pay a price for what had happened, and in the end Father decided it was to be the Greek poets.

It was a small wooden box, and we all knew about it. Susanna kept it hidden away under her bed, a modest thing, of almost fearless dignity. Inside was everything that made her what she was, her books, her Greek poems, all the fire which had ignited her young soul and shaped her into the person she had become. It even contained some writings of her own, for I knew she had begun to write poems and such of her own composition. A plain wooden box was all it was, yet Susanna had often resorted to it on the sly, making something of an effort to keep it concealed from us, though as I say, we all knew about it. Would that Zebedee had not been so intent on meting out punishment! Would that he had been a man of more reserved temperament! For it was into this box, in essence Susanna's private sanctuary, that he now broke, impervious to his daughter's pleas as he scattered the contents about. Hindered not by mercy's restraining hand, deaf even to the now-not-so-subtle remonstrations of Salome, he proceeded to render into pieces every leaf and scrap of papyrus adorned with writing of any kind. I should not describe it as a wanton rage, for it was not that, but rather a cold and methodical destruction. In vain did my mother, usually rational but now as unchecked in her passion as Susanna, plead for restraint. But it was not to be. Father, who could scarcely read himself, proceeded in ridding the house entirely of the language of ideas. Everything in Susanna's box, every verse of poetry, every commingled thought and romantic expression, were torn, cut, ripped, diminished, the writing made illegible. When he had finished producing this heap of wattled scrap, he tossed it all into the brazier and burned it.

"We'll have no more of this nonsense!"

Another edict was issued as well: no longer would Susanna undergo schooling from Rabbi Joel. She was to stay home, cook, and sew until Father found her a suitable husband. On this, he would brook no argument. Yet argue my mother did, for it had been her lifelong dream that her daughter should acquire an education. And Salome was a determined woman.

It took a full month, but finally Zebedee relented; Susanna once again returned to school. As for her books and poems, however—these could not be unburned.

Chapter Thirteen

In the three years following that night, my sister evinced an aversion toward our father that never left her completely. It was subtle, mind you. There was nothing any of us could point to, no overt sign, that is to say, of enmity, or even dissipation of congeniality. In all her exchanges with Father, she was polite, but I saw, or thought I saw, something in her eyes, a cry in protest from that remote corner of the soul where, by the grace of the Great Giver, peace tries ever to prevail. She never spoke of this of course. In fact, you could say there was an absence of communication all around. Indeed, not once, in all the time since that night of senseless destruction, was the incident ever discussed or even mentioned. Not by Mother, not by Father, not by anyone, including Susanna herself. It was as if we had deliberately buried it. Yet something was not the same, and I could not get over the feeling that Susanna, unable to contain the sky that was her mind, had cut the ropes that had bound her, that she was looking for some means, *any* means, of escape. Escape to what I could not imagine, for in the years that followed, she had several offers of marriage. These came mostly from older men. All of them, including one which Father arranged for her, she rejected, spurned, as if the suitors were afflicted with a leprosy. She wanted no part of them.

On a positive note, education at least ceased to be a thorny issue in our household. Susanna, like James before her, completed all of her instruction at the *beth ha-sefer*. Beyond this, there was the *beth ha-midrash* in Jerusalem, but the majority of Jewish children never made it that far. In any event, such a pursuit was not available to Susanna, for girls were not accepted. By the grace of my mother and Rabbi Joel, she had advanced in the world of learning as far as was possible for her to go.

As for James, even had he felt the call to attend the *beth ha-midrash*, little in the way of opportunity existed. Zebedee had determined such was a waste of time for a fisherman's son. There was an old saying. It was a sort of pun, and it turned the word *banim*, or children, into *bonim*, builders. It was James' destiny to build our family fishing business. And so it was that my brother took to the Lake of Gennesaret with Father and the other fishermen, plying their nets to the water. In this endeavor, he grew strong, utilizing that same natural, innate wisdom that had led us off the mountain. Over the next year, I watched him as he became increasingly at one with the lake. It was in him, of him, and at times, I would notice how often he gazed upon its waters, just in a certain way, with a studied judgment, its currents seemingly flowing in rhythm with the coursing of his own blood.

As may be expected, he and Father did not always enjoy the smoothest of relations, and the older James got, the more frequent their clashes became. James was a loyal and faithful son, and a courageous brother, and I can but attribute such difficulties as they underwent to the remorse Father's wrathful judgment ever seemed to inflict upon those around him. As I have noted before, there was simply an unwillingness to bend. The only exception in this regard was in Susanna's refusal of the marriage he had arranged for her—he did not force her to go through with it.

It became the match that wasn't. The suitor Susanna rejected was a farmer named Eliezar. He had accumulated considerable wealth in the growing of flax, Galilee's principle industrial crop, used in the manufacture of linen. The marriage would have been quite financially advantageous to us, and Zebedee was particularly keen to see it go through. With Eliezar's *mohar*, or dowry payment, we would have been able to fend off the depredations of the tax collectors while setting aside something for ourselves besides, yet Eliezar was three times my sister's age, and though he was plain spoken and of an agreeable nature, it was clear Susanna held no affection for him and above all had no intention of marrying him. Father, at least to his credit, had had the wisdom not to force the issue, though under our laws he would have been within his rights to do so. Perhaps he realized he would have faced a fierce reckoning, not with his daughter so much as his wife, for Salome would in no manner have stood idly by while Susanna was packed off into an unhappy marriage. But for whatever reason, Zebedee let the matter drop. Eliezar ended up wedding a girl even younger than Susanna and from a family even poorer than ours.

As for me, I was still in school and between Father and me, unlike the case with my two siblings, there were no fulminous clashes. The reason for this? I think it largely had to do with my being youngest, which earned for me most times nothing more severe than Zebedee's wholehearted indifference. I simply fell below his notice, which suited me just fine, since it made my life less complicated.

But there *was* something driving me to distraction in those days, something turning my world upside down as well as inside out. In a word, it was *girls*. I had begun to take a keen interest in them. They seemed to occupy my every waking thought, and many of my sleeping ones, for at some point on this short road I had traveled so far, it had begun to occur to me they were the loveliest of creatures. And yes—there *was* one girl in particular. Her name was Milcah. We were the same age. I would see her sometimes in the lanes of the village, and one day I finally worked up my courage to speak to her. But I should have foregone the opportunity. My discourse, as I stood in her presence, proved so clumsy and scantling I could not have looked any more foolish had I stumbled into a fire and set my hair alight. She even did me the honor of collapsing into giggles, and away from the painful encounter I limped, red-faced with embarrassment.

And I never got up my nerve to try with her again. I just couldn't do it.

Chapter Fourteen

That year on Gennesaret, a vessel carrying a Roman senator collided with a Galilee fishing boat. Two fishermen were killed, and despite drunkenness on the Roman ship, nothing had been done to punish those responsible. The unstated message seemed to be that as far as the Romans were concerned, our lives were worthless. By our conquerors we were put to the sword, imprisoned, crucified. More Jewish lives in fact were forfeited or brought to ruin than grains in a handful of dust, yet let a Jew kill, or even only smite, a *single* Roman, and a cry so fervid would be raised that you could not help but hear it echoing all the way to the sky and back.

My father had pushed for compensation for the families of the drowned fishermen, in the course of which he had become embroiled in a dispute with the local Roman-appointed tax collector, who was not a Roman, but a Jew. Zebedee had left something of a mark upon the fellow's institutional depravity, and in so doing, my father had re-earned his nickname, *Nasha Hadad*, Man of Thunder. The affair resolved itself in Father's favor, the small financial gain being given to the widows and children of the two men killed. It was a magnanimous gesture on Zebedee's part, and there were those who came to look upon my father, not without justification, as a defender of the downtrodden.

I have up to now portrayed my father as a hard man, a severe man, and most assuredly he was those things, yet I would be remiss if I did not mention also that there were noble qualities about him. It wasn't just the drowned fishermen or the dispute with the tax collector. Zebedee had a way of negotiating all the obstacles that can be constructed by the indifferent Furies of Fate, and of eventually finding paths around them. Looking back on it all now, I cannot help but admire his ability to hold us together body and soul in the times in which we were living. Eking out a living on Gennesaret was never easy, but the taxes we were forced to pay brought us nigh to the gates of desperation. It's well I should pause here and mention that wherever a tax collector could be found, misery was not far behind. We paid land taxes, income taxes, water taxes, city taxes, house taxes, boundary taxes, market taxes, plus taxes on fish, meat, produce, and salt—and that was only what we paid to the Romans. Besides that, there were the religious taxes. These included the half-shekel sanctuary tax, due each year on the 15th of Adar, and, for those who farmed or herded, the one-tenth tax. No more, no less, just one-tenth, except there were three different kinds of one-tenth taxes required. Culled were the *ma'aser rishon*, "the first tithe," given to the Levites, for as it says in the fourth book of Moses, "I have given the children of Levi all the tenth in Israel"; the *ma'aser sheni*, "the second tithe," taken from what was left over after the first tithe and carried to Jerusalem, where it was there consumed by the landowner and his family; and the *ma'aser ani*, "the third tithe," given to the poor. In every seven-year period, tithes were taken to Jerusalem each year but for the seventh. The *ma'aser rishon* and the *ma'aser sheni* were required in year numbers one, two, four, and five; and the *ma'aser rishon* and *ma'aser ani* in the third and sixth years. Those landowners who did not comply were shunned, the increases of their fields held as "unclean."

In regards to all these taxes, those paid to Rome were deeply resented by my father. Yet of the religious taxes, he took no exception, for of course it was all dressed up as "holy unto the Lord," and to Zebedee, who after all was a pious Pharisee, such a distinction made all the difference. In addition to benefiting the Levites, the one-tenth offering, as Moses had written, must provide also for "the stranger, the fatherless, and the widow, that they may eat within thy gates, and be filled," and my father, as I've already alluded, held a share of compassion for the downtrodden, as was the case with Pharisees in general, or at least as was mostly *presumed* to be the case. All too often, however, our leaders made it abundantly clear their prime concern was their own comfort and well-being. And as to those two factions, Pharisee or Sadducee, the "rivalry" said to exist between them was not really as pronounced in all matters as one might have supposed. A certain sympathy for the poor was *professed* by the Pharisees, but the fact was, neither party, Pharisee nor Sadducee, had been outlawed by Rome. This of course stood in marked contrast to the Zealots, or *Sicarii*, who really *did* have some concerns for the poor, and who had been branded by our conquerors as insurrectionists. Unlike the Pharisees and Sadducees, the *Sicarii* were routinely put to death...whenever Rome was able to capture them, that is.

But with regard to these religious taxes, one might ask, where stood our overlords, the Romans? Did they not look askance upon such collections as a rival system of taxation? Actually no. There of course had been times in the past, and would be so in the future, when the Temple treasury was looted with wanton abandon, but in those days of Caesar Augustus, and even into the reign of Tiberius, which soon was upon us, not only were our religious taxes condoned, but Roman soldiers frequently secured their transport. Meanwhile (despite all the tithing presumably done for their benefit) the poor became, in a word, *fleeced*, much like the sheep of the land, left ever poorer and poorer.

As I say, my father believed in the system of religious taxation, as he believed in the Pharisees, and refused to see anything faulty in either. Some people are born with a fundamental inability to see certain things, even though these things may be wavering glaringly in front of their faces. My father was one of these. It was natural, I suppose, that Zebedee should identify with the Pharisees, for the latter, as I say, made a show of concern for the poor, and my father was of course a poor man. But the fact of the matter is, the *real* Pharisees, the scribes and doctors of the law in Jerusalem, incarnated in their elevated and royal domains, coveting rather a lot but actually wanting for very little, gave little heed to the pains and miseries of the poor, and with the death of Hillel this had become even more the case. We, the poor of Galilee, were disdained for the most part as the *am ha'aretz*, and nothing about that ever changed.

Nothing about *anything* ever really changed—except for me. *I* was changing. Though my family was fleeced like the rest of the poor, I was growing older, finding myself beset with joys and desires that were new to me, my eyes exhilarating to a world rich in marvels.

Chapter Fifteen

"**A**s is befitting a true scholar, I have this small gift for you." And with these words Rabbi Joel produced a stone cup, lovingly carved by some craftsman, and handed it to me. I was nearly 14 years old and had just finished my schooling. "And as the scripture would have it, 'may thy cup runneth over.' Happily, then, do I offer this first filling." From a flask, he beamingly poured a thick, sweet liquid, a wonderful *shechar*, made from the fermented juices of pomegranates and dates.

"Oh my!" said Susanna, her eyes shining upon me as I took my first sip. It was fairly potent stuff, but sweet and delicious. And I was overwhelmed by the gesture of the rabbi—this kind man I had grown to love and admire so greatly. He was here. Along with the others. They had come to pay honor on what for me was a very special occasion: my last day of school.

"Drink deep, little brother, though, of course, you are not so little any more," James said.

"Here! Here!" exclaimed Peter.

We had gathered at a bend of the Jordan, though in no way to regret or repent. Here, only a short distance from the school, the water formed itself into the task of simply dwelling serenely and competently in a delightful little aerie of lush sound. It was secluded from the external world. We were near the school, the synagogue, the rest of the town, but far enough away as to be able to savor for ourselves, in some temporal manner, the deliciousness of this special moment. At the age of thirteen, I was now considered a fully-grown Son of the Law; the Torah had been taught to me rigorously, yet thanks to Rabbi Joel, my life, all of our lives, had been enriched immeasurably, beyond the boundaries of the Law's narrow criteria. He had challenged each of us, opening up the worlds of science, philosophy, poetry, and drama. Like any good teacher, he had helped us to spread our wings, and in so doing had shown himself as tolerant as the earth itself.

Must I mention it?—that in the despicable crime of teaching girls to read, he and my mother were still hinged together? They were. And just as in days of old, the practice was more oft-criticized than not. In fact, a small but vocal group of men in the town, like slavering dogs, had formed themselves with the hope of rallying one and all of the townspeople, and seemingly the angels of heaven too if were possible, against the efforts my mother was making. Undaunted, Salome had continued her mission, still carrying the hapless rabbi in tow. Joel, for his trouble, found himself forced to endure on occasion salvos of rebuke, which of course, in the trading back and forth of reprimands, tended to fall his way more or less by default. One particular encounter, with a man named Azariah, had been especially alarming, not only for Joel, but for all of us who had witnessed it. The aforementioned Azariah lived in a hovel some distance from Gennesaret along with his wife and thirteen children, including three daughters upon whom my mother had dared take pity. Placing them in school had been her solution to the family's poverty, but Azariah had not taken kindly. A copious burst of invective had been the extent of it, though there had been those witnesses to the incident who had feared for the rabbi's safety, if not at present, then possibly at some point in the future. *O Paraqlita!* Aggrieved at the rather nasty abuse heaped upon her accomplice, my mother, with a well-nourished measure of contumacy, had marched herself down that path of clamor and knocked upon the offender's door. Here she delivered the sternest of tongue-lashings. With remarkable stoicism, Azariah had contemplated the purpling streams of her anger, and only when she had finished speaking, then and only then, had he given his answer. It was in effect no answer at all, but rather a sudden and violent slamming of the door in her face. Zebedee, of course, found out about it. Astonishingly, no fault did he find with Azariah, but rather with Salome. She should mind her own business, quit interfering in other people's affairs. For my mother and father it was yet another case of their fundamentally divergent views on the entire world and just about everything in it.

"It has been a pleasure, Johannes, for me to have been your teacher these years," Joel said now. "You have been exceedingly conscientious and diligent in your studies."

"Thank you, Rabbi."

We looked at him with devotion, much I should think as Azariah, in inverse proportion, must have looked upon my mother as if regarding a three-headed serpent that day.

"Allow me to pour some more of this," he added, "and let us all pass this cup that I have given to Johannes, and let each of us take from it a drink."

There was something praiseworthy in the flow of his words, in the breadth of his giving heart. We, his students, seated in our assembly, were come to draw upon the floating jewels of his wisdom, although I'm sure he would not have viewed it as such. Yet to the gathering, there *was* a certain intimacy. James and Susanna had arranged it. In addition to the rabbi, they had invited Peter, Philip, Andrew, Nathanael, and Perpetua—a celebration in honor of my completion of my studies. Perpetua and Nathanael had come from Capharnaum and Cana respectively, a long way; I was touched that they had made the effort, and it was good seeing Peter again, for he had been spending increasing time of late traveling back and forth from Bethsaida to Capharnaum to visit Perpetua.

I thought back over the past three years. After our adventure on the mountain, Peter's leg had healed to a fair degree. There remained nothing more than a slight limp. In fact, so much time did he spend now in transit back and forth that we had seen very little of him of late. He and James were both nineteen now; and then there was Philip, who, at eighteen, was as creative, shrewd and resourceful as ever; finally Andrew, who, though only fourteen, had even at this time begun to meter the glory of heaven, for already he was on his quest for God, a quest that would define his life for evermore. We had all grown. We had all changed. Yet I could not help wondering: was there not something unchangeable about us as well in the way we all drew warmth and friendship from each other, much as the world draws warmth from the sun?

"Rabbi, we all owe you a great deal," said Susanna, who had survived another attempt by Zebedee at arranging a marriage. She passed the cup to him, and as she did so I wondered if my sister had ever given consideration to marrying the rabbi. Clearly, she thought much of him. Perhaps, under different circumstances...and if such a union had transpired, is it possible things would have turned out differently? But there were barriers to this potential happiness, not the least of which was Susanna herself. In all of her exercises of both body and mind, there was no rival to the daughter of the ocean, the Sothis of the golden stars, which had smitten her spirit in the name of those *dramatis personae* she savored in her poems and stories, those characters she had learned to see in every flower and stream, in every vein of every leaf. She had tamed herself only enough to make herself one with them. They were more real to her than this less-than-perfect world around her. At seventeen she was now of the age, yea even beyond the age, at which a great many of the girls in our town married. Alas, in marriage Susanna seemed to have little interest.

The rabbi refilled the cup, corked the flask, took a drink, and once more started the vessel around the circle. "You have all been good students in your time. A teacher can ask for no more than to be blessed with students such as you."

"Rabbi, what do you think of the Zealots?" This came from Philip, who had concluded of late that there was much about them, called *Sicarii*, or Zealots, he deemed dashingly admirable. The name *Sicarii*, "dagger men," had been given them by the Romans in reference to the curved, Persian-styled knives, or *sicae*, they carried. With their "zealousness" for the law, they had much captured the public interest of late. Under a new system promulgated by Rome and the new emperor, whose name was Tiberius, we now had *publicani*, or tax collectors, who were appointed for five-year terms. The contracts were given to those willing to perform the service for the least amount of money. It was a system ripe for abuse, a system the Zealots had pledged to resist by the sword. Nothing had so far come of this pledge other than a few minor and highly disputed incidents, yet it was enough to give rise to stirring in the breasts of those who, above all else, despised the Romans and longed to shake off the dust of their presence in our land. And of course of these there were many.

"I have listened much to what they say," answered Joel. "Some of it I agree with; most I do not."

By leave of the new system, gangs of brutal men were being hired by the new tax collectors. It was Hephaestus mounted upon a bier, and people were at their mercy. The Romans were tightening their grip upon our land and going about it in a clever way: they essentially had begun hiring our own people, for grand sums, to murder and rob their fellow Jews. Once Rome received its quota in taxes, whatever else the *publicani* could plunder in addition, seemingly, was theirs to keep. The *Sicarii*, on the other hand, had exhorted people to unite in opposition. And Rome had not taken kindly. Two dagger men had been captured in Sepphoris and crucified, yet the Zealots remained unbowed. Second only to YHWH, they revered the brave, and they urged others to do likewise. And some were starting to listen.

"It is very hard on poor families," said James. "Some have been told they must pay twice, even three times what they were forced to pay before." This was true, and people were hurting as a result. "The *Sicarii* are resisting this."

"There are those," added Peter, "who declare we should all, everyone of us, as a group, refuse to pay the taxes. I have heard this talk coming from Capharnaum and some of the other towns. It is said also that a delegation is being sent to Caesar."

"If all in the nation refuse to pay at once," Philip replied, "there would be nothing the Romans could do. What could they do, slay all of us? What do you think of this, Rabbi?"

"What do I think of that?" Joel replenished the cup and passed it forth again. "I will answer your question with a question, Philip: what if they only kill a few, and then the rest of the nation relent and begin once more to pay their taxes? If only you, your friend, and his friend remain standing in defiance, who will the Romans punish?"

"But something must be done, Rabbi! There is suffering taking place!" Philip protested.

Joel responded with a cautious smile. "Suffering has always taken place. The reason I answer your question with another question is that I cannot tell you what to do, Philip. It is not for me to tell anyone what to do. Each man— and woman—must decide for himself—or *herself*—how to direct the course of his or her life." I glanced at Susanna, whose eyes were fixed upon the rabbi's face; clearly what he had said had been spoken as much for her as for the rest of us. "The only thing I can tell you is that bloodshed is not the answer, for it never leads to anything but more bloodshed."

It was extremely unusual for a rabbi to say, "I cannot tell you what to do." Most had no compunction whatever about telling people what to do, as many people as possible, or as many as they could convince their interpretation of the Law was the only correct and true one. But Joel had always been different. We knew this.

"Rabbi," asked Andrew, "why is there always suffering?"

"Knave!" retorted Philip. "What kind of question is that to ask the rabbi?"

"Why do you call me knave when all I did was ask a question?"

Philip rolled his eyes. "For the love of the Lord!"

Philip was being overly dramatic. Andrew was a good soul, and while his enthusiasm was at times disconcerting, it could not be implied in all truth that there was about him any perversity of heart.

Nathanael spoke now for the first time, "It is a legitimate question, Andrew, but one which no one can know the answer to, isn't that right, Rabbi?" Nathanael—he was more massive, more physically large than ever, yet still he carried that ever-present smile along with that quiet, gentle nature we had come to know on our trip to the mountain.

"Well, *someone* might know the answer to it. Regrettably that someone is not I." The rabbi cast his deep, liquid eyes upon each of us in turn. "But here is what I *would* say: listen to your dreams. For it is written, 'And it shall come to pass that I will pour my spirit upon everyone; and your sons and your daughters shall prophesy; your old men shall dream dreams; your young men shall see visions.' Those, as you know, are the words of the prophet, Joel"—he gave up a modest smile—"for whom I was named. One day we may *all*, everyone of us, as the prophet has said, including women, as he also noted"— here the smile twinkled out and touched Susanna—"dream dreams and see visions. And we must listen, and watch, and be aware, so that we will know when that time comes. And when it *does* come, we must not flinch or fail to speak the truth of what we see."

"Sometimes bad things come from speaking the truth," said Peter.

"Worse things come from failing to," replied the rabbi. "Knowledge of truth is the way of *gnosis*, but truth is useless if you fail to speak it."

"What is *gnosis*?"

"*Gnosis*? Ah! Well...the short answer is that it is the search for things that cannot be seen..."

Every time I now hear the question *what is gnosis?* I think of the prisoners in the cave, in the story told by Plato. You are perhaps familiar with it, dear Quintus? It is a story, which, to a large degree, exemplifies what it is to gain gnosis, whether Plato intended it as such or not, for truth is often beyond what we are able to conceive, and when finally we do comprehend it, we become as the prisoner who has never before seen the sun. That is what it is like to gain gnosis, Quintus.

"What things are there which cannot be seen?" asked Peter.

"You mean what things besides God, brother!" put in Andrew.

The young teacher smiled. "Many things. But those who search for the secrets of the saintly will, if they are diligent, find them. That is your first lesson on gnosis. It is also likely to be your last. If Rabbi Hamul heard me discussing such things with you he would be displeased."

"Did you learn of such things in Alexandria?" I asked. The Egyptian city held much fascination for me, for I had begun to think of it as a place where immortals must surely sit, and in my imagination, I conjured a vision of its citizens drinking ever from a fountain of wisdom.

"Dear Johannes, listen to me! You do not have to be in Alexandria, or Rome, or anywhere else in particular, to search for what is real. It is right inside you. Follow your dreams wherever they lead, and do not be despondent if along the way you stumble upon darkness, for one who has never stood in darkness cannot know what it means to welcome the light."

"Rabbi," interjected Susana, "sometimes I think—oh, it will sound silly, I suppose..." Her voice trailed off.

"What, dear child? *Tell* me."

"I don't know...I just think sometimes that terrible things are going to happen...you know? To you, to me, to all of us..."

"Most likely terrible things *will* happen; they always do sooner or later. It is an imperfect world we live in, dear girl. Of course that doesn't mean we don't try and make it better."

"Rabbi, why did that man treat you in such a terrible manner?" This spoken by Andrew, whose curiosity about all things under heaven never lagged.

"You are referring to Azariah?"

"Yes."

The rabbi's features became thoughtful. "I think because of fear."

"Aye, fear alright, " put in Philip, "—fear that his ignorant brood of offspring might not turn out as grandly and fulsomely dull-witted as he himself."

"I think he fears much more even than that, Philip. I think he fears exactly what we all fear—that which he does not understand."

"Maybe to his list of fears we can now add one more—fear of another knock on the door from Mother," mused James.

Joel's face suddenly brightened. "You know, James, and you too Susanna and Johannes! Your mother has been a mainstay. She has made my life here tolerable. Without her, I think I should have left Bethsaida long ago. Yea, in fact, had possibly even been driven out. You are acquainted with the fact that three years ago Rabbi Hamul wanted to remove me?"

"No! We heard of no such thing! Tell us!"

"Yes. It is true. This was around the time that all of you scampered off to the mountain—against my better advice."

Our smiles were appropriately sheepish, as he continued,

"Rabbi Hamul had begun to find with me many faults. I am not sufficiently devoted to the law. I am not conscientious with my sacrifices. I am too much of a talebearer and a dreamer. All of which are true. In any case, he had made his decision, and I was in the course of packing my things and arranging for passage, when what do you think occurs?"

"Nay! We do not know. Tell us!!"

"To the school comes none other than—whom do you suspect? Can you guess?"

"You mean...Mother?"

"Precisely," he replied. "The very mother of James, Susanna, and little—but now big—Johannes!"

"She never *told* us!" said Susanna.

"I am not surprised, but in fact it is what happened. She knocked on the door, much in the manner, I should imagine, as she knocked upon the door of Azariah that day, and when Rabbi Hamul appeared, she voiced to him her feelings and thoughts; in the end, he relented. My tenure here was spared. But I was, as I say, on the brink of passage."

"What would you have done? Where would you have gone? Back to Alexandria?"

"Yes, I have a brother there, and was planning to move back in with him. But as I say, your mother intervened, and here I've stayed."

"Alexandria!" exclaimed Andrew. "The greatest city! Greater even than Rome...or Tyre."

"Not greater than Rome, at least not in some people's eyes," said the rabbi, "but yes, greater than Tyre."

"I am very glad you did not leave us," said Susanna. "We would have missed you."

"And I would have missed you as well," he replied. "But know one thing and that is this: there most likely will come a day when I shall leave this town, for my stay here, even with all that your mother has been for me, has not been a happy one."

"Nay, Rabbi, never! We would not want you to leave! Not ever!"

"Do not say such, for certain things are meant to be, and if they happen it is because they are meant to happen."

"But it would not be the same here without you!"

"Maybe not," he replied with the beginnings of a grin. "And maybe that is not such a *bad* thing!"

"*Nay*, Rabbi! We cannot believe that!" we all voiced in protest.

The sun was going down, willingly taking unto itself the foot shackles of slow death as it slipped into the land of fixed dreams. Philip commented dourly, "That Rabbi Hamul, he is such a *raca*!"

"Nay! You must not say such as that!" answered Rabbi Joel, genuinely distraught at Philip's comment. "You must not even think it, Philip! Try and understand, all of you, the rabbi is a man of great sincerity in his beliefs, and for that he is deserving of respect."

"But he wanted to get *rid* of you!" Susanna protested.

"For reasons which he thought were valid. Try to understand, the rabbi is a good man, and he is not to be faulted for failing to see a city built upon a hill when that same city is as abstruse and invisible to everyone else. Though he sometimes falls short, as do we all, he is a man guided by his principles, and that is not something you can say of all men. Some men are wholly devoid of principles, but the rabbi is not one of them."

"Nay, of course not, but—"

"Listen to me! Know this and know it well: Rabbi Hamul has his faults for the very good reason that humans are imperfect beings. Now, there are many ways we can respond when we see someone acting in a misguided way. Is it better to hurl recriminations, or is it better to respond with love? You and your father, James, have had trying times in your relation as father and son, times when peace and civility have fled. It is not for me to advise you in this, for I have not walked in your sandals. I can only speak to my own situation. Insofar as it similarly applies, I see love as the better way. I have come to regard it as my task, nay, as my duty, to *love* Rabbi Hamul."

"That is a difficult duty to place upon oneself!"

Joel smiled. "It is not as difficult as you think. For as I have said, he is a man of principle, even if he does not always see clearly. And that is a starting point. And besides that, he is a great sower! Even now, he is planning the construction of a new *mikvah*, the ritual bath; it is to be built here on this very spot, where we now are sitting, and I have no doubt that six months or a year hence, if you walk down to this bend of the river, you will see it standing here."

We all pondered these heretofore-unnoticed virtues of Rabbi Hamul. Empty now was the flask of *shechar*. The sun was gone to its final resting place; all that remained was a slinking band of purple light. I wondered how my life would be different now that I was no longer in school. I was thirteen, yea, nearly fourteen. I didn't feel any older, though perhaps to others I looked older. I glanced at the rabbi. He was quite obviously preparing to take his leave of us, but before he could do so, Andrew interjected another one of those irrefragable, soul-searching questions of his.

"Rabbi?"

"Yes, Andrew?"

"Well, what I wanted to say is, you remember when we went to the mountain?"

"How could I forget?"

Again we were sheepish.

"I guess it wasn't a great thing to do," conceded Andrew.

"Yes and no," answered our teacher, not without humor.

"Well," Andrew resumed, "what I wanted to ask you is...you remember when we got back, what we told you?"

"That you saw the yellow wolf."

"Exactly! And that is what I find puzzling! It has been three years now and yet nothing that has happened, to me or any of us, would make us think we have received a blessing from God."

Joel smiled. "Give it time. Perhaps it will come."

Chapter Sixteen

While older now, I was still no more successful in affairs of the heart. My unrequited love for the beautiful Milcah remained, but in the spring of the following year, she was betrothed to a young man named Ethan, who was eighteen. After their wedding I seemed to become like one of those love-besotted figures in Susanna's stories, forever doomed to stalk life's blind, windswept pathways while hiding the pain gnawing at my broken heart. Or so I fancied it anyway. I was, of course, helping Father and James. Though I had never particularly *wanted* to be a fisherman, now I was. The hours were long, and Gennesaret was fickle. Sometimes our haul was as vast as our nets could hold; other times we scarcely fed ourselves. My mother's garden helped make ends meet. Corn was harvested in the month of Ziv. We also ate locusts, usually cooked rapidly in boiling salted water, although sometimes Salome ground them into a powder, which she then mixed with wheat and baked into biscuits. They were actually quite delicious, and thus we adapted, utilizing what the earth provided.

But there were certain ravages from which the earth could not shield us. The tax collectors, for example. Under the new Caesar, they had become more emboldened than ever. Threats were issued and even violence unleashed, as people found themselves increasingly at the mercy of men grown strutting and boastful with their newfound powers. Inevitably, as we feared it would, trouble soon found its way to us. One day, a most unappealing man sought Father out on the quay. He was neither physically large, nor was there an altogether absence of civility, yet something about him suggested an inner disfigurement, of mischief unfettered. Long did he and my father converse, for most of the time it took James and I to sort our catch. We had pulled in to the *evra* at the mouth of the river where the Bethsaidan fishermen tied up every night. In the next boat over, old Jonah, Peter's father, went about his own duties, though occasionally, like us, glancing up at the stranger who stood engaged with Zebedee at the end of the quay. On this day Peter was helping his father, for this was one of the times our love-stricken friend was home rather than plying the road between Bethsaida and Capharnaum.

"Who was that man, Father?" James asked when Zebedee at last returned.

"The new tax collector."

"What is his business here? We have paid our taxes," James replied.

"Not according to him."

"For what reason does he say so?"

"We owe more." Zebedee, tight-lipped, began adjusting the sink-weights on our *sagene*, seemingly, to outward appearances, absorbed in this task. "We also paid taxes only on our property. Now he says we must also pay taxes on our persons."

"Say again?"

"Taxes—upon our persons."

"Our 'persons'?"

"Aye. We have bodies, each one of us. Now we must pay taxes on them."

"I have never heard of such a thing! It is of no sense!"

"It is against *God*, is what it is!" thundered old Jonah, who had wandered over from his own vessel. "These people, these *tax collectors*, they are sinners of the worst sort!"

"Aye, I'll not disagree with that, Jonah," replied Father.

"How much do we owe?" inquired James.

Father told him. It was a staggering amount—sixty-five shekels of silver.

"But why so much?" breathed James in astonishment.

Zebedee was again tight-lipped. "Because of the taxes on our bodies, and because we underpaid the amount of tax on our property."

"But do we have that much money?" my brother wanted to know.

"No."

"What will we do?"

"Ask for more time."

Peter walked over now. Of recent, he had been our main source for news from Capharnaum and the other towns and villages around Gennesaret, and the information he relayed now was not good. "The chief tax collector of Capharnaum greatly distressed one family there. They beat the man in front of his wife and children. Many families are being told to pay what they do not have. The family of Perpetua are very fearful."

"They cannot do that here...*can* they, Father?" whispered James.

But Zebedee had no answer.

In the coming days and weeks we doubled our hours upon the lake. Fishing. It was what we were born to do, it seemed. For there were few other options. Unless we were to go out and join the *Sicarii*, and while a few people actually did such, this was not Zebedee's way, and James and I were Zebedee's sons. And our way was fishing. So day and night, we did just that, and eventually we managed to save some money, but it was not enough.

In his travels to and from Capharnaum, Peter picked up a lot of news— mostly bad. Roman soldiers raided a second *Sicarii* house in Sepphoris. One of the occupants had been crucified; the others locked away in prison. And in the countryside just outside Bethsaida three men were killed, their bodies found in weeds a short distance off the road. Some said they were dagger men from the town of Gamla, a center of *Sicarii* resistance to the east of us; others said no, they had been assassinated *by* the *Sicarii*; still others thought them merely travelers waylaid by robbers. No one knew. But it was an ominous sign—that the ground was shifting under our feet. A messiah would come, a warrior king who would lead us in throwing off the Romans, some felt. Others threw up their hands, shook their heads, and said there was nothing to be done but pay the taxes. In Bethsaida the new tax collector, whose name was Zichri, set up a booth in the agora. His methods were callous, cruel even, and with his advent, those who looked to the scriptures did so ever more fervently. God would send his servant to his Chosen Ones, they assured everyone. We had but to wait. 'Why wait?' others said. Better to act now. Isn't that what the *Sicarii* advocated? Act now and trust to God's deliverance. Could we not, would we not, through the Faithful One's help, usher in our own hundred years of independence, just as the Maccabees had done? And so it went back and forth, a lot of talk that led to nothing.

Through it all, Rabbi Hamul continued work on the *mikvah* he was building by the river. Maybe he felt that if we were all simply *clean* enough everything would turn out agreeably in the end. And yes, to be sure, cleansing ourselves from contamination, like waiting for the messiah, had its proponents. And so the *mikvah* gradually rose. Occasionally, strolling nearby, I would see people standing in groups, nodding approvingly, as the workers put their stones in place. "That Rabbi Hamul," these would say, "he is such a good man!" And I would remember that because of Rabbi Hamul, we had almost lost Rabbi Joel, yea *would* have lost him had it not been for my mother. But of course I didn't say anything—and as it turned out, we lost Rabbi Joel anyway.

That searing morning in the middle of summer, James and I had accompanied Mother to the agora. The sun, though it was still early, burned hot as flame-crowned fat as we walked about the square, being amongst the first to arrive on that market day. Our agora was not large, neither noble nor worldly, but it *did* offer a fair number of staples if you were determined to find them, which on that morning my mother was—though I was not—and I trailed in behind both her and my brother in a state of lazy, lion-headed balminess. Browsing here and there, we came at last to a stall at the north end of the square wherein stood a linen merchant, who seemed sorely vexed, and for good reason, it turned out. Behind his ciborium, just moments before the agora had opened and before he'd even had time to arrange his wares, he had stumbled upon what he had at first taken for a corpse. Upon closer inspection, however, the body was discovered to yet have life, though not by much.

"Where?" Mother inquired urgently.

"Just behind the tent!" To the spot he led us, and there we found him— our teacher. Apparently on one of his solitary wanderings, he had been attacked sometime during the night. "A doctor should be sent for," said the merchant. "It would be well also to notify his kinsmen." Standing there looking upon him, we were taken by a feeling of horror as well as one of complete helplessness, my mother's face turning paler than I had ever seen it. Joel had been pummeled severely about head and upper body. Moreover, it had not been a robbery, for in his purse were coins which surely would have been stolen had his attackers been robbers. No sign of life was there other than a ragged scepter of breath.

Quickly my mother hired a litter and we removed him to our house, sent for a doctor, and tried to make him as comfortable as possible. A measure of wine was poured out by the *medicus*, who arrived in short order. He also made a poultice of fish brine, normally used for rheumatism, but it would also be beneficial for the swelling and the bruises, he assured us, and, after dispensing this, he then proceeded to spread honey over the open wounds. With the slowness of spring returning, our beloved rabbi began to regain consciousness.

"Who did this to you?" my mother asked.

Through swollen eyes, he struggled with the light from the open window. "I don't know. It was dark, and they wore *piljons* and had wrapped linen scarves about their faces."

"Did they say why?"

"Aye." He nodded, grimacing in pain. "All the generations...Abraham till now...it is against God's law to teach the Torah to girls...this reason they gave."

He also had been told to leave Bethsaida. And to show him of their seriousness they had beaten him with a feral and malicious relentlessness, sparing only his life in the end. His jaw was broken, several teeth were missing, and his face resembled nothing so much as a lumpy and discolored bale of straw. I suppose, if one chose, one could construe the attack also as a veiled threat against my mother, though of course no one had dared lift a hand against the wife of *Nasha Hadad*. And so rather than my mother, it had been the mild-mannered rabbi targeted for retribution. Suspicions immediately alighted upon Azariah, whose encounter with Joel the previous year was still much remembered. However, the rabbi laid this to rest. It had not been he. Though the attackers' faces could be little glimpsed, he was sure—though I'm not certain how—Azariah had not been among them. But then none other than the doctor himself confirmed this, saying he had only just treated Azariah for ague the previous day and that the man could not possibly have risen from his bed.

Chapter Seventeen

If the town had been in an uproar before, it was nesting upon the wide pastures of chaos now. A meeting was held at the synagogue. One after another, people got up and orated in florid and boundless manner on the affair. Everyone, it seemed, had an opinion—on the beating of the rabbi, the teaching of women, the paying of taxes, even on whether or not the messiah would come. Of course hardly any women spoke. One of the few exceptions to this was my mother.

"Well you may remember when not a single girl in this town could read or write. Now, praised be to the rabbi who has suffered this terrible assault, some are now literate!"

Salome, in her own way, was merely stating a fact, but one of the men rose to his feet in bombastic rebuke. "Nay! Nay! Nay! Thy praise must be unto the *one God!* No other!" Anyone who failed to give proper praise to God was, of course, an individual of suspect character, and no doubt he meant to imply that my mother fell into this category.

"A bad wife is a chafing yoke. He who marries her seizes a scorpion," commented another, leaving little doubt that in his view Salome was just such a deadly menace.

One of our more learned townsmen said that since the Torah listed wives, along with asses, cattle, and oxen, among the possessions of one's neighbor which one must never "covet," then clearly (he reasoned further) the Torah meant to imply that wives, by inference, were the *property* of their husbands, and hence girls also the property of their fathers.

"Here! Here!" exclaimed those who welcomed this efficient and sound reasoning. But then another purported to offer the more lenient view. "It is fine if girls learn, as long as they receive no *formal* instruction," he declared. "If they should teach each other though—*that* is acceptable!"

But such permissible attitudes—were they not mere foolishness? Indeed this was the view of some. "From a woman sin had its beginning," said one man with a great deal of weightiness. "And because of her we all die!"

Finally one corpulent fellow, having apparently more than a passing fancy for sages of the desert, expounded the novel idea that God had once asked himself, "From which part of the man shall I take the woman?" Resolutely he then gave what he asserted to have been YHWH's reasoning on the matter: "'Should I take her from the head? Nay! She would be too proud! From the eye? Nay! She would be too inquisitive! From the ear? Nay! She would eavesdrop! From the mouth? Never! She would be querulous! From the hand? She would be wasteful!' In the end the Almighty One formed woman from a hidden, inconspicuous part of the body—the rib. This he did in the hope of making her *modest*!"

Through it all, my mother stood her ground remarkably well. "In refusing girls the opportunity to read, you would deny knowledge to Wisdom herself! For Wisdom is a woman, and there is no one loved by God who does not dwell with her!" But in some respects, she had become like a rod that calls down lightning from the sky, and eventually she was shouted down. The tacit implication seemed to be that the attack upon the poor rabbi, while deplorable, had been nonetheless *understandable*. Some even suggested the abuses currently being wrought by the tax collectors were God's punishment upon us for having allowed the teaching of girls. But my mother was not entirely without her supporters, which, to our surprise, included even a few of the men present, and towards the end of the evening these too rose to their feet. Consequently, those on the other side regained their feet, attempting to shout even louder, until near total confusion reigned.

It was in the midst of all this shouting and braying that a most astonishing thing transpired, for suddenly the door of the synagogue flew open. Out of the night he came, his appearance frightening. As usual he was dressed in the filthiest of rags, his hair and beard of an untameable wildness, an unreluctant erdgeist in trance to the imperishable. Of course, I recognized him immediately. It was Rogah, our mountain man. His excursions through Bethsaida had been infrequent over the years. I had seen him no more than a smattering of times since our brush with death, yet I had never forgotten him. How could I? How could any of us? And often I had wondered what kind of life he had, living as he did, alone on that wild and strange mountain. Yes, this I had wondered about him, and many other things as well. He had saved our lives. But what in the name of the Heavenly Host was he doing here now? Had he simply been wandering by, heard the noise and confusion, and decided to step in? Perhaps. At any rate, into our midst now he advanced.

The shouting, which a moment before had filled the air, tumbled into a dilapidated and uneasy silence. Into the room the erdgeist shuffled, while all about people stared transfixed. Yet as he moved through them, it seemed to me he was possessed with a certain oblivious and sublime inveteracy, as though lord of his own vision, panderer to the eternal. At first, having entered through one door, it appeared he intended nothing more conspicuous or spectacular than crossing the room and exiting by way of the other, but just then his forward progress came to a halt as, without warning—and prompting a cry-soaking gasp of fear from the crowd—he spun, like an attendant to the boatman of the Styx, pivoting swiftly and agilely about, until he had executed a full and complete circle. Much like a stray thought that might have seized him, it was as if only now, at this diaphanous moment, had he suddenly realized he was not on his mountain, and that the light supplied by the sputtering lamps in the room was noticeably inferior to the refulgent dawns he was used to upon those faraway peaks. Blinkingly, he gazed about, peering through the textured layers of his darkness and bafflement. If it had been quiet before, it grew even quieter now. I wanted to go to him, say something, anything, maybe offer my hand in greeting, and I could see James and Susanna were entertaining similar notions, but before any of us could act, the visitor's mouth flew open and out came one of the strangest utterances I had ever heard.

"Now, O Nairyosangha, in the fall of a sparrow, there is *nothing* else to be known!"

They were the first actual words I had ever heard him speak. And immediately upon speaking them, he turned and exited the synagogue by way of the same door he had entered...leaving mass confusion in his wake.

"Huh? What does he mean, 'there is nothing else to be known?'"

"What is he saying?"

"Who is Nara-gansa?"

"To whom was he speaking?"

"Fall of *what* sparrow?"

No one knew what to make of the specter's sudden materialization, nor of his strange words. However, as before, a noisy tocsin of opinion-trading issued forth.

"He is *demon*-possessed!"

"He could be dangerous! We should not have this man coming around here any more!"

Demon possession. It was naturally decided to put the question to Rabbi Hamul, who was known to be an expert on the subject.

"Well...he *could* be possessed...that's–that's–that's–entirely *possible*..."

With this clear and decisive proclamation in hand, no one could doubt *something* needed to be done to render the community safe from such a menace, this despite the fact that Rogah, for years, had never been more than an oddly recurring manifestation, a relict, a shadow which came and went like the hyrax, the argali, and other such harmless creatures of the land. James, my fearless and resolute brother, was instantly on his feet.

"Nay! This is not right! He has never hurt anyone!"

"How do you know?"

"Because he helped us once!" There then followed a relating, in general terms, of what Rogah had done for us on the mountain. Following my brother's example, I rose to my feet and confirmed the account, even though of considerable timidity in the face of such tumult, as did Susanna, and yes, even Philip, whose temperament, we well knew, would not allow him to stand idly by in the face of such a misbegotten contretemps. And had Peter been present I feel sure he would have added to the testimony as well, for he had the most to be thankful for. But it was a moot point, and even had Peter been here I'm sure it would have turned out no differently. We were as if speaking to a synagogue of the deaf.

"How do you *know* that he has never harmed anyone? You keep saying that, yet you offer no proof!"

"That's right!" asserted another. "Think of the killings that have happened hereabouts! Do you not remember? *Three men* found beside the road! Murdered! Some say they were *Sicarii* from Gamla; others say merely travelers. I know not *who* they were! But someone murdered them! How do you know it was not he?"

"It is folly to even speak of this!" one man asserted with an air of resignation. "He cannot be prevented from coming into the town!"

"Aye!" agreed another. "What can we do to stop him? If he wants to come to the town, we cannot prevent him."

But this line of reasoning was angrily rejected by a square-jawed, pugnacious-looking young man, who voiced the opinion there *were* certain steps which *could* be taken to prevent Rogah from entering Bethsaida. Furthermore, the speaker let it be known that he for one, in the interest of protecting the town, of course, stood squarely in favor of taking them. I felt a certain tightening in my gut, for he giving vent to these ominous proclamations was known to me. It was Hodi. Yes, my old childhood nemesis was still around. And just as in those days of old, he was still surrounded by his adoring disciples, who, as ever, laughed on cue when he purported to say something funny, while following him about wherever he found it pleasurable to lead. The only difference now, they were able to bully and intimidate anyone they so chose, even up to and including grown men, which they had become themselves. If ever the term *am ha'aretz* could have been accorded, well might it have applied to them. They were the lowliest rabble around. Although, strange to say, few others were able to perceive this about them.

"There can be but God's rejoicing in the freeing of ourselves from such a dark and sable presence in our midst!" It was clear he well remembered the thrashing James and Peter had given him years before, for as he spoke his eyes sprinkled paradigmatically in my brother's direction, a mischievous half-grin planking itself, jackal-like, upon his curling lips, although this was not manifested in such a way as would have been especially noticeable to other than James and myself. "We cannot allow this man to wander about at will. There are *children* playing about. Even if he is not demon-possessed, as the rabbi says, he could nonetheless hurt one of them."

He who had lavished so many moments of misery upon my *own* childhood, now casting himself as a protector of children? It was a spectacle so sickening as to leave one gasping for the open air. Could not anyone, with a reasonable modicum of mental capacity, see the venality on display? But words soaked in lies are capable of procreation, and it was with a sense of foreboding that James, Susanna, Philip, and I left the synagogue that night, the four of us walking home together. We could not, of course, know what was to come, but our fears proved well grounded. Four days later Rogah's body was found face down in a shallow ditch near Gennesaret, his throat slashed. Did Hodi kill him? I suspect so, though nobody ever knew for sure. And I guess after all nobody really cared. Rogah had no family or friends.

Yet his death *was* mourned by someone—my sister. It was a day or two later I came across her at the Jordan. She had chosen that bend of the river where so often we had gone swimming when we were younger, and here, by the flowing water, in solitude, she had taken roost, about her some wildflowers freshly picked. But the arrangement was haphazard, the flowers in disarray. In the dirt in front of her, she had written his name. R-O-G-A-H. One of the uprooted flowers she twirled absently in her fingers while staring moodily at the water. Following a long silence during which neither of us spoke, she tore her eyes away from the river and looked up at me. "We should have gone out that night, you know?—*after* he left the synagogue."

While the body is transitory, the spirit is eternal, and there was, I well knew, something inviolable about that spirit of hers, for she had struggled through the years to make it so, perhaps for no other reason than as an act of self preservation in a world where her father, three times now, had attempted to marry her off. And as I looked upon her, it seemed to me that she sat, not as a forlorn or miserable creature, but as one who has firmly and consciously planted that banner of inviolability. "We shouldn't have waited, John. We should have gone right out after him the very moment he left the synagogue. We should have followed him and searched him out until we found him." Several of the flowers she now took up and tossed upon the water. "He needed us," she said, still looking at the water though choking back tears now. "We should have found him, and then we should have taken him out of this town. We should have taken him back up to his mountain. Just as he brought us down, we should have carried him safely back up."

Chapter Eighteen

U pon recovering sufficiently, Rabbi Joel left our house. He went home, he packed his things, he said goodbye. And he left Bethsaida forever. We all understood. We embraced him as a beloved friend...and wished him luck in Alexandria. That night my mother commented sorrowfully, "It is such a loss for this town."

Without the rabbi's light whatever would we do? I didn't know. But the lord of rays, the Eye of Ra, rises ever in the eastern sky by day, shining on both the good and the wicked, the just and the unjust, and through it all we simply try to keep going. I should mention that in regard to the near-death of the rabbi and its ugly aftermath Father had remained on the whole detached and oblivious. It was not that he was insensitive to what had happened, for this was not the case. It was merely that he was preoccupied. The extension of time granted us by the tax collector was nearly up. We needed money, and we needed it fast. From the stories reaching us, from Peter and others on the circuit around Gennesaret, it was clear that failure to meet the demands of the tax collectors could have serious consequences, and it was at this time I began to wonder to myself if some physical harm might come to my father, possibly even my mother as well; once I would not have thought so, but after what had happened to Rabbi Joel and to Rogah, such things were no longer hard to imagine.

Just when everything appeared bleakest, Father hit upon a plan, although you could say it was less a plan than a desperate throw of the dice. But throws of the dice were all we had left at this point. Zebedee's idea was simply this: that we should go west and fish the Great Sea. I had never in my life seen a body of water larger than the Sea of Galilee, and I knew little about the Great Sea other than it was big. But not only had Father seen it, he had fished there as a young man. Moreover, he had often longed to return, and one night after dinner, reminiscing on those days of old, he gave off a blustery smile that was as fulminous and battle-songed as the blustery sea wind. The Great Sea, he assured us, was the answer to our problems. Then a wink escaped his eye as he clapped me jarringly on the back. "You will see fish bigger than your whole body!" It was an androcentric slap of affection that came near to knocking me completely off my perch. Regaining my balance, I took note of the fact that he had used the words "you will see," which meant, apparently, I was to go too.

Now this whole endeavor was lifted from the hypothetical to the imaginable by the felicitous coincidence that a fisherman in our town had a kinsman in Tyre who owned a seagoing ship. The plan was that a handful of us from Bethsaida should pool our resources with an equal number of Tyrians, including the ship owner, who would join us in the venture. Meeting up in Caesarea Maritima, we would fish all the way up to Phoenicia, docking at last in Tyre. A great deal of expense, however, was involved; the ship was in poor condition and required much retrofitting. It was a foolhardy idea, but Father staked all. Of course, what other choice did he have? Zichri the tax collector darkened our doorstep with ever-greater frequency these days, the sword at his girdle seeming to grow larger and more threatening in proportion to his waning patience.

Curiously, it was at this point that our family drew closer, Salome and Zebedee, even Father and James, ceasing their bickering. Everyone realized the risk we were under. It was also at this point I began to understand for the first time in my life what injustice is, to grasp its shadows of contempt, and its disregard for the lives of the innocent. And this realization gave rise unexpectedly in me to one other, for there began to grow in my heart in these days a fierce loyalty to my father. It was something close to love, though of course it was as ever difficult to love a man like Zebedee. Maybe it is simply enough to say I under*stood* him now. I understood his thunderous though filial pieties, and that what he was doing, he was doing for all of us. I understood also that despite my father's pretensions at Pharisee-hood, we were nothing more than common folk, and when I considered what we were up against, literally the might and power of Rome, coupled with the unyielding plexus of tax collectors now in open collaboration against their own people—when I understood all this, it made me angry. And I resolved fiercely to stand at my father's side. It was something I think we all felt on some level, even Susanna, though doubtless she had never forgotten, nor forgiven, the destruction of her beloved books.

By what means had a repugnant creature like Zichri gained such authority over the people of Bethsaida? It had come about through the not-so-benevolent graces of the Sadducees in Jerusalem—this we now learned.

The Sadducees and their accomplices, the Herodians, were Rome's best friends, ever obliging in whatever suited their foreign masters, and well had they been rewarded for their fealty. The strength of the Pharisees, their ability to gain the loyalty of men like my father, lay in their championing the cause of the poor, and in expressing opposition to *some* things which Rome did. Mortifyingly, however, this opposition was often expressed, when it was expressed at all, with great timidity, in words possessing no more strength than the faintest puff of wind. Our leaders were but part of a system that was harnessed to Rome's sovereignty and dominion, a system which naturally created a certain complacency and indolence that were their own rewards. In short, we were not likely to receive any help from either Sadducees *or* Pharisees, despite my father's almost child-like faith in the latter. Neither were we likely to reap any assistance from the Zealots, who of course were an outlawed party and were thus in no position to help us should they even want to.

As dark as things were, it occurred to me nonetheless it could grow darker, for around this time another recognition hit me as well—that not only could some physical harm come to my mother or father, but the possibility also loomed that one or more, or even all five of us, could be sold into slavery. For that *too* was Roman law. Any free person could own a slave. And those who could afford to, usually did. And this is what the Great Sea held before us like the cup of Tantalus: the prospect of emerging from our difficulties with our lives, as well as our freedom, intact.

Chapter Nineteen

It was not long before we were to leave for the coast that Rabbi Hamul and his workers finished construction on the *mikvah*. In fact, we postponed our departure by a day so that we might attend the special *bur-ka-tha* that was held. Virtually the whole town turned out. The ruler of the synagogue was there, and even a few Pharisees and Sadducees arrived from Jerusalem. Mostly, though, it was ordinary people. They came because this was something new and fine, because it was an accomplishment for our town, and because a feast had been prepared and musicians were there.

There were a lot of pretty girls too. My lack of success with the opposite sex continued to haunt me. Because of it, in fact, I had been given, by the rowdy men of my father's fishing crew, a most humiliating sobriquet: "Johannes the Virgin." Gleefully the name would sing from their lips as we toiled with our nets and ropes. Full well they knew the chaffing it caused me, and naturally the more I chaffed, the more I was called by it, until eventually I began simply to accept as my lot in life that I should ever be known by this tiresome name. I hoped only, rather against hope, that regardless of what name others might call me by, I should not, please Lord, remain in my infernal state of virginity forever, though for now there seemed little likelihood of changing matters. Thus I moved through the crowd that day as good natured shouts of "Greetings, Johannes the Virgin!" followed me everywhere about.

An epicene stream in a flowery robe of autumn sunshine—in such manner did the crowd spill out of the synagogue and down to the *mikvah*, which stood upon a flat spot of earth just below the Jordan's shady pool. There was a lump in my throat as I gazed upon the marvelous structure, for it had been built, just as Rabbi Joel had said, precisely on the spot where we had celebrated my last day of school, now more than a year ago. Our *mikvah* was made of hand-hewn blocks, not basalt like the houses of the poor, but a high-quality syenite, and inside was a pool for the immersion of the body, plus a smaller one for washing utensils. The immersion pool held the prescribed forty measures of water. This of course had to be "living water," meaning rainwater, seawater, or river water. At no time could this living water have been carried in vessels. Being next to the Jordan, we were of course well placed with regard to the obtaining of river water, but then some of the Pharisees had held that the waters of the Jordan were too muddy for purificatory purposes. Hence had come the need for the new *mikvah*. Though situated near the river (mostly for sake of convenience), the building was actually equipped with a cistern for the catching of rainwater, holding a channel for releasing some small portion of this into the bath, for it was not required that all the water in the bath be living, only some. The laws governing ritual purity were complex and I didn't try to keep track of it all. Some of it, I knew, pertained to contact with Gentiles, although defilement could also originate from certain foods, exposure to diseases or bodily emissions, or to contact with the dead. Ritual immersion offered restoration from any one of these states of impurity. And thus out of such concerns was our *mikvah* born.

The crowd grew as the musicians played, and much joy was in the air, yet it was a joy I did not feel myself. Feeling out of place, I took my leave. For a great long time I simply walked. It had begun to seem to me that life on this earth was nothing more nor less than the act of *dumping*. Everybody got dumped upon—and then dumped upon someone else in turn. The Romans dumped upon the Jews; the Jews dumped upon each other; the Sadducees dumped upon the Pharisees; the tax collectors dumped upon the people; the rich dumped upon the poor; the free dumped upon the slaves; the men dumped upon the women. Around and around it went. And now here we were about to make our way to the Great Sea, where we would presumably, in a manner of speaking, dump upon the ocean's creatures. Could anything good come from all this dumping upon one another? And why did things always seem to turn out this way? Does not even bliss itself grow tepid eventually? All this dumping of the filth and slop of life's retributions, one upon another—on it went until you reached the end of the chain somewhere, beyond which there was no one weaker left upon which to dump. I thought of Rogah. Someone had certainly done an effective job of dumping upon him. He had been dumped right out of existence.

My steps took me further and further from the town until I ended up close to Gennesaret, a much-beaten footpath carrying me at last down to the shoreline. Here, unexpectedly, I encountered Philip. Cross-legged he sat at the water's edge, though as I approached he remained unaware of my presence, facing the river with his back toward me while ever so often picking up a pebble and tossing it, almost angrily, out onto the water. When I voiced a greeting he turned with a start. "Well well, if it isn't Johannes the Virgin."

Nothing of a needling had been intended in his calling me this. Yea, the appellation seemed to slip from his lips with hardly a thought, a measure, surely, of how fond others had grown of addressing me by this not altogether derogatory epithet. The pebble tossing resumed. I started to take my leave, for I detected about him an unmistakable gloominess of the spirit, though something held me back. A flock of birds skittered gracefully at low altitude, just above the water's surface, ornamenting the low-pearled sky with their antiphonic invigoration. The water of Gennesaret is sometimes veined with a strange marbling, and so it was this day. Looking out, I felt myself deeply moved by the beauty of it all. "You did not wish to attend the celebration for the new *mikvah*?" I asked.

He laughed a sardonic laugh. "Unless they plan to open their veins in the bath, the water shall never reach their hearts." Furiously he hurled out another pebble, then sighed and turned to face me. "You know sometimes I look at Nathanael and I think, '*Why* can't I be more like him?'" I did not know what to say to this, but he seemed not to notice or care. "Everything he does, he does with love. Everything he speaks, he speaks with love. Everything he touches, he touches with the heart. Me, no matter how I try, I just cannot seem to be like that."

I shrugged. "We are all different."

"Aye, so we are."

Chapter Twenty

It was the Plain of Esdraelon, in the western portion of Galilee—we were crossing it with our donkey and a voluminous quantity of supplies on a day on which the heat was oppressive. Over the shriveled land, the great sun held mastery, while my new rose-colored tunic, sewn by my mother, clung to my back with a firm and moist persistence. "Maybe we should stop here for a spell," Father said, taking out his *miktoran* and mopping his brow. Beside the road grew a gnarled oak under whose shade we halted. James drank some water and passed the skin to me, finally to Father. After slaking our own thirst, we watered our pack animal.

Before departing Bethsaida I had spied my brother kissing a girl named Abigail. The two had been keeping company of late, and their goodbyes were of the most tender sort. Father had refused to say how long we should be away, and as I looked upon them I saw, or thought I saw, something more than fashion and decoration in their embrace. Somehow, I knew this girl had come to abide regally in James' heart, and for a moment, furtively, I had gone on watching them—before turning discreetly away.

Dawn came, and Zebedee, James and I had set off, trudging tiredly by nightfall into the town of Arbela, where we had taken a room in an inn. Here we passed the night, only to set out early again the next morning—and now it was after midday of the second day. We were on our way to Caesarea Maritima and the Great Sea, but we were still many furlongs off. Departing Arbela quite early, we had traveled beneath Ra's sweltering hand until coming at last to a village named Nazareth; although somewhat near the major trade center of Sepphoris, it was an unassuming, out of the way place. Little met the eye save two great trees growing next to a spring in the center of town, with a few sedate stone buildings clustered about, and a small synagogue resting on the hill beyond, yet I had immediately sensed something in the air, a quietness, giving rise to a manservant's melody of the heart. It was cooler here than upon the broiling plain. Stopping at the spring, we filled our containers before sallying forth down the little dirt street, turning at last into a carpenter's shop.

"Father?" James finished watering our donkey as the animal began to graze unprofitably at some dried, withering broom sage. "Who *were* those people back there—back there in that town?" Having by this time found adequate recompense from water and shade, Zebedee opened one eye lackadaisically. As I waited for his response, I thought back to our encounter of earlier that day…

"We are in need of a gaff!" Father had announced in his customary louder-than-necessary manner of speaking as we'd entered the carpenter's domain. The fragrance of freshly-hewn wood gave a tantalizing nourishment to the air as I inhaled deeply. "It should be suitable for fishing on the Great Sea. Can you make one for us?"

"Of course!" Named Joseph, he was stooped at the shoulders, aging in years, and though he greeted us in an amiable manner, it soon became apparent he was not in the best of health; on a stool he rested as the work was performed in the main by his son. This latter, a young man perhaps a year or two older than James, selected several pieces of wood from a large stack, executing each movement with the studied grace of an eventide canticle. His name, we learned, was Jesus. I watched as he took a strip of juniper and smoothed it down, picking up a bow drill at one point and beginning to wield it with skill. The tool consisted of a bowstring wrapped around the handle of a drill bit; back and forth, he pushed the bow, creating a deep hole in the wood, then into the opening he fashioned an iron hook. With much interest, I watched, for it was the first time I'd ever observed a real carpenter at work. He must have sensed my curiosity, for at one point he paused from his work, looked up fully into my face—and smiled. It was wholly disarming. The smile seemed to master me with its humble reverence, yet also to hold up, in almost catopric manner, an image of my most secret and intimate thoughts, and I found myself blushing. *Shushantha*. The wildest and most worthy flower of sorrow's cessation!—and for some reason I wasn't quite sure of, I was proud he had taken notice of me.

By and by we had our gaff—a good, nice strong one! Zebedee, who had diverted himself in an almost haranguing manner with the pale and wheezing Joseph, set down a few coins, at which point we had thanked them and left. The road out of town led us finally to the River Kishon and set us upon the Plain of Esdraelon. It was the road we were on now—and it would eventually take us all the way to the coast.

Zebedee raised his head as he replied, "They're distant relatives on your mother's side,"—then re-mopped his brow before somnolently closing his eyes once more.

Prudence is the foundation of heaven, while zeal is the preserver of the earth. By and by, we resumed our journey, and as we did so, I mostly forgot about that chance encounter in a carpenter's shop in Nazareth. Moreover, it would be years before I would lay eyes on the man, Jesus, again. My thoughts, for now, turned toward the Great Sea, thoughts of glory, leaving me smitten with that old earth-preserving zeal, for it seemed to me, with the open sea beckoning like a king's chest of jewels, I was on the adventure of a lifetime. And in a way I was. Yet as things were to turn out, it was not on the open sea but in a teeming marketplace in a strange city, at the sea journey's end, that occurred what affected me to a far greater degree than anything I was to witness from the deck of that mighty sailing vessel. It was another *chance encounter*, you might say, not unlike the one in Nazareth; in fact, the two, coming at either end of the sea journey, were in a very real sense related, and I've no explanation for it other than to say that they were both, in a certain manner of speaking, magical.

"What is Caesarea like, Father?" James asked as, on our feet now, we once more merged ourselves with the road.

"A large place. Many people. The Gentiles are there in great abundance."

"Will we see lots of them?"

"Of course."

Gentiles. Yes, it was to be expected! For there were many Roman soldiers in Caesarea. Of course in Caesarea we were also to meet up with the crew of our fishing vessel as well. Yes, a great adventure, it seemed, was at hand, an adventure perhaps not unlike our trip to the mountain some years ago, but alas, Peter and Andrew were not here to enjoy it with us; the former, caught up in the throes of passion, was once again lodging in Capharnaum, while the latter, as befitting his incessant search for the Ultimate Truth, had left Bethsaida for the desert, where he now abided with an assemblage of ascetic sages. That the two, Peter and Andrew, were in fact brothers was a curiosity, for so completely different were their outlooks and temperament. Our friends must have been in James' thoughts as well, for my brother said now, "It is too bad that Peter and Andrew could not come to the Great Sea with us." But Zebedee, walking along with his heart of granite and the open road before us, evinced little agreement. "Them we can do without. One's head is filled with nonsense, and the other is guided by his loins." It was clear that Zebedee regarded Peter and Andrew as "worthless sons," unworthy of their father, old Jonah. For of course Peter and Andrew, in their respective wanderings from Bethsaida, had left the old man alone. For Zebedee, it meant they were sons of affliction. But that was my father, always quick to judge.

As for old Jonah himself, he of the risen moon with one wing already in heaven, it seemed not to matter greatly to him one way or the other. Though he was a fisherman of many years, and had tossed many a net into the sea's arching and spray-filled festivals, he had pronounced himself "too old" to accompany us on this occasion. But he had prayed the *Shema* on our departure and wished us well.

Chapter Twenty-One

A very long time ago, it had been called "Strato's Tower." Now, formally, it went by the name Caesarea Maritima, a large bustling port city of thousands of people. And no place like it had I ever seen.

Commanding parapets spaced along the city walls gave little hint of what might lie within, but making our way through the arch of the east gate, we suddenly found ourselves in a world of near-perfectly-squared, block-like streets. Crooked streets, winding whimsically this way and that, were the only kind I had ever known, and at first, it seemed stunningly unnatural and inappropriate. Streets that ran straight, in the manner of a flying arrow—who had ever *heard* of such a thing? But in navigating about the unfamiliar city, I came, after a while, to appreciate the pattern-like predictability.

Fed by a great aqueduct rolling in from the north, Caesarea Maritima was home to a theater, stadium, palaces, and workshops, some, like the tanner's, emitting highly disagreeable fumes, and of course many carts, thundering here and there, as they plied their spoked wheels to the geometrically linear lanes. Crowded along those lanes were merchant stalls filled with grapes, corn, palms, as well as wool and silks and other fabrics, and herbs of every healing quality. In the midst of all this stood a huge temple—dedicated, perhaps not surprisingly, to worship of the emperor of Rome, and hence the name "Caesarea." I was beginning to believe the larger world must be full of emperor-worshipers, for it seemed whenever venturing very far away from Bethsaida I ran into one of their temples.

It was a busy place, a bustling place, a port that was everything I had imagined it to be, but the most amazing sight of all was the Great Sea itself. It was vast; it was more than vast; it went on *forever*. But almost of equal wonder was that which had been created entirely by man—the great ship haven. The thing was full of the ocean, yet enclosed almost entirely by massive stone walls! Never before had I seen walls built upon water. They were huge, walls fit for enclosing a palace, only the palace in this case was the sea itself! The sea and the ships docked upon it! At first I could not fathom how the ships got inside, but then I saw it—a small opening at the northwest corner where vessels moved like slow-running sap, and through which the razor-honed meeting of sea and sky could be glimpsed. Framing either side of this opening were two towers of great height. I knew not the purpose of one, but the other was a lighthouse, named, as we learned, for Drusus, the son-in-law of the late Caesar Augustus. It was a tower whose flaming beacon extended far out onto the sea (as we were soon to observe).

In terms of size and population, Caesarea was not as big as Jerusalem, the only other city at that point in my life I could have compared it to, but it had one thing Jerusalem lacked: a prevalence of young women standing about the streets in revealing clothing. These painted creatures were especially numerous near the ship haven, and by and by, I came to understand their purpose was to offer themselves to the Roman soldiers and sailors. And many of these were about! For Caesarea is where the majority of the Roman legions who occupied our land were housed, and here within its walls the most enticing of fruits were surely available. I was spellbound at the sight of the seductive women, James too, for as we walked along, Zebedee clipped my brother on the back of the head and traduced sharply, "A wise man keeps his thoughts off the harlots!" True words my father spoke. A wise man *does* keep his thoughts from straying to such territory. But I was young, and God takes a thousand forms, and all in all, this great port city struck me as a place where decorum, as well as everything else I had ever been taught about the proper attitudes between men and women, had been set aside, and, if not completely abandoned, at least shrugged off and forgotten for a while.

We returned to the ship haven early the next morning, after spending the night in a Jewish-run inn, and this time I was confronted with yet another sight profoundly affecting my young heart, though in a manner far different from the prostitutes of the day before. It was a slave ship—a Roman trireme. Moreover, the vessel, at that moment, was being disencumbered of its human cargo. Presided over by an aedile with a whip, these men in their chains struck me as the most debased of creatures, a debasement reducing them, it almost seemed, from full blood-and-flesh human beings into mere *semblances* of humans. I watched as, with their leg movements severely limited, they were shuffled down a plank, the sight leaving me rooted to the spot, incapable of looking away, for it was my first face-to-face confrontation with the *commercium* of human misery. Something about those shackles denied all tidings of truth and decency. So disturbed was I by the plight of these poor beings, there came over me, there and then, the outrage of the unwounded, prompting me to vow with boyish fervency: "One day I am going to free them!" An innocent enough remark you might say, but it brought instant rebuke from my father and brother. "You must not say such things, John! Not in public, nor even in private," warned Zebedee.

"Nay, do not speak such, little brother!"

Now quite a staggering discovery was it learning that in the view of Father and James I was simply to forget what I had just seen! And of course I didn't forget it. The sight of those men, walking down that plank with their shackles, remained permanently fixed in my memory. Understand, Quintus, that what brought me to my newfound conclusions on this matter of human bondage wasn't only the fear of what might happen should our family fail to pay off the tax collector. No. It was more than that. Slavery, I came to feel from that day forward, was not only unnatural and repellent, it was a transgression against the Great Incorruptible One, God, the invisible spirit who had spoken the world into existence and created everything in it. And I vowed to myself that one day I would resist this evil institution with all my might.

Chapter Twenty-Two

We left there (with Father and James practically dragging me from the spot), lumbering down the quay where eventually we located the ship on which we were to depart, and what a ship it was! Unlike the cumbersome slave trireme, it was a magnificent sailing vessel, at least to my boyish eyes, as it sat there, fully outfitted, fastened by lines to the bustling, noisy dock, robed in a diamond of sunlight while seeming to yearn sumptuously for the freedom of the faceless winds.

Our crew was eighteen in number, some of us from Bethsaida, a few from Caphaernaum, the rest from Tyre—all fishermen, except for a carpenter, a lean, stalwart Tyrian who had seen to the outfitting of the battened ship. It was in reality an aged vessel, he explained, with detached objectivity, and had required much labor to make seaworthy. He was a friendly sort, in his twenties, who went by the name Jude Thomas, though some on board referred to him as "Didymus," which in the Greek tongue means "twin." As for my own cognomen, "Johannes the Virgin," rude voice was given it immediately by the Bethsaidans, and taken up just as readily by the rest of the crew, one and all, that is, save for the carpenter, Jude Thomas, who alone seemed to have no interest in making sport of me, a fact causing me to feel more than a little kindly disposed towards him.

And so we embarked, nose through the northwest gap in the sea wall, scudding to fore with an indwelling song of praise, propelled by the sea-bird-chattering breezes, at last into the swells of the Great Sea's staggering vastness. Soon the coastline became a blur. So much water! No measure was there for it, and its abundance made me feel small. Our ship had two masts, a cabin containing a galley situated behind the foremast, with sleeping arrangements below. Hardly more than an old, weather-beaten tub was it in the assessment of our Tyrians, but in my eyes it was a splendid ship! We flew along at a fast clip with sails at full, sails stretched to such unassailable tautness they seemed to possess a vigor (in spite of the vessel's age) equal, I rather thought, to the torrents of Gilgamesh, spun-flax sails inbreathing immortality. And the fish we took! Those creatures of the deep, authorities of Poseidon, numinous compeers of his Tritonic realm—they were just as Zebedee had predicted. *Bigger than your whole body*. If the Tyrians were the more skillful in the actual maneuvering of the ship, we of Bethsaida and Capharnaum were the casters of nets. We put out a double-layered *sagene*, the large dragnet, and soon it was full. There were fish with swords and sails, with jagged rows of teeth, and some with many and varied colors rivaling the robes of Croesus. Creatures such as could scarcely be imagined!

Into a routine we settled, trolling the sea all day, while dropping anchor late at night, our position on most occasions far out from land, so far the coastline could scarce be discerned, especially at night, other than by way of an occasional torch flicker from afar. Those who steered the ship did so in a manner I had heard of yet never before seen in actual practice: they plotted our course by points of reference to the stars, in such manner knowing at all times, to a remarkable degree of certainty, where in the world we were. Of much fascination did this hold for me, and keen was I to learn more of it.

In the event of one of the sea's more phlegmatic calms, we would loaf about deck, occasionally glancing overboard where the shadow of our keel would attract a calling of sea nettles; at the same time, however, our Tyrian sailors were always on guard for something called "the black north wind," a sudden, vengeance-seeking gusting of the more surly elements, rumored to be especially severe around Joppa, a place the Tyrians were particularly eager to steer clear of. And we *did* steer clear of it, but were not always able to evade the weather phenomenon altogether, a torn sail and broken spar being the result of an encounter one evening at late twilight. The damage caused Thomas, the ship's carpenter, to have to scale to the top of the foremast to free the splintered beam. Disentangling it from the halyards, he returned to deck and began the task of bracing it; it had to be braced, said he, for there was no extra spar with which to replace it. The sail would need to be patched back together as well. In these efforts, James and I assisted, and when the keen-eyed carpenter was finally satisfied with the repairs we had made, he scaled the foremast once more, rejoining the rounded and restored timber in a hopefully-now-indestructible manner. It was late when the job was finished. Everyone, or most everyone, had gone to sleep. Sleep indeed had a certain allure, but at the last moment, the three of us diverted ourselves to the galley, where we warmed ourselves over cups of wine.

"What will you do when the voyage is over?" asked Thomas.

"I don't know," shrugged James. "Go home, I guess, much as I would like to do otherwise."

"I, for myself, would like nothing better than to keep on sailing, never attaching myself permanently to port or land, abiding always on the sea." A spry smile found a home on his face as he yearned on, "Years and years would go by, and still I would be a sailor—*that* is what I would like!"

"The sea has been very fruitful," agreed James. "A great deal more time would I like to spend upon it as well." We each in fact confessed our desire to sail the world's oceans, to see what jewels they might hold out in their proffered hands, and as our talk stretched out, I divulged my long-standing desire to visit Alexandria. Even though Rabbi Joel had gone, the Egyptian city still held a special fascination for me, breathing its imbued golds upon my imagination from afar.

"Yes, Alexandria would be nice to visit some day, for sure," agreed Thomas, "but the place I should most like to see is *India*!" And with a wistful longing he now began to speak of that faraway land's antipodal greatness. "I once talked to a man who had read a book on India, a book supposedly written by a soldier who had traveled there with the army of Alexander, the king of Greece. He said it was a collection of strange tales, involving such things as you could not imagine!"

"What sorts of things?" asked James.

"Well, it is said that the people worship at a certain river, and that there are philosophers who engage in behavior most strange. Things like going about naked, or lying upon hot stones in the heat of the sun. In particular, he said, was a story of a man who stood upon one foot for an entire day. Further, it was reputed that what he did was not at all unusual, and that numerous others in India engage in such practices all the time! How I would love to find out why they *do* things like that! It is most strange! Yet in India, such persons are said to be held in the highest of honor!"

"It all *does* sound rather queer," mused James. "But if you believe in your heart you will make it there one day, perhaps you will."

"I would like to *think* so!" Thomas gave a pessimistic sigh. "But it is unlikely, for I am as bound as a tree with its roots in the ground. My family, my father and brother—well, I have obligations. You know how it is. And little can I ever expect to get out of them."

But boundaries are moveable, as the cosmos itself moves, and I felt that some day he would make it to that land of his dreams. However, for the time being, a fast friendship formed between us. We talked that night, and many others besides, late into the night, talked the dreams of patient gardeners, whose shoots push ever upward...upward...tender shoots, breathing the sun's brilliance through the crusted dust of the earth.

Chapter Twenty-Three

While that stretch of the Great Sea between Caesarea and Tyre made for only a small portion of the earth, it was an area of considerable size nonetheless. For three months we cast our nets in these waters and in the process took a bountiful harvest. In midwinter, we sailed into Tyre, and after our catch was sold, Father found we had earned enough money to pay off the tax collector, with even a small portion left over for ourselves. Time had come to part and return home. On our last day in Tyre, Thomas wished us a safe journey back to Bethsaida, embracing James and me in turn; our friendship with the carpenter had grown into a thing of suppleness and dexterity, and we vowed we would one day see one another again. It was one of those vows you make without any real expectation it will come to pass, but it didn't hinder us making it nonetheless.

With goodbyes said, Father, James, and I set out for home, but to exit Tyre we had to pass through a large, teeming agora at the city's gate. It was a marketplace bustling with noise and confusion, rich in marvels, and more than anything I wanted to linger and explore what it had to offer, but Father was eager to get home, and so, following his lead, we pressed through its crowds in muddled determination. As we made our way, however, I could not help casting my eyes about like a creeper-plant in the power of sunlight. This was fabled Phoenicia, whose seafarers had once journeyed to the farthest reaches of the earth. Even now, traces of its former glory braced the shadows and recesses of the marketplace. The city was the terminus of the great east/west caravan route. From its port, ships departed for all points upon the earth, and as we moved through there, we found ourselves engulfed in a whirl of strange languages and accents, the thought occurring to me that even Rome, with all its vast might, could not penetrate, and never would, the secrets this place held.

Maybe it was an abode of pure being, that agora, a creature wearing its endless shops and market stalls much as a necklace, and maybe these factors placed it within that imperishable, swift-horsed domain in which such things could not fail to happen—or maybe it was simply a chance moment in time, a moment when, in a chorus of theatrical applauses, heaven and seed-bearing earth, each on some itinerant peregrination, flowed together in two briefly merging streams. At any rate, it was here, amidst the bantering and bartering and noise, there occurred that second strange encounter to which I heretofore alluded. Zebedee was still of a determination to be away, and pushed us along at such pace as we might be capable of maintaining, but the street was narrow and crowded, and our progress was slow. At last, we found ourselves hemmed completely in as we tumbled, full fore, into the midst of a rather unusual assortment of pedestrians. Journeyers from the east by looks of them, possibly having arrived on one of the caravans from Palmyra. In any event, a rather anomalous dash of humanity. Clad in yellow robes, they encompassed us with the faculty of a bubbling and rising floodwater, until we found ourselves surrounded on all sides, a tinkling of bracelets and small bells calling forth a *musica* hieroglyph of heavenly-invoked alterity. I assumed we would simply extricate ourselves and be on our way, but suddenly a commotion laid claim upon the whole company. Among them stood an elderly man whom I took for their leader, and it was he now who began to speak—a torrent of words, rolling end over end, like gaudily-painted stars out of the heavens, as he raised one arm in the gesture of a herdsman, an arm held sedulously aloft, along with an extended finger, pointing, with a steadfast and decorous praise, directly at me.

The gabble of words continued, all of it utterly incomprehensible, for their tongue was quite foreign. Father was still intent on plowing his way through, though for now our way was blocked as the monks, with an aroused discourse, seemed to have commenced an impassioned debate amongst themselves. Meanwhile that extended arm, like the spear of Hecate, asserted an almost god-like power as it continued to point itself in my direction, bringing with it the curious and probing eyes of the others. Just when the whole affair seemed to be immodestly disrobing itself before me, a young member of the group stepped forward and addressed me in Greek. Now I did not speak Greek near as well as Susanna, and his was none too good either, but somehow I was able to get the gist of his meaning.

"He says that you are one day going to serve a great master—" here he paused, gesturing toward the elderly leader, who smiled my way and nodded in the affirmative. "He is a *bodhisattva*, an enlightened being, one who has freed himself from the cycle of rebirth yet who has chosen to reincarnate. At any rate, what he says for you is this—that there is one who has finished his journey, one whom you and many others shall follow, like swans who have left their lake."

I had no idea what he was talking about, and the whole thing was making me more than slightly uneasy, but equally, at the same time, the words evoked in me an incipient curiosity, a desire to know more, an inquisitiveness containing its own soul of sinew. I should also mention, my studious Quintus, that he was, all of them were, of that order of persons called *Sramanas*, they who believe that nothing which befalls a man is either good or bad, and who think it fitting and right to live their lives as poor wanderers. I have at odd times encountered others of this belief, and while I have always regarded their views as most exceedingly strange, I have nonetheless held a certain measure of respect for them. The God they worship, it is said, lived as a man some five hundred years before I was born.

"There are three jewels…" The young acolyte was speaking once more in his broken Greek, while Father, at the same time, tugged at my arm with a stubborn insistence. "…He whom you are to follow shall leave his home to walk in the bright state, and will lead others into that kingdom as well. You will be one of these." Suddenly, and with a graceful movement, he took a string of beads from about his neck, placed them around my own neck, and kissed my cheek.

Chapter Twenty-Four

Years later, looking back on it, there was no doubt in my mind he was talking about Jesus. I have no idea how those monks knew what they seem to have known, other than to say that it was magic, for you must try and understand that the magic of God runs parallel to what we think of as reality; it in fact overlays it. You may find this encounter in the Tyrian marketplace difficult to believe. If that is the case, you shall surely find other things which follow in this story even harder to accept, and in that event I would ask you merely to look into your heart. In so doing, know this—that the heart is sacred, and that as a sacred entity it is oblivious to such ideas as 'this is possible, while that is not possible.' And upon reaching this truth, you arrive at one other. Opening the sacred heart and looking inside, what we find, my knowledge-hungry Quintus, is the illimitable universe of space.

We were seven or so miles from Tyre when we came to a village and decided to halt for the night, the keeper of a comfortable inn serving up a savory and well-seasoned broth. Finishing my meal, I sat outside on a split-railed stoa, finding here a measure of long-sought solitude as I fingered the little string of beads the monk had given me. It was that wonderful time of day. Moon and sun were well on their way to trading positions in the sky, and I watched the evening shadows deepen, listening to the fashionable eyes of night, as the cedar-scented air poured over me.

The next morning the beads were still around my neck as we resumed our journey homeward. I thought of us as rich messengers of the sea's penance to our salvation, as, like restless Hyperboreans, we climbed through passes of cedar and conifer, pointing ourselves down that road to where the finest parts of earth and sky came together. After three hours of steady travel, Zebedee called a halt. Our *punda* still bulged with the money we had made from our three months of fishing, and there was danger of bandits along the road, Father for this reason determining we should linger for no great length of time. A few bites of food were all we ate, washed down by a few swallows of water, whereupon Zebedee roused us to our feet once more. A flock of birds winged across the sky, reminding me that the warmer months were not far away; we had been gone a long time, and I was now every bit as eager as Father to be home. Always toward home, with its anterior priorities, is the mind forever called, and my thoughts drifted happily in that direction...until a chance glance in my father's direction rocked me abruptly back to my senses. With the inflexibility of marble, Zebedee's hardened gaze was fixed upon the beads around my neck, in his eyes one of those looks I knew well—a look of zealous scrupulosity that ever so often transformed his face into the sternest of judges, a look that could come nigh, in its flint-like hardness, to slaying living things. Immediately I knew trouble was afoot. Trouble was no less arrived at table like an unfriendly guest, ready to partake of a meal.

"For the sake of the Lord, boy, take those off and throw them away!"

It was the beads he was referring to.

"W-Why?" I stammered. I was feeling suddenly alarmed, for I had grown to love the little necklace, with its strung-together perforated globules, and the thought of losing it was appalling.

"Because I have told you to do so."

"But they are mine!" I protested in some earnestness—yet with the sinking feeling that the best I could hope for was to forestall the inevitable. "They were given to me, and I want to keep them!"

"Take them off *now* and discard them."

James, knowing Zebedee only too well, pleaded on my behalf, "Can he not keep them, Father? What is the harm?"

"You stay out of this. Come now John! We must be going. Hurry up and do as I have told you."

"But I do not wish to lose them!" And I begged to be allowed to take the beads off, to refrain from wearing them, while yet keeping them. Words, however, were useless. For Zebedee, the necklace was nothing more than the product of an idolatrous faith. Swiftly his hand flew to my throat and ripped it away. It was an act of impetuous anger, committed with such force that it caused the string to break, sending beads victoriously fleeing the darkened colors of his wrath. My eyes fought their way back to his face in hot fury. I was thoroughly repulsed and wanted to lash out in anger, but my tongue was tied; in defeat and humiliation, I stood before him, silent.

"Come let us go!" He took the reins of the donkey and began to move off, leaving me standing there in a state of wounded indignation.

In a way, it was like Susanna and her books—it was something I never got over. That's not to say I ceased to respect my father or that all filial obligations to him were abandoned from that moment forward. It was just an awareness, that the gulf between us was wider than I could ever hope to bridge, and that there was no use in even trying. *Ar'a shukhalfa!* The world was changing in ways my father did not and could not understand, and that inability to understand, that unwillingness to allow human warmth to overcome the antagonisms and insults that fed upon his soul, eventually would tear us apart once and for all. As we resumed our travel, I angrily forced back the tears, but I could not cause to abate the sense of violation I felt. Leading our donkey, Zebedee strode well out in front, with James and me lagging some ways behind. My brother took the opportunity to confide, "It's alright, John. We'll be home soon." Dear, beloved James! How much I appreciated him at that moment! "It will be good to see Mother and Susanna again, don't you think?" he asked.

I did most assuredly. And the gloom in my heart was beginning to lift. "Mother and Susanna, aye, and I don't suppose you would also be thinking perhaps of Abigail as well," I teased. I was referring of course to the girl I had seen him kissing on the eve of our departure.

"Abigail?—hmm, what do you know of her?"

"I know you like her."

"Nay! It is *not* true!" He lapsed into silence before glancing once more, furtively, in my direction. "Well, maybe a little!" A grin spread slowly across his face; we walked a while longer before he ventured, "You know, John, for a virgin, I think you are pretty smart."

And so we made our way home to Bethsaida—but it was a Bethsaida, which, in the coming year, would be radically transformed. *Sicarii* unrest was to break out in Gamla, and come summer we would undergo what would amount literally to an invasion of Roman soldiers.

Chapter Twenty-Five

"The Lord be praised! You are returned!" My mother spared no effort in the preparation of our homecoming feast. We had autumn figs, pumpkin, a roasted kid, arum, millet, a relish made out of wild capers, and afterwards a confection consisting of dough flavored with rose, jasmine, and pistachios. It had always been one of my favorites. Zebedee waxed loud and long on our exploits on the Great Sea, obviously having forgotten the incident with the necklace. But I had not forgotten. It is funny how we remember certain things, as if the mind cannot let go even after the heart has pronounced itself willing to forgive. At any rate, we paid Zichri the tax collector the taxes we owed on our bodies, then we returned to our old fishing grounds at Gennesaret. We had been more fortunate than most.

Not many days after our homecoming, we received horrible news from Capharnaum; the father of Perpetua had been slain by his own hand. Vast amounts had he owed to the tax collector of that district, an individual known to be of the grossest inhumanity. Stunned at the news, James and I left for Capharnaum immediately. A scene of wailing and grief is what met us upon our arrival. At the family's home, friends and loved ones had gathered to eat the bread of mourning. Here resided an ashen, stricken Perpetua, who clung to Peter with a fearsome dependence; his so much as rising to his feet, or momentarily leaving a room, seemed to fill her with an irrational anxiety. She and her mother were alone now, and to lose Peter as well would have been unendurable for her, but of this she needn't have worried, for Peter had never stopped loving her nor cooled to the comforts of her body. Yes, she had made him the pillar of all her hopes, but not, it seems, without some plausible expectations in return. And indeed, once the period of mourning came to an end, the two were married.

James and I yet again made the trip to Capharnaum, and this time, needless to say, it was a happier occasion. The bride and groom stood under the huppah as they took their vows. With her father's death now behind her,

Perpetua looked radiant. The wedding even drew Andrew home from the desert, and I spent much time listening to his eponymous tales of the Shekinah, the radiance and glory of God manifested in a storm cloud, and as he spoke it became obvious that life among the desert sages agreed with him. "A group of us is going south, to the *Yam ha-Mela*, to abide for a time with the Essenes who live there." We were standing in the exedra amidst the flowing wine and laughter. "My heart grows heavy with the waiting, but even that is salvation, do you not know, John? One seeks...and eventually finds."

The Essenes—he had talked about them since we had been children. And now he was going to live with them! There was a serene joy on his face, and I wished him well.

Old Jonah, too, exuded contentment, the occasion affording him the rare opportunity of seeing both his sons at the same time. He didn't say much to anyone, mostly just wandered about the house and garden with rheumy eyes. Well on in years, he could no longer fish Gennesaret the way he used to. Nonetheless he mended nets and attended to other simple chores. He and Peter were to move to Capharnaum after the wedding. They were leaving Bethsaida permanently; Perpetua's family home would be their new quarters.

The pomegranate was crushed, and a vase of scent was broken, the couple being now officially joined. For a respectable while, they lingered amidst the measured discretions and mounds of food, but after a time vanished like yesterday into the night.

And so it was that Peter left Bethsaida. I did not know it, but my own family was to follow suit, with a sense of pedestrian urgency, quietly closing off the doors to our grief in the wake of the tragedy that was soon to come upon us, preferring instead, I suppose, a dry barren shell of a life and our own peculiar brand of bitterness. *Pronoia*, as the Greeks say—forethought. And I wish we had had some.

And so the wedding came and went, and there were flowers once more in bloom on the hills around Gennesaret, and I sometimes walked up there alone, thinking how wonderful it would be were there one alongside me whose hand I might take. It was a world of rapturous beauty, and there were dreams to be shared. Dreams—one item at least, if nothing else, I possessed in abundance! But alas! I was still as shy as ever. I had long ago shed my infatuation for Milcah, who in any event had two children now, but this had not cured my romantic heart. The difference was that the longings I felt now were for someone nameless, a beauty with the sweetest of lips, whose image distilled drop by drop into the narcissus of my imagination. She came to me, breaking through my shyness, and I would reach for her—whereupon she would disappear, leaving me once more alone in a world that never seemed to change.

But then in the lanes and streets of our town, I would see actual, *real* couples, lovers, like James and Abigail, and at such times something would whisper to me that love was out there waiting for me, that it was possible.

Chapter Twenty-Six

But if love was out there, so were all the other emotions that the human heart be capable of. That summer brought with it the emancipation of these emotions, a wave of them, traveling outward from a turbulent center like ripples upon water. The turbulent center was Gamla. There, in the little town nestled in the highlands to the east of us, on a hill shaped like a camel's hump, the *Sicarii* had attacked and killed two Romans. The incident was perceived, rightly or wrongly, as an assault upon the archons of public order, and it was an act that had its own spoils. The spoils were the reverberations, which spread outward, to Bethsaida, to Capharnaum, and even as far away as Sepphoris. In our own town, the mob that formed was not really an organized one; it was just a lot of people who were fed up and could take no more. Yet in an unruly appointment they came together, pouring forth the proclamations of hearts dwelling in fire.

I had been at the Jordan, at that place where we tied in each evening, making repairs on our boat, when Philip came running up with the news of what had transpired to the east of us. "In Gamla!" He was out of breath. "The *Sicarii* have laid claim to the city! Several buildings have been set alight!" His words cavorted with lauds and praises for they who had struck at our enemies. The image brought to mind was one of horses rushing dramatically to battle. In point of fact, however, I doubt what actually transpired in Gamla had ever been that raptorial in scale or scope. Like most things of this sort, it was an unplanned chain of events, which simply had "happened." But there *was* more. "Elsewhere people are heeding the call, in Capharnaum, Chorazin, Sepphoris!"

As he spoke, I squinted into the sunlight, trying to fathom what it meant. It was not long, of course, before we found out what it meant, found out that the winds raging in the hearts of people elsewhere, were blowing in the hearts of Bethsaidans as well. The mob which formed that night, as I say, was not organized at all. It was just a lot of people carrying a lot of seeds sown upon the emptiness of empty bellies. But they came like emanations out of the shadows of chaos. Men like Matthan, the potter's assistant; and like the sons of Gilead, who worked at the tannery; men who performed hard, grueling work, yet whom most seasons were barely able to feed themselves and their families. It was the hottest time of the summer, when people take to sleeping on their rooftops, and maybe it was for this reason the streets were so full that night. At any rate, in the center of town they gathered, contemplating heroic acts against the tax collectors. Contemplating a different world.

But there were other men in the street that night too, men like Rabbi Hamul, and like my father. Sober-minded men who feared where a rebellion might lead and the actions it would provoke Rome into taking. Even the ruler of the synagogue came out, only to disappear once more after a rock narrowly missed his head. Not so easily scared off, however, was Rabbi Hamul, and I say this to his credit. He was as persevering as a Nile mosquito come to feast upon the bare legs of Anubis, as he attempted to reason with them, pouring out his words of caution and prudence, this appeaser-of-wrath's maternal uncle. "Men! Consider your actions! What you are doing could bring the wrath of the Romans down upon us all!"

I'm sure Matthan and the others must on some level have realized the wisdom of what he was saying, but there was also that pent up anger—anger which, it became clear, would have to be vented, at least in some small way, before they would be ready to call it a night and go home. "Shut your mouth, Rabbi! Tired we be of ye rich, who live it up while we sweat and starve!"

"You cannot defeat the Romans yourselves," the rabbi continued with his message of even-tempered realism. "Trust in the Holy One and wait for him to send his messiah."

"Away with you!"

"Aye, we be our own messiahs!"

But determined to defeat the winds of rashness, the rabbi continued his appeals, and he might eventually have succeeded but for what happened next. Crashing like coursers into the street came now a third group of men. These, armed with clubs, fared forth hurriedly on scaraboid legs as they advanced upon the ranks of the agitated mob. It was an ominous sight, not least because their faces were all too familiar to me. It was Hodi and his followers. And to my horror they commenced, with their clubs, to bludgeon the poor tannery workers. The street at this moment erupted in chaos. In spoliation and hatred, the combatants seemed to unroll earth itself as they tore at one another, and a bloody battle ensued. By night's end one man, a tannery worker, lay dead.

This prompted more clashes the next day, and the troops of the tetrarchy were mobilized, but the fighting continued, Herod's forces being unable to restore order. And eventually Rome, just as Rabbi Hamul had predicted, took matters into its own hands. Two legions came down from Syria, one fanning out through the Galilee, and the other, the tenth, taking control of Gaulanitis and Batanaea. Whether such large numbers of soldiers were needed was disputable. Doubtless, however, the Romans well remembered the revolt of Judas the Galilean and were taking no chances. They arrived in Bethsaida early one foggy morning, filling the town and the surrounding mist-shrouded countryside with their mounts and weaponry, horsemen and foot soldiers alike. Striding at the head of each column, liberated from death, were the *signifiers*. These, upon their upper bodies, wore the animal skins of wild beasts, the heads still attached to the pelts, prescribing jaws, teeth, staring eyes. The effect was to give the wearer the appearance of being half man and half wolf, or half lion, as the case may be, each column cereclothed with a different animal tutelary. A frightening apparition it made, and there were those among the populace who believed the spirits of these once-living animals were invested in the *signifier*, who, it was said, took on its traits of savagery, a notion gaining much credence among the more superstitious, and which the Romans vested no effort to dispel.

But it was the horse soldiers who were the most frightening. Each carried a long spear as well as a javelin housed in a quiver attached to their four-horned saddles. Further armed with the long sword known as the *spatha*, these men and their mounts, with a motile urge to Adraestia, the Goddess of inevitable fate, could bear down upon an adversary with crushing speed. Laminated bronze helmets, corselets, and thigh guards left the opponent with little prospect of inflicting harm upon the rider, and even the horses themselves were outfitted with armor, each bedecked with the *chamfron*, a hide frontlet studded with decorations. Standards, borne by the *aquilifer* and bearing the image of Tiberius Caesar and the Roman eagle, were raised everywhere. Rabbi Hamul was aghast at the idolatry. One cohort of about 300 soldiers even quartered itself on the banks of the Jordan scarcely three furlongs from our house. Throughout the town, the sense of danger was palpable, while all thoughts of rebellion ceased. People, my father included, went about with eyes averted, conveying themselves along in a manner not unlike sullen children. The soldiers were numberless and spoke little. Some I guess had served in the most far-flung reaches of Rome's more sclerotic lands. They were armed with crossbows and swords and their shields and cuirasses bore the image of the gorgon, Medusa, whose hair was said to have been transformed into snakes. This was the army of Rome. And it was upon us.

Within our town, however, was one who seemed not of the opinion that the world had gone in any way awry or amiss. This was my sister, Susanna. In fact, her senses, with the arrival of the soldiers, seemed to have found the greenest clover on which to feed, and from the very outset, she, alone amongst our family, looked upon the columns in spellbound fascination.

Chapter Twenty-Seven

On the hills above Gennesaret were large stands of trees, great oaks, conifers, and terebinths. Not unlike a scree-filled wadi, the trail leading up wound over an indefatigable preponderance of bared rocks and trip roots, although one's efforts, when reaching the top, were rewarded as the path leveled off into a terrazzo of sublime beauty. Stepping into the aromatic terebinths, I paused a moment—and looked back. The glassy lauds of Gennesaret, mingling wealth with wisdom, sprawled out in rich vista below. From this height, I could see that the water was rust ocher close to the cliffs, giving way to shades of azure and jade farther out. All night we had fished those waters, and as I looked out, I felt weary but at the same time light and weightless, imagining myself almost as Sothis, the Dog Star, floating high in the sky.

But the sparkle of the Galilean Sea was put to flight as I turned once more and entered the grove of trees, feeling myself welcomed by its mysteries of height and sistrum-like wind-rustlings. Through patches of myrtle and acanthus, I began to step, making my way through emerald-tipped splendor, a lonely retinue of one. The solitude I usually found here is what I had sought, yet dimly now I perceived I wasn't alone; from somewhere farther in the grove I could hear voices. The tones were spirited and light-hearted. Wondering who it might be, I followed the sound through permutations of sun and theriomorphic shade, at last pushing aside a broad, prickly acanthus leaf as my eyes came to rest upon them. It was Susanna. And with her—a young Roman soldier. I could tell from his uniform he was an *optio*, a deputy to a centurion, making him one of the lower-ranking officers. Placidly they seemed to be sharing some amusement or other, their faces aglow. It was a beautiful day, and here on these hills the afflictions of the world below seemed to vanish in a whisper of divine favors. As a place for sharing a moment of closeness with another it was ideal, and clearly, they had sought it out for that reason.

The *legionaries* had been with us for some time now. The streets were calm, and while the soldiers were not by any means welcomed, I think most people by this time had grown accustomed to their presence. Nonetheless, it was a shock seeing Susanna in the company of this young Roman. Gazing upon the aborning little scene, I found myself in some confusion as to what to do. Would it be advisable to call out to them? Confront her, perhaps in anger? Or better simply to fade back into the world below, leaving them to their moment of privacy? I had not fully decided when suddenly the matter was settled—by Susanna herself. Looking up from her conversation with the Roman, she gazed into the near tree-growth where I had come to rest. If my sudden appearance caused her the slightest consternation, no indication did she show. Yea, it was as if it were no less than wonderful and auspicious, as she called out to me exquisitely, "John!" and with an archer's grace began to motion I should come over and join them. While still hesitant, I pressed forward. "This is my brother John. John—Maximinus Julianus."

The Roman and I greeted each other. "John the son of Zebedee," I said.

"It is a pleasure to meet you, John." He was tall, broad-shouldered, his face open and youthful, his eyes, though clearly cautious, holding for me a measure of warmth. I judged him in his mid twenties. He extended his hand, which I took. Yea, what else was there to do? Tethered to one of the trees behind them was a large, white horse. It was a magnificent animal, and I said as much.

"Yes, he is a good horse," Maximinus agreed. "Would you care to ride him?"

"Nay, I could not!" I felt hugely taken aback by the offer. On the one hand, never had I ridden a horse, and the idea of doing so now conferred upon me a tingle of excitement. But on the other, I thought to accept the invitation entirely improper, for this after all was a Roman, more pertinently a soldier, a hated foe of our people, and something about the scene I had just stumbled upon gave me an uneasy feeling. All kinds of exigencies shouted in my head that I should refuse the offer.

"Have you never ridden before? Come, I will show you—"

"Go ahead John! You will not believe the feeling it will give you!" urged Susanna. "We rode all over these hills this morning. You cannot imagine the fleetness of foot!"

"Nay..."

"He's really quite gentle," urged Maximinus Julianus. "Here let me help you up—"

"Nay, I will *not!*" I retorted sharply, backing away from them. Immediately I regretted my tone, feeling foolish, as they regarded me with what could only have been unalloyed bafflement. But then…

"It's alright, John…" Susanna's hand touched mine—a touch of reassurance, bestowed almost like an alm. Her voice, so clear and lovely, seemed to be saying, "Don't worry, he's different." She was twenty-one years old now, and had grown into a beautiful young woman. There was a subtle loveliness to her, the antimony darkening her eyes being shrouded only by the quiet chaos of her smile. It was easy to see the Roman was smitten by her. My outburst had given him no offense; on the contrary, in a curious way he seemed aware of my inner prerogatives. About his eyes, I detected a tactfulness, a keenness of discrimination that was content to let problematic ventures go unrealized. "I've got an idea," he said. "Let's go for a walk! In a place as lovely as this, it is preferable to riding anyway!"

"Oh, Maximinus, that is a wonderful idea!" From about the animal she took hold of the reins. "May I lead him?" The Roman readily agreed. Upon the horse's neck, Susanna placed a hand and spoke softly, calling him by name, "Come, Nebula." To the beast, the Roman gave an added encouragement of his own, by means of a clicking sound made from the back of his tongue.

And with that we set off, our footfalls buoying us through the wild, time-hewn hills, the horse clip-clopping along behind. The growth was dense at first, but then we stepped out into the open wind's billowing bosom. Off in the distance, ebbs of sunlight played upon the surface of Gennesaret. As we walked, the trees became thinner and thinner until at last we reached a bare ridge top where two lone terebinths stood like wise guardians, limbs outstretched to the eternity of sky.

"What a lovely view!" murmured Susanna.

"Aye, there is much here to please the eye." His gaze, however, was not on the surrounding countryside, but fixed upon Susanna, upon whom the innuendo was not lost.

"Flattery, thy tongue is named Maximinus!" she said.

"Nay, nay, *not* flattery!" he protested with a laugh.

"Magnanimity then."

"Further off still."

"I think it likely you have known many women—in every place you go as a soldier! I suspect you have them waiting for you."

"No. It is not true."

"Not *any?*"

"In truth, none that have cared."

"I must confess my doubt. I should not be surprised if many girls have given you their hearts."

"Hearts are funny things. They love one day, and in the next grow cold."

"With the weak of heart maybe...but perhaps not so with the strong?" She looked at him in serene appraisal.

"Maybe," he conceded with a smile. "Even the strong of heart require their fodder and feed, though. Take Nebula, for instance!"

"Oh, he is a wonderful horse! I think he is Prometheus, unbound at last, and with the gallant heart of a Titan!"

"Yes, he *is* pretty fiery of spirit, although I do not know if he stole his fire from Zeus."

"He is magnificent! Perhaps he takes after you!" Then she said: "Mmmm...smell of the hyssop?"

"Aye," he answered. "It is very lovely up here."

"I breathe sometimes this air, and then welcome the sun's caress upon my face."

"You do not welcome the sun's caress always?"

"Not always, no." She lowered her gaze, looked up at him once more, and confided, "It is hard for me sometimes. I often feel I am as Prometheus myself, though bound forever."

"Let's see now...'*Hurry thee from the land of Thebes with a fair wind behind...Out onto that formless deep where not a man can find...*'"

"You know Sophocles!" she exclaimed in delight.

"Some," he admitted. "Pray, let's see if I can remember the rest: '*Hold for an anchor-fluke...for all is world-enfolding sea...Master of the thunder-cloud...set the lightning free...*'"

Here he faltered, whereupon she supplied the rest,

"'*And add the thunder-stone to that...and fling them on his head...For death is all the fashion now... till even Death be dead!*'"

"Well done!" he exclaimed with a laugh.

"It is one of my favorites." The horse nudged its nose affectionately between her and the Roman as she began to recite another:

> '*Shimmering throned, Immortal Aphrodite,*
> *Daughter of Zeus, enchantress, I implore thee*
> *Spare me, O Queen, this agony and anguish,*
> *And crush not my spirit.*'

"Hmm…" He pondered a moment. "Sappho, I believe? And if memory serves, the rest of the poem is a prayer to Aphrodite for success in love."

In astonishment Susanna laughed, impressed that he knew Sappho—a woman poet.

"I have not seen her work performed widely," he confessed, "but what I have, I have enjoyed."

"I too! She is my favorite, but I like others as well. I like this one for instance:

> 'O heart of mine, pray tell me why thou goest on thy way?
> What is it that you seek, knowing winter's despair
> At each and every ruined road is destined there to lay?
> Blind, sad, tormented heart, why canst thee cease to care?'

"Hmm…I do not recognize it. Is it Sappho?"

"No, it is my own verse."

"Do tell! I like it *very* much!" he said, obviously impressed.

"It is nothing," she demurred.

"It is *not* nothing! Not at all! On the contrary, it is a verse of much beauty, like you yourself, Susanna, but may I offer to you my one wish?"

"What is that?"

"That your heart may one day not be constrained with such a terrible sadness."

She tried to hide a tender, yearning smile, staring at the ground where the saffron Crocus grew, as the great horse, that spotless white flame in the sunlight, continued to stalk our steps.

"So, Johannes!" The Roman addressed me heartily now. "I hear you are a fisherman!"

"O, he is a wonderful fisherman!" Susanna boasted on my behalf. "He has fished the Great Sea! And one day he shall become the greatest fisherman of them all! And poets shall write of his exploits upon the sea, and he shall even usurp Poseidon!"

"I think not," I replied.

"Do not be so sure of that," the Roman answered. "Fate is a whirlwind. It blows one in many directions."

"That is true," I agreed. "It blew you all the way here, you and the rest of your army." *Where you actively seek to keep us all under the yoke of Rome*—is the part I left unspoken. "How did you come to be a soldier?" I asked instead.

"My father was of the Equestrian order. Alas, he passed away when I was but seventeen. But he loved me very much, and before he died he wrote my letter of introduction to the army." At this, he picked up a small stone, walked a few paces before playfully flinging it. "I went before the *probatio* and was accepted—that is all there is to it. It is a very dull story basically."

"No, not at all!" objected Susanna.

It was obvious they wanted to be alone. I walked with them a while longer, at last politely excusing myself. But that night Susanna sought me out, her face conjoined by a host of confusing emotions as she poured out the whole story. That I should keep her secret she urgently beseeched. "We have known each other for a week." The two of us had positioned ourselves outside the house, where no one might overhear. Soft and subdued was her voice, trickling into the night like the stars overhead. "Oh John, I can't tell any of this to James! You're the only one I can trust not to tell Father. Please do not speak of what you saw today. I do not want to lose Maximinus!"

"But he is a *Gentile*," was all I could think to say.

"I know," she replied bitterly, forlornly.

"You know what Father would say, what he would do—he would—"

"Don't say it! I know!"

Were it discovered Susanna were consorting with a Gentile, she would be considered defiled, not only in Father's eyes, but in the eyes of just about everyone in town. But that was only part of the matter. The fact that Maximinus was a Roman soldier, and therefore an oppressor of the Jewish people, would make Susanna's transgression a multitude of times worse. In our town were those who would think it perfectly right and proper to stone such a woman to death. And even if Susanna escaped stoning, her fate, should she remain in Bethsaida, would not be a happy one. I didn't know what to say. Absurdly what came to mind was Rabbi Hamul's lovingly-crafted receptacle of living water by the Jordan.

"If Father and Rabbi Hamul find out about Maximinus, you will have to spend a good long time in the *mikva*."

"Aye," she replied miserably. "Ten *years* quite likely!"

Chapter Twenty-Eight

It could not be said that the love into which my sister fell was not equally returned. This at first I cynically did not believe to be true. But gradually I began to realize my error. Every waking moment that fate would allow, she and the Roman spent together, and as summer slipped into fall, I kept their secret. Of course, Father eventually found out anyway, as perhaps was inevitable. Some men chanced seeing the lovers walking together on a road outside Capharnaum, and duly reported it to Father. No use would there have been denying it, and Susanna didn't try. "I am going to marry him! He has asked me and I have said yes!"

This was true. He *had* asked for her hand. But her announcement was hardly mollifying to Father. "This man wants only one thing from you! He will offer you lies and you will believe him!"

"Nay! It is not so!"

"Foolish girl!" He slammed shut the window and barred it. "You have dishonored your family, dishonored the Torah, and dishonored God!"

"I have balanced my heart with all of my duties and have failed in nothing!"

"We granted you the faculty of book learning! Well would it have been had we never done so! Well would it have been had you never been born! A conniving, deceitful *harlot* you have become!"

And so anger tore through our house in gales. It is like a beast, anger, and it wrought beastly destruction upon us. After confining Susanna to one room of the house, securing the door with iron chains, Zebedee then proceeded out to the Roman encampment by the Jordan. By this time, somehow, he had found out the name of the soldier. I did not witness what transpired that evening, but from all reports it was a harrowing confrontation, with Maximinus and Father very nearly coming to blows. Tamping the commotion, the sentries then sent for the *tesserarius*. The latter, deeming Zebedee to be "out of control," ordered him clamped in irons. I should like there to be no confusion on the matter: the order resulting in Zebedee's confinement was *not* given by Maximinus. In fact, the young Roman had averred forcefully against it. But he was overruled. Zebedee was locked in chains, making for a rather curious irony, that of the daughter being confined by iron to one room of her home, while the father was bound likewise in the Roman camp.

It would be hard to say how long Father would have remained a prisoner had not Maximinus interceded. His requests for Zebedee's release were rewarded eventually, but what I feel compelled to point out is that throughout the entire ordeal, the young Roman's behavior was beyond reproach. Nonetheless, upon his release Father returned home in a state of fury. "You have disgraced us!" His words, in true thunderous fashion, made clear his opinion of his daughter. "Chirping lustily after Romans! All of your life you have tested us with your afflictions!"

Though the chains from her door were lifted, his orders were that she was not to leave the house unaccompanied. Another marriage was arranged, hastily, and this time Father was of a fierce determination she would go through with it. The prospective bridegroom was named Lud. He was a brute of a man who had accrued a certain prosperousness through the buying and selling of livestock, considerably less a prize than Eliezar, the genteel landowner Father had chosen some years previously, but then Susanna was damaged goods now and we were fortunate any man at all would be willing to have her.

"I will not marry him!"

But Zebedee had no ears to hear. Susanna had committed a grave sin, and Father began negotiating the *qinyan* with Lud. Quite literally, this amounted to the "acquisition" of his daughter by the ox breeder. A *mohar*, or dowry, was to be paid to us, twenty shekels of silver, a modest amount, yet more than money motivated Father just now. He was determined the family should not be marked by permanent disgrace, and if Lud were willing to take Susanna it was a sign to the world that no actual defilement had occurred, regardless of what the truth may have been. My sister had no say in the matter. Her only hope lay in Salome's being able to exert some moderating influence upon Father, which Salome tried valiantly to do, yet to no avail. Zebedee obstinately stood his ground. It was one of the few times I remember my mother failing, in her persistence, to gain at least some measure of indemnification in the face of Father's precipitous wrath.

If anyone were more unsuited for my sister, I didn't know who else it would be other than Lud. Though given over to a certain unintuitive baseness, he was nonetheless considered pious, a man of good standing who had elevated himself through cunning and who was known to pray regularly for YHWH to rain destruction upon the Gentiles and to make them all our footstools. His affections would have been spurned even if Maximinus hadn't been in the picture, but of course, at this point, Susanna's heart belonged wholly to the Roman. Sequestered from one another, the lovers grew frantic to communicate. Only transmitted reassurances could ease their pain and uncertainty, but naturally for this to occur a trusted go-between would need to be found. And not surprisingly I was prevailed upon to fill this role. It was a job I did not seek, and did not want. Yet upon me it fell.

Zebedee's daring adventures at the Roman encampment soon became common knowledge. The news of his being clamped in irons by the hated conquerors of our land, rather than diminishing his stature, had but enhanced his persona of *Nasha Hadad*, the thunder man, and of course all who heard the story accorded him much sympathy, for anyone with a disobedient, wayward daughter was certainly deserving of such. Everyone agreed Lud, should his marriage to Susanna go through, had bought himself a hellcat, yet it was a hellcat the ox breeder seemed determined to possess for himself; the plans for the wedding proceeded apace, and in those days Lud would show up at our door of evenings wearing a voracious, predatory grin.

I was nearly 18 years old now, hastening through the weedy tares of my youth. During this period of strife I mostly absorbed myself in my work, trying in some way not to think about what was happening, but fate was about to throw herself in my path, and the luxury of not thinking about any of it was soon no longer to be mine. At an inn I stopped one evening along with several other men of my father's crew, our work over for the day. My companions were of the rowdy sort, and the suggestion had been strenuously made that we should take refreshment together before departing for our respective homes. So we added some silver to the innkeeper's pockets, and following a round or two, a toast was made.

"Here's to *Nasha Hadad*!"

The conversation had given itself over almost exclusively to one topic, their great employer's skirmish with the Roman Legions, and the mood was jovial.

"Aye, but do not forget Johannes the Virgin, *son* of *Nasha Hadad*!" said another, slapping me affectionately on the shoulders. The contrast between a "thunderer" on the one hand, and a "virgin" on the other, was sufficiently ludicrous as to evoke much hilarity, and having grown accustomed to such ribbing, I took no offense. Seated at a table in back of the inn were three Roman soldiers. Little notice had I given them upon entering, but turning to regard them now I realized, with a start, one of them was Maximinus Julianus. It had been some time since I had seen him. Briefly, our eyes met—a tacit acknowledgement of each other's presence. It really was little more than that.

I was of the wine spirit that evening, it in fact it had become my custom to spend my nights in the inns until all hours of the morning, and easily I outlasted my companions, who in any event had wives and children to go home to. When, much later, I glanced at the table in the rear I saw that the Roman, too, was now alone; in fact, aside from the innkeeper, we were the only souls left in the place. It was late, and before long he rose as well, girding himself for a departure into the night, but just before exiting eased himself alongside my table. "I would have a word with you."

I shrugged. "So sit down." My tone was not in any way devoid of civility, or at least I hoped not. I had no objections to sharing a drink with him if that's what he wanted, but he seemed to have other ideas.

"Perhaps it is better if we speak outside." And so to the street we took ourselves, where the air, nimble and cool, began with a heralding limpidness to drive the effects of the wine from my head. "So they call you Johannes the Virgin."

"Among certain other things no doubt—is that what you wanted to ask me?"

"Nay!" He dismissed the comment, and for a long moment appeared lost in thought. "How is Susanna?" he ventured at last.

"How would you think?" When he did not reply, I added, "If I were to say she is anything but miserable it would be a lie."

"Oh alas the while!"

A shudder racked his body as I continued, "She is to be married in two weeks' time."

"So I have heard! And is this marriage something she wants?"

"No, it has been arranged by our father and the man she is to wed."

"I had thought as much. I must talk to your father."

"It will do no good."

"I love Susanna, and I know she loves me! Surely he must desire his daughter's happiness!"

"It is not that simple."

"I know—that I am a soldier in the Roman army makes me into the enemy of your people! May the gods be merciful, well do I know this!"

"It is not only that."

"It may come as a surprise, Johannes, but I *do* care what happens to your people. Do you honestly think I see what goes on around and yet have no compassion? Those men who work in that tannery—ghastly and appalling are their lives! Do you really think I have no pity?"

"But of course there is nothing you can do."

He took a deep breath. "Know this and know it well, Johannes: the man who employs those men and pays them their miserable wages—that man is *not* a Roman. He is one of yours!"

"Aye, and you and your fellow soldiers guard the gold that goes into the pockets of him and his friends!"

"Shall we just say, then, that certain uncomfortable truths are known to the *both* of us? But that is not why I wanted to talk to you; I would like to ask you to take a message to Susanna."

So finally we had come down to it. And indeed, the request came as no surprise. I had expected it all along. "Alright," I agreed at last. "What is the message?"

"Tell her I love her. More than life itself I love her! And tell her I will do everything in my power to see that we are reunited. I will move heaven and earth even. Please tell her this. And meet me here tomorrow with her reply."

Chapter Twenty-Nine

Ｎnd so I began to carry their messages. Two weeks remained before Susanna was to marry Lud. While relying on me increasingly as the bearer of their expressions of love, they beseeched at last I should also help in arranging a meeting. Susanna *was* allowed to leave the house *when* attended by a male member of the family. If some pretext might be devised requiring her to go out in my company, and if only I should play along, they would be able to set eyes upon one another for the first time in many days. It was the request they now made of me. Reluctantly I agreed.

Crucial to the whole endeavor was the fact that my having known about Maximinus, almost from the very outset of the affair, had never been discovered by the other three members of our family. Thus, insofar as I had pretended total ignorance of the matter, I retained Father's trust. And so the meeting was arranged—nine days before the scheduled date of the wedding. But carrying it off became a precarious endeavor in and of its own rite, as rumors began to circulate that Maximinus' legion was to return to Antioch. Indeed, the civil disturbances which had brought the soldiers here in the first place had long since subsided, and currently, as a consequence, it was not known when the new orders would arrive, only that they would be coming soon. Nonetheless, the agreed-upon day finally arrived. To the designated rendezvous point I took Susanna. My plan had been to leave them alone for an hour, after which I would return and escort her home. When Susanna and I arrived, Maximinus was already there, pacing back and forth. Overwrought by weeks of separation, they greeted each other in the heat of what even the most casual observer could only have imagined was a love of incomprehensible magnitude. If anything, this was even more so on Maximinus' part. "How I have dreamed of seeing you again! Night after night, dearest Susanna, I have looked to the stars seeking to see only your face!"

"Oh Maximinus, how I do love you! Tell me this is real, that I am actually holding you in my arms. For so long has my heart been broken that my dreams, yea my whole life, have slipped into darkness!"

"Yes, dearest, it is as real as the earth upon which we stand, real as the pain that has haunted my spirit day and night."

"You are the only light that I know, Maximinus. I cherish only the blessings of your love."

I was about to discreetly take my leave of them when suddenly the Roman caught my arm. "No Johannes, stay! For I have something to say, and it is proper you should hear it. Susanna—please, listen to me—"

"Yes Maximinus?" She looked up at him through the abundantly rich vermillion of her rejoicing thoughts, her eyes gazing deeply into his.

"Listen to me, both of you—Susanna—I put in a request that I might marry—"

"Oh yes! Yes, Maximinus! I will! Say only when! I will depart with you tomorrow...tonight...right now! Whenever and wherever you say, I will come with you!"

"Nay, Susanna, it is not that simple. Listen...please...there is more...something I must tell you. Something about the army. We are not allowed to marry. At least not as a general rule." He paused, stumbled really, his spirit subsiding into the despair of a grieving Glaucus longing for his Scylla. "Sometimes, however, special dispensations are meted out, and in this case I had thought that I might—well—that I might be granted this special favor in view of my father's years as an Equestrian."

"And?"

"I was refused."

"Refused," she echoed hollowly.

"What I am trying to say is I cannot marry you until my term of service is ended."

The sacred shrine in which her hopes were stored had just been punctured, and I could almost literally see the finitudes of light escaping her eyes.

"When will that be?"

"Our terms of enlistment are twenty-five years."

"And how long have you served already?"

"Five years."

"Five years..." Her voice came as but a whisper. "Five *years*—we cannot get married for *twenty more years*?"

"Susanna, listen, there is another way. I can take you to myself as my unofficial wife. You would be allowed to join me in that case. Our hearts would still be united in love. There would be no difference."

"Oh no..."

"Susanna, it is not how it sounds! Listen! It is an espousal that is perfectly legal, and quite a common practice in fact. Many of the men do it, and there is even a special provision for it—"

"Nay—"

"—and when my years of service are up I will be granted a *conubium*, giving me the right to marry a non-Roman citizen. At this time all of our children will automatically become Roman citizens, as will you yourself, with all of the rights that that entails."

"Oh Maximinus. I would go with you anywhere! I would follow you to the ends of the earth—but as your *wife*, not as your concubine."

"Susanna!" he pleaded. "It is not *like* that, please believe me! Do not squander our hopes in haste! With courage we can still commit ourselves!"

"What can I say to you, Maximinus? In what may my poor heart, here and now, at this moment, find hope? My father has sold me to a man who is to take possession of me nine days from now, and yet you tell me you cannot marry me for twenty years! Oh, into this world I wish I had never been born!"

"Nay!" Desperately he took hold of her arm. "Do not say that! You tear my soul with words like that!"

"All my life I did know sorrow, familiar friend, until you came along. And you drove him away with your eyes and your voice and your laughter."

"Susanna please, *don't* turn your back on us!"

"I must go. My father will be wondering where I am."

"Susanna, you do not have to marry this man! Believe me! Go with me to Antioch! The legion is leaving soon, in a few days. We can be together in Antioch. It will be as if we are husband and wife, and when I am away, you shall lodge with the other women. It is our life! Do not forsake it!"

But she was crying now. "I have to go, Maximinus..." It seemed there was nothing left to say; leaving the Roman standing there, my sister and I made our way home.

The next day the *legionaries* got their orders. They were to pull out in six days. The news came at the inn, where Maximinus and I met the following night. At his behest I relayed the information to Susanna. The marriage to Lud was still on. The directive from the legion command meant the Roman would be departing Bethsaida two days shy of the wedding. It looked as if Susanna's future was sealed. What, if anything, could be done I did not know. But I knew who I needed to talk to—Philip.

"It is true," he said the next day as we ordered wine. "The soldiers are not allowed to marry." It was a market day and the agora was extremely crowded, although here in the inn there was a surcease from the tinkling bedlam outside. I had taken Philip into my confidence, laying out the whole story. Of course he could be trusted, of this I had full faith, and I knew something else as well: that of the Romans and their methods of operation he was quite knowledgeable, for he had been keeping company with the *Sicarii* much of late. There were eyes and ears everywhere. The *Sicarii*, it was becoming clear, knew a great deal about their enemies. "But there are ways around it. They have what they call a *conubium*. You see, the length of service is twenty-five years. A long time. And they don't want fighting men whose thoughts are preoccupied with wives and children back home, men constantly wanting to go home for visits and such like as that."

"It seems a rule of hardness."

"True. But as I say, there are ways of easing the pain, so to speak. The Roman authorities understand the average soldier cannot go twenty-five years without a woman. Hence they are allowed to take 'unofficial wives,' as they are called. These women abide with the soldiers in whatever lands in which they are sent to serve. Not only does the Roman Senate allow this, but it actually encourages such arrangements. A soldier thus happily situated thinks less often of returning home, no matter how far across the empire he may be flung."

"I see."

"Then, at the end of his twenty-fifth year he gets the *conubium*, if, that is, he survives his military service. At this point, his unofficial bride and any children they may have produced become Roman citizens. For these women it serves as a pathway to Roman citizenship, there being considerable advantages to such as you know."

It was starting to make a sort of sense. We drank for a while in silence. "Have you heard the news?" I said at last. "The *legionaries* are pulling out and returning to Antioch."

"So it has been said. They will return. And even when they are away, they are never very *far* away We are a land under subjugation." He lowered his voice. "The saber strokes may not be over though. There is much of interest happening in Gamla just now."

If a renewal of civil strife hovered in the distance, it figured to start in Gamla; the place had become notorious of late as a center of resistance to Roman rule. "I have spoken with a Zealot named Simon. They are watching the Roman troop movements carefully. They even have spies inside the Roman camp."

"If more attacks occur against the Romans, the Pharisees will be much distressed."

"Aye," he replied with a rueful smile. "It is too bad they cannot bring themselves to take a principled stand."

"'Principled?'" I repeated. We both laughed. The notion of a Pharisee taking a stand upon 'principle' was about as unlikely as a three-humped camel.

"Have you heard about the tax collector in Capharnaum?"

"The one who drove Perpetua's father to his grave?"

"The same."

"No, what?"

"Someone killed him. It is said the deed was carried out by the *Sicarii*."

"You are serious?"

"You know, of course, the man's actions had become unspeakable. He had these mechanical devices he used to crush people's limbs." I had heard as much. The Capharnaum tax collector had become notorious, and the stories about him were legion. How much of this was exaggerated would be difficult to say, but if only a third of it were true, the man certainly qualified as a devil of the worst sort. "Simon believes the killing was done by *Sicarii*, but he does not know this of a certain, for the *Sicarii* do not speak of such things to one another except as there be a need to know. What is known, though, is that his body washed up on the shore of Gennesaret. Stab wounds were upon the chest, and his hands—the hands of a thief—had been severed."

"When did this happen?"

"Last week. The Romans sealed the area and made a search in hopes of catching the perpetrator, but the *Sicarii*, if truly it be they, had gone."

Over the next few days, a flurry of messages passed back and forth between the lovers. A number of options were considered, including desertion from the army by Maximinus. They even thought of saddling the horse Nebula and escaping east toward Parthia. While this would have placed them substantially out of reach of Rome, it would doubtless have brought other disasters upon them. Finally, in desperation, another meeting was arranged, another rendezvous point chosen, a secluded copse of trees on the bank of the Jordan near where the river empties into Gennesaret; here they clung to each other in desperation, and in the end, it was Susanna who relented. She would go with him to Antioch, she told him, at his side, as the unofficial wife of a soldier who had twenty years left to serve. And so it was settled. She'll have at least that chance for happiness, I thought. Yet even with this agreement sealed, a wind of discontent blew through the Roman's heart. Pained was he at being the cause of what would in essence become a permanent rift between Susanna and her family, although I did not realize how strongly he felt this until a few days later when he showed up at our door. It was a most unexpected visit. Little could be expected to come of it, which I could easily have told him and spared him the trouble, yet Maximinus had wanted a meeting with Father, and in pursuit of such had hoped for a healing. It was not to be, of course. No invitation did Zebedee even issue for him to cross the threshold of our house. Their words flew at each other on the street outside. Astonishingly, Maximinus had learned of the Jewish custom of *mohar*, and had brought 60 dinars. It was not near the amount promised, in fact now paid, by Lud, yet for a soldier it was a grand sum, as much as he made in a year. To get it, he had borrowed from virtually everyone he could prevail upon for so much as a single *quadran*. It was a noble gesture, yet its effect upon Father was as if it had been the deepest of insults. His thunderous incantations grew so thunderous in fact they brought Mother and Susanna to the door of the house. Seeing Maximinus, Susanna became instantly agitated. And now that he was here, now that it was all out in the open, she made no secret of her desire to depart with the Roman. That night. Right then and there even.

"I would ask you again to take this money." Maximinus held out the dinars before Father. "I would purchase with it Susanna's happiness as well as your own, for you cannot possibly believe you will ever be a happy man living with the knowledge that you have consigned your daughter into a life of misery."

Father replied that such "misery" as had fallen upon our house had been delivered from the Roman's own hand, and our recovery from its clutches would come only when he left us, never to return. Perhaps the Roman felt there was some truth to this, I don't know, but at last, his face creased with woe, he turned, venturing nothing further, neither to Zebedee, nor to poor Susanna, who in any event was in full flood of tears at this point and hardly capable of speaking. It was over. At least for now.

But that night Salome and Zebedee had one of their fiercest fights ever. "You must let her do as she wants! She wants to go with the Roman. You must let her go!"

"We will not sit in the seat of the scorned nor bear the yoke of indignations. Had there been a reverence for virtue instead of reading things in books, perhaps none of this would have occurred!"

"In light divine, Zebedee, I pray you turn from this course!"

"She will be wed in four days. Susanna will get used to it. Speak no more of this."

That Susanna and Maximinus had devised some means of communication with one another had become a matter of some suspect. Incredibly, suspicion still had not devolved upon me, although I did not know how much longer the deception could go on. Of course, time was running out anyway. In the final few days before the wedding, I was kept busy relaying a flurry of messages, and in the end the courage of the lovers did not fail them. It was decided that the night before the *legionaries* were to quit Bethsaida, Susanna would leave the house in stealth. With her belongings packed, she would make her way to the Roman camp. The troops would embark at dawn, and Susanna would travel with them. This was the plan. It was considered likely she and Maximinus would be well on their way to Antioch before Father even realized she was gone. For the main part, I was simply glad it was settled, glad also she was on her way to the happiness she sought. But most of all, I was glad to be absolved of any further message-relaying.

"My dear little brother!" That night with her things packed, we said what we imagined to be our final farewells. "My dreams could never have come true were it not for you."

Whether she would find the fulfillment she imagined, I didn't know. What I *did* know of course was that I loved her. Deeply and immeasurably. "I hope you will be happy with Maximinus." Then I added, "Maybe we will see each other again some day." We were both near tears now.

"I *know* we will, John!"

As it turned out, we *did* see each other again, and much sooner than either of us expected. The next morning I arose from bed, astonished to find her once more in the house, as if she had never left. "What happened? Why are you not with Maximinus?" I whispered in the courtyard.

Her features clearly troubled, she whispered in return, "There was no one there!"

"No one there? What do you mean?"

"Just that. The soldiers were gone! They were no longer at their camp."

Yes, by moonlight she had made her way to the Roman bivouac, only to find it deserted, and there in the empty darkness, her things gathered about her to ward off the chill, she had set herself down to wait...but her wait had been in vain. "I did not know what to do." A tear, pushed by another behind it, made its way onto her face, swiftly erased by a movement of her hand. "Daylight was not far off, and so I finally just came home."

Folly of all follies!

"But not until today were the Romans to have left!" I exclaimed.

"I know, John. What does it mean? Why did Maximinus leave without me?"

I thought for a moment. "He probably had no choice." This most likely was true, yet at the same time, I had a bad feeling about it all. Out to the camp I stalked that morning, to see for myself, but it was as Susanna had said—completely abandoned. All about were footprints, human and pack animals, bespeaking of a great torrent of activity. But no one there. Beset by a host of troubling questions, I did the only thing I could at the time that made any sense; I sought out Philip in the agora.

"Aye the Romans left a day early."

"But why!"—this I thundered in a manner, I should imagine, not so very different from my father.

"The *Sicarii* struck in Gamla."

"The *Sicarii*!" Dumfounded, at this point I didn't know whether to love them or hate them.

"The Roman cohort here in Bethsaida was sent to reinforce the one in Gamla. Two people in the city of Gamla were killed."

The idea evidently had been to give the Romans something to think about as they withdrew, and to make it seem, at least to outward appearances, as if the legion had been driven out. Such apparently had been the *Sicarii* leaders' thinking. "And maybe in a way," Philip sighed, "they succeeded. But from what I am hearing now, a portion of the town has been destroyed, apparently in retaliation."

The wedding was to be tomorrow at Lud's house. While I was sorry for the people of Gamla, I kept returning to that one thought. The *wedding*. That and the fact that Maximinus was off in—Gamla, Antioch, or who knew where. I wondered how much of this I should tell Susanna, but decided, when I got home, to tell her everything. Perhaps it was a bad choice, but the alternative was to leave her in the dark imagining the worst, and I figured the limited news I had was better than none at all. Perhaps, though, as I say, it was a bad choice. When we awoke the next morning, Susanna was gone. And by late afternoon, when it was time to leave for the wedding, she still had not been found.

Chapter Thirty

I t was to have been a festive torchlight procession carrying the bride to the groom's house. But there were no torches. Nor was there a bride. The scent of flowers filled the air, the canopy had been erected, the guests were adorned in their best dress, and an agitated Rabbi Hamul stood about with a nervous smile. Everybody was there in fact but Susanna. Father was beside himself, clumsily trying to explain—*what* I'm not sure. Lud, for his own part, was angrily demanding the return of his *mohar*. The guests were now starting to leave.

We had searched the whole countryside that day. And we searched it again the following day. Susanna was nowhere to be found. By nightfall of the second day I had concluded to myself she had traveled to Gamla on her own. These suspicions I now shared with James, and on the morrow, we set out. A city torn with grief is what we found upon arrival. The Romans had inflicted considerable punishment, and while a large number of soldiers still lingered about, Maximinus did not appear to be among them, nor was there any sign of Susanna. After much searching, we concluded it had been a wasted trip and started for home.

Bethsaida we found much as we had left it, with still no sign of Susanna. The only difference now was that Mother was near the gates of despair. We all waited, hoping to hear something—and finally we did. Five days later, Susanna was found by some young boys digging for mud turtles on the shore of Gennesaret; it was an area of the shoreline overrun by high reeds and stagnant water, a marsh long thought to conceal an unwholesomeness. Fishermen had taken to their beds after abiding there any length of time, and for that reason people avoided the place. Here it was Susanna, knowing that the place *was* shunned by the townspeople, had chosen to conceal herself. But like others, she had sickened. When brought home she was still alive, though delirious with fever.

I suppose she had planned to remain hidden in that somber fen until the Roman returned, and even after she had taken sick, she had been certain Maximinus *would* return for her. Indeed, at least in this, her faith had not been misplaced. Two days later, he *did* return, rushing into town at a gallop and heading straight for our door. Yes, he *had* been sent to Gamla, though from there his century had been dispatched further, to Jerusalem, and it had taken him this long to get back. Susanna had deteriorated to a severe ague, and a yellow pallor had settled upon her. Not only was Maximinus admitted to our house this time, but the animosity between him and Father was set aside. Even Zebedee sensed anger was a royal domain no longer affordable. All thoughts now were for Susanna, and nothing else.

The Roman entered the room and sat by her bed. When she opened her eyes and saw him a noble flame shot forth from her, her feverish lips parting in a half-smile. "Maximinus."

"I am here my sweet, my dearest." He took her hand and held it to his face, the hand of the Magna Mater, a hand which in the next few moments was cherished by his kisses, and then moistened by his tears.

"Do not cry, Maximinus, my darling, I love you." She placed her hand to his head. Yes, she did love him. This she repeated, over and over, in a vocation of single-hearted devotion. But already she was in the noose of a prosodic and garlanded Death...and that night he took her. In a torrent of tears, the Roman buried his face in her bedcovers. Throughout the long, dark night and into the dawn he stayed at her bedside.

That day was a crisp autumn one, and in the afternoon we laid her in the ground, for we were poor and could not afford a tomb. The spot we chose was a grove of terebinth trees, where sunlight splashed upon the Crocus in loving and protective dabbles. We buried her clothed in white—fire and light for the boundaries of heaven, even as she became one with the earth. Through it all, no words were exchanged between Father and Maximinus. None whatsoever. Afterwards, the Roman rode away to rejoin his unit.

In the weeks and months following, we went about our daily affairs mechanically, with a sense of emptiness, as if the vitality had been sapped right out of us. My mother especially seemed in a state of gloom, and I worried for her a great deal, for there were times I would come home and find her crying by herself.

Maybe it was the pain of being where Susanna's memory was so strong; maybe that was what drove us to sell everything and leave for Capharnaum, or maybe it was something else. Zebedee said it was only because the fishing would be better. But I cannot help thinking we were running from something, and in the process hoping to avoid some droll, uncomfortable truth about ourselves. Not long before we left, I took a day off, abandoning myself to one of Gennesaret's lonelier shores, hoping to construct for myself a sense of peace and healing. I remember the scent of redbud in the air that day as I ambled south in the direction of Gergesa. I had actually traveled quite a distance from Bethsaida when suddenly I spied three horsemen approaching from afar. Like me, they were transporting themselves parallel to the shoreline, though coming from the opposite direction. Further, they seemed to be moving at a fairly stiff clip, for tiny simooms of dust were raised by the horses' hooves, the riders seeming to hang halfway between earth and sky as they galloped. When the distance had narrowed, I saw that they were Roman soldiers, as I had felt all along they must be, and when closer still, I was able to make out that one of them was Maximinus Julianus. It had been several months since we had laid Susanna in the ground, and I had seen nothing of him in the meantime, but here he was now, riding up through that waterfront approach. Where had the soldiers come from, and where were they going? I did not know, but as they drew close, Maximinus lifted a hand in signal to the other two. At this point, all three reined to a halt. The Roman delivered a casual fiat to his companions, who remained in their saddles, as informally he dismounted.

"It is good to see you, Johannes," he said, walking up.

"Good to see you as well," I answered, truthfully. "Where have you been? We have not glimpsed you of late."

"We have come from the Decapolis, an incomparable place of earth and firm hills, where far fewer people wish us ill than in most places. Alas, it is now time for our return to Antioch." He smiled, a smile that seemed to grapple with the weight of recent events, and a part of me, the best part I hoped, smiled back at him.

"We are moving to Capharnaum," I said at last. "We have sold our things."

"Is that a fact?" He glanced for a moment at the sky, perhaps in search of the gods of consolation. "I rather suspect you may like it there. And of course, may you catch *many many* fish!"

We talked for a while, until it seemed we had talked ourselves completely around the cosmos, or a small part of it anyway, talked until there was nothing left to say, or perhaps, more accurately, until we realized we both had reached the boundary of things better left unspoken. Before we parted, he held out his hand...which I took in my own.

"I say goodbye to you Johannes." Then, perhaps, with a nod to Sophocles, he added: "And goodbye to the sun that shines on me no longer."

LaSalle 11

Antecedents

Time loses all meaning...

Looking up from the mass of papers for the first time in nearly two hours, LaSalle opened the window for air and massaged his eyelids gently. The computer was still on, though the device had long since reverted to screen saver mode. He glanced at the clock: 9:25.

In doing a translation of this sort you utilized everything you knew, not just about the language, its phraseology and fixed meanings, but also every other scrap of learning you had ever in any way acquired concerning the period of antiquity in question, knowledge of cultural values, symbolism, and religious influences, rites, and practices. And when you exhausted what you knew, you employed a lot of guesswork. In such manner did the translator attempt, with strong emphasis on the word *attempt*, to draw some logical conclusions about the ancient writer's original meaning and intent. LaSalle had had to employ a measure of such guesswork here, but one thing was clear. The reference in the story to "Sramanan monks" was unmistakable. *Sramana*. It was a Sanskrit word, meaning "ascetic," or one who "renounced," and it derived from the root *sram*, meaning "to toil." Originally, the term was applied to Hindu forest dwellers, denoting extreme deprivation in the search for God. Later it became identified with Buddhists, even though the Buddha's "middle path" was far less extreme than the self-inflicted tortures of some of the Brahmanic ascetics. At any rate, two questions came to mind: 1) is it possible monks of the Buddhist faith could have been present in the city of Tyre in the first century AD, and, 2) could a disciple of Jesus have encountered them in his childhood?

For a significant number of scholars, the answer to the first question would be yes. The edicts of Asoka would tend to bear it out, but even more than that, the historical timeline, beginning with Alexander the Great's invasion of India, speaks like a cipher calling. Nearchus, Onesicritus, and Aristobulus, accompanying Alexander's march into India, had one and all noted the presence of peculiar "philosophers" in their written accounts—

Gymnosophists, as the Greeks came to refer to them. "Naked philosophers." Whether specifically Buddhists would be debatable, and they may in reality have been Jains. But then Megasthenes, following Alexander by a mere 20 years or so, observed two additional sets, or subsets, of philosophers, quite distinct from one another, and which he identified as "Brachmanes" and "Sarmanes." That he was referring to Hindu Brahmins and Buddhist Sramanas seems on the surface clear. But Megasthenes went on to note that the Brachmanes were held in the "greater repute," a factor easily reconcilable to the timeline, given that in the day of Megasthenes, roughly 180 years after the death of Siddhartha Gautama, Buddhism was still a young religion, thought of as a Brahmanical heterodoxy.

The Diadochi, Alexander's successors...and the chronology leading up to the time of Christ—all of it speaks...

326 BC—Alexander crosses the Indus into the region of the Punjab and fights the Battle of Hydaspes, forming an alliance with King Ambhi of Taxila, a city which within a hundred years becomes a famed center of Buddhist learning, the Macedonian monarch establishing vassal states in Bactria (northern Afghanistan and Pakistan) and western India.

323 BC—The death of Alexander

321 BC—Partition of Triparadisus, dividing the empire among his generals;

311-302 BC—Seleucus I consolidates control of the eastern portion of the empire.

305 BC—Seleucus wages war against Chandragupta (referred to in Greek sources as "Sandrokottos"), emperor of the powerful Mauryan Empire of eastern India, but hostilities end with negotiation of a dynastic marriage alliance.

305-290 BC (approx.)—Seleucus dispatches the Greek historian Megasthenes as ambassador to the Mauryan Court at Pataliputra, on the banks of the Ganges.

281 BC—Antiochus I, son of Seleucus, begins to reign, though he and his successor, Antiochus II, both prove weak leaders. Various territories under independent Greek kings break away, giving rise, first, to the Greco-Bactrian Kingdom, followed by the Indo-Greek Kingdom, ushering in a period of syncretism between Hellenistic culture and Buddhism that continues up until the time of Christ and beyond.

273 BC (approx.)—Asoka, grandson of Chandragupta, becomes ruler of the Mauryan Kingdom, unites all of India from present day Afghanistan in the west, to Bengal and Assam in the east.

265 BC (approx.)—Kalinga War and Asoka's conversion to Buddhism.

260 BC—Asoka's rule by dharma and propagation of Rock Edicts.

250 BC (approx.)—Third Buddhist Council convened at Pataliputra, following which Asoka dispatches Buddhist emissaries to the west.

232 BC—death of Asoka.

220 BC (approx)—Greco Bactrians establish contact with the Sinkiang Uigur region of China on the Silk Road

185 BC—Demise of the Mauryan empire, replaced by Sunga empire, which, according to some ancient records, persecutes Buddhists.

180 BC—Buddhism, by contrast, begins to flourish under Indo-Greek kings, who issue coins combining Greek and Indian language and symbols.

150 BC (approx.)—begins the reign of Menander I, perhaps the greatest of all Indo-Greek kings. Referred to in Buddhist texts as "King Milinda," he is said to have achieved arhat status. During this period, Greco-Buddhist art emerges, as well as bilingual coins in Greek and Pali, the latter composed using *Kharosthi*—a script derived from the Aramaic alphabet. One coin from the era depicts a seated Zeus with a Buddhist wheel at his feet.

130 BC—Menander's death. Scythian and Yeuzi incursions into Indo-Greek territory commence.

80 BC-10 AD—Indo-Greeks continue to lose ground, culminating at last with the kingdom's collapse (although the Greek presence in India is believed to have lasted for several more centuries).

13 AD—(approx.) Indian embassy sent to Caesar Augustus; self-immolation of Buddhist monk in Athens.

The key figure in the above timeline (discounting of course Alexander, who initiated the whole sequence with his invasion) is Asoka. If it was Alexander who brought the culture of ancient Greece to the East, it was Asoka, more than anyone, who reciprocated, exporting Buddhist culture and teaching to the West. But in typical Asoka fashion, it was not an invasion force he sent westward; it was a force of *dharmavijaya*, "conquest by dharma." The emissaries he dispatched, by some records, even included Greeks who had converted and become Buddhist monks. And to what lands in the West did these envoys journey? To which rulers and kings did they present themselves? The Rock Edicts, particularly the incomparable Rock Edict XIII, give an answer far more precise than one usually finds in ancient sources, listing the kings as "Antiyoka"—"Turāmaya"—"Antikini"—"Makā"—and "Alikasundara." Scholarly consensus on anything is elusive, but the general view that has emerged is that the references are to five sovereigns of the Mediterranean world, respectively: 1) Antiochus II, of the Seleucid dynasty in Syria and western Asia, Asoka's immediate western neighbor; 2) Ptolemy II Philadelphus, in Egypt; 3) Antigonus Gonatas, of Macedonia; 4) Magas of Cyrene, in North Africa; and 5) Alexander of Epirus. Their dates range from 285-239 BC, placing all five contemporary to Asoka.

Asoka's *dharmavijaya* mission extended to lands as far away as 600 "yojanas," Rock Edict XIII also avers. Taking the yojana to be roughly seven miles (the precise conversion rate for the ancient Hindu distance measurement is unknown, but has been figured variously as 4-10 miles), the figure of 600 yojanas turns out to be the exact distance, as the crow flies, from Pataliputra to Macedonia, as well as from Pataliputra to Epirus, in modern day Balkans, and Cyrene in Africa.

So what is *Dharmavijaya*, or "conquest by dharma"? To answer that of course required familiarity with the root word *dharma*, and scholars over the past century and a half have had difficulty translating the term. Various definitions have been offered: *truth...justice...duty...natural righteousness...a universal law holding all life together in unity*. Perhaps the latter came closest, though no one had ever been able to nail it down precisely. Maybe Asoka hit it right. The rock edicts left in the Bactrian regions, written in Greek, translated it into the Greek *eusebia*—piety. But one thing was certain from even a superficial reading of the ancient texts of that age: the culture as a whole, if not everyone in it, placed a high value on dharma, as did Asoka himself, following, that is, his conversion to Buddhism. The rock edicts, should one choose to depart from the more cynical critics and regard them as other-than-royal-propaganda, bear that out. But propaganda or no, by the time of Christ there were more than just a few royal emissaries shuttling back and forth between India and the Mediterranean. The Silk Road offered Greeks of the East one means of maintaining contact with the greater Greek world in the West. The Indian Ocean sea trade provided the other. The Greek geographer Strabo, a contemporary of Christ, reports 120 ships setting sail from Myos Hormos to India each year, while an ancient periplus whose date is uncertain but is believed by some to be first century, describes Greco-

Roman merchants selling goods in the Indian port of Barbaricum and trading them for, among other things, nard.

The sea trade...yes, it was the sea trade that provided the balneum to the whole picture. The Egyptian Red Sea ports of Myos Hormos and Berenike made up one end of the periplus, while at the other, mariners found haven at Barbaricum, near the Indus delta—present day Karachi, Pakistan—and Bharuch (referred to by the Greeks as "Barygaza"), at the mouth of the Narmada River—in what today is Gujarat state. So was all of this to imply that Jesus was a Buddhist? Hardly. Theories of syncretism can be carried to the extreme. That is certain. But cultural contacts between central Asia and the eastern Mediterranean in the period in question were more numerous than many have reckoned.

LaSalle rose, stretched, and switched on the radio on the shelf above his desk. An allunisono of syrupy pop music filled the room. Following two hours of intense study, it sounded unusually loud, but the priest didn't adjust the volume. Instead, he followed his feet into the kitchen and returned with a plastic olive-green dinner plate covered with crisp apple slices, each slice smudged with a compendious dab of peanut butter. The two flavors in combination, apple and peanut butter, had always appealed, he supposed, to his more supple and childlike nature. He took a bite and turned his attention once more to the computer screen. Of course, the time line, he thought, contained other curiosities. The final item irretrievably caught the eye, perhaps more so than any other: the self-immolation of the monk.

The year is AD 13, or roughly thereabouts. If it's AD 13, it's the year immediately prior to the succession of Tiberius Caesar to the throne of the Roman Empire. Ostensibly sent by an Indian "King Pandion," the delegation to Caesar Augustus arrives in Antioch, in Syria, then journeys on to Athens, where the Sramanan, in a demonstration of his faith, climbs upon a pyre and ends his life. The incident is said to have created quite a sensation—as might well be imagined! Was not one of the most enduring and iconic images of the Vietnam War that of the Buddhist monk who immolated himself on a Saigon street? The image was emblazoned into the memories of virtually everyone who lived through that era. Would it have been any different in AD 13? Even without modern day photography or the reach of global media, the event would have been talked about. And remembered. The monk's fiery destruction is told of by two ancient writers whose works survive to this day: Strabo and Dio Cassius. Strabo for his own part quotes from Herod the Great's court historian, Nicholas of Damascus, who ostensibly joined the delegation in Antioch then followed it on to Athens. And then at Athens?...*Om Shanti Shanti Shanti*...Afterwards, the monk's remains are placed in a tomb, on which is inscribed the words, *Zarmanochēgas indo sap Bargosēs*, "the Sramana master from Barygaza in India." In Plutarch's day, a hundred years later, the sarcophagus was still visible and made note of.

Couched in the fabric of life...an apple...a human being...an exercise of charity...though underneath, as perhaps Parmenides might have noted, a fearful path extends. LaSalle turned back to his papers. The syrupy pop music had given way to a news announcer...

"In fears of a widening war in the Middle East...a rise in the price of oil per barrel...Hurricane Roxanne having formed in the Atlantic on Monday..." LaSalle tried to follow the announcer's voice, so conversant in its impetuous interplay of spoils and disaster, but instead his mind drifted back...to Asoka...

Born a prince (not unlike the Buddha himself perhaps?), his birth date is uncertain, but he was probably still a young man upon assuming the throne in 273. The name itself means "without sorrow," though later in life Asoka would adopt the more supernal *Devānāmpriya*, "beloved of the gods," perhaps giving fuel to the edicts-as-royal-propaganda point of view. The early years of his reign appear to have been characterized by a level of brutality not terribly incommensurate to other kings and despots throughout human history. But then had come the Kalinga War, followed by Asoka's adoption of the Buddhist faith. Remorse, *profound* remorse, at the war's carnage, the carnage that is described so vividly in Rock Edict XIII: 100,000 killed; 150,000 carried off prisoner; many others perishing from other causes. And the edict makes clear: the depravity of endless war is to cease. "Verily the slaughter, death and deportation of men which take place in the course of the conquest of an unconquered country are now considered extremely painful and deplorable by the Beloved of the Gods." Thus had Asoka's words been transcribed onto Rock Edict XIII—and left to eternity.

Maybe in the end it wasn't the precise definition of *dharma* that was important. Maybe in the end it was Asoka himself. Thirty-four texts and inscriptions, carved on rocks, pillars, and cave walls throughout the Indian subcontinent—this is the legacy. The inscriptions were first deciphered by scholars in the 19th century. More have been discovered and translated since. Through it all, emerges a portrait of a man, along with his system of government, which perhaps remains unique in world history. What other than that can one say?—of a man, arguably one of the most powerful on earth, issuing edicts deploring not only the killing of human beings, but also of animals; who asserts repeatedly "all men are my children"; who adjures the speaking of truth; who propounds the Buddhist philosophy that it is good to have few possessions? What else can one say of a monarch establishing an elaborate social welfare system, with "officers of dharma," whose task is to care for women, children, the aged and the sick? Yes, all this and more are there in the lithic records. Asoka's ministers even seem to have taken into account the different languages spoken in the various regions of the far-flung Mauryan empire. Bilingual edicts were left in a number of locales. Inscriptions discovered in the Hellenic areas of Afghanistan, for instance, were found to have been carved in both Greek—and *Aramaic*.

The critics of course have always said that even if these Buddhist missions of Asoka's to the west did occur, they obviously didn't make much of an impression on the Greco-Roman world. But is it possible they made more of an impression than is generally realized? The New Testament, with its God of love, mercy, and forgiveness—so different from the vengeful and jealous God of the Old Testament. The anomaly has always been there, but...

In the beginning was the Word. Was it now possible to deduce that Christianity had other antecedents besides Judaism alone, and is it possible that Buddhism was one of them? *Thus have I heard...becoming...he who has ears to hear?* A groundswell of conventional opprobrium would vociferously reject such a notion. But while God alone is eternal, neither does collective human consciousness remain in a static state forever. For scholars of the origins of Christianity, "syncretism" has often been a major bugaboo. Suggestions that the faith borrowed anything from the Greco-Roman religions or the spiritual traditions further to the east have often been rejected out of hand. But the unearthing, at Nag Hammadi and elsewhere, of decidedly non-orthodox texts, texts evincing a syncretistic embrace of other beliefs—Greek metaphysics, concepts of reincarnation, creation theories strikingly different from *Genesis—all* of this began to reveal dimensions to early Christianity never previously suspected.

Dreams have a way of reckoning through the aggregates of injuries...dreams in search of...what? Perhaps none other than what Jesus had said, as described in one of those very texts, the *Gospel of Thomas*: "I shall give you what no eye has ever seen, and what no ear has heard." Yet was not that very thing right inside you? And hadn't that really been his point? *Auscultare,* the Romans had called it—the art of hearkening and listening. Specifically, listening to sounds of the human body for purpose of medical diagnosis. Maybe the answer lay not so much in timelines, lithic inscriptions in India, papyrus texts from Egypt or Syria, or the like; maybe the answer lay simply in harkening, listening, and looking within.

The dreadful news segment, with its rumors of the next war, the next catastrophic act of nature, the next wave of suffering and death, its tidy capsulization of the undying greed, anger, and folly that now stoked the 21st century to its present audible, crackling, roar—*thankfully*—was over—while the syrupy pop music, equally dreadful in its own right, was back. Was it real, or was it all a dream, *maya*, illusion? There were certain parts of LaSalle's faith that, despite his being a scholar and an academic, he could not separate or break off from himself. One was the belief in Christ. The other was a conviction that the greater sorrows were far outweighed by the fairest eyes of love. The love of God. As he turned his attention back to the translation, it occurred to him that an auscultation and a translation were perhaps not so very different from one another; in carrying out either, you hearkened to what was within, and in the process, time lost all meaning—as the labor moved towards the door of the bridal chamber…

Fishermen

Chapter Thirty-One

I t is said that when the purpose of life is forgotten, when wisdom recedes and men become scarcely truthful in speech, God manifests himself on earth. Even now, I cannot say how I know of such things, for God is the Supreme Poet, and it is not possible to know all the verses he writes. But there is one thing I *do* know, and it has to do with *Kefar Nahum*, that "village of consolation," our new home—Capharnaum. I say this for I know it to be true, that it is a place where Gennesaret pulses in your blood. It becomes a part of your life. Like the beggar begging for food; like graceful village lanes lined with mimosa, jasmine, and oleanders; like snails in sunlight. All of it seeps into you and out of you again. Here. The village is also a stopover on the *Via Maris*, the "Way of the Sea," as it's called, that highway linking Damascus with Egypt. A place of peace. A place of consolation. A place of gleaming waters. This is Capharnaum, this and more.

There is much also I might mention of that road, the *Via Maris*, my beloved Quintus, for down it have passed innumerable armies, caravans, and travelers of all nations, some conquering, some conquered, each caravan and army leaving its imprint over time. We took a house just off this ancient road. It was a sun-cheery dwelling of pleasing sapidity, sturdy to the winds, modest in size though somewhat roomier than our home in Bethsaida. Its sleeping rooms were flanked by an orderly little courtyard which protected us to an extent from the dust of the road, but if we listened carefully we could make out the sounds of travelers. I thought about that road a lot, the *Via Maris*. To the north and east, it led to Damascus, but theoretically, you could go all the way to Mesopotamia, to Babylon, or Parthia. In the other direction lay the Great Sea, and eventually the road wound all the way to Alexandria, the city on earth I still longed to visit more than any other. And knowing there were all these points to which the *Via Maris* potentially connected me gave me a sense of kinship with it. I thought of it almost as a living thing. It was my friend. It understood me. And sometimes I would walk out, stand at its center, look up and down, and imagine I was going somewhere—anywhere.

Capharnaum was indeed a gateway of sorts. Traveling from east to west it was the first town you came to after crossing into the tetrarchy of Herod Antipas. Assuredly, it was not a large town. Magdala for instance, on the western side of the lake, was considerably larger, and certainly it in no way compared with Galilee's cities, Sepphoris, say, or Tiberias, which was now Herod's capitol, yet Capharnaum was in many respects a place of abundance, a place of benefaction. Fishing was the main livelihood, though there were also a fair number of glassmakers, but regardless of one's chosen trade, neighborliness and generosity found a home to a fair degree; there was a pervading sense amongst its inhabitants that while Capharnaum might not be the grandest spot on earth, plenty of worse places existed.

Being on the edge of Herod's kingdom meant there was a customs station here for purpose of taxing travelers and that a Roman garrison was frequently nearby, but unlike other locales, relations between Jews and Romans here in Capharnaum were peaceful. One could say *cordial* almost. This had been true since the arrival of a new centurion, a man who not only afforded the Jews a modicum of respect, but who had even helped build the town's new synagogue. It was a different time now, and even the tax collectors had grown more temperate. The terms of service of the *publicani* had been lengthened considerably by Tiberius Caesar, who had offered a wise though perhaps self-evident observation, that "gorged horse flies suck less blood than fresh ones." Exercising a noteworthy measure of wisdom, Tiberius had placed curbs upon the hated tax collectors—and yes, had also lengthened their terms of service. It seemed to have had the desired effect. The runaway abuses of several years ago such as had led to the death of Perpetua's father had become a thing of the past. Capharnaum, unlike Gamla, never had been a center of Jewish resistance, but now, with tax collectors having become moderately looser of grip upon the streaming udder, and given also the settling in of the new *primus* of centurions, who after all was a decent and just man, Capharnaum had evolved into a place where Jew and Roman, for the most part, got on peacefully.

Our house was northwest of the new synagogue. It was, as I say, near the *Via Maris*. Simon Peter and Perpetua lived on the far side of the synagogue, south of it, in between our place of worship and the lake, although in a general manner of speaking nothing was very far from anything else in Capharnaum. We ourselves were within easy walking distance of Gennesaret, including that point along the shore where the majority of the town's fishermen pulled their boats in at night. A word or two about this shore point, for here one found not only a robust amount of activity, but also an astounding panorama. When you looked out upon the expanse of that Galilean lake, you found yourself staring at a sparkling and wide vista. It was a vista containing movement, but a movement which at the same time was encompassed within a larger and greater stillness. Boats, in a bewildering farrago, were everywhere to the eye visible. Near and far, they crept stealthily across the sea on the winds of Callirrhoe, and yes, our own boat soon took its place among them; in fact with Simon Peter we formed a partnership, his vessel and ours abiding most days within range of each other.

Peter and Perpetua were still very much in love. They continued to live with Perpetua's mother and old Jonah, the four having made themselves into a harmonious little family in the comfort and safety in Perpetua's family home. It was a steady, timber-keel of a house with a roof of thatched branches, weathering the sea winds with an emmer stalk's perseverance. No longer of course did old Jonah help with the fishing, nor even the net mending, yet Perpetua, greatly solicitous of his care, and according him also honor and esteem as was his rightful due, concerned herself with his well being much as if he were her own father. Truly, she seemed to have found happiness in her marriage to Peter. Despite the rigors of managing a household and caring for two elderly people, she nonetheless packed a woven basket of food and carried it each midday down to the shore, for our hunger at this hour was great. It was invariably stocked with the most nourishing and tasty of comestibles, grapes, cheese, figs, eggs stuffed with olives and capers, breads, roasted fish, and more, and as she served out this wonderful food she would smile, occasionally saying sweet things to Peter, as we filled ourselves beneath the sky's humble praises. Greatly did we look forward to her arrivals, and even Zebedee became exceedingly fond of her.

Each Preparation Day, which is to say the day before Sabbath, she and my mother would work the day long, preparing a special meal for us to eat on the Sabbath, for of course no work of any kind was to be performed on the Sabbath, not even food preparation. Then at twilight came the blowing of the trumpets ringing out from the rooftops. All work at this point ceased. Sabbath officially began when three stars had appeared in the sky, and there were those who concerned themselves with the making of careful and precise observations as to this. After all, God went to the trouble of maintaining all of his intricate cycles and rhythms as displayed by the heavens, and in carefully attuning ourselves to these patterns, could we not but help find ourselves closer to Him? And of course it was known, or at least professed by some, that wisdom and health were determined by the sign under which one was born.

Then came the morn. To the synagogue we would steadfastly make our way with all the other believers. There was a great deal of love in that synagogue, flowing through our hearts, young as well as old. The *Shema* would be recited. Then the readers would come forth, seven in all, standing before the Holy Ark. Anyone, even a visiting stranger, could become a reader, anyone, that is except for a woman, for women, of course, were not permitted to read the Torah aloud. My mother on this matter held her peace. I think she had become resigned to the fact that there were certain things in life she would never change, or perhaps now that Susanna had gone changing them no longer mattered so much to her; wars of words with Zebedee were the price she had always had to pay for speaking her kernels of truth, and I think she had finally become weary beyond measure of it all.

With the conclusion of Sabbath, Gennesaret once more beckoned. In working its waters, we used three kinds of nets, the cast net, the trammel, and the *sagene*. The latter is sometimes also referred to as the "dragnet," and is by far the largest of the three. Employing it skillfully takes a crew of men laboring in concert, however. In teaming up with Peter and his helpers, we worked the north shore of Gennesaret to the west of Capharnaum, near an area called the *Heptapegon*, or seven springs. The springs were warm, and this warm water had a quite remarkable effect on the fish, drawing in a mysterious abundance of them in their various-hued schools, the waves surging in past the viridian shoals to lap gently at the shore-pebbled earth, waves bringing food to us, and life to a firmament of aqua vegetation. Arriving at the springs early in the day, two of us would emerge from the boat and pull one end of the *sagene* up onto shore. The rest of the net remained in the boat and would be lowered by those who steered the vessel—first away from land, then reversing back to shore; at this point, they too emerged, whereupon the two groups of us, working in concert, would pull the net in. When it was heavy and resisted our efforts, a joy leapt through our hearts, for we knew the catch was great and our toil had been rewarded. We knew also that a large number of coins would fall our way from the salters and wholesalers.

Even after the fishing was over, there remained the work of cleaning and mending the nets and sorting the catch. This latter task especially had to be adhered to meticulously, for it was necessitated by religious considerations. Trout, perch, and pike—fish with scales and fins—were acceptably edible to

Jews; creatures without scales and fins, catfish and eels and the like, were by Law of Moses unclean. These were usually tossed back, though some of the Hebrew fishermen set them aside and sold them, for it seemed that Gentiles, and especially Romans, were fond of such fare.

Old Jonah, whose hair had whitened to the color of wool, breathed his last in the second year after our move. He spent his final days peacefully enough, though a fatigued and rheumy weariness settled on him at the end. Dressed in garments of dust, Peter tore his clothes, and with the corpse borne upon a litter, we set out for the grave. At the head of the procession walked the women, as was the custom, for it was said that since Eve had brought death into the world, it was only fitting that women should lead death's victims to the grave. And so we spoke the Kaddish. *May the prayers and the entreaties of all the people of Israel be received before their father in heaven.* After Jonah was laid to his rest, we returned to the house and ate the bread of mourning.

Thus it was we settled into our new life in Capharnaum, and as we did, I became wise in the ways of Gennesaret, while my body grew hard, my hands growing as scarred and calloused as my father's. I was now in my twenty-second year of life.

We saw a good deal of Nathanael in those days. Ever so often, he would come into town, bounding along with his great bulk and his sprightly step. His face had matured but retained that warm, gentle smile, and with each of his passes through Capharnaum he would make straightway for Peter and Perpetua's house, for as kinsman to Perpetua it was natural he should lodge with them. Upon his visits we would gather, often at one of the inns, to talk late into the night, and much was there to speak of. While daily life in Capharnaum remained largely free of discord, this was not always the case elsewhere. The *Sicarii* and Rome were as ever like unto the fox and the jackal. The Zealots would strike somewhere, Rome would respond with a frenzy of savagery, at which the *Sicarii* would fade into the shadows; then when the Romans, feeling the threat had passed, relaxed their vigilance, the *Sicarii* would choose some locale and hit again. Back and forth it went. The Romans, despite their overwhelming power, could never seem to defeat their foes entirely, yet at the same time, the *Sicarii* did not enjoy widespread support among the population, at least not in those days. There would come a time when they would, but this would be long after Tiberius Caesar left the throne. And so on those nights we talked—of the Roman presence, the folly of our priests, the graft of the market inspectors who were appointed by the local Sanhedrin, and a host of other things, our tongues livened by the wine, livened also by Nathanael's visits, for we always found pleasure in the gentle giant's company. And so it was on one of these nights, as we kept the innkeeper busy, our friend related a curious tale of a wedding party he'd attended in his hometown of Cana. "There was a man there who, it is said, caused several stone jars filled with water to become wine."

"What? Are you daft?" Peter was gruffly amused. On the table before us rested a warm loaf of bread baked by the innkeeper's wife, while on the far side of the room a boisterous group of the inn's customers played Latrunculi. The game involved the moving of pieces around a board subdivided into small squares, and much laughter now emanated from the players, the sounds filling the fusty air with gaiety. We requested another decanter of wine, while Perpetua divided a plate of figs, and placed some before Peter.

"I didn't actually see it myself," Nathanael admitted. "But there are those who swear it happened."

"Water into wine—that sounds like something *Andrew* would come up with!"

"Where *is* Andrew these days, anyway?" The question was put by my brother James, who, though not normally a frequenter of the inns, had joined us this evening, for like all of us he was quite fond of Nathanael and looked forward to his visits.

"Still off in the desert, where he no doubt be learning how to foretell the future." Peter rolled his eyes and reached for a fig.

Seated next to my brother, and rounding out our number, was another by the name of James, a short man with a careful, studious air, who sat comfortably upon a rounded cask which he had rolled up to the table for that purpose. He was a mosaic artist. In fact, he and his father, Alphaeus, were considered the best of their trade in the region. Such was their renown, they had even been commissioned by Herod, in work which had been performed at the tetrarch's palace at Machaerus, near the *Yam ha Melah*. The project, for which they'd been paid handsomely, had been completed and they had only recently returned to Capharnaum.

"If ever he does so you would know which days to not bother casting your nets," said James my brother. The comment elicited much mirth, whereupon he added, "Give Andrew credit for one thing. He at least perseveres in his beliefs."

"He is one day going to be a great prophet." Perpetua cast a doting smile upon her husband, who, ignoring her look of affection, heaved a sigh over his younger brother's whimsical vagaries.

"How likely may he make a living selling his prophecies?" wondered the other James, whom we had in fact taken to calling "the other James."

"Oh, he never concerns himself with such mundane matters as that," Peter answered dryly. "Far more important it is to delve into the mysteries of God."

"Do they satisfy the hunger of the belly, these mysteries?"

"It is not especially necessary that they do so, not when *brothers* may be depended upon," Peter fumed.

"Andrew suffers from a deformed hand," observed the first James by way of humor. He smiled and then demonstrated: "His palm be forever extended outward and opened."

"Aye," Peter scowled. "Three times I have given him money, and what does he do? Takes it out to the desert and shares it with his fellow sages."

"Maybe he will one day discover the secrets of God," suggested Nathanael with a hopeful smile.

"And maybe he one day will not!" countered Peter. "He came to visit last year spouting some fool's notion about telling the future by looking at the stars. Likely even his prophet friends will soon be calling him starry-headed Andrew!"

Perpetua placed a restraining hand on Peter's arm, "Pray, don't speak so harshly about your brother."

"So who was this man?" Other James, exercising interest over the wedding in Cana, leaned forward on his cask.

"A stranger. And I really didn't get a good look at him. It was a very large feast, with many guests. A very big house, belonging to one of the wealthiest men in town, though a very good man, gracious, and kind to his servants."

"So how did the water get turned into wine, if it did?" inquired Perpetua.

"By some unknown means. Mind you, I did not see this with my own eyes."

"Then what makes you think it happened?"

"I do not know that it *did*, actually. I only know that *something* happened—because of people's reactions. *That* is what I witnessed, the measured reaction upon the faces. With my own eyes here is what I saw: first there was wine, then the wine ran out, then there was wine again; then I saw the servants, who have always been treated well, mind you, and had no reason to lie, looking very mystified. It was at this point that the host of the feast and the bridegroom came over, whereupon they too were mystified. Then it was whispered that a man had instructed the servants to fill some large water jars, and that afterwards the servants found the water in the jars had become wine. One person whispered the news of it to another, then that one to another, and so on, until the thing came to be whispered all about; no one, however, spoke of it openly, as if preferring to pretend it didn't happen, and maybe in point of fact it didn't. But it was a very curious thing."

"Bah! It was the wine put the notion in their heads—drunkards all!" Peter gave a laugh.

Nathanael grinned. "Maybe."

"Aye, wine shows no preference between rich and poor," Other James mused, taking a drink of wine.

"Wine into water—that's one even *Andrew* hasn't come up with!" Peter replaced his cup on the table with a loud thump.

"Well do I know that brothers can be a trouble to the heart, though," the mosaic artist resumed. "My own has chosen a path neither I nor my father are happy with."

"Your brother Matthew, you mean?"

"Yes."

"What path?"

"He has hired on with the chief tax collector. A booth he will set up soon on the *Via Maris*. You will likely see him there at some point."

At mere mention of the words "tax collector" a shadow fell over the table. No longer of course did the *publicani* commit excesses, yet memories still ran deep. "We have advised him not to do this, but he says he has no talent for artwork and must earn his way somehow. He has moved out and gotten a place of his own, and now spends all of his money on various women with whom he runs about."

"Can you not persuade him to work at something else? It is a job that will earn him much animosity."

"Well do we know this. He knows it too."

Throughout this exchange, Perpetua sat quietly with pursed lips. Before her, with her hands, she knotted and re-knotted a napkin of rolled cloth. I'm not sure if Other James knew of that which had been inflicted on her family by the previous tax collector, though my guess is he didn't; Perpetua for her own part maintained a bulwark of silence. Peter, however, sensitive to his wife's mood, changed the subject. "What was it like painting the mosaic in Herod's palace?" he asked.

"We went to Machaerus in the autumn, just after the Day of Atonement." Other James paused, the lines of his forehead creasing in sober reflection. "We were there for two months. Up here the early rains had begun, but when we arrived there it was very warm."

"Is it a fine palace?"

"More of a fortress. It is heavily fortified, but yes—once inside it is very lavish. It is here Herod fetes the rich and the powerful, and I must say, a more sordid and depraved lot you would be hard pressed to imagine."

"How so?"

"They speak continuously of those they plan to war against and subdue to their will. It is a most disgusting talk. Of course they can do nothing without the permission of Rome, but then many of those present are well-placed Romans. And not only Romans. The high priest from Jerusalem is a frequent guest as well."

"Caiaphas you mean?"

"Aye. He arrives with his assemblage of servants and bodyguards, *mebhinim* and *soferim*, all with their grand airs. Once within the walls of Machaerus his public display of piety is shed, for there are many delights to partake of and he forbids himself none of them."

"What *sorts* of delights?" This from Perpetua, who courted a mischievous smile, her somber mood of a moment before now over.

"Oh…" Other James gave a reflective shrug. "Dancing girls, prostitutes, exotic foods of all sorts, and of course the wine flows nonstop."

"In any of this did you partake yourself?" I asked. Immediately, I regretted the question, for it prompted an outburst of laughter. I should here explain that even now, at the age of twenty-two, I was still called 'Johannes the Virgin,' and for largely one valid reason: I *was* still a virgin. *Panem et circenses*. My question, and the context in which it had been asked, were sufficient to trigger the mirth of my companions.

"Nay!" answered Other James, still laughing. "We did our work. That is all." Thankfully at this point the innkeeper arrived; a spill was wiped up and pleasantries were exchanged. When he had gone, Other James expounded once more on the doings at Machaerus. "Over all the activities Herod presides with a regal air, but you can sense a brutal nature underneath."

"Of course by dallying with the prostitutes the high priest has now made himself subject to blackmail," my brother observed.

"Yes, there is that..." Other James broke off a piece of bread. His hands were delicate, the hands of an artist, as they occupied themselves in exiguous fraternity, first with the bread, then with his cup—near empty. It was getting late and we were all growing conscious of the hour. "There is much more that goes on as well; we saw, I'm sure, not even a tenth part of it. There is a young girl who is kept at the palace, not one of the pleasure girls, mind you, another purpose she serves. Most of the time she is locked away in one of the rooms. I saw her only occasionally the whole while I was there, very beautiful, but always upon her face a terrible sadness. Herod brings her out when he desires to know if someone is lying under interrogation, for it is said she has certain powers, and that she knows when people speak truth or lies."

"Think you will be called back there to work?"

"We have not been requested to, and in any case I have no desire."

"You and your father have plenty of work without the favors of the tetrarch?"

"For the most part. We start a project at the public bath in Caesarea next week." He paused, continued on a different note: "You know, something curious happened on our way back from Machaerus. Leaving off from the Salt Sea, we followed the Jordan north. After some miles, we came upon a camp belonging to a holy man of some sort. With him, there at this remote place along the river, were a great many people. Many of them he would lead into the water. The curious part is they came to the water naked, yet unashamed in their nakedness; once in the river, the holy man would take hold of them, lower them below the surface and bring them back up. We watched the goings-on for a good long while, for it was a most unusual sight. I remember also the way the man spoke, his words—they were of great power. Though named John, his followers mostly seemed to call him 'the Baptizer.'"

"I have *heard* of this man!" James remarked suddenly. "It is said he is an Essene, or used to be. Supposedly, he has some knowledge of magic. There is much talk going on about him just now."

"Magic! What nonsense! It is all trickery and foolishness," declared Peter.

"Yes, it might be that," Other James conceded. "I wanted to stay and hear more of what he had to say, but my father was in a hurry. Maybe I shall go back sometime. A great many people, perhaps a hundred or more, had gone there to be baptized and to hear his words."

Chapter Thirty-Two

It was a few days later when Matthew, the younger brother of Other James, set up his tax booth on the *Via Maris*, much as his brother had said he would; equally as predictable was the antipathy this earned him, but if he cared, little did he show. It was with some interest now I began observing young Matthew, who was also known as Levi. Whereas his brother James was average of looks, Matthew on the other hand had been blessed by the gods with tallness of stature and striking physical beauty. I began stopping by his booth hoping to cultivate his acquaintance for the very good reason that there seemed forever about him a bevy of the most beautiful young women. In time, I came to realize these were drawn as much by his comely features as by an ineluctable charm he wielded and which had a rather demonstrable affect on them; in short—I was in the presence of a master. I had begun to think of my virginity as dangerously close to becoming a lifelong affliction, and I suppose in ingratiating myself with Matthew I'd hoped to somehow acquire his skills. I didn't, of course. Around women, I remained as fumbling and shy as ever, yet in the course of these protracted efforts at self-improvement, I made the discovery that Matthew, despite his detested profession, was an altogether agreeable fellow.

In the spring of that year, Andrew came home from the desert. He was full of much spirit and exuberance, just like Andrew of old, yet after an hour or two in his presence, I sensed a new maturity, a new ripeness and sweetness of his nature. He talked of the desert, told of his teachers, extolled his *mishnath ha-chasidim*, his course of instruction for the pious, and marveled upon the wondrous mysteries of God; he even confided certain secrets of telling the future by looking at the stars, this as his older brother evinced an ill-humored wrinkling of the brow. But mostly what Andrew talked about, could not seem to even *stop* talking about, was the man known as John the Baptizer.

That he had made his way out to visit the new prophet was to be expected, for Andrew had always been attracted to new things and ideas.

What we were not prepared for, however, was his announcement that he had left the Essene settlement at the Salt Sea. It was of course amongst the Essenes he had made his vows, that all "knowledge, powers, and possessions" were to be shared equally with one and all in the community, a simple covenant, intended no doubt to convey righteousness and close the doors of vanity, but as I say, he had left, much as if in pursuit of an elusive star, in the process attaching himself to John the Baptizer, whose steadfast disciple he had now become.

"Andrew, for the love of the Lord!" Peter exploded. "You are like a moth that goes from one lamp to another!"

"Brother, you would not *believe* the things the Baptizer says! Much he speaks of is so very true! You must come out and hear him for yourself. All of you, come with me to hear his words and be baptized!"

We were taken aback by his intensity, but then not so. Perpetua smiled inwardly; it was, after all, vintage Andrew. But Peter was not pleased with his departure from the Essenes, for it was from the Essene community he had hoped Andrew would obtain a measure of stability.

"Trouble not your heart, brother. Once you hear the Baptizer, you will know that I speak truly of him!"

"Oh for the love of the Lord!" Peter groaned.

"Well, Andrew, at any rate—" Perpetua favored her brother-in-law with a tolerant smile, "—*welcome home*! It is good to have you back!"

"Thank you Perpetua! It is good to be back. And I should like it very much, Perpetua, if you too would come and hear the Baptizer!"

Still smiling, though this time not as much, Peter's wife replied, "Well...*perhaps*." I could see she had no intention of journeying abroad to have herself dunked into the Jordan by a wild man, and was trying only to facilitate peace between the brothers.

Yet Other James was of quite different mind, letting it be known he, for one, very much *did* desire to heed Andrew's invitation. "This is no doubt the man I was speaking of!" He turned to the rest of us, then back to Andrew, of whom he inquired urgently, "Where can the Baptizer be found nowadays?"

"Currently at Aenon, near Salim."

"I think we should go!" Other James turned once more. "I for one would very much like to see this man again!"

While his suggestion was made in all earnestness, it was my brother who actually tilted the balance—in favor of the journey. "So many people are now talking of this sage of the Jordan," he said, "I think it best we go see him for ourselves." But there was an exaggerated intensity to his words, detectable at least to my own ears, if not to others; James, I well knew, had never been particularly enamored of desert-wandering holy men, but there *was* something beckoning to him, for a trip away from Capharnaum would avail him the opportunity of diverting himself to Bethsaida, and in Bethsaida was someone my brother very much *did* want to see—his girl Abigail. The two had lost touch after our move to Capharnaum, but about a year ago, they had re-established the bond, and he had since been slipping away to her side whenever time would allow. I had no doubt that at some point, either on our way to Salim or coming back, he would find a way to divert himself to her door.

It took some doing, but Perpetua, too, was persuaded that an excursion in the fresh air of several days' duration would be a much-welcomed distraction for us, which left Peter as the final holdout, but even he too gave in, perhaps only for being outnumbered and wishing to put an end to the discussion. At any rate, he managed to subdue his more curative and overt cynicisms, and early one morning in the month of Tammuz, we started out. Across Gennesaret we made our way, landing at Hippos, and from there traveling overland down to the Hamet Gader hot spring. Crossing the River Yarmuk, we arrived finally at the Jordan. It was a full day's journey, and near Salim the road became noticeably heavier with traffic, both foot traffic and donkey carts. Arriving at the village of Aenon, we were astonished to find the lanes literally choked with travelers; it was a veritable surge of humanity. One and all seemed in route to the Baptizer's place of encampment. Andrew was no less surprised than the rest of us, for the throngs, he said, had not been near this numerous when he'd left. Indeed, by word of mouth from a passing traveler, we learned that the camp of the holy man had grown in essence into a small city.

Finally, a little ways out from Aenon, we reached our destination—a flat, sandy plain on the west bank of the river. At first, I could not believe my eyes, for there were quite easily five thousand present. Andrew led us to the Holy Man, who wore clothing of a utilitarian and rather eremic nature, made entirely of camel's hair. The prophet—for that, at least by reason of my vague notions as to what a prophet was *supposed* to look like, is what he struck me as first and foremost of all—took the time to greet each of us personally. "It is good you have come! You are most welcomed!" His voice boomed like some colossal animal. Unruly was his beard, yet there was something about him as he crossed the gaveled interstice of shallow riverbed to stand before us; it was as if he were a being set sail upon his own light ship, as he stood with a smile, the flapping, canopied archway of a tent behind him. Quite clearly, like Elijah before him, he was living on nothing more than the wild country around us might provide; this applied not only to his camel-hair clothing, but the food he ate as well—as we learned that night when he invited us to a meal. The fare consisted of wild honey, locust leaves, and carob pods from a nearby tree. No flesh of any animal, either wild or domesticated, ever passed his lips that we saw, an abstinence, which, as we learned, had rigidly been adopted by Andrew as well. "Much joy it brings me to see you again, Andrew!" His voice enveloped us now in jovial pieniloquence. "And a most especial joy it is to meet your brother!"

Peter was taciturn, offering no more than a few obligatory syllables in reply. Everywhere all about were people. The traveler who had spoken to us in Aenon had been right: the camp was indeed a city, and a remarkably peaceful one at that. There were tents, fires, musical instruments, and even an outdoor oven where a group of women were baking bread. Exploring our way about, we learned everything was shared in common; if you desired food, clothing, wood for a fire, whatever you might have need of, it was all amicably yours for the taking. There was movement and activity in abundance, yet I had the feeling people were no more than passing the time while waiting for the Baptizer to speak. For the moment, however, the Holy Man had disappeared, hardly surprising when you considered the numbers competing for his time and attention; consuls of faith and disciples of the breath of life, searchers of peace and seekers of God—these and more sought him out.

Around mid-afternoon, we took seats on the ground. I found myself sitting next to a man with a small child on his lap whom I watched for a time, a lovely lad, with a bright smile and graceful eyes that were almost feminine. As I watched him, Andrew, seated on my left, provided an ongoing commentary on various aspects of life within the camp of John the Baptizer. "Something of a curious nature happened about a month ago..." I wondered if he had better not be helping his master, but he seemed to prefer remaining in my company. "There was a man who came and was baptized, and as he stepped out of the river a dove flew down and landed on him. It was a most strange sight, for the dove and the man seemed to merge, and for the next few days after that, the Baptizer spoke very little. It was *very* peculiar."

The young father next to us unwrapped a loaf of bread and courteously offered to share. I accepted, intoning my thanks; eating of the morsel, a feeling of peace came over me, a contentment so complete I was markedly startled a moment later upon hearing my name called boisterously: ***"Well bless my soul! If it isn't Johannes the Virgin!"*** Swiftly turning, I found myself staring into the face of Thomas Didymus. Not since the day of our parting on the quay in the bustling city of Tyre, some years before, had I seen that stalwart ship's carpenter. Staggering was my surprise, so much so I could not disguise my delight. "Thomas!"

"In the flesh! It is good to see you again, John, and of course you as well, brother James!" My brother was every bit as delighted as I. Thomas clapped both of us affectionately. "I see you have already made the acquaintance of my friend Thaddaeus." He indicated the man with the child on his lap who had earlier shared his bread. The boy, a strikingly beautiful youngster indeed, regarded us in open-eyed wonder. "And his little son as well!"

"Thank you for sharing your bread with us." Perpetua, on the other side of Andrew, leaned and faced Thaddaeus. "What is your little one's name?"

"Gabriel."

"Gabriel! Like the angel!" she said, obviously much taken with the handsome child.

Thaddaeus smiled, "Yes, the same."

They had come south from Tyre, the three of them, Thomas and Thaddaeus with the boy, in a quest to see the new prophet, John the Baptizer, for yes, it seemed the Holy Man's fame had spread into Syro-Phoenicia. Arriving two days previous, they had simply merged with the thousands. "We kept hearing stories of this man who some say can perform wonders, and who speaks of God's coming wrath. 'So!' says I to Thaddaeus. 'Let us journey down and hear this man's words for ourselves!' But of course, you remember, I am a wanderer at heart!"

"Did you ever make your way to India?" I asked.

"Not yet," he answered with a wistful smile. "But someday!"

Past the outer lines of the cinnabar wash, I could see trails of people following a serpentine path along the road from Aenon. More arrivals. But something else seemed to be taking place as well, much closer; it was a hush. Across that field of thousands it descended, as if by means of some unseen cue, spreading by compartments, here and there, until it rose to a great height and seemed to produce its own cautious solemnity. John the Baptizer, it seemed, was about to speak. And then I saw him. He was seated on an acroterium, feeding a thousand dreams, much like a fire assuming different shapes, even as he sat motionless, swathed in the silence of Ptah, oblivious apparently to his surroundings. The front-most throngs gave call to him, but he seemed not to hear, perhaps giving ear instead to some faraway star, a star where his heart found mercy, for little mercy, of course, is there to be obtained in this world. At last, he opened his eyes, his thoughts diverted from the rainy season of his soul, his gaze settling in ascendancy over the crowd as he began to speak.

"Solace lies with Life Everlasting, who transcends not only the darkness, but also the light. Out of fire and of water was the one heaven spread out, but know this also, that *two* Kings were there, *two* natures were fashioned! A King of this world and a King from outside of the worlds! The King of this age girt on a sword and put on a crown of Darkness; a crown of Darkness he put on his head, and took a sword in his right hand; he stands there and slaughters his sons, and his sons slaughter each other; he stands there in his world of vileness, sown full of thorns and thistles, clouded over by clouds, with ten thousand times ten thousand dragons in each single cloud.

"The King from outside of the worlds set a crown of Light on his head, and took Truth in his right hand, and he stands there and instructs his sons and daughters, and his sons and daughters instruct each other. And he became a king for the Nazōræans, and on his name they mount up and behold the light's region. I myself came and found the Nazōræans, how they stand on the shore of the Jordan. I brought them myrtle and white sesame. Here we stand on the bank of the river; here we are also the fish swimming in the river, while the filth eaters come, beating on the waters to frighten the fish into the nets; and laying waste to the land of Jerusalem!"

I didn't know whether I was listening to fits of sobbing produced by a madman, or an unchained tempest, a rushing fountain of Spirit, providing both consolation to the bereaved and a baptism of water that hovered at the verge of incineration. He went on like that for the better part of two hours as scarcely anyone spoke or moved. We were the slaves of God, the disciples of those who name the Name, he said. Would God have compassion, forbearance, and mercy upon us? He beseeched that the Holy One should do so, for how stupendous, he said, is God's grandeur! Finally, he closed with a hymn. "The Song of the Poor's Exaltation." A sound within a sound it was, for the Poor were the *Ebyonim*. It was a song turning heaven and outspread stars into a mixing bowl of souls, as he raised his voice to sing:

> For thy sake, O Poor,
> Was this firmament spread out,
> And the stars pictured upon it;
> Blessed is he who is to the Poor one a father;
> Hail to him whom Great Life knows

It was near sundown when he finished. A line formed at the river of those seeking to be baptized. They gathered at the shore and then, one by one, merged into the water, naked, yet unashamed in their nakedness. "You must come as little children to the kingdom!!!" his voice boomed; and that is how they went. My eyes, as you may imagine, lingered especially on the women. Should I be ashamed of this? Perhaps. And yet angels and their mysteries seemed to command the whole proceeding, with the Baptizer himself serving almost as no more than a mere functionary. Women and men went under the water. Upon coming up, to each of them he would speak: "In the Spirit of Truth, I baptize you as a son (or daughter) of the Light."

When all had been baptized, he again addressed the crowd. "See that you do not abandon the slave to the hands of his master; abandon not the weak to the strong. Between the Spirit of Truth and the Spirit of Injustice God has set eternal enmity. The Light and the Dark are ever opposites. There will be no day in this world in which the dove loves the ravens. Those who follow the Spirit of Injustice are bound in the marshes of deception; they are dishonorable and pitiless. Love and instruct one another. Look after the fish of God; see that none of them fails. Let yourselves be instructed, you perfect, and ascend to Light's region. *Praised* be Life!"

Chapter Thirty-Three

I n front of me were two lights, one on top of another. The light of an exceptionally bright moon in the sky, and the light of the fire before me. Around that fire, I sat with the others, watching the Baptizer's face. We had been with him five days now. Throughout, he had shared his fire and food with us, but this was to be our last night; tomorrow we were to strike for home, and auspiciously now the sky was aflame with the stars of heaven.

After our meal (the usual unpalatable fare, though I was by now grown used to it) the Holy Man had launched into a strange discourse, although I might mention that over the five days we had been here I had observed how his words often took sudden and erratic turns of logic. It was something one simply got used to. But now what was emerging from his lips was strange even by his standards. "Coming is one of the Light, and you must understand this Light and make friends with it. The Spirit of Truth will be upon him. He will lead many away from their covetousness and vanity, and when he comes, you must go with him, for he will have great need of you." Was John the Baptizer saying we were to follow not him, but another? And who was this man of which he spoke? Could a gate be shaken by the four winds, or a living root pulled out of dried ground? There was something, as I say, peculiar about it, as if he were Thoth holding out the *utchat*, the eye of the sun.

"Master, how will we know this man?" Thomas, who had taken to calling the Baptizer "master," seemed, moreso than any of us, to have found this camp in the wilderness a scepter of flint upon which to strike his ingrained wanderlust. I wasn't sure if he would ever still his soul's inner restlessness, but for the moment the Tyrian carpenter had to all appearances claimed the blessings of the Lady of the Sycamore trees.

"When the fishers hear the call, their hearts will fall down from their stays." The Baptizer glanced first to Thomas, then at Peter. "I might for many be a loving shepherd, but if a lion comes and carries off one, how am I to retrieve him? If a thief comes and steals one away, how am I to retrieve him? If one falls into the fire and is burnt, how am I to retrieve him?"

Listening to his voice, I reflected...back...over the past few days. They had gone by quickly, and I must tell you, dear Quintus, that something extraordinary had happened to us in this oh-so-short time. We had fallen, yes fallen, under the spell of this man known as John the Baptizer. An inner light shone in him, you could see it at all times, and we had to conclude that Andrew had been right; on but our second day we were ourselves baptized, even Peter. With a great many others, we took our place in line by the river, making our descent, one by one, into that dirty brown water, only the moment I touched its surface, it transformed itself miraculously into a shining jewel, and stepping into it produced in me a sense of kinship with every man, woman, and child here. John the Baptizer's camp had become, in essence, the *adat ha'yahad*, the society of unity; this muddy Jordan, which I'd known in its more mundane aspects all my life, seemed suddenly to have wound, much like a living thing, round and round the hearts of us all.

We had never imagined, in our wildest dreams, John would find time for more than a few cursory exchanges with us as he went about his affairs. The numbers of people seeking him out in the backflow of the multitudes were too great. Yet from the moment of our arrival he had urged upon us the shelter and comfort of his own fire—*us* in particular. At first I thought it owing only to our being friends of Andrew's, though later I sensed something else, a product of some yet-to-be-formed asterism of grace.

"Since we have been here I have known much peace," Thomas said now. "I do not relish leaving tomorrow." None of us did. I glanced at Perpetua, who rested her head on her husband's shoulder. Of us all, the wife of Peter seemed especially to have developed a tender fondness for the wild man of this wild country, coming to understand, perhaps more instinctively than the rest of us, how God abides as much in the petals of a rose as in the inner sanctum of any vast, gleaming temple.

"You will know even greater peace to come, Thomas, and more joy than you could ever imagine possible."

"Rabbi," Andrew raised his voice hesitantly, "your words that we are to follow another are troubling, for I cannot possibly imagine following any but you."

"Andrew, you are a very dear one, and I love you much, but I would have you understand, all of you, my days will come to end. This camp will cease to be; to dust it will be rendered."

"No master!"

"It should not happen!"

"It should not, but it will." Even having pronounced this, John seemed strangely untroubled as he resumed, scarcely skipping a beat, "They, the Romans and the Jews who are their servants, will never allow this to continue, for it threatens them. You saw the ones who came the other day..."

I had seen them. We all had. It had been our third day in the camp, at around the fifth hour; in they came, an armed party on horseback, trampling over the brown earth, into the Baptizer's peaceful multitudes, a large cohort of heavily armed solders, and safely protected in their midst—several members of the Jerusalem Sanhedrin. "These have little humanity in their hearts." The words were whispered by a man who happened to be standing next to me at the time, a Samaritan who had resided here several months and had seen the same group of riders before, or, I suppose, one similar to it. We watched them press through, the horses urged to no more than a trifling pace, yet there was a sinister presence to mounts and riders as they sundered the crowd like dark angels. At last to a halt they came, in front of the tent of John. The latter emerged much as if having expected them. In the nodules of his wild and untamed visage I detected something sharpened, poised, like an arrow getting ready to fly. "Does God clothe you with meekness and fear as befits those who would become righteous?" The words were neither Saturnian, nor prelude to an amiable veneration, but there *was* a curule seat set down for a shepherd's dog; contained within the question was a bold and artlessly concealed scoffing. For a moment nothing could be heard but the clink of armor as the soldiers shifted in their saddles. Not Roman regulars were they, but troops of the tetrarchy, answerable to Herod. The three Sanhedrin councilors in their midst gazed upon the Baptizer with contempt. Jews yes. And so was John. But other than that, I could not see what he and they could possibly have in common other perhaps than the flame of the wrath of the scorching wind of which each was made. "This is an iniquitous and unlawful gathering. Why do you not send this rabble on its way?"

But the Baptizer was not about to be reduced to servitude. "I lay down in Zion a living stone of probation, and yet you, you brood of vipers, care nothing when the earth groans out of season. What makes you think you can escape the wrath which is to come?"

"Who do you think you are—*speaking* to us like that?"

"One who recognizes falseness and deceit."

"A prideful blasphemer, who thinks himself a prophet but shall one day receive a grievous chastisement!" blurted the second.

"What can a dirt-girdled, soot-stained drunkard who fancies himself a hierophant have to say that would possibly interest all these people?" the first wondered aloud to his fellows, this while glancing scornfully around the camp.

"You think you are some jeweled and lordly king of this rabble, but what are you, really? You are nothing!" averred the second.

"I am a voice crying in the wilderness."

Seated on the horse next to the second, the third councilor, who until now had remained silent, affected an air of merry-making. "Are you the 'Messiah'? Is that what you claim to be?" The comment kindled amusement, even amongst the soldiers.

"Do the lost lambs of God look to the coming of a Messiah, when they receive justice from those who rule over them?" Gradually, as the remark sank in, the laughter was replaced with stony silence. John, however, had not finished. "The man who has two tunics should share with the man who has none; why is it the likes of you, with all you supposedly know of the law, can never remember a rule even as simple as that? And don't bother saying to yourselves, 'we have Abraham as our father,' for the fact is God can raise children of Abraham out of these stones lying on the ground. What advantage is there of earthly things? Look about you. The ax head is already at the trunk of the tree, and every tree that doesn't produce good fruit is going to be cut down and thrown into the fire."

"Do you perhaps see also a skull floating on the water, Prophet?" It was one of the soldiers, speaking now for the first time, a threshing-sledge of a man; from his saddle, he suddenly raised a long-bladed *spatha*, bringing the point to bear against the Baptizer's barrel-like chest. In the soldier's face, deep within the gibbously hardened eyes, was a smoldering intensity, a look so dark one would have thought it capable of sending down rain from the thunderclouds. With a remarkable fearlessness the Holy Man did not flinch from the contact, instead returning the man's hardened gaze measure for measure. Still seated astride his mount, the soldier pressed the *spatha* further...and further...until a trickle of blood appeared, yet the Baptizer seasoned himself inert, his eyes become chips of feldspar as they burrowed back into the soldier's own smoldering orbs. For a long moment the two held their ground; at last, with a painfully slow movement, and with eyes still fixed biliously upon the Holy Man, the soldier lowered the sword. As he did so, I realized suddenly I had been holding my breath, and as air resumed flowing in my lungs, I experienced a sense of regaining something that for a brief moment had been lost to me—the ability to differentiate between existence and annihilation.

The soldier and the Holy Man continued to appraise each other, in the cold eyes of the former a hint that the business between them remained unfinished. Yet no further words were spoken. The only sound was that of hooves as reins were loosed. Men and animals turned in a line; retracing their steps, the riders culled a path back through the crowd, exercising again that same methodical gait as their horses pressed forward. John, despite his now-steadily-bleeding chest, remained where he stood, motionless, until the last of them disappeared over a ridge, whereupon he collapsed, haggard, onto a camel-hair blanket spread for him on the ground as Perpetua, a panicky Andrew, and several others rushed to his assistance.

Chapter Thirty-Four

After a meal of boiled groats and sections of fruit, we spent the rest of the day and that night recovering from the incident—only to have the desert, the following day, deliver up yet another party of visitors whose passage through our midst was to be a somewhat unsettling one—although here all similarities ended, for the encounter turned out to be of a far different nature from the one of the day before. Not on horseback but on foot came the new visitants, traveling over the cracked land like a scattering of grasshoppers, blown into our midst by the desert wind. Or that, I should imagine, is how it must have seemed to the child Gabriel, who took it upon himself to wander, enchanted, into their midst. "Please excuse him," apologized Perpetua, taking hold of the boy, but in the view of the new arrivals, no offense had been committed. "It is quite alright," said a gray-bearded one, who carried a walking stick, a placid smile settling on his face as he gazed upon the child, while his companions, all considerably younger than he, unburdened themselves of their packs. I was beginning to think the boy's instincts had been right, that there *was* something unusual about the group, when suddenly Andrew's voice rang out. "Father Hilkiah!" I turned my head in time to see he of Jonah's blood bounding forward. "It is good you are here! Much have I longed to see you and the other brothers again!" Did Andrew know these people? It seemed he did.

"We have missed you as well, Andrew."

The travelers evidently were known also to the Baptizer, for moments later the Holy Man's voice erupted with its characteristic volcanic delivery. "Hilkiah, words of blessing to you in all truth!"

"May everlasting peace be yours, John."

"Welcome to our humble camp! I see you have already made the acquaintance of little Gabriel!"

"Ahh..." The aged one smiled and ruffled the boy's head. "The Holy One's light shines ever forth from the eyes of a child!" Much like a bee collecting honey, the old man seemed to draw some libation of power up through that touch to the child's head.

In due course, we learned they were in route to the *Yam ha Melah*, on whose shores they lived. They were Essenes. Or at any rate, this seemed the case with Hilkiah. As for the others, I wasn't completely sure who they were, and something suggested they had merely attached themselves to the elder somewhat in the manner of restless clouds following the wind. Simon Magus was the name of one; though only in his twenties, it was said he had studied magic in Egypt; next came Dositheus, a young man of slender of frame, clad in a tunic of coarse wool, who had a studious air though with eyes of unruly fermentation; following Dositheus was the woman in the group, named Helen, though she was called "Luna" by the others; an auspicious beauty rose through the layer of dust on her face. And then finally Darda—of them all, he seemed the most cut from the same cloth as the old man, Hilkiah, and it was given that he was an apprentice healer, one in the process of learning, from others at the *Yam ha Mela* settlement, of the many, varied plants, herbs, and rhizomes, all provided by God for relief of the sick, and to be administered only by those of innate wisdom. Though bound for the Salt Sea, with its pained spirits and caves of seclusion, they rested now. And of course we all ended up at the Baptizer's fire that night.

I was to see things around that fire I would not come to understand until years later. It wasn't just Simon Magus, whose magic was as a moon-bird singing to its kinfolk; it was also the elder, Hilkiah, aged and cynical, who gave off, much as a plectrum's striking of a single lyre string, the note of a slightly ill-tempered rain cloud watering the earth.

"Are you Essenes?" I asked when we had finished our meal, for my curiosity had gotten the better of me at last.

Sipping a bitter infusion, the young physician-in-training, Darda, gave an impassive smile. "That word follows us around quite a bit."

"What he means to say," explained Andrew, "is that the name 'Essene' is simply a term applied by others, mostly for not knowing what else to call them."

"Names are nothing more than external forms, placed upon objects for sake of convenience, and of course the world felt it necessary to do this in our case, as it does in all others." Hilkiah pronounced this with a bored expression, and proceeded to ease himself into a seat near the fire.

"The word 'Essene' means 'pious one,'" Andrew went on. "And as far as names go, one may suppose it as good as any in this case. But it is not how they refer to themselves." From his seat before the fire, the Baptizer followed this exchange with a bemused expression. A puzzled Perpetua risked a question, "So what *do* you call yourselves?"

Hilkiah shrugged. "We are the *Nozrei ha-brit*, the Keepers of the Covenant."

"We are The Many," added Darda.

"They are also The Few," put in Simon Magus.

Here John the Baptizer gave a hearty laugh, and said, "A long time ago, one of Hilkiah's forbears became disenchanted with the powers in Jerusalem; he felt they had become corrupt, that they were engaging in all kinds of falseness and deceit and leading the country down a crooked path, and of course he was right in that." The Holy Man picked up a branch and contemplatively stoked the fire. "Well," he said, setting aside the branch at last, "the 'Righteous Teacher,' as Hilkiah's great grandfather came to be known—he was a priest of the Zadokite line—had a number of interesting ideas. For one thing, he taught that people should renounce wealth acquired by wickedness. They should be hospitable to strangers, treat the poor with compassion, and most irksome of all, from the point of view of the rich rulers in Jerusalem, he said that everyone should own everything in common, and that no one should acquire more than anyone else.

"But these things, admirable as they may be, were not enough; as long as people continued to live within a corrupt and iniquitous kingdom there was no way, no matter how sincere and honest their hearts, they could avoid becoming corrupt and iniquitous themselves. So what Hilkiah's great grandfather proposed was that they should completely separate themselves from that kingdom, no longer live in it. Or even anywhere near it. Of course, by this time, the Teacher's words had so aroused the ire of the leadership in Jerusalem that separation had become more than a moral imperative; it was a practical necessity from a safety standpoint. Had he remained in Jerusalem, his life would almost certainly have been forfeit.

"So they left the holy city, the Righteous Teacher and his followers, heading out to the wild country. First, they went to the wilderness southeast of Damascus; later they settled at the Salt Sea, though by this time Hilkiah's great grandfather was no longer with them. His old enemies in Jerusalem, fearing he would one day lead a revolt against them, went up to the Damascene wilderness, hunted him down, and killed him. Shortly before he died, however, the Righteous Teacher looked up at the stars, for Hilkiah and his followers have long believed that the moon and stars portend the future.

Fishermen/239

So he studied carefully what the stars had to say; in addition to his own death, which he *did* in fact see clearly, he also divined that in forty years time the land of Israel would be overrun by foreigners, and he issued a prophesy accordingly. Almost exactly forty years later, close enough, at any rate, to convince a lot of people the Righteous Teacher had known what he was talking about, the Romans came."

Silence greeted this rather astonishing tale. But before anyone else could get a word in edgewise, the Baptizer resumed, "That was a long time ago, of course. Now Hilkiah himself is the *mebaqqer*, and all these years he and his people have been steadfastly keeping God's ordinances." He paused, smiled knowingly. "Alas, though, the *Kittim* are still here, isn't that right, Hilkiah?"

"May the shining javelin of Adonai smite them where they stand."

Still smiling, John went on, "Hilkiah and his people don't much care for the Romans, that is except for their way of measuring time. You see, down where Hilkiah lives, they don't look for the new moon as marking the arrival of a new month. Instead, they reckon time chronologically based upon appearances of the sun. Each year has exactly 364 days—52 weeks of 7 days each. And it's all discerned by the movement of the sun, rather than the moon."

"Why this strange manner of calculation? It is a thing of no sense," asserted Other James.

"On the contrary, it makes an infinite amount of sense," Simon Magus declared evenly.

"It gets back once more to Hilkiah's great grandfather." The Baptizer's voice boomed in time to the dancing flames. "The people of Israel, said the Righteous Teacher, were not in tune with what he called 'the Great Light of Heaven,' which of course is the sun. In fact, he said, not since their return from Babylon had they been in tune with it, not even once. Not only were all the feast days, including Passover, out of kilter, but the priests in Jerusalem weren't even observing the Sabbath on the correct days, which the Righteous Teacher considered a grievous sin against God. Is that about the size of it, Hilkiah?"

"You speak correctly, John."

"In fact that's how they managed to kill him," the Holy Man went on. "They went up to Damascus and crept into his camp on a day they knew the Righteous Teacher and his followers would be observing the Sabbath—not a thing they ordinarily would have considered acceptable, except for the fact that of course for them it *wasn't* the Sabbath."

"But the sons of the dawn shall triumph." Darda placed his cup down, his youthful features taking on a look of pride. "Adonai shall lay His hand on the neck of His enemies and His feet on the pile of the slain. Then He shall gather up the spoils for His people."

John stared at and through the young disciple, turning morosely, after some moments, to face Hilkiah, "You will resurrect Antiochus Epiphanes teaching them such as that."

"There is war coming with the *Kittim*, John. This I have told you many times."

"You are quite right. There is. And for those who refuse to clothe themselves in the righteousness of the meek there will be no end to this war. Fire has dust for its abode."

"Spoken very well, John. As you are always prone to do. But remember that Belial has been unleashed. As the prophet said, 'terror, the pit, and the snare are upon you, O inhabitant of the land.' The priests shall sound the trumpets of Massacre, at which time Belial shall come to the aid of the sons of darkness. Then the war will come; the stars even now foretell it."

To this, the Baptizer made no reply. In silence, we watched the fire crackle until my brother ventured, "This looking into the future by means of studying the stars—I do not see how such a thing is possible."

Peter chimed in. "He is right! There is no believable logic in it. The sun, the moon, the stars—they are far away. How can they have any bearing over what transpires here on earth?"

The Baptizer grinned, but it was Hilkiah, who answered. "The sun, the moon, and stars were made by Adonai. Not only did he make them and place them in the sky, but he also set them in motion. Now, why did he do this last thing? Why not simply let them hang stationary?"

"I don't know," Peter shrugged. "Why did he?"

A thin, satisfied smile spread over the aged face, as if the answer was all too obvious. The Baptizer, grinning wide as ever, supplied, "Hilkiah will tell you it's so God could speak to us." He shifted his weight, threw another log on the fire, this time a very large one. A shower of sparks went shooting upward. "The idea is, God uses the movements of the planets as a sort of language of communication, there being no verbal language between humans and God, beyond the mere pronunciation of the Holy Name, that humans are capable of. Have I got it right, Hilkiah?"

"Your truth is of a certain, John. It was the archangel Sariel who taught men about the course of the moon, and he it is whose name shall be carved upon the shields of heaven."

"Hilkiah and his disciples have been carefully keeping records on the stars, the angels, and all sorts of things for years. How many scrolls do you have now, Hilkiah?"

"More than a hundred," answered Darda.

Thomas looked perplexedly at the old sage. "I never thought of the movement of moon and stars as a 'language' before."

"Adonai established it to show us the ways of His heart."

"It sounds fascinating," said Perpetua.

But Peter was unconvinced. His skepticism prompted Andrew to remark, "Brother, you have to know that with God *anything* is possible!" And at this point, like two birds working in tandem at building a nest, Andrew and Darda commenced valiantly trying to illuminate Peter's thinking on the matter. The Baptizer, for his own part, seemed content to let the matter lie. As for the old *mebaqqer*, he too had withdrawn from the conversation. His thoughts, behind the lids of his now-closed eyes, seemed in search of an arrangement or order that could only be thought of as dreadfully lacking in the outer world. At some point, he began to issue forth a humming; subdued initially, this grew steadily in volume over a period, a curious reverberation, journeying from somewhere deep within the old man, and after some moments, it began to claim our undivided attention; to all intents and purposes, it was as if the *mebaqqer's* senses had become wholly disengaged from the world around, as his mouth poured out that clairaudient intonation, at which point something astonishing occurred. It commenced as a whistling sound, a wind, arriving at our fire site with a turbulence, craving and ignorant at first, but then beginning to direct itself by way of movement, turning, coiling, advancing this way and that, as would a serpent. From nowhere it seemed to have sprung. Was it simply a random gust of wind? My faculties of reason assured me that this, and only this, could be possible, yet on it went, winding about like a spirit, hungry for its seat within the Seven Poles, as it executed a tighter and tighter ambit around the fire and ourselves. At last, the turbulence, much like a living thing, gathered itself into a fierce and formidable presence several cubits above our heads, whereupon, without warning, it catapulted itself with a dive straight into the fire. *Khayla!* Stoked only moments before with a fresh log laid upon it by the Baptizer, the blaze died immediately, the flames choked into a vapid darkness as the wind serpent literally sucked off its life;

save for moon and stars, night's blackness enveloped us. But then, precisely as the *mebaqqer* ceased his all-infernal humming, the blaze, to all appearances previously expunged, leaped to its original height; hereupon, Hilkiah opened his eyes.

"You have been wounded, John."

His tone was of genuine dismay. "It is just a small cut," assured the Holy Man, upon whom the display of wind and essence seemed to have made no impression.

But at this point, their gnomish punctilios were savagely interrupted by Other James.

"Wait a moment! Did you just—" he paused, realizing the absurdity of what was about to be suggested—"make the *wind* blow?"

Like the rest of us, Other James had witnessed the peculiar interplay of fire and wind; unlike the rest of us, however, he had observed it with the careful, contemplative eye of an artist, and now, possessed of the thirst of the thirsty, nothing less than a full explanation would suffice.

"I don't know, did I?" Pressing a finger to his chin, Hilkiah seemed to consider the matter objectively. "Perhaps I *did*."

Here, frothy gales of laughter erupted from the Baptizer. Had we witnessed a comedy? Was it a farce? But John's amusement was not shared by Hilkiah, who, if anything, seemed to regard freak acts of nature unworthy of even remarking upon. "Allow me to see, John," said he with a tired sigh, as the Holy Man, continuing to laugh, began to remove his camelhair tunic.

Hazardous and slow is the path to the Unrevealed. Like Other James, I too tried to make sense of what we had seen, and, like him, awaited an explanation; none was to come, however. John and the *mebaqqer* had moved on.

"How came this upon you, John?" He was referring to the wound, that angry vessel of turpitude carved madder-like upon the Holy Man's chest by the soldier the previous day. More than twenty-four hours later now, the skin was red and suppurating.

"We had a little visit yesterday..."

"May the *Kittim* be cursed without mercy!" commented Hilkiah indignantly when the Baptizer had relayed the details "—along with that Assembly of the Wicked that ever consorts with them!" Having rendered this malediction, the old *mebaqqer* nodded curtly at Darda, who rose. From a pouch, he withdrew leaves of a jagged shape and ruddiness. Breaking these up, he placed them over the fire to boil; meanwhile from a second pouch, he withdrew what appeared to be tree bark and crumbled this as well. Hilkiah, content to watch with an air of detachment, his deft interplay with the wind now a thing of the past, wheezed phlegmatically, "The serpents are the kings of the people, justifying ever the wicked, while unceasingly condemning the just..."

"This needs to be purified." The young physician began to cleanse the wound. I was soon able to smell the aroma of rosh, the pain-relieving narcotic which the Romans sometimes referred to as gall, as Darda's mixture began to boil. At last the liquid was given John to drink, while from the second potion a poultice was formed and applied to the wound. Watching him at work, I found myself contemplating yet a new mystery: how had the old *mebaqqer* detected the break in the Baptizer's flesh? "You have been wounded, John," were his words—but had not the wound been covered by the Holy Man's tunic? Was it possible the Baptizer had removed the garment, say earlier in the evening or afternoon, possibly affording the visitors a prior glimpse of the broken skin upon his chest? Perhaps, but I had no memory of it. It was simply another mystery out of the veritable bouquet of mysteries the evening had handed us.

As John passively accepted the healer's ministrations, Hilkiah waxed volubly over the evils of the *Kittim*, but at last, the tirade seemed to collapse of its own weight. At some point, the child Gabriel, who had fallen asleep in Perpetua's lap, awakened and turned his gorgeous eyes on the once-more-crackling fire. To his sweet, angelic face, Perpetua pressed a kiss. "So what *is* going to happen in the future? What *do* the stars tell you?" she asked.

Hilkiah's reply was aloof. "Think not of the future. It is more important to know the time you are in now."

"I do not understand," said Thomas. "What is the time we are in now?"

"We have come to the end of the old age. Many changes are in store."

"It is now the dawn of the new age"—this spoken by Simon Magus, who seemed to effortlessly weave together the domestic strains of the night. "We have entered the time of the fishes."

"It is more than the time of the fishes." The Baptizer replaced his tunic. "It is the time when darkness will return to its regions and a poor fisherman will call out to those who hunger and thirst for righteousness and gather them together."

The words were opaque, yet it seemed to me John, the wild man of this estranged, wild country, had climbed to the top of his own mountain of dark judgment. In doing so, curiously, he had looked out upon light's regions whereupon he had discovered what is eminently worth discovering—how to press his way forward in way not of iron.

As for the astrologers of the *Nozrei ha-brit*, they stayed one night only, hastening themselves onto the *Yam ha Melah* next morning. In the early sunlight hours, the Holy Man emerged from his tent to see them off, yet it was the now-embarking *mebaqqer* who became the giver of parting advice.

"Watch well your back, for you are in grave danger, John. I have looked at the stars and the future does not augur well for you."

"It matters not if I die now, Hilkiah, for the waters of the spring have already begun to flow."

But the *mebaqqer* was not pacified. "Give all this up, John! You waste your words on those who have no ears to hear; I see no reason why you continue with this!"

"Faith and truth are advancing the world over, but it is a slow process. That's what you have always failed to understand, Hilkiah. *Panta rei*, all flows, as our Greek brothers say. The wicks shift. You, a watcher of the stars, should know that better than anyone."

"The Gentiles are not our brothers. You will rue your actions one day, John, and that day is not long off. The *Kittim* wish only to conquer and kill."

"When the table is prepared, is not the priest the first to stretch out his hand to bless the first fruits? There is a harvest waiting to be gathered and one to gather it."

"You flood the heavens with your words, John! A *king* as would be!—but what *kind* of king? A king first and foremost destroys his enemies. The *Kittim* are the enemies of all, John. And they will one day fall prey to a terrible anguish, with all of their wise men swallowed up by the howling seas!" And with that, the old sage pivoted as he and his young companions set off. After but a dozen paces, however, he turned once more, "If the soldiers come, make your way south to us, John! King Herod owed us a debt, and his son will not attack our settlements. Come to us. You will find safety with us."

The Baptizer merely smiled, raised his hand in farewell. Then they were gone.

Chapter Thirty-Five

And as I say, come morning we were to be gone as well. At the moment, however, we continued our vigil before the Holy Man's fire of penance as the moon vaulted across the sky in its quest to find the dawn. That I should not be getting any sleep tonight, I had already come to accept as my fate. It was of course a long way back to Capharnaum, and we were leaving at first light, but sleep seemed impossible. "It is the Spirit of Truth that you really seek, and the One who brings the Spirit with him." The Baptizer's voice had grown uncharacteristically soft now.

"This man you speak of, Master, is he the Messiah from God?" asked Andrew.

"Nowadays," my brother interjected, "people look for a Messiah everywhere, in this place, in that place, there have been those who claimed to be him and were not. As for me, I am tired of it all, for it is all mere words. Words that borrow and never repay."

"It is not words, or even deeds you need to look for, but Light." The Holy Man gazed, not at any one of us, but into the fire, much as if sitting alone talking to himself. "Those who await a man of war will be disappointed, for that is not what this One is about. He is about teaching the world to love, and he brings the Light of a glass reflecting the sun, the Light of a dove singing its praises to the morning."

"You sound as if you know him," said Other James, "almost as if you've *met* him."

"I have. He has been to this camp."

"No!" we chimed in unison. "When?"

The Baptizer raised his eyes from the fire, turned to Andrew, "You were here that day, Andrew—remember?" Everyone now looked at Peter's brother. "Think hard."

"Do you mean..." stammered Andrew, "—that man! The one the dove came down and landed upon that day?" The Baptizer was silent as Peter's brother pursued, "*He* is the one—the one of which you speak?"

"The Spirit is in-breathing and out-breathing, Andrew. He will show it to you. He will make it come to life for you. Walk with him. He will lead you on the pathway to peace."

"Who is this man?" asked Thomas. "Is he here in your camp now? Can we meet him?"

"Oh no. He's not here now."

Thomas, expecting further clarification, frowned when none came. "Teacher," said Other James, "those astrologers—how is it that the wind was made to do what it did? You declined to speak of this when I asked you of it before; is it possible you would explain it to us now?" Still plagued by the mystery, the artist stared across the dancing flames into the Holy Man's face.

John seemed lost in thought but at last said, "It is the pronunciation of the Holy Name, Adonai. Although there are many names for the Holy One. One name is four letters long; another is 22 letters. The latter I suspect is the one Hilkiah called upon. But there are others besides. There is the 42-letter name. There is even one utterly stupendous name that is in 72 parts of three letters each, and which supposedly Moses used to part the waters of the Red Sea, though no one, not even Hilkiah, knows how to pronounce it any longer. The knowledge has been lost."

"You mean merely by pronouncing this name—the *wind* was made to blow?"

John's booming laughter returned momentarily, "The blowing of the wind was inconsequential; what Hilkiah was trying to do was to see into the *pleroma*, and in doing so he was able to sense the wound upon my chest, but he had no control over the wind other than that it simply happened in the course of his calling upon the name."

A hundred questions followed this, but the Baptizer, it seemed, had said all he intended saying. The sun was coming up. Despite a night without sleep, I wasn't tired. In fact, I felt buoyant, optimistic, as we prepared to leave, yet discord was soon in the air, and it broke out between Andrew and his teacher. The brother of Peter had all along intended remaining here in service to John, but in this desire he was firmly rebuffed. To no avail did Andrew appeal for the Baptizer to change his mind. With a brusqueness of manner that bordered upon rudeness, the Holy Man made clear his preferences: he wanted Andrew gone. Peter's brother did not take it well, but it was Perpetua who voiced the concerns I think we all were feeling: "I fear for you, *Abba*."

"Fear not, for there is a kingdom of heaven on earth where treasures are stored up like the forms of God. To enter it you must seek the narrow gate. *Always* seek the narrow gate."

And with that we struck out for home.

Chapter Thirty-Six

As anticipated, during our return trip, my brother James broke off and traveled to Bethsaida, for his heart, as I say, had become deeply bound to the young woman, Abigail. I in fact fully expected the two would marry. His parting words to us were brief, in such haste was he to be off; the rest of us bade him a safe journey to Bethsaida, and then we pressed on homeward to Capharnaum.

It was to be some days before Jesus (for it was indeed he the Baptizer had spoken of) would turn up on the shore of Gennesaret, and even when he did, we still, rather densely, did not make the connection. This would require a well-timed prod from Andrew. Even after I began hearing of a man named "Jesus" going through some of the towns and villages, I still did not make the connection to the youth I had met years ago in that carpenter's shop in Nazareth, a failure which persisted, incredibly, even after I heard him spoken of at one point as "Jesus of Nazareth." But then it was a fairly common name, Jesus, and I had yet to cross any divides of the mind, or come to understand the tracks of daylight over the horizon.

As expected, James and Abigail indeed wed. Zebedee restored and repaired one of the rooms in our home for the couple to move into, a work he performed with a great deal of methodical, handcrafted tenderness. It was a tenderness which spoke volumes, in a way he had never been able to communicate with words, of his love for his eldest son. An exceptionally self-assured woman, Abigail, for her own part, settled easily into life as a fisherman's wife, and everyone said James had chosen well. But if the marriage was something to rejoice about, and it was, the same could not be said of the fishing. For in these days, Gennesaret took, rather resolutely, to one of its more fickle moods. It may have been the "time of the fishes," in the sidereal words of Simon Magus, but very few fish were landing in our nets. Long days and nights we toiled, with little to show for our efforts. Even the warm waters of the *Heptapegon*, normally so abundant, were empty and lean.

"I have never seen it this bad. It is as if the very waters themselves are drying up," said Peter when we had taken consolation one night at one of the inns.

"Perhaps the fish have all swum to Egypt," offered James glumly. The inn where we were sitting was close to Peter's house, and an aromatic wine rested on the table before us. The two wives, Abigail and Perpetua, who had become natural allies, divided a loaf of bread as the innkeeper hovered nearby, inquiring if there was anything else we needed; he was a relative of Perpetua's who sympathized with our scarcity of catch, as well he might, for the majority of his customers were fishermen who were in identical straits as ourselves.

"I ran into Philip last week in Bethsaida," said James when the innkeeper had gone. "His days are spent increasingly in the company of the Zealots."

"When do they plan invading Rome?" quipped Peter morosely.

"Probably never." James offered up a knowing smile. "But something apparently is stirring in Gamla, where of course the *Sicarii* have always been strong."

"It is the talk of fools! That is all it ever is."

Other James had also joined us this evening, as had Thomas, who had elected to abide for a time in Capharnaum, even as Thaddaeus and his young son, Gabriel, had journeyed on to Tyre. "You know," Other James lowered his voice, "sometimes I think I can almost *taste* the freedom our land would know were we ever actually to rid ourselves of these Romans." The comment was not without its measure of irony; Other James' brother, Matthew, as we all knew, worked for the chief tax collector, next to the soldiers, the most visible symbol of our subjugation.

"What do you think about this Messiah the Baptizer says is to come?" Thomas inquired with a half-grin.

The comment had been put to Other James, but it was my brother who answered. "The Baptizer seemed pretty sure about it. Maybe he will prove right. Who knows?" James shrugged.

"He will have a long line of Anointed Ones to stand in," Thomas pointed out humorously.

"I wonder how the Romans would react if he *did* come," said Other James, ignoring the Tyrian's somewhat irreverent remark. "If he is truly anointed by God one would have to wonder—would they even be able to *stop* him?"

Peter gave an exaggerated yawn. "God has gone to sleep, as I must soon as well." Whatever glimmer of the eternal the Baptizer had tried to inculcate in us, Peter had not taken much of it with him. Since returning to Capharnaum he had reverted very much to his old churlishly rough edges.

"God in his glory cannot fail those who abide by his laws, or at least one would like to suppose so." Other James was growing increasingly annoyed with the direction the conversation was taking. "Would the Baptizer have told us of his coming if he were not reasonably certain? I think not!"

"Your faith in the Baptizer is touching. As for me, I've had it up to here with so-called 'wise seers.' I've got a brother who won't lend a hand on the boat because he's too busy contemplating the mysteries of heaven. All I can say is spare me. I mean God bless the Baptizer; he's a nice man; but what does it all mean?" Peter spread his hands apart as if to say it meant nothing. "Show me a 'wise seer' who can put fish in my nets and I might listen to what he has to say."

"You ask too much, Peter. Nobody can put fish in your nets but you."

"Well, I think the Baptizer was a dear man," said Perpetua "And I'm glad we went."

"Yes. And as to whatever doings the *Sicarii* be about—" Other James shrugged—"All I can say is it would be nice to see freedom come and the Romans leave, Messiah or no."

"From the talk I hear from Philip, there may be many who would be willing to fight at his side if the Messiah were to come," said James.

"'Fighting?'" Perpetua retorted. "You are *confused*, I think, about the one spoken of. Remember John's words—those who look for a warrior will be disappointed. Men! Why is it all of you are always ready to solve things with war and killing? Me, I am a woman, and I say there has been enough bloodshed; the time has come for a different way, and that is why I found the Baptizer so dear."

Thomas flashed a quizzical smile. "Do you think it's possible to make the wind blow by saying the name of God?"

"Who knows?" My brother grinned.

"No!" Peter adjudicated the matter firmly. "It is not!"

"Then how did it happen?" Other James demanded with a measure of petulance.

"It was a coincidence! The wind simply blew when it blew. That is all." Peter rose abruptly. "I've had enough wine. I'm going home to get some sleep!"

Chapter Thirty-Seven

W	e all, in fact, retired to our homes, but for those of us who made our lives on Galilee's great inland sea, our sleep was not long. With the moon still high in the sky, we rose and headed for our boats. Through the remaining hours of night we worked, throwing our nets to the indefatigable currents, drawing them back through the portals of darkness, and grieving for what was not there. On and on we toiled, but our luck in no way changed; the lake had become like a burnt seed.

Zebedee was still the master of our boat and crew, yet he was growing older now, his hair having become gray to a quite fair degree, and the long hours were taking a toll on him. His arrogance had grown somewhat subdued, his gaze seemingly not so hard. This was not to say his customary rancor was completely gone and dried away. It wasn't. Yet those of us who knew Zebedee well, who had tread the rivers of callousness that flowed from his breast, could sense his oppression of spirit. Our weeks in the shadows of lean uncertainty were wearing him down; they were wearing us all down for that matter. Our luck had to change soon, but it didn't. Not that night anyway.

The world was awash in noonday sun when we made our way, empty-handed, back to that Capharnaum shore. Arriving there, I noticed an assembly of people hunkered together not far from the water's edge; at first, they seemed partaking of nothing more than the whistling, incoherent harmonies of the sea winds, but then I noticed one and all appeared to give ear to a lone orator seated at their center. The overhead clouds parted as I watched, at which point a flame of sunlight fell upon his shoulders. His listeners leaned forward. Curious, I drew closer.

"You know the commandments," said the man in the center of the circle. "Do not commit adultery. Do not kill. Do not steal. Do not bear false witness. Honor your father and mother."

"Master, all these things I have observed since my youth."

"Yes, but there is one thing you lack. Sell everything you own, give the money to the poor, then you shall have treasure in heaven. And then come and follow me."

I tried to fathom the almost majestic audacity required to produce such a demand, but it eluded me. Even at that level of whimsicality, there was more. The poor, he went on, were blessed by God, and as he offered this curious assertion his voice took on an efferent quality, as if extending invitation to the lowliest and most destitute of peasants who might stumble along that shore and join him.

"Whoever heard of the poor being *blessed?*" grumbled Peter, who had wandered over as well. Never one for mourning or lamenting over a world sown so thoroughly full of thorns and thistles—this was Peter. Yet in a sense, one could not argue with him, at least on this point. The poor's being "blessed by God" was a queer notion. There were of course those who felt varying measures of sympathy for the poor, some even who championed their cause, but to say the poor were blessed by God? It was a strange manner of thinking. For most people, it was the rich who were blessed by God, while the poor were simply—*poor.* The man who had offered up this simplistic-but-edifying notion to the contrary was about thirty years of age; he wore a faded tunic, his face lean and narrow, yet with a weathered quality, as if to suggest that the greatest heart is the one moved most by compassion, and that that which ripens slowly is the sweetest. His words, moreover, were being given consideration beyond all measure, for the crowd about him grew until it became impossible for all to hear. Girdled by the sea on one side and those pressing closer to hear on the other, the man in the faded tunic inquired of Peter if he might stand in his boat. I fully expected Peter would send him on his way with a sharp retort, but to my surprise, my friend merely shrugged, offered him a seat, and pushed a short ways out into the shallow water. Here, from the stern of the vessel, he continued to pour forth that curious homage to the poor, along with other peculiar utterances, all of it seeming to rise, and rise, all the way to the summit of human destiny, where his words strode the heavens in peace. The poor blessed by God! *Khayla!* A harmoniously born spirit! And was he not thought-surpassing in his extolling of that spirit! Yet at length it all came to a light-refracting end. Concluding his remarks to the crowd, he turned to Peter and urged, with a rather ungainly and sackcloth sort of royalty, "Launch out into the deeper water and cast out your nets."

But Peter had grown impatient. "Nay! Along with you! You've had your set-down in my boat. Now be on your way!"

"You will not cast out the nets?"

"No use is there in it," Peter grumbled. "We have toiled all night with nothing to show for our troubles."

"Try it anyway," the man coaxed, his weathered face parting in a smile.

For a moment, Simon Peter seemed infuriated, but then, with a cautious dignity, he relented, taking up the oar and pushing out just past the shoals; over the side went the circular trammel net, the net which so often had returned to us empty of late. I had to agree with Peter. No use was there in this. But of course the man old in days, if he is wise, will not hesitate to ask a small child about the place of life. A moment later, the son of Jonah signaled frantically to the rest of us for help; the net was literally bursting with fish!

Quickly James and I raced to Peter's aid. It took all three of us to pull the trammel out of the water. Inside were enough fish to fill the vessel to the bowlines! Astonishment beyond words. Peter gazed upon Jesus, for indeed it was he, and hastily offered up a humble propitiation to the gods: "Master, go away from me, for I'm a sinful man!" The seaside wonder-worker in the faded tunic seemed to take this as a literal command and an instant later was out of the boat, striding along the shore. Dumbstruck, we stared agape...but then I abandoned the boat as well, in hot pursuit—too late, however, for by this time the crowd on shore had swelled to an even greater number, and in the knotted mass of humanity I lost sight of him. In the confusion, I stumbled, rather dyspeptically, upon Andrew. "I see you *found* him!" said he.

"No, I *lost* him" is what I almost sputtered in reply, but of course I realized his words, in any avenue of context, made no sense; instead I shouted, "What are you talking about—found who!?"

"Him!" Andrew pointed; at precisely this moment the crowd parted, briefly, but long enough for me to catch a glimpse of a man's back. A man in an old faded tunic. "It is he! The one the dove came down upon that day!"

I was incapable of responding, yea, incapable of any speech at all. I could but stand with eyes bulging, even as Peter's brother galloped off in pursuit. It was at this point I felt, rather than saw, Peter and James catch up with me, yet even then was incapable of hailing or greeting them, incapable of performing even the paltry service of a watchman calling out in the night. But if my voice was lost to me, my legs were not, and suddenly, as if in repentance for stupidity, they were commanding me forward. Peter, James, and I, began to trail Andrew, who in turn was in hot pursuit of Jesus, and we became like a flock of pelicans in the desert, all following one upon another.

Through the choppy and hale wind, so strong that it was itself a wind of brightness and glory, we followed that retreating back as it slung itself along, followed it on our stampeding feet, while harboring something in our hearts, a retrofitted urgency that turned us suddenly into light vestures, greater than the world around us. On we went, driven by a compelling need, yearning for the substantial as well as the insubstantial, the absurd and the sensible, until at last that face, that weathered face with its comfortable tangle of emotions, turned itself around, gazed back at Andrew, while inquiring most companionably: "What is it you seek?"

Andrew stopped dead in his tracks. "Rabbi, where do you live?" At this point, arriving abreast of Andrew, we too stopped dead in our tracks.

"Come and see," he replied.

Chapter Thirty-Eight

Far down a wash we walked, along a sandy trail leading past an ancient menhir, out beyond a deserted quay—to a place where he was alone with God. Here a grebe modulated its voice and gave a mournful call as we stepped through the high couch grass. An abandoned fishing boat camped on its side served as his only shelter from the elements that we could see, yet there could have been cupbearers and courtiers awaiting his beck and call. About him was a child's life and vigor, coupled, curiously, with an old-age-like fortitude, which seemed neither aggrieved nor made joyous over vicissitudes of fate and harmony.

We were perhaps a mile away from Capharnaum, but we may as well have been somewhere else entirely, a place as eternal and million-toned as the far side of the sun. I could hear the roaring of the sea, and a gong sounded somewhere far off in the distance; all that was visible to me, however, was the sun, waxing great, a carouse across the great palaestra of the sky, but it was an inner sun, pouring into my heart.

"It is a long way out here." Peter gave an appraising glance to the basalt-bundled earth, where, a few cubits away, a wandering hyrax had left the tracks of its passage.

"An ass which turns a millstone does a hundred miles walking. When it is loosed, it finds it is still in the same place." Jesus spoke in a dismissive manner, as if he'd no more concern over our present remoteness than might a rock-splitter over a stray pebble. Moreover, it was as if the world were something more divine than the cumulative total of its separate parts, and that while a mere blade of grass might seem insignificant, it might also buttress the heavens.

"Master, what did you mean when you said the poor were blessed by God?" inquired Andrew.

He picked up a pebble, juggled it in his palm before replying, "There will come shame one day upon those who are secure in things which do not last, and upon they who hope in the flesh, and in the prison that will perish. For those, their hope is based upon the world, and their god is this present life; they are destroying their souls with the wheel that turns in their minds."

I had of course by this time realized he was the same Jesus I had met years before in that carpenter's shop in Nazareth, then so young and sturdy and nimble, grown now into a man. He, as well, remembered, for as we walked out here, I had caught, not so much a flash of recognition, more like a knowing remembrance, a grain-ripened understanding, and in that moment, that identical smile he had favored me with years before had reappeared on his face, reappeared as if our last meeting had been only yesterday and he were inquiring, "Where have you been?"

"For those who cannot see and have not ears to hear, the poison and blows of their enemies are a delight; they have surrendered their freedom to slavery and their minds to foolishness, prisoners bound in caves, laughing and rejoicing in their mad laughter; in them darkness rises like light. But know this, that in light the Father's one desire acts with ours. It always has, eternally. Even so..." and here he sighed, a long, expansive, lugsail of a sigh, "even so...it is easier for a camel to get through the eye of a needle than for a rich man to enter heaven; and because of this, the poor are blessed by God."

Chapter Thirty-Nine

And so it began. The months of the roses of Jericho, which is to say summer. Both the finite and the infinite are the creation of God, and that's what overtook us, a summer of the finite as well as the infinite. Ah, but there was one shadow upon that summer, the shadow of the hand of my father, that became necessary for me to counter in my own way. Even in those early days, they who were without ears to hear were not shy in flaunting their truculence and disapproval of the Nazarene. For such persons, and Zebedee was one of them, anything this ripe-fruited tree might put forth, no matter how amazing or wonderful, was but evidence of malign intent. It has of course been many years, and my father has long since gone to his final passage, but mostly what I remember about those days is a fractiousness that grew upon him whenever Jesus was around. He was getting on in years, and the grayer and grayer he became, the more he propounded his writ of *exigi facias* upon the world and just about everyone in it. From his childhood he had drunk the *canicula* of life, and little patience did he have for matters beyond his understanding; in such regions lurked hostile and vagrant forces. For Father, truth resided in the spoils of war. This was Zebedee, and toward Jesus, as I say, he exhibited an almost visceral antipathy. *Go down one of you, the enemy of the other.* I, on the other hand, was drawn toward a different truth. I had met the Baptizer. He had stirred a sumptuous broth, and poured that broth into the willing bowl of my heart, and as a result, I had become, in many respects, a mustard seed in the palm of the Fisher of Great Life, waiting to be planted in the ground. And so it came about that I moved out of my father's house entirely that summer, took my few things, and moved into Peter's.

But are there not gardens beneath which rivers flow? Our days became as the shape of water on the hand of Zaratust, for the prodigy Yeshua had performed with the fish repeated itself many different times, in many different ways. In Bethsaida he healed a blind man; in Chorazin a girl was lifted from a malaise of blood sputum; and in Capharnaum a man with a crippled and useless hand was rendered whole, which things, wonderful as they may be, seemed to earn for the Nazarene nothing but more wrath from the maligners and malingerers. He was accused of healing on the Sabbath, which he in fact did. But the charge became a weapon used against him by liars and hypocrites, often those very same people most infuriated by the parables he told.

He was also tall and muscular, though it was not that redoubtably imposing muscularity found in the Greek athletes at the paelestra; it was more a muscularity of stamina, carrying him to walk great distances. And something else: though people were drawn to him, at first by hundreds, later by the thousands, he was paradoxically given over to solitude much of the time. "Many who are first will become last," he said to me one day. "Recognize what is in your sight, and that which is hidden will become plain to you." What was in sight, he tried to make me to understand, was nothing less than the kingdom of God, but the kingdom wasn't only in the heavens; it was on earth, and even, quite literally, inside us, and if you had faith even as large as a mustard seed you could make your way to it, knock, and open that door. Because God wanted us to open it. Because he yearned for our love. The Nazarene explained this yearning thusly: "Just as a person who is not known to other people wants them to know him and love him, so it also is with the Father."

We began to walk with him. Everywhere. Peter, Andrew, James, my brother's wife Abby, Other James, Thomas—and when we got to Bethsaida, Philip too joined us. He was married now and had a child, and along with us came his wife and small daughter, as well as his friend Simon, of the *Sicarii* band from Gamla. An accomplished player of the cithra was this Simon, who went everywhere with that instrument slung over his shoulder...as we soon discovered; others came along on that walking journey as well, some as disciples, some merely as givers or takers of succor, but all found delight in the momentarily leveled piece of ground that the Nazarene's words seemed ever able to carve out of the chaos of life. In Bethsaida, for instance, where we had met up with Philip and his family, we encountered Rabbi Hamul. Like my father, the rabbi was aging in years, and I would have thought him quite averse to this new teaching. Much to my surprise, however, he warmed to it, and that was the peculiar thing about our teachers and doctors of the law, for not all of them were against Jesus. Rabbi Hamul said the *Shema*, smiled upon us, and wished us well.

But let me tell you of what happened with Matthew, the brother of Other James, for it was the most unexpected turnaround of all. A chance encounter one day resulted in an invitation for Jesus to dine at his house. The Nazarene gratefully accepted, although the charge of consorting with tax collectors and "prostitutes" became his inescapable reward for entering the house in question, yet it seems not to have mattered. Either to Jesus or Matthew. By all accounts, the dinner was enjoyable for one and all. The "prostitutes" in question, of course, were Matthew's young lady friends, of whom, in the main, were three: Elisheba, whom Matthew was quite serious about and planned marrying, a winsome, blossomy girl with a sensuous radiance, who seemed thoroughly devoted to him; and then there were Dinah and Tirzah, her two closest friends. The latter especially became an ardent and devoted follower of Jesus, and a rare individual indeed. Decidedly a cut out of the ordinary, Tirzah not only was enchanting to look at, but had been raised in Rome and could fluently speak the languages of the Greeks and the Romans, as well as the common Aramaic of the Jews. It was a skill that had proven useful to the local Roman praetor, who had employed her as a translator, in which capacity she had met Matthew. As for Jesus' coming to dinner that night, the evening seems to have turned into an affair of set-aside predispositions, as well as, surprisingly, some considerable gaiety and mirth, but the most astonishing part of all is what followed the next day, for suddenly and without warning Matthew resigned his position as tax collector, an office from which he had derived a respectable income. But in a moment it was gone. A remarkable turnabout, to say the least, and no one had been more surprised, or pleased, than his brother, Other James.

Lachma. It is the Aramaic word for "bread"—but it can also be interpreted as "understanding," for it is a word rich in meaning. Know this, my hungrily serene Quintus. God opens his bosom to all, pouring out his *lachma*, this bread of understanding, to those who seek, ask, and knock, and I think it was this which Matthew came to realize that evening that Jesus spent at his house. Of course make no mistake, what God pours out for his sons, he also pours out for his daughters, which brings me back to the woman, Tirzah, for I have no doubt she had procured for herself, somewhere along the way, a measure of that divine bread. I have already mentioned her adeptness with languages, but having been educated in Rome, she was also well versed of the poets, could produce written discourses on one subject or another, and had even studied geometry. The latter, she insisted, had been given to the Greeks by the Egyptians, who had invented it for purpose of measuring their lands during the Nile's flood times, which is perhaps neither here nor there. My only point in mentioning it is to illustrate that she was learned in so many, many things. Now it was extremely rare, for all the attempts at uplifting girls made by tender and caring souls such as my mother, encountering a woman in who was accumulated an apportionment of knowledge greater than that held by most men. In terms of followers of Jesus, however, Tirzah wasn't unique. On the contrary. It was not unusual for people with rare and wonderful gifts to simply show up. In fact, it seemed to happen wherever he went, but in Tirzah's case there was more, for this woman who had adorned herself in the robes of knowledge was to end up offering a special gift. Wholly of her own accord, she began carrying about books and scrolls upon which she proceeded to record events, including a great many of his sayings, an undertaking which became a matter of some diligence for her as we traveled about; a fragment of this she would snatch, another of that, as she pursued not only the light the Nazarene held forth, but also, I rather think, something deep within herself. *I am the swallow, I am the swallow, the scorpion, the daughter of Ra.* In a way, she was that indeed. That and more. An admixture of fire and cold, light and dark, as she fought her way into the pronaos of her devotion to the Nazarene, a devotion which in the end proved, in a strange and sad way, almost noetic.

So many joys, passions, sorrows, delights—all of it fell our way as we traveled. Capharnaum to Bethsaida. The *Via Maris* to the kingdom of heaven. And back again. How many trees do you create when the sap is running throughout the entire land? Take Bethsaida for instance. During a return trip there late in the summer we discovered Nathanael staying at the house of Philip, and what a delight, for not since before our journey to the Baptizer's camp, and well before Jesus showed up, had we seen him, this mainly being due to his occupation of late in service to a rich man on the other side of the lake. But here he was now, long lost friend and brother of prevailing peace!

"Upon my word!" exclaimed Jesus when the two were introduced. "An Israelite without guile."

"You seem to know me," replied the gentle giant, puzzled.

"I saw you earlier when Philip called out to you under the fig tree."

It was that odd caress of the eternal to which we were growing accustomed in all doings where the Nazarene was concerned.

"The odd thing about it," Nathanael confided in me later, "is I really *had* been sitting under a fig tree earlier that day, and Philip at one point really *did* call out to me."

Chapter Forty

I had brought along a great deal of food packed into a jute sack. The sack was slung over my shoulder, and others were similarly burdened, some with two or more sacks. A thousand or more people were expected to show up, and we had been told to prepare for a long outing. It had been Jesus' custom to speak in the synagogues, but the numbers had grown to where this was no longer possible, and that is how we came to be climbing that hill above Bethsaida that day with the songs of bluebirds ringing in our ears and the scent of black aloe and frankincense in the air. In essence, the outdoors had become our synagogue. It was our last day in Gaulanitis—we were returning to Capharnaum tomorrow—and the hilltop we had chosen lay just beyond town, with the Jordan and its feathery vegetation just visible in the distance.

Dear Quintus, incomparable is the offering of life, and beyond contemplation the great diversity of that life. In the audience that day were young and old, men and women, weavers and sandal makers, shearers and tanners, fishermen and tillers of the soil; there even was a trickling of *Sicarii*, for a group of them had come down from the camel's hump of Gamla. It was a *locus communis*, that hill, a hill of walking sticks and sunshades, where the primal power of the earth could be felt as much in the spreading boughs of the terebinth as in the cry of a baby. It could also be felt in Jesus' words. Something about that day calls out to me even now, the way it formed a support for the leafy branches of manumission, a day full of *lachma*, that bread of understanding, as I've no doubt the Nazarene knew full well it would be. The poor, as he always asserted, were blessed by God, and that was how it began; but then also blessed, he said, were the meek, the hungry, the merciful, the mournful, and the peacemakers, and what then poured from his mouth was a discourse of almost hyperboreal resplendence. "Show me the stone that the builders have rejected. That one is the cornerstone." I am able to recount much of what he said that day because of the written record left by Tirzah. Her words, or more precisely his, reached a magnificent height on that occasion, soaring like a bird with wings, soaring like Grace's Athena. Since I long ago memorized to heart that tract she left us, I will simply recount some of it for you here, Quintus:

"Lay not up for yourselves treasures on earth," he said, "where moth and rust corrupt, and where thieves may break in and steal."

And this:

"Instead lay treasures in heaven, for where your treasure is, there will your heart be also. Unless you are more righteous than the scribes and Pharisees you will not be able to enter the kingdom of heaven. No one can serve two masters: either he will hate the one and love the other, or hold to one and despise the other. You cannot serve God and money. Therefore, what I say to you is this—take no thought for your life, or what you shall eat or drink; or for your body or what you will put on it. For is life not more than food? And is the body not more than clothing? I say to you: behold the birds of the air! They neither sow, reap, nor gather into barns. But doesn't your heavenly Father feed them and care for them? And will he not do the same for you?"

This also:

"And look at the lilies of the field, how they grow! They don't toil! They don't spin wool into clothing! And yet even Solomon in all his glory was not arrayed as they are! And if God so clothes them, will he not do the same for you? So endeavor not to be of such little faith. Do not worry yourselves over such things as 'What shall we eat?' or 'What shall we drink?' or 'How shall we be clothed?' For your Father knows you have need of these things. Instead, seek the kingdom of heaven. Ask and the kingdom will be given to you; seek and you will find it; knock and the door shall be opened. For all who ask receive; and they that seek will find; and to those who knock, the gate to the kingdom will be opened."

And this as well:

"You have heard it said, 'Do not commit murder,' but I say to you whoever is angry with his brother without cause is in danger of judgment. You have heard it said, 'Do not commit adultery,' but I say that whoever looks upon a woman with lust has already committed adultery with her in his heart. You have heard it said, 'Love your neighbor and hate your enemy.' But I say to you *love your enemies*, bless them that curse you, do good to them that hate you, and pray for them which spitefully use you. You have heard it said, 'an eye for an eye.' But I say to you, do not resist an evildoer, and if someone strikes you on the cheek, turn to him the other also, and if someone asks for your coat, give him your cloak as well. Therefore, and most especially, do to others what you would have them do to you, for this is the law and the prophets."

There was much more besides. He went on like that for more than two hours. I'm not sure how much of what he said was taken to heart by those present, or whether the *Sicarii*—O yes! They in particular—could in any way have been favorably disposed to that part about loving your enemies. On the other hand, I would not want to imply that they who sought to free Israel through the shedding of blood, including the blood of Jews, had anything specifically *against* the Nazarene, for that was not the case either. Much of what he said, about the Pharisees for instance, the *Sicarii* were in wholehearted accord with. Yeshua after all had not been the first to call the Pharisees hypocrites and would not be the last. Moreover, one Zealot, as I mentioned, had even begun to sojourn amongst us, but Simon was an exception to the rule. In the end, we were never joined to any significant degree by they of the curved dagger who would one day place their shields in a row against the Romans.

But there is one aspect to all this, Quintus, I feel I have not explained adequately, and that is that part about loving your enemies. Much about this was very similar to the assertion about the poor being blessed by God. In other words, it was a difficult concept for people to grasp. Monumental shifts were required, not only in the way you viewed the world and just about everything in it, but also in the way you viewed yourself. One simply did not, as a matter of course, love one's enemies. Rather, one hated one's enemies while reserving love and favor for one's friends. To believe otherwise demanded a drastic alteration of the mind, an alteration even of sight, sound, and the senses; you must in fact learn to dismantle the external senses and learn to sense with the heart and mind. Some were ready to make such leaps, or at least attempt them; others were not.

But as I say, that day on that hilltop stands out in my memory. The discourse Jesus delivered up was as the golden apple of the Hesperides, and each of us took a piece of that apple, and even the *Sicarii*, I dare say, could taste clearly of its sweetness, and Tirzah filled up a good portion of an entire scroll with her writing.

We stayed at Philip's house that night, and the following day made our way to the quay at the mouth of the river where it emptied into Genneseret.

We were to depart for Capharaum in two boats. A great deal of gear, much of it roped together in bundles, was stacked upon the quay and required loading into the two vessels. A man who happened to be present at the time offered some most welcomed assistance, in the course of which he informed us he had heard Jesus' talk the previous day, a talk which had been "strewn with magnificence," as he put it. He was exceedingly polite, this as he willingly placed his shoulder to the heaviest of loads. Finally, with our efforts concluded and our boats loaded, he inquired if he might sail with us to Capharnaum. We had no objections. Urgent business in Capharnaum required his immediate attention, he added by way of explanation, and again we assured him we didn't mind.

"What is your name, stranger?" asked Philip.

Deftly the man extended a hand. "Judas—Judas Iscariot."

"Welcome Judas, it is nice to meet you," said Philip.

Other James, of a more cautious bent, gave the newcomer a filmy glance, not offering to take his hand. Even so, I doubt Other James could have anticipated the havoc that was to be wrought upon us by this man. None of us could have. What we didn't know then, but found out later, was that Iscariot had formerly served as a Temple scribe but had been dismissed from his position, after which he had gravitated over to the *Sicarii*; after a time in the company of the dagger men, however, he had been cast off from these moorings as well. Not unlike Tirzah, he was highly schooled and learned, but despite his learning, and despite all his elaborate civilities, there was an inner maliciousness about him. I'm reminded of these things when I think of the silent proclamations laid down by shadows astir before dawn, or of how the darnel takes root in the plowed field. I suppose, however, none of this could have been foreseen that day.

Matthew showed up next, followed by Tirzah, carrying, as was her custom, a basket of scrolls. She was lovely enough to arouse the almighty sun, and as she handed her basket to Philip, Judas Iscariot's gaze fell on her appreciatively, roaming up and down the length of her body as she settled herself nimbly in the boat. The rest of us boarded also, whereupon we cast off, coasting lazily downriver, merging with Gennesaret and picking up a strong wind. To our home shore it took us in due course.

I suppose Judas finished whatever business he had in Capharnaum; he never did say what it was, and maybe he simply found our peristyles and domains pleasing and maybe that is why he decided to linger. But measures and seasons bind us with their fetters, much as they do with angels, demons, and the gods of heaven no less, and five days later when we departed Capharnaum, once again by boat, Judas Iscariot, rather with the fusibility of wax, was still with us.

Chapter Forty-One

We crossed from one side of Gennesaret to the other and back again, as many times as there were eternal secrets in the hearts of naked children. The crowds eventually grew vast; people with fevers, boils, and other misfortunes came to us, materializing out of their gray obscurity, as they sought the Nazarene out for healing and a stripling of pity. Even in those early days, there was talk of making Jesus king, not that kingship was something he wanted. Never once in all the time I knew him did I hear him proclaim himself a messiah or king. Neither did he claim to be the "son of God," other than in the general sense, which is to say in the sense that we all, every one of us, are children of God. Instead he was, in his own words, *bar d'nasha*, the "son of man." It was the only claim to rank or sovereignty I ever heard him make, and it was not really that at all, for in calling himself this he was essentially saying he was one of us, he was *of* us, we were of him, and the universe freely laid upon each of us its blessings of *hayye d'alma*, eternal life.

I must tell you of one of our crossings of Gennesaret, for it was a day on which a quite curious incident took place. Into a single boat we were crowded, and a marvelous breeze cosseted the vessel, pushing us along at an exhilarating pace. From the northern town of Chinnereth we had set sail, bound for the more southern regions of the lake where the earth unrolled into the intuitive peace of the resumed river. A layer of clouds covered the sky, but these occasionally broke, allowing scattered groves of sunlight to spill earthward. It was near summer's end. With us was Tirzah, who as usual cut a ravishing figure; and Judas Iscariot, who seemed unable to keep his eyes off her; Thomas also, with his windsong voice and love of the sea; large-but-gentle Nathanael seated next to Thomas; Peter steering the boat with help from my brother James; Andrew, Simon, Other James, and Matthew—it was a vessel of some considerable length, but we were large in number that day, and our sheer strake was riding low in the water. Yeshua had settled in at the stern, but shortly after our departure fell into a deep sleep. From somewhere above, a sparrow, unhobbled from earth as its wings plied the solitude of the sky, called out, voicing its forlorn and holy Arcanum to the universe. Upon the waters of Gennesaret, especially the farther out from land one gets, one can feel one's bonds being loosened from this earth, much like that wayward bird above us, and so we sailed, our bow riding upon the fishes and the grandmotherly waves, until the archangels of the wind began to change substantially their song. At first, it was only a spirited buffeting, impulsive and draconian, but then the sky became eternity grown lachrymose as the clouds began to deliver moisture. Softly the drops fell at first, but before long, we were being lashed with rain. It was a fierce storm, containing about it the scent of power. Would the monster Typhon have found inspiration in its aptitude for bullying? Well he might have, for the force was that great. Smitten by winds, fisted by waves, our heavily laden vessel reeled dangerously, thrashed from right and left, as the elements maintained their assault. Incredibly, Jesus was still asleep, though someone in the rear of the boat at this point shook him urgently, "Lord, wake up, for we are in terrible danger!"

What I saw at this moment was Jesus raising himself, his face an unmolested repository of perfect calm; beholding the surface of the lake, now as uneven as a boiling spring, beholding also the boat taking on water like a hungering mendicant, he issued a sharp directive to the sky—"Be silent!"—as if skies and winds were in habit of obeying human commands. It was a shout that might have rivaled the thunder—and at precisely that moment, the storm abated. *Te Deum.* The winds stilled; the clouds broke; and a pale sliver of blue shone through. "Do not be afraid," he said with a perfunctory gesture. "Storms come and go, but faith stays eternal. Just as you are in God, so he is also in you."

And that is how it happened, Quintus, exactly as I have described it. We camped that night, and for the next two, close to the Hammat Gader hot spring, with Simon the Zealot strumming his cithra as we sat before the fire. The instrument had drunk large drafts of rain, yet incredibly, the thing was still able to make music, and as Simon played, we sang an old song we knew, *The Song of the Sea.* Considering the storm we had just come through, it seemed an appropriate choice, for the Sea of Galilee had indeed sung us a song. It had also plied us with an offering of omnipotence, although this feat had been matched, if not altogether surpassed, by the Nazarene himself. Thomas seemed to find the words most of us were thinking. "Master, my mouth is wholly incapable of saying what you are like."

And that was how the summer drew to a close. The Aramaic word is *datz*. We had lived in abundance that summer. But life is ever changing. All the days grew short, and in the fall of that year, John the Baptizer was arrested.

Chapter Forty-Two

For some reason it did not occur to me, at least not right away, how the news of the Holy Man's arrest would have affected Andrew. It was only later, when I saw him grieving alone, I realized how deeply anguished he must have felt, but of course it wasn't only Andrew. The imperator of the banks of Aenon had been seized. And many were those, numbering in the tens of thousands, who had tread through his wondrous *pinacotheca* of love and penance.

We were back in Capharnaum, that village of consolation, and much were we in need of its consoling graces. "He was the very genius of *hokmah*," commented a pained and somber Perpetua as we sat in her enclosed triclinium. Several of John's disciples were present as well, still fearful, though largely recovered from the soldiers' assault upon their camp. Loose talk had begun to emerge, from here and there around Galilee, of storming Herod's fortress at Machaerus, where it was known John had been taken, although for now wiser heads seemed to prevail.

"He was Elijah and more." Yeshua raised a pair of calm, limpid eyes, gazing in turn around the room. "What did you go out to the desert to see? A reed shaken by the wind? A man clothed in fine garments like your kings and great men? Upon them are the finest raiment, yet they cannot discern the truth. So did you perhaps go to the desert to see a prophet? *Yes*, I tell you! John is great among men, but understand that those least in the kingdom of heaven are greater than he." Then, oddly, he seemed to speak directly to John, a thing not possible since the Holy Man was many miles off, locked in the dungeon of Machaerus, yet that is how it seemed, as if Jesus were somehow speaking to him face to face: "O John, you are a fisher among fishers. Your ship is not like our ship. It is not tarred over with pitch. It shines by night like the sun, and wondrous standards are unfurled above it. Our ship sails on the waters, but your ship sails between the waters. O John—*hakana ninhar nuhrakun qedam bneynasha*, let your light shine before men." He paused and resumed, once more to the rest of us, "As one candle lights another, so does the teacher pass knowledge onto the student. Whoever has ears, let them hear."

But Peter's grief-torn brother could see no profit in the contemplation of candle flames, and was, even should it mean taking up sword, vowing to attach himself to any endeavor which might lead to John's freedom. "I should never have left him that day; it was not righteous that I did so." Fleetingly I thought of the Essenes. Would a force from the *Yam ha Melah* now seek to free the Baptizer from his imprisonment, and would Andrew join them?

"What do you mean not righteous?" Peter frowned. "He *asked* you to leave."

"He didn't mean it! He wanted me to stay!"

But this prompted a tender riposte from Perpetua. "Andrew I was there that morning; I heard everything John said to you. His words were that you should leave there and come home with us to Capharnaum."

Peter too began to coax, in a voice almost as tender as his wife's, "Brother, listen to me. If you had stayed, you also could have been taken prisoner—or worse. The Baptizer knew this. This is why he sent you away."

Peter's words were likely true, but Andrew rose to his feet in anger, vowing that "this time" he would not abandon his teacher. The statement drained Peter's quickly ebbing patience. "'This time?' What do you mean 'this time'?" He was concerned, as were we all, for Andrew's safety.

"Andrew," Perpetua broke in, "he taught you, as he taught all of us, to be strong, and that understanding is one of the powers of the soul. It seems to me, Andrew, that you are not using this power."

Their entreaties, however, were spurned. "So! The trumpeters have thundered their grandiosities and the flautists have played their supine melodies! But let them know this, that God is all powerful and unceasing in his gifts. Let them know also that there are those who, in birth and bound to passions, shall never fail as Keepers of His Covenant, and that *I* am one of them!"

"You are letting your grief control your actions!" Peter was still angry, yet layered in his voice now was something I had never heard in Peter's voice before—a soul-wound of love.

"God is indeed unceasing in his gifts," Jesus broke in quietly. "But would it not be folly to mourn and pray for the seed to appear again, in order that it might again be consumed and mourned for?" The words were as a well of living water, waiting to be drunk of. But Andrew had no thirst. Glaring furiously at the Nazarene and regarding the comment as an affront, he turned and stalked from the room.

The Egyptians have a story that great Thoth cut out the sinews of Typhon and used them as lyre strings, thus teaching us how the discordant elements of the universe can be brought into harmony. Yet it is also said that Typhon struck the eye of Horus, the son of Isis and Osiris, and then proceeded to take out the eye and swallow it. *Kosmos desmoterion.* The world is a place of chains. In the end, it was decided to dispatch Andrew and Other James to Herod's palace at Machaerus to plead for the Holy Man's release, Andrew because he was so obviously in need of doing *something*, and would surely have set off on his own anyway, perhaps to court some disaster upon himself; Other James in hopes that his level-headedness would restrain Andrew from the more extreme forms of himself. But in the case of Other James, there was another, more practical, reason for packing him off to Machaerus, for this would not be his first visit there. Both he and his father had done a series of mosaic rosettes at the palace, and while it had been some time ago, quite probably someone in Herod's court would remember him. But even if this turned out to be the case, would it win the freedom of John the Baptizer? Or would they find, on announcing themselves at Machaerus, a serpent waiting to strike?

"Go with God, brother." In tight embrace Matthew clasped his brother. A tenderness most noble had settled upon the two sons of Alphaeus in the days since Matthew had quit his job as tax collector. Now, rather than an agency for tenseness and spleen, their connection as brothers had evolved into a tree whose branches supported them in mutual celebration of their common blood. Matthew seemingly had set aside his forays of courtship and pursuit of one woman after another, and now fully intended marrying Elisheba, and perhaps an even riper date to fall from that tree of brotherly divinity was that Other James had given the match his unqualified blessing. So much had changed in so short a time!

"I know that by the grace of *El Shaddai*, I shall see you again, son of my father." Other James placed a hand on his brother's shoulder.

"The hardest thing of all," Matthew replied, "is to love someone and have need of that person. Such need have I of you, my brother, and for that reason I know you will return."

Goodbyes were exchanged as well by Peter and Andrew, though considerably more reserved ones, for a wedge had come between them. Yet even so, I think both of them, even Andrew, realized the precarious nature of the journey that was about to be undertaken. At last, with farewells said, the travelers set out, a patina of blue sky fluctuating malleably between their shoulders as their footsteps carried them over the darkened stiles of the *Via Maris*. It should not be imagined any of us neglected to pray for their safe return.

Chapter Forty-Three

Having seldom been of similar accord on much of anything else, Salome and Zebedee had their differences over Jesus as well. As I believe I've mentioned, Quintus, Father had no use for the Nazarene, disliked him all the more the longer he stayed around. Jesus for the most part seemed unbothered by this; aware of my father's reputation as the thunder man, he had taken, in a mild vein of humor, to calling James and I the "sons of thunder," though rather than softening my father's heart, it seemed but to intensify his animosity. Whenever the two of them chanced to meet, Father's ill will would scarce be concealed.

As for Salome, the opposite held true. She had observed the trail of the Nazarene's procession through our lives and had found there something most pleasing to the ear and eye. Whereas everyone else had trouble making sense of such notions as the poor being blessed by God, concern for the less fortunate was a thing my mother understood readily and instinctively. The upshot was that while Zebedee thundered away about Jesus' "deceitfulness," Salome gave us money. And so by subtle grace and artistry, all in time comes to pass.

Did you know, Quintus, that while the mustard seed may be the smallest of all seeds, there is great power in it? Somewhere along the way, perhaps as a boy, Jesus had taken up a cup, discovering that the inside and the outside were one in the same, both being made by God. In making this discovery, he had then gleaned one other: that the kingdom of heaven is like a mustard seed. It is the smallest of all seeds, of course, the mustard seed, but when it falls on tilled soil, it produces a great plant that becomes a shelter for the birds of the sky. In other words, Quintus, a mustard seed may not look like much, but what it can give is quite a lot. *Detrahm l'marya Alahak men kuleh lebak*...Love the Lord God with all your heart. It is the commandment God gave to Moses, and Moses gave to the people of Israel. The mustard seed is nothing less than the narrow gate; it is the kernel of the palmito, the indivisible point, the door between the physical world and the kingdom of heaven, and that door opens both ways. In Aramaic, O wisdom-seeking Quintus, we have a word, *hayye*. It means "life," but it can also mean "life energy," and as such, it is the life force within us; as we love God, with a love so strong it becomes as a stab wound to the heart, that mustard-seed door opens and *hayye* begins to flow and move inside us. My mother, with her strong heart, had no difficulty, as I say, understanding these things, and probably for this reason was compelled to declare to Jesus one day, "I am your disciple."

And so she was, and so she became.

That is not to say Salome took the step of leaving Zebedee and beginning to travel with us. At least at this time she didn't—although later she *did*. And in so doing she would accompany us on one last sad and fateful trip to Jerusalem, but that as I say was later; for the present, she contented herself with holding the dipping ladle of coins that kept us going.

In the weeks following Andrew's and Other James' departure for the south, we journeyed from Capharnaum to Sepphoris, to Safed, to Chorazin, and back to Capharnaum again. The crowds were growing, yet in just about every place we went, we came upon people who believed Jesus was evil. If he had healed anyone, they were quite certain, it was because he had derived his powers from Beelzebub, yet conversely, there were those as well who wanted to crown him king. Never in my life, either before or since, have I encountered such wildly conflicting opinions arising over a single man. In some respects, those wanting to crown him king were every bit as misguided as they who held him as Beelzebub incarnate. An insurrection against the Romans—this, more than anything else, such men longed for. They were aggrieved Jews, who cherished fond dreams of a slaughter of our enemies and of Jesus leading it. It was, of course, a complete failure to understand who Jesus was and what he had sought to make the world, but the most unfortunate part of this let's-crown-him-king frenzy is that it blinded people; it prevented them seeing the wondrous jonquil of God in plain sight before their eyes. But for they who have no ears to hear, and no eyes with which to see, all that is of beauty is shorn and all the jonquils are cut down.

We spent that winter, or a portion of it, at the mount of Carmel, but in some respects, it was a sad winter, for we were few in number. *Mikroteros poimnion.* The winter skies remained gray and austere, and when we returned in the early spring, the news was even sadder. It was that graceful swan Perpetua who met us at the door, she who, like my mother, had come to regard herself a disciple of the Nazarene, but of course Perpetua had an elderly mother of her own to take care of, and for this reason, she did not travel with us. It would be a mistake, however, to think her role was insignificant, for Perpetua had made it her solemn duty to clean and care for that house in Capharnaum, to see to it that it remained essentially livable, and an admirable job she did of this, especially in light of the crowds that incessantly stalked Jesus. I never once saw her composure break—not, that is, until that day.

It was, as I say, she who met us at the door, and one look at her face told us the news was not good.

"It is John the Baptizer," she informed us now. "They have killed him."

Chapter Forty-Four

Other James' entrée at Herod's palace had at least won them something. The body parts had been returned. With head and trunk no longer joined, they had taken the Holy Man's remains and buried them in a tomb. Machaerus had actually been the second stop on their mission of deliverance. Prior to venturing into the southernmost reaches of Perea, they had, at Andrew's vehement insistence, paid call at the Essene settlement on the Salt Sea, but here they had found the valiant *Sicarii* unwilling to spring to battle on the Holy Man's behalf. Why? Perhaps the answer lay in those parting words spoken by the *mebaqqer*, Hilkiah, that year previous at the Baptizer's camp: *King Herod owed us a debt, and his son will not attack our settlements.* Neither would they attack his apparently.

And so as options fell, one by one, the two footsore travelers came at last to Machaerus itself, not as warriors, but as two humble penitents who would appeal to a tyrant's mercy. No sooner had they arrived than Other James was indeed recognized and remembered, but the "courtesy" shown them consisted, as I say, of having the remains handed over, this by a kindly steward who informed them also of the whereabouts of a tomb. It was not far away, which was just as well, for an extended journey burdened with such grisly cargo would have shattered poor Andrew's soul. The tomb was on the shore of *Yam ha Melah* in a cave, with Mount Nebo in the distance; inside, they laid the Baptizer in to his final *salus*, sealing up the fissure at last from the sea's reek and stench.

Chapter Forty-Five

We ate the bread of mourning, after which Jesus went off alone and we didn't see him for several days. The Baptizer's death made me angry, but unlike Andrew, I didn't blame Jesus, the *Sicarii*, or anyone really except maybe Adrasteia, the Goddess of inevitable fate. But then *Petskha* was approaching, and there wasn't time for blaming, for we were making plans to go to Jerusalem.

All things precious shine from the horizon, and for us Jews, few things were more precious than Jerusalem. With the certainty of good blessings awaiting them, the offspring of Abraham would be converging upon the Holy City from every direction, carrying in many cases their moveable property, arriving with a religious fervor, yet at the same time courtly and spry with the winter gone and the warmer season come. No less than the rest of us, the beheading of John had had its impact on Jesus; I had always known there was, running deep within him, a passion valiant in its theft of fire, but that *Petskha*, with more people in Jerusalem than I had ever seen before, that fire was on display like never before. What came to pass was, in a sense, a duel of words, a contest of wills, between Jesus and the chief priests, and with one chief priest in particular, but in a more roundabout manner, it also became a contest between Jesus and Herod Antipas, though I doubt Herod ever realized this or that it was Jesus who had robbed him of the eyes through which he had been able to view the world's terrible radiance. But from truth the cowardly shelter, and riches come to those who live upon the blood of the dead, while the lion becomes man—and so we started out.

Down through the city of Jericho we went, then up the deep, steep pass towards Jerusalem, a single file line of beetles making its way along the coruscated crust of the earth, yet in a sense walking The Nile of the Sky. Before reaching the Holy City, we stopped at the village of Bethany, here being welcomed most hospitably into a house belonging to a man named Lazarus and his two sisters, though many others were present besides. It was a large house, fragrant and nicely appointed, and prosperous with flowing wine. The guests included several members of the Sanhedrin, of who I was slightly in awe. Here, after all, were we, the filthy, dirty *am ha'aretz* from the north, mingling in such company! Incongruities further abounded insofar as Simon's being with us, for the *Sicarii*, quite naturally, were the implacable foes of the Sanhedrin, but then that was one of the strange things about the house of Lazarus: it was a place where all disparate types came together, including those from opposite sides of the affairs of treachery, not in a spirit of reconciliation exactly, more like wary acknowledgement of each other's presence. Quite simply put, it was a place where one could glance to the far side of a room full of guests, glimpse one's mortal enemy, and simply resume some intimate conversation of a moment earlier. In such manner did the house seem to be afforded the sanctity of neutral ground. High-ranking Romans, even Pilate himself, were not unknown to the place—and yes, *Sicarii* as well. As the householder in such an establishment, Lazarus seemed, at least on the surface of it, to tread a dangerous line, as did his two sisters, Martha and Mary. I have no idea how or at what time Jesus had made the family's acquaintance, although Mary, the youngest of the three siblings, seemed quite besotted with him. "I feel as though I could look up in the night and see a comet blazing by and you would be on it, waving to me," she remarked to him that evening, in her voice a note of longing as she held him in the mirror of her gaze; few women would not desire to marry a king, yet here, with kings abounding all around, was one whose sights were set on a poor man of no standing. No doubt were those who would have dismissed her as a foolish young woman.

As for Lazarus and Martha, never could I determine with any degree of certainty just where their political sympathies lay, that is to say whether these might be with the Pharisees, Sadducees, or the *Sicarii*, with those who collaborated with our enemies, or with they who sought to overthrow them. Or perhaps even with the Romans themselves. In the prism-like abattoir that is Roman rule, one exercises great care in one's locutions, and where Lazarus and his family were concerned, the advantage could lay only in preserving that cautious ambiguity. We stayed that night in their house; the next day we made Jerusalem. It was the eighth day of the month of *Nisan*.

Lo, the sublime favor one could feel casting eyes upon this wondrous city with its Temple richly adorned in gold almost as bright as the sun itself! When you approached Jerusalem, especially from the east, the light reflecting from those golden surfaces was as a spiritual nuptial to the eyes. *Ha La Beit,* the Mountain of the House. It was the instantaneous smile of YHWH, as if he had chosen this fiery splendor as an epicene reflection of his very own beauty, and we were here at last. Inside the city proper, the noise went from loud to deafening. Pilgrims. Revelers. The cries of water carriers carrying skins on their backs. And the streets—virtually impassable. We took lodging in a small, tumble-down dwelling on a steep, winding lane in the heart of the Lower City. The house belonged to friends of Simon's, and over the course of that week, we came to refer to it obliquely as "the *Sicarii* house." Within its walls, you were forever acutely aware of the festival going on outside, for they were thin as reeds, but in a way, thin walls and all, it was the cynocephalus, that house, the dog-headed ape, sitting upon the beam of the scales, weighing life and death as measures of wheat and barley in the balance.

On the street outside, the never-ending flow of pedestrians caught one up immediately. The Temple and the Huldah Gates were to the north, the perfume factories directly south, and the Pool of Siloam to the east. We were pretty much in the thick of it all. A great many Roman soldiers were in evidence as well, though for the most part they kept a low profile, not wishing to spark disturbances. At the same time, however, a careful watch was kept over the citizenry, and especially, it seemed to us, over the citizens of the Lower City. The morning after our arrival, Jesus led several of us up to the Temple, and of that day, I must now speak in some detail, for what transpired earned for us the lasting hatred of the highest religious leaders in the land.

It started with Jesus overturning the tables of the moneychangers, a reputed act of violence seized upon by his detractors, who used it to brand him a hypocrite—for after all had he not failed to turn the other cheek? But to fully understand what happened that day, you must first of all understand what it was like simply to walk into the Temple. Big and bustling would be a good description for starters. After ascending a number of stairs, you came to the Royal Porch and the Court of the Gentiles, the most exterior areas. These were accessible to anyone, including even, as the name would imply, Gentiles. Here were the *nummularii*, with their sacks of coins and their careful hands, here also the sellers of live animals with a goodly number of creatures, some tethered, some caged, bleating as they awaited the spilling of their blood. The altar was in the Court of the Priests, the innermost court, but even here, in the outer courts, you could smell the smoke of burnt flesh; often it seemed in no hurry to depart or dissipate, hovering over the Temple Mount like some graysooted floriculture, a cloud from which, when the wind was right, there was nowhere in the city one might escape its scent entirely. Atonement of sins through the shedding of blood—the more sins, the more atonement, the more blood, until human vileness was finally vanquished, *if* it ever was.

Blood—the life of all flesh. So it is said. In his demand for blood, YHWH of course is not alone. It is a *pro forma* thirst shared with the Gods of the Greeks and the Romans, both of whom parade their own festivals of blood, but I am speaking here and now of Jerusalem, so let us consider that. During Passover celebration, the city's population swells to three or four times normal, which means a lot of sins to atone for, a lot of smoke, a lot of blood. The Hebrew word for sacrifice is *korban*, which derives from the words "come close." We were supposedly coming close to God through all this slaughter. And those bringing their sacrifices did, in a manner of speaking, come close, if not to God, then at least to the priests, who were always, quite naturally, eager to receive their offerings.

Further on from the Court of the Gentiles was an area called the Court of Women, a large and spacious quadrangle where both Jewish women and Jewish men were allowed to congregate, although beyond this point wives and daughters were forbidden from passing. Men, however, were given leave to advance into the *next* court, known as the Court of Israel, where they handed over their sacrifices, and from here it was possible to cast their eyes, finally, over into the *furthest* court—the Court of the Priests—and view the *kohanim* at their holy tasks. Be assured, they were not allowed to physically enter the Court of the Priests, but they *could* observe, and the enterprise they looked upon was often one of considerable activity. The "heavenly fragrance" of the incense, along with the pungency of the holocaustal pelage and flesh, mostly obscured the smell of blood and entrails, even though the gore was rather voluminous—so voluminous a drainage system had been constructed for diverting blood away from the altar, as well as from the shambles with its eight marble tables for washing entrails. Slaughtered upon the altar were birds only. Larger animals had to be taken to the shambles, where their heads were secured in a ring placed snugly around their necks. *And thou shalt put the mercy seat above the ark*. Then the creature was killed and flayed. When the killing was over and the sacrifices had been performed, the priests stood on the porch of the Holy Place, just in front of the golden-vined doorway, and with hands in the air they would recite the Benediction of Aaron: "The Lord bless you and keep you; the Lord make his face to shine upon you, and be gracious to you; the Lord lift up his countenance upon you and give you peace." Amongst them stood the high priest himself. His own hands, too, were raised, though not as high as those of his fellow *kohanim*, for he wore the priestly crown, a crown bearing the letters YHWH, the name of God, and for this reason it was imperative his hands never rise above his head. And thus were our people's sins presumably atoned for. Afterwards the purgative process began. Through two holes at the southwest corner of the altar, the *hins* of blood were flushed away by water into the Kidron Valley.

So many people seeking forgiveness for so many sins naturally required an almost unending supply of animals. While some Passover pilgrims brought their own sacrifices, others, particularly those journeying from afar, found it impractical transporting live creatures all the way to Jerusalem. By happy coincidence, however, the Temple officials were able to remedy this problem, and so yes, the sellers of these miserable creatures was one of the things Jesus saw with his boundless eyes of *nuhra* as we entered the Holy House that day.

The other sight confronting him was that of the *nummularii*. Like the live animal sellers, these also, for a price, were willing to assist pilgrims in keeping on the right side of the Law of Moses. Coins had to be changed if they were not shekels of the Tyrian variety. The latter were made of silver and deemed of reliable value, but Jews came from many distant lands, where often Tyrian shekels were unavailable, and so a stop at the tables of the *nummularii* had to be made. In any rate, after fattening the purses of the moneychangers, *and* the animal sellers, you were now ready to make your sacrificial offering. Depending on your status, it might be a sin offering, a vow offering, a Nazarite offering, cattle tithe, or other; you conversely might also wish to purchase wine, oil, or fine meal for a meal offering. Opportunities abounded to appease God in other ways. In the Court of Women, for instance, were fifteen receptacles called "trumpets," for thus were they shaped, and yes, into these trumpets, coins could be dropped as well. As may be imagined, a lot of money changed hands, much of it ending up in the Temple treasury where it was put to use in a variety of ways. There was maintenance, purchase of service utensils, hiring of teachers to instruct the priests in the art of slaughtering, payment of those who investigated blemishes in the sacrifices. Vast, in other words, were the expenses.

I recall a story, my beloved Quintus, about a priest engaged one day in the "wood chamber," an enclosure located in the northeast corner of the Court of Women and which, as the name would imply, was used as a storehouse for wood to be burned upon the alter. In the Wood Chamber certain specific priests were assigned to work, in the main those with physical blemishes of one sort or another. Blemished priests were forbidden from duties at the altar, but they could be useful in other ways, and one of these was by assisting in the Wood Chamber where they were tasked with inspecting pieces of wood for the presence of worms. Worm-eaten wood was of course unsuitable for the holy fire and had to be culled from the stockpile. Well, as the story goes, a blemished priest was thus engaged one day inside the Wood Chamber when he noticed a paving stone askew; somewhat excitedly, he emerged to inform his fellow priests of what he had found, but before he could get the full story out he was struck dead on the spot. More than simply stunned at this development, the other priests were, shall we say, *rhapsodized*, for it could now be presumed with confidence that the Ark of the Covenant had been hidden, on that very spot, deep beneath the Wood Chamber, hundreds of years earlier when the Babylonians had laid waste the city. A tall tale to be sure, although perhaps a kernel of truth to it, even if the poor fellow had done little to deserve his fate.

From all these and many other doings inside the Temple, Gentiles were firmly excluded. Gentiles were in fact barred from entering any part of the Temple at all other than that outermost court that bore their name. This was made very explicit, for separating the Court of the Gentiles from the inner courts was a *soreg* ten handbreadths high. Upon it were columns at equal distances one from another declaring the laws of purity, and here could be found notices forbidding non-Jews from proceeding further. So there should be no confusion on the matter, the notices were written in both Greek and Latin, and non-Jews were well advised to take heed: the penalty for any Gentile caught violating the rule was death. And thus, dear Quintus, we sought for the divine in measures proportioned with the passions of self-adoration.

You would think that of all the creatures consumed upon those assertive flames of sacrifice, at least one might have been offered up that Passover in atonement for the murder of John the Baptizer, but I think this is not likely the case. Of course, John's killer, Herod, was not a Jew strictly speaking, but then that's a somewhat separate issue. Hither and thither did our leaders flutter freely about in their divine boats of hypocrisy, often outdoing themselves in their collaborative unctuousness. The Essenes had a name for them: the "seekers of smooth things." And yes, you could watch as they ascended and descended smoothly through the various gates and terraces of the Temple, often sweeping by amidst encomiums of praise.

So that all, in a very general manner of speaking, is what confronted Jesus and the rest of us as we arrived at the Temple that day.

There were five of us that day, with Jesus making six. In the Court of the Gentiles it was very crowded, and I recall now a marvelous beauty to the set of the Nazarene's jaw, how it shook, twitched really, as he surveyed the scene before us. I'm not the only one who noticed it. "Master, what is it?" someone asked, for we were all oddly puzzled at the sudden withdrawal of the zephyrs that so often frolicked in his weathered face. Without answering, Jesus turned to me and confided quietly, "Observe carefully, Johannes, and I will show you how to make a spring of living water burst from a stone." And then without saying a word further, he left us, making his way to one of the broad flat tables occupied by the moneychangers. On this table, stacked in rows, imbricated like the scales of a fish, were a great many coins, enough money to feed a family like mine for a year. Sidling up to the table, the Nazarene gripped its polished edge firmly, and, perhaps not unlike Horus of the rising sun, in one sweeping thrust reversed it broadsides—so that the assiduous, level top of the table went from resting comfortably just beneath the moneychanger's hands, to collapsing like a great sea wave down upon his head. O misery of man! It was as if an earthquake had rocked the Temple. Another table went likewise, and then a third.

First there is order, but order is invariably transient, do you know, Quintus?—and out of it arises chaos. But chaos is many things, and one man's chaos may often be another man's order, and vice versa. Being younger than the Nazarene, and far more timid by nature, I could not possibly imagine doing what he had just done, and I stood gaping in disbelief, but there was no time to contemplate. At Jesus' urging we strolled calmly away, tutelary spirits of the sovereign forest, leaving behind a row of upturned tables and a gaggle of moneychangers paddling in the chaos, as we made our way into the Portico of Solomon. Here, amidst the columns, beneath the cedar-lined ceiling, Yeshua began to teach the crowd in earnest. He told them there were those who wished to turn the Temple into a den of thieves; he told them God desired mercy, not sacrifices. He was something luminous, a celebrant of the magnified and unsurpassed, and he rose in that inspired moment to greatness. He had not yet mentioned John the Baptizer, but it was on his mind, I knew. A great number of people were in the portico, and soon I could hear whisperings all about. "Who is this?"

"It is *Jesus*, the new prophet from Galilee!"

In due course, as was inevitable, the Temple authorities arrived, along with a detachment of Levites that included the master of the Temple Guard, all of them quickly assuming the choleric prerogatives of the Mighty and the Wise. "Who gave you the authority to come here like this?" Florid and with a very moist and bulbous face, the speaker of this last seemed to have a penchant for a great deal of spurious tongue wagging. I did not know until later that he was Annas, a former high priest and father-in-law of the current high priest, Caiaphas; at that moment, all we knew was he was a very florid and bedewed gentleman who stood, with his phalanx of watchmen, crowding us in a most intimidating manner.

Given what had just transpired in the Court of the Gentiles, I could only think we were in deep trouble. If you imagine I was frightened, you would be correct. I was about as frightened as any twenty-three-year-old young man could be. No doubt, Annas knew his presence was intimidating, as he fully intended it should be; accustomed to having his authority obeyed, the former high priest glared at us with a look meant to demolish and demoralize, but Jesus, bearing a spade of gold, was on the verge of scooping live, hot coals into his lap. "I will answer your question," replied he, speaking loudly enough for everyone in the Portico of Solomon to hear, "if you will first answer one of mine." No doubt, the witnesses to this exchange fully expected "the new prophet from Galilee" to retreat in the face of the official bullying, and I certainly would not have blamed the Nazarene had he done so. But this is not what happened. "John the Baptizer—was he a prophet from God, or just an ordinary man? What is your answer?"

Now the last thing the chief priests wanted was to be asked any questions about John. This could have been true anytime, but was especially so just now, with the city filled with thousands of pilgrims. Any hint that our chief priests had condoned or colluded with Herod in the Holy Man's death would be unceasing trouble for them. But the question had been asked. And now that it was out in the open it was as a loaded catapult waiting to be sprung. If Annas answered that yes, John was a prophet from God, the obvious response would be, "Then why didn't you follow him?" If on the other hand he opined that he was an ordinary man he risked incurring the wrath of the people, for to them John very much had been a prophet, perhaps *the* prophet, *Eliahu ha-Navi*, Elijah, for such had been suggested more than once since his death; moreover this was Passover, *Zeman Cherutenu*, the season of our liberation, and of course Passover tradition included a special prayer that

Elijah might make a speedy descent from heaven and immediately begin combating injustice. It was the right question at the right time. Annas and his watchmen were suddenly in a boiling cauldron, with every eye upon them. The Mighty and Wise old hypocrite groped awkwardly for the middle ground. "I, that is to say, we—don't know." *We don't know.* It was a humiliating admission for someone who ostensibly had a direct link to God and had once worn a crown with the name YHWH stitched across the front; a loud and slightly disdainful guffaw rang out.

"Then neither will I tell you by what authority I come here." Jesus turned dismissively from Annas as if he had fully washed his hands of him; at the same time a self-conscious titter swept through the crowd, smiles suddenly kindling even in the faces of the children. Annas, his dignity shrunk to the size of a windlestraw, grew increasingly florid and bedewed, but Jesus didn't wait to savor the victory. Without a word, he shouldered his way through the detachment of Levites, jostling them every bit as rudely as they had jostled us earlier. As for the people, including the children—ah, that was a different matter! "Hosanna to the son of David!" someone shouted. And smiling now in admiration—yes smiling!—the crowd parted for us.

With the Nazarene in the lead, I felt an enormous sense of pride, as well as a number of other giddy emotions, as we made our sweeping and dramatic exit from Solomon's Portico. It could have been because of these welling emotions, or perhaps in spite of them, that I chanced glimpsing something out of the corner of my eye while trailing Jesus through the crowd. Do you know how it is, Quintus, in one of those moments of confusion? You see something; it comes at you; then it is gone. Its appearance is so fleeting you're not sure you even saw it—just that quickly did it happen, so quickly I wasn't even sure but what I might simply have imagined it. Imagination of course is like the friend who comes to meet you; he may bring you a fragrant gift, or a dark tale to trouble your soul, but what I'm getting at, the thing which seemed to flash in front of me, was a face. A human face. Not just any human face, however, but one from my long-ago past, bringing with it a hedgerow of deeply unpleasant memories. I could not be sure of course, but the face I saw, or thought I saw, was Hodi's—but then, like a fish disappearing into deeper water, it was gone.

Out of the Temple we emerged, down through the Huldah Gates, into the bedlam of the street. It was dusk, and yes, it was Passover, and there was excitement everywhere. Surrounding us was much clamor, in reality nothing more than the general ambience and noise of the street, but because it was

Passover and because so many people were about, it was really quite something to be surrounded and engulfed by, and I soon forgot about things like shadowy faces and ghosts of my childhood. Breathing in the warm air of eventide, I could feel the joyous emotions of the season, and best of all, I was walking beside the greatest man I had ever known in my life.

Chapter Forty-Six

Returning to the *Sicarii* House, we were met with a scene bordering on pandemonium. A young girl in the grip of some inexplicable terror was the cause of this commotion, although no one could say with certainty what had brought her to her current state. The girl herself, unable or unwilling to speak on her dilemma, or apparently communicate at all for that matter, gave forth but a series of screams, these being liable to erupt at most any time, and rather jarringly. Had Rabbi Hamul been present, no doubt he would have pronounced it a case of demonic possession. Perhaps he would have been right. A few of the women, Tirzah among them, had taken charge of her, or tried to, but had been unable to calm her, and now the young thing crouched within a rampart at the east end of the house, staring warily out at the rest of us.

This house was inhabited of course mainly by *Sicarii*, not one of whom, I feel compelled to mention, had laid a hand upon her, or given her the slightest cause to take fright. So of what was she troubled? More particularly, where had she come from and why was she here? Some of this began to be answered piecemeal—*piecemeal* for no one could get more than a small part of the story out before yet another ear-splitting scream erupted—as we learned that at some point during the day, while Jesus had been overturning tables in the Temple, a middle-aged woman had arrived at the house with the young girl in tow. After depositing her solicitously, one might say almost daintily, though at the same time with hardly a word of explanation, she had then departed, *not*, however, before vowing a return in the evening. Presumably, if she indeed showed back up, she would offer a full account of her actions, or at least collect the noisome creature and be gone with her. For the moment, however, the girl was left on our hands, and we were at a loss to understand the nature of the black rain, which had so without question shattered her mind into pieces. The gist of all this was laid out in desultory tones by our artful artist, Other James, who was in something of a land of exile over the matter, for, as he now began to confess, the woman and the girl were not completely unknown to him as we had all along assumed; coincidentally, along with this intriguing admission, came a knock at the door. "I will get it," he said. "It is probably Joanna."

We were, it seemed, on the verge of mysteries revealed...

The woman who entered was veiled, circumspect, reserved, though upon gaining entry to the house she removed her head covering, revealing a visage both brave and gallant in equal amounts, grayish at the edges, with ample touches of ruthfulness. Yet it was not a joyful face; in the eyes in fact were covert flickers of fear. After composing herself, she turned, facing Jesus fully headlong, and inquired abruptly, "You are the prophet from Nazareth?" First giving the woman a cursory appraisal, Jesus next shifted his gaze onto Other James, upon whom he conferred a long, brittle look of ennui. The son of Alphaeus fumbled for words, "Well, it's—that is to say—" but was quickly cut off by the visitor—

"I'm sorry. I did not mean to be rude." Sweeping the artist aside, somewhat rudely, she extended a hand to Yeshua: "Please forgive me and allow me to introduce myself. My name is Joanna. I am the wife of a man named Chuza; my husband is chief steward in Herod's household."

Here Other James regained his tongue. "Perhaps it would be best, before Joanna goes any further, if I were to explain how all this came about..."—and so our eyes returned to him—and in fact that is how it all eventually got told, with a sort of back-and-forth acuity shared between the two of them...

"It was some two years ago," Other James began, "that I first went to the fortress of Herod at Machaerus. A few of you even know the story. My father and I had been commissioned to do a mosaic for the tetrarch, for which we were amply paid. At any rate, it was at this time, on my first visit to the palace, that I met Joanna. She it was who saw to our comforts, and a most praiseworthy job she did of this. We worked steadily, my father and me, and finally completed our job. Our time under the tetrarch's roof comprised roughly seven weeks altogether. We returned to Galilee where we found other work, secured other commissions, and at this time I thought I had seen the last of Machaerus, for I had no desire to return there, but then in the fall, after the Baptizer was taken prisoner, I saw Joanna again. This of course was when all of you sent Andrew and me to Machaerus to seek John's release. Everyone by now has heard the story. He was not released but...but...brutally murdered.

"Andrew and I were staying in the village of Machaerus, although there is little we would have known about actual events inside the fortress had it not been for Joanna, for it was she who came regularly and sought us out, relaying news of what was taking place. In addition to this kindness of Joanna's, her husband, Chuza, turned over the Holy Man's remains after he was put to death. Otherwise, we would not have even had these to take and bury. You are aware of the rest. Andrew and I placed the Holy Man in a tomb, sealed it up, and we returned to Capharnaum.

"Well anyway, yesterday, when we came to Jerusalem, I chanced seeing Joanna again. A few of us here went up to the Xystus, the upper agora, to purchase bread, but as you may know Herod's Jerusalem palace is not far from there; wandering that marketplace, I happened to see Joanna again, or rather she saw me first, at any rate, we recognized one another immediately and greeted each other warmly. It was while standing there in the marketplace that she told me of the strange state of affairs regarding the girl whom you see in yonder room. For most of her life, she has been kept slave and prisoner by Herod. In the seven weeks my father and I were in the palace, we would occasionally see her. Very beautiful, very lovely to look at, but always upon her face a sadness, and always she passed us by in silence. In our dealings with Herod, he never bothered to explain who she was, and we never asked, but occasionally in the palace we would hear whisperings from the other servants. It was said she possessed strange powers, the ability to know certain things, and to see things that cannot be seen. Joanna can speak more to this than I, since she has lived in Herod's court for many years, while I was there for only a short while, but what I *did* observe and what I *can* speak to is this: while many young girls could be found about the palace, women of great beauty, kept there for the pleasures of Herod and his guests, this girl was not one of them. *This girl* Herod seemed to keep separate and apart from all the others.

"Well...by and by, my father and I finished our work; we left the fortress, and as I say, I thought I had seen the last of the place, but then came the arrest of the Baptizer, and at your request, I returned to Machaerus. I've related already how Joanna informed us of the fate which befell John, but what I did not mention was what she said concerning the circumstances of that evening. It seems the girl, she who now seeks safety in this house, was present in Herod's dining hall when...when..." the artist gave a shudder, "when they brought in the severed head."

It was at this point Joanna took up the narrative.

"Laid they the gruesome thing upon the table, it having been carried in upon a platter by one of the servants and placed not more than three cubits from where the girl was seated. The beasts all gloated upon the prize. Done with her dance, the wicked little daughter of Herodias picked up the head and delivered it to her beastly mother, while meanwhile Mariamne, poor sad girl, gazed straight ahead, hands folded in her lap. Herod had ordered her to the table that evening, desiring an exercise of her powers, for these are great, and I have seen them myself."

"What sort of powers?" The question was asked by Matthew, but I think by now we all awaited an answer to this; even Jesus sat in rapt attention.

"She knows whether people speak falsely or truthfully, for she sees through all of existence; it is for this reason Herod keeps her. That night he had her at his side, having sent for her because he suspected one of the guests of treason. The triclinium was full, a great feast having been prepared by the cooks. Though the head's arrival had prompted vulgar amusement all around, for Mariamne it was as if some evil incantation had been exercised; even after the thing's removal, she continued staring at the very spot where it had been, as if it were still there, and in a way, for her, it *was* still there, for she sees not only what is present, but what is past and future as well, for as I said before, she sees through all of existence. As she stared at the spot, all vitality drained from her face.

"Her troubles started that night, but you have to understand that these demons did not come upon her all at once. At first, we noted peculiarities in the way she talked, a stray word here or there that simply didn't sound right. Then, most unusual of all, she began to speak in rhyme. Every sentence rhyming with another previous to it. We asked her why she had begun speaking in such a strange manner, but she could give no explanation. Herod became furious, casting her away from his table in disgust. To her quarters she was consigned under lock and key. Only my husband Chuza and I were allowed access, and only for purpose of bringing her meals, but worse was to come. Mentally she began to disintegrate; as if the rhyming were not already curious enough, she commenced, after a week or so, to speak in the tongue of the Romans. Never before had I heard her converse in this language, and I have known her since she was a child of six. I do not myself speak Latin, but my husband does, for he must deal with the Romans regularly. He said her words were ramblings, making a strange sort of sense, but at the same time bespeaking of foul, horrible things. Herod became frightened of her at this point. Physicians were called, but none could help. Over the next week or so her illness took yet another turn as she ceased coherent speech altogether; what came out instead were screams, as if she were confined in some chamber of horror from which she could not free herself. The outbursts became more frequent, erupting whenever anyone would touch her, or even venture too near. The sole exception to this was I. I alone she would allow close.

"Herod called more physicians, but again they were of no use. Her condition continued to worsen, and it has now become a thing most heart wrenching. I was at a loss as to what to do, at a loss, that is, until I saw this one in the marketplace yesterday—" here she gestured at Other James. "I remembered of course his visits to Machaerus, and I recalled an occasion in particular when he had spoken of a prophet, one greater than the Baptizer; as we stood at the marketplace talking, I told him the story you have now heard, and I beseeched his help."

"But who is she?" asked Peter. "Where did she come from? What is her name?"

"Her father was Greek, her mother a Jew. In the village of Magdala they lived; when still only a child, strife broke out in their town and her father was slain. The violence eventually had to be quelled by Herod's troops. With the family's home in ruins, along with much of the rest of the town, her mother became the tetrarch's unwilling concubine. Herod established her comfortably in the palace, but she died not long after; the girl was only six years old, but it was known even then she possessed a strange gift, and so Herod kept her. She became a virtual prisoner in his household, and it has been thus all these years. She is now the age of nineteen, with beauty most fair, yet a more miserable child you could never imagine. Her name is Mariamne, but Herod's servants refer to her for the most part as the Magdalene, for as I say, she was from Magdala.

Joanna paused, leaned forward, and gazed intently at Jesus. "Please understand, sir, in bringing her here I had no other choice. I alone know of her whereabouts. Both of us arrived veiled. Herod is much distressed, thinking she has escaped the palace on her own, perhaps to court some damage to herself, and has dispatched soldiers through the city. If they find her there is no telling what may happen. I fear for her as only a mother can, for over the years she has become very much like a daughter to me."

Outside, night had fallen. Through the thin walls of the *Sicarii* House we could hear the festival, noising itself dithyrambically on, yet here inside the house, not a soul stirred; the candlelight, the stillness of air, and the face of this woman who had come to us with this story of desuetude, this love letter so tenderly written—all of it had a strange effect on me. "Sir?" Joanna's eyes lingered on Jesus: "If you can do so, heal her. *Heal* her, sir, and when you leave here, you and your friends, take her wherever you may go, but take her far away from here. I beseech you, free her. Free her from her demons. Free her also from her bondage to Herod. You are her only hope."

Even the maddest sharers of existence must sometimes lodge in the grove of pure heart. We had all instinctively kept our distance from the girl. Still at this moment she remained caught up in that far corner of the house, crouching, her body coiled, staring out at us with the black eyes of Hecate, staring yes, though I'm not sure she really saw any of us. Tirzah, moved by Joanna's story, as were we all, tried reaching her, presumably in an effort to offer comfort, but this elicited such a violent shrieking it sent our poor, frightened scribe retreating skittishly away. While the screaming subsided at this point, the young thing continued to offer up dour looks, thrown in our direction like wildly strewn seeds; to my nostrils came a sour odor of unwashed flesh, even as I remained careful to keep my distance. Upon her head was a wild, tangled mass of hair, yet at the same time, it seemed to me she evinced a strange, animalistic beauty. The Egyptians say that when Nut, the sky Goddess, arched upon all fours above her loving consort the earth, chaos was brought to an end, but that if she should ever be removed from that position it would return. Perhaps something of the sort had befallen this born-and-destroyed ethereal flower; perhaps somewhere deep inside her, her earth and her sky were cleaved horribly apart. Warily and suspiciously now she peered at Jesus as he calmly entered the room, obtaining perch for himself a short but respectful distance away from her. The gaze transposing his face reminded me of an image of the moon as his eyes met hers, met them with an echo of the wind carrying the sound of the human voice. And then came the Nazarene's *actual* voice—as to the palsied maid he began to speak. To my astonishment, however, the words were Latin. I had never heard him speak such before, and did not even know he could. "*Maria, si tu insisto me abeo, solum insisto me tu vivo.*" I knew no Latin myself, but our scribe did. She it was who, later, translated for me the words. *Mary, if you die with me, you also live with me.*

What had he meant by such? I could not say, but the girl responded in a wholly astonishing manner; with a fluid and motile spring, pausing long enough only to cover a bared shoulder with a slipped thread of her garment, she plunged directly at Jesus. At first, I thought she aspired to attack him, though quickly realized her intentions were otherwise. Her plunge was nothing so much as a desperate leap, straight into his arms, as if nowhere else on earth offered shelter as safe. And then came his embrace—an embrace she snatched hungrily to herself as her avalanche of black hair covered the two of them.

Chapter Forty-Seven

We were still trying to absorb what had happened. The girl had been given food. Tirzah and my sister-in-law, Abby, had taken her to a *mikvah* three doors up the street. There they had bathed her, and yes, she *had* allowed herself to be touched. The screaming seemed to have abated, in total, and at this moment, the young thing lay sleeping in a rear room of the house.

At the *mikvah*, Tirzah and Abby had found her cooperative, while noticing one other thing as well: her speech, though perfunctory, had evidenced a peculiar tendency toward rhyme. It was as if the successive stages of her illness, described so vividly for us earlier by Joanna, were starting to reverse themselves. The irony was not lost on Joanna. "Never before have I seen the like!" The steward's wife was about to depart for the palace and had secured once more her head covering. "It is like she is going backwards, as if she searches for the self she once was before all this happened to her." We were in the main room of the house; outside the festival clamored on, and I was bone weary. It had been a long day, yet incredibly Jesus was about to go out again, to Bethany, something evidently to transpire at the house of Lazarus and his sisters. James and Peter, firm in the opinion he should not travel the road alone, were preparing to accompany him. A great exodus or departure seemed imminent, and the dwelling had that bustle that houses get when they are about to disgorge large numbers of their occupants. "Be of great care, all of you," said Joanna. "Know this also, that throughout the city are spies in the employ of Pontius Pilate; they know the city well; they know this house; they know it is inhabited by *Sicarii* sympathizers, and they are watching it closely. Whoever comes and goes—all of this is reported back to Pilate. Heed my warning. Herod too has his own network of spies. It is a city filled with much treachery."

Listening to her speak, I became aware of a number of things, the tender power of her voice, the movement of people in the house, as well as my own random and confused thoughts, but most of all what I became aware of was the noise of the city outside, a city that tonight, especially, seemed as if it were spinning like a wheel of fire in a vision of gold.

"It is known that Herod and Pilate are not friends. Indeed, toward each other they harbor a deep antipathy, yet in respect to one thing they share a common interest, and that is you." Here Joanna broke off to look squarely at Jesus: "Talk of the miracles you perform has reached them. They are intensely curious about you, and their spies are watching you. I had to be very careful when I came here today. A long and circuitous route I took in an effort to make sure the girl and I were not trailed. Herod does not know she is here, but be aware of one thing, he wants her back, and he will stop at nothing to get her. It will not be easy for you and your friends to smuggle her out of Jerusalem. They know she must yet be somewhere inside the city gates, but they know not where. Be assured though, when Passover ends and people start to leave, they will be watching; they are watching even now." With those words, she lowered her veil and departed.

The web of life exercised its satyrion as the festival beckoned, and others began to depart the house as well. Jesus, Peter and James went next, followed by Thomas and Nathanael a moment later, then Tirzah, Judas Iscariot, and several others, all taking flight into the night. Eventually I found myself in the dwelling alone—alone, that is, except for the sleeping girl. My fatigue was such I had been certain sleep would overtake me, but instead, I lay awake thinking of this strange creature sleeping in the next room, my ears still ringing with the echoes of her hamadryadic screams. These musings took a delicious turn as I thought of her lips, and her flowing hair, hair the color of water under the enraptured gaze of midnight, and despite my exhaustion I remained wide awake for a great long time. At some point, however, I *must* have drifted off, for the next thing I knew it was dawn, and James was settling down on the mat beside me. He had just returned from Bethany with Peter and Jesus. All night they had been away. Sleepily I asked, "How was your journey?"

"There is so much to speak of, John!" He whispered so as to not awaken others in the house, yet I could detect an amorphous note of excitement. "There were these two councilors, Pharisees, one named Joseph, of Arimathaea, the other Nicodemus; to the house of Lazarus they came in secret, not wishing it to be known they were meeting Jesus. They are of the

Sanhedrin, John! Think of it!" My brother, I could see, was in one of his loquacious moods. "Several hours they spent, John—talking to Jesus! Something is happening, little brother! I can feel it! With powerful men such as these on our side who knows what will happen? Yeshua could end up being made king!"

I doubted it would come to that, and said so. James, like so many others, seemed to have fallen prey to the dubious let's-make-him-king fever. In a way not surprising. My brother had always been more easily swayed and enthralled by the aura of power, a trait I think he had inherited from Zebedee. "You should have been there, little brother! Had you been there, you would know there are wondrous seeds being sown!"

Perhaps, I conceded. But as I lay there, I also considered what Joanna had said, that the city was full of spies, that an intensive hunt was underway for the missing girl, she who now lay under our very roof, and whose status under the law was technically that of runaway slave, and thinking of these things, I decided that, far from being disciple to a newly-crowned king, I would settle for us simply getting out of this city in one piece.

Chapter Forty-Eight

Aday after these events I returned to the Temple, where in the Portico of Solomon I again saw that face in the crowd. This time there was no mistaking; it was indeed the bully who had tormented me in my childhood. What was Hodi doing in Jerusalem? Was he a pilgrim, here only for the festival? Or did he live in Jerusalem now? And his gaggle of followers, why were they here? For as I perceived now, they were close about him as well, many of them the same faces from years before, boys once, but now men, grown heavy with the pungent condiments of life. In what was left of Passover I would see them, lounging in the rear shadows of Solomon's Portico, smirking as Jesus addressed the crowd. Cruel faces— which if anything had grown even crueler with age. And it wasn't only at the Temple. The streets of the Lower City are amongst the curviest in Jerusalem. They wander sinuously, crossing one another's path, absconding into the shadows of channels, buttressed walls, and a hippodrome; diverging; converging again; managing their feats with a menial and sometimes displeasing casuistry. In the next few days, I began seeing Hodi and his followers a lot on these streets; they would appear in the industrial quarter, or along the Way of the Cheesemongers, or sometimes we would even see them beyond the Lower City, in the upper agora for instance, or loitering in the shadows of the Three Towers. After a while, I began to feel none of this could be by accident.

The chief priests had grown sorely provoked with Yeshua's appearances at the Temple. *Petskha*, now nearly over, had been a rough ride for them, for Jesus had spared them little in the way of scathing remarks. It had prompted one of our *Sicarii* hosts to observe musingly, "He is one who confuses those in power." It happened to be so. The chief priests had the authority to order the Nazarene's arrest, but clearly, they were reluctant to do so in the face of such large crowds. Meanwhile he kept right on speaking, telling parables of rich men being cast into hell, while branding Jerusalem "the city that kills the prophets."

Finally, Passover came to an end and the festival crowds began to depart. "We should just put a veil over her. That is how Joanna got her here after all." The problem of how to get the girl out of the *Sicarii* House, let alone out of the city, had yet to be solved. The suggestion of veiling her had been made, cast aside, and then made again, this time by Thomas, who was just as anxious as everyone else to leave, for the city had grown extremely dangerous.

"It is not that simple. All women are being scrutinized, and veiled women are being told they must lift their veils before being allowed through the city gates." This came from Tephtheus, one of the *Sicarii* who had put us up in their house. "It is an outrage, but it is going on at each exit point from the city."

Standing behind him was Simon, flashing a grin, the wooden neck of his cithra balanced jauntily upon one shoulder. "Maybe we should just play them a tune." Meanwhile a series of pronouncements, rendered in poetic meter, poured forth from she who just then was the object of our concerns. Prosodies, syllabic and rambling, went on largely nonstop, prompting Tirzah finally to emit an exasperated sigh, "It has been like this all morning—chirping away in rhyme!" And even as our scribe spoke, the girl, Mariamne of Magdala, chirped once more:

> In course of wind and creature's turning night,
> The heart of dust, the fallen star redeemed to pay,
> Hath opened knowledge to the Prince of Light.
> In mire of spectacle, the echo's on its way.

The peculiar lines fluttered, looking for a place to land in the form of a receptive ear, though none was about. We mostly by this time had grown oblivious to the incessant rhyming. If Mary of Magdala noticed, however, she didn't seem to care. Barefoot, balancing slightly forward on the balls of her feet, she smiled eagerly as the strange utterances, one by one, took flight from her lovely mouth. Like rich tapestries, they unfurled themselves, though tapestries which none of us, in our earnest strategizing, bothered to regard too closely. Yet on the chipped walls of the *Sicarii* House they hung themselves, awaiting signification of their meritoriousness. One of the women, I assumed it was Tirzah, had dressed her in a pearl-colored *istomukhvia* that laced up to her throat; she was breathtakingly lovely, yet it seemed to our overburdened ears she might never cease with her constant summonses.

"We have to do something soon. The crowds are leaving the city." Thomas, with a spare tunic draped over one shoulder, strolled to a window and peered cautiously out.

"Aye," Peter agreed. "The more people leave, and us remaining here in the city, the more likely we shall be arrested."

"Arrested and beheaded as well! We shall meet the same fate as John the Baptizer!" In addition to being fraught over the matter at hand, as were all of us, Philip was anxious to get home to his wife and child.

"Herod has a century of soldiers combing the city for her," Tephtheus put in grimly. "If she walks out of here she will certainly be captured, and the rest of you with her."

"There is an easy solution." At these words spoken by Jesus, the house grew silent. "If it is a woman they look for, then we simply make her into a man."

Before anyone could reply, the girl unfurled another tapestry:

> *Into a man stuff pieces of corroded heart and lying lips,*
> *And the idols of Ophir will mock as the driven thing rips.*
> *There shall be lost hope in the greatness of this trust,*
> *But ever hope shine forth, then this man become I must!*

"'Make her into a man?'" Peter frowned. "I don't follow you."

"*I* think I know what he means," said Tirzah with a knowing smile, her voice barely above a whisper; she glanced hesitantly at the Nazarene, who nodded. "He means cut off her hair. Give her a change of clothes, and...well...maybe even put a beard on her face. I've seen it done before. We did it to a friend of mine in Rome once."

The idea was simple yet ingenious. For a long moment no one spoke. An expository whistle issued its way out of our artist, Other James. "It just might work!" The words were again a whisper. No one moved. The next voice was Abigail's, the volume level this time raised a notch: "Honey, come over here!" My sister-in-law spoke as if beseeching someone of simple mind, gaining the young girl's attention and coaxing her finally onto a settee. With a long, calculating appraisal, Abby ran a hand through her thick, lovely tresses. Certainly, they could be cut, and the result would be a somewhat more boyish appearance. Placing a "beard" upon that face would be the more important component to the disguise, but could such a thing be done, and if so would it fool the soldiers at the city gates? There was only one way to find out. Abby, with razor in hand, went methodically to work. The locks, in all their wealth, began to drop to the floor.

> Chop it thin and chop it lean
> But let not thy instrument chop flesh or skin—
> My locks now fall to please a king.
> To him I now my poor heart bring,
> The hidden fountain—it lies within.

"What is she babbling about now?" muttered an annoyed Peter.

With a perceptive smile, Matthew replied, "I think she is saying she *likes* Jesus!"

Abby gave a weary sigh, "That much has been evident from the start!" And with that, a spectacularly large cluster of hair fell mendicant-like to the floor. Through all this, the girl was pliant, remaining curiously still, "sensing," I rather believe, if not fully understanding, the goings-on, until eventually her head was shorn, and quite adeptly I might add, into a field of neatly-trimmed thatch. Abby had done a superb job. But at this point she made an announcement: her contributions to the alteration had reached their limit. Giving a haircut was one thing. Growing a "beard" on the face of a young maid was quite another, and, in my sister-in-law's opinion, a task far beyond her simple capabilities.

Yet in this, we had an Apis engendered by a moonbeam...in the form of our artist, Other James, and I sometimes think he was destined in a way to rise to that moment. Rise he did. "It is really no different from doing a mosaic," he said, bending forward while studying the girl's face. "In fact, it *is* a mosaic. We simply build up shaped sections of hair so that they fit neatly together on her face, more or less like tiles." He was no longer the affable companion to the rest of us; the artist had taken over. "Take some of the hair you've just cut and pare down the strands until they are no more than two digits of the finger in length." Taking direction from him, Abby assisted as he commenced assembling the scaffolding of our deliverance—*our* deliverance, as well as Mariamne of Magdala's.

The rest of us also helped. In addition to sizing individual strands of hair, there were pieces of cloth to be cut, sewn, shaped. These strips of cloth would have to fit seamlessly around the contours of the face. A paste mixture had also to be made. The work was quite tedious, but eventually it all began to come together. Throughout, the girl sat still, willingly allowing herself to be transformed, until the beard was quite full. No patchy chin-growth, this! When it was done, we stood back. The amazement I saw reflected around the room, I'm sure, was matched in my own countenance; Mariamne of Magdala's face, framed in its hirsute adornment, evinced a squareness pronouncedly masculine. Moreover, she had crossed an Ocean of Being, becoming in the process a shy fellow who might well have passed as a young noble's subaltern. Other James had truly created a masterpiece, but we had lost time. A *great deal* of it. While lingering behind these walls hunched over cloth strips and unruly hair strands, Passover pilgrims, droves of them, had poured from the city. It was imperative we move and move quickly. Unfortunately one problem still remained. "What are we going to do about these?" It was Matthew who put the question, a simple yet somewhat suggestive inquiry regarding a point of reference so obvious I don't know how we could have missed it: the girl's breasts. With her new beard, and her mind seemingly transported off in some faraway land, Mariamne exhibited a rugged, if somewhat distracted, bearing and manner, and might indeed have been mistaken for a male—from the neck up. Yet jutting out below her tufted chin whiskers were those breasts. While not what I would describe as ample, they were nonetheless, shall we say, *conspicuous*, a slender but pleasing measure of ambrosial paradise wrapped in the sateen fabric of her *istomukhvia*.

"You men get out of here!" commanded Abigail. "Tirzah and I will take care of that!" We were shooed from the room like a pack of jackals. The door was closed, but when it opened again a quarter of an hour later, what emerged was a handsome and beaming young man. The breasts had been tightly bound, and making the transformation complete, Tirzah and Abby had also clad her in a man's *ma'aphoret*. Gone was the marriageable young maid; in her place, a spry and commanding, if somewhat petite, prince of the realm. All in all rather superbly handled. But still there was one rather worrisome matter—those rhymed incantations. From her mouth, albeit encased now in a beard, the verbiage continued to spill, and giving ear, we became aware, *painfully* so, of the most perplexing incongruity of all: that while the physical features were distinctly male, the voice remained stubbornly and persistently feminine. Philip took the overly pessimistic view, as was his customary wont. "This is not going to work! It never was going to work! Her voice is going to be a dead giveaway!"

But Other James seemed to place a certain amount of faith, either in divine providence, or his own artistic achievement, if not both. "As long as she doesn't speak to anyone," he surmised, "we should be alright."

"Honey, listen to me!" Abigail took the young thing by her shoulders. "We're going to be leaving the house here shortly. When we do, you've got to be very quiet, do you hear? Don't speak to anyone on the street. Don't say any poems. If someone speaks to you, don't answer them. Let one of us do the talking. Do you understand?"

> My heart is blanched, my soul is keeled,
> Have thee no fear, my lips are sealed.

It was Matthew who detected linguistic purpose in the seeming poetic gibberish. "I think that means she understood"—and suddenly we were laughing, the girl, amazingly, laughing as well, proving that if she were demon-possessed, she at least had a sense of humor about it. The laughter eventually swept over *all* of us; it was like a therapeutic flood, but we did not, we *could* not, savor it for long; we were in dire need of haste. "Alright," said Jesus when the merriment had begun to subside. "Is everyone ready?" As difficult as making a girl into a man may have been, the more formidable task lay yet before us—getting out of the city.

We bade goodbye to our hosts, Tephtheus and his friends, whose safety we had put sorely at risk. Nothing we could say could possibly be adequate, so we simply embraced them as friends. Then we emerged from the house accompanied by our living, walking mosaic. Brilliant sunlight trammeled the streets. Shouldering our way along through the diminishing but still-considerable crowds, we made for the Essene Gate. So as to lessen the chance of her speaking to anyone, Mariamne was kept positioned at the center of the group. It was perhaps an unnecessary precaution. Just as she had promised, in that odd and eccentric manner of hers, she remained cooperatively silent, but I knew the real trial lay ahead, and I vowed to thank Adonai from the depths of my pounding heart once it was over and we were out of the city, *if* we in fact made it out.

There was something munificent about the sky as it hung above us, and I took comfort from the fact that there were still lots of people around, though as the Essene Gate came into view, I thought that in choosing it as an exit-way we surely had made a poor choice; it was choked with pilgrims and an abundance of soldiers, with a lengthy queue of people standing in wait. I tried to signal to Jesus to turn around, but either he didn't see or affected not to notice, and before I knew it we were there, in the queue ourselves, under the hardened glares of the soldiers. Too late to turn back. Camels, noise, travelers heavily laden with their belongings—it was as copious as perdition. Tantrumlike confusion held sway: a mass of people under close scrutiny, all caught in a line that moved with excruciating slowness. Two hours it took us to get to the head of the procession. The man in front of us, when we finally got there, pleaded to be allowed to pass, but for some reason the soldiers had taken an interest in him. As they searched his belongings, we waited, the moments growing ferriferous with tension. Then it was our turn. Phlegmatically the soldiers looked at us, speaking first to Jesus, then James and Peter, their pointed stares like sharpened scepters. A centurion with a hard declension in his face fastened his meddlesome eyes upon us, boring into each of ours in turn, until coming at last to rest upon the Magdalene, whereupon they halted. Unblinkingly, he studied her, much as one might regard an oddly shaped scale on the side of a fish. What had aroused his suspicions? The girlish frame perhaps? The whiskers I knew were pretty convincing, but were the shoulders a bit too narrow? What about her hands, were they not too delicate and small for a man's? And of course her *voice*. Merciful God, just don't let him ask her a question! It was beginning to look like we were found out, and I felt a punctilious sweat trickling down my back as I wondered what our punishment would be for attempting to escape with a runaway slave from the House of Herod. The soldier's gaze held fast, unabated; moments passed. At last, however, those eyes, so dreadful in their sheer composure, flickered ahead to the next person in line. God be praised!

Then we were told we might proceed. Suddenly we were moving again…

Merciful Adonai, we had made it!—out of the mob, out of the gate, out of the city. The relief was as a dagger of bliss, but I didn't begin to breathe easier until we got up into the hill country. Finally, we were there, however, in those wonderful hills, precious panoplies of restraint and solitude, with Jerusalem safely behind us. It was early evening. We stopped at a spring at the base of some cypress trees and quenched our thirst. "I think it's safe to take this off now." Other James began deftly to deconstruct the Magdalene's putative whiskers, doing so in an amount of time, thankfully, not near as great as putting them in place had required; away also came the *ma'aphoret*, revealing hair shorn boyishly close. I looked at her now. Her face was tinged with redness, the result of chafing brought on by the paste and hair with which she had come in contact. It had left the skin splotchy and discolored. The effect, all in all, was quite ugly, but as I beheld her, gazing toward her with a mixture of wonder as well as a rather puzzled interest, she struck me, rather oddly, as more ravishingly beautiful than ever.

LaSalle III

The Apocalypse

LaSalle looked at the clock: 10:37. Outside, a stately full moon hung in the sky, a trembling blossom, treading gingerly on an elongated and receding plume of cloud, just above that purple band of stratosphere where its own light melded with the spectral flush of the city. He regarded it for a moment— the sight of waves of sound and light, the sight of earthly light colliding with heavenly light. As he stared out the window, the Aramaic words *bar d'nasha* came to his mind. Son of Man.

Son of Man/*Bar d'nasha*. The term appears more than 70 times in the gospels, but what does it mean? When used, it is almost always by Jesus, seemingly for the most part in reference to himself. Elsewhere in the New Testament, we encounter the phrase rarely, once in Acts, twice in Revelation. So why so prevalent in the gospels? And are those gospel sayings in which the term appears truly authentic sayings of Jesus? Or were they fabrications added later by the early Church? If authentic (a dubious notion for a good many scholars), what would Jesus, assuming he *did* in fact say them, have meant by them? Was he claiming some sort of title for himself? Or were the words *bar d'nasha* merely a nontitular, Aramaic idiom? If the latter, was it a circumlocution for "I"—as in, *foxes have holes, birds of the air have nests, but I have no place to lay* my *head?* Or was it an indefinite, generic reference to "man"—as in, *whoever speaks a word against* **man** *will be forgiven, but whoever speaks against the Holy Spirit will not be forgiven?*

On the other hand, if it was a title, what sort of title was it? Perhaps an apocalyptic/messianic one, and if so, did it derive from the figure in Daniel 7:13? Possibly. But the "one like a son of man" referred to in Daniel is triumphant, a supernatural being, who comes "with the clouds of heaven" and is given sovereign powers. Was Jesus not more likely invoking his humanity? And if that was the case, was the son of man Jesus had in mind perhaps closer to the suffering servant of Isaiah 53? Or could we establish a link to the son-of-man-figure from 1 Enoch, a figure represented as a pre-existent, divine being who constitutes, like the son of man in Daniel, a rather more heavenly than earthly messiah? But then maybe it wasn't a messianic title at all. If not, then could it be a genealogical indicator? The word *adam* in Hebrew means "man." Was Jesus referring to himself as the "son of Adam?" Or did it perhaps mean "Son of Joseph" or "Son of Mary?" Did it designate a "lowly human?" Or did it perhaps designate, rather, the primal man, the "ideal human?"

All of these theories, and many others, had been put forth by scholars over the years.

LaSalle lingered at the window for a moment longer. At last he turned his attention back to his work on the translation, but for some reason he could not focus on it; even now, the words kept running through his mind. *Bar d'nasha.* Most likely, it *was* an apocalyptic reference, he thought. And most likely it *did* derive from Daniel 7:13. So how, in turn, did the author of Daniel intend for the title to be construed? In chapter seven of the book, Daniel has a dream in which four beasts, viewed as four world empires, rise out of the sea. In verses two through eight, they emerge, one by one, with the fourth beast described as "different" from the other three, a creature both "terrifying and dreadful." Daniel is "troubled in spirit" and seeks an explanation; an angelic figure tells him, "The fourth beast is a fourth kingdom that will appear on earth. It will be different from all the other kingdoms and will devour the whole earth, trampling it down and crushing it."

Many scholars today, probably most, reject the view that Daniel was written during the Babylonian exile of the sixth century BC, as the text itself asserts. The widely held belief is that it dates to around 170 BC during the reign of Antiochus Epiphanes. Antiochus was a Seleucid. After the death of Alexander the Great in 323 BC, the Macedonian ruler's vast empire was divided up among his generals, with eventually the Ptolemies taking control in the west, and the Seleucids consolidating power in the east. Israel at first came under the Ptolemy sphere, but later was ruled by the Seleucids. It was the Seleucid ruler Antiochus IV, or Antiochus Epiphanes, who desecrated the Temple and attempted to force the Jews to undergo Hellenization; the Book of Daniel is largely thought to have been written in response. So what, then, of the fourth beast, the one which would trample and devour the earth? Was the writer of Daniel referring to the empire of Alexander the Great, or to that of the Seleucids, or perhaps Rome? Take your pick. The Roman conquest of Palestine didn't occur until 63 BC, a century *after* the death of Antiochus. Thus, a choice of Rome as the fourth beast that would "devour the earth" would require philosophical acceptance of the notion that long-range prophecy is possible. Perhaps it is a moot point. In any event, we come to verses 13-14. Enter the son of man:

> In my vision at night I looked and there before me was one like a son of man, coming with the clouds of heaven. He approached the Ancient of Days and was led into his presence. He was given authority, glory, and sovereign power; all peoples, nations, and men of every language worshipped him. His dominion was an everlasting dominion that will not pass away, and his kingdom is one that will never be destroyed.

A regal figure, yes. A king. One given "authority, glory, and sovereign power" directly from God. So how does this figure square with the one described by Jesus in Matthew 8:20 (and paralleled in Luke 9:58):

> Foxes have holes and the birds of the air have nests, but the Son of Man has no place to lay his head.

Did Jesus intend for it to be the anomaly it appears to be? A heavy dose of irony perhaps? The phrase "Son of Man" appears nowhere in the letters of Paul. Yet it proliferates throughout the gospels, and then crops up again in the Book of Revelation, where the son of man figure speaks to John of Patmos and instructs him to write down in a book the visions that come to him. And what then follows is "the nightmare of God," as St. John's Apocalypse has been termed.

Heavily impregnated with symbolism, the Book of Revelation is puzzling and mysterious. A mystique in fact has come to surround it. Despite its many ambiguities, the tract has been, and continues to be, interpreted in creative, often absurd ways. It is regarded as history, end-times prophecy, or even both, by categories of expounders to whom such names as "preterists," "historicists," and "futurists" have been applied. In modern times, mainstream Christianity has tended to deemphasize the Apocalypse; church lectionaries seldom feature it any more, yet its passages have been evoked in countless books and movies. Moreover, for all its mysterious qualities, it *does* seem to resonate with disparate branches of the faith, from fundamentalists at one end of the spectrum, to liberation theologians at the other. Scholars, for their own part, have viewed the Woman Clothed with the Sun as representing the Virgin Mary, or, alternately, as the heavenly or earthly church, or Israel, while exegetes of various stripes and hues have struggled to name the beast, or decode the number 666. In all of history, perhaps no other piece of writing, including the works of Plato and Shakespeare, has held such sway over the human imagination, or the Western imagination at any rate. This has shown no sign of slacking off in modern times. On the contrary, if anything, with the world entering the nuclear age in the 20th century, the reverse has been the case.

In 1970, Hal Lindsey published *The Late Great Planet Earth*. Translated into 53 languages, the book became something of a manifesto for Christian dispensationalists, eventually selling more than 35 million copies and generating an astounding amount of mainstream attention. Essentially Lindsey's interpretation of biblical prophecy, *The Late Great Planet Earth* is filled with cold war rhetoric, with the author casting Russia as the biblical "Gog" and warning of "the vast hordes of the Orient" who, in Lindsey's view, would probably become "united under the Red Chinese war machine" in time for the final Battle of Armageddon. These theories were finely tuned in a follow-up book, published in 1973, entitled *There's a New World Coming*, a chapter-by-chapter, verse-by-verse analysis of Lindsey's interpretation of the Book of Revelation. In it, he speaks of the "merciless, sweeping tyranny" of an Antichrist who would rise out of Europe. Significantly, the European Common Market, in the early 1970s, stood at just under ten members; Daniel's fourth beast was described as having ten horns; likewise the "Beast from the Sea" that appears in Revelation 13. Lindsey took it all as evidence that the European Common Market (now with 27 members and known as the European Union) would morph into a "Revived Roman Empire," that would supplant the United States in power. As for the latter, America suffered from a weakness in its will to resist communism, and "is nowhere intimated in the Bible's prophecies of the last war of the world."

In yet another best selling book on prophecy, John F. Walvoord, chancellor at Dallas Theological Seminary, also warned of a coming world conflagration in his *Armageddon, Oil, and the Middle East Crisis*. The book was originally published in 1973, but was reissued in 1990—just in time, seemingly, for the U.S. invasion of Iraq in the first Gulf War. Walvoord, too, saw a revived Roman empire shaping up in Europe, but he also regarded the "power of Arab oil" as being destined to play a deciding role in what he referred to as the "Armageddon countdown." *Armageddon, Oil, and the Middle East Crisis* cites a number of passages from Revelation, including its references to the Euphrates River (16:12); Walvoord also depicted Saddam Hussein as having "the ambition of establishing a new Babylonian Empire with himself in the role of Nebuchadnezzar." But as for any role America might play in the planet's coming "death struggle," Walvoord seemed to agree with Lindsey: "No specific prophecy whatever is found concerning the role of the United States, indicating that its contribution will be a secondary one as the world moves on to Armageddon," he said.

Revelation's use of "Babylon" as a code word for imperial Rome was of course key for evangelicals watching events unfold in the Middle East. But some Christian dispensationalists took the literal view, that is that a *literal* rebuilding of ancient Babylon, on the site where it once stood in today's Iraq, was a necessary precursor to the final Battle of Armageddon. Saddam Hussein's alleged plans to do no less than just that were revealed in *The Rise of Babylon: Sign of the End Times* by Charles Dyer of the Moody Bible Institute. Arousing considerable public interest, particularly in the evangelical community, the book was originally published in 1990, and then reissued in early 2003—apparently timed for the advent of America's *second* invasion of Iraq. "Prideful" and "barbaric"—these are some of the adjectives Dyer used to describe Saddam Hussein, in a book whose front cover artwork featured an image of the Iraqi leader's face, with a mushroom cloud adorning the back. And what of America? How did it figure into Revelation's prophecies? Again, like Lindsey and Walvoord, Dyer felt the United States was "strangely absent" from biblical predictions of the end times.

But of course nothing captured the public imagination quite like the *Left Behind* series by authors Tim LaHaye and Jerry Jenkins. The books hit the mass-market fiction audience starting in the mid 1990s, serving up the adventures of a "tribulation force" of Christian believers who do battle with the Antichrist Nicholas Carpathia. The latter assumes control of the "Global Community" (the newly renamed United Nations), and moves its headquarters to "New Babylon," which has been erected—where else?—on the ancient site in Iraq.

In reading the Book of Revelation, university scholars generally part company, and in significant ways, with evangelical authors. One such scholar has been Elisabeth Schüssler Fiorenza, a Harvard professor of religious studies and author of two books on the Apocalypse. The Book of Revelation's main value is the insight it provides into the thinking of Christian communities of the late first century, argues Schüssler Fiorenza, who cited Walvoord in particular as an example of "how a fundamentalist reading of Revelation and imperialist politics intertwine."

"Biblical scholars do not read Revelation as a code by which to decipher events of our own time," she adds.

Writing in 1991, Schüssler Fiorenza viewed the Apocalypse as exhibiting "bizarre language" as well as a "grotesque world of vision," yet she also felt it was an "outcry for justice." To look upon the book as a prediction of future events, she reasoned, would be "disastrous," however. Instead, Revelation should be regarded as a "vision of a just world." Schüssler Fiorenza also considered the premise of authorship by John the disciple of Jesus to be "not tenable."

In his 1993 book, *The Theology of the Book of Revelation*, UK scholar and professor Richard Bauckham viewed the Apocalypse as a work "composed with astonishing care and skill." In his view, "we should certainly not doubt that John had remarkable visionary experiences," yet Bauckham, too, dispelled the notion of the book's being a picture of the future. Rather, he said, the ancient author's intended purpose was "to counter the Roman imperial view of the world," but the way he went about this is what aroused Bauckham's admiration for the text; the Apocalypse, he noted, "creates a complex network" of literary cross references, parallels, and contrasts, all put together in an "astonishingly meticulous" manner. The grouping of various things into sevens—cups, seals, churches, and the like—is only a small part of this picture. In addition to these more obvious groupings, Bauckham discovered "numerical patterns" in references to God, Christ, and the Spirit scattered throughout the text. These references often fall into factors of four or seven. For instance, seven designations for "Lord God Almighty" (found at 1:8; 4:8; 11:17; 15:3; 16:7; 19:6; and 21:22), are complemented by seven beatitudes (at 1:3; 14:13; 16:15; 19:9; 20:6; and 22:7 and 14), and fourteen occurrences of the name "Jesus." In addition, the word "Lamb" in reference to Christ, occurs twenty-eight (7 x 4) times. Seven of these are in phrases linking God and the Lamb together (at 5:13; 6:16; 7:10; 14:4; 21:22; and 22:1 and 3); while there are also *four* references to the "seven Spirits" (1:4; 3:1; 4:5; 5:6)...and *seven* references (5:9; 7:9; 10:11; 11:9; 13:7; 14:6; 17:15) to what Bauckham referred to as the "four-fold phrase" ("peoples, tribes, languages, and nations")—a phrase used by John as an indicator for all humanity. Baukham felt patterns such as these were "likely to be deliberate." It was a skillful, meticulous analysis, and a not-unreasonable conclusion, LaSalle thought.

In the ancient world, the number seven represented completeness, while the world, with its four wind directions, four corners, etc., was depicted by the number four. For Bauckham, Revelation addressed the "worldwide tyranny of Rome" in a manner that made it essentially "the most powerful piece of political resistance literature from the period of the early Empire." Of course, Rome isn't the only thing at which the Apocalypse takes aim. The words "synagogue of Satan" are found at two points in the text (2:9 and 3:9). For Bauckham, the phrase sounded "dangerously anti-Semitic," and in fact "would be, if repeated outside its original context." But Baukham regarded 2:9 and 3:9 as evidence of an "intra-Jewish dispute," rather than an outpouring of anti-Semitism, a dispute which he described as "a rift like that between the temple establishment and the Qumran community, who denounced their fellow Jews as 'an assembly of deceit and a congregation of Belial.'"

Indeed the Apocalypse does have "insiders," as well as those who seem clearly and pejoratively regarded as "outsiders." Scholar Cameron Afzal felt the tract's intended audience was the *insiders*, and that as such the Book of Revelation was not, per se, a missionary text intended to convert others to the Christian faith. Furthermore, Afzal, in his 2008 work, *The Mystery of the Book of Revelation*, contended that the author, whichever John it may have been, was possibly the most revolutionary thinker of his age.

> Among us are artists, visionaries, thinkers with creative minds
> that help shape our communal perspectives. Their work becomes
> a part of culture and helps us to perceive and apprehend both
> ourselves and the world around us. These cultural artifacts don't
> necessarily create reality in order to flourish and grow.
> Sometimes one of us will attempt to radically reconfigure the way
> in which we look at the world. St. John of Patmos was one such
> man.

Afzal felt John had intended his narrative of world cataclysm to function as a "future trace," as Afzal put it, an indication that something is to occur in the future, much as a glow in the sky before dawn indicates the sun will rise. "In a sense the future trace lies at the foundation of all modern physics in the form of probability theory or even quantum mechanics," he said. He also noted the book's extensive grounding in Jewish literature and culture, and said there is an "emerging consensus" that the author was indeed a Jew.

LaSalle was no physicist. But his understanding of the basic concept of quantum theory was that matter possesses a particle-wave duality, exhibiting characteristics of each. This in turn gives rise to a level of uncertainty over a particle's precise position, creating in effect a "range" of possibilities. The wave is what determines the range, but when the position of the particle is measured, the range narrows, creating what scientists refer to as "wave collapse." Why the phenomenon occurs has not been understood. Is it the mere act of observing? If so, would there then be no wave collapse without consciousness, and would the collapse therefore be deemed a result of "downward causation"? LaSalle was a priest, yes, and he dealt with matters of the spirit, a dubious concept for most scientists, yet in the world of quantum physics, dubious concepts often materialize into reality, the experiments of French physicist Alain Aspect and associates in the early 1980s being a case in point. Aspect proved that two particles emitted from the same wave function remained inextricably correlated. A change in one produced a similar and instantaneous change in the other, even when the particles were separated by a distance of more than a kilometer. Communication normally occurs by means of signals carrying energy. But in this case, there was none. The effect was referred to by some as "spooky action at a distance."

Or, LaSalle thought, as Jesus might have said to Mary Magdalene..."Touch me not."

To no great surprise, actual victims of oppression read the Book of Revelation in a manner far, far different from ivory-towered university professors, or even pulpit-pounding evangelicals, and LaSalle considered now the power of the Apocalypse and its relevance to the South African struggle against Apartheid. This in fact had been the subject of a 1987 book, *Comfort and Protest*, by Allan Boesak.

> I heard from family members how a mother and her four-month-old baby and six-year-old handicapped boy were driven out of their shack by tear gas. As they ran out they were driven back again by gunshots. While they were inside, the shack was set alight and they were burned alive. The police looked on without lifting a finger. The young man who told me the story was barely eighteen. I had no answer to his burning anger, nor had I comfort for the tears of the old woman who stood next to him.

The "comfort" Boesak finally elected to offer was that of Saint John's Apocalypse. Boesak, a minister in the Dutch Reformed Mission Church of South Africa, initiated a series of Bible studies for his congregants on the Book of Revelation. The latter, he held, has "much to say to our own times, and especially to those of us who, like the churches of John's time, must live under political repression." Boesak rejected the futurist interpretation of Revelation adopted by evangelicals, but likewise he also found fault with scholars who read the work solely in terms of its first century setting. Instead, he put forth a "contemporary-historical" understanding of the work:

"No prophecy receives its full and final fulfillment in one given historical moment only, or even in a series of events. If the prophecy is the expression of an undeniable truth which comes from God, it will be fulfilled at different times and in different ways in the history of the world."

But South Africa wasn't the only place people were reading Revelation and drawing solace from it. In 1994, the Chilean priest Pablo Richard published his book, *Apocalypse: A People's Commentary on the Book of Revelation*, following a series of workshops held primarily in Central America. The gatherings averaged eighty persons each, including peasants, indigenous people, leaders of Christian Base Communities and the like. Richard's conclusion was that Revelation is having a "decisive influence" in the Third World, where it is "coming to be the preferred book of the Christian Base Communities" and other ecclesial movements seeking social change. Its appeal, he said, is that it "unveils the reality of the poor and legitimizes their liberation." Richard furthermore felt that the Church ignores or downplays Saint John's vision at its own peril. "Over the long run, it was disregard of Revelation that opened the way for the incorporation of the church into the dominant imperial system and the construction of an authoritarian Christendom. To retrieve Revelation is to retrieve a fundamental dimension of the Jesus movement and of the origins of Christianity."

Unlike Richard, Catholic lay writers Wes Howard-Brook and Anthony Gwyther, writing in 1999, went so far as to attach a modern-day name to the beast: "global capital," they called it. The co-authors regarded Revelation's imagery as "lurid and violent," but then the beast of global capital also exerts a "systemic violence" that is "visible and apparent," they said. "We have also noted the 'war against the poor' waged on behalf of global capital in Latin America and other places when people are murdered for daring to seek dignity and the basics of life."

But the violence capable of being unleashed upon the planet by those of wealth and privilege was not only sensed and intuited by Third World peasants. Others saw it as well. In the United States, the Jesuit priest Daniel Berrigan wrote *Nightmare of God* while jailed for his anti-nuclear activism in the early 1980s. Berrigan takes his own country to task for "preparing for ever more lethal incursions" against other countries and peoples, while he also issues a withering criticism of biblical scholars: "To most scholars of the Bible, the crimes of the U.S. Air Force are forever beside the point. Thus does crime multiply and scholarship rot." The Apocalypse, in Berrigan's view, contains a "social bias" in favor of the victims of oppression, *unlike* America, which Berrigan felt was bent upon "carving the earth" through war. "Bellicose, selfish, self-deluded, icy, absolutely resolute—behold the Rome of the Book of Revelation. Behold also America?" For Berrigan there was only one choice: "resist the state."

With the publication of *Nightmare of God* in 1982, Berrigan may well have become the first American to draw a public analogy between modern day United States and the beast in Revelation, but outside the United States, others were making identical comparisons. One was Guatemalan exile poet Julia Esquivel. Her poem, "Thanksgiving Day in the U.S.", was written in November of 1981 and published the following year in her collection *Threatened with Resurrection*; here the poet speaks of being "led by the Spirit" on the "eve of Thanksgiving Day" into the desert where she has a "vision of Babylon."

> The Spirit told me:
> "In the river of death
> flows the blood of many peoples
> sacrificed without mercy
> and removed a thousand times from their lands...
> the blood of Kechís, of Panzós,
> of blacks from Haiti, of Guaranís from Paraguay,
> of the peoples sacrificed for 'development'
> in the trans-Amazonic strip,
> the blood of Indians' ancestors
> who lived on these lands, of those who
> even now are kept hostage in the Rocky Mountains
> and in the Black Hills of Dakota
> by the guardians of the Beast."
>
> Later another Angel showed me
> the plains of California,
> and I heard a great cry
> which poured from the earth,
> rising above the smoke
> from the skyscrapers,
> until even the Father could hear it,
> and it reached the throne of the Sacrificial Lamb.
> It was the cry of the blood
> of thousands of innocent martyrs.
>
> Then I recognized the Beast
> which has a thousand faces
> and a different mark

on the forehead of each.
The marks blazed with arrogance
in colorful, scintillating lights,
imitating the stars
and wasting the energy
stolen from the world's poor.

These marks
deceived the ignorant
and those who flee from the truth:
those who worship the Beast
in the Bank of America
or in its many other temples.

The marks offered them
sure and peaceful sleep,
a way to acquire prestige
and a thousand unnecessary things.
To continue along this path,
they had to harden themselves
against the Lamb and against
His Kingdom of Peace and Justice...

Then the Spirit
opened my ears and I was able to hear
the voices of the false prophets
continually vomiting falsehoods:

"The Government of the Babylonian States
will protect Western Europe
by positioning powerful missiles..."
"Haig...and the minister of Israel
sign a pact to ensure the bloody-peace
in Palestine..."

They twist the truth,
calling their intervention into Central America and the Caribbean
"peace and development,"
in order to silence the outcry of the thousands
crucified in El Salvador and Guatemala.

The years 1980-81 were bloody ones in the particular region of Central America, El Salvador and Guatamela, Esquivel speaks of. On January 31, 1980, a group of Mayan peasants occupied the Spanish embassy in Guatemala City, protesting the kidnapping and murder of peasants by the U.S.-backed government. Over the objections of the Spanish ambassador, Guatemalan police stormed the embassy, touching off a fire that left 36 people dead, including the father of Nobel laureate Rigoberta Menchú. The act was described as a "defining moment" in the Guatemalan Civil War, a conflict in which an estimated quarter of a million people were killed or disappeared. In neighboring El Salvador, on March 24, less than two months later, Archbishop Óscar Romero was assassinated while celebrating mass—one day after delivering a sermon calling for soldiers to obey God's higher order and to cease human rights violations on behalf of the government. The assassination was believed to have been carried out by a death squad operating under the orders of Salvadoran Army officer Roberto D'Aubuisson. Romero was shot while holding up the Eucharist. His blood spilled over the altar.

Then some eight months later, on December 2, four American church women, nuns Dorothy Kazel, Maura Clark, and Ita Ford, along with lay missionary Jean Donovan, were raped and murdered by members of the Salvadoran National Guard. At the time of her death, Donovan, just 27 years old, had been doing missionary work in El Salvador for three years. Her duties had included burying the bodies left behind by the death squads. She was said to have been an especially devoted follower of Romero, and reportedly had stood next to his coffin. During the bishop's funeral, attended by thousands, a bomb exploded, followed by shots fired. Some thirty to fifty people died in the resulting melee. Donovan survived that experience, but wrote to a friend in May of that year: "Everything is really hitting so close now."

Then, as the timeline goes, comes November of 1981: Esquivel writes the poem, "Thanksgiving Day in the U.S."

In the ancient world, "prophecy" and "poetry" were often regarded as one and the same, and maybe, LaSalle thought now, there was indeed something akin to "prophetic insight" in Esquivel's writing of the poem. Or at least in its line about the "crucified" of El Salvador. On December 11 (with the ink on the poem perhaps not even dry), the Atlacatl Battalion of the U.S.-trained-and-supplied Salvadoran Army carried out a massacre in El Mozote and surrounding villages. Just over a thousand people died. Women and girls were raped, houses burned to the ground, animals slaughtered. The attack seemed to have been part of a counterinsurgency strategy of "draining the sea to catch the fish." The idea was that the people were "the sea," while the guerillas were the "fish" that swam in the sea. Arriving after the soldiers had left, a detachment of FMLN guerillas, along with reporters from the rebel station Radio Venceremos, found that the attackers had been thorough; inside the village church were overturned pews, scattered saints, walls pockmarked with bullets, and "a mountain of rotting bodies." The guerillas would come to refer to it as "the saddest Christmas." Before leaving the village, they discovered graffiti left behind by the soldiers:

The Atlacatl Battalion was here
The Angels of Hell

Several years later, by which time El Mozote had become an abandoned graveyard, a contingent of guerillas made a return pass through the area by night, noticing a curious phenomenon: the entire ghost-village lit up by fireflies. Years later, one of them would remark upon it to the author José Ignacio López Vigil:

> It was a dark night and when we approached the abandoned village thousands of fireflies lit up at the same time. Thousands and thousands, the entire woods glowed. Then, as if by some mysterious order, they all went dark at the same moment. Then they all lit up again with that spectral light. Then they all went dark. I swear I've never seen anything like it in my life. I don't imagine anyone who was in the column that night has been able to forget the call of the fireflies.

But Esquivel wasn't the only Central American dissident combining the poetic and the prophetic at this time. In 1977, Nicaraguan poet and priest Ernesto Cardenal penned the poem "Apocalypse," in which seven angels come down to earth "bearing cups of smoke in their hands." One angel pours forth a "neutronic cup," while another's is of "Cobalt," and so on and so forth, and in the apocalypse which ensues, "Hiroshima's fate was envied." And hence, writes Cardenal, "BABYLON THE GREAT IS FALLEN"—a "great whore" who had come "clutching all manner of checks and bonds and shares and commercial documents."

Thus, has the Book of Revelation been read, perceived, and interpreted by a wide range of Westerners, Westerners grounded, in most cases, in the Christian tradition. But perhaps not surprisingly, the Apocalypse has also generated commentary from non-Westerners. One is India's Paramahansa Yogananda. Unlike many others to pen discourses on Revelation, this twentieth century Hindu yogi never questioned the authenticity of authorship by John the disciple of Jesus. In fact Yogananda, who, upon his death was given the title *Premavatar*, "incarnation of love," held John to be the most advanced disciple of the "Christ-man" Jesus.

> The records left by Saint John, among the various books of the New Testament, evince the highest degree of divine realization, making known the deep, esoteric truths experienced by Jesus and transferred to John. Not only in his Gospel, but in his epistles and especially in the profound metaphysical experiences symbolically described in the Book of Revelation, John presents the truths taught by Jesus from the point of view of inward intuitive realization.

For Yogananda, John's words contained a measure of "precision" not found in other books of the New Testament. Revelation's various septenary groupings, for instance, he viewed as representing the seven cerebrospinal centers of divine consciousness in the body. Expounding on one passage in particular, Revelation 2:26-28, with its reference to the "morning star," the Indian spiritual teacher said the words therein contained John's description of the *ajna chakra*, the spiritual eye, located at the center of the forehead. "The 'morning star' or 'star of the East,'" he said, "is the spiritual single eye in the Christ or *Kutastha* center of the forehead (east), a microcosm of the creative vibratory light and consciousness of God." In the passage in question, the author of the Apocalypse has Jesus promising the light of this star to those who remain steadfast. He also inserts a quote from the second Psalm.

> To him who overcomes and does my will to the end, I will give authority over the nations—*he will rule them with an iron scepter; he will dash them to pieces like pottery*—just as I have received authority from my Father. I will also give him the morning star.

For Yogananda, it was yet another example of Saint John's *precision*. "Through the spiritual eye, the adept yogi attains mastery over the forces ('nations') in his physical, astral, and causal bodies, and gains entry into the realm of Spirit," he said.

It was certainly an *interesting* interpretation, thought LaSalle, a far cry, to be sure, from evangelical views of Revelation. Alien as well from the elevated but starched discourse of Western academia, and as he considered this, a new thought came to him: is that what had happened to Cateline? Had God given her the 'morning star'? And in the process had she somehow, as Yogananda put it, gained "entry into the realm of Spirit"? He adjusted the Tiffany lamp and rubbed his eyes tiredly. Yes maybe that. Or maybe something else. But somehow the child had been able to see a wall, a wall containing *faces of the dead*, five thousand miles away in Sri Lanka. Somehow, she had. He looked at the budding screen saver on his computer screen and thought suddenly of what Jesus had said about love. *As I have loved you, so you must love one another.* Words from the Gospel of John. Yogananda was right. There *was* a remarkable "precision" here. Of all the sayings ever attributed to Jesus, by all the ancient gospel writers, this was probably the most important, the most vital not to lose track of. *Love one another.* The human heart is capable of many wonderful, and not-so-wonderful, things, but the most important of all, the one supreme feat of its many, many capacities, has to be, can only be, love; suddenly the Jesuit's thoughts turned toward the two people whose presence in this world he cherished most, Denise, a nun of the Ursuline Order who had answered her calling early in life, yet who had a great heart for children; and Cateline, a vivacious young girl inhabiting a world of darkness yet who somehow possessed a gladdening spirit of light. And he knew that what he felt was more than simple friendship; it was love. But he was a *priest*. He had pledged his life to God. Yes, but did that mean he was not supposed to have human feelings? For have them he did. If he was honest, he had to admit it. Love—it was what he felt for Denise, *had* felt for a great long time, and in the time since Cateline had entered their lives it had grown rather than diminished. And so it was to this, the reality of an unfulfilled love, that all his years in the priesthood had brought him finally. But what about love for God? What about the holy bridal chamber? Did not strong feelings for other human beings complicate that? Surely they did! Love for God, divine devotion, or *bhakti*, as it's referred by some—it had always been his main reason for taking the vows he had. What else, fundamentally, was being a priest all about? How could he now turn his back on such a love? He couldn't. But strangely, over time, he had noticed his love for Denise, rather than detracting from his love for God, had somehow *increased* it—by making it more powerful and real. Yet what was he to do with these feelings? What was he to do with that section of his heart where Denise had gained entry? He had no answer. He knew only that giving your love to God is like dying a little bit each day.

The clock—10:55.

Bar d'nasha. The Son of Man. The future, the past, the present...and an ancient apocalyptic writing seen through the prism of each, as viewed and exposited by only a *few* of the Book of Revelation's many, *many* expositors.

But *what if*—what if the author *himself*, John of Patmos, were suddenly to materialize out of the fog of time and obligingly offer up his own thoughts on the text he had written? An abstract, academic question surely, yet frighteningly, it was precisely what the Dura-Europos scrolls may tell us. Yes, he thought, and what then? What if this exposition of all expositions were made public? How long before the world would drink from the "neutronic cup"? Two weeks? Two months? Two *years* maybe? Yes, maybe two years...*if* humanity were very lucky. For how much longer could he and Arthur keep the content of the scrolls hidden? And were they justified in assuming they even had a right to? *Moral* questions, questions he had never dreamed of before, much less considered he would ever have to try and answer. But soon an answer would have to be found. In 1991, the Society of Biblical Literature had passed a resolution calling for open access and availability, to *all* scholars, of *all* newly discovered ancient manuscripts. "If the condition of the written materials requires that access to them be restricted, arrangements should be made for a facsimile reproduction that will be accessible to all scholars," the resolution states, and already the pressure was on; already Arthur was getting hammered on why the policy was not being adhered to. Arthur's solution, to imply to the media that the problem lay not with him, but rather with the Syrian government, was extremely unfair to the Syrians. Besides which, it was a charade that could not continue much longer.

LaSalle picked up the plate that earlier had held his apple slices. He took it to the kitchen, washed it, returning to his desk, where, seated once more, he leafed through his translation. He was ninety-nine percent certain the "John" named in the gospels as the disciple of Jesus and the "John" of the Dura-Europos scrolls were one and the same man. But was this man also the "John of Patmos" of the Book of Revelation? *This* he was less sure of. It required a great deal more study, more time. But how much more time did he have?

"I ate the book"—it was a Semitic idiom meaning, "I committed the book to memory." In chapter 10 of the Apocalypse, John "eats" a book that tastes sweet but turns bitter in his stomach. LaSalle had arranged to take a year's sabbatical from the University. At some point in the upcoming twelve months, he realized now, he would have to "eat" the Dura-Europos scrolls. But once he did, how long before they turned bitter on his stomach?

Adjusting the lamp once more, he resumed his work.

Sell Everything You Own,
Give the Money to the Poor,
And Come and Follow Me

Chapter Forty-Nine

We made for the last place we figured any Jew would try and follow—Samaria. And arriving in that distant-but-close land we learned a few things about loving your enemies. It was a lesson I had not expected. For most of us, there was no time in our lives when we had ever been taught to look upon Samaritans as anything other than the lowest of the low, and as regards the Samaritans we now encountered, and their lifelong prejudices toward we who were Jews, much I should have thought was the same. Why Samaritans and Jews were so despised of one another I'll not go into. It is a history of hatred, long and sad, and this, after all, is a story of love. That we had thought we should find ourselves in hostile territory in Samaria, somewhat less hostile maybe than Jerusalem but hostile nonetheless, goes without saying, yet it did not turn out this way. In the wake of an encounter between Jesus and a woman at a well, we were led into the town of Sychar and here were shown a rare measure of friendship.

Given we were in essence fleeing the authorities in Jerusalem, none too choosy could we be about whose hospitality we accepted, even if it meant abiding under the shelter of a Samaritan. For Jews, holiness has always meant separation from everything unclean, and the inhabitants of Samaria had long ago been established as among the most unclean creatures around, but for us, what transpired in Sychar was a bit like looking down at one's navel and finding there the heavens. I don't know which was the more astonishing for the villagers, having a young girl turn up in their midst speaking naught but rhymes, or a group of Jews willing to eat at the same table with them. But not only was the Nazarene *willing* to share their table, he was actually *eager* to, as they soon discovered. It was not to be expected our stay would be harmonious, yet that is precisely what happened, and I am happy to relate as much.

Yet I must also relate something else even more unexpected. If the Samaritans were astonished at having a rhyme-talking rebus turn up in their village, we on the Jewish side were no less astonished when that rhyming, as if it had finally outlived its usefulness, stopped. All along, I had assumed Yeshua had done what he could and that the Magdalene's speech peculiarities were more or less entrenched and permanent. But I was wrong. It was late on our first evening in Sychar when it happened. The meal had for some time been finished, the dishes cleared away, the fire burned down to a contented glow. With a small number of the villagers, we continued to occupy a seat in the presence of the embers, but it was late. Most had long since turned in. The Nazarene and Mariamne of Magdala, however, abided still in that fading light, as did I, Peter and James, along with four of five of the villagers. Side by side sat Jesus and Mariamne, and at one particularly fluid moment, their faces turned to each other, as their lips met; it was not a long, lingering kiss, but there was a sparkling radiance to the moment, as if it had risen up from some birthplace deep within the ocean. A kiss, yes. Yet it was also a key inasmuch as it seemed to unlock the girl's heart, tongue, and mind, all three, along with a conjunctive door leading to each; from that moment on, the rhyming, every bit of it, ceased, and as her speech fell into the commonplace, the mystified Samaritan villagers looked on approvingly.

We left that happy region soon after, whereupon Jesus began telling a new parable. It was about a man waylaid by robbers, a man found on the side of the road and cared for by a good-hearted Samaritan. If you love your enemies as you love yourself we all become one, a fountain of gold inside the gestating heart of God. And *that* was the invaluable lesson we learned in Sychar.

Chapter Fifty

It was unclear how active Herod's pursuit of Mariamne might still be, but upon leaving Samaria, we affected quick passage through Galilee, steering clear of Tiberias, the tetrarch's capitol, and skirting Gennesaret by night. At dawn we arrived in Bethsaida. Philip was at last reunited with his wife and child, but even here in the familiar and relatively safe environs of Bethsaida we resolved to linger only a short while, and that evening we set out for Gaulanitis and the lands of Mount Hermon, which were well outside Herod's jurisdiction; to stay as far out of the tetrarch's reach as possible seemed advisable for now.

With little let up we pushed deep into Gaulanitis, coming weary and footsore by the second day to a rushing river. Jagged rocks surrounded it on either side, as it stove through pine and holm oak, through a forest so dense it provided a canopy above our heads. The water was cool and sweet, and we set about raising tents and making a camp. Holes were dug for food scraps, as well as for bodily wastes, one for the women, one for the men. To the south lay Bethsaida; Gischala to the south and west; Damascus north and east, yet it seemed, by fortune, we had found an abode not only lovely and habitable, but remote enough to provide us with a measure of safety. We did not know it then, but the secluded little spot was to remain our home for the next three months.

Having secured our tents, we set out in exploration, penetrating the tall tree growth, looking for firewood, while encountering before long a little-used trail; deeper and deeper it led us into this sylvan world, until at last we reached a narrow break in the canopy, where the sun was able, just barely, to cast down uraeus-shaped dapples of itself into a mossy clearing. Here Thomas' feet exercised a brief but graceful series of skips. "Feel of this moss! It makes you want to remove your sandals and dance around!"

Tirzah, also noting the sumptuousness of the ground, added, "Aye, and tickle your toes until they dream happily."

"Perhaps," suggested Judas Iscariot, "other parts than your toes might be tickled as well." Tirzah ignored the comment, made with an obvious dose of innuendo, but in a way, Judas' remark set the tone for the querulousness which ensued. Despite Thomas' carefree dance steps, we were tired, our tempers on edge. Many miles had been traveled with little let up, and of course, no one had forgotten the rather harrowing scene at the Essene Gate in Jerusalem. While we seemed, for now, to have found secure landing, having a runaway slave in our midst nonetheless was asking for trouble. Or that at any rate was the feeling of some, and of this view especially was Judas Iscariot, for whom any obligations we may have incurred as to the woman, Joanna, should rightfully be regarded as hereby fulfilled. It was an opinion he had ventured more than once since the onset of our risky flight: Mariamne of Magdala ought to be cast loose and left to fend for herself. It was a harsh view, an uncharitable view, yet it was a view not rejected completely out of hand by the others, and to my surprise, most of all had Peter seemed in accord with it. And here and now, resting upon the soft moss as we recuperated from our fatigue, it was Peter, and not Judas, who rounded upon the girl with a sudden antagonism. "So tell me, what are these 'powers' of yours? After risking our lives bringing you out of Jerusalem I think we have a right to know that." The word "powers" had been rendered with a porphyrous heat, as if he were skeptical of their existence. A rancorous interrogative, to be sure, yet I'm not convinced Herod's would-be right of ownership over Mariamne was the chief thing just then on Peter's mind, for we were, after all, a long way from Galilee. At least part of his discontent, it seemed to me, stemmed from that fire lit kiss in Sychar and the bond of tenderness between Yeshua and the Magdalene that seemed to have begun to develop at that point. Perceptions, of course, may sometimes be erroneous, but there was among the group as a whole a perception, taken rather for granted, that Peter, James, and I were the Nazarene's closest confidantes. I of course was much younger, therefore far less taken into account, thus it was widely viewed that the highest positions of trust and influence were held by Peter and James, and I think Peter was loathe to anything threatening to upturn that view. I would like to be clear, though; Peter was not an unkind man. Never did I know him to hurt or deliberately cause pain. Yet in the months to come, this antipathy toward Mariamne never left him entirely, and the end result was that no closeness of any kind ever evolved between them.

"It is nothing really," she demurred softly in her new, non-rhyming mode of speech, but even as the words came out, that formerly cornered animal we had seen back at the *Sicarii* house leaped once more to her eyes.

"No!" Peter persisted expansively. "I hear you have these extraordinary powers! Tell us more! Maybe you could even give us a demonstration!"

The Magdalene backed away, looking for all the world as if she might turn and run, and perhaps she would have done just that had not Jesus intervened. "Do those who hunger gather grapes from thorns, or figs from thistles?" It was a question he seemed to hold out, much as if shining a lamp into a darkened triclinium. Turning now, he regarded the Magdalene with a cautious smile. "He who places a shackle upon doubts observes the light of the rising sun."

He was in a sense, I think, challenging her, and if cornered before, she was thoroughly trapped now, yet detectable upon her also was an inner mettle, as if she would not go down without a fight; and so she didn't. "I have not done that which is abominable! I have not caused terror, nor have I caused any to weep!" The words, spoken fiercely, were nonetheless an apology of sorts, though what she was apologizing for I could not imagine. No one had accused her of such, and certainly she could not be held responsible for the brutality of Herod.

But far from blaming her, the Nazarene's gaze softened even further. "Earthly empires are as walls of sand. From the inside to the outside, from the desert to the sea, those who would become the humble servants of God focus their hearts on him."

At this point, despite being the object of a multitude of stares, she regained a measure of calm:

"I–I sometimes see and hear things. Things I often don't want to see or want to even know about. Where they come from and how they get there I cannot say, they just fling themselves into my head sometimes."

"Meaning," he asked by way of reply, "if I know something...you know it too?"

"It's not that simple."

"Let's try." This spoken with a playful grin as he pivoted, "Peter! Whisper a type of flower into James' ear! Then come over here to where I stand." The benevolent zephyrs which had vanished that day he had upset the tables of the moneychangers had returned once more to his face. Much as a physician now, he took matters in hand, and looking back on it, I'm sure he must have foreseen how this exercise was going to turn out. As for that cornered-animal look formerly on Mariamne's face, it appeared to have jumped mysteriously and effortlessly through space and planted itself upon Peter's. The Capharnaum fisherman, belatedly, seemed to regret not having left well enough alone; with a great deal of very noticeable reluctance, he followed Jesus' directive, leaning close to James' ear.

"That's right, just whisper the flower," coaxed the Nazarene, "whisper it very quietly so only James can hear—yes excellent!—now come over and stand here before Mariamne." Yeshua, taking Mariamne's arm with one hand, and Peter's with the other, proceeded to stand the two face to face. "Now Peter, look directly in Mariamne's eyes and think very hard of the flower you whispered." Whether Peter was thinking of flowers, I could not say. All I can say for sure is that Jesus placed a hand on Mariamne's shoulder and urged softly, "Now Marianme, if you know the name of the flower, tell us."

"Rose," she replied with scarcely a hesitation. It was as if she were yoked to the Seven Gates of Arit. As you may know, Quintus, in that last Gate of Arit, where starlight is poured from the nettled remains of ages whole, the Egyptians tell us the doorkeeper is Sekhem-Matenu-sen, the watcher Aa-maa-kheru, and the herald Khesef-khemi, the three cosmic prayer-givers in the house of many mansions, and perhaps it was their voices had softly whispered to her. Or maybe she simply made a lucky guess, but somehow she had named the correct flower. I knew this even before James confirmed it, *knew* because Peter's eyes flew wide open like the mouth of a baby cormorant, and James' verbal confirmation a moment later came as but a mere formality.

Nonetheless, the results were deemed only partly satisfactory, and a need for repeating the experiment was assessed. With a slight modification—this time it was James doing the whispering—the procedure was reconstructed, though with similar results. Somehow the girl correctly guessed the new flower: lily. Even so, skeptics remained.

"Roses and lilies are far too common. Such flowers she may simply have guessed with luck!" adduced Other James. "Do it again, only this time pick a flower far more peerless and rare."

Jesus was openly laughing now. "You can name anything with a stem growing out of the ground! It does not matter! She will get it every time!"

Indeed his words seemed to be borne out:

JASMINE

HIBISCUS

CABBAGE FLOWER

With each new test, and no matter who came to stand before her, the Magdalene intuitively stripped away the hidden kernel of Anahita. Through it all, this formerly forlorn and damaged creature of that wan corner of the the *Sicarii* House began to bask and glow, not because she had turned the tables on Peter, not even because of the sheer level of amazement she had sparked in the rest of us; the cause of her deepening satisfaction, and it was oh-so-obvious, was that she had won Jesus' approval. It was as if guessing flowers correctly were infinitely less important than that she had found a way to make the Nazarene like her.

We had reached the conclusion it simply was not possible to thwart her mental peregrinations when suddenly Judas Iscariot intervened. "Let me try it." Toward Tirzah he leaned, closer than was necessary, and, wearing a lubricous smile, began to whisper. This accomplished, he strolled toward the Magdalene with an ease of dominion. "I'm thinking of the flower, Mariamne," he announced in a tone very much, I should imagine, like that employed by Elijah while taunting the priests of Baal. "Tell me what it is."

With everything that had transpired, I fully expected her to put a quick end to this man and his high pretensions, but it was not to be; after many successes, her powers seemingly failed her.

"I don't–I don't know...tulip, I think," she said.

To Tirzah all eyes turned. Everyone, I'm sure, expected the same automatic confirmation, for the girl's performance up to this point would seem to preclude any other possibility, but it was not to be. Hesitantly our scribe stammered, "No, it was—carnation," here breaking off, as if she had perhaps misunderstood the flower type spoken and throwing a quizzical glance to Judas. The latter, for his own part, looked as if he had laid hold of the necklace of Harmonia.

"I *did* say the word 'carnation' to Tirzah, but then I thought of no flower at all; in fact I put flowers far out of my mind. I just wanted to see if our little slave girl could be confounded and brought down from her lofty perch. The answer is she obviously can be. On the whole a rather *fascinating* discovery." Having spoken this, he stroked his chin whiskers with a glint of amusement.

Chapter Fifty-One

Abwoon d'bwashmaya

I t was a prayer Yeshua taught us during our stay in Gaulanitis, and the first words were those. In your language, my grammatically astute Quintus, they would perhaps be rendered as, "*Pater noster, qui es in caelis,*" but in our native Aramaic things are not quite so black and white. There is great flexibility of meaning, and words often have much playfulness about them. *Abba*, of course, means father, but it's root, *ab*, refers to *all* fruit regardless of what source from which it is germinated. The word *abwoon* is a derivative of *abba*, but it is ungendered, at least insofar as its original roots, *ab* and *bwn*, are concerned, meaning that in the precise manner in which Jesus taught us the prayer, its opening words could just as easily be rendered as "divine parent" rather than the more masculine "our father."

I should also make you aware, Quintus, that when conversing in Aramaic every statement must be examined from at least three perspectives: the literal, the metaphorical, and the universal. The latter can also be thought of as the *mystical*. But in other words, you ask yourself three questions. One (the literal), what is the face value of the words? Two (the metaphorical), how do they relate to you as an individual as well as to the life of your community or society as a whole? Lastly you must also delve into the feelings that are evoked by the *sound* of the words; what is the truth of the experience they point to, and what do I perceive as justice and duty based upon this new understanding? This is the mystical or universal. With these elements taken into consideration, the Aramaic words *Abwoon d'bwashmaya* might in reality be translated as, "O birther! Father-Mother of the Cosmos, you create all that moves in light." *Unus sonus.* There is a sort of music in unison here, my young Roman friend. Just as humanity is both male and female, does it not perhaps follow that God, in whose image we are created, is also both male and female?

We were in those days of course learning to live simply on what was available from the forest, and it was quite hard sometimes, *hard*, that is, thinking of one's favorite foods (as most all of us are prone to do), and not being able to handily lay hold of them, because of course we were far away from any marketplace. But what Jesus was trying to teach us was that food should be regarded as nothing more than maintenance for the body, and that our real food is God. Thus...

Nethqadash shmakh,

the prayer continues. And indeed, God's name is hallowed, but in the metaphorical and the mystical veins of understanding that I spoke of we would also remember that the name is the eternal Sound, the sound that created all others. The Holy Name—we tune ourselves to its tones. They are above, below us, all around, residing within our hearts, our own "holy of holies."

Teytey malkuthakh,

or "*Advéniat regnum tuum,*" though here again, Quintus, your language is limited. What is being called for is not simply that God's will be done, but that God create an actual reign of unity on earth, a *kingdom*, in which we live in harmony with all life. The psalmist put it rather nicely when he said, "Even the sparrow finds a home, and the swallow a nest for herself where she may lay her young, at your altars, O Lord." God's kingdom springs into existence as our arms reach out to embrace all of his creation, and I should perhaps mention that during our stay in the forest of the Gaulan we left off, like the *Ebyonim* of John the Baptizer, the killing of animals for food. We did this I think because—how shall I put it?—because, just as the psalmist made clear, the entire world is God's altar. As the eternal Sound resides within each of us, so it resides also in God's other creatures, animating each with life; if we are to lie cradled in God's lap, safe and sound in His bosom, we must cause no grief, no pain, and while the Nazarene never, during his short time in our midst, specifically decreed that the many creatures of earth, air, and sea should be spared, always and forever, and on all accounts, I have since come to realize largely that this is the best way, for you see it is like this: the mustard seed cannot be watered with blood. And those who persist in believing otherwise are merely deluding themselves.

Nehwey tzevyanach aykanna d'bwashmaya aph b'arha.
Hawvlan lachma d'sunqanan yaomana,

Ah yes, we're back to food again, but of course there are different kinds of bread. There is the bread you eat, of wheat, zeia, or barley; there is the bread of wisdom and understanding. The word *lachma* may refer to either. But if our daily bread becomes the latter kind of *lachma*, there is nothing hidden which will not ultimately be revealed to us, and while the word *sunqanan* refers to "needs," it can also imply "an illumined measure." You are beginning to see? Thus...

Washboqlan khaubayn aykanna daph khnan shbwoqan
l'khayyabayn, wela tahlan l'newyuna
Ela patzan min bisha
Metol kilakhie malkutha wahayla wateshbukhta l'ahlam almin.
Ameyn.

But Amen is not really the end of it. It is in fact only the beginning. If I were to say to you that inside of our bodies is a garden and that through that garden runs a river, you would probably think me deranged, but indeed it is true. To find your way into that inner garden you place the mind in the heart. And in doing so, you almost inevitably find yourself entering a narrow gate, a gate leading you into a garden, a garden watered by a river of *hayye*, life, or life energy. God is the supreme Poet, and this river of *hayye*, can be made to flow in two directions, and when you reverse its direction you are in a sense born again. Did Jesus have the power to do this? *Meus amicus* he had the power to do anything! It was we, the rest of us, who were struggling to grasp so very many things, struggling to understand that the river even existed in the first place! And yes, I might also mention that there were among us those who equally failed to perceive the true meaning of that word *Abwoon* from the prayer's very first line. For they of such limited understanding, a Supreme Poet and Sovereign Ruler, in whose image we are created, could not possibly be other than "Our Father." But the fact is, as Mariamne of Magdala realized instinctively, and as I later came to realize too, she is also our Mother.

Chapter Fifty-Two

It was the day I became the wind, which is to say the day I fell in love. Already the month of Sivan must have been upon us, or so I now recall it at any rate, for it had become warm already, even here in the high-forest country of Gaulanitis.

Our camp at times grew dissonant with a certain adjunct of noise and confusion, not surprising given the close to thirty of us sharing its small confines, yet upon the surrounding timber paths one might easily lose oneself under that bewitching canopy of woodland boughs and here find peace in the tranquil whispers of the forest. On just such an excursion had I embarked on that strange and wonderful day, carrying myself off alone through viridian shadows, as the noise of the boisterous camp receded behind me. A world rich in offspring, broadleaves contented with an occasional stroke of my face as I passed amongst them; birds and squirrels foraging—this and more greeted me as I made my way deeper and deeper into the forest. I had grown to love it here, and was not looking forward to returning to the land of Galilee and its hot and dusty villages with their palpitating temperaments. All of it seemed far away now, and I was content it should remain so. Here the forest created its own seasons, or perhaps more accurately non-seasons, and absorbed in its hylic abstractions, I continued to wander along. The din of the camp was by this time long since undetectable. Fully alone I assumed myself, and so quite startled was I when, arriving at a clearing, my eyes came to rest upon two fellow wanderers, and in just that instant I was hailed.

"Shlomo!"

"Shlomo," I replied politely, trying to hide my surprise.

"We were just looking for anything edible. Abigail sent us out to see what we could find for dinner!" A redolence of berries blended with the forest pine on that ribbon of multi-textured ground I now occupied with them, Tirzah and Mariamne. The latter it was who had hailed me. Both, however, evinced a keenness of bearing as towards me they made their way, divagating through the ferns and bracken, carrying upon their arms baskets, one apiece, the presence of which attested to the fact that they were indeed employed in the search for food; as they arrived fully before me and I was able to peer within, the emptiness of those selfsame baskets declared their spectacular lack of any success in the endeavor. But hearken! Two lovely women wandering the forest alone! There was a winning brilliance to it, enough to fire the imagination of any young man.

"Here let me help you!" I plunged forward, offering my assistance, for of course they were most exquisite. The Magdalene, I felt, was especially beautiful. Since that very first night in the *Sicarii* house, she had been scarcely out of my thoughts, occupying one of those far corners of the human heart, *my* heart, where sinners are prone to burst forth in song. "Do you know much about foraging for food in the wild?" I inquired doubtfully. Taking up pace alongside them, I suddenly felt my old shyness threatening to trip me up, just as it had so many occasions in the past, yet at the same time, conveniently, I found myself in the rather manly and exalted position of being able to fulfill a need for them, for as it turned out, neither knew the first whit about ascertaining what might or might not be edible hereabouts. This was not terribly surprising. One, after all, had been raised in Rome, while the other had seldom, until recently, stepped foot outside a pampered tetrarch's palace. Tirzah skillfully delivered up a hypersensitive giggle. "We were thinking we might have to stop and re-evaluate the likelihood of a great feast around the campfire tonight."

"Nothing much grows here other than trees!" remarked Mariamne petulantly. "And who can eat a tree?"

"What sort of food were you looking for?" I inquired.

"We don't know."

"Something *delicious*—ah! but not too hard to reach!" suggested Tirzah hopefully.

"Well"—and here I gestured expansively at the surrounding woods, "there—there *are* edible foods in a forest like this." Pronouncing this, I racked my brain trying to remember what, but I was drawing a blank. Mostly, it had been my mother and sister who had done this sort of thing; my father, brother, and I had simply fished. But in earnest I thought of what comestibles Mother and Susanna had often gathered from the wooded areas along the Jordan. Wild *bananas*. That was one! And saffron crocus. And I began now to be alert for such. Any other time I might have paused and wondered what Abigail could possibly have been thinking sending two such ill-suited creatures out to gather food, but for now I was too inflamed by their nearness to give it much thought. "Have you seen anything that looked at least promising?" This I inquired of the Magdalene, but again it was Tirzah who answered:

"Aye, I saw a berry a while back."

"Only one?"

"Yes. One."

"They usually grow in clusters."

"This one was by itself."

"Perhaps a bear came along and ate her companions," suggested Mariamne. They were engaging in harmless sport with me, but Wisdom be intoxicated if I didn't take the bait! For the next hour, I climbed trees for them, shaking down shoots of this and that. We were fortunate enough to come across an acajou tree, and the young women made a game of trying to catch the raw nodules I tossed earthward. The forest yielded up other treats as well, wild mustard, locust beans, and most delightful of all, a patch of aneth, which makes for a mild but excellent seasoning.

"You are a regular Pythagoras," commented Tirzah when we stopped to rest under a holm oak.

Rabbi Joel had taught us Plato, Socrates, and Aristotle, but if he had ever mentioned Pythagoras I had long since forgotten. "Who is Pythagoras?" I asked.

"Famous fruit gatherer," she replied with a long, sensuous breath, then smiled, "At any rate, thank you for your help, Johannes!"

In our hour-long trek through the woods, beads of perspiration had formed upon Mariamne's forehead, and just now that moisture seemed to adorn her skin with a raw sexuality. "Abigail and the others will be most impressed with what we bring back." She looked at Tirzah confidently and grinned, "We shall be regarded as the victors of the forest!" I was spellbound by the up-and-down tones in her voice. In our haste to affect an escape here into the high country, still had no "appropriate" women's attire been procured for her; at that moment she was clad, somewhat dubiously, in a set of trousers such as might be worn by a Parthian peasant, as well as a shortened and scruffy-looking men's chiton. Even so, I found it hard to take my eyes off her. "And tonight we will all become kingly feast companions!"

"Yes," put in Tirzah, "they will all doubtless think we are of *great* mettle."

"Do you think we have enough food now?" Mariamne inquired, turning to me studiously for advice.

"Of course! plenty!" replied I, "unless there lurk gluttons back at camp who desire to eat the fruit and the baskets too." Both thought this extremely funny, and suddenly it occurred to me that at some point over the past hour my shyness had vanished. It had simply wrapped itself in its worn out old cloak and slunk disreputably off into the shadows. In those days I was still occasionally called "Johannes the Virgin," by my more bombastic acquaintances naturally, but suddenly I didn't *feel* like a virgin any more, and as we rose to return to camp I did something I never expected in a million years to do; I took the Magdalene's hand. "Here let me carry this for you!" and with one hand I snagged her basket. Meanwhile, her other hand fell easily into my own, and that was how we walked, side by side, hand in hand, all the way back to camp.

Upon returning to the boisterous hub of the camp, we emptied out the two baskets before the austere eyes of the cooks.

"Great work Tirzah and Mariamne!" commented Abigail, whose approval we seemed to have won.

"Oh, it was nothing, really!" protested Tirzah.

"No, no, it looks like you have quite a lot here!" disagreed my sister-in-law as she sifted through the contents. "To tell the truth, when I sent you out I really wasn't sure either of you would know what to look for, but you have done remarkably well, the Holy One be praised!"

"We simply drew upon our vast knowledge of deciduous biomes"—but at this point Tirzah was elbowed sharply to silence by her friend.

"Tirzah and I can't take credit for any of this, Abby; it was really Johannes who found the food, all of it. All Tirzah and I did was help."

"Really!" My sister-in-law's arm slinked around my neck, giving me a ferociously affectionate pat. "Good work, little brother!"

The meal served up that night was adequate. It was *more* than adequate. It was quite good. Yet such were my thoughts I ate little of it. Mariamne of Magdala—throughout dinner she was all I could think of. Even later, lying upon my blanket, her loveliness resurrected itself in a piquancy of memory, along with that feel of the touch of her hand, as I realized that the pavilion of my heart, in but a few short hours, had become beset with pangs of love.

Chapter Fifty-Three

The mere sight of her was able to fill me with the most irrational hymns to Paradise. Like a friendly and eager dog, I showed up daily at her side. We were sent together on food foraging trips, while other occasions we simply wandered off on our own, exploring the forest's substrata. Much to my pleasure, I came to know her light-hearted teasing, while at the same time I found myself trying to fathom that strange territory of her mind, and how she had been able to do the thing with the flowers; eventually we became closest friends. Each day, as her hair returned, she grew increasingly lovelier to look at. I adored the sound of my name flowing off her tongue, and I knew I wanted to be more than just her friend. At the same time, I thought of that kiss she had shared with Jesus that night in the Samaritan village, and of how, whenever we were in his presence, a certain faraway look would lay claim over her; at such times, it was as if I had suddenly turned into a piece of wood. I was falling deeply in love with her and was, even without the ability to know the unspoken thoughts of others, pretty sure her feelings for me were not the same. Yet I could not stop sculling, in my pride, into that enclosed circle of creation, or trying to give birth, in my own way, to that which was rent in twain.

"What was it like living in Herod's palace?" I inquired one day.

"Lonely." To the forest we had taken once more, a lovely day, and for a long while we had wandered the dense undergrowth, skirting lichens, mosses, and tree ferns, the camp by this time some ways behind us. "Would you like to sit down, John? We could maybe just talk for a while?" I thought it a delightful suggestion. Under a graceful mimosa, we located a pomegranate-shaped rock, here seating ourselves as the forest breathed around us.

"Did you live there all of your life?" I asked, for I was greatly curious to know more of her past.

"Almost. I became a ward of the palace when I was very young. At first Herod paid little heed to me. It was my mother he had eyes for. But I was frightened of him. I remembered the violence in our town, the night my father died. Even though Herod had had nothing to do with Father's death, I was still afraid, afraid of what might happen to my mother, afraid also for myself."

The town of *el Mejdel*, Magdala, it was a place dappled of hue, harnessed upon the northwest shore of Gennesaret not far from the newly-constructed city of Tiberias. The child had come of mixed union, the father being Greek, the mother a Jew. Jews and Greeks both lived in the town, though not much in the way of peace had ever existed between them. In joining themselves in marriage, the young couple had defied accepted bounds. It was a risk taken solely for love, a risk that had had consequences.

"We were never really accepted, either by Jews or Greeks. To her own people my mother was a harlot, one who had given herself wantonly to a Gentile; to my father's family, on the other hand, I was little more than the product of a mistake he had made. I guess they thought he had succumbed to temptation in a moment of weakness. My mother was very beautiful, but the feeling was my father was a fool who had purchased himself a load of trouble. Neither of their families had any use for me I guess."

Yet no two parents ever doted on a child more than this. As the little girl grew, she became especially attached to her father. He was a stonecutter; often she traipsed after him as he went about his work, positioning herself as much as possible in his shadow, listening for his good-natured croonings as he toiled with hammer and chisel. She had learned to love the figures he carved, Olympian deities, river gods, and nymphs. They almost spoke. Her mother too was a song of virtue and kindness, a fearless woman who imparted wisdom as roses. It was a home that literally abounded with love, yet before long the parents began noticing an abnormality in the girl, the discovery of which was not unlike standing in a great tide of augustness while suddenly observing a subtle but inexplicable error.

"My mother was still in the house that morning. I must have been about five years old at the time. Father was at his bench carving, and I had followed him out as usual, but as he worked, I knew something was wrong; he and my mother had quarreled that morning. Suddenly as I watched him at his workbench I saw clearly what was in his heart, and what I saw was bitterest remorse. It was because he had made her cry. Understand, it wasn't merely that I sensed, or had some *feeling* of his pain; I *knew*. I knew because everything in his heart, I could feel in my own. It came over me so quickly I fell forward on my face. 'Daddy, please don't cry! It's alright!' I pleaded with him, even as I lay sprawled on the ground. I wanted to comfort him, but I couldn't get up from the dirt, and I couldn't stop crying, because I hurt so much for him.

"Totally bewildered, he picked me up. 'Child! Whatever on earth is wrong?' And though he held me in his arms, my tears wouldn't stop. I was afraid he was going to die from his sorrow. I really thought that. I thought the intensity of it would kill him, because it seemed so intense to me, and I kept saying, 'Daddy, it's alright! It's alright! Mama still loves you!' And suddenly this, too, wasn't a matter of belief or speculation, for suddenly I could hear my mother's thoughts too; just as I had known my father's anguish a few moments before, now I could feel hers as well. It did not matter that she was in the house while my father and I were in the work shed."

"Well, he took me inside and handed me over to my mother. 'She is *very* upset!' In their concern over me, they forgot their anger toward each other, yet they needn't have grieved on my account. Once in the house I realized, and like everything else, I knew this to be true as well, that all would be right. And so I stopped crying."

The incident seemed over. In reality, it was only the beginning. Other episodes came and went, taking different forms, colored in many tones and hues, yet all shared one thing in common; all thoroughly defied any rational attempt to explain them.

"We had this friend, more my mother's friend actually, but one day she lost a necklace. I heard them talking about it and my mother telling her it would be all right, that it would probably turn up. No, the woman said, she had looked everywhere and had given up hope of finding it. Suddenly as they were talking, I saw the necklace in my mind; it was silver, with several pieces of smoky quartz attached. Very clearly I could see it, and I told her where in her house she should look for it. Later she came back saying it had been right where I had said."

Events of this nature became common as clover. The parents could not understand it. They knew only there was something extraordinary about the child they had brought into this world. It seemed a gift from heaven almost, but bad times were on the way.

In the little town of Magdala, life went through periodic upheavals of strife between Greek and Jew, usually nothing to worry about, but the following year internecine warfare broke out when a group of disorderly Greeks placed a crudely carved statue of the Roman emperor in the doorway of an alley, demanding passing Jews stop and pay worship. Worship or be reported disloyal to Rome. Nourished by long-simmering hatreds, the incident set off five days of clashes worse than anything anyone could remember.

"A house was set on fire that night, and then the next night another. My mother and father were both afraid. My father had told me, 'Never let anyone know about the things you can do with your mind,' so I didn't; I never spoke about it to anyone, but there were some, like our neighbor whose necklace I had found, who already knew, and it had begun to be said I was a witch of some sort; my mother, a Jewess, had had intercourse with a Greek, and evil was the result. And so the next night they came when we were asleep, and our house, like the others, was burnt to the ground.

"When we awakened we found ourselves already cut off from the door, and it was only by my father's taking an ax and chopping through the wall that we were spared burning alive. Others were not so lucky. Do you know how it is, John? Once blood is spilled, it goes on spilling. I knew my father was going to die before it was over; I knew, because I had already seen it.

"It was two nights later. His younger brother had become involved with one of the mobs, and my father wanted to stop him before he killed someone or was killed himself, and so my father went out that night. He was trying to make peace, because he was a Greek married to a Jew, and because he was simply a peaceful man and he didn't want to see any more blood shed, but his own blood was the price he paid. I begged him not to go, but he went anyway, and of course, just as I had known he would be, he was killed. My mother and I found his body the next morning. Two others died that night as well. I was six years old at the time."

Herod Antipas sent soldiers to put an end to the rioting. Six people were crucified, three Greeks and three Jews, as peace was restored, but the unfortunates who had been burned out were reduced to living in the rubble of their homes. In just such circumstances, the young mother and her child were noticed. The woman, being of striking beauty, was promptly brought before Herod.

"She was very beautiful, my mother. Herod was very taken with her, and while she had no intention of sharing his bed, her will was broken when he threatened to kill me in front of her. But you know, I don't think he really would have done that. He had heard of my powers, and already the notion of using them for his own ends had entered his mind. In the weeks that followed, he began showing me little favors, letting it be known he would be grateful, and by implication kinder to my mother, should I cooperate. He had us both under his power that way. I found that because of the things I could do, I was becoming increasingly of interest to him. One thing was certain; I wasn't a normal child anymore, if ever I had been."

"So what finally happened to your mother?"

"Within a year she came down with fever and died. Heartbroken and miserable it left me, but then I came to know the loving kindness of Joanna, the wife of Chuza. She would comfort me, take me into her arms, tell me stories, and in a very real sense she became my second mother. I, in many respects too, became her child, for she and Chuza have no children of their own. Had it not been for their love, I should have sought my own death, for I was a prisoner in the palace, and with both my mother and father gone, I had no further wish to live, but Joanna would place her arms around me and tell me everything would be alright. Only she had the power to make my tears go away.

"Of course, when Herod beckoned, I had no choice but to go. My relationship with the tetrarch became a complicated one. I was called upon to discover plots against him, and there were plenty of these. Prisoners were often brought in; as I grew older, it became my role to observe their interrogation. Herod came increasingly to trust my judgment, for I always knew when they were lying. Whether they were criminals, officers in the royal entourage, even members of the tetrarch's own family, it did not matter. At a word from me, they were taken out and executed. Times were, much later, I would occasionally feel sympathy, and would lie to save this or that one from punishment. But if, looking into their hearts, I saw only blackness and murder, I had no qualms about letting them go to their deaths.

"Herod issued orders I should be given the best of everything. Anything I desired was mine, yet at bottom, I was still a prisoner. I could not leave the palace unless accompanied by Joanna. I want to tell you something, John, just so you'll know, Herod never sought me out for sexual gratification. *Never.* And there's a reason for that. He believed carnal desires would deplete my powers. He's a very superstitious man. Always was and still is. Anyway, I–I just wanted you to know that. You asked what it was like growing up in Herod's palace. That's how it was. Yes, I was totally at Herod's disposal, but his sole interest in me lay in my winnowing the guilty from the innocent and finding out the plots against him. So that was my life, from the time I was a child of six all the way up until roughly nine months ago, but then everything changed; I began to regard myself as stained beyond redemption.

"It started in the fall, a day the palace was in something of a state of havoc because Chuza was ill. In the afternoon, they brought in a prisoner, a holy man of some sort. I knew nothing of him, only that he was unlike any prisoner I had ever seen. As I looked upon him, I saw the face of the sun in all its glory. At the same time, his body was a compendium of ruin. They had tortured him. While able to hold up his head, he could not stand; his legs had been broken, yet as he looked at me, I heard him speak. The words were, 'Enter through the narrow gate.' It was a peculiar thing to say, but beyond merely puzzling over what he meant, I realized suddenly that no sound had come from his mouth. He had spoken, but not verbally. Rather, he had somehow 'placed' the words in my mind. 'Enter through the narrow gate.' It was the first time I had ever been spoken to like that, and would also be the last until I met Yeshua, and at this point I *tried*, John! I tried *everything* I could think of to save this man's life! I told Herod he had mystical powers. This was not a lie, and indeed Herod believed me; he always believed whatever I told him, and under different circumstances I'm sure the tetrarch would have spared his life. But the prisoner's misfortune was that Herodias, the wife of Herod's brother, harbored some terrible animosity toward him."

It was John the Baptizer of course. In fact, the encounter took place during the Holy Man's last hours on this earth, and what she would witness that night would send the young girl careening into a world of overreaching darkness...

"They were having a feast, and I was brought in because there was a man at table whom Herod suspected of treachery. Before I could render a judgment on him, however, the entertainment started. Music and dancing went on, more than an hour of it, and I knew they were planning something because I could feel the subterfuge in the room, even as the lamps and torchlights illuminated the faces of the guests. The daughter of Herodias came in and danced. Everyone was much enraptured with her, especially Herod, for she is quite beautiful. When she had finished, the tetrarch spoke a foolish pronouncement, and the girl went to her mother; moments later she returned and said, 'Bring me the head,' and within the hour, the head of the *qadisha nasha* arrived. They had dressed it up on a platter, and all were much amused. I wanted to leave the table but I dared not. I felt that by witnessing and being party to such monstrous grotesquery I was rendered foul and corrupted beyond any hope of redemption.

"That's when it started. Later that night I began to hear voices. They flew at me like pebbles in a whirlwind, and from that moment on I could no longer tell the real voices from the ones in my head."

The hallucinations began to feed upon themselves until the Self that was the young woman disintegrated; Herod's physicians were called, but her condition grew worse. The tetrarch became frightened. Convinced he had murdered the reincarnation of Elijah the Prophet, he was sure the girl's misfortunes were his punishment, and suddenly there was a terrifying and dreadful weight to his diadem. Through physician's consultations, day after day, the madness went unchecked, indeed, it worsened; in the end, the girl was completely caught up, locked behind the gates of *sheol*, as her ravings spewed forth. So it remained until Joanna's escape with her and the pair's covert journey to the door of the *Sicarii* House—a day, of course, I would never forget. But there was one aspect to it all that still puzzled me.

"Your words, the way they came out as flowing verse, it was a most curious thing to give ear to. What caused you to speak in such a manner?"

A smile caught hold as she replied, "There were these—*beings*, I would call them. Wife companions, maybe. Each had a lovely luster to her skin. They told me form and emptiness are no different from one another, that all creatures love life and fear pain, and that thoughts and physical events conform to one another. They quite simply saved my life, and whenever they spoke to me, they did so in rhyme, and soon afterwards my own words were coming out the same way; I could not stop it. I was in a heaven of stars, but all the while, throughout the entire time, the wife companions were there beside me, nodding, blessing me. They saved my life, literally, and that night when Yeshua came into the room, they instructed me, 'Go with him.'"

I knew not of the rewards or punishments of spirits, nor could I say whether such things of which she spoke had any foothold whatsoever in reality. But in a way, it did not matter to me. She was a multitude of successive emanations of light and voice, and I knew only that here, now, sitting beside her, I was wholly under her spell. "May I kiss you?" I asked.

"I don't know." Blushing furiously, she looked away into the shadowy trees. Turning back, she said simply, "It is getting late. We should probably return to camp."

We started back, adorned with the grief of a forest's fading daylight. I tried to hide my feelings at being rebuffed in my desire for a kiss, but the disappointment, as it turned out, was only temporary. Nearing camp, there came stealing over her, I suspect, one of those chance incitements of the mind, an impulse, fallen, like a stray petal, into that delightful realm known as the "possible." I could already hear the rising and erratic brew of the voices of the others in the distance when suddenly we enkindled a huge broadleaf's embrace. At this precise moment, she stopped, turned, threw her arms wildly around my neck, while placing a kiss tenderly upon my lips. Then, just as abruptly, she broke free, a struggling mass of ill-contained energy, and sprinted quickly ahead into camp.

Chatper Fifty-Four

L ife is like a sieve whose contents drain away a little each day, each hour, each moment. Finally it came time for us to vacate our sanctuary in the forest, though not for a retrun to Galilee, at least not yet anyway; instead we went north, toward the great mountain, Hermon. Much I regretted leaving this hallowed ground whose trees had been our protectors. In their midst I had become unrestrained of voice, a benevolent finder of the light, but we are loosed and we loose. We are born and we bear. We are wounded and we wound.

And love inflicts its own blissful wounds. With the full force of a thousand suns, the realization came to me that Mariamne was in love with Jesus. It was impossible to miss. When alone with her, I sensed she that held, certainly, *affection* for me, but anytime the Nazarene was nearby, it was as if I were rendered invisible to her. Her eyes were for him alone. Before long, Quintus, I will lie in the ground, a moldering log. I must say, however, prior to shedding this cloak, that never in my life have I known such hand-me-down sorrow as I knew in those days. Try and understand though: there is marvelous thunder in the rapture shedding thought of the poets, and God is the greatest poet of all. And Yeshua too was a poet in his own way. He was *bar d'nasha*, the son of man, filled with the power of *hayye*, life and life energy, flowing toward the kingdom of heaven, leading us ever to those five trees in paradise whose leaves do not fall; this I came to realize, not so much from listening to his words, or gazing on his face, but rather by beholding the sky as the sun rose of a morning. *Abwoon d'bwashmaya*. If God was the Great Birther, the creator of all that moves in light, Yeshua was the son, a distinct part of the cosmos that the Mother-Father had given birth to. And of course he would say, "but so are you all!" And that is a fine bit of truth, an exquisite truth, outpoured from Heaven and imbued with a soul of marrow and flesh. But the fact was, it was not I, nor anyone else, Mariamne was in love with. It was Yeshua. He only.

By the rushing water we gathered on our last afternoon, that *river*, our steady companion, who had faithfully quenched and cooled us in its Eden-spilled bliss. For the most part, men and women had taken to bathing at separate points along it, although a few, married couples like James and Abby, had come to harbor a friendly togetherness at a bend further upstream. This particular day, however, we were down close to the camp, near the tents, with the melody of its flowing currents audible nearby. A permutable wind gently stretched its wings over both the stream as well as the scented gorse, expounding a sapiential cheerfulness as it changed into a swallow at last, guiding others of its like. Jesus bade us form a circle. When we had complied, he stood himself at the center of it, and what then transpired was a dance of sorts. Thomas, in his supple and bending hand, held a rattling sistrum, and to its rhythm, we raised our voices in song. For some reason, I thought of John the Baptizer's sunlit prytaneum by the Jordan. In a funny way, it seemed we were not so very far from there, either in distance or time, and as the circle began to move, Jesus looked skyward, calling for praise and glory for the Divine Mother/Father, *Abwoon*.

"Ameyn!" we responded.

He next said we should give praise and glory to Wisdom, but he was speaking naturally in Aramaic, so instead of the Greek *Sophia*, he used the Aramaic *Khek m'tha*, but once more we responded, 'Ameyn!" As the circle continued to move, I found my eyes returning ever and again to the Magdalene. I have to tell you, my beauty-loving Quintus, I have no words adequate to describe her. Still was she clad in that same ragged chiton and trousers, yet I had come to realize she regarded it a matter of little importance, in this respect being not unlike John the Baptizer in his camel hair vestments, or even the Nazarene himself, for allow me to mention: just as the Baptizer before him, Yeshua too exhibited an almost pathological lack of concern with material comforts. One who covets nothing is, of course, unfettered, a truth seemingly realized instinctively by the animals of the wild, yet one we humans perpetually fail to grasp. Mariamne, it had suddenly dawned on me, was, very much like the Baptizer, much like the Nazarene too, a thing of the wild; I tried to understand it, but couldn't, for my thoughts were entangled by the feelings I felt for her. Yet *t'var sheryana*! Broken breastplate of my heart! It was not only her I knew love for. It was he, Jesus, as well. And untangling it all seemed nigh impossible.

"Now, whereas we give thanks—I would be saved and I would save!"

"Ameyn!" we answered...and despite my confused emotions, I began to feel *hayye*, the wine of love, flowing in me.

"I would be loosed and I would loose."

"Ameyn!"

"I would be wounded and I would wound."

"Ameyn!"

"I would be born and I would bear."

"Ameyn!"

"I would eat and I would be eaten."

"Ameyn!"

We were doing the dance of God, gymnosophists of the tympanum, *Nethqadash shmakh*, hallowed be thy name! We were emancipated and erased in a universe that belonged to the Dancer, for hear me now, Quintus: those who hold love in their hearts are the dancers of God.

"Whosoever doesn't dance, does not know what shall come."

"Ameyn!"

"I would flee, and I would remain."

"Ameyn!"

"I would adorn, and I would be adorned."

"Ameyn!"

"I would be united, and I would unite."

"Ameyn!"

"I have no house, and I have houses."

"Ameyn!"

"I have no place, and I have places."

"Ameyn!"

"I have no temple, and I have temples."

"Ameyn!"

"I am a lamp to you who behold me."

"Ameyn!"

"I am a mirror to you who perceive me."

"Ameyn!"

"I am a door to you that knock at me."

"Ameyn!"

"I am a way to you who travel with me."

"Ameyn!"

At last, we reached the end. The circle cleaved first apart, then in on itself. We were exhausted, laughing, happy. As the formation broke up, Mariamne made her way to Jesus, and with a maiden's dreamy gentleness, laid her face against his shoulder. Thus the dance ended, and so too the day as well. On the morrow we did indeed travel, like migrants, dripping through that great sieve of life, as the ground moved once more beneath our feet.

Our next stop was Panias.

Chapter Fifty-Five

The city hadn't changed much, other than its name; it was now called Caesarea Philippi. *Caesarea*, in recognition of its Temple to Caesar, still standing, and *Philippi* in honor of Herod's brother, Philip, who ruled the area as tetrarch. Otherwise Panias was much as I remembered it. And yes, the Goat God, that tumescent proprietor of the city's *other* temple, still did a brisk business. We in fact ended up at that end of the crowded acropolis, surrounded by porticoes of mighty strength, cylindrical drums, and urn-shaped capitals, all of these dallying flamboyantly amidst lofty statues that seemed to whisper, even in their intoxicated stillness and unabashed nudity, of calumny and glory. Whispers, amongst kings long dead, induced surely by the draughts of Selene. By and by, we found ourselves no less at that same grotto, which was the Jordan River at its source. And above it still the same inscription: "The Court of Pan and the Nymphs." I suppose, likewise, I should not have been surprised at crossing paths with the same priestess, and so indeed, it came about; she was fifteen years older, and looked it, but unmistakably it was she. Of course, we had aged too, and little wonder, then, that at first glance she did not recognize us. But then, after several fumbling moments: "Servant of the Immortals! *Now* I remember thee!" Yes, she remembered...and the chariot of my *own* memory found its way back as well, to Peter's broken leg, those treacherous snows, a sobbing Andrew, but mostly what I remembered was how we had traveled to the mountain's summit, beheld the yellow wolf, and descended to the blessings of our priestess of Pan—Pompeia. "He who aspires with a longing heart may one day set free the mountains! Please...come to my house!" And suddenly it was as if the years had melted away, and we were enjoying her hospitality once again.

Of course it was not the same house as before; it was a much larger one. She had done well for herself over the years. We introduced her to the Nazarene and passed a pleasant evening together, our hostess serving up food, including those sweet, tangy fruits I remembered so well from before, called mandarins. "The tetrarch used to have them brought in from India. Now he grows them himself, in a house made of glass!" A hearty laugh she delivered up at the absurdity of such a thing.

Philip, the tetrarch over Gaulanitis, I should perhaps mention, was a different creature from his half-brother, Herod, who ruled Galilee. He was to die childless a few years hence, leaving behind no heirs. Throughout his life, however, both in his personal affairs as well as in the administration of his government, he showed himself a man of quietness and moderation. In addition to Gaulanitis, he also reigned over Ituraea, Batanaea, and Trachonitis; it was by and large rugged country, populated in the main by Syro-Phoenician folk; Jews were in a minority. *Vis consili expers mole ruit sua*, someone once said. Brute force, bereft of wisdom, falls of its own weight. Philip, though born of the House of Herod, was the antithesis of brute force, and neither he nor his land fell to ruin in his lifetime. And so we passed several days here in his city of Caesarea.

Of course above the *polis*, with its pagan temples, its divine consolations, and its glass house full of mandarins, loomed still that eternal mountain. It peered down every avenue of the town. Even indoors, you sensed its power. Now I had no longing to be up there again; once amongst those treacherous peaks had been enough, but after several days it became apparent that Jesus, for some unknown reason, desired gaining the top, and upon three of us he prevailed to accompany him: Peter, my brother James, and me. As I say, I had no desire for such a journey. Mostly what I regretted leaving behind was the much-beloved face of she whom I adored, even if she *didn't* quite adore me in the same way. Her now rapidly-returning hair had begun to resemble tight bundles of grass, and I was more in love with her than ever, and while I knew she would be here on our return, still it was difficult tearing myself away. But as I've already said, there was something binding me to the Nazarene, something almost as strong, if not stronger, than what I felt for her. I couldn't put it into words, other perhaps than to call it simply *lachma*, the bread of God. What I'm saying, Quintus, is I could no more refuse or say no to him than I could hop like a star over the moon.

And so on that day...a cluster of clouds loomed and lingered above our heads with a sutler's remorse; taking one last sad look back at Pompeia's house, I slung a jute sack over my shoulder, as the four of us set out.

Around midday of our second day, we gained one of the mountain's three summits, and though my heart felt heavy, my mood brightened considerably as I viewed the world from those future-annihilating prominences, a world engulfed in the Oreads' dazzling spaces. It was mid summer and no snow was to be found here on top, although the air *did* seem to hold a tutelary coolness, a wind-breath that marched upon you footless and free and caught you up in its anxious, reed-flower calculations. A dalliance of sunlight rested upon the earth's pieties as well as its desires, that world down below I'm speaking of, from which we had journeyed, and which lay now sprawled before us decorated in a mantle of obliviousness. Jesus implored we stop for a while. We were on a narrow plateau decorated with a patch of bindweed, its funnel-shaped flowers swaying in scoffing in amusement, as to our left palisades of marcosite and monzonite skipped into the upper mantle of the summit. Dwarfs we were, beyond reach of the Pleiades and Orion, yet at the same time bounded by them. Some water we drank from a skin while speaking of commonplace things, and as we tarried I had the sense of our voices carrying like duck feathers on the wind. I felt, perhaps from sitting this high up, a nourishment being poured into me, filling me with a tamarind fruit of cognition. This increased a moment later as Yeshua began to speak of how we might seek God through the dwelling house of prayer. "God hears your cry, he treasures your toil, and he says to you, 'O Poor Man, don't be alarmed or fearful.'" We are the *meskina*, the poor, and ours is the kingdom, *malkuta*, and God is joined to the heart. This we already knew, for he had spoken of such things before. But now there was something new in his voice, a search for birth, parturition, which he seemed to seek on all our behalves. "Think of God, and let him be the love of your heart until he spreads forth abundantly inside you and you feel him as movement and rest." At this point, he put a hand upon me, me alone, and spoke close to my ear: "Radiance, Johannes, is standing in front of you in plain view. Recognize it." Then abruptly he rose, took himself off some ten steps, and sat himself down, frighteningly close to a precipice. Much as a young blade of grass, flowering lambently out of adamantine rock, he began simply to *preside*, king-like, over sky and earth.

Feel God as movement and rest. As surely as the dove is the sacred creature of Aphrodite, I attempted just that, but after half an hour or so I commenced to fidget. At similar loose ends were James and Peter. Finding God's writing upon the tablet of the heart is not easily accomplished. We wetted our tongues and began to talk amongst ourselves, careful to keep our voices low out of consideration for Yeshua, who sat on still, high upon his perch, tinctured, oblivious, as if rooted there by thunderbolt. In this manner an hour went by, then another; at last, we decided to rouse him, for it was getting late, but to our surprise, we found him unresponsive, his body rigid. No matter how we tried, we could not shake him to wakefulness. "What should we do now?" Peter asked, abandoning the effort finally.

My brother sighed tiredly, giving glance to the fading sun. "It is too late to start down now. We will have to spend the night on the mountain." A few bites of lamb we ate, food from Pompeia's table brought along with us; it was cold but palatable. As total darkness set in, we fought off the chill best we could, my thoughts turning, inevitably I suppose, back to those nights we had spent up here years before. Perhaps James and Peter were nurturing similar ruminations, for an uneasiness settled upon the three of us, though eventually we slept. For me, it was a sleep of sweetness. I dreamed of Mariamne, and of Jesus, and I; wearing identical cloaks, we walked, the three of us, in tandem upon a lonely sandspit robed by the sea, under a clay-colored sky, going where I didn't know. Just walking.

When I awoke and saw Jesus, no longer seated but standing and talking with two men, I thought it must be a continuum of the dream. That the men possessed a peculiar attribute was the first thing I noted about them. Of varying color was their skin, like the skin of snakes. Graceful and light also were their movements, but beyond this, the whole mountaintop seemed bathed in a supernal light, bright enough to light up the ground. Most startling of all, one of the men bore no small resemblance to John the Baptizer. In fact I thought it *was* he, and felt an urge to rush forward and greet him. At this point, however, much to my consternation, I found I was unable to rise from the ground; my legs simply would not function. I lay, gazing fixedly at Jesus and the two men, observing the scene much as if from inside a knot within a tamarisk tree. James and Peter awakened, but, like me, were unable to move; yet my eyes were drawn irretrievably back to the scene before me, as Jesus continued to converse with the two visitors at his side. At this point, the summit began to be enveloped in a fog-like mist. It came on us, potent and volitional, and for a while I could see nothing, but I could *feel* it, the smith's bellows of the mist's intellect! *Materia medica.* It was alive, active, both male and female, light and life subsisting. For a while it lingered, but then at last passed slowly to the east of us; further away I watched it travel. When I looked again at Jesus, the men were gone as well. Only he remained. Beside us now, he knelt, telling us not to be frightened. Somehow I wasn't, but James and Peter were. Their trembling tongues attempted to converse, but were having trouble getting anything to come out. In any event, talk was unnecessary. *Khesem*, as we say. A bewitching! The whole thing had been just that, a bewitching. Peter would swear later the two men had been Elijah and Moses, though how he arrived at this conclusion I've no idea; yet continue to insist on it he did, until the day he died. For his own part, Jesus would say only that there is a place where light comes into being by itself, and he requested we not speak of what we had seen. Why, I wasn't sure, and still am not sure till this day, but it was a request we honored until well after his death.

Speaking only for myself, the *nasha d' nuhra* seemed to have stepped, as Yeshua said, out of some realm of light. Who were they? John the Baptizer? A singer and a bard? Or maybe a simple oblation poured out from *shemaya* upon poor, sundered earth. My own personal preference is to believe it really *was* John, his spirit anyway, come perhaps to reminisce with his old friend. Or maybe simply the *malaka* of God, a glimpse of what is preexistent, another dance of the great Round. Perhaps it would even be accurate to say it was "all these things." Or as Jesus would later come to say, *Wa kulheyn halneyn mithausepheyn*, "And all these things shall be added unto you."

Unlike fifteen years ago, this second trip of my life to the Sacred Mountain of the Snows was happily devoid of falls and broken bones, yet we did walk into a calamity of sorts—on our return to Caesarea Philippi the next day. Arriving at Pompeia's quarter, we were met with considerable tumult and perplexity, the cause of all this disorder amongst our friends being a young boy said possessed of a demon. This at any rate was the conviction of his father, who had carried him into town in desperate search of help. Upon a pallet, the small fellow lay writhing, and with much drooling and gnashing of the teeth. The town *medicus* had been called but had been unable to control the seizures, and even to get to Pompeia's house, he had had to make his way through a crowd, which by this time had grown considerably. It was the reckoning of the *medicus*, and pretty much everyone else besides, that not much longer could a child's body withstand such violent convulsions. But *yida*, as we say in Aramaic. Into his arms, Jesus took the boy, whereupon the convulsions subsided. Beginning to breathe normally, the boy relaxed, turning his eyes, so resembling two small jewels strung upon a thread of consciousness, upon Jesus. Divine consolations! We were by this time in the center of an assiduously straining crowd, many of whom stared with open mouths at the scene before them. Perhaps no one was more astonished than the father, however. Delightedly, he took his revived son into his arms, and thanked Jesus, while again reiterating his belief the boy had been in the grip of an evil *diwa*. This comment prompted a rather odd, seemingly off-topic response from the Nazarene, "Into the hands of men the *bar d'nasha* is going to be betrayed," yet I'm not sure anyone, even the father, heard it, for in the general commotion, virtually all had begun to talk, exclaiming loudly over the boy's sudden deliverance from his lfe-threatening infirmity.

You will recall, Quintus, for I have heretofore made mention of it, that as school children long ago we would oft make merry over Rabbi Hamul's considerable fears of demonic possession. Children are invariably given over to such distillations. But consider this...that I no longer mock in fun those who proclaim the existence of these gambeering spirits, for I have come to realize they are in fact real. Oh, not that they cause young boys to roll upon the ground, and the like. They are far *too* clever for that. But they are out there. Don't doubt it, Quintus. And they are ruled by the Prince of this World, the red dragon, Melkiresha, he of the reeking collyrium, the enemy of truth. For know this: there is Melkiresha and there is Melkizedek. The two stand eternally in opposition to one another. One's name means "my king is wickedness." The other's means, "my king is justice."

Chapter Fifty-Six

Pompeia sold her house and came with us when we left Panias. What word, what aspiration of virtue, can express the merit of a great disciple living in kindness and good will? That word, I tell you, is "Pompeia." A bright dawn of the morning, who knew how to live on this world and shine, such was she. The money from her house made us rich...temporarily. Returning to the Galilee, we purchased food for the hungry and gave it out for many days at a time, and in such manner went through the sum rather quickly, but of course in the process thousands of the region's poor came to us.

It was midsummer, and more than three months had passed since our flight from Jerusalem. Was it safe now returning to Herod's tetrarchy? No one could know for a certain, but among us was great longing for missed loved ones. A lengthy time had passed since Peter had laid eyes on Perpetua, while James and I had come to worry deeply over our mother, as did Other James and Matthew for their father, Alphaeus. The prevailing feeling, moreover, was we had to go back *sometime*. Of course Capharnaum, emblematic village of consolation, would forever be home for me, yet our return was more than a simple homecoming. The bread of life remarried our affections to the *meskina*, and theirs to us. Love for the poor creates its own straight path to union with God, and in the process the poor rise like the mariners of Ra. And so to us they came like mariners, including one day on which we fed more than five thousand. It made our return to the Galilee nothing less than a construction of sorts, of a palace; it was a palace surrounded by green foliage, cool shade, and every blossoming hue; it was the dexterous formation of archways, parturition of a conch shell of the universe in which the merciful obtain mercy and the poor are blessed by God. We were become chariot wheels. And those wheels would one day take us all the way to Jerusalem, where the earthenware pots of our own lives would shatter into pieces, and where those without ears to hear would act with no sense of shame; and even in victory, which in a way it was, none of us would emerge unscathed. But all this was to come somewhat later...

When we arrived at Peter's house, the door was unlatched by Perpetua, who welcomed us home with great delight. Peter instantly swept his wife up into his arms. O God of the stars in the sky, such gifts of love! For Peter's and Perpetua's love for each other was just that, a gift, a perfect ear of corn, braided and sweet; much was this the case even in those days before the birth of their daughter, and became so even more afterwards. So yes, they were overjoyed at being reunited, yet abruptly Perpetua broke free of her husband's embrace and confided, "There are some people here." Composing herself, she gestured toward the interior of the house, adding, "They say they are relatives of Jesus."

In profoundest curiosity, we entered; as we did so, they stood—two men of pious and noble bearing, along with a woman, and a young girl of perhaps fifteen years. The men smiled politely, cautiously testing the air, yet it was the woman who immediately caught my eye. She stood like Moira, one of the three sisters of the seasons, surveying us with a directness and boldness of heart that seemed to shout *shubakha!* to both earth and sky. "Her name is Mary." Perpetua lowered her voice still further: "She says she is Jesus' mother."

Before we could react, Jesus stepped forward. With nothing in any way resembling elaborate formality, he greeted her, yet it was a greeting containing a measure of deference nonetheless, deference to a tabula of tender beginnings, terraced against erosion, as he reached forth, took her hands in his own, and with alacrity said, "*Ema.*"

Chapter Fifty-Seven

I t was later that evening. We had nestled ourselves in Peter's triclinium, by which time one thing, above all others, had grown apparent to me: if ever was a mother who adored her son it was Ema Mary.

"You've been well?" she asked.

Perpetua, with the help of Abby, Pompeia and Ema Mary, had baked bread and a cake flavored with cinnamon and sweetened with the thickened juice of dates. It was a meal of no scanty succor, dolloped into a robe of riches for the auspicious occasion of our homecoming, and Perpetua, who had supervised the whole thing, had truly surpassed herself. Jesus, breaking off a piece of bread and dipping it into a sauce made of fish and muries, delivered a taciturn nod of the head. "Endowed with strength, *Ema.*"

We listened as the family gave an account of their journey from Nazareth. Not knowing if they would even find Jesus, they had nonetheless set out, feeling it of importance to try. Yeshua's *adversitas* with the chief priests, and his careening of the tables of the moneychangers, were now widely known, talk of the episode having reached even the little out-of-the-way village of Nazareth. Hearing the story, the family had in great haste set out for Capharnaum, being directed, after a series of inquiries, finally to the house of Peter and Perpetua. "One man told us you have 'passion,' 'courage,' and 'audacity.'" Here she smiled fondly on her son, then added hesitantly: "Others were not so pleasant."

I recalled the aging carpenter, Joseph. At mention of his name, *Ema* Mary brightened. "That was my husband! Alas he was taken from us eight years ago. The final dissolution was an endurance of much turbidity, but envy never found a place in him, and in the end Adonai suffused him with the nectar of sweetness." She favored me with a glorious smile. "It's so kind of you to remember him!"

The two men, Jesus' brothers, were reserved; I sensed about them an ingrained resilience, one perhaps much tried and tested. James, the elder of the pair, was sufficiently affable when engaged in conversation, yet about him was that same gallant dignity evinced by *Ema* Mary. He seemed a man who avoided rocking boats, but there were also telltale hints, even at that dinner table on that long-ago night, of the "James the Just" he was to become, the leader of the church of Jerusalem who would one day tread the pathways of righteousness determined to keep sorrow at bay.

The other brother, named Jude, had that sort of brooding nature common to the more stoutly fanatical devotees of Jewish Law. I could see he disapproved of both his brothers, though Jesus by far the more so. And then there was the girl, named Yona, which means "dove," though try as I might, I could discern nothing particularly "dove-like" about her. Upon her rested a great weight of the spirit, or seemed to, nourished perhaps by a brooding calyx of anger; through dinner she spoke hardly at all, and remained silent afterwards. Of the three siblings, James was the eminently more conversant, yet couched within his words was a reproof toward Jesus. "Coming from the south is news that the chief priests seek to kill you." *G'va* is the Aramaic word—to make a choice. For James, in bringing upon himself the wrath of the powerful, Jesus had chosen unwisely. "Must you always butt up against them like a ram with horns?"

The "news" that there were those about who sought to kill Yeshua was not really news to us at all, and indeed the Nazarene seemed unperturbed by the announcement. "Should a man repent for speaking what is true? Does a saber kill the spirit, or a javelin destroy a song? God's kingdom is here and now."

"God is the God of Abraham, Isaac, and Jacob, and *we* are their children! And 'we' includes the Pharisees and the chief priests!"

"God is not the God of the dead, but of the living."

"Fine words!" answered James. "But is it necessary to speak them to those with the power to kill you?"

"Does my Father love me because I lay down my life, only that I might take it up again? Remember, righteousness doesn't arrive upon one because one is born a Jew. It is strived for and earned. You are a poor man. Do not say, 'Since I am poor, I shall not seek knowledge.' Shoulder every discipline, and refine your heart."

"You so easily speak of shouldering disciplines! But what for your discarded mother? Does the Holy One will that you cast off all links to your family?"

This prompted a softly-spoken admonishment from Ema Mary, "James, don't." Upon his arm she placed a restraining hand. Flushed and angered, he turned back to his meal.

The younger brother, Jude, gave a reflexive pull to his chin whiskers at this point, offering up what was actually a rather cogent observation. "It is wise not to envy the prosperity of the wicked."

"The wicked will have their *own* worries!" *Ema* Mary replied in earnest agreement. "Adonai has scattered those who are proud, brought down the powerful! He has lifted up the poor! We are the *meskina*, and the son of the Living One will *not* be afraid!" As she made these remarks, suddenly I thought I knew where Yeshua had gotten all of his peculiar ideas about the poor being blessed by God. In a strange way, it seemed, he had gotten them from her.

Chapter Fifty-Eight

T he Galilee we had returned to at this time was a land in turmoil. A *Sicarious* named Barabbas had instigated a rebellion in Gischala. From there it had spread southward. It was an insurgency whose one notable characteristic seemed to be pillage. Waylaid travelers were murdered, their belongings plundered, all ostensibly to finance the coming war with the Romans, though of course there were those who pointed out, rather reasonably, that in a fair number of cases it was Jews themselves, and particularly poor Jews, fallen victim to the marauders. An enterprise of compassion and loving kindness it was not. The name Barabbas of course means "son of the father." Another case, it would seem, of a new would-be *anointed one* passing himself off as God's warrior-messiah.

But with every last *ruha* we pray for felicity and a mother's arms. My own mother included. I should here mention that Salome had taken greatly to heart Yeshua's words about loving your neighbor and giving to the poor; I should also mention this was not a thing my father was truly happy about. If Zebedee had disapproved of the Nazarene before, his feelings evolved now into outright contempt. But felicity has a thousand hearts, and my mother, as is to be fully expected, persevered in the face of his disapproval, handing us shekels as well as clothing woven from her own loom. And she wasn't the only one. We in fact were showered with gifts, of a great variety and from many people, so much so Jesus appointed Judas Iscariot to take charge of our bag of coins for purpose of keeping track of it all; it was an unwise decision, I remember thinking. A man may fly like a hawk in the heavens, or cackle like a goose in the underworld, but if he is a double-minded man he will be unstable in all his ways. Perhaps the most that can be said is that time runs all courses.

Which brings me, in a sense, to Mariamne, for time, you see, had run a certain course with her as well. So far as I knew, it had yet to be discovered she had been abetted in her escape from Jerusalem by the very same Nazarene who just then was causing such consternation in priestly and royal circles, and I was resolved to try and keep it that way. Realistically speaking, however, there was little I could do if Mariamne herself were determined to be indiscreet, which she at times was. There were occasions she would accompany Jesus abroad, even during daylight hours, often wearing no head covering or making any other effort to disguise herself. The most I could do was console myself with the thought that in Barabbas and his band of robbers the authorities had more, a great *deal* more, to worry about than a mere escaped slave, but Capharnaum, though only a small spot upon the earth, was a vital point along the Via Maris; all those passing through it, did so under the watchful eyes of the Romans.

The depredations of Barabbas lent Yeshua's parable of the Samaritan a somewhat added resonance in those days, and for more than a few people, it was a resonance unpleasing to the ear. A self-apparent sort of wisdom is what the parable evinced on its surface: *care for your fellow human being.* Yet its capacity for arousing antagonism quickly found root in its tendency to undermine Jewish notions of chosenness. In the parable's telling, of course, it is the Samaritan who helps the man in need, *after* the priest and the Levite have left him to die, a factor arousing considerable ire among Jews; the upshot was that those who despised the Nazarene to begin with, did so all the more now. Even the *Sicarii*, largely our friends heretofore, began to take umbrage. But the Samaritan parable wasn't the only one with the power to provoke. There was another, a story of penitence concerning a man's two sons, a most stirring tale, and I shall relate it for you here: a man had two sons, the younger of which made a request one day of his father—that he might take possession of his inheritance immediately rather than having to delay until such time as his father should die. Out of a bottomless well of love, the father granted the request, and the son wasted no time enjoying his newfound riches. To a distant land he took himself off, freely spending his wealth on wordly pleasures, only to find himself in want when the money ran out (as inevitably it was bound to). Hunger pangs began to gnaw upon him, eventually becoming so severe he hired himself out to a swine farmer, and in the process came to realize what he had never believed possible: that his lot in life had sunk lower even than that of the men who worked as his father's hired hands. And so toward home he turned, daring to hope for no more, of course, than that his father might take pity upon him and allow him to labor as a field hand alongside the other men in his employ. Ah! But the young man underestimated his father! Seeing his son approach from afar, he ordered his servants to bring forth the best robe and slay the fatted calf. "This my son was lost, and he is now found again," said the father, and a feast ensued.

It calls for wisdom, Quintus: the father in the parable represents God, of course, but it was a God unlike any we had ever known. Our God of course is YHWH, the One God, Adonai. But could this be the same YHWH who had commanded Saul to slay every last single soul in the Amalekite nation, including women, children, and even babies? Or was it perhaps a *different* YHWH?

A God of infinite love and forgiveness was a notion whose time had come. The parable of the home-returning son went largely hand in hand with the story of the Samaritan and its message that we must begin to see all men as our brothers. In fact, they were the Twin Siblings of Destiny, those two parables, or that is how I came to think of them at any rate. This doing away of divisions amongst humanity, learning to love one another as brothers and sisters—it *must* come, and it *will* come, for in a very real sense it is *inevitable*, Quintus. For when the sun is darkened, when the moon no longer gives off her light, and the stars fall from the sky, when *all* the tribes of the earth mourn, then the notion that we are Jew as opposed to Gentile, Greek as opposed to Roman, or this as opposed to that, will be seen for what it is—an *illusion*. And when that day comes, God, the God of love, will wipe the tears from the eyes of his children. But as I say, this parable, like that of the Samaritan, sparked much anger and belligerence. Could such a God be relied upon to restore Israel to its former glory, or would we actually *prefer* the YHWH of old, fully accustomed, as he was, to raining destruction down upon our enemies provided we only obeyed his commandments? They who frowned upon the parable of the son, like those waxed to anger over the Samaritan, were numerous, but there were also others, those with ears to hear, as Jesus would say; using their ears they were able to detect the melismata of sublime bliss, and with these parables and many others flowing from the lips of the Nazarene that summer, this bliss was everywhere to be partaken of. Alms from where immortals sit! We had awakened God as a lover! A God whose touch was tender as that of a lover!

As I say, a God of love was a notion whose time had arrived. Our "little group," such as it was, grew first into the hundreds, then the thousands. We began sleeping in fields, caves, along Gennesaret's shores, and many other places, for no house was big enough to hold us, and the chief priests became ever more vexed. And yes, Quintus, the river does indeed flow through the garden. That summer I began to hear and see everything with a vibrant clarity, every little bird's voice, every leaf, feeling myself more fully awake and alive than ever in my life.

Chapter Fifty-Nine

The emperor Tiberius, who would end up reigning for a total of twenty-three years, was once asked why he allowed Roman prefects to remain in office for extended periods. His answer, as I believe I've already mentioned, was that gorged horse flies would suck less blood than fresh ones. There were indeed gorged, blood-sucking horseflies around in those days, *bandits* if you will, and Barabbas wasn't the only one. Pontius Pilate was then busy achieving his own dust monument to immortality. By that summer, Pilate had been prefect over Judea for three years, and his tenure in office had not been a period of cheer for the Jews, his subject people. In Judea, prefects were responsible for collecting tribute for Rome, and it was fully expected anyone holding that office would skim off as much for himself as he could reasonably get away with, yet from the first, Pilate, more so than his predecessors, had seemed particularly intent upon putting his boot upon the neck of the Jewish people. His very arrival in the land occasioned the first of many strophes of dudgeon between ruler and ruled. Making his way into Jerusalem by night, he had smuggled in military standards bearing medallions of Tiberius CÆSAR. Jews begged and beseeched removal of these idolatrous images from their holy city, but he refused. In response, a large number of his subjects surrounded his residence in Caesarea, and for five days they stood in protest, encompassed by soldiers who threatened to kill them should they not disperse. The petitioners, by way of response, threw themselves to the ground and bared their necks, stating in essence they preferred death to the iniquitous idols hanging within sight of their Temple. Unwilling to kill so many, Pilate succumbed to their demands, removing the ensigns, but he and the Jews would never be wholly reconciled to one another. On another occasion, after he had seized a portion of the Temple treasury to pay for an aqueduct, they again became troublesome with their protests, but this time the prefect was ready for them; his soldiers were ordered to dress in civilian clothing, mingle amongst the crowd, and attack the troublemakers with staves at the first sign of unrest. It was an effective strategy. The protest was crushed. Thus was Pilate. His tenure in our land was marked by graft, insults, robberies, and executions. Eventually his cold, calculating heart took him to the slopes of Mount Gerazim where he massacred a group of peaceful Samaritans in an act so outrageous it ultimately became his undoing. This, however, was still some years off.

In all fairness I should mention Pilate was mild compared to the outright looters Rome appointed to rule us in the years afterward, but his time amongst us was not a happy one. And so—leafless, shadowless, and swift as heaven, the mornings came to us. We must have passed through just about every town and village in Galilee that summer, slipping in and out of each under the long, twin-shadows cast first by Pilate, and then by Herod. So many villages I cannot recall them all, only that we were on the move constantly; part of the reason for this of course was that, with rumors of Jesus' death being sought from certain quarters, it was becoming increasingly dangerous for him to linger in one place for too long.

While Ema Mary remained with us, the two brothers and the sister departed once more for Nazareth. And what of the Magdalene? Her closeness to Yeshua began to grow ever more apparent as she commenced taking pains to see to it he never went anywhere alone. Of course, we *all* did for that matter, but with Mariamne there was more to it. The poor being blessed by God was a truth she had taken very much to her own heart, and by this time it had come to the stage where she never missed an opportunity accompanying him into their midst. However noble one's intentions may be, the smell of the poor may at times be overpowering. Dirt, bodily wastes, leprosy—all are to be endlessly encountered, yet to these things Mariamne seemed oblivious; it was a curious immunity in one who had lived much of her life in a palace. How was one to explain it? Some asked that very question. The commonly accepted answer was she was in love with Jesus, and so was willing to put up with certain disagreeable conditions, for love's sake, as it were, yet I think she was not being given her due. There was this tendency, particularly on the part of Peter, to denigrate her, to not take her seriously. She was a woman. She was only half Jew. On top of all that, was the undercurrent of talk that she had been Herod's *pillages*, his concubine, and little did it matter she had denied this. Judas Iscariot had given up trying to have her discarded from our midst, though their relations were hardly cordial. But Peter and Judas were only two. This antipathy they felt was shared by others. From our viscera, O Lord, please tear out the disease of jealousy, for this I think had much to do with it. The sacred science of love finds bed and food in a young girl's heart, which is perhaps as it should be, and Mariamne, as I've said, was in love with Jesus, but what was clear, so clear few could miss it, was the Nazarene was also in love with her—or perhaps it would be more accurate to say he *had been* in love with her. For around this time things between them *did* begin to change. Of this, I shall speak in more detail later, Quintus, for it greatly bears reflecting upon. For now, let me say only that such jealousy as may have been felt, by Peter and others, became as water for the sipping, and that there were those who sipped from the left hand, while failing to notice the wonderful morsel of food available in the right.

In sum, yes, the road traveled by the Magdalene was not an easy one; hearts may be callous, intentionally or otherwise, and indeed, there was a measure of callousness on display in her regard. In none of this did I take part, however, for as I've said, I was deeply in love with her. I was also young and innocent, *young* in years and *innocent* in the ways of the heart, and because of this, the jaded suspicions that came so naturally to others did not enter me; I was Mariamne's friend, and I remained so. But even I, yes even I, had no clue as to the depth of the devotion that had taken hold inside her. None of us knew it then, but her love for the Nazarene was as vast and untamable as the ocean itself. This she was to demonstrate oh so well, on a night not far off in the future, when she would walk, almost literally, into a lion's den wherein she would witness one of the most shameful episodes of Peter's life. It was an episode, in certain respects, he spent the rest of his days trying to make amends for.

But I have to remind you, Quintus, that all life is flow. Flow of that river through the garden. From flowers in spring to the smell of the poor, the flow is everywhere. We are in it and of it. *Pante rei*, as the Greeks say. All flows.

Chapter Sixty

Indeed, there is much to be said about this channel of life that is called the flow, or at any rate Yeshua felt there was, for he spoke much of it in those days. But whenever doing so, it was always to us alone. The flow, he felt, was beyond the understanding of the multitudes, who were incapable of perceiving its subtle graces. You asked, Quintus, how it came about that day on Patmos, after you were struck down by that beam, and your lifeblood did moisten the earth, how it was you continued to live? By what means such a happy yet unlikely outcome? The answer lies in that great ocean that is known as the flow. Here is gnosis, Quintus: the flow is everywhere, and it is nowhere. It is pensive by nature; it is the palm turning downward, laying fuel upon the fire; it is the arrow loosed by the bowstring; it is food in a bowl; its approach is bliss. Its potter's wheels are the reins of a kingdom. Despite all this, it is hard to see. Harder still to reverse. But know this: when the Great River is flowing downward, there ensues a generation of men; but when it changes direction and flows upward, a generation of gods takes their place. Mastery of the waters was known by Moses; by Joshua; by Elijah and Elisha; they reversed the flow of water, as did Jesus. By water of course I mean not only earthly waters. There are also waters of the soul. Their reversal brings us into the presence of the Holy Spirit. Yes, Jesus could do this, but so could we, he assured us. If you like, then rain, O sky! For mastery over the flow meant we could do such things as even the Nazarene himself could do! We could heal the sick. Cause the blind to see. We might even, as Yeshua himself told us, say to a mountain, "Go and throw yourself into the sea," and watch it be done. It takes faith to move a mountain, just as it takes faith to reverse the direction of the flow, but rest assured, Quintus, you yourself can do these things. But to do so you must first learn that the flow is in everything.

None of us in those days, of course, had moved a single mountain, nor cured so much as a mild cough, but our time was coming. Indeed, it did come. And, I should say, in a manner of speaking, it also *went*. Now, in these bitter days, and the even more bitter to follow, are those who will take the keys of knowledge. They refuse to enter the kingdom of heaven, while also hindering others from entering.

But be of faith, Quintus, and know this: the flow is there...always waiting for us...

Chapter Sixty-One

In fall of that year, after *Sukkoth*, we once again wrested ourselves from the boundaries of Galilee, this time making our way to the land of Tyre, home of Thomas, home also of his twin brother, whom we were soon to meet. Before getting to that story, however, I should pause and mention that in these days a deep and abiding friendship had come to exist between Thomas and Nathanael. *Khavra—friend*. While Knowledge and Truth abound together, appointed brave sons through a hundred winters, so too with this pair, their friendship having solidified through all our time in Gaulanitis, bringing them to a closeness much resembling two barleycorns resting side by side. Whenever one commenced a chore, both applied themselves; whenever one transported himself to this or that place, the other invariably went along. In Gaulanitis they had shared the same tent. They were as alike as Knowledge and Truth, and just as Knowledge and Truth are liberal givers, so too Nathanael and Thomas. "Whoever asks for your coat, give him your cloak as well," Jesus had said. For some, this was a hard teaching to follow, but not for them. The gentle giant in particular was forever giving away coat, cloak, sandals, food, and more, in a manner a prudent person would consider extravagant. His friendship with Thomas might have served as something of a brake on this tendency but for the fact that the two thought alike on the matter: that possessions were useless other than as objects to be dispensed of freely to whomsoever should have need of them. Yet the lilies of the field had no finer raiment that they, and in ceaselessly casting off all that they owned, they were but following their master, for you see our bag, that day as we started out for Tyre, was empty yet again.

Yes, the shekels came and went, as commonplace as blandishments, but oddly it seemed not to matter. If we gave away a lot, and we did, we also received, usually in equal or greater measure. In this village a *kor* of wheat. In the next a cart full of fresh melons. That's how it usually went. It was especially true on that journey north; through every village we passed, we were graciously received, all the way up and to the city of Tyre itself, at whose gates we arrived in short order. And so I came once more to that fabled Phoenician city of old, once more also to its mysterious agora, whose impervious market stalls I had first laid eyes on so many years before. It was good being back, and we ended up tarrying for three weeks, safely out of reach of Herod, the chief priests, and Pontius Pilate, safely beyond the land of Judah with its bandits and anomalous warrior-messiahs. And yes, as I mentioned, we made the acquaintance of Thomas' twin brother, Nestor. We also met Nestor's gallant employer, Astatius Eutyches, a master of ships whose vessels sailed in and out of the port of Tyre with the regularity of stars crossing the heavens. In fact, we were invited to stay in his spacious home by the seaside.

It was also at this time I became fond of the Roman baths, their solaces, varying degrees of temperatures, and strengthening animations. Our stay in Tyre thus became a respite of sorts, though not one entirely without its etesian winds of disquiet. The home of Eutyches was a most comfortable dwelling, yet an inability to sleep one night took me by impulse beyond a cenaculum where we had supped the night before, out onto an open-air peristyle where I chanced overhearing a conversation between Matthew and Tirzah—concerning Judas Iscariot. Please understand. I had had no intention of eavesdropping. It was roughly an hour before dawn, the absence of the sun keeping my peregrinations concealed as I had made my way amongst the slumbering colonnades, my footsteps taking me by chance in the vicinity of the forlorn pair, and yes, there was a somewhat distracted forlornness upon them. I had been on the verge of hailing them when something about the scene suggested my intrusion would be of little welcome; huddled together in quiet but rapt conversation, they sat with a candle burning between them, and while I hastily made the decision to withdraw, my ears were unable to cancel or abrogate the words I now overheard: that Judas had been stealing from the bag Jesus had given him to keep. Could there possibly be some mistake? Hardly, given that the witness to his misdeed was none other than Tirzah, who was now carrying his child.

In the consummation of night, in the company of a trusted friend, the human heart feels freer to open up than at other times. Tirzah was currently engaged in an outpouring of clamant sorrows, voicing scorching indignation at the machinations of a thief on the one hand, while on the other—in light of her present predicament of being with the thief's child—lamenting mournfully over what she was now to do with herself. It was a tangle of emotions from which she sought to free herself by laying them on the shoulders of her longtime friend, Matthew, who, with his ever-present sensitivity to the female heart, offered such comforting certitudes as could reasonably be extended given the state of affairs. Feeling as if I had heard too much already, and surely more than I had bargained for, I withdrew, leaving them to their shared commiserations.

Our Tyrian nights were filled with sea tales, told by Nestor's employer, Astatius Eutyches, stories of his life, parts of the world he had seen. A master of many ships, he resided more frequently in Alexandria than Tyre, but insofar as he was ordained with the far-flung regions of Osiris' song, you could just as easily say he was a citizen of the world. "To all of they who are the lords of the spiritual creatures!" he toasted one night. "And to they who are the lords of the earthly creatures, and from the lords of those who live under the waters, to those who live upon the land, and to they which strike the wing—I with my own lips have fashioned these words: O Heroes, befriend us with no scanty succor!" The gods seemed to have heard his request. Upon his table were damsen plums, pomegranates, poppyseed, Syrian dates, and opimian, which was the finest wine on earth. The part of the Great World Euthches' travels had taken him to included India, and by his tales of that faraway land Thomas was especially spellbound, for it had long been his desire to go there. Quite willing was Eutyches to expound on the matter, too. And *khayla!* Did we ever listen! We listened as he described the port of Barbaricum, the Indus River, as well as a seasonal wind that made the journey there possible in under a year, that horned lion of nature now called the *mausem*, or *monsoon*, and which was referred to at one time simply as "the Hippalus" (after that ship captain in Eutyches' employ who had discovered the weather phenomenon), winds that could be harnessed like a fast-moving chariot! We human beings, it seems, have mounted the oceans as the shoulders of Apis, and become Serapis in the process! And I, who am called naked into this world, stretch out my arms in wonder at it all!

In such a manner did Thomas, too, stretch out his own arms, and I knew, just as surely as I was sitting here, he would one day make that journey to the land of the Indus. His twin brother knew this as well, which brings me back to the subject of Nestor, for as I have said he was Thomas' twin, and we were here in the monsoonly presence of Eutyches by virtue of his being the latter's valiant and trusted employee. While Mount Olympus had given us Castor and Pollux, the root in the hard earth from which the twins Nestor and Thomas had sprung had been far less decorous and garlanded. In terms of the general weal, the family were as the holes in the wall into which the roof beam is inserted. That is to say, they were the builders, laborers—carpenters in the main—from their father before them, to his father before that, and so on. Shipbuilders. Builders of palaces. Rugged capstans, turned upon the iron forge of duty, where the sweat of the brow is assuaged only by belated and reluctant benediction of the archangels. Yet both boys, in reaching young-manhood, had longed, in their respective ways, for something more. Nestor had been the *bukhra*, the first born; in fact, Thomas had not been expected at all; his arrival, a short time after his brother, had been such a discommoding flash of the supernal that upon the baby's birth everyone thereafter had referred to him simply as "the twin." And the name had stuck. Inside him was a natural curiosity, seeking to activate him every bit as much as his own physical arms and legs. For both twins, life became a quest...for something beyond the planting of a seed or the first fruits of the ground. It was a longing to lay hold of some handsome, ugly, powerful, or weak aspect of the Great World that could at least be understood as uniquely theirs, but there the similarities ended. While this trait had compelled Nestor into the more conventional vestures of family, duty, and devotion, it had led Thomas to seek gnosis in the land of Judea where he had heard tell of a great prophet and holy man by name of John the Baptizer. The rest was as Herodotus might have written it.

And thus were our Tyrian nights. But for me, by far the most delicious thing about Tyre was having an opportunity to bathe regularly. The public baths, the *thermae*, became my daily passion. It is said that everything known to us is known by virtue of the harmonious relationship of all things, one to another. I've often thought the Roman baths, with their gradational measures of heat, provide an excellent example of this principle. Step into the *frigidarium* and one finds featherless space, freshly sprung from the ether; move into the *tepidarium* and characteristics of color begin to appear; finally in the *calidarium* one becomes omnipresent, both eternal soul as well as a lump of salt, this as you begin to taste the sweat of your brow, while the faces of your fellow bathers take on the flush of your own crimson heart. Thus it was in the *calidarium*, in these visits to the baths, that I lingered especially, for always I found there the beloved guests of both mortals and gods. Serenity. Bliss.

Chapter Sixty-Two

I t might be well, Quintus, for me to pause now and elaborate on what I alluded to earlier regarding the affections of Mariamne and Jesus, for their love for one another at this time *did* begin to to devolve, to wind down in a sense, and it was on our journey back to Galilee, likely even a little toward the end of our stay in Tyre, I began noticing it. Oh, mainly the change was in the Magdalene. It was a tendency toward brooding, toward long silences, and it transformed her into a very different Mariamne from the one I had come to know during our passage in the Gaulinitis forest, those days when she had seemed close to mounting the heights of heaven in her newfound love. But why? Upon what was she troubled? Once back in Capharnaum, and presuming upon our friendship, I put to her that very question, however, it availed me little. On the matter, she refused to speak, insisting rather pointedly that "nothing" was amiss. I knew better—knew because I knew her so well and loved her so much. I presumed at bottom it had something to do with Jesus, and though disappointed in her refusal to take me into her confidence, I was by now growing used to such things. While few conclusions could be drawn on it all, I did do one thing: the knowledge that *something* was wrong I kept close to my heart, kept it concealed there, as a half understood truth, locked away in its own chamber of the ephemeral.

But for the most part it was good just being back in familiar surroundings, the flickerings of those fair streets, the easy movement of Gennesaret, and the sound and fragrances of Capharnaum's sturdy little marketplace. As always, the agora was a hub of activity, and just there on a crowded day I chanced upon one whose face was in some respects an extension of that sequence of familiar surroundings, yet it was also a face evoking for me deep memories because, for all its piquant familiarity, I had not laid eyes on it for a startling number of years.

Into a sandal maker's for purpose of looking at footgear I had wandered, my own sandals, due to endless traipsing from mountains to seas, having deteriorated to the point of being now suitable for casting into the infernal regions of Tartarus. My meager funds would have to be spent on new ones—this I had finally concluded. The shop smelled of freshly tanned leather, and there were several styles to choose from, though I wandered about in great humility, for much of it was beyond my means. Of course the open-toed *solea*, the rudimentary "common-man's" sandal was the most affordable. But the merchant also had the newer *calceus*, the closed boot which I had seen on members of the higher classes of late. Nice but expensive. More expensive yet was the *caliga*. It afforded excellent protection for the feet and was much worn by Roman soldiers, and while I had no idea if Jesus planned taking us back up to Mount Hermon, it would be ideal for such a journey. I had often admired them, but I was only kidding myself. I could not afford a pair. Absorbed in these thoughts, I became only vaguely aware when someone entered the shop, commencing, like myself, to browse, a customer to whom I paid little heed until suddenly finding myself yanked, almost physically, from my reverie. Quietly had he stolen up behind me, his mouth scant *unciae* from my ear, and in this manner began to impart, in a tone of moderately glib cheer, advice on, *of all things*, my selection: "If you're thinking of going with a boot, the *calceus* is sufficiently adequate, although I think you'll find the *caliga* wears much better." In the sound of the voice, I detected a note of kindly condescension as well as an odd ring of familiarity. Quickly I spun and found myself staring into the face of Maximinus Julianus.

"Maximinus!"

It was all I could think to say, for so staggering was my surprise. Suddenly I was back upon those hills above Bethsaida amidst the fragrant terebinths, with Susanna and Maximinus walking hand in hand—how long had it been now? Five years ago? Six maybe?

"Although," he went on deliberatively, oblivious to my gaping expression, "for the money, the *solea* makes for an attractive, all-around, general-purpose sandal." Pausing, at this point he smiled slyly. The word *solea* baffled me until I recalled that a moment earlier—a moment or was it a lifetime?—I had been browsing for footwear.

Absurdly I laughed. "I guess it will have to do! It's all I can afford!" Even though it was impolitic in the extreme for me to be seen embracing a Roman soldier, a hated enemy of our people—even so—we embraced, as a thickness gathered in back of my throat, "It's been a long time, Maximinus. How have you been?"

He was in military attire, which meant obviously, still, he was in the Legions, and of course I knew his twenty-five years could not be anywhere near up; yet I saw, from the greaves on his uniform, he had at some point attained the rank of centurion. The designation gave him a command, most likely over a hundred or so men. While I detested the Roman domination of my land, and nothing ever would or could change that, I was pleased to see him, and yes, pleased also at his good fortune.

"Surviving what they throw at me mainly."

"You're a centurion now."

"A minor one, *decimus-hastatus-posterior*. Usually what that means is I get to pull escort duty when the other centurions are too busy." He smiled self-deprecatingly. A fine powder rested on his clothes, the dust of the Via Maris perhaps, or the digests of some village through which he had perhaps ridden. We left the sandal maker's, strolling past a merchant offering necklaces, robe fasteners, and pins for fastening tunics, the wares hanging on strings as they clinked and clacked in the breezy lassitude; at last we ended up in a crowded inn. "You are one of those with Jesus, the prophet from Nazareth?" It was less a question than an assertion, an accusation almost, though not gilded with the baggage of vituperation; rather it held almost a touch of mirth.

"That's right," I answered guardedly as we ordered wine. "How did you know?"

"I saw you with them one day a while back," he responded without elaborating.

I contemplated this momentarily, and then mentioned, "We are stopping here in Capharnaum for a few days. It is home for a number of us."

"I know. The whole town seems to be in a state of bubbling-over propinquity."

"It gets like that sometimes."

"More than sometimes apparently," he replied as the wine arrived. "From what I hear, everywhere this Jesus goes he creates a tumult, with crowds and what-not coming out to see him. It's become quite unnerving to your religious leaders. They keep hearing stories of 'miracles of healing' and the like. I understand they're quite fit to be tied at this point."

Jesus' uncanny ability to molest the tranquility of our rulers was one of the things I most admired about him, though of course I voiced no sentiment of this sort just now. Despite our past connection, Maximinus was at bottom a Roman overlord. What I did say was: "He doesn't intend them any harm. They simply weave their own conceits and intrigues."

"Do tell."

"He says things that are true. And that's what they don't like to hear, the truth."

"Truth means many things to many people."

"There are abiding truths, truths which find complement with other abiding truths."

"Are there? I wouldn't know."

"Does army life still satisfy you?"

He shrugged. "It gets tiresome at times." Then with a sigh: "Of late we've been providing a great many armed escorts. A ring of bandits has been quite active hereabouts—"

"Barabbas, you mean—"

He smiled ruefully. "Precisely."

"Have you not heard? He is a great 'hero' of our people, or so it is said at any rate."

"Things are not always what they seem, Johannes."

"I will agree with you on that."

"Your mother and father, how are they?"

I felt he was leading up to something, though I could not guess what. "They fare mostly as ever, carrying on in their respective ways." We finished our wine and called for more. After it had arrived and the innkeeper had gone, I allowed a sigh to escape my lips. "My father is not terribly fond of Jesus."

He laughed—laughter containing a note of bitterness—"I'm not surprised. Your father's approval is not an easy thing to win."

With a sad smile I replied, "I guess not."

"Your mother, on the other hand," he continued evenly, "I remember as being a rather kindly and courageous soul. I hope she has fared the years well?"

"She has."

"Listen, Johannes," he said after a protracted silence, "I would ask of you a favor."

"Ask it then."

A long, probing look he cast into my eyes. I had not the slightest idea what was on his mind, only that he had the appearance of a man attempting to concoct some means of constructing shelter for the incomprehensible, while at the same time entertaining doubts as to whether such shelter was architecturally possible, and whether it might be best to simply abandon the whole matter. "I am an ordinary soldier," he spoke at last. "Such things as prophets and miracles of healing—these things I know not of. But there are many rumors about this Jesus. Such stories and talk, one never knows what to believe. Are the blind made to see again? The crippled to walk? I do not know." Maybe he was simply searching for a post in the earth that could not be shaken by the four winds. At any rate, he turned upon me a deep, liquid gaze, entreating, "If such things are possible, Johannes, there is one for whom I would request it. My commanding officer, the *Primus-Pilus* of the centurions, he is a very decent man, and has always treated your people with civility and respect. Alas he is currently in great need, and I would ask...only that..."

"You're asking for the Nazarene to heal him? He is sick—is that it?"

He was startled into confusion. "He? No! I'm sorry, I didn't mean to imply that—no, it isn't the *Primus* who is in need of healing; it is his servant. *He* is the sick one! It's a young boy, Johannes. The camp *medicus* has been able to do nothing for him and says it is only a matter of time." Giving vent to pent up emotions, he issued forth, "This is a *young* lad, Johannes! One imbued with so much promise, so much in the way of life's auspicious graces! The *Primus* is very fond of him, and is much distraught over the current situation, for Marcus is literally wasting away before our eyes. If you, that is to say if Jesus—if there's anything that can be done—"

"I will speak to Yeshua." With this small reassurance, his features relaxed, though not by much. "Where can I find you tomorrow?"

He told me.

"That is not far from the synagogue." I paused, while considering, "Meet me there, at the front of the building, shall we say the fifth hour? I will bring news. Perhaps Jesus shall be with me. I can't say for sure."

"The fifth hour then. I will be there, Johannes." He grabbed my arm as we rose. "Tell me, these stories—what do you know of them? Can your *Christos* help the *Primus'* servant? What is your fairest estimate?"

"I can only speak to Jesus and tell him about it; what takes place from there is up to him. As for whatever stories you may or may not have heard—" I broke off, not knowing what to say or whether it was advisable to say anything at all, "—you will simply have to judge for yourself."

Bafflement and doubt mingled in his face as he answered: "Until tomorrow then."

Chapter Sixty-Three

The shuffle and crush of humanity post-rippled along the front steps of the synagogue as the crowd hovered, their eyes peering into the sun-casqued sound of Yeshua's voice. It was the typical sort of crowd that formed whenever he went out these days, and they had followed us all the way to the synagogue. The day was in its fourth hour, though judging from the shadow-slant of the gnomon, I could see the fourth was waning and the fifth was near. I had not mentioned how I had become acquainted with the Roman soldier we were about to meet, nor had Jesus asked, neither had Thomas or Nathanael. The four of us were here alone. Mariamne, having occluded herself in one of her daily bowers of gloom, had remained behind, while Peter, James and others were fishing Gennesaret. As we stood in wait, the crowd grew more garrulous, calling upon Jesus to show them a sign from heaven, a request we had all come to regard as tedious. I was growing bored and restless, but then I saw him. He was standing casually in the sunlight, a gaunt, bronze cuirass covering his chest, his weight shifted slightly to one side, upon his head the helmet of a Roman centurion. Despite the uniform, I could not hate this man. Seeing me, he shouldered his way through the crowd. "Greetings, Johannes." After responding likewise, I introduced him to Jesus, to whom he extended his hand: "It is an honor sir. I have heard much about you!"

For a moment their eyes met, but then a Jewish elder tugging at the hem of Yeshua's tunic caused the Nazarene's gaze to slide downward. He was a small, slightly stooped man, with that priestly, alms-giver's look they sometimes get after a lifetime of purifying mind and body. The point of his beard billowed slightly in the breeze as, looking upward into Yeshua's eyes, he urged, "Reproach him not, for he has helped many of our people." At first, I thought he was talking about Maximinus, though after a moment's confusion I realized it was the *Primus-Pilus* being spoken of.

"Where is the young man?" asked Jesus.

"I will take you," answered Maximinus.

Still followed by the mob, we shambled through winding streets, presumably, I thought at first, to some military bivouac of some sort, but it was at the front step of a modest home we finally came to a halt. "We've been lodged here a week; I'm sure we've outstayed our welcome. Unfortunately due to the lad's condition we have been unable to resume travel."

"You are only passing through Capharnaum, then?" Jesus asked. Adjacent to the house was a stable, its door slightly ajar. Inside I glimpsed a number of horses—equestrian military mounts. No family of even moderate means could afford mounts such as these.

We entered the house, Nathanael momentarily filling the doorway as perhaps no one else could save for the stoutest of soldiers, and then only fully armored. Maximinus turned, slamming the door shut on the throngs outside, bringing blessed relief from the clamor. "Yes," he answered. "You want the straight story? I'll give it to you. We're guarding a shipment of 100 talents of gold, taxes collected for Rome." Seeing no reproof in Jesus' eyes, he went on, "With the bandits that have been operating hereabouts, nothing can move through this country without a heavily armed escort. Unfortunately, after we arrived here in Capharnaum the servant of the *Primus* became too ill to travel further." The family who owned the dwelling were somewhat known to me, individuals of solid reputation, yet their house could in no way be regarded as their own any more. The soldiers had taken it over in full; they were in the vestibule, on the balustrade, everywhere, menacing looking men, yet somehow I could sense a suspension of that menacing quality, as we filed past them. "I'll get the *Primus*. Please, wait here," said Maximinus.

He left us, returning some moments later in the company of a man in his late fifties. It was a manly face, hard, lined by many winters, yet one suggesting at the same time a certain craggy gentleness. He would look natural, I decided, riding at the head of a cohort of 500 men, armed and battle ready, or delighting in a beloved grandchild bouncing on his knee. In his eyes, I noticed fatigue, as well as something else: raw pain. "You are Jesus of Nazareth." It was not a question but a statement. The words were clipped. Flagged in a formal military bearing, the eyes fixed themselves rigidly upon the Nazarene.

"I am Jesus." Like a snake uncoiling, Yeshua turned to face him. His eyes were bold, defiant, in a way the Roman commander probably was not used to. Not to be outdone, the *Primus* returned the insolent stare with a look of iron. "They say you're a troublemaker." The words were barked. "You go through the towns stirring the people up!" He spoke in the manner of the sternest of judges, but Jesus, possessor of both the visible and the invisible, gently laid down a reed mat upon which the judge might sit:

"Gathering a harvest into the barn requires the cooperation of water, earth, wind, and light."

"Is that so?"

"Likewise, the harvest of God also depends on four elements: faith, hope, love, and knowledge. You summoned us here for a reason?"

The *Primus's* eyes softened slightly. "Yes. There have been strange reports, that you have some sort of power over sickness."

"And did you believe these things?"

"Frankly, no."

"Yet your heart now carries a heavy burden."

He gestured toward a bench, "Please sit down."

"I'll stand."

"Suit yourself!" The eyes rekindled momentarily in flame. "What I want to know is are you a charlatan? Some fraudulent fortune teller? Or do you really have this power, because if these reports about you are true..." and here the stern judge suddenly began to crumble, "...we have in this house one who, one who barely clings to life...and if you can help, I would ask only that you do so." Looking haggard, he now sat, upon the same bench he had urged upon Jesus a moment earlier, as Nathanael and Thomas held their positions at the door, their eyes upon their master.

"I will, and in doing so I will show you a power greater than Rome."

"And what power is that?"

"The power of God that lives within the human heart."

Blank stares emanated from the soldiers about the room; the Primus heaved his shoulders, conceding the territorial prerogative to Jesus. "Alright."

"Show me to your servant."

Down a hallway we were led, to a *cubiculum*, in which lay a young man unconscious upon a bed. His emaciation made it difficult to guess his age, though he might have been fourteen or fifteen. The sight of him brought a visible stab of pain to the Primus. I'm not sure what the Romans were expecting. Some drum-and-feather dance of a sorcerer's magic perhaps. Without a word, Jesus gathered the boy in his arms, touching one pallid cheek, his finger then moving to the lips; still as a corpse before, the boy at this point drew a deep breath, and then it happened; color flooded into the cheeks with the constancy of summer's ripening. It was the color of the flow.

The color of *hasha*, or now. The eyes flew open. The boy called out for his master, whereupon the *Primus* sprang to life, "I'm here, Marcus!"

In the moment was a joyous immortality; the Nazarene rose from the bed, the Primus, his entire manner changed, rising likewise as he said, "I don't know how to thank you..."

"Treat the people with justice," replied Yeshua. "That is how you can thank me."

The Roman officer made no reply. The Nazarene said no more. Toward the balustrade we turned, Jesus in the lead, followed by Thomas, Nathanael, and myself. A dozen silently staring soldiers parted, as if on cue, making way for us; moments later, we were back on the noisy street.

Chapter Sixty-Four

"He's now eating regularly and this morning was up walking around and helping the *Primus*, just as of old." The half-empty cup left a dark ring on the heavy planks of the innkeeper's table as Maximinus picked it up, but no sooner had the liquid touched his tongue than he lowered the vessel, wiping his mouth delicately with the back of his hand. "The medicus reports never having seen such an amazing recovery. We should be pulling out tomorrow."

It was two days later and once again I found myself seated across a table from my longtime friend—could I call him that?—friend? Is it possible I could think of a member of the Roman legions in such a manner? But I did. Strange to say I did. "Yes, we also are leaving Capharnaum, at first light tomorrow."

"Where will you go?" he asked.

"Jesus has his sights on the wilderness east of the Jordan. We shall be passing by a village called Aenon, a one-time favorite tarrying place of John the Baptizer's." Indeed we were bound for that old familiar region, with its elderberry solicitudes, its dalliance of light upon quietude, repentance upon mercy, bound to there and even to further reaches, for from Aenon it was planned we should make our way into the eastern desert beyond. I had no idea why we were going so far abroad. Perhaps for no other reason than staying one step ahead of those plotting to kill Yeshua. Hearts are like vessels in some respects. Empty ones are always easier to carry than the full. As I thought about that chestnut-colored ground once tread upon by John and his multitudes, I felt compelled to make a declaration of sorts. "What days those were! Now, instead of John the Baptizer, I guess we have Barabbas. Funny how times change, and often for the worse."

My words were spoken offhandedly, yet Maximinus took up the comment in a wholly unexpected manner. "Let me tell you something about Barabbas," he offered now. "He is an agent of Rome."

"*What*?!"

"Oh yes. You mean you had not figured that out yet?"

"I don't *believe* you!"

"Believe it. He and his band of *Sicarii* are working for Pontius Pilate, the Roman governor of"—

"Yes, yes! I know who Pontius Pilate is!" I waved the words aside. "But why? It doesn't make sense!"

"Doesn't it?" Maximinus leaned back, regarding me. "Pilate wants to extend his authority into Galilee; if he can make it look like Herod's a bona fide incompetent, incapable of controlling the rabble rousers, he's got a good case. Barabbas, for his part, develops a reputation as the most notorious murderer in the land, useful currency in the circles in which he travels. Rome, naturally, has a stake in all this as well. Tiberius, certain high-ranking members of the Senate—they're all concerned about what's going on in Galilee, and they're not convinced Herod can handle the problem."

"The problem of the revolt started by Barabbas, you mean?"

He waved a hand, dismissing my words. "Nay, Johannes. You keep forgetting, Barabbas is working for us." He raised his eyes, regarding me evenly. "The problem they're worried about is Jesus."

"*Jesus*?" I was thunderstruck. "Why are they worried about him?"

"Thousands of people have begun to follow him. Anyone who commands that kind of a following worries them."

While the heart may be the abode of the spirit, it was suddenly my head that was spinning, as I tried to fathom the implications of what he was saying. O multitude shamed by greatness of Heaven and Earth! If he was correct, then the only serious armed resistance to Roman authority was not really *resistance* at all. It was a requiescat for the dead, a massive pretense aimed at nothing more than furthering Rome's power over us. I didn't know whether to laugh or cry. "Is he in danger—Jesus?" I finally asked.

"You might say that."

"We have to *protect* him!" But what was I thinking? How could Peter, James, or any of the rest of us provide any sort of "protection" when we were all but apertures, threaded together by a light that had become infinitely copious. I looked at Maximinus, fearing what he might reveal next, but our conversation lapsed into the commonplace.

"I'm going back to Rome," he said at last, "maybe for as long as a year."

"Why?"

"I'm to serve a stint in the Praetorian Guard before returning to the Tenth Legion." The Praetorian Guard! Of all of Rome's Legions, it was the most feared. They wielded enormous power, at least in Rome itself, the power to take life, or to give it, or to turn truth into lies, and I wondered how much of what he had revealed could confidently be regarded as fact; yet somehow, I felt my instincts about him had not been wrong. He was still the same Maximinus I had known years before, the same Maximinus who had loved Susanna. And what need, after all, had he to lie?

"I have to go, Johannes." He finished his wine and rose to his feet. From my worn *punda* I dug a few coins for the innkeeper, but he pushed these aside. "Let me get it."

Being down to my last few *prutas*, I didn't argue with him. We walked through the door out to the street, where his horse stood tethered. A quiver containing a light javelin clung to the animal's back, attached to the usual four-horned saddle favored by Roman equestrians. Here, from one of the saddlebags, he retrieved something, a small cloth bundle of misshapen shape. It appeared to contain coins—and judging from the sound it made—a *lot* of them. "The *Primus* sends this as a gift for your *Christos*."

"Keep it," I said, thrusting it roughly back into his hands. "If it's tax monies taken off of poor Jews I don't want any part of it, and neither would Jesus."

With a weary sigh, he regarded me evenly. "I didn't think you would take it," he said at last. "But I promised the *Primus* I would at least try." Up into the saddle he heaved himself. From this lofty height he gazed down, looking regal in a careless sort of way. I regarded him with a sense of deepening estrangement, wondering if I should ever see him again. "I'm glad the boy is better now," I said.

He nodded, absently, but he didn't smile. The sun was behind him, leaving his face partially in shadow, yet even so, I could see the look of worry etched there. "You asked me before if Jesus is in danger. The answer is *yes*, Johannes, from every conceivable direction." I had guessed as much. The flanks of the horse twitched as the Roman gazed...at the market stalls, the busy street beyond, finally back to me. "A word of warning about Pilate. He's an extremely foul man. Should you, Jesus, or any of the others venture into Judea stay out of his way, better yet, stay out of Judea altogether. That is the best advice I can give you." Sensing its impending embarkation, the great animal, nostrils flaring, began to skitter. Still regarding me, the Roman gave one last lingering look of misgiving. At last, with head high, he bade, "*Vale*, Johannes!" while reining hard, turning the beast around. Then, like hawk-headed Horus in courtship to the wind, he galloped away.

Chapter Sixty-Five

I t took us three days to make Aenon near Salim, where John the Baptizer had once camped. And when we got there we bathed in the river. Being in that place, with its ghosts of the past, held for me a miracle of sorts, a miracle of hope. Hope of course is the eternal bard of the stars, the golden kiss of God through which we ripen. Between the poles of the conscious and the unconscious—just there does one find power a thousandfold, and as we bathed in the Jordan, the water flowed both up and down. Do you know how it can be, Quintus? The light of the body is the eye, and if your eye becomes single, your whole body fills with light. From within the water I saw this occur, and at the same time from far above. Chanted praises, O Son of Strength! And this is why I sing to you, be of good courage, and if you are discouraged, don't be. Rather be *en*couraged. Take heart. Reach forth to what is before you, for we are in the presence of the different forms of God. *Pante Rei*, all flows.

We left the Jordan and journeyed east. Though elsewhere winter had come, here the days were still warm. Upon us were the khamsin winds. After three journeys of the sun, we came to a wheat field, already harvested, but left were a few grains, which we took of and ate, for we were hungry; then we pressed on again, into even emptier country. Finally, in the *midbar* at the edge of the desert we arrived at a village, a dusky, sleepy little place, called *Mia*, as we found out, remote to be sure, remote from *everything* other than the eremic land's own recitations of low sensuality. Soldiers, Roman prefects, bandits, and warrior messiahs seemed of another world altogether. About the village was a protective air as the khamsin blew in, kindling it in dusty splendor, a village perched on the edge of the desert of the great white raven, as the winds whispered greetings and compliments to its unblenching eyes. Finding our way to a rattling well, we came upon a sight of stately peace. Seated on a veranda were several mothers delicately nursing their babies. Other than occasional glances in our direction, they seemed quietly absorbed in their maternal nurturing. Jesus viewed them for some moments, turning finally before remarking to the rest of us, "Those babies are like they who enter the kingdom. When you make two into one, and you make the inner like the outer and the outer like the inner, and the male and the female into a single one, then you will enter the kingdom of heaven."

Like as not the center was round. In truth, O Quintus, in entering the kingdom, one comes very much as a newborn baby; and arriving there you find, just as Yeshua said, that the inner is like the outer. From the well we slaked our thirst, which, following our long trek, was considerable. Gazing distractedly up and down the silent, dusty street, I noticed a flamingo strolling undisturbed through its center, a series of mud huts, shaded by the occasional Palmyra, bounding either side. At the far end of the byway was a dilapidated, four-cornered sheep pen, but from this vantage point it appeared unlevel, tilting penuriously into the shade of a protective grove of aspens. Yet my attention kept returning to the mothers on the veranda; a scene straight out of eternity it was. We had come to a remote village, but in a sense, we had also wound our way up to a star, for it was from here that Jesus planned sending us out on our own. Mia, this village in the middle of nowhere, was to be a point of embarkation. From it, we would go forth and teach the kingdom; to it, we would return.

"Take nothing," he said, "no money, no bag, no bread, no staff, no extra tunic. When you enter a town and are welcomed, eat and drink whatever is placed before you. Heal the sick and say to the people, 'the kingdom of God is near you.' In whatever house you are welcomed, give that house your peace. Stay in one place. Do not move around from house to house. If any town fails to welcome you, as you leave, shake the dust off your feet as a testimony against it."

The inner, it seems, had become like the outer. We were to go in pairs, Peter and James, Thomas and Nathanael, Philip and Andrew, it did not really matter as long as we went in twos, yet the instructions filled me with a certain foreboding. The notion that I, or any of us, should be able to heal anyone's sickness seemed but a heron's cry of folly. Given, however, we possessed the unalloyed confidence of the worthy one from Nazareth, what else was there to do but to take our leave and go as instructed? We were as at the entrance to an anthill. The anthill was the great, wide world beyond. There was nothing to do but enter it, and so we set out, all of us, or *almost* all of us, for there were *two* of our number who were to travel a different road, or rather were to travel *no road* at all; two who were to remain behind in Mia with Yeshua, for yes, the latter himself intended staying here; and as I say, he chose two to linger and abide in his company. As you might guess, Mariamne was one of those. I was the other. O gentle Quintus, have I not already provided accounts aplenty as to the manner in which I was powerless to refuse him in anything? In this, it was no different.

And so the others started off while we remained. While we remained, they went south, west, and north. While we remained, they doffed gazes upon forests, fields, towns, villages. While we remained, they extolled the call of the wind, loud voiced and eternal: *The kingdom is spread out on the earth and it is ours*. And so going...going...they left, carrying no money, no food, no extra tunic, yet each in a sense as gods, bearing a share of heaven's munificence. *The Son of Man hath not where to lay his head*...yet the Spirit does not lie, and all things in due time attain a sort of *tuva*, blessed ripeness. That night, with all the others gone, Yeshua the Nazarene, Mariamne the Magdalene, and I, John of Capharnaum, lay down our heads in Mia.

Chapter Sixty-Six

We took up lodging in the wooden-plank home of an aged man and his daughter. How Jesus had come to know them, I don't know, but lingering on in the village, I developed an affinity for the pair. The man was quite advanced in years, while his daughter, about the age of my own mother, possessed a warm smile coupled with a decisive simplicity she seemed to exercise in everything she did, whether it be gathering pinion nuts, chopping stalks of nettle, or caring for her father. That Jesus had had some purpose in asking me to stay behind had already occurred to me, yet he gave no clue as to what this might be. But purposes are like pathways. You follow them until they lead somewhere. Whatever it was, I assumed it would become known in due course, and so bided my time. Indeed came a day, roughly a week after the others had left, he beckoned for Mariamne and me to follow him; into the surrounding countryside we took ourselves, through one field after another, unopposed by the restraint of rules, as the sun bent over us in seasonable favor. Surely Mariamne and Yeshua would prefer being alone was my first thought, and briefly I considered turning back, yet had he not specifically entreated I should join them? And so, for better or worse, I continued apace, though feeling uneasy.

Strewn sparsely with myrtle and broom, the crest of land we found ourselves on rose and fell with the unyoked ardency of a ram's desire, its spiny plants pullulating nostalgically in the gentle sunlight. A grove of coniferous trees rose up on our right as the path took us up into the lofty hills south of the village, winding further and further, until at last a gentle wind applauded as we assembled ourselves on a cheery little ridge top. A view made for the gods it was. Like rival spirits, earth and sky were wedged asunder by a horizon of infinite sharpness and distance. A tawny, hard-looking loaf of bread made an appearance from a woolen fire sack carried by the Magdalene, which Jesus took, gave thanks for, and divided. "Here, Johannes." Suddenly I was hungry, my mouth watering. "And you, Mariamne," he said next. She folded the fire sack and laid it aside. I was enthralled to her mortal shape, fascinated by the curve of her wrist, as, with the tender station of an amiable queen, she persuaded a section of the bread to part. This accomplished, she pushed the loaf back upon Jesus, "Now you take some," giving him a consecrated look of pure devotion.

It was rough fare, but tasty. We ate as Jesus, strangely, shared memories of his early life growing up in Nazareth. I say "strangely" because normally he didn't talk much about himself. But this day he did. Much of it was of a personal nature, his brothers and sister, his days as a child growing up in Egypt. We heard of a young boy, named Zeno, who fell off the roof of a house, and how he, Jesus himself, had been unjustly accused by the boy's parents of causing the fall; heard also of the revolt of Judas the Galilean which broke out during the family's return to Jerusalem and continued on through their settling in Nazareth. Though still a boy at the time, he had vivid memories of the affair. "The Romans crucified hundreds of people and lined the roads with the crosses." Later his father, uncle, and he found work helping rebuild the city of Sepphoris. The stories he told that day, the words he spoke, were like a chariot drawn by four white horses. Marianme and I listened quietly all the while...and thus began one of the most arrestingly singular and unusual periods of my life, for there were just the three of us, and it was close, intimate. The days stretched into weeks, and then into months. We were biding our time, awaiting the return of the others, and in this period of calm I got to know him, I mean *really* know him; hours came and went in which I found my peace in the moonlight of his more pensive nature, while at other times rejoicing in the pomp of his reflexive and more exuberant moods. It's a period I shall always be grateful for, for it sped me toward a reckoning of sorts, a reckoning with myself. *Palgutha.* O Lord, mend my poor heart! Yet I wasn't the only one to undergo a self-reckoning at this time. Mariamne did as well.

For all my soul, Mariamne continued, even still, to subsist in her despondent malaise, lost to life's harmony like the spirit of a withered flower. It was that same sullenness of the heart I have previously described, and I wish to be precise: it had followed us all the way up to our arrival here in the desert, persisting even afterwards. Nothing seemed capable of shaking her from it. Of course, I knew, in a roundabout way, it all had something to do with Jesus, but no spoken confidences had I been favored with, even still. This, however, was about to change, and it began with a chance encounter one evening around dusk.

Leaving the home of the old man and his daughter, I had taken a leisurely stroll about the village, having no particular destination in mind as I ambled about on this early evening, absorbed in my own foolish ruminations. At one point, my steps veered off onto a path leading around the rear of the sheep pen, just down past its water trough, beneath its secluding aspens, and here it was I came upon them, Jesus and Mariamne. Alone, face-to-face, they stood. Low were their voices, though as I readily perceived, it was not a moment of tranquility; an audible note of discord hung in the air, although I should hasten to add that this was mostly on the Magdalene's part; even at that indelicate moment, nothing seemed to upset the charmed courtiers standing at the roundhouse of the Nazarene's formidable spirit—a fact which seemed to infuriate her all the more.

"Who!" she was imploring of him now, "*Who? Who* will ever love me? *Tell me that!*" The words tumbled out in anger, yet at the same time, she was a house of ennui built upon a heap of ruins. Standing with her back toward me, she was unaware as I approached, although he *did* see me, and as he did so he offered up a rather startling reply to her query.

"He is right behind you."

And with that, he served up a rather courtly gesture; outward it sailed, over her shoulder, dipping and swooping in my direction, whereupon suddenly she turned; becoming aware of my presence for the first time, she blushed, a furious, carmine flush of a blush, running through her face all the way up to the roots of her hair, as first at the ground she looked, next rounding suddenly upon Jesus, and then finally, as if having been caught in some unforgivable act of shame, turning pointedly away from the both of us. In that moment I saw what was unmistakable—that she knew. That she, this woman/child, for she was little more than that, was aware, probably *had* been for a long time, of my ardent passion for her, that radiance-of-fire and fragrance-of-earth conflagration so unquenched by the fluid elements of my dexterous-handed dissolutions. Of *course* she had known. How could she *not* have? And he as well.

It was one of those squalid cages of confusion I seemed forever to blunder my way into in my dealings with the opposite sex, a cloddish footprint in time leaving me grappling to reclaim custody of my own stupidity, while wishing I might be swallowed up by the ground on which I stood. Able to bear it no longer, and feeling quite naked before the both of them, I fled, wild-bull-like. Behind me, I could hear Jesus calling urgently, "Johannes!"—but it was a cry I ignored, my legs hastening to deliver me as far away from them as possible.

Chapter Sixty-Seven

For the next two days, Jesus absented himself from the village, presumably wandering in the desert somewhere, though I could not say with any certainty where he had gone. Mariamne during this time tactfully made no mention of the embarrassing encounter under the aspens, but then that was the least of things then on her mind, as I was soon to learn. In fact, I found out quite a lot, and in very short order. It came, this knowledge, not with the fanfare of trumpets blowing, but rather like the flutter of a butterfly's wings, for that was how the sound of her sobs reached my ears that morning, so softly my ears at first did not register them.

I had risen early, folding my blanket with a shiver, feeling hungry, but the house was still sleeping, so I took myself outdoors. It was dark still, though dawn, I estimated, was not far off. The nights had turned cold, and the desert stars shone down in their millions, golden palominos, driven on the footsteps of a God whose face was hidden. At the veranda, where we'd seen the nursing babies on our first day here, something, I'm not sure what, gave me to pause; feeling myself bound to the night, as if some immortal tale were being imparted by the chthonian wind and it were incumbent upon me to stop and listen, I stepped up onto the veranda and stared out at the sky, which far off in the distance supported a medley of bewildering cloud formations. Reflecting upon the heavens, so vast and distant, I only gradually became aware of a faint sound—very close by. It was brief, little more than a laconic sluice of an indrawn breath, seemingly girt in sorrow, though of this latter I could not be sure, for the breath, or whatever it was, had been of such short duration. Quickly I turned, and that was when I saw her, seated in shadow at the end of the veranda, less than six cubits away. It was as if, poised in stillness, she had taken root here, keeping watch over the night, her arms hugging herself for warmth as she gazed out at the darkened village, neither looking at me nor acknowledging my presence in any way. A sycamore tree, growing just off that end of the veranda, seemed to reach for her, its branches hoping to gather her as one gathers a forlorn waif, but she gave no heed, maintaining her self-appointed vigil over the moon's vacant shadows. Still there was no sign of the dawn, and I wondered: had she risen even earlier than I? Or had she perhaps been out here all night? I was astonished at finding her here, and spoke her name. As I did so, I thought of the Egyptian Goddess Hathor, but this was a Hathor robbed of joy, a corpse-carrying Goddess of the sycamore trees, and suddenly I realized the sound I had heard had indeed been a sob.

"What is it, Mariamne? Won't you tell me what's wrong?"

I half expected another evasion, another half-hearted assurance that "nothing" was amiss, but this is not what I got. Acknowledging my presence for the first time, she turned and spoke in a voice as gloomy as the darkness around us, "It is Jesus. He plans to go to Jerusalem." The words seemed born of destitution as she continued, "Upon arriving, he will be arrested and put to death. He fully expects that. No—wait. That's not correct. It's *more* than that. He *knows* that this is what will happen, but yet he intends going anyway."

The assertion seemed preposterous. I took a seat next to her and demanded, "How do you know this? Did he tell you this?"

"No."

"Then how do you even know it to be the case?" I inquired peevishly. "It is lunacy!"

"Witness is in the hearts of all men, as one pervading the sky!" She turned once more away, staring back into the night, though at the same time continuing to speak, "I'm male, female, hermaphrodite, a goddess, a harlot. I've argued God out of the universe. I don't know what I am, or *who* I am anymore!" This, I realized, was in reference to all the talk that had been going on about her. It was beyond merely uncharitable, that talk; it had been mean-spirited. And it persisted. "All I know is that he is Higher than the Highest, that I bow to him! That he is my providence and that he touched my soul like no one ever did!"

Jesus, of course...yes *he* had touched her soul. And despite his talents for healing the sick and causing the blind to see, he had been unable to hide, from her panoptic eyes of *nuhra*, his intentions on journeying to Jerusalem. Or perhaps, for whatever reason, he'd had no desire to. Is truth found in the immutable light of a cold dawn? Suddenly I understood it all. We were caught up in a wheel of joy and sorrow, pride and vanity, wisdom and folly, rest and travail, fairness and foulness, remembrance and forgetfulness—all of it endlessly turning on and on. Yet when the sun's power is focused through a glass, it creates fire. He, the Nazarene, was that glass; the fire he had created was in the hearts of all of us. It was a heroic and cleansing fire, a fire that could slow that wheel, and even stop it altogether, yet suddenly I was angry with him. Could he not see that Mariamne loved him, loved him so much her poor heart was breaking? Did he not realize what his being taken prisoner in Jerusalem would do to her, should it come to that? I tried to understand why he would court such a danger, but I couldn't. Yet there was more…

"Judas Iscariot plans to betray him to the Sanhedrin. Jesus knows this. Furthermore, Judas is aware Jesus knows. Each knows of the other. Faith? *Belief?* What does it mean? Love is like lightning until the lightning finishes striking, it seems."

"It *can't* be," I said, though I knew it was. There were a hundred, nay a thousand spikes and edges to the thing. Of all the disciples, I was the youngest, or I *had* been, but now, sitting next to me on this veranda, was one even younger, one who had come at us out of a cathartic darkness, a waif, yet a waif possessing what is beyond pride and hatred and blindness, the power to see what others cannot; at the same time she carried with her a childlike vulnerability, and alright, I'll say it—it filled me with a longing to *protect* her. A pull, it was, stronger than any I had ever experienced. Alone of itself, it would have been almost more than I could handle, yet complicating things even further was the anger I felt building within me, anger at the Nazarene for causing her sorrow. This was probably illogical on my part, but there it was.

"Oh, Johannes," she whispered. "He is going to *die.*"

I refused to believe this and told her so, but I may as well have been talking to the wind, for to her it was all a lingering echo, a *redivivus* of that traumatic episode from her childhood that had claimed the life of her father. Jesus was to die as her father had. She was sure of it. And nothing I could say could make her believe otherwise. Who are the protectors of liars? And who shall reap a harvest in a day of grief? What I was feeling for her was deep. It was *alma*—eternal. It was *khadaw*—everything extreme. It was wild and far beyond my ability to control, and I knew she felt it too, and suddenly we were in each other's arms, clinging desperately to one another, as the dawn announced itself with a brutish lassitude.

Chapter Sixty-Eight

*B*lessed is the one who has suffered, and who has found life.
I did not care for those words then—why should anyone have to suffer?—but I have since come to realize their timeless truth, most noble Quintus. Within that truth is the incomparable mansion of the Lord's presence, for to suffer for God is most divine. The more you suffer, the less you suffer. There is paradox to it.

It was a day or two later when Jesus returned from his wanderings on the desert, extending a venerable courtesy to the old man and his daughter, as well as to Mariamne and me. His mood was jovial almost, as if he had found *huba* in the golden garden of the Hesperides, but of course, blessed is the one who has suffered, and in the days leading up to his return I had done some suffering of my own. By neither his probity, nor his pleasance, was I to be assuaged. Still angered by what I viewed as his thoughtless infliction of pain upon Mariamne, I had decided to confront him, and it was later that day I got my chance.

"Hosanna that you have returned!" I began, trying at first to still the commotion in my heart with a few fleeting banalities. We were standing alone on a rocky escarpment, with a reddish-gold half dish of a sun sinking on the western horizon. Jerusalem, I knew, lay out there somewhere, engulfed in its noise, its turpitude, and its hypocritical fervors. Here, however, all was quiet; the deafening sound in my ears was the pounding of my own heart.

"Do you utter words of genuine hospitality, or does the Son of Thunder expound upon a leaf?" His face held a trace of mirth. Heaven is shadowless and swift, Quintus, and just as one cannot hide from heaven's gaze, neither could I hide from his. The mother stands as the youngling, loosed, feeds. If I was the youngling in this case, and I was, then he very much was the mother. I had come, intending to vent my anger, though in the face of his gaze my anger receded into helplessness. "The man whose labor is wisdom," he said, "considers all the oppressions that are done under the sun, and beholds the tears of the oppressed."

By 'tears of the oppressed,' did he mean Mariamne's? I didn't know. But at this point something happened. We began simply to talk. We talked of Mariamne, of death and life, of passing out of one existence into another. Much of what he said, particularly of the latter, was lost upon me, as I'm sure he must have realized. For like the flow of the river turning back, my mind, with a single-hearted devotion, kept returning to she who was incapable of ill will, she who was the essence and source for me of all life—Mariamne. In every expression of joy or sorrow that poured from my mouth, in every step my tired feet carried me, in every attempt at grasping some kernel of sublime truth, she was the one thing always before me. Suddenly I could not help myself. My eyes, as if become a fierce-flaming weapon, streamed scalding tears. "I cannot help it, I love her so much!" The confession lurched out of me with an impotent fury, while my sobs, despite my efforts at holding them back, burst forth as a dam. I could not bear to look at him. Though the miseries in my chest were infinitely vast, curiously I felt, rather at the same time, as if I had become a finite grain of sand, as I recalled to mind something he had once said: that an ass who turns a millstone a hundred miles walking, when loosed, finds that he is still in the same place. In Aramaic, we have a word...*sam*. It means to lay down something; it was time to simply lay down my misery. O beautiful and gorgeous Quintus, my friend of the lofty path (for I know you will one day find that lofty path and take it), I say to you that honied is the song of the angels as well as the work of the bee. In both is a certain magic. A similar preponderance of that same magic came in the next moment as Yeshua stepped forward and knelt—he had to kneel because by this time my knees had buckled; in my sobbing, like a leaf curling at the edges, I had crumpled to the ground. But gathering me in his arms, he cradled my head as if it were a bough of madder. "Johannes," he whispered—and then placed his lips to mine. In that moment, he drove away my darkness. He even vanquished the sun, by becoming the sun itself. In short, he healed me, healed me of all my squalor of soul, just as surely as he had healed the *Primus'* servant and so many others I had seen him heal.

Chapter Sixty-Nine

I wasn't the only one he healed; he healed Mariamne as well. *Khayla!* He lifted both of us, with that mysterious might of his, into the eye of Ra, so that from our night of bitterness and sorrow we awakened. *Ma're Khab.* O Lord of Love. The Good Shepherd he most certainly was, for he led us to a place beyond betrayal, where the winds are undivided, where we grazed in perfection on divine and spiritual nuptials. And here he received us unto himself, merged his being into ours. Looking upon him now, I saw myself. I saw myself likewise in Mariamne. They were in me, and I in them. And God dwelled in each of us, accomplishing the baptism of our hearts, watering the mustard seed, giving growth...*pante rei*. And the birds of the air came and built their nests.

All flows.

Chapter Seventy

I t was winter, and the Feast of Dedication came and then went, yet we remained in Mia. But of course we were living on borrowed time. I realized now how he had been trying, in his own way, to prepare us. Not just Mariamne and I, but the others as well. Comments about kernels of wheat falling to the ground and dying but then bringing forth much fruit, and such like as that, little more than subtle purgations they had seemed at the time, but now they took on a new meaning...and as our friends began to arrive, returning like Tammuz in the spring, these remarks increased in frequency.

Yes, our scattered flock began to unscatter itself. They returned like fire and air, sun and moon, lightning and stars, filling Mia with a strengthening life. Brimming with stories, tired, and happy. As regards their travels, you may think there is nothing of great import to relate, but not so. At the lake of Semechonitis, a crippled young girl was healed and made to walk. The one performing this miracle? The gentle giant, Nathanael. Neither gods nor magi comprehend or realize all the beauty of the flow, in all of its mysterious aspects, but one thing I've noticed. Those most steadfast in love find it and enter it very quickly. *Det haboon had l'had aykana d'ena ahabtekoon.* "Love each other as I have loved you." It is God's handmaiden, the flow, and in entering it, one comes to know how great are its dignity and loveliness; and within that embrace one especially such as Nathanael, a man whose heart aches with a love so great he is fully able to will himself to sickness, might easily hear the words, "It is I; be not afraid."

Chapter Seventy-One

T he message of The Preacher here comes to mind: *The thing that hath been, is that which shall be; and that which is done is that which shall be done: and there is no new thing under the sun.* Shall I say The Preacher was very wise and knew whereof he spoke? There is the alpha and the omega, the first and the last, and the closing of the circle (even though one's tears may fall at its closing). Understand, Quintus, that in all of the things I am about to relate there is nothing new...for did not Adonis of the Phoenicians pass from death back into life again? As also Dionysus of the Greeks? And was Tammuz of the Babylonians not resurrected from the dead? Yes, Osiris of the Egyptians too. And what of Horus, who was born of a virgin? For what reason did you wonder these things, Quintus? Is it the begotten of the dead, or the torment of a scorpion? The world is the river of God, flowing from him, and flowing ever back to him. And as The Preacher said, there is no new thing under the sun. And in just such manner as that river flowing back to God, so likewise did we make our way in the coming days back to Caphernaum. O little village of consolation! *Dilatasti cor meum.* How thou dost dilate my heart! Even now when I remember thee, I delight in thy sweetness!

Our homecoming was a joyful one. Or joyful in some respects, I might say, and less so in others. Upon our arrival I discovered that my mother and father had become antipodes of a sort. Salome had taken up lodging with Perpetua in the house of Peter. It was not entirely unexpected; she and Zebedee had hardly ever agreed on anything. There was something about my mother's heart that had learned to sing, I suppose, now that the battlesong of the thunderer was over for her, for the thunder man, my father, had, in a very real sense, blown her, like a seed grain on the wind, completely away from him. He was carrion for the birds of malady with his unrivaled gusts of rancor. She had spent a lifetime blunting his sharp points, purposelessly to my way of thinking, and her leaving him, I felt, had been long overdue. In a way, I was glad for her. Even with all she had endured, the female mystery that was her heart, that spirit of *khenuta*, the inner and outer sense of justice she had always carried and which creates its own rein of unity, had never died in her. In fact in the welcomed absence of Zebedee it blossomed forth more grandly than ever. She was with us now completely! And as such, she ended up traveling with us all the way to Jerusalem.

A pulse of life, Quintus. The prophet Isaiah said that God would speak with strange lips and foreign tongues. Indeed he has. And in seeking and speaking the Word of God one gazes along the forefront of the dawns to what is both near and far, ZEESAR, to the Knower, to He intoxicated by the bubbling spring of living water. ZEESAR is the river of living water, flowing back to the source. One may drink from *this* cup, or, conversely, one may drink from the cup of Melkiresha, "the goblet out of which the king draws his omens." And certain omens, may it now be said, had been drawn in our absence by the kings of our land. The most significant piece of news to reach us at this time was that Barabbas and a number of his followers had been captured by the Tenth Roman Legion. The insurrectionists (or might it be better to say the *putative* insurrectionist in the case of Barabbas?) were being held in an underground dungeon in Jerusalem. And so the kings had drawn their omens.

But there was a servant, of at least *one* king anyway, who had caused the burning bush of Magdala to lift up its voice. That servant I am referring to is Joanna, wife of Herod's steward. In her own way, she was a wholesome plant that had taken hold in the difficult soil of Obadiah, and just before Passover, she appeared in Capharnaum. Her showing up had a joyous effect on Mariamne. The light in my love's eyes outshone the sun! We learned that Joanna remained, as ever, a trusted member of the tetrarch's household, and the news she brought us was as a myrtle plucked out of a whirlwind. The son of Herod the Great had heard of Jesus. Aye, beyond all measure he had heard of him! And the tetrarch was anxious to learn more. Was Jesus the risen John the Baptizer? This was one story going about, and Herod Antipas had not ruled it out as a possibility, but there were other stories going around as well; with characteristic cunning, the tetrarch had begun toying with the idea of engaging the Nazarene in some capacity which might vaguely be described as "court diviner." Did the new prophet from Nazareth possess certain powers? Everyone said so. With Pontius Pilate actively seeking to undermine him, a fact of which he was only too painfully aware, Herod was in need of an ally. The need could in fact be described as urgent, for one thing our leader was not in short supply of was enemies. In addition to Pilate's subterfuge, Herod's own father-in-law, Aretas, was bent also upon his destruction. With such forces arrayed against him, Herod, the fox, was seeking desperately for a meeting with Jesus.

So that was one bit of news. Another, of equal or greater interest, had to do with Mariamne. Still was the tetrarch "furious" at his slave's escape, but with the various dangers pounding at his door, he had given up pursuit of her. *D'ma*. The blood scent had grown cold. There was now breathing room. Nonetheless... "This one"—and here Joanna placed an arm protectively about Mariamne—"should stay as far away from Herod as possible."

Chapter Seventy-Two

Would that we had taken Joanna's advice. Would that we had stayed away from them all. The Pharisees. Scribes. Chief priests. *Delatores.* Tetrarchs. Prefects. Far better would it have been had we shunned them entirely and kept completely out of the walled-in impluvium full of muraenas that was Jerusalem in those days. But of course we didn't, for it was Passover, *Zeman Cherutenu*, the season of our liberation. Years ago, God had taken a band of runaway slaves and led them out of the land of their captivity. An achievement of no scant measure, to be sure. Yet perhaps, in The Preacher's words, all comes down to vanity. The word 'liberation' does indeed ring with a certain sense of folly to me now. But we remember you, dear Lord, and we remember that what happened over this Passover did, in a sense, give being from non-existence. For consider, Quintus, that in the many years since Jesus' death it has been the slave population, both in Rome itself as well as Rome's conquered lands, who have overwhelmingly grasped that cord of existence now traveling freely under the name of "The Way." And should a rising up of slaves be any less feared by Roman masters than it was by Egyptian ones? For what other main purpose were the lavish spectacles of Nero than in putting a stop to this? *Nero citharoedus*, Nero the harp player. Perhaps it is nothing more than my love for him who spoke of freedom for the captives, but I say to you that what we gazed upon that day at the place known as The Skull were the hopes and doings of a liberation, a liberation that was desired by Love.

And so we started south towards Jerusalem, including my mother. Including also Tirzah, who was now heavy with child. Miles lay before us. But the Father makes his sun to rise on both the evil and the good, and his rain to fall upon the just and the unjust alike, and we are all children of the Father. "Sell everything you own, give the money to the poor, and come and follow me," said Yeshua to a man whose name I don't now recall but who'd accosted us on our way out of town—and suddenly I thought back to that day on the shore of Gennesaret when I'd first laid eyes on this extrusive and anomalous wanderer from Nazareth, a long time ago now, but in a way we seemed to have come full circle. The disheartened, dumbstruck man, unwilling to part with his treasures, abandoned us before we even reached the edge of town, prompting Jesus to express, not without a trace of amusement, that other tested and familiar aphorism: "It is easier for a camel to go through the eye of a needle than for a rich man to enter heaven." So it was; so it shall ever be.

And then we were out of Capharnaum, unconstrained on the open road, and it was indeed as if the circle was complete. In leaving Galilee behind, we were moving into the next circle. And so we traveled, without fear, steadfastly south...

How can I speak to you of the things that occurred during this last journey, and how in the process make sense of it all? When I tell you of a tax collector climbing into a tree in Jericho, or blind Bartimaeus sitting by the side of the road, or of one of the sisters at Bethany anointing Jesus' feet with nard, no trouble will you have, Quintus, following the musical notes one upon another, but when I speak of such things as the raising of Lazarus from the tomb, the music becomes disharmonious to the perceived and accustomed order. The idols of Ophir might mock. But in the beginning was something undefined and complete, something known as the Word, a force which came into existence before the earth itself. In the beginning was the *Word*, and the Word was God. It was Mariamne who discovered the truth of this and later wrote it in a book, Mariamne, who was now with child herself, though we did not know this at the time. But to come back to what happened at Bethany— yes, O Quintus, I should mention that a misbegotten and wholly ill-omened tragedy had befallen the little family there. Lazarus had taken sick and died. The darkness became dense. But understand, BEL bows down and Nebo stoops. The maid carries the honey in her mouth, and brothers and sisters will clasp arms together and remove the spiteful tree stump standing in the path. "Lazarus come out!" And suddenly the tree stump was removed. But once done it could not be undone, for the house of Lazarus and his sisters was such a public place; the fears, jealousies, and hatreds were loosed as if flung from a box, for the fact is, the raising of Lazarus was witnessed by too many to be dismissed as wild rumor. The Sun came out, truly and completely, and showed itself on the eighth day of Nisan, and it would not take the world long to begin to show its hatred of its Light. But then those weak of mind are always easily preyed upon by the Prince of this World, which explains why the tide turned so quickly against us, for it turned as quickly as the reflection of sun upon sea wave, or a lion in pursuit of prey. No one, I'm sure, understood this more so than Jesus. But it was also understood by Mariamne, by Thomas, Nathanael, and even by myself.

And so, two days later, after the raising of Lazarus, we left Bethany, with Jesus riding on a donkey. ZEESAR. The Jordan had flowed upward. Coming down the hill towards Jerusalem, we were met by ecstatic crowds. I didn't know if there was a needle's eye somewhere in the universe big enough for a camel to pass through, but as we made our way through the Golden Gate and finally into the city itself I felt myself, if not in the eye of a needle, then certainly in a screeching vortex of sight and sound. Here we have flowed like falcons' wings on the winds of time. Jerusalem. We have arrived in thee!

Inside the city, the festival was already going in earnest. There were musicians, dancers, and yes, beautiful women, a cacophonous reverie everywhere to be found. Jesus, perhaps sensing my confusion, leaned close and whispered, "Know that what sees and hears in you is God's Word"—here he used the Aramaic *miltha* rather than the Greek *logos*, though either would have applied—"and that your spirit is God itself. Not separate are they, one from the other, for just in their union does Life consist." Then he added with a smile: "So understand the Light, Johannes, and make friends with it." There was something divinely intoxicating in the words. They were touched by the beauty of the beautiful, and immediately he had spoken them a stab went through me, a stab in which I sensed his love for me stronger than I had ever felt it. Let me tell you something Quintus, for there is one Truth I have come to understand above all others and that is this: that God, El Hanne'eman, the Faithful One, is in every heart, and we are in him. *Abwoon d'bwashmaya.* The Father. The Mother. The Divine Parent. All in one. And did you know, Quintus, that the Hebrew word *rahm*, which means "womb," is related to the Aramaic *rahma*, which means "friend"? So you see, we not only are God's children, we are also his *friends*.

As are you yourself Quintus!

Chapter Seventy-Three

The Zealot House was no more. Or that is to say, the Zealots who had lived there were scattered long since to the four winds. Some had been hung on crosses; others slipped into concealment. With no place to stay inside the city walls, we made our way to the Mount of Olives, where we found ourselves by no means alone. Many thousands were camped out for the *Petskha* celebration, both here on the mount and throughout the Kidron Valley. A spot we chose, simply calling it home, and from here made our way into the city, day by day through the festival, returning once more each night, a pattern that prevailed all the way up to the eve of the Day of Preparation, when he named Joseph of Arimathaea at last provided us a house with lodging. You will recall Joseph was a member of the Sanhedrin, an intimate, too, of the family in Bethany, and about him I shall have more to say in due course, for he befriended us at very real peril to his own self. By the feather of Maàt, though, I would have you understand, Quintus, that there was a virulent poison in the air from the start. It was a certain flavor of calumny, in light of the happenings at Bethany, coming from the Pharisees in particular, that I would describe almost as an amiable burn. There were not more than 6,000 Pharisees in all of Judea, and even fewer Sadducees, but then there were no rules for the size of a tomb, and the city that kills the prophets bore their imprint. So yes, perhaps inevitably, we found ourselves at odds with the Pharisees. But they weren't the only ones.

Scarcely had we arrived in the Holy City when I spied that very same ignominious minion I had chanced upon in the Portico of Solomon last year, he who was more like unto Barabbas than perhaps even Barabbas himself. I refer of course to Hodi. Yes, the bully and his rabble were upon us again. It seemed, from my singular perspective at any rate, that they had no less than run amuck throughout my life, pursuing me, intentionally or not, down every harbor and roadstead of my time here on this earth. Were we currently of any interest to them? Assuredly we were! It would appear in fact they had no purpose other than monitoring our every move. That they were operating as functionaries of the Sanhedrin, I felt certain. The chief priests had set the waters in motion, and those waters now longed for their freedom, yet the hand of Pontius Pilate was surely visible as well, for such favors as might come to any Jew were invariably granted, or not granted, by the Romans. Our counselors and priests were as little more than playthings to be manipulated. Thus the dice were thrown. And whenever the Romans threw the dice, it was always the Jews who came up with the *canicula*.

O shimmering dolorosa! I no longer needed Mariamne's eyes of *nuhra* to see what was happening. It could be heard through the blowing of the shofar; seen through the false smiles of false prophets; smelled through the perfume of burning flesh. But yet there was Jesus...teaching crowds daily in the temple! The kingdom, the power, and the glory were more fully upon him than ever! Gold, as you well know, Quintus, is a tempting bauble that hangs before all humanity. And can one serve both God and mammon? No! Think it not for a moment! And I can hear our Nazarene's voice, even now, rising through the Temple courts, telling them this, telling them also they cannot serve two masters, for they will hate the one and love the other; telling them they must lay up treasure for themselves in heaven rather than on earth, for where your treasure is, there will your heart be also. And yes, teaching *forgiveness* too. That if you forgive others their trespasses, your heavenly Father will forgive you, but that if you do not forgive others, neither will your heavenly Father forgive you. From morning till night he spoke to the crowds, argued the law, even with the most fearsome of his detractors, and yes, told the twin parables of the Samaritan and the lost son. He told them again and again. And they amazed just as they had done in the past, yet also—just as they had done in the past—they aroused to fury the purblind, the unseeing, the unhearing. But it did not seem to matter to him. His words would not stop; his tongue would not hold itself.

Chapter Seventy Four

In the beginning, God created man, along with the obligation to selfless service. This was the pearl. But very few in Jerusalem that Passover wanted pearls. What were wanted were miracles. Miracles of course may sometimes be large or small, but what really needs to be said is that the human soul becomes unfettered when the dart of God's love wounds the heart. This, if I had to point to one true miracle, is the *one true* miracle.

That evening we emerged from the Temple into a night of burnished wonders. I was very tired, for we had been with Jesus in the Court of the Gentiles since early this morning, yet even now, these many hours later, the Nazarene's eyes of *nuhra* seemed to hold back the gathering gloom. Mariamne as always followed in his shadow, though by this time, in deference to the spies trailing us, she had taken to wearing a head covering. Tomorrow at sundown would begin the Day of Preparation. Like tumbling leaves, we descended into the mad, noisy street, into a throng as fat as the god of the Nile. The Passover meal was to be in less than forty-eight hours. In the tumult just beyond the Huldah Gates, in the Ophel square, we came upon two Greeks, evidently acquaintances of Philip's. For a few moments Jesus spoke to them, though I had trouble making out his words, for everywhere around us were revelers filling the night air with the emblematical bursts of *Zeman Cherutenu*. I looked for Judas Iscariot but I didn't see him.

When at last we turned from there, headed for the city gates, the Greeks were still with us, accompanying us even all the way back to the Mount of Olives. Peter, James, Pompeia, my mother, Thomas, and Nathanael all were along as well. Someone remarked on the city's wondrous buildings, for without doubt, a true magnificence rested upon them, and though it was intended as an offhand remark, it brought from Jesus a foretoken.

"A time will come when not one stone you see will be left standing on another," he announced with a measure of conviction that seemed to flavor the night with a cameo of jasper. "Every one of them will be thrown down. Watch out that you are not deceived, for false messiahs and false prophets will arise. Nation will rise against nation, and kingdom against kingdom, and there will be great earthquakes, famines, and pestilences. You will hear of wars and rumors of wars, but do not be alarmed, for such things must happen."

Prophecy, Quintus, is largely a matter of recognizing what is right in front of you, for when you open your eyes and see what is plainly in your sight, those things which are hidden inevitably become visible as well. This is a very basic and simple truth, though one unrecognizable to most. But please give ear and try and understand—that what Jesus saw that night was nothing more than that which already was in plain sight. It was clear as earth, air, water, and fire. And I should mention that, very much as he described it, the destruction of the Temple and the city of Jerusalem did indeed come to pass. It was the formlessness of outpoured chaos, and I lived to see it. But then what are stones? What are buildings? Where indeed does YHWH abide?

With a good measure of dread, and of course feeling terribly exhausted, I laid myself down to sleep. In my dreams I sailed over ocean's streams, to far white cliffs, and perhaps would have kept sailing, on and on, but for what occurred roughly around midnight—a hand shaking my shoulder. Though gentle, it was a shake no less of firmness; I opened my eyes to the sight of Mariamne leaning over me, the night sky and her dark blue head covering barely distinguishable from one another, leaving visible only the whitened shadows of her face, as to her lips she pressed a finger, beckoning me to rise and follow. Groggy with sleep and still very much fatigued in my bones, I got up nonetheless, my curiosity piqued as we slipped out of the confines of the camp. A short way down the hill, we came to Jesus standing and talking with someone, one of the Greeks, I thought at first, but upon more careful inspection realized it was his brother James, who acknowledged us with a slight nod of the head as we drew near. Many months had passed since that evening at Peter's house in Capharnaum, and I wondered at his sudden appearance here tonight. "Shall I lead you?" asked he who one day would become known as "James the Just," his gentle tones enclosing us like a Garden of Eden rustling under the canopy of heaven.

"Those meek before God shall find what is beyond sorrow," came Yeshua's reply in the darkness. "Please lead on." And with Mariamne and I following close behind, they started off down the slope. Why had Mariamne awakened me? No doubt Jesus had asked her to, but why? Where were we going? And what is it which lies "beyond sorrow?" Though still sleepy, suddenly I felt an even greater need for food, for it had been many hours since I had eaten, but putting these thoughts from my mind, I continued to walk as the four of us set course for the city. Skirting the tombs, I could smell hyssop growing, a delightful smell, yet it was the back of James, who strode a scant distance ahead of me, that absorbed most of my attention. There was something new and different about him, and I could not place it at first, but then it came to me: he had, in a sense, slowly ripened, *tubwaykhon*, just as a water pot filled one drop at a time. *Jacob ha-Zadiq.* James the Just—even in those days it was said of this brother of Jesus that his tongue savored the taste of God's love. He was to be put to death by the Sanhedrin some years hence, and I weep for him now, almost as much as for Jesus himself, as I weep also for my dear wife Mariamne, for out of the four of us making our way under that flaming sky that night, only *I* am still alive.

Past the Gihon Spring, we entered the city through the Tekoa Gate, known also as the Ashpot Gate. Perhaps due to the lateness of the hour, there were no guards. Indeed, the much quieter streets led us softly past the Pool of Siloam, and deep into the bowels of the lower city with its now-shuttered buildings. Still lit, though presently silent, was the great Temple, rising into the air on the hill ahead, to outward appearances abandoned, though with a patina of smoke and ash persistent in the sky, hovering, just above the massive structure, like cherubim above the mercyseat. The flesh of the innocent burned to purge the sins of the guilty. Into the Valley of the Cheesemongers we made our way. Here were scattered people about, though most seemed absorbed in the churning rod of their own late-houred ruminations. Cautiously I glanced back to see whether anyone might be following us. There didn't seem to be, yet if ever the authorities were to arrest Jesus, now, with so few witnesses about, would be the perfect time. But the Street of the Trumpeting Place remained silent as we ambled down its row of closed shops, hobbling as cast outs, staying close to the Temple wall, finally crossing underneath the archway. Mariamne and I walked in silence, though the two brothers conversed in subdued tones. They had taken the lead and strolled out ahead of us now as we skirted the Hasmonean Palace with its coned cupolas, by and by finding ourselves on a rise affording a spectacular view into the Temple. The vantage point was truly breathtaking, and it would have been nice to pause and take in the sight, but we kept moving, coming at last into the shadow of the fearsome Antonia Fortress; at this point all talk ceased. Stoutly built, the fortress, with its raised walkways and torch-lit towers, gazed over the Temple and the northern part of the city with the lofty air of a deity. Inside were Roman soldiers, probably five hundred or more. Like much of the rest of the city, the imposing fortification was silent at this hour, yet the very air, around it and us, seemed to coagulate in the embalming stillness. Quartered within those walls, I knew, was Pontius Pilate. What would he be doing now? Sleeping? Lying with his wife? Or perhaps quaffing the best of wines or eating a succulent dinner? And if he knew we were out here in the night, just beyond these walls, what then? How quickly would we be surrounded? Would we live to see the sunrise? There is something about being in such close proximity to the thing you fear most in life that heightens each of the body's senses. I could feel whole worlds colliding in my heart. But we passed without incident. Emerging from the shadow of the Damascus Gate, we found ourselves on the outside of the city's extended wall, following as it bent first northward, then eastward, until we came to what was known as Bezetha, or "New City." Initially, like the other areas of Jerusalem through which we had passed, it seemed to be sleeping, though by and by I began hearing muffled voices, so *someone* was awake. Quite a number of someones from the sound of it. At last, we sauntered up to the Sheep Gate, so called by reason of the animals herded through on their way to the altar, discovering, as we arrived, a market lining its entrance, though of course everything was now closed. Passing through the silent stalls, we approached at last the Bethesda Pool, the location, I now perceived, from which the voices emanated. Walking abreast of James the Just, with the Magdalene and Jesus directly behind us, I entered the first line of colonnades, finding myself completely encompassed in a whispering hush...of murmurings, groans, idle chatting. It was, all of it combined together, a confused chorus, though a rather subdued one. When my eyes had adjusted to the light, I was able to make out, lying all about me, the most wretched of creatures; clothed mostly in rags, they comprised, I realized at once, the city's vast population of beggars. Amongst them were the sick, the blind, and the halt. Stepping further underneath the peristyle and into their midst, I perceived an eerie stillness to the place, yet combined with this was a sense of expectancy. It was as if the people all about were waiting for something to happen. And indeed they *were*. For amongst the poor of our land was a legend, that at odd times an angel would appear at the Bethesda Pool, possibly by day, possibly at night, but its appearance would cause the waters to stir, at which the first to enter those restorative waters was said to obtain cure from his or her affliction. Whether true or not, it was a legend nonetheless *believed* by a great many, and for this reason they gathered;

twenty-four hours of every day they gathered, in great numbers, forlorn and abandoned, waiting for the *malaka* of God, waiting for an angel. We passed into the next peristyle and the sight was the same. There were five peristyles in all. In each the same.

These, Jerusalem's poorest of the poor, were those who would one day follow Jacob ha-Zadiq, James the Just, and it was he who walked easily amongst them now, stopping ever so often, giving comfort here and there. The peristyles were filled to the rafters, much as if a great sea wave had swept through, leaving behind bodies, in some cases riddled and diseased, as it had receded. In amazement, I gazed about. The pool was empty; no one was in it. Yet the entire scene, pool, people, and colonnades, seemed livened with a serpent-like fluidity. As we stood squarely in the middle of it all, a man of strikingly odd appearance approached us and began to speak. Wide were his eyes, every bit as wide as an owl's. This feature was complimented, enhanced you might say, by a curved beak of a nose so dramatically bird-like I could not help but thinking of him as a talking bird. A vaguely proprietary note resided in his voice, suggesting a connection of some sort to this "House of Mercy," as it were, though whether he was an appointed caretaker of some kind, or perhaps one of the sick and diseased himself, I could not guess. In either event, he assured us, rather amiably (chirping at us *affectionately* through his beak), that the angel was real. "She is the water's Child." This he pronounced ponderously, like some night-weary owl beholding the first light of dawn.

Dawn, by my reckoning, was still some ways off. Indeed the sky outside was quite dark. But suddenly I *did* become aware of a light, coming not from outside the peristyle, but from within. It was less a light, actually, than an *embryo* of one, yet seemingly with the power to dispel what darkness might rest upon the earth's estuaries...avarice, want, pain, hunger, disease— multiplied, increased, broken, diffused. I did not recognize it at first, but after a moment, a strange thought came to me: that the glimmer I was seeing was the jewel of God's blessing for the poor. "This man here." Within the surrounding hush, the words seemed inordinately loud. I looked about in time to see Jesus kneeling beside a man. A good way back from the pool he lay, and even in the poor light, I could see his legs were useless, this as he attempted to stir himself, blinking up at the Nazarene in some confusion. For 38 years, he had been coming here to this pool. (This we were now informed, in somewhat confidential manner, by the Owl Man). I started forward, intending to kneel by the man's other side, opposite Jesus, but Mariamne got there ahead of me, leaving me to peer down upon the scene from just over her shoulder. Leaning closer, I detected the strong stench of urine as she placed her hands gently upon his filth-encrusted legs.

"Do you want to be made whole?" asked Jesus.

"I have no one to put me into the pool," the beggar answered impassively. "When it is stirred, someone always gets to the edge of the water first."

A slight silvery light seemed to diffuse itself from Mariamne's hands, as also from those of Jesus, which gently now touched the cripple's shoulder. The man *would* walk. That much I already anticipated. What I did *not* expect, could not in any way have imagined possible, was the tympanum of God's treasure that in the next moment materialized, here, in this House of Mercy, in this river's bend of the flow. I think it may be, Quintus, much in the way that spring always comes. There is war, famine, plague, nation against nation, kingdom against kingdom, yet through it *all*, all that has been, and all that is to come, there has shone, and will continue to shine, that embryo of light-within that is God's love for the poor. It is much like spring returning each year. Blessed are the Poor, for theirs is the Kingdom of Heaven. Amidst the reek and stench of the man's befouled legs, Mariamne's hands were as tongues of love—and in the next moment the beggar gathered together those spindly, weakened legs, rose, and stood upon them. As this happened, at precisely the same moment in fact, the pool stirred; off we looked over the water, and the sight there was nothing short of stunning. Up from the reservoir she ascended, and it was just as the Owl Man had said—the *Water's Child*. Slightly above the surface she hovered, visible in faint outline, yet I could see her! We all did. Jericho. Balsam. The thing the Wise One holds in his hand, or tries to, although what he is left with, if he is lucky, is humility. For only a moment she appeared. When she had gone, the waters returned to their previous calm. But she had come. She had shown herself. I glanced out between the colonnades. Off in the distance I could make out he who had been healed moments earlier by Jesus and Marianme; in the direction of the Sheep Gate he now walked, still carrying his blanket, embryonic pinpoints of light twinkling about his head and shoulders as he stepped through that empty, open-aired marketplace where the wind was as a stolen angel.

We left the Pool of Bethesda, navigating in a southerly direction, reaching the Ashpot Gate just as daylight was beginning to creep into the sky. With a sudden fit of coughing, James took his leave, though not before embracing his brother, kissing him, his voice conveying a note of grief. But had he not, had we *all* not, glimpsed what is "beyond sorrow"? The eternal flow flows eternally through us. As it does, so it will. And I had now seen it, God's handmaiden. She has a bodily shape, or she took one in that rarefied moment. *Khayla!* We had all seen it. Or had we? What really was it we saw?

It is very hazy to me, Quintus, but I can think now only that what appeared above the pool that night was indeed that which is beyond sorrow, the reality that lies in the eternal, and which makes this world seem so temporary and pale by comparison. It is the sight I will remember and cling to as I die.

As we made our way back toward the Mount of Olives, I could hear a cock crowing. Dawn. The Day of Preparation would officially begin at sundown that evening.

Chapter Seventy-Five

Ｗe crossed the brook Kidron, at last reaching our still-slumbering camp. I was wide-awake and sleep seemed impossible, yet miraculously it came. When next my eyes opened, I made the startling discovery that the sun had journeyed far, far up in the sky. Over the Mount of Olives it poured in stunning valor. At first, I thought myself alone in camp, discovering my error only upon stumbling clumsily over Mariamne's sleeping form, or what *seemed* to be her sleeping form. Upon her back she lay, yet something odd. Looking closer, I saw that her eyes were open, staring, transfixed almost, upon the sun. Was she awake then?—yet my tripping over her might have gone completely unnoticed for all the response she gave. We were alone in camp. The others, including Jesus, presumably, had gone into the city. "Mariamne," I said, and when no reply came knelt by her, repeating her name. Still she did not move. It was as if some critical part of her were missing, leaving only the empty vessel of her body. Furthermore, her skin was cold to the touch. This I discovered on attempting to shake her awake. "Mariamne!" I cried—and with a sense of urgency took her in my arms. Gradually, like fire dwelling in mist, her eyelids flickered, the orbs beginning to disengage from that portion of the sky upon which they had been fixed.

"Whoever has come to know the world," she whispered, "has discovered a carcass. And whoever has discovered a carcass, of that person the world is not worthy—he *said* that!" Suddenly she sat bolt upright, blinking.

"Who?"

"Jesus! He spoke just now!" I looked, but no one was there. "Jesus!" she repeated, and pushed me away, scrambling to her feet. "We've got to find him!"

"He's not here!"

"They are planning to arrest him. Judas is with the Sanhedrin right now!" On her face a look of alarm, though one mingling, it almost seemed, with the bitter herbs and salt tears of Passover. "Judas is before the chief priests right now! They are going to pay him. They *are* paying him! They are giving him silver coins—he is *accepting* them!"

It took a while to sink in. Could such a thing be? Judas, at this very moment, at the Chamber of Hewn Stone, betraying Yeshua for money? "Are you sure? Because if it's true, we have to warn Yeshua!"

"They are going to arrest him! It's going to be tonight after the sun goes down!" Hastily, she wrapped her head covering in place. "Come on!"

Earth and sky suddenly became chaotic dance partners as we raced across the Kidron Valley, hoping against hope to excise time and its more malevolent qualities, death, sorrow, lamentation, pain. At the city gates, our progress slowed, and while we finally made it through and into the city, we found ourselves, before long, jammed in the throngs at the Xystus. Shrieks of children rent the air as noise and confusion flew at us with outstretched talons. "Wasn't there a house at which we were going to eat the Passover meal?" She had to shout in my ear to make herself heard.

"The house of Joseph—yes!" I shouted back, remembering suddenly.

"Do you know where it is?"

As it happened, I did, for I had accompanied James and Peter there only the previous day. "Yes!" I said, and through the dusky firmament of bodies around the theater I took the lead now, as we pushed along the crowded street, turning upward at last, mounting the storied slope of the Upper City, where carriages were prohibited and only pedestrians and rich men's litters were allowed. It was farther away than I remembered, but at last we were there—walking up toward the front of the house of Joseph of Arimathea. And such a house it was! An upper room elevated the dwelling, regally extending its roofline, but long before reaching that, you passed through a colorful entry way laced with intricate mosaics. Inside we found the more subdued tones of a man who bore the grief of eloquence. The Pharisee from Arimathaea was in fact there, calmly addressing Jesus in the presence of a number of others.

"While not necessarily setting aside John's baptism of water..." Mariamne and I moved across the tessalated floor of the atrium as he spoke... "...nonetheless, I have always given credence to the goodness a man may obtain by praying."

I knew little of this man Joseph, only that he lived somewhere else in the city with his wife and children, and that this house was but a spare one, one of several he owned. I knew also, of course, that he was of the Sanhedrin. Yet despite feasting upon the waters his station in life entitled him, something in his eyes spoke of having navigated numerous of those episodes that are as cloud unaccompanied by nourishing rain. In encountering Jesus, by way of chance at the house in Bethany on a night long ago, it seemed to him he had stumbled upon what he'd long felt existed though had never found evidence to prove: light in darkness. But even before that night, even before coming to the home of Lazarus and his sisters and encountering the Nazarene, something had begun to gnaw at the heart of Joseph of Arimathea; it was a song, a repartee to the cosmos perhaps, telling him he should take unto himself the title of *m'shamshana wameskina*, servant of the poor. The feeling never left him, and on that long-ago night, and in the presence of that light-in-darkness at the house in Bethany, the world and everything in it seemed suddenly to turn completely about. As it did so, YHWH, the wrathful God, shrugged and lowered his head like a docile king of elephants. *Pante Rei.* All flows. And where the flow leads, this Pharisee had followed. The house in which we were standing was a composition of beauty and orderliness. By making it available to us for Passover, Joseph had demonstrated his innate generosity, but befriending the Nazarene was not without its risks. Had he befriended Barrabas himself his social standing could not have been more imperiled.

As we crossed the room, I had the feeling that the conversation Mariamne and I had managed to stumble into the midst of had reached one of those pregnant moments in time.

"They would consider taking the way of Cain," Joseph was now saying. "For Caiaphas, it is better that one man should die than that a whole people should suffer."

"What shall I say, 'Father, spare me from this hour'—even when it is this very hour I have traveled far to reach? Look at the fig tree, Joseph. When its twigs grow tender and its leaves come out you know that summer is near. In the same way, you know that what's in a man's heart determines his speech, that happiness is the outcome of good, while pain is the outcome of evil."

"The ways of God are equal, while the ways of man seem always so very *un*equal." Joseph expelled a weary sigh. "I can only weep for the daughters of Jerusalem, for I fear that one day bad times will come upon us."

"Yes, the Law is twisted, and even ignored when convenient., and because of this there will come a time when those of Judea will flee to the mountains. But know this: that the Father is the origin of all; and he lifts the veils of those who are his." The Nazarene paused, fingered a sprig of *jeezer*, and then casually handed it to Joseph as if it were a bouquet of the most beautiful flowers. "There was a man who made a great supper and invited many. He sent his servant out at suppertime, saying to him, 'Ask them to come, for all things are now ready.' But they who were invited each had an excuse. The first said to the servant, 'I have bought a piece of land and I must go and see to it.' Another had just purchased five yoke of oxen and also asked to be excused. Another said, 'I have just married a wife, and cannot come.' So the servant came back and told his lord all these things. The master became angry. 'Go into the streets and lanes of the city and bring in the poor, the maimed, the halt, the blind." Yeshua paused again—and this time he smiled warmly at Joseph. "A parable for the Passover. Take it home and share it with your children."

"Well yes, you're right. I must be home to my family." He smiled as well, strode forward, and clasped Jesus firmly by the shoulders. "My friend—we will talk again tomorrow."

Joseph, I am sure, sincerely meant those words, for of course how easily one may gaze upon the sands of the desert and be lulled into believing them to hold water. By way of reply, the Nazarene merely nodded.

Chapter Seventy-Six

*I*esvs Nazarenvs Rex Ivdaeorvm. Those were the words the Romans wrote upon a sign and affixed to the cross. I could almost see that sign in my mind's eye, even then, even here in this house, with its upper room of astringent lathers. And I know Mariamne saw it. For she saw much.

I don't recall whether by this time we had forgotten about Judas Iscariot, or whether, recoiling from the griffin's gaping jaws, we had looked over the abyss into the ungrudging womb of metamorphosis. We all knew. Not just Mariamne and I alone. Everyone in that house, from Ema Mary to my mother, from James, to Philip, to Andrew, and all the rest—all of us had seen the far-fleeing sun. And we knew, in seeing it, that anything Judas did or didn't do was of scarcely any matter now. In our tongue the word that comes to mind is *beka*. It means to weep.

Outside the house, the last daylight was fading from the sky. Inside, the lamps were now lit, and the evening meal was being served. The whispering trees of life tear no holes in the sun, neither here, nor in the mansions of heaven, where a place has been prepared...I remember Yeshua's voice that night. It flowed forth like the balm of Gilead, comforting, consoling, as he spoke of one thing and another, of beautiful lips and braided hair, of Love, shining radiant like gold, but before he spoke, aye, before he even partook of the meal which had been set, he got up, removed his outer clothing, wrapped a towel around his waist, and poured a basin of water. What sort of curious affair was this? We were not long in finding out. Around the room he took the basin, arriving, one by one, before each of us, whereupon, methodically and with immaculate care, he began to wash our feet. Something of a tumult it caused, for there were those, even then—might I say it?—who thought of him as a conquering warrior messiah. Peter, for one, registered much distress at this humble show of abasement, but at a word from Jesus—"if I do not wash your feet you can have no part of me"—the Capharnaum fisherman allowed the washing to proceed, though on his face a look of having just lost a benediction from the archangels.

And so around it went. When it came Mariamne's turn, no protestations did she make; rather, it seemed to me she "endured" the lavation, for that is how I would describe it really, as an *enduring*. An endurance of a pain as articulate as night as, with tears on her face, she looked down at he whom she loved above all others, kneeling before her with that basin. I don't think anyone really understood why she was crying. Except of course Jesus. And I— I also understood. No sound came from her, no sobs. By way of some boundless might, these she kept muted. There were only those silent tears of *shrara*.

Then to James, Thomas, Nathanael...carrying his basin he went, binding each of us to him with this small, fragrant flower of humility, until at last all was made rich in sweetness. "Do you understand what I have done for you? You call me 'master' and 'teacher,' and this is well, for these things I have been to you, and now that I, your master and teacher, have washed your feet, so you should also wash one another's feet."

What can I say of this night? How speak of it without tears coming to my *own* eyes, just as they came to Mariamne's? It is not because my death is near, Quintus, that I cry. It is not that I am old and have lived my time. It is because death did not come and claim me long ago. At night, when all is peaceful, many, many birds gather. They settle upon majestic, moonlit boughs, some happy, some sad. Their aspirations bring joy and death. And when the life-night comes to its end, they look to the sky, at which time they fly away, in all directions, according to their destiny. On the day that now lay before us, we became as those birds—flying off from Golgotha in all directions, silhouetted by the sun. It was not my destiny to go to the cross with Jesus that day, even though there were times later I wished I had.

But I am getting ahead of myself, for I must finish the story of that night, and I must say something especially of the things which he said in those hours just prior to his arrest, for in this relatively short time he built for us the abode of God's Spirit of Truth and Love. And, so that he would not leave us as orphans, he revealed for us the shining beauty of *Paraqlita*.

"If you love me then obey my command—and my command to you is that you love one another. In this manner, all will know you are truly mine. Greater love has no one than this: that he should lay down his life for his friends. I no longer call you my servants, for a servant does not know his master's business. I now call you all my friends."

Yes. He *had* called us his friends. And *Paraqlita's* birth was as the bud of life plucked by the dove from the terebinth tree, for among the last words he spoke to us that night were those concerning *shlama*—peace. "Peace I leave with you. My peace I give you. I do not give to you as the world gives. So don't let your heart be troubled, and don't be afraid."

Chapter Seventy-Seven

I f the world hated us, it also hated him. For as gusts of the wind come and go, so also the tides of the human heart. But in the father's house there are many mansions. *Tauta'va*. We are all sojourners in this exile.

In order to give a reckoning of the events of that night I must rely in places upon accounts by others, Mariamne and Peter for what took place at the high priest's house; Joanna for what occurred at Herod's; and a Gentile steward known to Joanna who was able to relate the gist of the scene between Jesus and Pilate. Of and in my own witness, I can say only what transpired on the Mount of Olives, for it was to there we retired, later on in the evening, leaving the *house* of Joseph, in order to make our way out to the *garden* of Joseph, called Gethsemane. It was here the soldiers, led by Judas Iscariot, found their way to us. Overall, they were not the most disciplined of ranks. Swords came unsheathed as Jesus was seized roughly and bound, a violent handling that leveled off at last into a confused exchange over whether the entire lot of us should be arrested, or the Nazarene alone. The low-ranking guard commander in charge of the group settled in favor of taking Jesus only, "for now." Yeshua stood chained amongst them. The rest of us were ordered to disperse, an order promptly complied with. Cravenly off into the night I scampered, in the end taking cover amidst the tombs, hunkering down in the cold as Philip and Andrew came stumbling moments later into the same area. Here it was, concealed amidst those markers of death, the three of us kept company through the cheerless hours that followed. Meanwhile, unbeknownst to us, Peter and Mariamne, after initially hiding themselves, began an intrepid pursuit of the arrest party back to the city, trailing the flickering torches all the way across the Kidron Valley. No way could I then conceive of it, of course, for in no manner would I have thought her capable, but this runaway slave from the House of Herod not only followed the soldiers and their prisoner all the way back to the city, right up to the high priest's door, but even managed to get *inside*. And upon gaining entry, arranged for Peter to be admitted. *Me'on arayot.* She entered it...entered, and led Peter inside as well.

And so yes, it was at the palace of Caiaphas, the high priest, they ended up, a locale by chance known to my love, for she had visited many times as a member of Herod's retinue. Most especially was she recognized by the serving girl at the door. Once Mariamne requested entry, the girl readily assented. It was that easy. Having gained admittance herself, my clever and resourceful love then prevailed upon the same girl to open the door for Peter.

King-like and heavenly was this high priest's palace, though within its viridarium Peter and Mariamne witnessed a series of punishments inflicted on Jesus. Present was Annas, father-in-law to Caiaphas, the man whom Yeshua had publicly humiliated a year previous. His expression through it all remained one of steadfast and supreme satisfaction. But perhaps the greatest obscenity of all lay in the person of the high priest himself, a toady who owed his position to Rome. Caiaphas had been appointed by Valerius Gratus, Pilate's predecessor, yet it's fair to say that without continued patronage from Pilate his profitable sinecure would be lost to him. So low had we Jews sunk that the choosing of our own high priests was now done by our Roman overlords. A "trial" of sorts was the main order of business, and it was completed rather quickly. Caiaphas and Annas were ably assisted by the paid *delatores*, namely Hodi and his rabble, who testified as to various untruths regarding Jesus. Having given ear to their calumnies, the toadying worm of a high priest leapt to his feet, rent his clothes, and demanded, "What need have we of further testimony!"

Yes, Hodi and his rabble formed the foundation of the decision to convict Jesus, but there was one other little sacrilege the bully was to perform before the night was over, and this had to do with Peter. Hodi had well taken note of the Galilean's somewhat furtive arrival earlier, the same Galilean, of course, who had thrashed him so soundly as a youth, and an opportunity for retribution soon presented itself. A smug smile spread itself across his face as he devised his plan, or that is how I like to imagine it. In any event, as the son of Jonah and a number of others stood warming themselves by a rich fire in the atrium, the aforementioned serving girl was prevailed upon for yet another favor. This time, however, the request was made not by Mariamne, but by Hodi. To walk up to Peter and inquire, "Aren't you one of them?"—this the young woman was instructed to do. Furthermore, she was to issue her accusation in a manner most shrill, calling as much attention to herself and to Peter as possible. Like all good servants, the girl sought to win favor from her masters, and in playing along with Hodi's charade, it seems she excelled beyond all expectations. Peter, the same Peter who had once professed a willingness to die for Yeshua, denied even knowing the Nazarene. But the girl was persistent, unwilling to let it go at that, and the Galilean fisherman was obliged to issue fully three denials in all, all of which took their toll. Realizing he had succumbed to fear in a moment of weakness, he raced from the building, stumbling bitterly into the night. An amusing spectacle no doubt for Hodi, but for Peter it turned into a soul-shattering experience, and in a very real sense he spent the rest of his days on earth trying to atone.

With the crowing of the cock, Jesus was taken before Pilate, transferred to Herod's, and then, sometime later, back to Pilate's. But we are as we are, and we are of ourselves, and I should here like to backtrack to the Mount of Olives and relate very briefly something of our night of squalor there, a night which delivered, to those of us who had remained behind, a sober recognition of our *own* need for atonement and recompense, as, with dawn approaching, we slowly regrouped ourselves.

Chapter Seventy-Eight

E ven after the soldiers left with Jesus in their custody, I feared, as did Philip and Andrew, to emerge from the tombs. No fire did we build, for so great was our fright we dared not call attention to ourselves. But the night brought with it a tenacious chill, driving us finally, in the hour before dawn, into a state of much restlessness. Working up our courage, we ventured from our hiding place. Almost immediately, we came upon James and my sister-in-law Abby, followed, a short time later, by Thomas and Nathanael, the seven of us drawing comfort from each other as we re-summoned our fortitude. Others began falling out of the night as well, Pompeia, Matthew, Other James...at last Peter, whom we found, in the first wretched flight of dawn upon the land, weeping beneath a holm oak in the Kidron Valley. What had become of Jesus? All we knew was that the state of affairs was a grim one. Had there been any doubt of this before, the sight of Peter's tears of impotence eliminated it.

The sun, Ra, the eye of the world, had been risen most of an hour when finally we spied three women walking together on a distant ridge—Ema Mary, my mother, and Mariamne. Our cries rang forth, and almost immediately the trio saw us, yet the reunion held little hope or happiness.

"They are going to crucify Jesus." Mariamne's doleful monotones informed us of the encroaching catastrophe as she relayed, very briefly, what had taken place at the high priest's house. Her remarks were addressed to one and all, although as she spoke, there came over me the feeling she was speaking to me alone, for her perilously solemn eyes bent repeatedly in my direction, eyes which, it occurred to me now, would never be completely cried out of love's tears.

Chapter Seventy-Nine

"**S**o you *are* a king then."

"'King?' It depends on how you use the word."

"You stand accused by your own people and their chief priests." Pilate gave up a half-grin. "If you are a king, apparently you're not a very *admired* one."

"I am not an earthly king. Were I, my followers would have fought when your soldiers came. But my kingdom is not of this world."

"Ah! Now we're getting somewhere—then you *do* admit you are a king."

"I was born for that purpose, yes. It is why I came into the world, to bear witness to the truth. Those who are of the truth hear my voice."

"What is truth?"

It was the servant friend of Joanna who related the gist of this conversation, but after all what did it really mean? Maybe the Roman prefect was trying to say there is no such thing as truth. Or maybe he was saying that the truth is whatever we, the Roman conquerors, say it is. Over my life, I have heard many people proclaim many things. I have heard things spoken in great wisdom; I've heard other assertions born of folly and madness. But in the eye of Hubris everything is burning. The senses burn. The mind burns. Even the world itself burns. And the world was burning for Pontius Pilate.

We were standing just then on the *Gabbatha*. Jesus was not present yet, nor was Pilate, yet a considerable crowd *was* there, perhaps as many as six hundred or so, mostly common people, seeking respite from their daily boredoms in the whimsy of a moment's public diversion. *May the Lord hear thee on thy day of trouble*. Though the sun was high, the morning grew steadily pierced and darkened. All about was a sort of listless, carrion-like energy. A group of *tephillin*-adorned Pharisees hustled by in the direction of the Xystus, yet the doors to the Praetorium, Pilate's residence at the Antonia Fortress, remained shut and beveled in stillness. Even then I clung to my hopes, even as the crowd formed itself into increasingly discordant clusters and more people arrived, people perhaps sensing the posh gut of hatred soon to be torn. Someone commented that the "deceiver" had been taken away to Herod's palace. Another said no. A third averred he indeed *had* been taken to Herod's, but that that had been earlier and he had since been brought back to Pilate. By chance and a nebulous sort of glory Hodi was there, he and his rabble making for an evil and ill-smelling presence on the *Gabbatha*. Even a man with no wound on his hand might occasionally touch poison and be sickened by it. I am referring to the poison of the Spirit of Injustice, which is of course Satan, the Prince of this World, for it seemed to me it was this poison that had infected Hodi, even as far back as when we were children. Now, here, our paths were crossing again. Of course he spotted us as well, and we had not long to wait before he strolled by to gloat. "Pilate slays with the arrow. Your master shall soon sojourn in *Sheol*." I suppose all the fight was gone from us. Peter, even my valiant brother James, allowed the comment to pass unchallenged, for Heaven help us, we were afraid.

The doors to the Praetorium burst open suddenly and quite noisily, and there he was, the governor of Judea. Across the balustrade he swaggered, a man of middle years, graying somewhat about the temples, yet eyes alert and cautious, the mouth twisted into a closed, tight phalanx of a grin. As prefect, he was the highest-ranking Roman official in the land. No one in Judea held more power. Gazing out upon the Jews, his mortal subjects, he seemed to savor the moment. The show, in a sense, had begun.

Pilate alone occupied the balustrade at first, though a short time later Yeshua was brought out, yet it was a Yeshua from whom my eyes recoiled in horror. He had been beaten badly. Physically weak, it appeared he required assistance, though when let go of by the two soldiers on either side, he managed to stand on his own. The crowd found the sight risible. Beside me, Ema Mary stifled a scream, as instinctively I placed an arm about her, trying, in some manner, to shield her from the sight, for her son had been intentionally made to look a figure of ridicule. A crown he wore on his head, yet one plaited together out of thorny jujube branches. Draped about him was a purple robe—purple being the preferred color of the Roman upper classes. It was as if Pilate were saying to his Jewish subjects, "Here is your king!"

But there was more. The thorns of the jujube had torn into his flesh, bringing blood to his face, a face corked and welted in a dozen or more places, though beyond even that, his beard was gone, at first I assumed shaven off, though closer look suggested it had been ripped away in handfuls. Patches of hair seemed to be missing from his head as well. Whether he had earlier been taken to Herod's, as the whisperers on the *Gabbatha* professed to know, was unclear. At present, however, he stood solely in the custody of Pontius Pilate, "an extremely foul man," as Maximinus had once described him, and at that moment, as I watched the spectacle, Maximinus' words came to back to me.

But the *barbaricus spectaculum* was only just beginning. "Behold the man!" Pilate accompanied his words with a generous sweep of the arm. It was a haughty moment, a public moment, a moment of captor and captive. Whatever you may think of this man's performance of miracles, rumored or otherwise, he was in essence saying, no one, but no one, can stand up to the power of Rome. But it was his next words—"Here is your king!"—which came as a calculated shattering of dignity. Hodi and the human refuse about him erupted with cries of "crucify him!", the refrain quickly taken up by the gullible and incitable crowd. Ah, but the show was not yet over! Another farce had yet to be unveiled. "This man stands before you convicted by your own chief priests. However, as you may know, we have a custom of releasing a prisoner to you each year in honor of the feast. I shall now release him." But no such thing was to be, nor had it even been contemplated. Dropping their cries for Yeshua's crucifixion, Hodie and company issued a new imperative: "Away with this man! Give us Barabbas!" And low and behold, onto the balustrade a moment later came the great "insurrectionist" himself. Purposefully he strode forward, pumping his fists, a man steeped in arrogance, whose very name was his bounty, bespeaking his churlish proclamation: "Son of the Father."

So now we had the two most celebrated and famous, or should I say infamous, prisoners in Jerusalem, one standing on the one side of Pilate, subdued and beaten, the other on his opposite, a picture of robust strength, one might even say cockiness. Is it hard to imagine which the crowd preferred? Shouts of "Barabbas! Barabbas!" filled the air.

"But what about Jesus, who is called Christ?" replied a manifestly bewildered Pilate.

"Crucify him!" shouted the crowd.

"Crucify your *king*?"

"We have no king but Caesar!"

It was precisely what the prefect wished to hear. In releasing Barabbas, he had skillfully fostered the illusion that the crowd had achieved a "victory," painting himself in the process as a benevolent governor who had bowed to popular will. And so Jerusalem became once more the city that kills the prophets, and if Barabbas, the murderer, felt any remorse that two of his own followers were to be taken out and crucified as well, he gave no sign. For the first time in my life, I was ashamed of being a Jew.

Chapter Eighty

O f that walk out to Golgotha, I shall speak little. It was a disparaging procession up to a bleak, barren knoll outside the western walls of the city. Of course, the prisoners were stripped of their clothing. With the Romans, it seems, merely *killing* their enemies is never sufficient. Death must take for its twin brother humiliation, and in these public spectacles, both may be prolonged, by hours, sometimes days. Affixation to the cross does not mean bodily functions cease. Respiration, passage of wastes—all must go on. But in this case a somewhat speedy end of the matter *was* desired, for Passover was approaching, and it was deemed expedient that all traces of the execution be erased by sundown. For that reason Jesus and the other two prisoners were nailed, rather than tied, to their crosses, for it is widely believed multiple piercing of the flesh in this manner hastens the oncoming of death. To bleed, my Lord, for thee. *Iesvs Nazarenvs Rex Ivdaeorvm.*

When the crosses were raised, the women stood back some distance, deliberately averting their eyes. How pitiable their lot, thought I, though far more pitiable were those who had followed the procession to Golgotha for no other purpose than to jeer and taunt, such people having forfeited all claims to humanity. And then of course there were our chief priests. A wise man recognizes the proper moment for all actions, but our chief priests were not wise by any means. At the raising of Jesus on the cross they broke out in vexation—oh not at the injustice, mind you. Rather, their grievance was over the wording on the sign.

"Change it to read, 'he *said* he was king of the Jews!'" Determined to be toadying worms to the end, it seemed, but Pilate granted them not even this modicum of respect.

"What is written is written," he dismissed airily.

Ah! The naked spectacle of sorrow and dross. But among the last words I heard from the Nazarene was a prayer, not for himself, but that they, his tormentors, should be forgiven by God. Understand, Quintus, I could *hear* him speaking. Close to the foot of the cross I stood, and these words I heard him say: "Father forgive them for they do not know what they do." It was more than astonishing; it was a sacrifice, unto something immaculate and terrifying, whispered before a mad and ulcerous multitude. There is one other thing he said I'll also relate, of a personal nature, a request he made of me—that Mariamne and I should thereafter care for Ema Mary. I gave him my solemn promise we would. It is a request, I'm happy to say, we carried out fully.

Finally, what can I say of him? I know not from where he came, for I did not see him earlier in the procession out here, but it was sometime not long after I had assured Yeshua I would care for his mother that I saw him, my gaze falling by chance on those oddly and unmistakably accipitrine features. It was the *Owl Man*. Not since the night at the Pool of Bethesda had I laid eyes on him, and as I say I didn't see him during the procession out here, but as I watched now, he methodically affixed a sponge to a hyssop stalk. The sponge had been dipped in the milky white juice of the gall plant, or what the Hebrews refer to as rosh. It is a potent pain reliever. To Jesus, near death now, he offered it. Had the Owl Man come all the way out here from the city for no other purpose than to perform this act of mercy? As I watched him, with the hyssop held aloft, he seemed to me much as a guide from the far bank of the Acheron, ferried perhaps by Charon. Much later, when the bodies were being removed from the crosses, I happened to see him again, still holding to his gall-moistened sponge...crying.

Chapter Eighty-One

O f the events of later that day and the night which followed I must hereby give an account, for more tragedy awaited us. In the afternoon, the body of Judas Iscariot was found hanging from a tree. His covenant with death, made perhaps with his usual avarice and biliousness, had been in some ways nonetheless a redemptive act. Or, if not that, at least an expression of his tragic merit as a human being. Much has been made, and continues to be, of his act of betrayal, but what I feel compelled to say is that his role in all this was less a lightning flash than a random drop of rain. Did he, for instance, before his final act of self destruction, pause to consider that those who sought Jesus' death would have found a way to bring it about regardless of anything that he, Judas Iscariot, might have done or said? I feel reasonably certain he did, and I prefer to think somehow that it did not matter to him.

But that was not all.

In the evening hours, we returned to the house of Joseph. Approaching the dwelling from the north, we saw that a candle had been left burning in one of the upper windows. It was yet another signature of death's holy rite. (Enough for one day, surely!) I remember one or two of our number puzzling over who could be in the house, for we knew that Joseph, after laying Yeshua in his family tomb, had retired to his home. That it might be Tirzah did not occur to us, for so tumultuous had been the day's events, we had not even noticed her absence.

"Tsevâchâh!" wailed her longtime friend Matthew when we entered. It was a wail of grief and despair, well understandable, for the sight which met us was a grisly one. The floor was soaked in blood, copious, monstrous amounts of it. Heavy with child, so much so she would surely have given birth within a matter of days, if not hours, the scribe had taken a knife and severed her veins. Not far from her body, yet resting sufficiently above the floor as to remain unsullied by the voluminous spillage, were her scrolls. Or her *precious* scrolls, I should say, for in all of our travels they had seldom left her sight, these books in which she had faithfully recorded words spoken by Jesus in virtually every town and village through which we had passed. Later, upon opening and reading them, we discovered some Aramaic words and phrases here and there, but found by far the majority of it had been written in Greek. She was the most educated among us. I had always known that. But wretched is the body that is dependent on a body. In the end, rather than bring the child of a betrayer into the world, she had taken her own life. A harsh judgment, to be sure, no less for herself as for the child.

But what of these scrolls and the words therein? Quintus, they were a wild haunting. It was Jesus writ large. And yes. A lot of what I remembered him saying was there...*blessed are the poor...foxes have holes...the kingdom is like a mustard seed.* Neither was John the Baptizer omitted. Strange this, since to my knowledge, Tirzah had never met the Holy Man. But there it was, details about things like Yeshua's baptism, which, as far as I can figure, only Andrew, or possibly Jesus himself, could have told her of. Omnipotence resided in these pages of hers, an omnipotence that had come to consume the world and all the war makers in it. My assumption is that in putting it all in Greek she had harbored the ambitious goal of spreading Yeshua's teachings beyond Judea to the wider world. She succeeded. For these volumes of hers became the source of much of what was later written about the Nazarene. Of course, she was an adulteress and the consort of a betrayer, and I knew even then she would never, in a million years, receive credit for any of it. No one would even hear her name. Ever. But I proclaim it here and now: Tirzah! Tirzah! May the Immortal Gods sing thy fame!

Perhaps good and evil are but different parts of the circle of life, and just as the different parts of a circle flow eventually into one another, so, too, do good and evil. It is a circle around which we travel in endless repetition...birth, suffering, death...on and on...until we pull ourselves out of its murky waters into the arms of the Radiant One.

O Tirzah. The tears you cry are our own.

Chapter Eighty-Two

Day is to night as night is to day, and the golden bird drops from the side of the world and becomes a shooting star. Foreseen only was the bitterness, but our bitterness turned to joy, for just as day becomes night, and sorrow becomes joy, so too does death become life. Given his raising of Lazarus, what transpired perhaps should have come as no surprise. Yet who could have foreseen it? Who would find fault with us for failing to imagine that Immutable Truth, in all of its wild tribes and reciprocities, might carve, file, and polish itself in such a manner? It was Mariamne who first saw him, early on the third morning, at the tomb of Joseph, where she had gone to wrap his body in spices. Only no body was there to be found. Rather she found someone very much alive. Later she would write a poem about the encounter, scribbled in her hand, onto a leaf of papyrus that I kept for many years, right up until the time of my second arrest, but then it was lost, as were so many other things out of my life at that time. Yet no matter, for strangely I still remember the poem, every word, in its entirety:

Noli Me Tangere

There, by the tomb in the light of morning, I saw what for me
Could not have been earned or thwarted—
You desiring to become perfectly lonely;
You living—your face transformed like the peak of a golden
   mountain,
Yet still your face;
You standing—your voice with its magic power, telling me all is
   expedient,
Yet still your voice;
You—enamored of the witch;
You—triumphant.
O madness, seek for me—with the rich generosity of a king
Kind to his slave—in this place, there or here;
Find a treasure house for your disciple, kindred in sorrow,
And pray never adjure, *noli me tangere*.

But she did not go mad again. And for this I was grateful. And maybe it was the love she felt for me that saved her. I should like very much to think so. Maybe also the directive he imparted to us—*Go out and teach*—had something to do with it as well, for *yes*, he *did* eventually appear to all of us, and *yes*, there *was* a difference. It was a matter of him looking more like "himself" than ever before. It was he, evolved into something more quintessentially *him*. He spoke with us, and even ate with us. We saw him in Jerusalem, and again at Gennesaret's shore, and then we saw him no more. His body dissolved. But he had called us his friends. And he had laid down his life. And God had wiped away our tears.

O *Ma're*, all we have is yours and all you have is ours.

Chapter Eighty-Three

T he hills near Bethsaida overlooking Gennesaret are a place for lovers. I can state it no more plainly than that. The tranquility, the sweet terebinths—so much about it is conducive to romance. So it had been for Susanna and Maximinus years before; so also for Mariamne and me now. Hills lovely in *form* and *fragrance*—these were my thoughts as we climbed that slope in the gentle sunshine, with Gennesaret's ever-conquering blue-wisdom at our backs.

So much around us, we do not wish to see happen. Yet at the same time, dreams, like raindrops, remain firmly fixed in our minds. Mariamne was starting to grow noticeably heavy with child, and there was much about which to be happy. Bringing Ema Mary with us, we had come to Bethsaida, paying visit to the home of Philip and his wonderful family. Life is an embellishment of many colors, but where had those colors all gone? I thought of the others, of Simon the Zealot for instance, embarking off down that road back to Gamla, his cithra strapped across his back. Though he could not read or write, in the years that followed, Simon ended up singing and playing songs, musical stories really, celebrating the life of Jesus, throughout the Galilee and Gaulanitis, even up to the lands of Damascus, Antioch, and beyond. I thought also of Thomas and Nathanael, leaving by ship for Ephesus, and of those others who had dispersed to Tyre, Caesarea, and elsewhere. The birds had indeed scattered from Golgotha in all directions. This applied to the women as well as the men, though in the case of my mother it had been merely to fly home to once-familiar territory. Yes, I should mention that she who gave me birth had returned to Zebedee, returned to the barren, withered garden of their marriage together. I had been against the move, but to no avail. "It is normality," she'd insisted with a shrug. And in the end perhaps normality was more important to her than happiness, though I could not help feeling she had made a bad bargain with life.

"The sacred times are not passed away, John," said Mariamne now, as we climbed the last rise leading up to the top of the hill. "They are only beginning."

Sacred? Who knew? Yet I could not help thinking she was correct, for in Jerusalem, from where I had just returned, there was indeed something resembling the sacred, or if not that, at least a steady rising on the horizon day by day. I had accompanied my brother and Peter there for *Shavuot*. Another journey, another promise to the darting flame that was my memory of the Nazarene. Yet it had been a miserable trip, and all because of the desperate longing I knew for she who now walked at my side. And so, upon my release from prison, I had left them, Peter and James. A case of abandonment it surely was! But my stay in the Holy City had been at least of sufficient duration to convince me something momentous was happening.

"As a favor to me John, would you...take my hand?"

Winter was past and the rains over. O Solomon and your beloved, before us you stand with the greatest of hearts! Like a reed in marsh water, my voice thickened, "If you would entrust your hand to me, Mariamne, I would gladly take it, for your hand is of the kingdom, as is your heart." And in the kingdom of heaven, I knew, flew the crane and the eagle, just as flew my love for her. A delicious sea wind gusted at our backs as we reached the crest of the mountain, and just beyond it, a little stone hut I remembered from years and years ago. Once used by wandering shepherds, it was now abandoned. We took seats on the little stone stoop in front, basking in shady subterfuge as we stared out, not only at Gennesaret, but at all the rest of the earth we could see from here, which included the town of Bethsaida.

"It is so very beautiful!" Her words seemed to fly with the bluebird that lifted itself off even as she spoke, loosening its own cry to the marooned of speech. For several more moments we sat, talking quietly, finally rising and entering the hut. Here, in a corner, we found a straw broom, thoughtfully left behind by some previous occupant, and making quick work of a layer of dust, we opened the shutters to allow an airing.

"Kinsman to the poor and the wayfarer—that is us." Upon the casemate windowsill I leaned after we had dispensed with the sweeping. She stood beside me and together we stared out upon a tiny, faraway cluster of fishing boats. Gennesaret, that great and vast lake—it had always had the power to evoke in me a variety of moods, including sadness, which in part is what I felt now, for I knew Mariamne had to leave here. And I knew I had to go with her. We were destined to become wayfarers for sure.

"Even the wayfarers might love one another, for God made all things," she said. God indeed made all things, and never did I feel this more acutely than when I looked into her eyes. God's kingdom is in us and all around us. There is the amygdalus, the almond, the mustard seed. Life to life. And Attis—from the blood of his self-mutilation sprang violets. Is it not so? And did I not see those violets in Jerusalem? I did, during the *Shavuot*, or, as the Greek-speaking Jews refer to it, Pentecost. Forty-nine days. Forty-nine violets. It was subtle, this flowering. In the Law of Moses, as it was handed down to us, God was unknowable, his face far too awesome to behold. But this was no longer the case. Not since Yeshua. God was now known. All you had to do was knock. With the command "love one another," the established order had been turned upside down. Yeshua had dismantled reality, dismantled the law, reassembling both as something the chief priests no longer recognized. It had angered them, and in forty-nine days, their anger had far from abated.

As I thought of these things, I looked deeply into the eyes of my beloved, and said, "Just as the sea and its waves are one, so you are the song of my soul, Mariamne." It was true. She exerted a pull on me stronger than the ocean, a fact to which I had reconciled myself, for the road to *Shavuot* and back had taught me it. Before departing for Jerusalem, I had beseeched, pleaded with her, to make the trip with us, but she had refused, and little wonder. While her relations with Peter had never been amiable, after Golgotha they had degenerated further. Though greater than great, God had found not yet a way to make them other than as bird and snake, contemplating one another warily in the loneliest reaches of wilderness. I think mainly it was that she was so completely different from us. We were fishermen, while she was—well, it was hard to say *what* she was, other than something *other*, something almost impossible to define. The rancorous discord between her and Peter left me, quite naturally, caught in the middle. I had set off for Jerusalem with Peter and James, while she had remained in Galilee, staying first with Pompeia, until the priestess of Pan departed for Caesarea of the Mountain, then alone, carving out an anonymous solitude for herself as her womb grew ardent with love.

In Jerusalem, little did I find but cheerless gloom, which the city, I'm sure, found in me as well. Oh, that is not to say the numbers seeking to know of "the Christos" (as Jesus had now come to be known) weren't larger than ever. They were. Greater by far than ever when he had drawn breath. But our chief priests, having helped rid the city of his physical presence, sought to eradicate his memory as well, and in their service, a pernicious man named

Saul. He was an individual of much anger and wrath, though later it would be said he had changed.

Standing here with Mariamne, however, here on a hilltop, in a shepherd's hut, with she who was the shepherdess of my very own star, all of that seemed remote. My love and I were united once more. She edged closer to me and I took her into my arms, thinking, as I did so, how yes, we are *all* colors, every one of us. We grow out of the ground, full of the spirit of God, turning into blossoms of every speckle and hue. "O Mariamne..." I whispered, and with the palm of my hand touched her face, placing my other hand upon her breast. As sheaths dividing and falling—so became our clothes, until only our *kolburs* remained, and then they too were gone. I breathed the heady, nocturnal scent of her as I placed my cheek against her belly, now noticeably rounded like the gourd, feeling myself in heaven as she spoke in whispers, "Hold to me, O my beloved, O dearest one." Her words were as the prayer of a martyr before death, for it *was* a kind of death we subsequently reached. *Abwoon d'washmaya*, O Mother-Father, birther of the universe, seal us with your kiss!

When our lovemaking was over, I sat outside the hut; after some time, she joined me. It seemed to me that God, *Alaha*, the Oneness, is not only the maker of bonds, but the shatterer of them too. I thought of this because I knew there was one bond Mariamne and I had left to shatter, and that was our bond to this land. She of Magdala had to leave Galilee, leave Judea. The sooner the better. Legally she was still Herod's slave, and remaining here could but only increase the chances that one day, sooner or later, she would be captured and taken. Already, it seemed to me, she had borrowed heavily upon what limited time fate ever seems to allow in such matters.

"John?" Her voice contained a lusty tenor. Suddenly I thought of the two lions of the Egyptians, seated back to back from each other and supporting the horizon. One of the lions' names is "Yesterday," the other "Tomorrow." We presently were caught, it seemed to me, in that narrow space separating the two. But not for long. "John, do you love me?"

"More than anything, Mariamne," I answered.

"Much love do I feel for you as well." She lapsed, musing in silence. The silence was broken, however, when all at once she turned once more and inquired with a sudden coltishness, "Would you like to get married?"

"Yes Mariamne, more than anything."

The motive of all is love, and when we stream towards God, we see our love become an ocean. Had it, I wondered, been that way for Yeshua? Close to the end, I mean, after he had offered up that prayer for forgiveness for his enemies—had the love in his heart simply swelled and become as vast and boundless as the Great Sea? Is that how it happens when the nettle of the heart is pricked? "You have a wondrous light in your eyes." She smiled as she said this, gazing at me intently.

"I feel like I'm dancing inside," I replied. Yet even as the words came out, I sensed something else inside as well, an endemic rainy season arising to receive that light as its dancing partner. And this she was quick to perceive, for that was another thing—every joy or sorrow entering or exiting my heart on whim or chance seemed in some way detectable to her.

"Tell me," she urged, pushing closer to me.

"While in Jerusalem I saw a man stoned to death." This indeed was the case. A man named Stephen. And I tried describing to her something of the affair, but I'm not sure my words were able to convey the full disgrace and depravity of it.

"Do not think about it," she said when at last I had finished the story. I took her hand in mine and thought: perhaps she is right. Perhaps some things are better simply not to think about. Of course, we had no way of knowing it then, but Herod's days were numbered, as were those of Pilate, also Caiaphas. And even Saul, the man of persecution, would one day walk the shining way to the fields of Aaru. A journey, maybe not of our choosing, but a journey nonetheless. And all journeys begin with the first step. I stood up. "We should get back to Philip's house. Ema Mary will be wondering where we are." She rose to follow, but abruptly we found ourselves in each other's arms again. "One who can sing the song of God is very fortunate," I managed to whisper as we kissed.

"I am in love with your grace, John."

Alma haymanutha. Faith eternal. And so we broke apart at last, and started down the hill, I with my future wife at my side.

LaSalle IV

Cateline

It was as much as LaSalle had translated so far. More remained, but it would have to wait. *Love one another, as I have loved you.* The Gospel of John's essential message. A thought suddenly struck him and he rose from his desk.

Making his way to one of two giant bookshelves he had purchased last year from a furniture shop in Cormontreuil, he paused, scanning the various-colored spines, pulling at last a volume from the second shelf from the bottom: *Pistis Sophia*, translated by G.R.S. Mead. The *Pistis Sophia*—"Faith Wisdom"—it was a Gnostic tract believed to date to the third century purporting to relate conversations between the disciples and the resurrected Jesus. He didn't know what exactly had made him think of it, and he wasn't sure which part of the text contained the quote he was looking for, but hastily he began flipping through the pages. At last, in chapter 96, he found it:

> I have said unto you aforetime: 'Where I shall be, there will also be my twelve ministers.' But Mary Magdalene and John, the virgin, will tower over all my disciples and over all men who shall receive the mysteries in the Ineffable.

Mary Magdalene and John the Virgin. *Johannes the Virgin.* Will tower over all my disciples and all men. So often in scholarly research, the heart, blind intuition, call it what you will, proves the most faithful counselor. LaSalle returned to his desk with the book. *Mary Magdalene and John the Virgin.* Interesting the *Pistis Sophia* author placed Mary Magdalene's name first. Hastily adjusting the Tiffany lamp, LaSalle picked up the last page of his translation and read the words again: *And off we started down the hill, I with my future wife at my side.* What we had here in the Duro-Europos text, he realized suddenly, were the *seeds*, the *beginnings*, of what came to be known as the "Johannine Community," or "the Community of the Beloved Disciple," the body of Christians who later produced the Gospel of John. The John of the Dura-Europos scrolls and the John of the gospels, the disciple of Jesus, were one and the same. He was sure of it now, and the thought made his heart pound. He looked at the clock. 12:38 a.m.

The Gospel of John. The one that stood out, that didn't conform to patterns of the other three. The one with its polemics against "the Jews." Of course, the gospel was likely written in stages, with heavy redactions along the way. The entire twenty-first chapter seems to have been added by a later hand. Moreover, a sequential problem exists in some of the earlier chapters. Four through seven, for instance, place Jesus variously in Galilee and Jerusalem with no logical order of progression from one place to the other, while his words "Arise, let us go hence" in 14:31 are not in fact acted upon until 18:1. Internal disorder is prevalent. So when, one would need to ask, did the redactor, or redactors, enter the community and do their work? Mid first century? Late first century? Early second? And most crucial of all, what purpose were they hoping to achieve?

Among early Church fathers, Bishop Irenaeus (died *c.* 200), became one of the first to champion John's Gospel. The bishop felt Matthew, Mark, Luke, and John were the only legitimate gospels because they alone had been written by eyewitnesses to the events described, and he referred to them collectively as the "Four Formed Gospel." Irenaeus was convinced, despite little internal evidence, that John the son of Zebedee was the author of the fourth. *Ironically*, the bishop was also a fierce opponent of the Gnostics, whom he branded as "heretics"—*ironic* because the Gospel of John appears to have been known, read, and accepted in Gnostic circles well before it reached Irenaeus and the "orthodox" branch of early Christianity. The Valentinians, a second century Gnostic group centered most likely in Egypt, evinced familiarity with John in some of their earliest writings, while a fragment of the Fourth Gospel is in fact preserved on a piece of papyrus discovered in the Egyptian desert and dating to the first half of the second century—quite possibly the oldest fragment of any Christian writing ever recovered. Perhaps even more striking, the gospel seems to have been highly favored by the Naassenes, a Gnostic group said to have been led by a woman named Mariamne. So there *does* seem to have been a certain familiarity with John's gospel in Gnostic circles. By contrast, in the orthodox wing of the church, Ignatius of Antioch and Papias of Hierapolis, whose deaths occurred in the first half of the second century, and Polycarp, who died *c.* 155, all seem unaware of it. Nor is it mentioned by Justin Martyr (*c.* 100-165), writing from Rome.

"A two-level drama"—thus have modern scholars described the Fourth Gospel, the idea being it relates the story of Jesus while also conveying, in between the lines so to speak, something of the saga of the Johannine Community as it unfolded later in the century. The view has been challenged, but in a nutshell the theory is that strife came upon the community mid-to-late century, most likely after the death of the Beloved Disciple. One of the thornier issues seems to have been the group's relationship with Judaism, though other questions were certainly argued as well, such as whether Jesus had been human, divine in some respect, or even God himself. Eventually (as the theory goes) a schism takes place. One faction of the group gravitates toward the Gnostics; the other toward the "orthodox" branch of Christianity, although of course in that day what was "orthodox" and "heterodox" had yet to be firmly established; it all depended on your point of view. In either event, the age-old question has been and remains: *who* was the Beloved Disciple, and why was his or her name redacted from the gospel's final version? Theories that it was John the son of Zebedee, John Mark, Lazarus, or simply a church elder named John (all put forth by scholars at one time or another) do not explain why the name need have been kept secret, since all of these would have been dead by the time of the Gospel's final redaction. So was the Beloved Disciple merely a fictitious character? That too has been suggested. But the Gnostics, for their own part, seem to have placed the mantle of "Beloved" squarely upon Mary Magdalene. The *Gospel of Philip* depicts her and Jesus as exchanging kisses; in the *Pistis-Sophia* she becomes the "inheritor of the light"; while the *Dialogue of the Savior* holds her as a "woman who had understood completely." Compelling evidence, maybe, to support a theory of Mary as the Beloved Disciple. But could it possibly be, as the *Pistis Sophia* also seems to imply, that John the son of Zebedee was, shall we say, *present* all along, just as Orthodox tradition has long held? LaSalle read the words again: *Mary Magdalene and John, the virgin, will tower over all my disciples and over all men who shall receive the mysteries in the Ineffable.* Was it farfetched, LaSalle now wondered, to presume that the character crafted in the Gospel of John was in reality a "composite" so to speak, a fusion, of both husband and wife, into a single character, a character who then came to be known as the Beloved Disciple? It was at least worth pondering. Worth pondering also is whether there might not have been attempts by the early church to in some respect "shortchange" Mary Magdalene of the credit due her. The author of the Gospel of Luke seems complicit in this. "The Lord has arisen and has appeared to Simon!"—this ground-shaking announcement, in

Luke 24:34, is neither preceded nor followed by any mention of an appearance to Mary Magdalene. Luke, then, seems clearly to have a prejudice in favor of Peter. But the same certainly cannot be said of John, who consistently favors the Beloved Disciple, often at Peter's expense. So then the ever-perplexing question remains: why would a community of Christians produce a gospel in which its founder's name is deliberately withheld? What would have been the motive?

One answer, and LaSalle had to admit it was plausible, is the male members of the sect were embarrassed at the community's having been taught and led by a woman. While Jesus seems to have recognized women as more or less equal to men, and while Paul, too, evidently valued certain women as co-apostles, by the end of the first century a far different view prevailed. "I do not permit a woman to teach or to have authority over a man. She must be quiet," says the pseudo-Pauline author of I Timothy. Tertullian and other church figures held similar views. In the years after the death of the Beloved Disciple and the resulting schism (assuming a schism indeed occurred), would the breakaway group pressing for acceptance into the orthodox church have felt compelled to hide the fact they had been under a woman's authority? And would the knowledge that the gospel they were bringing with them had been authored by a woman—would that need to have been kept under wraps as well? The answer is quite likely yes on both counts.

LaSalle switched off the lamp, rose from his chair and reached for his jacket, the world inside his flat grown suddenly stifling. It was a feeling that came over him this time each night. Normally, he worked himself into a static fatigue, but with the onset of this weariness arrived, incongruously, not drowsiness, but rather an uneasy restlessness. It was an oppressive, nagging unquiet that could be satisfied with no less than a half-hour's excursion into the sublative night air, where the tingling coolness became, strange to say, the only soporific for him. Pulling closed the door, he inserted his key, turning the lock, making his way along the vestibule to the stairs. As he entered the street, muted echoes, the predominant sound produced by the city at this hour, quickly surrounded and engulfed him. Distant echoes—of nothingness. Yet they contained sound vibrations, vibrations abounding with life, albeit life of a perhaps more exotic variety. At this time of night, the city was never fully awake, neither fully asleep.

Turning towards the Canal de la Marne, the Book of Revelation came to mind. *When he opened the seventh seal, there was silence in heaven for about half an hour.* So who, he wondered, was the mysterious "John" of the Apocalypse? And, for that matter, who was the mysterious "Mariamne" of the Naassenes? First question first. Author of the Apocalypse—was it John the disciple of Jesus, or would it have been an obscure presbyter by the same name, as some have contended? Much like the Gospel of John, the Apocalypse views the world as ruled by evil, but the Apocalypse does something the Gospel doesn't do. It takes the theme of messianic war, a theme running through much of the Jewish apocalyptic literature of the period, weaving and combining it with an exodus theme, or liberation from slavery, and does so while presenting Christ as a witness. The result is something of a hybrid form of literature. The long-awaited Jewish Messiah, a descendent of David to be anointed by God to lead his people into a war against Gentile oppressors, is reinterpreted—as Messiah *Jesus*. He is a king victorious without military conquest, his victory universal, attained not in the narrow interests of a single tribe or nation, but on behalf of the *international* People of God. But how, if not militarily, can such a victory be secured? By Jesus' work as the "faithful and true witness." The Greek word for witness is μάρτυς, or *martys*, from which the word "martyr" is derived. Jesus, the sacrificial lamb, the Lamb of God, bore not only verbal witness by his teachings, but offered further witness, of an even more powerful variety, in the act of his death. Bearing witness, or what the Apocalypse refers to as "overcoming," is what Christians are called upon by this "John" to continue. And indeed, many did! Not only as verbal witnesses, but also going that extra mile and taking the path of martyrdom. There was Ignatius, whose execution was said to have been ordered by Trajan; Blandina, a slave woman who confessed her belief in Christ during the reign of Marcus Aurelius and was, according to legend, subjected to a series of tortures that included roasting on a hot grate and goring by a bull; and then of course Justin; Felicitatis; the brothers Plutarchus and Serenus; Rhais—all said to have been martyred for the faith. And the list could go on. Christianity. It was a faith with a doctrine that rich and poor, slave and free, were equal unto God, and it seems to have been an idea people were willing to die for. That the faith eventually came to serve the empire as the state religion of Rome, making it a useful instrument of the very "beast" the Apocalypse had warned against, is surely one of the supreme ironies of history.

So were the "John" of the Gospel of John, and the "John" of the Apocalypse, one and the same? And what of Mary Magdalene? How did she fit in? If she was slighted by the author of Luke and others, the question then becomes to what extent? What *really* was Mary Magdalene's role, if any, in the early church? Her final appearance in the Bible comes in John 20:18, in which she tells the other disciples of having seen the arisen Jesus. After that, nothing. Did she simply drop from sight at this point? Curiously, she is never mentioned in the Lukan Acts or the letters of Paul, a conspicuous-by-its-absence kind of thing, not unlike Paul's failure to visit Alexandria on any of his missionary journeys, also quite curious. Rome, yes. Corinth, yes. Athens, check. Ephesus, quite naturally. All great cities of the empire, all visited by Paul. The apostle even discusses his intentions, in Romans 15, of journeying to Spain, some 2000 miles distant from Jerusalem. But no mention anywhere of a stop in Alexandria, a city which lay, parenthetically speaking, "just around the corner." Home to a world-famous library. A city that would have been regarded as one of the most advanced on earth. Yet for some reason, Paul felt disinclined to evangelize there. Why? Could it be because someone of equal or even greater stature was already there? If so, who? Might it have been the Johannine Community?

The author of the Gospel of John seems to have been intimately familiar with the geography of Palestine, considerably more so than the authors of Matthew, Mark, and Luke. Yet modern scholars are divided over where it was actually composed, some arguing for a Syrian origin, others Ephesus, while still others have theorized the group may have been centered at different locales at different times in its history. Also posited is that contact between the various Christian communities in the Mediterranean world may have been much more widespread than previously thought. At any rate, strong ties to the Egyptian city within the Johannine Community were certainly possible. But then come the side questions. What about the Naassenes? What of their *own* connection to the city of Alexandria, and their early acceptance of the Gospel of John? And most especially, *who* was the Naassene teacher known as "Mariamne"?

The name 'Naassene' seems to derive from the Hebrew word *nahash*, or "snake." A more generic term (applied often not only to the Naassenes but to other Gnostic sects as well) is "Ophite," from a Greek word also meaning "snake." For Gnostics of the Ophite persuasion, the serpent in the Genesis story was symbolic of *gnosis*, or knowledge. That they were "snake worshippers," however, seems to have been an unfounded presumption or misnomer, at least in the case of the Naassenes.

But be that as it may, still—who *were* they?

What we know of the Naassenes comes to us from one of their chief critics, Hippolytus, an early third century bishop whose avowed purpose was to "exterminate the monster" of heresy—*not*, one would think, a reliable or impartial source of information on a group like the Naassenes. Yet in his *Refutation of All Heresies*, Hippolytus does us the invaluable service of quoting extensively from a Naassene document that evidently had come into his possession. As he tells it, the Naassenes believed "the serpent is a fluid substance" and that "Eden is the brain, as it were, bound and tightly fastened in encircling robes, as if in heaven." The bishop seems to have had little understanding of the words, dismissing them largely as the "crazy notions of fools." Yet is it possible, as some have theorized, that members of the Naassene sect were practicing a discipline similar to Kundalini yoga? A fascinating thought, perhaps, yet of course entirely speculative. However, there *are* some things about the Naasenes that can be reliably gleaned from the bishop's text: a) that they were a Jewish-Christian sect; b) that their teacher was named Mariamne; c) they were centered in Egypt, most likely Alexandria; and d) that they highly prized the Gospel of John. Indeed, Hippolytus has them quoting the gospel at some length.

LaSalle crossed the Canal de la Marne, ending up on the Boulevard Paul Doumer. Strolling by the neighborhood apartment blocks, he thought of something one of his students had said the other day: "Eternity is a hard thing to embrace. All most people think in terms of are short, centimeter-long sections of it." A thoughtful young man. One of his more promising students. And perhaps Anton was right. Concepts such as *immortal, preexistent, self-begotten*, are difficult ones for people to come to grips with. Sometimes, to LaSalle, it seemed he learned as much from his students as they did from him, but life, after all, is a learning experience. Indeed, does one ever truly stop? "There has never been in the whole history of the world what could be called an entirely new religion. Every religion we know presupposes another religion, as every language presupposes an antecedent language." Those were the words of 19th century scholar Max Müller, one of the first western scholars to translate ancient Buddhist texts into English. As a devout Christian, Müller was able to make such comments because, rather than feel threatened by the numerous parallels he discovered between other faiths and his own, he celebrated them. Or as he put it: "Surely truth is not the less true because it is believed by the majority of the human race."

Leaving Rue de Thillois, the priest found himself on the Place Drouet d'Erlon. Something about the air in this part of Rheims always filled him with desire as well as a ceremonial sense of wonder. An hour or two earlier and the district would have literally been packed, yet even now in the late night hours it was still very much awake and pulsing. Glimmering streams of water cantilated forth from the pluvial fountain as music drifted through the doorways of those restaurants and bars not yet closed, the street, despite the late hour, remaining populated by scattered nodes of people—rakish and dapper young men, sequined young girls in tight fitting tops. It all had a somewhat gothic atmosphere. With a bass note that tingled the cerebellum, the unmistakable strains of "War" lumbered through the doorway of one of the bars, its argumentative but graceful beat flung, aphrodisia-like, into the night's ambience, only in this case, in true syncretic fashion, the classic hit by the American rhythm and blues singer Edwin Starr was rendered tumultuously in French:

Guerre ! Huh ! Bon Dieu, y'all !
Pour quoi est-ce bon ?

Through every age, it seemed, lessons were learned, forgotten, and relearned. And just as quickly forgotten again. Anton was right. Most people never saw more than occasional flashes of the eternal. Every day the news was full of the humanitarian crisis in the Middle East, but did any of it matter to those continuing to give the orders to drop the bombs? Probably not. To them the flash was invisible. *Good God, y'all.*

Bede Griffiths, the Benedictine monk who spent 25 years in an ashram in India, said that the truth of the imagination was a primordial one, and that the power which pervades the universe and the mind had been revealed with marvelous insight in the Vedas some 15 centuries before Christ. "The human imagination," he wrote, "has always been haunted by the feeling that we must die in order that we may live; that we have to be born again." Creation. Preservation. Destruction. The three persona of the Hindu trinity. In the Hindu scheme of things, successive world ages come about in which humanity grows increasingly corrupt and dissolute, until finally comes the Kali age and destruction. It is a concept the author of the Apocalypse would surely have understood.

Leaving the Drouet d'Erlon, LaSalle turned homeward, moving down Rue Buirette past the Holiday Inn Garden Court, a facility honorably and generously stocked with the region's most famous product: champagne. "*Bon Dieu, merci de la carbonation,*" he thought with a smile as the sparsely trafficked street flowered briefly with a young girl and boy darting by on a motor scooter. Merging from Rue Payen back into Boulevard Paul Doumer, past the restaurant at the underpass, he reflected once more on the Society of Biblical Literature's resolution—in which those in control of newly-discovered ancient manuscripts had been called upon to provide open access. Adopted in 1991, the resolution had been eminently reasonable, motivated moreover by the noblest of sentiments, that knowledge should be shared, that the written records left by ancient peoples are humanity's collective birthright. Further, it had been prompted by a sad history, dating back to the 1940s, of scholarly rivalries, of secrecy and jealousies, spawned by the discoveries made, within a few years of each other, at the Dead Sea and at Nag Hammadi in Egypt. These difficulties had delayed full and open publication of these ancient texts, not by years, but decades, and there were understandable fears of a similar wall of secrecy being thrown up around the Dura-Europos discovery. The impasse on the Nag Hammadi Gnostic tracts had been broken finally in the 1970s when the Egyptian government and the United Nations Educational, Scientific, and Cultural Organization, or UNESCO, came together and named an International Committee, leading to publication of a twelve-volume facsimile edition. Could that perhaps serve as a model for how the Dura-Europos scrolls should now be handled? *Perhaps UNESCO and the Syrian government then...*and in fact Arthur had already sent out exploratory feelers in that direction. But aside from such a project going forward, it would have to be established how, and under whose auspices, the scrolls were to be secured from the war now raging in the Middle East. Syria was currently flooded with upwards of a million refugees from Iraq. Even assuming the project could go forward under these circumstances, there was the impact publication would have upon the world at large. What would the reaction be in the "Christian" west? And what would be the reaction elsewhere, for that matter? Reverberations were sure to follow, dramatic ones. *Infinitely* more so than those which had accompanied publication of the Nag Hammadi or Dead Sea texts, so dramatic there would be no possible comparison. What, he wondered, could have induced the earth to give up such a secret? More importantly, how would it all be perceived, rationalized, interpreted? What portion of humanity would consign a nineteen-hundred-year-old document into the realm of "truth" in all its fiercely falling blows?

What was it the English poet William Blake had said? "Everything possible to be believed is an image of truth." Blake—who had embraced the concept of the human imagination as the body of God. But this wasn't a product of anyone's imagination; it was, unthinkably, an actual voice from antiquity. Such a voice emerging suddenly, without warning, and with a terrifying clarity, in the twenty-first century—what would be the consequences? Say it was determined positively that John of the Dura-Europos scrolls, and John of Patmos, the author of the Book of Revelation, were one and the same. What price would the earth pay? A third world war perhaps? Perhaps. But retribution and violence on a wide scale most likely, the full impact of which would be *beyond* predictability.

It was this which Arthur wanted to avoid, and so far, he had been successful. But sitting on the Dura-Europos discovery was like sitting on a live volcano. And LaSalle suddenly felt as if he had joined Arthur on the volcano's top. How long could publication of the scrolls be delayed? Indefinitely? If the past was any indication, the answer was no. Eventually, the dam would break. The scholarly world was in no mood for another "academic scandal *par excellence*," as the debacle over the Dead Sea Scrolls had been termed. Calls for publication of the Dura-Europos material had been growing increasingly strident. Only recently, an editorial in a scholarly journal had singled out Arthur for attack, and in an effort to deflect the mounting criticism, his friend had taken to issuing statements to the press, vague comments hinting that the problem lay not in London, but with obstacles imposed by the Syrian government. In LaSalle's opinion, it was an evasive action that could not help but collapse of its own weight, and when it did the mess would be even worse. Besides, mischaracterizing the situation in such a manner was extremely unfair to the Syrians. *Everything that can be believed is an image of truth.* An image of the truth...or an image of the beast? Take your pick. Either way the choice was unpalatable. And so it was, as all these forces had begun closing in on him, and feeling the rumbling of the volcano beneath him, that Arthur, his old friend, had reached out to him.

Continuing down the Boulevard Paul Doumer, parallel with the canal, LaSalle thought back to a summer of many years ago when he and Arthur, young college students at the time, had bicycled the Côte d'Azur. At St. Tropez they had begun their journey, following the coast all the way to Menton, rambunctiously taking to some of the hills in the Estérel, later gliding past the shops, pedestrians, and flower boxes along the Rue d'Antibes. Somehow, he had known life for him was going to change that summer. And indeed, it *did*. It was the summer he had finally decided to become a priest. It was also the summer he had fallen in love. And he remembered it well...

She had come upon them in the Place Masséna, the palm-tree-lined, red stucco square at Nice's Old Town. Around her throat, she wore a tasseled necklace, with one link in the chain in the shape of a rose. *M'excusez-vous, mais avez-vous le temps ?*—and from the first he had been powerfully attracted to her. Could one's heart, or even time itself, stand still? It seemed in this moment they had. But he was giving serious consideration to the *priesthood*. How possible?—that he could be caught up in love so unexpectedly? Yet that is precisely what happened. Arthur too had puzzled over it, but his British friend had also humored him, agreeing to linger on in Nice longer, a total of five days longer as it turned out, than they had planned. As any good friend perhaps would.

He and the girl in the rose necklace walked across the street to the beach, later into the Old Town, and that day they fell deeply in love. But it was not so much a physical love, or even a romantic one. Rather it was more a *psychical* bond, which is to say a love of both heart and mind. A trial of the heart and a Clementine Romance of the mind, he mused. And that was the thing. The girl informed him her mother had died the previous year and she was now considering entering the convent. Naturally, he confessed his own aspirations to the priesthood. Strangely, both of them had reserved that summer as a "last fling," a moment to be savored and experienced before making that sharp departure from those prevailing currents of life that claimed most people. Furthermore, she understood something he himself had come to understand: that without God we suffer and die, like a plant without water, or a prisoner without light. How fair! They had much in common, it seemed! Soul mates, one could almost say, and that indeed is how Arthur came to view it. In fact, Arthur's instincts were not far off.

She had returned to Paris, while Arthur and he had finished their bicycle journey. But he had kept in touch, continuing to see her whenever time would allow, either in Paris or the south of France. The love he felt for her remained strong, even after she entered the convent that fall. But another love claimed his heart as well, and it also would not let go—his love for God. And so he joined the priesthood. But he had never forgotten her or that day in Nice they had fallen in love. It had been more than 20 years ago, and though they had never consummated their love, a river had entered the ocean nonetheless. The girl was still around. She had of course grown older now. However, in all this time he had never stopped loving her. It had been Sister Denise—or Denise Michallat as she had been known then.

He had served the priesthood in Thailand, supposing, by removing himself to another continent, she might somehow become less a part of his thoughts. The refugee crisis was overwhelming. Days at a time, he went without sleep. Thailand—it had changed his life physically and emotionally. It had changed him spiritually as well, for it was in that far-distant land he had picked up the practice of *bhakti*, or devotion to God. "The best thing anyone can do, Lord, is to love you, for there is no greater love than this"—this was bhakti. It was love, a love for God, that grew and grew, carrying over eventually from meditation into daily life. Yet through it all, through the crisis years in Thailand, she never strayed far from his thoughts, the girl with the rose necklace from the beach in Nice. Who in the meantime, still in France, had become an Ursuline nun.

Nearing his flat now, LaSalle stopped into an all-night market. The inside of the store was carpetbagged in a sickly fluorescent light, as well as drowned in the hypnotic cadence of an unusually loud radio. The noise box, for all its persistent polyphony, seemed to have little impact upon the half-closed lids of the sleepy clerk. In America, what you got was the prestige of one mouthwash over another. Here radio tended simply to be boring, and in a certain manner of speaking, he had to sympathize with the tired young man. Wandering the aisles, he picked up coffee and laundry detergent. Finally a package of frozen *feuilles de brick*. Perhaps he would get time to whip up something special in the kitchenette, though he couldn't for the life of him say when, so better to get the frozen variety. As he wandered the aisles, the music gave way to the voice of a news announcer. (Was it the same one he had heard earlier in the evening or did they all simply sound alike?) Hurricane Roxanne again, bearing down on the Gulf Coast of the United States...followed by a sou's worth of news on the war...and of course another international conference in another out-of-the-way place to head off another crisis on this or that. *Oderint dum metuant.* Seek forgiveness and woe unto the axis of evil. The monotony of it stood poised like a Hurricane Roxanne hovering offshore from the underworld. *When the hurlyburly's done, when the battle's lost and won*...the second witch in Macbeth. LaSalle took his groceries to the counter, handed some money over to the bored clerk, and departed.

When Cateline, the young blind girl, had come to the orphanage there had been questions as to her medical history, what illnesses she had had, whether rotavirus, antibiotic side effects, allergies, or other difficulties had been encountered in childhood. The mother had left nothing by way of records, and maybe after all there were none. A complete workup had been done, just as a matter of course, but the child's health, though she was sightless, appeared generally good. Nothing more serious than occasional sleep problems. She was "bright," "gifted"—the usual adjectives had applied. Yet at the same time, there was a pronounced reclusiveness from the other children. Inside her own world of darkness she had enclosed herself, and thus she remained despite all efforts at bringing her out of her shell. LaSalle had been the only one capable of penetrating that wall, LaSalle and Sister Denise.

The sister, of course, had never told Cateline of the long-lived friendship between herself and the priest. Neither had LaSalle mentioned it. It was a discreet matter between the two of them. There had been no reason for the child to know, and certainly they had never given her any cause to suspect, yet as in the case with Arthur, her instincts on the matter had been unfailing. By hook, crook, or whatever imaginative means she could devise, she had begun to "push" the two of them together by degrees, bringing about a series of disquieting and occasionally embarrassing contretemps, engineered quite comically, in many cases, by the child herself. In a way he supposed he and Denise, perhaps subconsciously, had begun thinking of her as the child they had never had, and to that extent had become passive accomplices in her game. Thoughts of what *might have been*...

Reaching his building, he mounted the stairs, inserted his key, and entered the flat, ready for about four hours sleep, his usual most nights. Upon the table in the kitchenette, where he had brewed his coffee earlier this evening, he placed the bundle of groceries, the blinking light on the phone informing him a call had come in while he was out. "A strange time of night for someone to call," he thought. The groceries needed to be put away, especially the frozen bricks, but before shedding his jacket, he picked up the phone and dialed the code. The message was from Denise, and the words hit him like ice-cold water to the face.

"*David, it hasn't occurred to me to call you until now. I'm sorry for the lateness of the hour, but I know you're usually up late. It's Cateline, David. Earlier this evening, as inconceivable as it may seem, the blood from her eyes started up again. And something else as well: she began complaining of a burning sensation on her skin. It was at first simply exasperating, but then...Oh God, David, the burning. The tears. It started out as no more than a drop or two but then it became a torrent as before. Je suis à l'hôpital. The doctors are with her now. That's all I can tell you at this point. The situation has been chaotic. I rode in the ambulance with her. Again, I'm sorry to call you so late—mon frere, David.*"

Without bothering to unpack his groceries, he was out the door, flying down the stairs. His car he used but seldom, but it would be the fastest way to the hospital this time of night. Seat belt. Keys. At the end of the block he made a right, then another, navigating the mostly empty streets, navigating with the cherished thought that one could live a life without resorting to casuistry or infatuation, and that there were no threatening clouds that could not be pushed back with a well-conceived and determined effort. Hastily he tried Denise's cell phone. No answer. Equally as hastily he threw the phone into the passenger seat, still steering the car, praying to the Holy Virgin, to the Angels of the Presence, to God most high, to anyone with ears to hear, to become close united friends, to stream to the side of Cateline, to the side of Denise, to those he loved, and to those he couldn't quite muster love for but tried in his own inadequate way.

Arriving at the hospital, after committing more than a few traffic violations along the way, he thought of how one may be brought into the vicinity of death without ever knowing or seeing it. Either going or coming. Into that hospital waiting room he strode with a rush, having arrived with an all-out sense of urgency. But suddenly he felt drained, tired, overcome. Agitatedly his eyes searched the room—and then he saw her. She was on her feet, striding towards him. The choking, strangling, whittling-down-the-spirit look of worry he saw on her face was, he knew full well, reflected in his own. In her own face, it was a look telling him, assuring him, that whatever duty, whatever distinction, between the past or present, between the pure or the impure, they shared together. Did circles close? At some point maybe they did.

"How is she?"

"The doctors are with her." Something in her voice longed for reciprocity, something appeased and yet not so. Suddenly he had the sense, here in this hospital waiting room, they were partners in a slow-motion duet, a glorious, still-life waltz that climaxed as they came together and touched. The communion of saints; forgiveness of sins; resurrection of the body; life everlasting. For a moment, they simply stood in silence as she leaned her head against his jacket, he offering the succor he knew she felt at the touch of his hand. Then—

"She says a 'rain of fire' is falling upon her from the sky and that the fire is burning her skin. The doctors have been with her for the past two and a half hours—but David, it is just as before. No medical reason for what is happening to her, they say. But there are endless welts on her skin. Whether the fire is real or imagined, David, the burns are there! It shouldn't be happening, the doctors say, but it *is*."

"Maybe they'll find something. There is always the possibility of more tests. They've only had her for one evening! They can't have covered everything!"

Were there medical answers? Or were the answers to be found elsewhere? He didn't know, but it seemed he had climbed to the top of this hill before, as, he knew, had she.

"It's nice that they can give reassurances, and I'm sure they will have plenty. I'm sure also that there are moons mounted on comets as well, for God's sake! But what's coming out of her eyes, David, is blood red, and it's been flowing like that all night. Oh David"—and suddenly this sister, this woman he loved so much, this soul bride who had looked his way so many years ago upon the Place Masséna in Nice, was sobbing now. "Oh David...she is...crying *the tears of God*."

Glossary

Of first and second century terms and expressions
Aramaic–Hebrew–Greek–Latin

Abwoon [*Aram*] from the root word, *Abba*, our father, our mother or father of the cosmos; our God

Adonai [*Heb*] Lord

aida [*Aram*] hand

Alaha [*Aram*] God

alma [*Aram*] forever, eternity; may also mean world

am ha'aretz [*Heb*] literally "people of the land." Usually used derogatorily, and often by Judeans in reference to the people of Galilee

ar'a [*Aram*] world

atsat ha'yahad [*Heb*] society of unity

aukama [*Aram*] black

bar d'nasha [*Aram*] son of man

bayta [Aram] house

beit [Heb] house

beka [Aram] to weep

bereshith [Heb] "in the beginning"—the creation; also, as *Bereshit Rabbah*, refers to a compilation of early midrashim, or interpretations, on the Book of Genesis

beth ha-sefer [Heb] literally "house of book." Refers to primary school, attended by children up to the age of 13

bukhra [Aram] first born

bur-ka-tha [Aram] blessing

canicula—the lowest throw at dice

chara [Heb] shit

cubiculum [Lat] a sleeping room in an ancient Roman house

datz [Aram] to live in abundance

diwa [Aram] demon or devil

d'ma [Aram] blood

dramatis personae [Lat] literally "masks of the drama", refers collectively to characters in a drama

ebyōn [Heb] destitute, poor; one who is needy

ebyonim—a group of early Jewish Christians who opposed animal sacrifice, were vegetarians, and viewed Jesus as human, rather than divine, though who felt he had become equivalent to an archangel upon his baptism and being landed upon by the dove. The word derives from the Heb. *ebyōn*, meaning "poor."

El Shaddai [Heb] A Hebraic name for God, translated as "God Almighty," or "God of the Mountains"

ema [Aram] mother

evra [Aram] landing place

Gabbatha [Aram] denotes a paved area in Jerusalem believed to have been located next to the Praetorium, the building thought to have served as Pilate's residence at the Antonia Fortress

gamla [Aram] camel

gatha [Aram] a vehement cry

gehenna [Gr] comparable to the English "hell." Originally referred to the Valley of Hinnom, outside Jerusalem, where refuse was burned

g'va [Aram] to choose

hadad [Aram] thunder

Hathor—Egyptian goddess of love, motherhood, and joy, also known as the "Lady of the Sycamore Trees."

haymanutha [Aram] faith, belief

hayye [Aram] life, or life energy

hin—ancient unit of liquid measure, roughly equal to 4 liters

hokhmah [Heb] wisdom

huba [Aram] love

Iesvs Nazarenvs Rex Ivdaeorvm [Lat] "Jesus the Nazarene King of the Jews"—inscription on the cross placed by Pilate as described in the Gospel of John, often represented today by the acronym INRI. The letter "J" was not added to the Roman alphabet until the Middle Ages, while the letters "u" and "v" were often used interchangeably—again up until the

Middle Ages. The synoptic gospels (Matthew, Mark and Luke) also speak of an inscription on the cross, though with slightly different wording

istomukhvia—a shift, or robe, worn around the body by women; the garments were often made of flax, Galilee's principle industrial crop

jeezer—wild rosemary

kethuba—[Heb] a prenuptial marriage agreement, sanctioned by ancient rabbis, that was designed to protect the rights of the woman. Generally under the terms of the contract, the wife was to be paid a sum of money should the marriage end in either divorce or the death of the husband.

khab [Aram] love, or to love

khavra [Aram] friend

khayla [Aram] might, miracle, power

Khek m'tha [Aram] wisdom

khenuta [Aram] sense of justice, righteousness

khesem [Aram] bewitch

Kittim—name used by the Essenes to refer to the Romans

kohan [Heb] priest

kolbur—undergarment

kor—also called *homer*. Hebraic unit of dry measurement, approximately equal to six bushels

korban [Heb] a sacrifice

lachma [Aram] bread

ma'aphoret—head covering

Ma're [Aram] Lord

Ma're d'huba [Aram] Lord of Love

malaka [Aram] messenger

malkuta [Aram] kingdom

mebaqqer—leader of the Essene sect

mebhinim [Heb] scribes who served as a jurists or interpreters of the law, as opposed to *soferim*, actual writers or scribes

me'on arayot [Heb] lion's den

meskina [Aram] poor

midbar [Heb] an area suitable for pasturing flocks, often translated as "wilderness"

mikroteros poimnion [Gr] little flock

miktoran—breast scarf

mikvah—[Heb] Jewish ritual bath

mithausepheyn [Aram] shall be added unto you

mohar—[Heb] an amount of money paid as part of a marriage contract. As a general rule, the sum was paid by the bridegroom to the father of the bride

muma [Aram] spot or blemish

nasha [Aram] human being

nehwey [Aram] your

Nile of the Sky—the Milky Way Galaxy

noli me tangere [Lat] do not touch me

Nozrei ha brit [Heb] literally "keepers of the covenant." A name sometimes applied to the Jewish sect known as the Essenes

nuhra [Aram] light

nummularii [Lat] money changers

Oderint dum metuant [Lat] let them hate us as long as they fear us

Oread—in Greek mythology, any of a group of mountain nymphs, companions to Artemis

palgutha [Aram] discord, division

panem et circenses [Lat] bread and circuses

panta rei [Gr] all flows, or the universe is constantly changing, a phrase associated with the Greek philosopher Heraclitus

Paraqlita [Aram] comforter or advocate; the Holy Spirit

Petskha [Aram] Passover, the Jewish paschal feast

piljon—a type of cap worn by men

pinacotheca—a gallery, or "picture room," in ancient Greece and Rome

pleroma [Gr] literally "fullness." The term is found especially in Gnostic literature and refers to the totality of all divine powers as well as a realm of light, above the earthly or cosmic realms, in which such powers are thought to exist

pronoia [Gr] forethought, providential care

punda—purse

qadisha [Aram] holy

raca [Aram] an empty-headed person; may also mean "to spit"

risha [Aram] head, leader

ruha [Aram] spirit, breath, or wind

sam [Aram] to lay something down; also to ordain, commit

Shavuot [Heb] "weeks"; name designating the Jewish Festival of Weeks, which came later to be associated with the Christian "Pentecost"

Shekinah [Heb] divine presence, esp. the feminine presence or attributes of God

Shema [Heb] or Shema Yisrael, a prayer recited twice daily and beginning with the words "Hear O Israel," from Deut. 6:4

Sheol [Heb] place or abode of the dead, comparable to the Greek "Hades."

sheryana [Aram] breastplate

shlomo [Aram] peace, or "hello"

shmaya [Aram] heaven

shrara [Aram] truth

shubakha [Aram] glory, praise

shukhalfa [Aram] change

shushantha [Aram] flower

Sicarii [Lat] plural of the Lat. *sicarious*, or dagger. Literally the term means "dagger men" and refers to a group of first-century Jews, closely connected to the Zealot Party, who sought to end Roman occupation through armed violence

sofer [Heb] *pl.*-SOFERIM—scribe; skilled calligraphers who were charged with transcribing Torah scrolls—as opposed to MEBHINIM, who were jurists or interpreters.

soreg—a wall in the Jerusalem Temple that served as a boundary separating the Court of the Gentiles from the rest of the Temple; Gentiles were forbidden to pass beyond it, an offense punishable by death

spatha—a long sword used by Roman cavalry

t'var [Aram] to break or crush

tauta'va [Aram] sojourner, foreigner

tawdi [Aram] thank you

te Deum [Lat] thee Lord

tefillin [Heb] phylacteries

tesserarius [Lat] a Roman soldier or officer in charge of sentries

tsevâchâh [Heb] an expression of anguish

tubwaykhon [Aram] that which is in tune with divine reality—often translated as "blessed"

tura tsa [Aram] correction

tuva [Aram] a blessing

uncia [Lat] Roman unit of measurement, roughly comparable to one inch

yahad [Heb] unity

Yam ha Melah [Heb] sea of salt, the Dead Sea

yona [Heb] dove

yida [Aram] to know the way, and to have in your hands the means to act

zadiq [Aram] just, righteous

zeman cherutenu [Heb] season of our liberation, Passover

Excerpt from

The Memoirs of Saint John: The Infinitesimal

Forthcoming from:

Once There Was A Way

OTWAY Books

Mariamne and I were married over the strenuous objections of my father, Zebedee. His hair had turned overwhelmingly white in those days, his face evincing the beginnings of tallow-like pouches, though these had not removed the edges from his rancor or uncharitableness. Most of his objections to Mariamne centered on the fact that she was part Gentile and therefore of inferior status. She had no family, no one even knew her father, and initially it seemed my love and I would have to journey elsewhere, away from Capharnaum, should we wish to secure for ourselves the bonds of holy matrimony. But then my mother stepped in. Salome was perceptive enough to realize the state of my stricken heart and determined that Zebedee, through his bigotry and foolishness, should not destroy the life of another of her children. With passion and contumacy she let it be known he would have one major fight on his hands if he did not culminate his pestilent objections. The objections subsided, and the wedding took place.

To our house, Mariamne was brought in a torchlight procession led by Philip, who later stood under the chupah with a raised cup of wine while reciting the blessings of God. Present that evening were, of course, my mother, along with my dear brother James. Present as well was Peter, up from Jerusalem, in whose company I felt slightly shame-faced. "I'm sorry I left you and the other brothers in Jerusalem," were my apologetic words to him at one point.

"John..." he shook his head as if marveling at my nonsensicality. "You always did worry about the silliest things!" It was an expression of unreserved friendship, and as the evening progressed, he exhibited, even toward Mariamne, a measure of free-flowing affability. This was Peter. From the earliest days of my childhood, when he had rescued me from the not-so-tender mercies of a bully, all the way up to our travels with Jesus, and even to that bitter morning we had found him crying beneath the holm oak tree in the Kidron Valley, I had always looked up to him. Friendship. It is sometimes nothing more than a cumulative total of poignant and unbearable griefs, and I knew that wherever in this world I went, to whatever land and upon whatever sea I might travel, I would always meet, like the doe of the morning, that feeling of allegiance to him.

"Be happy, John..." He embraced me, placing a kiss on the side of my face. "*Had m'shamlaya*, let your joy be full."

"*Tawdi* Peter," I whispered.

Besides this dear and very *old* friend, present that night was a much, much *newer* friend, one whose showing up at the wedding feast came as a complete, though pleasant, surprise. James, the brother of Jesus, I'm talking about. I had not seen him since that night at the Pool of Bethesda, when Jesus and Mariamne had healed the cripple underneath the colonnade in the presence of the Owl Man. We stood together and chatted, and doing so I felt a quiet strength emanating from him. Oddly, as had Jesus before him, he now made a request of me—that Mariamne and I should care for Oma Mary. It was a request I wondered about for long afterwards. Would he not, only naturally, wish to care for his mother himself? But he seemed to have other plans, and I can only conclude that he had determined to go where his mother could not follow, for yes, he had chosen to embrace the poor, to speak out against the villainies and transgressions of our leaders. As, of course, his brother had done. And concerns for Oma Mary's safety were much on his mind, I think. The rich, Quintus, are one day to weep and howl, make no mistake on it, for that day is coming; and James, much as one holding up a mirror, was intent on forcing them to realize this. I should add, too, that he came near succeeding, and perhaps very much *would* have had his life not been expended.

Besides these, many other guests filled the house that night—Matthew and Elisheba, now married themselves, and Matthew's brother, Other James. They were there along with Philip's wife and children, who were of splendid vigor, and the evening seemed to favor this illustrious assembly of family and friends with a marvelous bliss and bravado. Finally came the moment when my bride made her appearance, her hair hanging loose to her shoulders, a veil covering her face. We stood together, she and I, underneath the huppah as she looked at me and recited the words, "A kiss from those lips! Wine cannot ravish the senses like that embrace. Draw me ever after you, where you will. See we hasten after you by the very fragrance of those perfumes allured!"

To that was joined my response: "Rouse and come, so beautiful, so well beloved, still hiding yourself as a dove hides in a cleft rock or a crannied wall." With no talent for singing, I somehow managed nonetheless to trill the line, "How beautiful you are, my beloved, how beautiful!" in what was, one might suppose, a halfway respectable manner. Then the pomegranate was crushed, the vase of scent broken, and it was done: we were husband and wife.

During the feast afterwards, my mother took the opportunity to convey upon us a present, handing it to me in a fleecy rucksack made of sheep's wool. Untying the string, I saw there were silver shekels inside, many, many of them.

"There are a hundred in there," she said. "I want you to have them."

It was a grand sum of money, and suddenly I realized where she had gotten it; it was her life savings, the product of a long span of years, from youth to maturity, years of efficiency and obligation, years brimming with the trials and endurances of her marriage to Zebedee; this small bag was what she had to show for it all. My brother James had a gift as well: he and his wife Abby were vacating their house for the night, leaving Mariamne and I alone to enjoy the diversion of its comforts and privacy. His voice was gentle as his hand took mine. "Congratulations, little brother!" I embraced them both at this point, my mother and James. Words could not express the love I felt for them, and so I didn't even try.

The evening had grown late. Guests were preparing to leave, while time had come as well for Mariamne and me to depart—for James and Abby's house, where we were to spend the night. Not once throughout the entire festivities, neither during the wedding, nor the feast afterwards, had my father paid us the compliment of presenting himself and offering to us his good wishes. We simply had not seen him. All in all, his absence, quite truthfully, had been more one of welcome than cause for disappointment, but suddenly, as the door to the house was opened and the guests began spilling into the street, I spotted him. At a point directly across the street, conspicuously visible from the front gate, he had fixed himself, here standing, poised and erect, next to a weighty object I immediately recognized as a barrel of fruit, one of several my mother had ordered to feed the guests.

Seeing us emerge from the house, he picked up the barrel—it must have been quite heavy—raised it above his head, and hurled it to the center of the street where it landed with an audible smack, sending melons, figs, and the like, eddying here and there. The meaning of the wasted fruit was clear, but just to make sure no one missed the point, Zebedee opened his mouth and discharged a salvo of umbrage, the words of which were aimed exclusively at Mariamne and me. The offspring of our union, he informed us, would in no way be considered family; our children he would never regard as his own blood or kin. It was a jangling and dissonant end to what had been an otherwise pleasant evening. Three days later Mariamne and I departed Caesaria by ship. Our destination—Ephesus.

We sailed with Oma Mary and little Yona, the somewhat sullen younger sister of Jesus, and I must say it was hard leaving Galilee, but to do so seemed the lone sensible course. Mariamne was still a runaway slave, and while no location could be considered totally safe, we had calculated that distant Asia, so very far from Herod's realm, might provide us at least a *somewhat* reasonable hope of avoiding her capture. But this wasn't the only determinant for choosing the bearings we did. Out of the more than quarter of a million inhabitants of the city of Ephesus lived two who actually were *known* to us: Thomas and Nathanael. There was another reason also. The sea. In Ephesus, I could make a living as a fisherman, a good one, and with the money my mother had given us, it would be possible to purchase my own boat, nets, and gear.

Thomas and Nathanael had not been able to journey to our wedding, but they came out and greeted us upon the landing of our ship at the great Ephesian harbor. Suddenly we found ourselves in a giant megalopolis. It was by far the largest city I had ever laid eyes on; we saw gymnasiums, baths, statues (nude and otherwise), brothels, taverns, inns, shops, and everywhere people, people, people! Most of the city lay among and between two peaks, Pion to the northeast and Coressus to the southwest, with the sea jutting up against Coressus near the mouth of the River Caÿster, and the harbor angling in, almost up to the door of a large gymnasium. The *polis* seemed to have been built almost as an adornment to the two peaks, with the grand homes of the rich terraced on their vertical slopes and the Great Theatre carved literally into the side of Pion. From Harbor Street, you could make your way past the largest agora in the East, and into the fabled Street of the Curetes.

LaVergne, TN USA
17 October 2010
201092LV00004B/2/P